First Edition

REBEL KING

BANNOK-BURN

BOOK THREE

[signature]
Carolyn Hale Bruce
Loon Mountain 2006

REBEL KING

BANNOK BURN

BOOK THREE

Chronicles of Robert de Brus, King of Scots

A NOVEL

CHARLES RANDOLPH BRUCE
&
CAROLYN HALE BRUCE

AHEAD OF THE HANGMAN PRESS

2 0 0 6

AN
AHEAD OF THE HANGMAN PRESS
BOOK
PUBLISHED BY
BRUCE & BRUCE, INC.

Copyright © 2006 by Charles Randolph Bruce & Carolyn Hale Bruce

Published and Distributed in the United States by
Bruce & Bruce Publishing
PO Box 64007 Virginia Beach, VA 23467-4007

www.RebelKing.com

First Edition

Hardback: ISBN 0-9721674-6-3
Paperback: ISBN 0-9721674-7-1

Manufactured in the United States of America

Cover design and illustration and character drawings by Charles Randolph Bruce

To our children and their spouses
and our grandchildren,
present and future,
with our love.

Your ancestors were at
Bannok Burn.

Vici and Bobby
Randy and Tammy
Docie
Ian
Kacie
Morgan
Riley
Randy

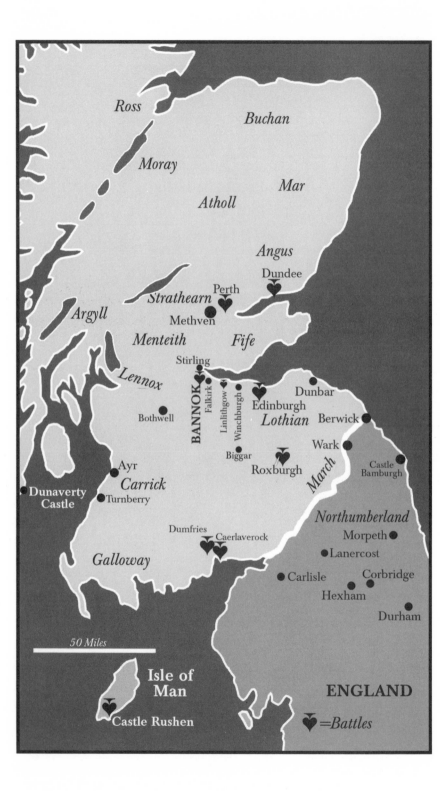

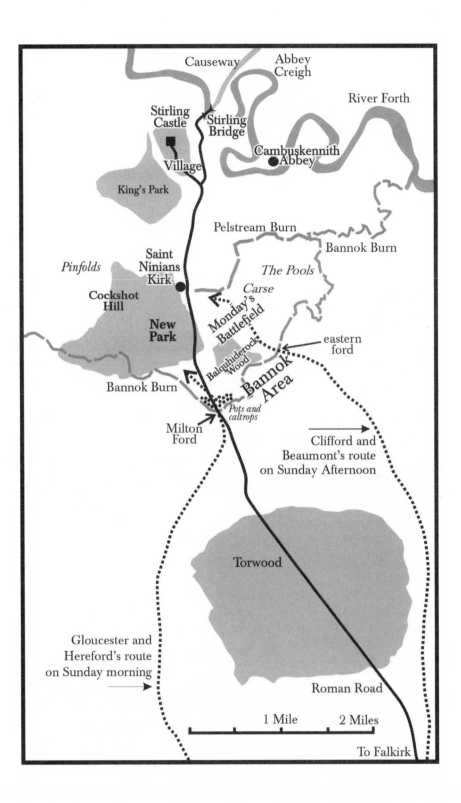

THANKS TO
OUR MODELS

Dean A. Ablowich
Mark Allen
Tim Bennett
Andrea Bruce
Steve Bruce
Richard Christy
Alex Clydesdale
Roy L. Conn
Mary Elizabeth Hale
Josiah Wallace Hunter, Jr.
David Irwin
Richard Jenkins
Jamesie Johnston
Edmund Langevin
Benjamin Lee
Michael Maddox
Jon McCollum
Mark McLain
Jesse Mellema
Donovan Murray
Harry Neeson
Kacie Ouellette
Robert Ouellette
Victoria Bruce Phelps
John Plausie
Ryan Robinson
Serg 'si Robton
James Sarver
Nathan Schroedter
Pablo Scruggs
Stephanie Seddon
Mike Sharpe
Robert Major Stewart
Tu-Bardh Wilson
Rickie T
John Wallace
Brian White

AND THANKS TO
OUR ADVISORS

Thomas C. Burns
Robert Lockwood
Thomas Allen Bruce
Rita and Oliver Hamilton
Alexsis Mansisidor
Donovan Murray

THE AUTHORS

Charles Randolph Bruce was born and raised in the highlands of southern West Virginia, where his Scottish ancestors settled in the late 1700s. Family lore holds that his immigrant ancestors left Scotland one step ahead of the hangman, having been on the losing side in one of the Scots' wars with the English.

Carolyn Hale Bruce is a native of the mountains of Southwest Virginia, where her 18th century ancestors include those with the surnames Agnew, Fraser, and Thompson. She has written and had published two pictorial histories of her home town, Roanoke, Virginia, and an illustrated history titled Virginiana, A Visitors' Guide to Virginia History & Other Stuff.

SEPTEMBER 26th 1310
LOTHIAN

Wan autumn sunlight filtered softly through mist shrouded hardwood trees, their leaves drifting about in flashes of yellows and reds with the slightest breeze. Quietly, a column of mounted soldiers moved among them, the ground covering of wet leaves muffling the horses' ponderously rhythmic gait. As they neared their objective, the leader of the column silently drew his sword and held it high as a signal to his troop to do the same. Finally, their weapons at the ready, the small army bolted forward almost as one, charging down upon a tiny hamlet that lay ahead of them in a corner of a broad clearing.

A woman with a baby on her hip stepped out of the darkness of her smoke-filled hovel and immediately heard the rumble of the numerous hoofbeats. Sweeping the clearing with her eyes she caught the flashes of light off metal at the edge of the woods beyond the tilth of her garden plot, and calling an alarm, ran toward the nearest stand of trees, clutching her baby tightly. A man and another child exited the same hovel to hie in the woman's footsteps toward the trees, and perhaps a dozen others left their homes to get away from the oncoming death. Adults shrieked and children wailed as they fled in terror.

The last to leave the clutch of wee thatch-roofed, mud and stick huts saw the raiders coming in two separate columns, merging together as they charged toward the village. Knowing there was no escaping such a horde, they ran on anyway, to die with their own. Reaching the tree line, they turned their great round eyes toward their crude huts to watch the end of the world approach.

But the advance had stopped, and instead the soldiers were engaged in a noisy combat amongst themselves. A writhing mass of men and mounts were flailing at each other with vicious and noisy intensity, and as far away as the people in the woods were, they could see the bloody results as men fell to earth to be trampled by their fellows.

What madness was this, an army falling upon itself in such a deadly struggle? Yet the battle raged before the villagers' incredulous witness until only the victors remained standing. It was then that they saw the rampant lion flag of the Scots king come to the fore and, with a handful of men, move away toward the direction from which the second column of riders had come. Those remaining behind picked through the dead and wounded, taking what they would from the defeated foe.

. .

"He killed them all! All!" stormed King Edward.

"Save the six that limped in here this morn," answered Sir Robert de Clifford, nodding slightly in agreement.

"Who gave permission for them to go plunderin'?" barked Edward, scowling blackly.

"'Twas the Welsh... mostly," answered Clifford, "They do as they get the notion to do. Impossible to teach them discipline, it seems."

The king slumped into a chair. He and his staff occupied Shieldhill, an amply supplied manor house in the region of Biggar, while his camped army encircled the grounds of the house and the village it abutted.

"Damn them!" the king hissed. "Did they not yet know that Brus awaits such forays? It is not that they were the first to suffer such slaughter!"

"Sire, these oafs pride themselves upon their prowess at arms, and if they thought of it at all, no doubt held that the Brus and his band would not dare face them. Not an uncommon error in men of their ilk, without officers of worth to lead them."

Edward glowered at Clifford, but said nothing to contradict the statement. After a moment's thought, he offered, "Fear for his own hide keeps the damned coward from comin' to do battle like a true knight, instead of attackin' without warnin'!" Propping his head atop his fist as it rested on the arm of the chair, he looked out over his stagnating army.

"Fear... perhaps," replied Sir John Seagrave, a large man who had instigated the failed attack on Rosslyn Castle some seven years earlier against a band of Scots led by Sir William Wallace, Lord John "The Red" Comyn, Sir Henry Sinclair, and Sir Simon Fraser. He continued, an edge of doubt in his voice, "More likely, Sire… it is merely what he has chosen to do."

"He'll not *have* a choice once we meet up with John Macdougall and Richard de Burgh, come from Ireland with *their* armies," proclaimed the king confidently. "*Then* we'll flush them from the underbrush and into the open!" He grabbed at the air with one hand, catching the Brus in absentia.

Clifford sighed deeply. *He can run circles around the likes of us,* he thought.

"Send out more spies!" ordered Edward, his temper flaring, "I want to be rid of that baseborn coward before I leave this godforsaken land!"

"Why not send envoys under a banner of truce to find Brus and invite him to battle here at Biggar where we hold the high ground?" offered Sir Henry de Percy.

"*You*, who were run, huddled and whimperin' in the bottom of an oxcart, from the Brus' own Turnberry Castle … you *want* the Brus to come here?" chided Clifford.

"Better that, than hiein' south as you did when you heard Black Douglas was lurkin' in Douglasdale," gainsaid Percy. "Did ye fear his father's ghost was guidin' the young whoreson's hands for your throat?"

"Cease this bickerin'!" shouted the king, standing and throwing his hands in the air.

The lesser men glared at one another but none went against his king and spoke.

"I shall ask the Earl of Cornwall his thoughts. He's far more strongly witted than the three of you together!" announced the king, and he held his head high and walked from the solar. The knights bowed appropriately at his exit.

"Cornwall! May he rot in hell! Will we never be rid of that goddamned Piers Gaveston?" wailed Seagrave once the king was beyond earshot.

The silence that lay like a barren field between them foretold their answer.

Henry Symonds

ÒECEMBER 9ch 1310
CASCLE BERWICK

It was dank and cold and an almost constant barrage of snow showers spat icy barbs into the faces of all who ventured forth, yet spies were plentiful over the whole of Lanarkshire. King Edward's spies would locate the Scots and report back to their liege, and King Robert's spies would guide him to strike the occasional knot of English that had broken away from the main army for plunder or on orders of King Edward.

More than once marauding English troops found themselves against the well-honed blades of Robert's mounted soldiery, yet when they searched for him and his army, they were not to be found. Edward and his English and Welsh forces constantly combed the fields and forests around Biggar.

Well over a year since March 1309, when Robert de Brus presided over his first Parliament, and almost two years since the Earl of Ross came willingly to his peace, the King of Scots was at last making solid gains toward getting the realm pulled together under his banner. He would have easily done so had it not been for King Edward's constant abrasion to that cause.

In late summer, with an army of six hundred knights and three thousand infantry scraped from anywhere he could manage, the English monarch had once again invaded Scotland. Only four hundred of his army were of English origin, the remainder mostly Welsh. Three English earls followed their king into Scotland in this invasion: Gloucester, Warenne, and Edward's constant companion, Piers Gaveston, Earl of Cornwall, who was but recently brought back from his temporary exile in Ireland. The veteran barons Sir John Seagraves, Sir John Saint John, Sir Robert de Clifford, and Sir Henry de Percy also followed.

King Robert, however, had an entirely different war in mind than did the English monarch.

Realizing at last that the Brus was not going to engage him in a pitched battle, Edward left Biggar within a fortnight. Attempting to reduce Robert's ability to starve out those small pockets of support in the royal castles still stubbornly held by the English in Scotland, he first took supplies to Castle Bothwell. By doing so, he was also enticing Robert to challenge him along the way, to no avail.

Edward then led his army to Renfrew, situated on an estuary near the western coast, where he awaited the arrival of John Macdougall, Lord of Lorn, and King Robert's father-in-law, Richard "The Red" de Burgh, Earl of Ulster. Both had thus far failed to deliver promised men and supplies to the English monarch, and this time was no exception. After a week of waiting, he turned his army back to Berwick on the eastern coast. Utilizing a route designed day-by-day from the constant reports of his many spies, he arrived in Berwick at the end of November. By then his three thousand infantry's time of feudal service to him had elapsed, and the conscripts thus left Scotland on foot and made their way home to diverse places in England.

The Scots' constant attacks on unsuspecting groups of Edward's army had taken a toll of almost five hundred dead. His hit-and-hide tactics were nearly always successful and provided a regular pinprick to Edward's wit and spirit, and most of all, his pride.

Robert had not been found except where he had not been expected.

• •

"The Scots 'king' will be lookin' for a truce," said Piers Gaveston, thoughtfully playing with a sword, tossing it from hand to hand, up and down, swinging it as in battle. Edward watched lustfully, fascinated with the graceful movements of Gaveston's still youthful form.

"You have a notion?" he asked, rotating his head on the upturned pillow to follow the movements of his companion.

"A plot, actually," replied Gaveston, placing the sword handle against his crotch suggestively. Its effect was not lost on Edward.

"I have the most beautiful necklace for you, Dear Brother," bribed the king teasingly.

"Is it as pretty as the one you gave me that came to you with your

French whore?... pardon, I meant 'queen'."

Edward giggled. "Oh, it has many more jewels than that trinket, I dare say," described the king. He took his index finger and, leaning far out of the bed, drew a pretend necklace on Piers' hairy chest, and traced the ripples in his muscles to his navel. Then he tried to grab the sword, but Piers' reflexes were far too quick. He had the blade by its handle instantly and swung it lightly away, feigning to cut Edward's hand, but instead he smiled. He knew he was by far the superior swordsman, but it pleased him to prove it again. He sat on the edge of the bed and used the silk coverlet to wipe the sweat from his face.

"My 'notion' is this. When Brus comes to parlee," explained Piers throwing the sword to the flagstone floor with a resounding clang and suddenly rolling up on knees and hands to be atop the king, "we'll spring our trap and bring him back to Berwick!"

"Break our word?" Edward feigned being startled at the proposition. "You want to catch Brus?"

Edward again giggled. "I ain't goin' back to London without having the son of a whore in my pocket." He reached up and grabbed Gaveston's by the long locks at the back of his neck, drawing him down to kiss him hungrily on the mouth.

• •

Within three days, Robert had granted a request for a meeting to take place on the seventeenth of December at Saint Michael's Kirk in Linlithgow. Its purpose, he was told, was for consideration of the cessation of warring for the winter, citing a chance for the English to leave Scotland without being attacked. However, Robert knew that, in truth, Edward needed to withdraw to the south due to a lack of fodder for his horses and the loss of his feudal infantry.

He also knew that Saint Michael's was attached to a large earth and wood fortress, then being used as a storehouse and sometimes residence of the English king while he was on campaign in the vicinity.

Suspicion gnawed at Robert's finely honed distrust of Edward, and he sent James Douglas and Henry Symonds to Linlithgow to see the disposition of the area around the kirk. Soon the two spies wandered the narrow streets of Linlithgow as ordinary folk looking for their next meal, something that was nearer to the truth than either of them wanted to dwell upon.

As they bargained with an old hag for a small loaf of bread, they found the English on whom they had come to spy.

"Make way for the king's men!" shouted the gruff voice of one accustomed to giving orders to thick heads. Like those around them, the spies did their best to move quickly to the side of the muddy track as forty English soldiers made their way through the crowd in the marketplace and headed straightaway for the road to Saint Michael's Kirk.

Symonds placed a half-penny in the withered hand of the old woman and took a small round loaf from among her wares. It was nicely browned and crusty, and as his mouth began to water he broke the bread in two, handing Douglas his share.

"More a'comin' yonder," said Douglas quietly, and he nodded in the direction of Robert de Clifford and Henry de Percy just emerging on horseback from a cross street. The two Scots kept their heads down, eating from their purchase and not wanting to be noticed, all the while watching as the two nobles' horses pushed their way through the crowds, bumping any who dared make way too slowly.

Then trumpets began to blare and English soldiers pushed the people farther from the main part of the street.

"Must be their king," said Symonds with a sneer. He washed down his bread with a swallow of whisky from a skin he carried in his kit. He offered the same to Douglas, but he refused, watching instead to see who qualified for such a display.

"Nae, 'tain't Edward," said Douglas as he saw coming toward him, in the finest clothing he had ever seen in his life, the cocky Piers Gaveston. Arrow straight he sat, his horse's trappings riffling across the great beast's broad chest and down its sides as Gaveston's cloak flowed gracefully around him. He was the image of a noble king.

Symonds whistled softly. "Wonder who he is, the fancy one."

"That be the Earl of Cornwall ... Robert wants no harm to come to him... e'er!"

"Why?"

"King's orders," said Douglas, leaving Symonds wondering why this lavishly costumed English earl was different than any other.

After watching the pomp and power trail off Symonds observed, "'Ppears they're headin' for the kirk." He took one more swig from the skin before returning it to its hiding place in his kit.

"Aye. It does." He paused a moment and asked, "But why are they goin' to the kirk today? Robert won't be here until tomorrow, soonest."

"Maybe doin' the same thing we are, havin' a look about," Symonds suggested.

"Maybe," Douglas answered. "But why so many? There's only two of us. Why all the soldiers, and the earls and knights?" He turned to look at Symonds as if awaiting an answer, but Symonds merely shrugged his shoulders, at a loss for a reason.

"I'm thinkin' our wily king was right. He knew somethin's rotten about this 'parlee', and you and I are goin' to find out what 'tis that's a'stinkin'." Douglas started off through the mud and mire toward the kirk, and Symonds fell in line behind him.

• •

As they drew within sight of the kirk the pair heard a smith at work, or maybe more than one. Whoever it was working the smithy kept up a steady rhythm with his hammer, and the sound of it grew louder the nearer they were to the kirk. The two Scots decided to skirt around the area at a good distance, to see if the smithy was actually there.

After a half hour's walk, they had their answer, and decided they must get into the kirk, but that was impossible until after the sun set. English troops posted at intervals on the road and more within the kirk made it so. So they wrapped themselves in their heavy cloaks, and waited.

The spies made not a sound, nor did they speak even in a quiet voice until "The Black" Douglas reached inside the folds of his kilt and drew out part of the bread they had purchased from the hag.

"Where did ye get that?" whispered Symonds.

"Ye bought it yerself this morn," replied Douglas, biting down hard on the stale crust.

"Are ye goin' to eat the whole of it?" demanded Symonds, his belly feeling especially empty now that Douglas had food.

"Did ye not eat yers?"

"Aye, but..."

"And did ye not divide the loaf fairly between us?"

"Aye, but..."

"Then ye cannot begrudge my eatin' my share, can ye," asked Douglas rhetorically, and he took another bite. Symonds pulled up his hood and sat dourly, fairly tasting each morsel that crossed Douglas' tongue, until the last of the bread was chewed and swallowed. After that, they both regretted that it was gone.

It was a long, cold wait, and Douglas arose after dark, chilled and stiff, and not in a good mood. "Nearly froze to death," he grumped, stretching the stiffness out of his back and shoulders now that he could move without being seen. While they worked the soreness out of their bones, the blacksmith continued apace, his hammer ringing hard against the anvil. Now that an almost inky blackness enveloped them, they could see the light from the forge making the windows glow brighter each time the smith worked his bellows.

"Could have made a fire to ease the cold", grinned Symonds, "but our spyin' days would surely have been o'er when the English came to see who set it."

"Don't know that it makes much difference if we cannot get closer. We can't see a damn thin' from here," Douglas complained.

"You go. I hate the stink of English," lamented Symonds with a sour face.

"Smelt yerself of late?" grinned Douglas, though his face could barely be seen in the faint light from the English torches around the kirk.

"Let's go," groused Symonds.

The two crept silently from their sanctuary and worked their way through the shadows to get closer to the kirk wherein the meeting would be held on the morrow. Here and there they found themselves wading through wispy curls of mist, risen off the nearby loch, but not heavily enough to hide the Scots from English view. Suddenly, Douglas held out his arm to stay Symonds' movement, and both froze. No more than ten yards ahead were English soldiers carrying something long and heavy into the kirk. Slowly the spies sank noiselessly to the ground and remained still.

"These be the last of 'em," said one to the soldier at the door as they passed through into the building's interior.

"The last of what?" whispered Douglas to himself in frustration.

"Couldn't see," responded Symonds, just as softly.

Drawing short swords from their sheaths and tucking them close under their cloaks, their hoods pulled over their heads, the Scots silently darted their way from place to place, edging ever closer to the humble stone structure. At last they were close enough for "The Black" Douglas to peer through a window while Symonds kept watch.

Straining to see through the hand-sized, heavily rippled glass panes, he could barely make out the actions of those inside, and what he saw confounded him at first. There in the middle of the nave was the smith, pounding a long, flat strip of iron against his anvil... no, he was punching a hole in the iron as might be used to attach something to the bar, or the bar to something. As he watched the smith, his eyes unscrambled the blurry forms he could almost make out and he whispered, "May God damn 'em all to hell!"

"What is it?" Symonds whispered in return.

"We must go and warn the king!"

"What is it?" Symonds insisted.

"We must leave this place now!" Douglas turned away from the window, but Symonds grabbed his sleeve and signaled him to be quiet. For a long moment, both men stood immobile and Douglas glanced around until he sighted two English soldiers lighting a fire alongside the road. He hissed, "Ach! If we had only left moments ago! Move 'round the corner of the building!" They crouched below the level of the mullioned window and crept around the corner.

Once there, the two sat on their heels against the wall of the kirk and breathed a bit easier, but they were still trapped. Symonds peeked back around the corner to see if they had been noticed, but apparently they hadn't. The fire builders were squatting, too, warming their hands before their growing flame.

Symonds whispered. "There's only two of 'em. We can handle them without any trouble."

"Aye, but what about their friends in the kirk?"

"Well, fog's risin'. We could wait 'til it's thick enough to cover us."

Douglas shook his head. "In the mornin' Robert will be comin' and the 'parlee' is naught but a trap. We cannot wait."

While Symonds kept a watch on the pair at the fire, his companion searched about for an escape route. In a few moments he returned with no solution. They were surrounded by Englishmen. Suddenly, Douglas asked, "Do ye yet have yer skin of spirits?" Symonds nodded. "Is there anythin' in it?" queried Douglas.

"'Bout half full," Symonds replied.

"Let me have it!"

"What, the whole thin'?" Symonds grew a bit testy. Douglas shushed him.

"That's what will get us out o' here if my plan works."

"What plan?" Symonds asked, all the time reaching for his whisky cache, and handing it to Douglas.

"Can ye sing, Henry?" Douglas broke into a wide grin as he pulled the stopper from the skin and poured some whisky into the palm of his hand.

Moments later two obviously intoxicated men appeared on the road and staggered toward the English soldiers by the fire. To any who witnessed their stumbling gait and heard their singing the disheveled pair appeared intoxicated, and the English guards accepted their initial observations, especially when they caught the strong smell of spirits on the men.

"Hold on, Seamus," said the first guard as they started to pass him. "Where did ye come from?"

"My mother's womb, sir," slurred Douglas with a puzzled frown and Symonds broke into laughter. "What?" Douglas looked to the giggling Symonds, "so I did. What d'ye think?!"

"No, no, no, no, no," Symonds shook his head. "The lad means, how did we get here!" Pointing to his feet, he ostensibly lost his balance and fell to the ground, followed by much struggling to get up again.

"Oh, well, I came by shanks mare, o' course!" Douglas directed the answer to the burly Englishman, who roughly grabbed the much lighter Douglas by the front of his surcoat and slapped him hard across the face. Douglas shrunk back as if helpless and put his hands up to his head protectively, but the guard held fast to his clothing.

"Pay attention, lackwit!" shouted the guard. "Where were ye before ye walked here!?" Douglas acted as if he were trying to think. The guard hauled back as if to strike him again, but Douglas yelled and fell to his knees.

"I – I don't know, Sir!" he wailed. "Please don't hit me again, Sir, I can't remember!" He groveled and moaned at the man's feet as if he were completely at the guard's mercy.

"Look here!" the guard gloated to his companion, who was yet standing by the fire. "This is the kind of losels we're up against. Both of 'em fit only to wallow in the dirt with swine!" He laughed derisively, then put his foot on Douglas' shoulder and pushed the Scot over to lie flat.

Symonds had at last made it lurchingly to his feet, deciding that the discussion had reached the point at which a dram of whisky was called for. Taking the small skin from under his cloak, he removed the cork and started to take a swig when the guard stepped over and seized it from the man he saw as a drunken Scot. Smelling the contents, the guard smiled, quickly deciding that the fiery liquid would be just the thing to warm his belly while he stood guard on this icy black night, and he took a hearty draught from the skin. It burned all the way down, and made him feel warmer in the process. He signaled his cohort to join him.

"There's but one thing good about this bunch of half-witted savages; they do make fine, strong spirits," he said, handing the skin to his mate. As the second guard filled his gullet with Symonds' whisky, the first chased the two Scots away, giving Symonds a kick as he fled with Douglas, still reeling and pitching.

Once they cleared the area of danger, they took off trotting toward the place they expected the Scots king to be waiting on the western side of the town. It was a good run for the two of them, and Symonds got winded after about three miles. He started to hold his side and limp along.

"Another mile or so, Henry... we'll be there," Douglas gasped. By the time they reached the encampment, neither man could talk except in one and two word bursts. The night pickets stopped them, but one man recognized the Douglas and showed him directly to Robert, while Symonds laid himself down and tried to recover his wind.

Arriving at Robert's tent Douglas thought to wake his friend with a touch to his shoulder but was surprised that his friend was soundly asleep and stirred not at all.

"My King," he spoke and Robert awoke with a start.

"Jamie!" he said at last, sitting up and shaking his head as if removing the last bits of sleep from his mind. "Jamie, I am glad ye're returned safely. I hope yer journey was successful.

Douglas was still breathing heavily, but could at least speak normally. "Aye, Sire, 'tis as ye thought 'twould be. The English surround the kirk and lands, and inside the kirk they are constructin' a cage of iron, large and strong enough to hold a bull. Last I saw, they were still at the task."

• •

All was ready at Saint Matthew's on the morning of the scheduled parlee. The king, having arrived earlier from nearby Linlithgow Castle, was in a mood nearing giddiness. Sitting on a cushioned chair by the window in his residence in the adjoining fortress, he waited to see Brus ride up to the small stone kirk and enter to meet, not with his king, but with his confinement and ultimate doom.

Lord Gaveston had seen to the placement of troops and the installation of the iron cell, though it was early in the hours before sunrise when the undertaking was finished to his satisfaction. He had managed only a short nap before the winter night's sky again saw the sun, but his excitement at the imminent capture of the rebel 'king' was almost more than he could bear. He would be the one to catch the Scottish fox after so many others had failed. Rather than feeling tired, he was exhilarated.

Sirs Henry de Percy and Robert de Clifford were far less so. Sitting with Gaveston and the king to await Brus' arrival under the false promise of a state of truce was tedium itself as far as they were concerned. And the more the wait lengthened, the greater the ennui.

As noon passed, the foursome grew less and less convivial, until there were times when no one spoke, and when someone did, he was answered with mere grunts if not silence. Even the midday meal could not enliven the melancholy as it became evident that their prey had escaped the snare.

Afterward, his belly full and his exhaustion pressing him downward, Piers Gaveston finally went to sleep.

By twilight, Edward, king of England, was forced to admit, at least to himself, that he had been awaiting the arrival of a will-o'-the-wisp. When that notion took hold, he abruptly stood and strode out of the room without even looking at the bows being hastily proffered by Percy and Clifford. Lord Gaveston snored peacefully on the cushioned bench.

Left alone except for Cornwall, the weary knights gathered up their paraphernalia and left as well. As they exited the sitting room, Percy said, "When the king decides the blame for the failure of this adventure, ye and I shall be the primary candidates to play the goat, Sir Robert," and they both looked back at the slumbering earl.

"I think, Sir Henry, that I shall return to my own bailiwick this night. I have urgent matters I must attend at home." And the door closed behind them.

Nigel Brus

JANUARY 6th 1311
DUNDEE

Five pilgrims had made their way through the snowy high country, skirting around Perth toward Dundee. Their clothes were sorely worn, with many layers to keep the cold winter wind and snow from their skin, and their mounts were hard-used and scrawny, but well behaved in the environment. What sparse weapons they had were hidden amongst the rags to draw no suspicion as to their identity or purpose.

The little troop came down the mountains toward the sea where the countryside was dotted with farm villages of a few simple houses, and byres surrounded by acres of fallow ground awaiting the warmth of spring to bring it back to life. On the northwest side of the town of Dundee, with its castle still in English hands and acting as the hub of English activity for the area, stood a fairly large and substantial house, compared to its neighbors, complete with glass in the windows and a heavy thatch on the roof.

"Who comes, Mother?" asked a boy of about eleven when he noticed his mother at the window and heard a muffled commotion just beyond her barred door. She hesitated but a moment before deciding the best course of action.

"Ye and Christian get in the cat-hole! Now!" she whispered harshly to make sure her son knew to obey without question.

As the boy and his sister slipped through a small hole in the wall behind a storage box, they heard a loud hammering at the front door.

They glanced at their mother, who shooed them on their way with a wave of her hand, and the boy slipped the box back over the entrance to the recess.

Christina reached through the slit in the side of her skirt and gripped the handle on the dagger strapped to her leg. She went to the door and listened.

She jumped away at the return of the hammering.

Fear at first grabbed her heart in its fist, but then anger replaced it, flushing her face and fortifying her will. She and the children were alone except for an aged farm hand and the boy who kept the stables, and she knew all might be killed by these unknown raggedy men, including her children, were they found in their hiding place. She drew her dagger and flung wide the door, ready to take on the demons of hell if need be.

The large masculine frame silhouetted against the light snowy background gave her pause at the sight of him, yet she was prepared to strike at him if he moved. Instead he spoke.

"Christina," he said in a husky voice.

"Aye?" replied she, suspicious of the tattered man before her but finding his tired voice vaguely familiar.

He pushed the hood away from his face to reveal a bearded man with auburn hair showing just a hint of gray at the temples.

She melted, "My God, Robert! Ye have lived for me to lay eyes on once more!"

"I have," he said as the four other tatterdemalions pressed to his back. "Ye havin' us in, Milady?"

"Ye are well come, Milord King, most well come!" said Christina, almost giddily.

The two children quietly peeked from their hiding hole, reluctant to emerge for fear they might yet be in danger of being killed on the spot.

Robert took two steps into the room and Christina could not contain herself any longer and reaching up, gave Robert a grand hug and kissed him on his cold, chapped lips. Robert hugged her as well, for he had missed her company for the last two years.

"It is that good to see ye, Robert!" She said a bit breathlessly. "Last time we were together was when ye were recoverin' from..." Christina suddenly realized the possible need for her nursing services and, quickly looking him in the eyes asked, "Ye aren't feelin' poorly again, My King?"

"Ne'er better, Lass," returned Robert, smiling. The others of his band bent down to step under the door's low lintel as they moved over the threshold and inside the doorway. "And ye?"

"Ne'er better," she repeated, too excited for anything more clever.

"Ye recollect Andrew?" asked the king as the squire pushed his hood back to expose his face.

"Aye," she said hugging the lad. He was a little embarrassed even though she had a comforting hug similar to one from his own mother, whom he had not seen for more than five years.

"Reckon they hain't fixin' to kill us," whispered Nigel to his sister as they peeked at the events from the pair's hiding place.

"And who are these lads?" asked Christina as the other three pushed away their hoods and stood dripping on the floor as the snow melted from their clothing.

"These are all that are left of yer high landers ye lent me," said Robert sadly.

Christina looked at each of the men and sought recognition of them. The first, she paused before saying his name, but shortly it came to mind and she smiled, "Parlan, ye have grown such a fine red beard!" The young man's face broadened out in a toothy grin. "He was just a lad when he left here," she said to Robert.

The second man had dark features and clear green eyes. "Like meadow grass in springtime," she said. "I'd know those eyes anywhere! I am so happy ye've come home, Brodie."

Finally, she gazed at the third fellow, nearly as tall as Robert, with rosy cheeks that belied his somber mien. "And this one is no doubt serious little Dirk, though not so little anymore! Ye were near seventeen years when ye left, and ye must have grown twice as fast as ye had before to get so tall!"

Then she stood back and looked at the three of them and tears filled her eyes for those who were not coming back. Still, she smiled for the three and said, "Well come to my home. Well come all of ye."

Andrew shut the door and the room was again darkened but the blow of cold winter was left outside.

"Are we to come out now, Mother?" asked Nigel from behind the box that hid the children's sanctuary.

"Oh, aye, children! Of course ye are to come out," she said, and moving the box from the mouth of the hole, motioned them to emerge. The children scrambled out and stood close by their mother's skirt, just in case. She was having none of that, and pushed them forward toward Robert, who seemed like a fearsome hulking thing to them.

"Robert, these are Nigel, just turned eleven, and Christian, almost ten. Yer children, Sire," she introduced them with obvious affection and pride.

Robert knelt on one knee to get a better look at the pair, who still wouldn't stand too close to the stranger. "Madam, ye have beautiful, strong children," was his first comment. Then he motioned to the boy to come closer, which he did after glancing at his mother for permission.

"Nigel, ye are a hardy lookin' lad. Are ye a hunter?" asked the king and the boy nodded. "What d'ye hunt around here?" Robert asked.

"Hares and pheasants, mostly," the child answered. "Sometimes I shoot at a wild shoat, but they be harder to hit, and ye must have a care that the old sow be not nearby." Robert smiled in agreement.

"While I'm here, will ye take me huntin' with ye?"

"Aye, if mother says I might," said Nigel, looking at his mother, again. She winked at him and he smiled. "Mother says it be alright."

"I shall look forward to it, then," said the king, reaching out and gently slapping the boy on the arm. He then looked to his daughter, still clinging to her mother's apron, her big eyes filled with worry.

"Will ye come here, Christian, and join yer brother that I may see ye?" Robert asked, but softer than he had spoken to the boy. She shook her head and pursed her lips as if about to cry.

"I'll nae harm ye and yer mother is right there," he coaxed. She just looked at him but didn't move. Her mother moved slightly closer to Robert and since the child would not let loose of the apron, she moved closer as well, though reluctantly.

"Christian is a pretty name for a pretty girl like ye, don't ye think?" The child still wouldn't speak. "Are ye afeared of me, Lass?" he prodded. That got a silent nod in reply.

Then the child spoke with no prodding. "Ye don't look like a king," she said in her small voice.

"What does a king look like?"

She stared at him intently. "A king would nae wear raggedy clothes like yers," she said hesitantly, as if afraid he might be angry.

"Oh, but he might, if he were tryin' to travel about and not be seen," said the king.

"Why would a king not want to be seen?" she asked. "He is the king!"

"Aye, he is the king, but some would have another man be king. So, to be safe, the king sometimes travels in raggedy clothes." Robert smiled, but the girl was still not satisfied.

"Ye mean, they might hurt the king?"

"Some might."

The child's face grew very sad. "But I don't want you to be hurt," she said, and chin quivering, she moved into his arms and hugged him around the neck as large tears formed in her eyes, and her mother's.

Nigel yet stood back as his father hugged Christian for a long while.

Later, after four chickens were killed, dressed, and roasted, they all gathered around the table for a fine supper, including the old man and the stable boy.

"Any one of us would have kilt ten English for a single bird as fine as this at Slioch," remarked Andrew holding a joint up in front of him.

"I could have kilt ten on our way here, for this fine meal," gainsaid Parlan. They all laughed at the observation.

When supper was over and Christina had seen to the comfort of the new arrivals and her children for the night, she and Robert sat quietly together, only partially lit by the fair flickering light coming from the fireplace before them. She offered a cup of mulled wine, which he accepted with thanks, and after a few sips of the warm drink, began to relax, saying little, and then nothing.

As the silence stretched longer, the moment became awkward.

"What binds yer wit so, Sire?" she asked at last. The fire was even less warm and bright than when they first sat in front of it, and the chilled darkness closed in around them

"I was just thinkin' about seein' ye…" he paused taking a deep breath, "and the bairns, once more."

"Hardly bairns any more," she replied.

"Aye, hardly," was all he said, and grew silent again.

"I heard England's Edward is here'bouts, again," she said calmly.

"We've managed to stay clear of his trail, so far."

"Do ye not want a fight!?" she asked.

"Oh, I do, but on my terms. If I meet him and his great army as he wants, we cannot win. We haven't enough men and arms to meet such a number as he commands. We will surely lose, it will all be over, and Edward will rule Scotland. But, if we continue as we are, bein' a thorn in his side that he cannot escape, he will get bored with it and we shall win… eventually."

"If yer health holds, Robert," she said, almost in a whisper.

"Edward'll not bother us for the winter, I've seen to that," he said, trying to allay her concerns. "He'll tire of his games and get back to his comforts in London soon, I'm sure."

"What d'ye mean, 'he'll not bother us for the winter'? How do ye know?"

"I've drawn his attention in another direction, and he's apt to follow any trail we lay down for him." He looked in her eyes and realized he would have to explain more thoroughly. "I sent brother Edward and a goodly portion of our men, most on horse, down to Galloway, passin' close enough to Bothwell that the English got a good whiff of 'em bein' in the neighborhood."

"Won't they attack Sir Edward and his men?"

Robert shook his head. "Nae. I next sent word to the Macdonalds to bring a number of their galleys to bear on the west coast of the Isle of Man," he continued.

"Edward is goin' to assault Man?"

"He's goin' to make the English think so. It's a feint that will force King Edward to send ships and most of his army to protect Man, leavin' Berwick all but undefended. As the English hasten to the west coast they will leave all of Lothian bare naked of his succor."

"So Edward is not actually going to do any fightin', just make Edward Plantagenet think he will."

"Aye."

"What did Edward think of that?"

"He was none too pleased at first, thinkin' it was a long bit of travelin' for no gain."

"How did ye convince him that he needed to go?"

"I told him he could take his inamorata, but that he was not to saddle her with the likes of another, but bring her home safely. She is not just another of his tarts."

"Who is she?" asked Christina.

"Remember the Earl of Atholl, John de Strathbogie?" to which Christina nodded her head, "...she's his young daughter, Isabella. Her brother, Earl David, is not pleased with Edward paying her court." He stretched his long frame out so that his feet nearly reached the waning fire before he continued, saying, "But his quarrel is with me, not Edward."

"I wish John were here with us."

There was another long awkward silence as Robert grieved for his loyal friend. Christina's hand found its way to touch his in sympathy. Then from the depths of his sorrow, he said, "I need you, Christina."

"Do ye, Robert?" she asked, and smiled. Truth be known, her heart skipped a beat at this confession.

"Aye," said Robert, his face still gravely serious. Before she could think of what to say, he continued. "I need ye to raise horses."

"Horses?" Her abrupt response was not what he anticipated, and he hastened to let her know he didn't expect her to accomplish this all on her own.

"That's why I brought yer high landers back, to help ye and do as ye bid."

"Damn ye Robert Brus!" She was obviously disappointed, but he didn't know why, and his shock was evident in his widened eyes.

"I've brought money," he added. "Ye'll not want for anythin'."

"Money!?"

"Aye! What's wrong?"

Christina suddenly realized that he had not yearned for her as she had for him. She had hoped that he had come for her, not for her horses. She longed for him to talk about something far more dear to her heart than money, or horse breeding.

"Ye've always provided our needs for money, Robert," she said with sadness in her voice.

"Ye can have whate'er ye want," pleaded Robert.

No, Robert, I cannot, she thought. It was not the way she envisioned the conversation's path, but there it was, and she had to deal with reality.

She sighed deeply, sat upright in her chair and looked at him as she said, "My high landers and their horses? Ye want me to raise those nimble-footed Arabian cross-bred horses that we brought when we came to ye in Carrick?"

"We have only four of them left, and we need more."

"Raise them? Right under the English noses?"

"The English will not be in Dundee much longer, I promise ye."

"That, My King, is well come news... I hate them lurkin' about in the neighborhood."

Christina sat back into her chair. She thought of the possibilities of the horses and said, "We have others in the high lands."

"Others?"

"Other similar lines, in the mountains... where they must be reared."

"Then it can be done?"

"Aye," she said wistfully staring off, "it can be done."

"I knew I could count on ye, Christina," Robert took her hand and kissed it.

Ye can count on me to my very last breath, she thought, but instead she said, "Come, I'll show ye to yer bed, Robert. Ye have long days ahead of ye."

Thomas, of Lancaster

CDAY 12ch 1311
bAGGERSCON CASCLE ~ eNGLAND

It was the recent death of Henry de Lacy, Earl of Lincoln and acting Keeper of the Realm, that suddenly turned King Edward's world upside down. Henry's mild manners and likability kept the lid, though precariously placed, atop the boiling pot created by the king's refusal to forsake his favorite, Piers Gaveston.

The Lords Ordainers, powerful magnates formed to limit the powers of the monarchy, had for the time being kept civil war from breaking down the whole of the government. They continually badgered Edward for his dogged tenacity in holding his "dear friend" close to his person no matter how insulting and abrasive Sir Piers Gaveston continued to be toward them.

The king's dawdling at Berwick, ostensibly to bring war against Scotland after his army had dissipated and Percy and Clifford had left for the south, was primarily a simple ruse to keep some distance between the Ordainers and Gaveston.

However, the fortunes of Thomas, Earl of Lancaster, turned quite propitiously at Lincoln's death. Married to Lincoln's daughter, he acquired both of Lincoln's earldoms in right of his wife. Added to his previously existing three, this made Thomas of Lancaster the most powerful man in the realm, but for King Edward.

As was Edward, Thomas was a grandson of Henry III. At thirty-five he had been an earl since the death of his own father some fourteen years earlier. Rather tall and muscular, he was also devious to the bone, and those who realized it too late were soon cut down by his scythe of politically ambitious deception.

Thomas was required to pay homage to his royal cousin for the new earldoms and so, with a retinue of a hundred knights and numerous men-at-arms, he began his journey to accomplish that formality.

Refusing to kneel to the king on Scottish soil, Thomas threatened to take the lands without paying homage if the king, ensconced in the castle at Berwick, did not travel the several miles down the coast to Haggerston Castle in England, where the ceremony would take place. The king at first refused, but a man commanding five earldoms was difficult to rebuff.

Thus, on the appointed day, Edward and Piers sallied forth as grandly as their sparse wartime resources would allow. Though the youthful Earl of Gloucester and his retinue accompanied them as well, the total of their household knights and squires were no match for Lancaster's accumulated military mass.

Upon his arrival, the king dismounted and strode toward Thomas, already standing in front of his destrier with his guards close. He cursorily bowed as the king approached.

"You caught the Brus as yet?" he asked of Edward, fully knowing the answer.

Their entourages followed closely in their wake as the king and Lancaster, side-by-side, entered the tower castle of Haggerston.

"A coward he is!" interjected Piers, following near to Edward's heels and trying to come abreast of the king. He was hampered in the attempt by Lord Thomas' orders to his close guard to do just that.

Thomas ignored Piers.

"'Tis as the Earl of Cornwall says," agreed Edward, trying to put a likable edge on Pier's attendance. "Brus refused to meet us and do battle, but struck from hiding."

Thomas smiled knowing Edward's abject failure was embarrassing to him.

"Even so, our forces repelled him at Man," lied Edward, attempting to reinforce his position. "Brus is *finished* in Scotland!"

"Excellent news, My Liege. Then what earldoms in the realm of Scotland do you have in mind for me?" asked Thomas, calling the king's bluff.

"Five *English* earldoms should be quite enough for you, Cousin," replied Edward with bantered ease. "Should you have more you might have designs on my crown."

"And be subject to the Ordainers?" gainsaid Thomas, "I envy you *not* your station, Sire."

"But, you are among the Ordainers, Milord," reminded Piers from behind.

Thomas snarled, "Can you not keep your lapdog muzzled, Your Majesty?"

The king smiled meekly but did not answer.

Everyone took their places in the great hall as Thomas bent his knee to Edward, droning by rote the words that officially turned the earldoms of Lincoln and Salisbury over to him.

Edward nodded and Thomas rose to his feet.

Thomas reached out to Edward and embraced him, kissing him on both cheeks. Piers, standing to the left of Edward, prepared for similar treatment but received a cold, disdainful glare instead.

"You must kiss brother Piers as well, Milord," chided the king.

The newly pronounced Earl of Lincoln and Salisbury stood tall with his eyes darting from Edward to Piers. He was not unaware of his unique strength. His hand rested on the pommel of his sword, and he said, "My King, at best he is Lord of Cornwall by your decree… not *my* brother, not *my* lover, and certainly not one that *I* care for in the least."

The tension in the hall raised the hairs on the backs of the necks of many standing within earshot of their lieges.

"Tell him, Edward, that you are the king and he *must* do as you bade him!" Piers insisted angrily.

Edward opened his mouth to speak to Thomas, but noticing the man's fingers dancing on the hilt of his sword, he found the words chose not to leave his throat. Instead, desiring not to start something he might regret, he whispered into Gaveston's ear.

Gaveston's eyes widened as they darted toward Thomas. "God in Heaven! Will we never be rid of his kind!?" he bellowed that all might hear.

Edward glared at Piers in disapproval.

Turning away, Thomas coughed to hide a cunning smile. He had pricked a wound that would fester to his advantage and he knew it.

He turned back and bowed deeply. "Please accept my regrets, Majesty, but I am constrained to repair to London, forthwith," he deliberately fawned.

Taken aback at the abruptness of the man and his lack of civilities in not providing a customary celebratory meal, Edward frowned, saying, "No feast, Milord?"

"Much to my regret, no, Sire. Alas, but my added estates' business forbids my tarrying longer."

Edward raised his hand with his index finger upright indicating another element to the conversation. "I am appointing Gilbert de Clare my new Keeper of the Realm," he announced.

"Young Gloucester?" replied Thomas with mild surprise. "An excellent choice, My King! Of course, he is very young, but... an excellent choice," he added obsequiously.

"May he travel to London under your protection, Milord?"

Thomas again bowed in servitude.

"Make him honor *me*, my Brother, I beg you," insisted Piers in Edward's ear.

"Shut your mouth, Piers!" replied Edward sternly under his breath. Disappointed and incensed, Gaveston flushed with anger.

"Ye will rue this moment," he vowed to Edward.

The embarrassed king again smiled weakly at the Earl of Lancaster and tried to ignore his peevish paramour altogether, at least for the time being, for he knew the temperament of the newly empowered earl and certainly did not want to tangle with him on this occasion. He would make the affront to Gaveston's pride go away by gifting him some bauble or elegant piece of clothing.

• •

Edward was forced to hold parliament on the sixteenth of August, and so made his dreaded sojourn to London at the end of July. Fearing that Gaveston's insolence with his peers was building resentment and anger among them to the point that he could be in mortal danger, the king hid the Earl of Cornwall in the castle at Bamburgh and promised to send for him as soon as he could assure his safe return.

CDARCh 7ch 1312
york, england

Second only to London in size and in its importance to the wellbeing of England, York was adopted by William the Conqueror as his northern center of government. There he erected wooden motte and bailey castles of the Norman style, one on the southern side of the River Ouse atop Baille Hill, and one on the opposite shore. The castles, like the town itself, were subjected to the recurrent uprisings against the Normans, followed by William's terrible revenge, the "Harrying of the North". He not only retook the town, but for two years ravaged the roundabout lands, villages, and farms so thoroughly that two decades later, in the Domesday Book, the stretch between York and Durham was said to be "wasteland".

Some of it had not regained its total population hundreds of years later.

The wooden castle on the northern side of the river was long gone, replaced by the Great Tower of stone in a generally round shape displaying four lobes of the outer walls atop the site's high mound. Within the center of the quatrefoil was an open court that offered access to every side and remained constantly busy with the inmates of noble and common blood alike.

Strong and powerful walls encircled the entire core of the town, entered only via one of its massive gates, the grandest of which was Micklegate Bar on the south wall.

King Edward and Piers Gaveston had been holed up in the luxurious Great Tower since the eighteenth of January, when they arrived by boat with a small accompaniment of men-at-arms. The Ordainers, fueled by Thomas of Lancaster's hatred for Piers, were on the brink of civil war in England because of Edward's refusal to banish Gaveston from the kingdom and strip him of his title. The pair had come to York to raise an army far from the epicenter of the Ordainers' influence.

"You, little king, *must* do *something!*" Gaveston was livid. He paced the parameters of the large solar like a caged animal.

"But here we are together, Dear Brother," hopefully replied the king.

"Reckon this to be... together?" whined the earl, kicking the substantial chair in which Edward sat while watching Gaveston continue to encircle him. Edward steadied himself and wondered what more it would take to satisfy his beloved.

"I like bein' together at *Westminster!* I like bein' together at *London*

Tower! I like bein' together… when you are not whipped by that goddamned Lancaster! I like bein' *KING*!" screamed Piers, his nerves frayed to breaking. "That's what I goddamned well like… not this hidin' out in the *wilderness*!"

"Come, Dear Earl, one hardly would think of York as the 'wilderness'," replied the king.

"Where is the gaiety? Where are the barons and earls kissing our toes and groveling for more lands and power? Where? Where, I ask? Certainly not *here*," he said waving his arms across an imagined vista.

"Brother… Piers… we are waiting here for our armies to arrive… our missives to be answered. These things take time, that's all. Now, while there is nothing more we can do, shall we retire for play?" asked Edward attempting to assuage his lover's ill temper and end his tirade.

"You'll *not* get my affections 'til you again make us king!" countered Piers.

Edward sighed knowing he would have to cast Piers to "the wolves"… the Ordainers… in order to reassert himself as King of England. *Perhaps there is another way,* he mused, but his thoughts were interrupted by his companion.

Piers suddenly strode to the door to the solar, unbolted the lock and lifted the latch, then dramatically turned to announce in his most spiteful tone, "I shall have another tonight," adding sarcastically, "My Brother!"

"I have done nothing to drive you away, My Earl" pleaded Edward.

"Ah, but by your inaction you have done exactly that," he sneered.

"Brother!" shouted Edward shrilly as he stood to try and stop him from exiting.

Piers paused as a particularly disdainful thought passed his mind. Turning to face the king, he all but whispered, "I shall pick the prettiest man in the whole of the castle to bed this night!"

Edward shivered at the thought, just as Piers had anticipated and he smiled cunningly.

"I care not a jot," feigned Edward.

Piers knew better but thought to drive the point deeper, saying, "Perhaps, I will…" started Piers, accompanied with a grand flourish, "go to London and bed your queen."

"Hah!" the king was relieved, now knowing Piers was but baiting him. "Oh, Dear Brother, I would give the wench to you if it so pleased you," replied Edward merrily.

"You do not believe me?" Gaveston asked in anger, thinking the king mocked him.

Edward was stunned, not knowing how to play the conversation to his advantage.

"You *shall not* hold me prisoner!" shouted Piers puffing his anger more.

"… prisoner?" Edward did not understand the use of the term.

"Not in London, are you?"

"I am trying to keep you alive, Dearest One!"

"Then let us return to the Tower where we can again be *king!*" begged Piers.

"I tell you, I cannot protect you there, My Sweet," coddled Edward.

"You cannot protect me *anywhere* because you will *not* be ruthless with your *enemies!*" antagonized Piers, loudly.

"You think I would not do anything to keep you, of all people in this whole world, safe from death?" asked Edward, hands swinging wide to his sides showing the extent to which he was willing to spread his dwindling power.

Piers turned and placed his hand on the handle of the large door to illustrate his intention to leave and carry out his threats.

"Piers… Don't go!" implored the king.

Piers smiled and started to open the door.

"I have sent to London for Bishop Lamberton," Edward hastened to add.

"Lamberton?" said Piers wrinkling his nose in curiosity. "That ancient Scot clergyman you've been keepin' in the donjon?"

Edward nodded, again hopeful.

"And of what value…." Piers began again. "Will he pray the hateful Ordainers to hell?"

"I am sending him to Brus," bragged Edward, thinking that he had made a wise decision; his paramour had turned from the door.

Piers laughed aloud.

"You mock me, Lord Gaveston?!"

"No, My King," replied Piers smirking. "While he's at it, might as well have him pray Brus to hell, too!"

"I am offering Brus exactly what he has been wanting, in return for your safety," returned Edward.

Piers paused, his eyes wide. "For *my safety?*" he groped for more descriptive words, but none were forthcoming. "You would send me to that dreary, godforsaken Scotland… for *my safety!*?"

"Yes, Brother, you will see," explained Edward, "all will be… be…"

"Gone!?" thundered Piers.

Edward sighed. "I can no longer *protect* you! You have flung your arse in the faces of the Ordainers and returned to me too many times."

"It is your *duty* to protect me!" insisted the earl.

"The more I protect you, the less power I have!" gainsaid Edward in an uncharacteristic flash of verbalized insight.

"You but blame me for your own lack of will! Were you half the king your father was, the so-called 'Ordainers' would be looking down upon London Bridge from the *pikes* holdin' their heads! *He* knew how to deal with his enemies! But *you* haven't the stomach for takin' heads, have you?" He looked at Edward's face, agape, drained of all its color. He had known an unflattering comparison between the king and his father was a killing blow. "You will *never* feel my warm body against your cold clammy one... ever again!" hissed Piers as he stormed from the solar.

Edward sighed and stared a long while at the backside of the door, somehow still wanting... even expecting, Piers to suddenly return with a smile saying all was well in his world. But it didn't happen.

Edward Plantagenet, king of England, took to his bed alone and cried bitterly.

William Lamberton,
Bishop of Saint Andrew's

march 10th 1312
york, england

In three days, Bishop William Lamberton, having been escorted from London, arrived at the king's residence. He was grateful for his release from the prison cell in which he had been held since the spring of 1306... even before the devastating battle at Methven. His pale, drawn face mirrored the lost time and he appeared aged far beyond his mid-life years. He was a willing pawn in Edward's hands for he wanted not to return to his spartan, dank hole.

"How may I serve My King," said Lamberton with a gravely voice.

"Take this to Robert Brus," ordered Edward tersely as he placed a sealed document into the bishop's hand.

"The Brus still lives, Milord?!" Lamberton asked, surprised.

"He is at Castle Ayr," said Edward, glancing into the shadows of the great hall for a glimpse of a lurking Gaveston.

"Aye, My King," said Lamberton bowing low.

"You must convince him that it would be most beneficial for him to agree," pressed Edward. He held his head high, as if everything around him stank and he was trying to rise above it all. "A contingent of knights and followers will accompany Your Grace to see that your mission is accomplished."

Lamberton again bowed his aching back low. "Aye, My King."

• •

Five days into Scotland, the missionaries were suddenly, almost eerily, surrounded by two dozen Scottish warriors on horseback.

"Who be these spies?" questioned James Douglas.

"Men of King Edward," answered the captain of the contingent's soldiery as the knights sat astride their mounts unflinching. "Though we be not spies. The white flag of truce goes before us, Sir James."

When he called him by name, The Douglas realized he knew this Englishman from prior times. The voice was familiar, but he could not place it immediately. That did not stop his verbal assault on the trespassers. He sniggered and jibed, "Generally, ye dog-tailed whoresons are a mite tougher to catch than this," at which his men laughed openly. He obviously wanted a blood-letting at this encounter, and the English captain was of a mind to grant one when a gravely voice spoke up.

"We bear a missive for the Brus, young Douglas," interjected Lamberton, pulling the hood back from around his head.

"Milord Bishop?!" said Douglas with a great deal of amazement.

"Aye, 'tis, Jamie lad," croaked the cleric.

Douglas walked his mount to the side of Lamberton, looking at him hard, studying his changed face and his stooped condition.

"Ye know me not?" asked Lamberton.

Douglas smiled. "How could I not know the man for whom I was a squire?"

Lamberton returned the smile.

"Tell me, Lord Bishop," asked James Douglas, turning his rowdy horse toward the opposite direction, "Do ye condemn me to the devil for killin' yer groom when I hastily left yer service?"

"Killin' is always a poorly thing to do, my son," replied the bishop.

"He was fixed on killin' me for the takin' of my own father's destrier, Milord!" said Douglas in protest.

"Hot headed and in a hurry, killed the groom," returned Lamberton. "Too much hate and murder have I seen, and too much of sweet Scotland have I missed these past six years. I fear little stomach remains for the condemnation of any man for his actions these days. I would pray only that God help, and forgive, us all." A solemn Douglas nodded agreement, and thought a moment before taunting the English captain again.

"I see, My Bishop, that ye come to us surrounded by our enemies... How can I help your cause in our land? Would ye seek relief from yer wee escort?"

The captain and his knights quickly drew their swords, as did Douglas' men. The moment seemed to be frozen in time.

"Hold your tongue, James Douglas, or I shall teach ye some manners. Seems neither the bishop nor yer father lent them much attention when ye were a lad," the captain snarled, "and ye have great need of a proper spankin', which I can deliver with my sword here and now!"

It was then that The Black Douglas pulled the captain's name from the recesses of his mind and he blurted it out.

"Umfraville!"

"Lord Umfraville, to ye, Sir Brat!" Ingram de Umfraville hissed through gritted teeth as the ires of both men reached the boiling point.

"This will not accomplish my mission!" growled Lamberton, standing high in his stirrups. His office still commanded the soldiers' respect, and his eyes flashed in the expectation that he would get it. One by one the soldiers commenced returning blades to scabbards, though some didn't like it. Douglas and Umfraville held theirs, neither man wanting to be the first to put away his weapon.

Douglas looked at the bishop, and realized he had lost much of his robust physique during his years in the English prison. Rather than saying such, he offhandedly said, "Ye 'ppear to have lost some o' yer belly weight, Your Grace."

Lamberton returned to the seat of his saddle heavily, as if very tired. "Nothing to it, Jamie. Merely reduce your meals to one per day, and make it mostly inedible. Ye would be surprised at how quickly ye can shed a stone weight or two." Douglas set his jaw and was silent for a moment. He was far more somber when next he spoke.

"Ye said somethin' of a missive for King Robert?"

"We are told he is in Ayr," said the bishop.

Douglas answered him not but turned to Umfraville and said, "We'll take yer gillies and yer food and the bishop with the message to King Robert. None more."

"The bishop is under English protection!" growled Sir Ingram.

"That was well… when ye were in England!"

"We are still in England," provoked Umfraville, "but in the part that is in rebellion against its true king!"

Instead of rising to the provocation, Douglas stared at Umfraville and said, "No matter the name ye put to it, ye are in my bailiwick now, not yer own. The bishop is not well. He needs to rest."

"Lead the way and *we* shall accompany the bishop to where Brus is to be found!" insisted Umfraville.

"I'm not negotiatin'," said The Douglas. "As I said is how it shall be, and I'll give ye one chance to camp here and live, or fight here and die."

He couldn't hear what was being said, but one of Umfraville's lieutenants seemed to be urging that they fight.

"Before ye decide, ye had better look yonder," he said, and several in the English ranks looked across the field in the way he pointed. There waited more of Douglas' command. "Ye see my twenty-three to yer … not so many," said Douglas.

Umfraville surveyed the reserve group and realized that he and his men were fortunate in that they yet lived. It was written on his demeanor that the negotiations were over.

"Ye'll be findin' yer own food for the stay," said Douglas.

"Ten days," said Umfraville firmly.

"We'll be back when we get back, and we'll be takin' our sweet ol' time gettin' to where we're goin'... while eatin' yer victuals, sleepin' with yer cook women..." chided the grinning Douglas. With a quick nudge against his horse's shoulder, he spun around and at a trot led the column west.

The captain glared at the Scots as they departed, but sheathed his sword without having to admit verbally that the Scots got the upper hand.

• •

"William Lamberton?" asked Robert glancing around the large great hall of castle Ayr looking for his old friend, "The Bishop is here?"

"I have him in a wee room near the front," said James Douglas. "He bears a message from King Edward, Milord."

Robert looked Douglas in the eyes wondering what possible reason Edward would have for sending a message to him in the hands of Lamberton.

James nodded as if to say 'let's find out'.

Several passageways later Douglas swung wide the door where he had placed the old man a quarter of an hour earlier.

Lamberton arose almost feebly when he heard the door slam open and he saw King Robert standing before him.

"My Bishop," whispered Robert, "ye are alive!"

"Aye, My King, still among the quick, am I." Robert crossed immediately to the bishop and gave him a great hug. He noticed how thin the once stout man had grown but said nothing.

"They let ye out of prison to come here?" asked Robert.

"Accordin' to them, I am not imprisoned," started Lamberton, "and when I am allowed to wander the castle grounds, I believe them... but too soon am I returned to my 'apartment' and to my... reality."

"What of Robert Wishart?"

"The bishop is older than I and far more frail," he responded.

"But he lives?"

"As last I heard, My King," he replied, "They threaten me with his execution if I fail to return."

Robert's eyes brimmed with tears, for he had a special place in his heart for Wishart, the rebellious little cleric who encouraged and aided him at every step of the way in the early days of the fight.

"And ye are here at the behest of Edward, I ken," said Robert as he drew a large chair to the front of Lamberton's own and bade him to sit.

"Aye, a messenger I have become in my dotage," sighed the bishop.

"Ye are always Bishop of Saint Andrew's to me," encouraged Robert.

Lamberton smiled hoping the statement wasn't just so much patronizing.

James Douglas closed the door, leaving the room in only the light coming through the window from the diminishing and overcast day.

William Lamberton reached into his tunic and withdrew the now crumpled roll from the English monarch. "Not much of a messenger, My King," he said handing the document over.

"'Twill still read," replied Robert, breaking the seal and unrolling the parchment. He tilted the paper to catch the light and began to read.

Douglas and Lamberton were silent.

Robert finished reading and looked wearily into the grayness of the window.

What's it say, Robbie, Douglas wanted to ask, but didn't. He knew that the king would tell him what it said eventually, if he needed to know. 'Eventually' became immediately.

Robert sighed. "Edward is ready to acknowledge me as King of Scots."

"And about time, 'tis," replied Douglas, grinning broadly.

"What's he want in return?" asked the more reflective Lamberton, "I'm to convince ye that 'tis good for Scotland."

"'Tis not possible, My Bishop," said Robert.

"Will one of ye tell me the gist of it?" growled Douglas, unable to hold his curiosity longer.

"The gist," replied Robert still with his eyes fixed on the window, "is that Edward wants us to take in the Earl of Cornwall... Lord Gaveston."

"Gaveston!?"

"Aye."

"The Ordainers are determined to get Gaveston out of the way, to... destroy him one way or another. Edward hain't the army to keep them from doing anythin' they want," interjected Lamberton.

Robert gave a low whistle and asked, "Thomas of Lancaster behind this?"

"'Tis whispered so," answered Lamberton quietly.

"Then... convince me how this is good for Scotland," said Robert sighing deeply and looking at his old friend, this brave man who had spend years in prison for his sake.

"Yer queen still lives," offered the bishop.

Robert sat on the edge of his seat, eyes wide. "Where!?" he demanded.

"I wish I knew, My King," he at last said, and put one hand to his forehead and nervously massaged it as if trying to rid himself of a sudden headache.

"Then why did ye say such?!" growled Robert. "Ye know nothin'!?"

"Only rumors," whispered Lamberton. "Rumors have it that she is held under house arrest... somewhere north of London... nae more."

Robert sat back deeply into his cushioned chair and remained silent for a long moment before saying, "I thank ye for the rumor... at least I..." his voice trailed off as he realized he knew no more than he had known all along.

"Maybe we can get her back," suggested Douglas, always ready to confound the English.

"Not by this agreement," replied the king.

"We could ask," offered William.

"We cannot, my friends," said Robert sadly, "because I will not accept the offer."

"And why not?!" asked Douglas mystified. "Hain't he the one that ye ordered we should ne'er harm a hair on his head?"

"Aye, he is, but Edward will keep any bargain only as long as it suits him." To illustrate he holds up the communication brought by Lamberton. "He goes against his own liegemen to offer this pact so that Gaveston might remain with me until he can win over the Ordainers. If he manages that, anythin' he promises in here will be worthless." At that, Robert tore the missive in half. "So it is worthless, now. Besides, Lord Gaveston stirs up plenty of trouble for Edward right where he is."

"Shall I return to say ye refuse?" asked the bishop.

"Piers Gaveston has unwittingly been my best ally for many years, keeping Edward's mind occupied with whim and fancy... if it were possible to use him thus to Scotland's greater advantage by bringing him here, I would do so with no other reason."

"Don't ye reckon we could get Elizabeth out of England, and maybe yer daughter, and then send Gaveston to someplace else? Or better still, kill him?" asked Douglas.

"Edward would see through that ruse right quick."

"Then ye will not accept this offer by Edward to recognize ye as King of Scots?"

Robert threw one leg over the arm of the chair and smiled in the waning light. "Edward must already have put himself in the *most* dire of circumstances, else he would nae have made this offer, and that's for sure. If my refusal confounds him further, that is where we should leave our most dangerous enemy, don't ye think?"

Lamberton chuckled, at first, but then thought better of it. "Remember, the whelp has an unusual propensity for survivin', and e'en thrivin'."

• •

"NO!?" screamed Edward, unable to believe his ears, "What does NO mean!?"

"King Robert refuses your offer," reported William Lamberton. "It is written in his own hand, here!" He thrust the crumpled and torn parchment into Edward's hand.

"Then why did you return to me?!" ranted the monarch.

"Ye are my liege, Sire," replied the cleric bowing his head in servitude.

"Cease your prattle and be gone!" he commanded, and Lamberton left as quickly as his tired legs would carry him.

"You could have killed him... being the herald of unsuitable news," said Piers, feigning interest.

"One doesn't kill every messenger who brings bad news," replied Edward softly as he mulled over the ramifications of the answer.

"But that message *was* about me, was it not?" returned Piers.

"That is not business of yours," growled the king. "Besides, you haven't been here for days! Therefore the greater question is, where *have* you been?"

"No business of yours," said Piers smugly. "Although... if you must know... I went to London."

"London?!" Edward echoed, his eyes wide with disbelief.

"Yes, London," he said, still sporting the supercilious smile.

"That is where our enemies reside, Dolt!" argued Edward, passionately.

"And do you count your queen among them? She resides there... if I remember correctly," added Piers.

"And did you find the most beautiful man in London to bed?" carped Edward switching to the subject that was really plaguing him.

"I changed my mind," he said, and Edward felt much relieved until he added, "I chose instead to mount all of the beautiful women I found," offered Piers. "It was quite refreshing after having lain only with you, all these many months."

Edward turned near purple with rage. "You've just been on a goddamned orgy!"

"Jealous?" said Piers reaching for a nerve. "Have you never had an orgy with your queen and her lovely young handmaidens?"

"Damn you to hell, I am required to produce an heir! I *must* impregnate the goddamn wench and produce a little whoreson to sit on my throne when I am dead! It is my duty!"

"But, Majesty, you are their *king*! *Your* will is what must be done. Have you never, even on a whim, pulled one of her ladies-in-waiting into bed with the two you for a ménage a trois?" He was hanging over the king's chair, breathing heavily on his ear, trying to cause him anxiety and pain, and desire. "Not even once? Of course, four is better... or five..."

Edward jumped out of his seat and with a disgusted look shouted back, "Only the queen!" He then admitted distraughtly, "Only the queen... and quietly... in the dark... to make an heir. Just to make an heir... it held not the least bit of gaiety or pleasure for me."

"And did you speak to her in sweet tones and of... of love?" Piers asked.

"I thought only of you," was the soulful reply as plentiful tears ran down his face.

Piers smiled. "And is your French queen swollen fat with her royal lover's future pride?" he continued his taunt.

"Goddamn your skin!" shrieked Edward in agony. "Why do I put up with the likes of you!?... You who have cost me my kingdom!"

"Because without *me*!... Dear Brother, you... are... nothin'!" answered Piers, and coldly turned his back on the king.

"And you are nothin' without me!" retorted the king viciously.

There was silence between the two men until Edward said sadly, "I fear we are both right. God help me... I am roasting on two spits!"

ꝳAY 19ꞇh 1312
CASTLE SCARBOROUGH, ENGLAND

Edward and Gaveston had moved northward to Newcastle around the eighth day of April, trying desperately to raise an army to fight the barons and earls amassed against them. Neither man was willing for the earl to be exiled again, yet they continually exacerbated the Lords Ordainers' vexation by ignoring all of the lords' attempts at curbing the extravagances showered on Gaveston by Edward.

Thomas of Lancaster was the ringleader of the group opposing the king and his paramour. Almost by accident, Lancaster and the Earl of Pembroke had found the fugitives holed up at Newcastle. The elusive pair barely skinned out with their lives and, fleeing to Tynemouth, took a galley down the coast, returning to York. There, Edward had garnered a modicum of support in his attempt to get men-at-arms to fight for his cause and sent Piers, though reluctant, farther down the coast to Gaveston's castle at Scarborough in hopes of his quietly hiding out.

The fact that it stood on a dramatic stone headland projecting three hundred feet above and protruding into the North Sea, made the citadel difficult to assault, but made it also difficult from which to escape. Upon finding out from a local fisherman, his tongue loosed by a shilling of the king's coin, that Lord Gaveston was sheltered in Scarborough Castle, Lord de Valence laid siege to it.

Coordinating with de Valence, Earl Thomas encamped along the road between the town of York and Castle Scarborough and effectively stopped all communication between the king and Gaveston. Isolated, each not knowing what the other was doing for or against him, the lovers' hearts and minds filled with distrust and fear.

For nearly two weeks the strong walls of Scarborough were surrounded by troops of the Ordainers. At that point Pembroke sent a message to King Edward in York telling him that "…unless Cornwall surrenders to me immediately his safety will not be guaranteed. Furthermore, if I must sit on this molehill another week eating naught but beans and biscuits, I shall personally kill him at first sight!"

This shook the king to his core, prompting him to reply immediately with a hurriedly drafted message to Gaveston to give up, and to submit himself only to Pembroke.

Scarborough had proved to be unprepared for even this short siege, and Lord Gaveston certainly unprepared for his own surrender, but his choices lay somewhere between none and death. The provisions within the castle were completely exhausted and even he, the lord of the castle, was feeling the pinch of hunger. Thus, he succumbed to his own fear, Edward's plea, the lack of alternatives, and his empty belly.

He agreed to meet with de Valence.

"You swear to my safety 'pon your God in Heaven, Pembroke?" asked Piers, preparing to hand over his sword to the veteran warrior. They stood before the triangular barbican that was the only ingress to Scarborough Castle proper and served as foreground for the massive twin towered gatehouse and stout curtain walled fortress.

"I'd just as soon squash you here and now," threatened Pembroke, "but because I made oath that I would deliver you safe to parliament and the Ordainers if you surrendered peaceable, that I shall do."

"Then you do swear to my safety?" Piers pressed, wanting his fellow earl to guarantee his arrival, unharmed, at parliament.

"Not to you," retorted Pembroke, irritated, "but I'll see you get to London alive and unscathed."

"I prefer my castle at Wallingford," said Piers.

"What say?" replied Pembroke pressing his brows tight to his squinting eyes in displeasure.

"It is not far from London, Milord. Perhaps I would be allowed to remain there… under house arrest, of course… until I am summoned to vindicate myself before the parliament… if it would please My Lord," cajoled Piers, smiling and bowing slightly.

"Wallingford?" said Pembroke suspiciously.

"None are there save my house servants and a meaningless contingent of armed men," prattled Piers, "certainly no match for your own army."

Pembroke scratched his beard and looked at the meek and courteous but conniving man before him. *This is no fool,* he thought. *He would deceive me into appearing for him at parliament if I allow it! On the other hand, at least 'til his trial, house arrest in Wallingford might just keep him far enough away from London that his mere presence doesn't stir a riot. Besides, after parliament convicts him, he will be exiled to the continent or Ireland and trouble none of us more.*

"A'right," agreed Pembroke, "Wallingford 'tis."

Piers smiled and bowed graciously and with a grand show, handed his fancy jeweled sword to Lord Pembroke.

Pembroke inspected the elegant weapon before handing it to his closest minion with the direction, "Keep this as mine!"

"Yes, Milord," chimed the man, who handled the sword sweetly, almost reverently, as the richest booty he had seen in years, if ever.

"As the castle was poorly provisioned, I have not eaten since night afore last. Would that I might have meat and wine, Milord," said Gaveston, his belly smarting and growling from hunger.

Pembroke laughed, startling his captive.

"My Lord Pembroke, I presume you do not intend to starve me all the way to Wallingford!"

"Indeed not, Cornwall," Pembroke chuckled, "I shall have beans and biscuits brought to you."

"Surely My Lord..." Gaveston began, insulted.

Pembroke turned sullen, his eyes fiery, "'Tis that, or nothin'."

Piers knew he had reached the end of his conversational profit and, for that moment, kept his mouth shut.

They set their course southwest for Wallingford, a fortnight's ride away. Pembroke had sent for Lancaster, with his contingent of one hundred knights and triple that number of foot, to help escort the prisoner. At that time, Pembroke was obliged to dismiss a goodly portion of his feudal troops for a lack of sufficient funds to continue their service beyond their obligatory forty days. For his own concerns, he kept twenty knights close to his person, for he knew there was bad blood between Cornwall and Lancaster and he wanted nothing to do with it.

JUNE 9th 1312
CASTLE DEDDINGTON IN OXFORDSHIRE

The slow moving train of earls, knights, and foot warriors was making its way toward Castle Wallingford when Lord Pembroke, by happenstance or by design, suddenly realized how close by was the manor house wherein his wife was visiting for the summer.

"I'll be takin' temporary leave of you, Milord," announced Pembroke to Lancaster.

"And where, pray tell, will you be takin' leave to?" asked Earl Thomas surprised, "Deddington is but two leagues ahead and 'tis almost dark... we shall sleep there tonight!"

"I shall arrive there on the morn."

"Wench?" asked Thomas being nosey.

"Wife," said Aymer, wheeling his mount out of line and motioning to his twenty knights to follow. Then he paused and turned again to the earl. "About Cornwall, Milord. I have given my oath that he shall arrive before parliament alive and well."

"My Lord Pembroke, think you that I would allow your sacred word to be broken?"

Aymer chafed. "I have been privy to your schemes before!" He hesitated as if he might change his mind and stay.

"Rest well, Milord. I shall see to Cornwall myself."

"Just you keep my word!" said Aymer, adding, "I shall hold you responsible, Lancaster!"

"I'll send a messenger right away to make sure there are appropriate quarters for the king's favorite." Thomas turned in his saddle and shouted, "Forward a runner!"

Aymer de Valence led his knights down the hill. Lancaster smiled foxily and shook his head as he watched Pembroke depart.

"Yes, Milord," answered a slender young messenger as he rode to the earl.

"You must take a message to Lord Warwick."

"Yes, Milord."

• •

A short while after sundown, the waning quarter moon rising high in the east, Thomas of Lancaster arrived at Castle Deddington with his armed escort and the Earl of Cornwall. Though little remained of the stone castle as it once was, its remnants stood atop a high motte, thus making it a defensible position in which the earl and his men might safely encamp overnight. There was a habitable section of the old tower keep in which some comfort might be had, for it was warmed by a great fireplace and yet had some furnishings. But the remainder of the former stronghold lay scattered about the hilltop's inner bailey in heaps of rubble and great stone slabs.

Even so, Deddington was yet held by a keeper whose task it was to maintain a presence and protect all that was not already in ruins. The castle's other denizens included a cook and his helper, a groom or stock-tender, a handful of men-at-arms, a few farm animals, mostly chickens and sheep, and a mule for moving anything heavy about the place.

Piers Gaveston slid nimbly off his stallion and stretched the wrinkles from his bones. The groom from the castle took his horse and Lancaster's and led them away to a pasture with ample grazing for all the earl's cavalry horses.

"I hope you can provide supper of a decent sort," sneered Piers to Earl Thomas.

"We have supper for you," answered Lancaster.

"Beans and biscuits, like Pembroke's offerin'?"

"Not this night. This night you're fixin' to get just what you've asked for."

Piers smiled but from one side of his mouth. Somehow Earl Thomas' delivery of those words sent a chill over his heart. 'Tis nothin' he thought, dismissing the notion, but he could not help casting his eyes across the lonely, darkened landscape below.

"Where's Pembroke?" asked Piers as he was being prodded into the donjon's doorway by the blunt poke of Lancaster's long, spatulate index finger.

"Went to pay a visit to his wife," answered Lancaster, adding a satisfying chuckle under his breath. "Left you in my care 'til he returns."

In the great hall the earl's men were fed sparsely on the orders of the keeper, who did not trust them but was fearful of turning them out, not that he had the men to do such.

"'Twern't even a bit of meat in that small supper," complained Piers afterward.

"You hain't seen all of what we have in the storehouse for you as yet, Milord of Cornwall," sarcastically replied Lancaster.

"What might that be?" said Gaveston, sensing his troubles were just beginning.

"We have a mule for you to ride from here on," egged on Lancaster, near to a reverie of sadistic excitement.

"But, I have a fine destrier, a gift from King Edward!" objected Piers, just before two large men of Lancaster's troop grabbed his arms and pushed him against the door jamb. A third swiftly wrapped his wrists with rope and fastened them tightly behind him.

"Broke his leg, poor beast," lied Lancaster, sympathetically. He turned and led the parade of capturers and captured out to the fore lawn of the castle where a large draft mule awaited, fitted with only a blanket for a saddle.

"I *am* sorry, Gaveston," he feigned commiserating, "but I fear your testicles will be right ruined by this mule's bony backside by the time we get where we're fixed to go…" then changing his tone to one of unconcern added, "but… it can't be helped!" Adding menacingly with a turn directly into Gaveston's face, "Still want that kiss on the cheek from me?"

A man completely under another's control, Gaveston began kicking and screaming to the top of his lungpower like a wild animal in a trap. Two more minions of Lancaster's joined the group at his direction, and held their victim's legs so that he could not further resist the inevitable.

"Goddamn you all! Where are you whoresons taking me!? I will have my revenge for this hideous crime! Wait 'til King Edward hears of your ill treatment of me!" On and on he ranted, but his threats and curses were to no avail.

He was thrown across the back of the draught mule, his head pulled to its neck, and he was tied six times around with a rope so that he could not fall off no matter how much he wiggled and writhed.

The captors then mounted and went north toward Castle Warwick, leading the mule by a halter rope.

• •

Midday next, Pembroke arrived at Deddington castle. He knew instantly that Thomas had left with his troop since there were so few people about in the baileys.

"Where be Lord Lancaster?" he gruffly asked upon drawing rein in the midst of the inner bailey.

"Left, Milord," answered a near-standing youth as he worked about in a small vegetable patch.

"Gone?!" he asked surprised.

The fellow nodded, "Yes Sire, last night."

"Did they take Cornwall?"

"Took everybody that come with them, Milord… all rode south after supper… that's all I know," replied the boy.

"Were they headed for Wallingford Castle?" the earl asked, growling.

"South, I say, Milord, only south." The youth pointed in a southerly direction as if he thought the earl knew not which way south might be.

Pembroke turned in his saddle toward all directions with no sign of their disappearance. *South could mean anywhere! Damn you, Lancaster! Perhaps they did go on to Wallingford?* he mentally posed. "Damn!" he exclaimed aloud realizing his undoing was his lust for his woman, causing him to ignore his instincts. He knew not to trust Lancaster. "Damn! Damn! Damn! Heads will be piked on London Bridge for this day's shenanigans!"

The young page stood agape with nothing more to say.

Pembroke angrily jerked his horse's bridle and, followed by his knights, headed south toward Oxford, hoping to pick up their trail on the way to Wallingford.

• •

It was Lord Gaveston, Earl of Cornwall who got the royal welcome at Castle Warwick, many miles north of his own stronghold at Wallingford. The entire staff of Warwick and the local villeins turned out to line the sides of the road leading up to the castle, cheering, jeering, and throwing pig slop, stones, and sticks on him at every step of the poor mule's pace.

Gaveston knew then, if he'd had any doubt, that he had entered the very den of his greatest enemies and it would take every ounce of his beguiling ways to extricate himself from this mess.

Guy de Beauchamp,
Earl of Warwick

JUNE 17th 1312
WARWICK CASTLE

Originally in wood, a motte and bailey of the Norman style, Warwick Castle had been rebuilt in stone in the 1200s. Abutting the old motte, the imposing fort almost appeared to be part of the cliff rather than merely being erected of sandstone blocks cut from it. Below, on the south side of the cliff, peacefully glided the broad River Avon.

Guy de Beauchamp, Earl of Warwick and Lord of the castle, warmly welcomed his superior, the Earl of Lancaster, into his home. He openly relished the opportunity to play inquisitor to Gaveston for whom he had held a loathing for many years. Arriving shortly, sent for by Lancaster, were members of the Lords Ordainers Sir Edmund Fitzalan, the Earl of Arundel, and Humphrey de Bohun, the Earl of Hereford, to serve as judges in the trial of Sir Piers Gaveston. Both men were quick to accept the invitations and arrived at Warwick as soon as the legs of their destriers could carry them.

"Where is the little snivelin' prig?" asked Earl Edmund, a thin but muscular man of thirty-one years whose family had been prominently associated with the royal family in numerous ways for decades. His most distinctive physical features were the unusually large folds of sagging skin under his eyes that marred an otherwise not unpleasant face.

"Gaol," replied Warwick.

"I want to see him," came back Arundel.

"This way Milord," offered Lord Guy with a smile of satisfaction. He pointed to the passageway and stone spiral staircase leading downward. Lord Guy was large and swarthy, with dark hair that laid about his brooding face in ringlets.

The two nobles, led by the torch carrying gaol keeper, wound their way through the bowels of the castle.

"Right ripe smellin' down here," said Sir Edmund, wrapping his elbow over his nose.

"'Tis but the usual smell of prisoners, Milord," remarked Sir Guy.

"Which is Gaveston?"

"Just ahead we have him cooped, Sir Edmund," bragged Guy.

The gaol keeper came to a dirty wooden door and set his torch in the holder on the wall. He opened the small observation shutter to the cell. "Look lively in there!" he shouted as he pounded loudly against the wood.

Earl Edmund peered inward.

"Hain't escaped, has he, Milord?" asked the keeper knowing full well there was no way to get free.

"Can't see much with no more light than shows in that tiny window," said Sir Edmund, "but smell him, I do." And he turned his face from the doorway.

"No doubt shit his britches," teased de Beauchamp.

The two men laughed raucously and the gaoler smiled, enjoying the joke as well. He had seen that unpleasant circumstance more than a few times in this place.

Suddenly a bloodcurdling scream emanated from within the cell. "You shall all be beheaded for your crimes against me when King Edward hears of this! I swear it!"

Guy smiled and shut the observation hole though Piers still yelled obscenities and threats. "Still alive, I hear," he said to Edmund.

"If he lives 'til the morrow, we'll have his trial," Lord Edmund affirmed.

Recovering the torch, the keeper led the men back the way they had come.

"Why wait?" asked Edmund.

"We've one more to arrive by tonight," returned Guy.

• •

Mid-afternoon the next day, the four men supposedly acting as a committee for the Ordainers gathered in the great hall for the trial of Sir Piers Gaveston, Earl of Cornwall. Even if he were a member of the nobility by having been appointed such for his prowess in the bedroom rather than for his brilliance and courage on the battlefield, or for his having been born to it, he was entitled to a formal hearing of his accusers and his responses... a trial before his peers.

For the sake of their own noses, the lords had allowed a single bucket of water to be delivered to Gaveston's cell just off the great hall, where he had been kept awaiting the trial since the morning dawned. He had been voraciously hungry ever since leaving Deddington, and the smells of food wafting from the great hall drew him close to madness.

Three of the judges, the earls of Warwick, Arundel, and Hereford, took their places upon the dais behind a large, ornate walnut table. The area in front of them had been cleared of benches and trestle tables, and a single bench was placed squarely before them. Humphrey de Bohun, the Earl of Hereford, was the oldest among them by a couple of years.

"Bring in the prisoner!" demanded the Earl of Lancaster. He drew his sword and laid it beside the shallow bowl of apples and pears on the table. Then he sat in the middle chair and looked toward the door through which the Earl of Cornwall would enter.

Gaveston was a wreck to look upon. The old and worn clothes he had been given in captivity were ill-fitting, the trews dragging the floor over his bare feet, and the shirt seemed to be in its last stages of rotting directly from his body. His hands were bound with rope and his feet tethered so that he could take but small steps when he wasn't being dragged by the two burly soldiers flanking him. Piers' eyes were steadily on the fruit bowl as he was roughly put onto the lone bench.

"Are you Piers Gaveston?" asked Lancaster curtly.

Piers continued to look at the fruit.

"Milord Thomas, I fear our Lord Cornwall's wit is upon food," suggested Hereford, "can we not offer our prisoner a simple apple?"

"Of course, Dear Hereford. Would you care to fetch it for him?"

Hereford nodded and motioned for a close squire to come get the apple and give it to Piers.

Piers ate the apple greedily as the charges of breaking his exile, written in the most formal of language, were read. He did not look up toward the table until he heard Lancaster in his almost constant drone say, "sentenced to death by decapitation."

"Death?!" said Gaveston looking at the four men. "You would not dare!"

"You have been duly tried," said Earl Guy, smiling.

"Tried?!" said Piers in amusement, thinking to participate in the sham 'trial', "I have not had my say!" Apple juice and bits of the apple's flesh sprayed about as he spoke.

Guy de Beauchamp stood ponderously and looked down on Piers, "Do you remember once, when speaking to the king, you referred to me as 'the black cur' while I stood not two feet from you?"

Piers laughed in pleasure at his own cleverness, adding, "Rather apt, I should say!"

"I told you then, that dogs have teeth and one day my teeth would give you a goodly bite!" said Earl Guy. "I have voted you guilty, and that is my bite for you this day, Lord Piers Gaveston!"

"Very well, Milord, I consider myself chastised for my bad manners," Piers paused before adding, "I should have waited until you were out of hearing!" He smiled and looked from face to noble face, but found no hint of humor in any.

"You, in fact, have had your say with all of us here and many who are not here," added Lancaster.

"The king and I discuss nearly everyone at court, at one time or another. It is a monarch's duty to be aware of his friends, as well as his foes," he averred, and looked menacingly at his judges.

A knock upon the door halted the proceedings. With a wave of his hand, Thomas indicated to the soldier at the door to open it, but was surprised when Sir Roger de Mortimer, Baron Wigmore, entered the room and crossed to face the dais.

Thomas Lancaster, almost having completed the process of eliminating Piers Gaveston, was not pleased. "Mortimer, you are interrupting a proceeding of momentous import! Why come you here?"

Sir Roger curtly bowed to the four at the table and said, "I have come just to say let us be aware of acting in haste, Milords," he spoke calmly.

The four men glanced back and forth at each other as Mortimer walked to where sat the accused man they would condemn.

"Lord Gaveston was my guardian for some years, and though I don't agree with what he has done to the monarchy, I will vouch for his kindness to a fatherless boy, and for his prowess as a knight on the tourney field."

The Earl of Hereford fingered a long slash across his face, a permanent reminder of Gaveston's lance.

"That, however, is not the issue, here," stated Lancaster, only to be interrupted by Arundel.

"He is a sodomist!" yelled out Earl Edmund without provocation.

"Oh," said Roger, followed by, "and which of you has he sodomized?"

The men looked aghast, dumbfounded.

"The king!" blustered Edmund, "We all know, that! He... the king!"

"Then the king shall be hanged on the same tree?"

"The king is not guilty of such!" interjected Earl Guy.

"But, Milords, how can Edward be *not* guilty, when Sir Piers, is?"

"We don't have the authority... the king is not found so!" retorted Guy.

"Then don't kill Piers Gaveston for being a sodomist!" insisted Mortimer.

"We have condemned the Earl of Cornwall to death because he has disobeyed our decree to exile," offered Lord Fitzalan.

"He *keeps comin' back!*" added Guy de Beauchamp.

Piers finished the last of the apple, core, seeds, and stem, and was licking the palms of his hands and fingers.

"Enough of this!" shouted Earl Thomas as he stood and pounded the table with the hilt of his sword. The fruit shifted in its bowl and a lone apple rolled off the board and toward Piers who watched it come to rest half way between the renegade Ordainers and his chair. With a grunt against his aching body, he flung himself to the floor near the fruit. The others stopped to watch as the famished man grabbed the apple and began to eat it as hungrily as the first.

Thomas continued, "Regardless of his beneficences in the past, or his proficiency as a knight, he has been found guilty of breaking his exile, and he *shall* be put to death at tomorrow's dawn!"

Piers suddenly stopped eating and looked up to the table. Could he believe his ears. *Dawn? So Soon? There would be no chance for redress!*

He got from his knees and forced himself to stand, all the while clutching the prized apple.

"You men are simpletons, dolts! You cannot behead *me!*" His old haughty self had returned. "I am your master, brother to the king and, indeed, king in my own right! Do you not know how Edward listens to *my* words ere he makes any decision?"

His hubris pouring forth he continued, "Edward Plantagenet could not rule his kitchen without my giving him the menu! You *will not* kill me because you dare not leave him on our throne alone!"

The room became still as the arrogance of the man sealed his fate.

Roger said to him, "My Lord, I am a Marcher Lord with my own powers, but I cannot save you from these ravin's."

"I *need* no savin' from you!" shrieked Piers, his eyes wild with indignant fury. "Edward's army will be crashin' through these walls within minutes. *He* will save our throne on which *I* shall sit with him for the remainder of *our* reign!"

Piers looked at the men behind the table, their faces set in stone. Glancing from one to the next, his ire began melting and his courage faltering. He had known each of the four men at court at one time or another, and recollected lording over each of them his position as the king's favorite. Realizing his imperious outburst had only stiffened their resolve, he began to understand the precariousness of his plight.

His tactics then changed as he began to whimper, and tears filled his eyes as he dropped to his knees and began trying to recover control of the situation. "My Lords, I am a vain man, I admit, and at times I may overstep my actual place in life, but I beg you, do not put me to death for such folly!"

Warwick, Arundel, Hereford, and Lancaster were unmoved.

Bordering on hysteria, the Earl of Cornwall pleaded more, bowing his head before them. "Spare my life and I will speak highly of you to the king. I shall praise you at court and treat you as my brothers for ever after, I warrant… please… spare me!"

He looked up to see if any of his peers seemed to be taking pity on him. None did. He had humbled himself before them and even that had failed to touch them. Insulted, he again took a superior attitude, and the direst of threats roiled from his mouth and fell upon them. He blasted them with epithets and, trussed as he was, thrashed about like a madman. He lost all control and even wet himself in his rage.

Lancaster waved for the guards to take him back to his cell near the great hall. The men dragged him, foaming at the mouth, from the room and down the passageway, still shouting curses at full voice.

For a long moment the five men sat silent and unmoving, listening to Gaveston's ravings grow fainter. When at last they heard the door slam, closing him in his cell, Lancaster took a deep breath and looked about him at his fellow conspirators. "Give him a supper that's the best we have," he suggested to Warwick.

"Why waste a good supper on a dead man," somberly asked Earl Guy.

"Have it done, nevertheless," came back Lancaster.

Roger Mortimer was certainly in misery, for he had failed to save Gaveston in spite of his reasoning, though his efforts were only slightly out of appreciation for the warrior or the foster father. Rather it was that a living Piers covered Mortimer's secret tracks perfectly. Now he would have to seek other diversions for the king in order to accomplish his goals.

As arranged, Gaveston did get a supper to his liking and thus convinced himself the Ordainers had indeed had a change of mind about killing him. Again his superciliousness came to the fore, and as he sat lapping up the last of the rich sauce in the bottom of the trencher, he began to think of how he would take his sweet revenge on each of the judges when he was again free.

• •

When, on the dawn of the nineteenth of June, guards came to remove Gaveston from his cell, they roused him from a sound sleep that left him confused as to whether he was awake or yet dreaming.

"I thought you would never come get me," he said to Lord Lancaster as he approached.

"We had every intention of releasin' you from your cell as early as possible this morn, Lord Gaveston," said Lancaster.

"May I have my own raiment for my journey?" asked Piers being magnanimous.

"You'll not need clothin' more," said Lancaster, smiling.

Piers suddenly realized what was afoot and slung the dirty trencher at the earl.

Lancaster quickly raised his cloak and easily deflected the flying platter.

"You'll burn in the fires of hell if you perpetrate murder on me!"

"I suspect you'll be no more that a smolderin' cinder by my arrival time, Milord Gaveston," Lancaster said sarcastically.

Struggling against three large guards, Piers was dragged from the cell, his hands tied.

"If not for that supper ye ordered for him, his fight would be much less," said Earl Guy, observing the dragging and kicking and screaming.

"You wouldn't want to execute a starveling would you?" replied Lancaster. "He would be too delighted to die just to get beyond his belly."

Piers was taken to the bailey. His mule awaited him with the same blanket on its back as before. Neither of them was happy about seeing the other, sensing their entwined fate was coming to its end.

"Goin' with us to Blacklow Hill?" asked Lancaster, standing at the door of the keep.

"Much as I hate the whoreson..." Warrick said with a shiver, "I fear this will come back to haunt us one day soon. Arundel and Hereford will be goin' along, you need not more witnesses."

"Reckon I'll have a'plenty," agreed Lancaster. He bowed his head slightly, biding Warwick adieu.

Sir Guy watched the entourage form up and make its way single file down the path. All behaved as if in a pageant, maintaining the look of men completing a divine assignment. The liveliest of the bunch was

Gaveston, who continually screamed curses upon all their heads. As the last of the onlookers went beyond his sight the Earl of Warwick sighed and peered in the other direction toward the River Avon. It was peaceful in its meanderings below, and he wondered how God saw their day of judgment.

• •

The distance traveled was about a mile northward to Blacklow Hill. Piers Gaveston yelped hullabaloos for the first half of the trip until he wore himself out. He plotted to save his remaining strength for any opportunity to escape when he was removed from the mule's back. He kept looking to and fro for King Edward and his army to suddenly appear to chase off his enemies and save him.

At last the mule was halted at the foot of a wooded hill and the ropes harnessing Gaveston to the beast were untied.

Now's my chance, thought Piers. He began to kick the animal's sides with all his might, trying to make him run, but the startled animal backed up, instead.

Six large soldiers grabbed Gaveston on the orders of Lancaster and held him relatively still.

The executioner appeared, his head masked with a leather covering, and he held the axe in front of Gaveston to taunt him until Lancaster roughly pushed the axman up the hill. "You had best be fixed with a stout log yonder, axman!" he said gruffly.

"Yes Milord," said the executioner, "all is ready. Just follow me." And as the burly executioner trod heavily up the hill, he was followed by the priest, the earls, the soldiers dragging the condemned, and lastly, a handful or two of the curious.

Piers once again began his tirade, but with little effect against the six strong men holding him.

By the time the trailing assemblage reached the place of execution, Gaveston's voice had completely given out to a hoarse, gravely whisper and his mind would no longer form words intelligibly. Yet he continued to yell as loudly as he could as they tied him in position, his head on the block, so that he could not avoid his fate.

He wept uncontrollably, his face drenched in tears from his eyes and nose. Finally he could only make a barely whispered sound, like a baby that consoles itself. The executioner stepped into his place, having previously measured the distance from the chopping block to his stance so that he did not err in his stroke and cruelly injure, rather than kill, the condemned. He awaited the reading of the pronouncement, his axe head resting on the soft green turf of the hill. When Lancaster completed the document, all waited calmly through the priest's ritual for the dead, and at last, all was ready.

The executioner lifted his axe from the grass, and Thomas of Lancaster held up his hand to pause his action. Lancaster then bent down beside Gaveston's ear and whispered coldly, "If you return from this exile, Milord Cornwall... you can stay!" He grinned and moved away before motioning for the axman to complete his task.

Piers did not quiet until the blade fell clear through his neck and bit deeply into the log upon which his shoulders yet rested. It was a clean and well-placed cut, as the observers were wont to comment later.

Hereford and Arundel gasped at the precise moment the blade reached its target, each one thinking grimly about his own neck.

Lancaster, in his exuberance, lifted the lifeless head of Piers Gaveston aloft for all to see. The curious peasants who had joined the procession pushed close and some held their fingers in the dripping blood with a sense of excitement.

One of Thomas of Lancaster's men sallied forth with a plain wooden box built just for the occasion, and the earl lowered the head into it and closed the hinged lid.

"It is finished," replied Hereford almost sorrowfully.

Arundel nodded his head in agreement, turned and made his way back down the hill to his destrier. The others followed.

Two peasants who had been paid to do the chore buried the body of Piers Gaveston only a few feet from where he died, on Blacklow Hill.

JUNE 30th 1312
LONDON TOWER

Having heard with great relief that Lord Gaveston had given himself over to Lord Pembroke at Scarborough Castle, King Edward hastened to London with plans to mend broken alliances with the magnates. In the attempt, once again, to save his friend from exile, or worse, from punishment for having already returned from exile, he would be humble and receive their verbal scathing for a while. Then all would be well for a time.

"Send a messenger to Lord Pembroke to bring Cornwall here to me," ordered Edward in the comfort of his private apartment within the castle.

"My Lord King, it will be done," replied Hetherington in mid-bow.

"And send for every lord in the kingdom that has crossed me of late and bring them to a royal feast within a fortnight... and you take charge of the affair, Hetherington."

"It would be my honor," replied his advisor.

"Now leave me; I shall be alone."

With that, Edward rose from his chair and walked into the sitting room of his solar. After he had cleared the doorway, Hetherington left as well, closing behind himself the heavy door to the king's apartment. "The king is resting and not to be disturbed," he ordered the two guards standing at the king's door, but his statement had barely left his tongue when the three men suddenly heard a most horrible shriek coming from beyond the door.

"The king! Go to his aid, quickly!" Hetherington directed them, unnecessarily since the guards had burst through the door of their own volition before his short sentence was complete. He summoned the sentinels from the end of the hall, and swept back into the apartment thinking to find the guards with an attempted assassin by the scruff of the neck. He prayed the scoundrel hadn't been successful.

Instead, he found the king crumpled on the floor in a faint before a small table, upon which was set a plain wooden box with the hinged lid thrown back.

• •

For the remainder of the day Edward stayed in a fetal position atop the bed on which Hetherington had him placed. Numbed by shock and grief, he was near catatonic until he began cry, and then he cried, he cursed, he swore revenge, he cried more. *Pembroke shall pay dearly for this!* he vowed to himself as he sulked. *There be no punishment too great for the damned traitor!* And all the while his brain burned with the knowledge that it was he who told poor, helpless Piers to surrender himself to Pembroke, saying that only with Pembroke would he be given sanctuary. Oh, the guilt that consumed his heart and mind!

Before the day was out, the stench that emanated from the horrid box infiltrated every nook of the room, and once the foul air was ambient, the apartment itself demanded a wide berth. As the daylight hours waned, no one came near the room save those whom Hetherington ordered there for life's mundanities to be performed.

It was dark, and Hetherington had ordered candles lit by the time the distraught king at last arose and took another wrenching look into the box before reverently closing the hinged lid. Tears streamed steadily down his face. *Vengeance will be mine!* he swore silently. "Vengeance will be bloody *ours*, Dear Brother, Piers!" he said aloud, and sweetly caressed the top of the lid.

Calling for Hetherington to attend him, he ordered, "Send five hundred knights if you must, but… *get Pembroke in here!*"

"Majesty," bowed Hetherington as Edward swished by him and out the door to the hallway, through the gathered crowd of curious inmates, and down the passageway to the queen's chamber.

"Come alive, My Queen!" he prodded as he looked upon her sleeping form. *This is no time to lie aslumbering; murder has been committed!* He had hardly to glance at the several ladies-in-waiting for them to slip quietly out of the room and close the door.

Isabella roused and shook her head to clear away the sleep when she finally realized the king was beside her bed. She placed a plump eiderdown pillow between her back and the elaborately carved and gilded headboard and leant against it.

"Have you heard?!" he most urgently asked in a voice that broke.

"Everyone in the castle has heard, My King," she said stoically.

Edward began to cry afresh and fell across her lap, throwing his hands above his head and clutching and tearing at the elegant French coverlet much as mourners in Biblical times had rent their clothes in sorrow or repentance. "They have killed My Dear Piers!" he sobbed, obviously immersed in the pain of loss.

Isabella gazed upon him and secretly wished again that she had been apportioned a small measure of the devotion he had focused on Piers. As he lay across her thighs she ran her fingers through his locks to console him. On the night of the coronation banquet, when he ignored her and her family and played adolescent games with Piers, Edward had cruelly slain the innocent young girl's love she had held for him. Humiliated and affronted, she had then sworn revenge upon him, and have it she would. But as this wound was not of her making, it was not satisfying to that desire for retribution.

Thus, on this night and at this moment, her mothering instincts told her to have pity on him, though her hatred abated anything more.

After he allayed his tears and he went to sit up, his hand moved carelessly across her belly. His eyes suddenly opened as he realized she had grown considerably in girth.

"What is this?" asked Edward, his brows knitted in displeasure. "Would you bring yourself into court as some great cow wrapped in silks?! I will not have you fat and unattractive. You must eat less and regain your elegant form, My Lady. I demand it."

"I do not add girth because of what I eat, Majesty."

"Then you must see the physician and get a purgative. Your bowels need release."

Isabella sighed. She had hoped to keep the news from him for a little while longer, but since it had attracted his notice, now must be the appropriate time for him to hear of her condition. "I am in perfect health, Mon Roi. I gain weight in my belly because I am... enceinte. What is the right word? Enceinte?" Edward's confusion did not lessen.

"'He is your heir," she said calmly with a smile.

Edward sat up. "My heir?! When..."

"'He will be born in November, Sire, with the help of La Madone," she said and crossed herself.

Edward was stunned. He slowly stood, wiping the tearstains from his cheeks with his sleeve as his heart leapt to something akin to joy. His heir! His son! *But how could she know the babe would be a boy? Before the year is out! Oh, why could he not have been told before Piers was... Piers...perhaps we shall name him Piers!*

But something suddenly nagged at his wit and his thoughts turned from excitement to suspicion. He looked at the Queen, admittedly a beautiful dark-haired woman, no doubt desirable to numerous men... and a woman he had not been with for some time. How long had it been? Without saying a word to her, he calculated the months until the baby was expected on his fingers, and counted back to when the child must have been conceived, and he realized things were not as they should be. This could not be his child!

"How so November? I have been in York and you here in London since January!"

Isabella was silent. A smile of certain revenge played upon her face, completely wiping away her mothering pity. "Did you think I would just wait quietly, like a nun, for you to come to my bed, pinching your nose and taking me like a dose of some foul tasting herbal tonic, like the 'purgative' your physicians concocted? I? Isabella of France?" Her soft, feminine features were suddenly cold and hard. "I am no more to you than that! A medicine you must take so that your people will no longer think of you as incapable of producing an heir! You should be grateful. Now you shall have your heir and retain your crown! I have done you a favor!"

His glaring eyes weeping no more, Edward stepped back and slapped her across the mouth. She cried out, but recovered quickly and laughed cruelly through bleeding lips, delighted to have found something that pricked his heart so.

"My queen... a whore?!" he was aghast.

"My King, a sodomist?!" she gainsaid, dabbing at her smiling lips with a linen handkerchief.

"I will not claim this whoreson, you know!"

"You will," she returned.

"And why would I... it clearly is *not* mine!"

"And if it is not yours... whose is it, Milord?" she taunted.

Edward was silent, having no knowledge of her activities whilst he was in York.

"I will say to you that... this child will be of noble birth. You will be proud to call him your son!"

At that his legs grew weak and he was compelled to sit on a nearby chair while his mind whirled at who the man might be.

He is of noble birth, thank God! But who!? Perhaps my cousin Lancaster? Thomas Plantagenet? He hates me enough to fornicate with my queen behind my back! It could indeed be he, for he was not always in the north while Piers and I were. He tried to picture the two of them together, but couldn't. Lancaster was not charming enough for her taste.

It must be someone young, like Gloucester, Gilbert La Clare. I sent him to be regent in my absence. Did he think that entitled him to connive to commit adultery with my queen? He is a hothead; as beautiful as she is, she could have seduced him easily... but he hates the French. He could not abide listening to her with her French speech and her silly French ways. No, it must be someone who likes the French, or perhaps someone who is... the thought struck him like a thunderbolt.

Piers was a Gascon! Piers was born in France! And he was angry with me when he left and came to London! He could have done as he said and cavorted with this trollop and her 'ladies' four or five in the bed! He would 'appreciate' her French wines and her fine clothes. My God, it was...

"Piers?" he guessed.

"Piers was with you in York, Mon Roi," she said.

"But, he left York… in March… said he had come to London," gasped Edward remembering Gaveston's words upon returning to York.

"I recollect", said she, coyly. "He did make a surprise visit to his wife, non?"

Edward spun around. "And to you?!… Did my brother Piers also make a surprise visit to you?"

The queen swung her legs over the edge of the high bed and dangled her toes, swinging them to and fro. A slight smile played on her swelling lips, her eyes darting in his direction, that she might taste her sweet revenge on its first serving.

"Oh, God! It was Piers," he sighed, nearly gagging on the thought.

"What do you care who beds me?!" she retorted quickly. "If it was Piers Gaveston, he was a most sensual lover. He made me feel… perfect… a happy woman, at least for that moment. That is more than I can say for you!"

"It cannot be!" cried the tormented Edward. "You but mock me with the thought… in my hour of full sorrow! What a damned whore you are. Piers was *my* lover!"

"So he was," Isabella nodded, "and at last, in our infidelity," she remarked as if having found a bar of gold in the bottom of the guarde robe, "we have something in common!" She laughed gaily, no longer the shy young princess from France, but a young woman holding her own in the machinations of court life.

Edward sighed, feeling sorry for himself. "Yet, the child is not mine."

"But, Mon Roi, you will claim him, all the same… and he will be king when you are dead."

Edward reeled. What manner of God's trickery has ruined his total life in this single day? He remembered his father, and how, for as far back as he could remember, he had wanted the old man to die so that the kingdom would be his. *Now there's going to be a little cur sitting around and waiting for me to die so he can take over!* thought Edward. It was horrible. It was worse than horrible… it was… perhaps what he deserved.

Isabella interrupted his thoughts, "You will claim him as yours for as long as I do not confirm *your* secret to another soul on this earth. We will be civil to one another at court. We will fool even those closest to us, into believing that you are not a sodomist and I am not an adulteress. We have a twisted bond, you and I… your seed is no good, Edward. To keep your throne, you need an heir … and I have him, here, within my grasp!" She stretched the cloth across her abdomen to show the fullness between her hands.

"Oh, Father in Heaven," lamented Edward, putting his hands over his face. His head was spinning and he just wanted to get away from her. He got up and wandered aimlessly into the hall where he found Hetherington awaiting him.

"May I be of service to you, Your Majesty?" he asked politely.

"Are you sniffing me out at *every* turn?!" growled Edward.

Hetherington bowed in servitude.

"You will be well pleased, Hetherington," asserted the king, suddenly feeling a certain sense of relief in giving the queen what she proposed, and thus accepting his fate.

"I beg your pardon, My Liege?" replied the man, not understanding.

"Our *heir* abides in the belly of that *she-beast*, yonder!" he grumped, huffing down the hallway.

"Wonderful news, My King…" Hetherington's voice trailed off as he realized the disinterest of the king, who was nearly beyond earshot already.

One of the queen's ladies-in-waiting unobtrusively closed the door to the queen's chamber before turning to Isabella to converse in French, "Will he keep your secret, Mon Reine?"

"Oui, I am sure of it," she replied. "He has much to lose and nothing to gain if he doesn't. Besides," her face grew somber, "how could he not love the child of his goddamned favorite, Piers Gaveston, who turned the entire English kingdom on its ear?"

AUGUST 13th 1312
LANERCOST SANCTUARY

The political maelstrom roiling to his south between King Edward and the Ordainers over the murder of Piers Gaveston created ripe conditions for King Robert. Once again, he thanked Lord Gaveston's poor fortunes for much of his own apparent good fortune and he planned another raiding party into the north of England, certain that King Edward could not, or would not, send help of any kind. With these opportune incursions he acquired monies and other useful or valuable items to help support his government.

Robert rode south with a fairly large contingent of Scots warriors, his first stop, Lanercost, from where the old King Edward had directed his war against the Brus. Using his son, now King Edward, and his willing minion, Sir Aymer de Valence, Earl of Pembroke, Longshanks had wreaked much death and destruction on the Scottish people with all-out invasions as well as multiple murderous and terrorizing raids over many years.

Now Robert headed into northern England to extract reparations for the horrors of the reaving, ravaging forays both Edwards had brought upon the Scots.

There was no resistance of import, and the Scots easily laid claim to the village, after which Robert turned his attention to the Augustinian priory in which his wife, daughter, and sisters were "tried" for having been his family members, and Countess Isabel Macduff for having given him aid. All were here sentenced to heartless confinements in which they yet languished these six years after, unless they were dead. Lanercost had much to fear from the Brus.

Yet he was able to lead his army through the open gatehouse without incident, and the cloistered monastery lay spread before them.

It wasn't long before the humble canons of Lanercost Priory were dragged into the courtyard, many in bare feet and all in their drab, gray-brown hooded robes. Their hands were then bound behind their heads, the bindings tightly but not fatally around their necks. They were a quiet bunch, of uniformly downcast visage, naturally so under the circumstance, uttering no words of protest lest it give satisfaction to the hated Scots.

"They have tongues only for their prayers, My King," said Thomas Randolph coming on foot to Robert, still astride his horse.

"Put them in the dovecote," ordered Robert, dismounting. His feet felt a tingle as they touched the ground. He knew this had been a hotbed of hate for him, and was so even now, but revenge was not on his mind at present.

He stood a moment and gazed about him at the gentle, rolling landscape surrounding the priory. Fields were ripening with what should produce a fine harvest of bread grains, and orchards were heavy with apples and plums which, with the nearby vineyards he had ridden past, offered a good year for the monks to produce dried fruits and fermented drink for their use.

Turning back to the cruciform church, he was reminded of the reddish walls of Castle Kildrummy. Reaching well above the tallest trees, the stone front of the church was intricately windowed with three soaring pointed arches and much decorative stonework, and a wide rounded arch doorway recessed into the massively deep, solid stone walls. Robert walked through it and into the cool darkness of the nave, which stretched from him perhaps a hundred feet forth to the transepts, with windows on every side. Once his eyes adjusted to the reduced sunlight, he could see there were rows of eight smaller windows up high along the north and south walls, and larger, fewer windows below them. Beyond the transepts, at the end of the chancel were two sets of three tall windows, one set above and one below.

He also noticed that the priory was not a wealthy one.

"Go through the place, piece by piece," said Robert as he and Thomas removed their helms in God's holy place.

"Ye takin' ev'rythin'?" asked Thomas.

"Ev'rythin' they don't *need*," he replied, and he walked through the venerated landmark to understand the layout and the contents, his footsteps echoing off the towering stone vaults above.

"Randolph!" he called suddenly while Thomas stood at the door talking to one of his lieutenants.

Thomas came to him quickly along with the lieutenant and several others, weapons drawn. "Aye, Robbie!?"

Robert grinned and, realizing there was no need for alarm, the Scots sheathed their blades. "Bring one of those monks to me here... the prior, if ye think he might be willin' to chat. If not, then someone else," he said. "I have some questions about what these canons do here."

In about ten minutes Thomas returned with the prior and found Robert sitting in a large, well-padded chair behind a heavy oak table that had been well used as a desk.

"Ye fixin' to make an example of this'un?" asked Thomas, roughly pushing the monastic to his knees on the floor in front of the desk. With his arms tied, he lost his balance and flopped forward, landing with a solid thud.

Robert stood and peeked over the front edge of the table to see how badly the monk was injured.

The hefty man groaned and rolled over and labored to his feet as Robert watched him struggle.

Once up, the monk stared at Robert fiercely. Thinking he was about to be beheaded or disemboweled by this excommunicated devil before him, he was not intending for Robert to gain any satisfaction by watching him beg for his life. Still, he trembled, from ire or fear none could tell.

"Leave us, Thomas," said the king quietly, and pulled his dagger from its scabbard at his waist.

Thomas obeyed, closing the door behind him.

Robert approached the prior whose eyes were affixed to the blade in the king's hand. As he drew nearer, the Scot brought the blade up to the cleric's throat and the man could not completely stifle a sort of humming nervousness as he awaited his expected death. To his relief and surprise, the blade merely sliced through the painful bindings and released his hands. The dagger slipped silently into its sheath.

The monk rubbed his throbbing wrists, hoping for a swift return of feeling to his fingers, while Robert sat again in the chair. He quickly took the measure of the person standing before him. Though nervous, the man remained just where Randolph had left him, and showed little emotion. *A brave man*, Robert thought, but said nothing, instead he started examining the papers on the table before him.

After a spell of waiting before the Scottish king, the cleric grew tired and spoke. "How may we serve you, Milord?" Robert seemed to ignore the question for a moment, but then he looked up at the prior.

"Show us to yer wealth, wherever it be, and yer cellarium," replied Robert coolly.

"Wealth?" The prior's eyes twinkled with amusement. "Milord, we are among the poorest priories in England! If you came to steal our gold and silver, you have driven your ducks to a bad market. We have no such treasure to show you."

"Ye will forgive me, cleric, if I do not believe ye."

"Believe what you will, Milord. We were nearly spent out of our robes while keeping King Edward within our walls for over five months! Even now, years later, many of my brothers have no shoes for we cannot provide them."

"Then we shall take what we need other than gold and silver."

"Does that include our lives?" asked the canon suspiciously.

"And what would I do with yer lives?" frowned Robert.

"Holy blood on unholy hands?" retorted the monk.

Robert ignored the insult and spoke in low tones, "Ye were here when

King Edward was in residence?"

"I was…" he proceeded cautiously, "though we had naught to do with your queen and the others."

Robert's heart quickened at the mere mention of Elizabeth, even by reference. "Tell me what happened… that *ye* had naught to do with."

"There is not much about the affair that I know," he said, and stood silently again.

Robert commanded loudly. "Say what ye know, prior!"

The monk jumped at Robert's order, licked his dry lips, and opened his mouth ready to speak but nothing was forthcoming. Then, softly, in an almost whisper, he said, "The trials were here… right here, where we are now. King Edward sat where you are, and I…" he adjusted his stance slightly, "stand in the place of your queen, and your daughter held tightly to her. The other ladies, your sisters and the Countess of Buchan beside them, stood just back of your queen… and…" he paused, remembering the sad condition of the man, "…and… the Earl of Atholl… just about here." He shuffled quickly to where he remembered Atholl, hunched over and in pain. He made the sign of the cross at the spot and said, "All heard their fates bespoken within this very air, Milord."

Robert sighed, fighting back tears, *Had I only known it then,* he wishfully thought, *I could have rescued them and done away with Edward in the same raid.*

"They were not to be ki… I was told they would not be killed, Milord," said the monk, his head bent low.

Robert already knew that and was quick to return to the event at hand. "Where was the king's abode?"

"Yonder," replied the monk pointing to a door to Robert's left.

"Show me."

The monk walked to the door, opened it and Robert followed down the corridor to a large door on the left. He opened it and Robert entered.

"Where is his bed?" asked Robert.

"As I recall, his bed was in that corner, but has been long since removed elsewhere. We now use this room for the scribes' work," answered the monk almost politely.

"What do they inscribe?" asked Robert.

"Here we make copies of the Bible, Sire, and there are some manuscripts of church matters."

Robert stood over a writing table holding the neatly printed work of a master scribe and shuffled through the parchments. "When Edward was here," he asked, "were there any such writings?"

"You'll not find anything of them among those papers."

The king looked at him, "And where will I find them?"

"London, most likely," the clergyman replied. "They took ev'rything with them when they left."

"Ye mean documents?" to which the prior nodded, sympathetic to the king's sadness.

"Yes, there was a stack of parchments rolled up and taken out when the king left. Your kin were long gone by then."

Robert suddenly stopped his random shuffling when he saw his name written on one page. He held it up to the soft light coming through the lone large window. "What is this?"

"You read Latin, My Lord?" asked the monk, not wanting to reveal anything more than was necessary to this raider. The Scot was studying the parchment closely.

"'Ppears ye have taken a likin' to my life story!" he said.

"Not you, specifically. These pages are chronicles of our place and our days," admitted the monk, somewhat sheepishly.

Robert drew a chair to the table of randomly stacked parchments and began to read further. The cleric stood awkwardly, thinking his fate rested upon the way the war was portrayed in the writing. It was several hours before Robert looked up from the desk. "Ye see things a bit amiss from my reckonin'," he said.

"We know nothin' save what others tell as their tale," humbly replied the man.

"Then I will tell ye my part of the story," his brow furrowed. "Ye will refer to me henceforth, as Robert, King of Scots."

The monk bowed low, greatly relieved at realizing that if there was a "henceforth" spoken, death for him and his fellow monks was not on the agenda of Robert the Brus.

"Yes, Milord… King," meekly replied the man.

Robert sighed deeply. The air in the room had grown stale. He felt as if he were suffocating, and quickly stood and left without a word more. Unsure of what he should do, the cleric remained standing for a short while, absorbing the encounter, then sank to the floor on his knees to give thanks for his survival. Later, he was found there asleep, his crumpled body bathed in the failing light of the very long day. The uncharacteristically high drama seemed to be at a temporary lull.

• •

Within two days the monastery had been picked clean of anything that could be conveniently converted to money on the Isles or the Continent. Robert had it packed into three wains and, under trusted knights, sent it to Castle Ayr where the items would be catalogued and valued.

"Go to the dovecote and release those shiverin' monks," ordered Robert.

Thomas Randolph, without a word, turned and headed to the outside rear of the sanctuary where the monks, except for the single one, had been kept since their capture. The rusting hinges creaked as the small door opened. The birds fluttered in fear. The men inside squinted at the brightness of the sunlight.

"Come out," growled Thomas harshly, having no use for clerics.

"They're fixin' to kill and eat us!" yelled the most timid of the group.

"Hold your words!" argued another.

"Come out and get untied," said Thomas getting exasperated.

There was silence within.

"Out, goddamn yer skins!!" cursed Thomas, knitting his eyes and mouth into a scowl.

The stiff and sore monks hobbled out as quickly as they could, and stood with their toes in the sun-warmed dirt, happily enjoying the fresh air. Someone among them started to laugh, and then he fell to his knees and cried, he was so highly strung over having survived the visit from the Scots. The one monk Randolph had untied was working at untying the others as the Scots mounted their steeds and rode toward the gatehouse.

"Where to next?" asked James Douglas, guiding his horse alongside Robert's.

"Hexham," said he, and his spurs urged his horse quickly forward, nearly bolting the stallion to the head of the column.

"Hexham! King Edward hain't goin' to like this," muttered James to himself, and he put spurs to his own mount to follow Robert eastward.

AUGUST 18th 1312
hexham, northern england

A young man casually came from his thatch-roofed cottage with a bucket in his hand, heading for the town well. The fog was unusually thick for the time of year and, while he traversed the roadway as he had done a thousand times, an apparition slowly took form ahead of him in the fog. He became fascinated with what he figured was a visual twist on a clump of bushes or trees in the distance.

How odd, he thought, *it looks like a man on horseback. Perhaps a knight, perhaps a...*

Suddenly he was struck step-less. It was a knight on horseback, not an illusion. A large man, surely a knight, was sitting astride his horse in front of him. He continued to stare as other vague wisps slowly turned into knights as well, and joined the first.

The leader clicked his mouth and nudged his horse's flanks, and the tired horse walked toward the youth. "Laddie, can ye tell me where the town burgesses are to be found?" the great man asked, and the boy knew in an instant that he was a Scot.

The youth suddenly flung at the man the bucket he carried, turned, and ran as fast as his legs could, shrilly screaming all the way, "It's the Scots! The Scots have come to kill us!" He continued to give the alarm all the way through the town.

"Reckon they'll be woke soon?" asked Edward Brus.

"With that lad's voice, I'm sure it won't be long," said Robert smiling.

"Shall we commence awhoopin'?" asked his brother as James Douglas came to Robert's side.

"Not yet," answered Robert twisting in his saddle to see the disposition of his troops.

"They'll be out with their pitchforks and scythes afore long... this fog could kill us," said Edward.

"Stand yer ground, Brother. We're no dead, yet," said Robert.

Only moments passed before the roadway ahead was crowded with villeins armed with their farm implements. They gathered mid-road, huddled like sheep, hoping to secure safety in mass numbers, jeering at the armed knights blocking the west end of town.

Robert moved forward toward the mob. "Resist and ye will be slaughtered by my knights!" he shouted. "I do not want to lay waste to yer town and leave yer women and children without their menfolk. 'Tis yer burgesses I want. Have them come to me, now!"

One man suddenly stood forward, "We'll not let ye in!" he yelled, and held his guisarme, really the long-handled hooked pruning blade he used to trim dead branches out of his trees. He looked as if he knew how to use it, even when facing a knight on horseback. The other men with their farm-tool weapons loudly agreed. But Robert didn't want to allow the situation to become a brawl with the ardent, but untrained rustics.

He waited until their yelling had somewhat abated and simply whistled. Instantly, armed Scots on horseback and foot emerged from every quarter out of the fog. The townsmen looked around and quickly and realized that they had no chance against so many toughened soldiers. They swiftly lost their zeal until they were standing quietly, but they were obviously afraid they would be killed anyway. In the quiet, some of the women could be heard crying in their houses.

"Ye will want to get yer burgesses from their beds," said Robert soberly, "else ye may bleed in their stead."

The man who had stood forward turned to his next at hand, saying, "Get the burgesses... quickly... drag them from their sleep if need be!"

Robert waited as several of the men ran to fetch the town fathers from their rests. The people began to commiserate amongst themselves. The Scots warriors stood their ground silently.

At last the seven town leaders were reluctantly shuttled to the fore of the gathered crowd and stood to the front, some still adjusting their clothing to be presentable.

"I am Robert the Brus, King of Scots, and I am here to remove all of value from Hexham town," he announced. Hexham was a prosperous market town, and held considerable wealth compared to its neighbors.

"What d'you mean?" shouted an insulted voice in the crowd. "Is the 'King of Scots' merely a robber, after all?"

The entire group began to shout and shake their weapons menacingly in the air again.

Robert sat quietly until the clamor lessened and shouted, "I am no thief; I am a tax collector!"

"We pay taxes to Edward of England and none other!" said one of the burgesses.

"And what does Edward do for ye with the taxes he collects?" Robert gave his horse a nudge with his knee and the horse walked slowly toward the crowd. The Scot began talking to the assembled men in a patient and reasonable tone. "Does he prevent yer bein' raided and pillaged by the Scots to yer north? I would say nae! The only time ye catch sight of yer king's men is when it's time to gather the taxes, or when yer son is needed for his army! Is that not so?"

A murmur went up from the bystanders. Robert knew he was right, for there were many Scots lads who had fought in his army and now and again made a run at the more prosperous towns along the border. He continued walking his stallion.

"I, on the other hand, can put a stop to the Scots troublin' ye further, 'til..." he made a great show of giving the matter thought before saying, "the nativity of St. John the Baptist, next." Another ripple of discussion went through the gathered townsfolk, for the harrying Scots were a constant threat. Having peace from them would be worth a great deal.

"What do you want, then?" asked another of the burgesses.

"Two thousand pounds will save yer quiet, pleasant town," said Robert loudly enough so all could hear. His face was dispassionate.

"Why, that ain't even a year!" protested the first burgess, frowning.

"We will fight you to the death!" shouted another, he being the wealthiest of any in the town and thus having the most to lose.

The crowd grew suddenly silent.

"To the death?" asked Robert riding calmly up to the man.

"To the death!" he repeated belligerently.

Robert dismounted and, axe in hand, said, "Very well, then. *You* fight me."

The fellow's eyes grew large and round, and his face lost all its color as he realized how grand and imposing a man was this king. "I... I... I..." he stammered, without being able to say another word. He looked around to see who among his fellows would help him, but there was nobody willing to take on this knight.

"No?" Robert looked at the burgess with contempt, and turning his face to the assemblage said, "Yer burgess, brave lad that he is..." Robert paused for his gibe to have full effect, "... is quite willin' to have *ye* fight to save his purse, but *he* won't. So, I ask ye... are ye willin' to die to save his fortune?"

The mob was silent as they eyed the encroaching warriors.

"Two thousand pounds!" announced Robert loudly. "How many of ye would it be worth? Five? Would the lives of five of ye be worth two thousand pounds? How about ten? Or twenty?" he paused again before adding, "... of yer sons, yer brothers, yer neighbors... would ye sell them for two thousand pounds? If nae, how many must I kill to make two thousand pounds seem small enough a price to pay?" Robert looked at the burgesses and awaited an answer.

"We will get your money," suddenly said an elderly, white bearded burgess. "It... may take a day... or two... to collect it," said the old man. Even so, the burgesses were yet unsure of whether they would be safe from the swift and terrible axe of Robert the Brus, and they watched as he weighed the elder's words. After a moment's pause, he climbed back upon his destrier and took up the reins, holding his axe in the other hand.

"We are goin' to Corbridge," he said. "Bring the money to me there within two days... or we will return and burn the town... startin' with *your* houses." With the axe he indicated the burgesses, and wheeling his horse, led the way back into the fog. In moments, the people of Hexham were alone again.

Upon leaving Hexham, Robert and his men traveled east the several miles to Corbridge, named for the bridge going across the Tyne River, a common, navigable flow connecting the two towns to the North Sea. Robert traversed the bridge and rode through the town so that all could see he was there for business, and set up camp on the north side of the village to await the burgesses. They knew he was there; they knew his purpose. He wanted to get by without burning the village to the ground, if he could, but he had known that eventually, some town would determine to make him prove his threat.

Suddenly, it seemed that Corbridge would be that town.

James Douglas sighted a long string of villeins moving toward the Scots' camp. "Here they come!" he shouted.

"Form up!" shouted Robert shaking his head in disappointment. "Watch our backside, Randolph!"

"Aye," Thomas replied and tapped several men to turn and keep vigil on the fields behind them, just in case the villagers got ideas beyond their abilities.

Within mere minutes, the armed Scots had formed a line between the approaching men and the camp, a solid wall of chain mail and sword blades punctuated here and there with pikes standing tall and deadly. Robert pushed through the line and walked a few steps beyond to have some space between him and his men.

The townsmen formed a ragged line across the way. They were an angry mob, not much different in character than the ones in Hexham the day before.

"Where are yer burgesses?" asked Robert in a loud voice.

Seven men stood forward of the crowd and one yelled, "We heard about Hexham!"

"We'll not pay, ye damned robber!" offered another. The other villagers agreed vociferously. Robert remained calm and waited until he could be heard.

"Though two thousand pounds is a lot of money, it is not worth losing yer lives and homes!" he shouted.

"We have a king to protect us… we pay his taxes!"

Robert stood for a moment in disbelief. "Look about ye, men of Corbridge! Where is he?" questioned Robert looking about in serious jest. "He is not here to protect ye! Nae! He sends his army to Scotland, to thieve and rampage as it will... but it tarries not here to safeguard ye and yer town!" He looked at the faces of those before him, full of sullen scowls and anger.

"Yer 'protector's' army has reaved much wealth from us over many years past, and it is time for ye, and Hexham, and other Englishmen to repay us," he realized his words fell on deaf ears, "or we shall take it from ye in the same manner it was taken from us!" At that, he pulled his axe from his belt and held it low at his side.

"You shall not have it!" said the leading burgess, a wealthy man, so Robert judged by his clothes and demeanor.

"If ye know of Hexham, ye know they have come to my terms without bloodshed."

"We heard, but we are awake... and ready to fight!" said yet another of the burgesses.

Robert raised his axe and placed it in the crook of his arm, saying, "Who among ye will fight me, then?"

This time the threat failed to cool their ardor. The unsettled crowd grew angrier.

"We are not here to kill ye, nor harm yer women... we want only money, or cattle and grain," he pressed. "We will have it or we will destroy ye!"

The armed burgesses, most of them merchants living lives of relative ease, moved foolishly toward the Scots, who plainly were fully armed and toughened by years of war. Edward Brus and several staunch warriors moved forward to stand with the king. The outspoken burgess began to run and nearing the king, raised his sword.

Robert's axe rose as if by its own volition and deflected the man's weapon before coming down hard, removing the offending limb at the shoulder. His face registered only surprise, just before he collapsed at the feet of the Scots.

The fight was swift and deadly. In few moves, the handful with Robert brought down another five of the seven burgesses and four other villagers. The remainder scurried away yelping down the hill, either wounded or fearful, splattered with their neighbors' blood.

"What now, Robbie," asked Edward, wiping blood off his sword onto a dead man's tabard.

"Burn the town," said Robert. "Start in the center and burn the merchants' wares first. We must make them hurt the most. When we come next year, we'll have less argument."

"Aye."

"Somehow, I thought it would be easier this trip," said the king wistfully. "These men were not soldiers. They were like rabbits amongst wolves, and to what purpose... they should have stayed at home with their womenfolk." The brothers stood looking at the corpses until Edward broke the spell.

"I'm off to put the torch to their warrens. Want to come along?" asked Edward.

"No more killin', ye ken?" growled Robert. "And save the abbey!"

Edward nodded, turned, and climbed aboard his horse. He whooped and many of the others followed, setting prepared torches ablaze in the campfire as they went.

"Don't like this business, much, Robbie," said Thomas, coming to him and looking down at the bloodied burgesses, sprawled in the grass. "Tain't like war, when ye face soldiers." Robert nodded agreement.

"But our own survival depends on our goin' home with grain and meat, and money to buy weapons. Else it will be us lyin' in the bloody grass afore long."

"Aye, I understand," replied Thomas, and he spat on the ground near the bodies. "Shall I go to Hexham and collect the money there?"

"If we don't hear from them by in the mornin'. That will be quick enough. We told them two days," replied Robert as the town along the riverbank began to burn. The neatly thatched roofs began to smolder and soon columns of dark smoke rose into the already gray sky, doing nothing but making it grayer.

Through the dusk and into the evening hours the fires' glow made the whole area bright as a full moon, but with a reddish cast, like sunset. The thick smoke hung through the whole of the village and blew down the Tyne with the wind.

In the morning Randolph and two dozen knights made their way back to Hexham to collect their ransom. That afternoon the lone surviving burgess of Corbridge and his sons approached the camp of King Robert. Ahead of them they drove eleven beeves, a wain pulled by a yoke of oxen and loaded with sacks of grain, and eighteen hundred English pounds.

Robert accepted the terms and granted the town its treaty.

Thomas Randolph returned with the news that some of the townspeople of Hexham had run off to the forest with all of their cattle, and the burgesses, not wanting their cherished manor houses destroyed, had managed to come up with twelve hundred pounds. He had sent it on to Ayr.

He added that he had set the rest of Hexham alight, and when the king looked toward the west, there was a black smear above the horizon.

Robert sent the surviving burgess of Corbridge to Copland and Cumberland to tell them of the fate of his town. He carried with him the King of Scot's demands for money, cattle and grain. Another man was sent to Durham with the same message.

About a mile north of his camp was a large manor house belonging to a wealthy Suffolk merchant by the name of Robert de Reymes. The Brus had his camp moved there before nightfall, and the exhausted king and his lieutenants slept inside for a change.

Word spread as quickly as the smoke from the fires and the towns remaining downriver, not wanting to be burned out, sent emissaries to King Robert with the required monies and goods for a treaty until the following June. Those who could not pay the full payment sent hostages to act as sureties. Though this king's demands were stern, they were always treated fairly while awaiting being ransomed.

The local resident that Robert had sent to Durham returned badly beaten and empty handed and bearing the message that the Brus would dare not come so far south into England.

August 28th 1312
Durham, in Northern England

"Young men! Have need of a new saddle?" called out the saddle maker to Edward Brus and James Douglas as they wandered down Market Street shortly after midday. Farmers' baskets were full of fresh vegetables and there was plenty of meat displayed on the bow-legged shambles of the several butchers.

By everything they saw, Durham was indeed a town of wealthy merchants and prosperous farmers.

"He ain't a horse! Jus' looks like one!" quipped Douglas, smiling broadly and indicating Edward, who was in no mood to be teased.

"Sell you a horse, too, Scotsman, to match the saddle," replied the vendor upon hearing the northern accent.

Douglas glanced through the open shop and he saw silhouetted inside a swaybacked nag, probably unfit to ride. He paused, nevertheless, to look at the saddle the worn, bony fingers yet worked at sewing. The man and the horse in his shop were well suited, one to the other, James thought, but on looking closely at the fellow's handiwork, he saw it was as exceptional as the saddler was ordinary.

The saddler smiled, pulling out a wee knife to cut the sewing thread after tying off his last stitch. He watched James Douglas' eyes and thought, *First sale of the day, provided he has the coin.*

Douglas stood by the rail on which the saddle was slung and stroked its smooth leather, soft as a lady's kidskin glove. It was finely cut and perfectly sewn upon its wooden frame, with tooled flowers and swirling vines along the sides, and the high cantle of a knight's saddle. It was too carefully worked to have been made on the mere possibility of a sale.

"This is a noble's saddle, made by a master saddler," he commented appreciatively. At this the older man grinned pridefully. He liked this young Scot.

"So it was, young sir."

"Then why would ye sell it?"

The saddler's gap-tooth smile faded as he said, "Sadly, the great knight who ordered it... an old but distinguished warrior in service of King Edward and his father before him, died in his young mistress' bed a fortnight ago." He crossed himself before continuing, but his smile returned when he said, "But, by the saints, we should all wish to die as he did, an honored old man, breathing his last whilst riding hard on a softer saddle than this one!" And he laughed at his own cleverness.

James laughed, too, but Edward merely smiled and asked, "Did not the aged knight pay ye for the saddle?" The jollity was instantly gone from the fellow, replaced by a look of surprise, as if he knew not how to respond.

"Well, he... he... paid some... so that I could buy the leather of his choosing... but he still owed for the remainder, and now... I'll have to meet him in heaven to collect it!" He shook his head sadly.

"Let's go, Jemmy. The fellow is tryin' to sell ye another man's property!"

"It is *my* property... he never paid for my work, don't that count for somethin' after all?" He looked from Edward to James, who was the more likely buyer. "Feel the seams here, my friend, you can ride all day and never know it's there!" He glared at Edward as James' fingers traced the almost undetectable join.

"How much d'ye want for it?" asked James.

"Well, since you are obviously a man who appreciates a good saddle, I will settle for three and six," he smiled.

"Three and six!" Edward jumped into the bargaining. "For a saddle that's already been paid for? What about the man's son, or his grandson? Would they not demand the saddle if they knew the old knight had it made?"

The saddler grew angry, but controlled his temper. "I tell you, young sir, that the saddle is mine to sell! And if the old man's son wanted it, he would have to pay me three and six!"

"Well, I haven't three and six anyway, so I can't pay yer price," James turned and started to walk away.

"Three and two!" The saddler said quickly. James turned to look at him and he again said it. "Three and two. I can let you have this fine leather saddle for three and two... but I can go no lower."

"I'm sorry, saddler, but all I have is two and seven. I haen't any more." Again James turned to leave and the saddler changed his asking price.

"Three pounds even! I'll probably cut my throat when I think about it later, but for three pounds, you can ride like a king."

"But I haen't got three pounds. All I have is two pounds and seven pence!" Then a thought struck him and he said, "I'll be doin' some tradin' today, and if I'm successful at it, I can come back and get it later."

"Later?"

"Aye, later! I'll be finished here, and I'll have yer three pounds. Will ye hold it for me 'til I return?"

"'Til you return, eh?" The fellow scratched his chin beneath his scraggly beard and looked at the pair of Scots a bit before saying,

"Alright… but you can put some money, say… a pound? with me… just to prove you really will come back?"

James thought about it, and looked at Edward who shook his head as if to say "no", but in spite of Edward's warning, he reached into his drawstring pocket and pulled out a one pound coin and slipped it into the saddler's calloused palm. "Now, ye'll not sell it to anybody else? Ye'll hold it for me until I return?" Douglas asked. He really wanted the beautiful saddle. The older Englishman nodded.

"I'll put it back here in the corner, so no one else will see it. It'll be here when you get back. And, what of the fine horse?" pushed the man, "You have no horse, you said?"

"I'll have a horse afore I pick up the saddle," said Douglas walking away. Edward slipped his head and shoulder through his bow and followed.

The saddle maker took the straw out of his mouth and spat, saying "Damn sneakin' Scots!" and splenetically, he placed the saddle out in front of the shop, the better to attract a buyer.

The pair turned the corner onto Gillygate where the market stalls continued. The smells wafting from the various shops intermingled with other, not so pleasant ones, so a delicious whiff of baking goods would be completely ruined by the stench emanating from the tannery.

Dogs ran the streets in packs searching out whatever they could find. The more manageable ones served as guard dogs for various businesses around.

Some shop merchants had many fine imports from far away places brought to them by River Wear into the arm-crook of a bend in which the town nestled. Numerous craftsmen supplied the locally made items that people in the close countryside came to town to purchase, mostly with products of the farms. With enough trading one could usually get his desired supper with perhaps a bit of cheese left over for a morning repast.

As Edward and James continued their saunter they watched as a large sow was strung up by her hind legs. She had been clouted on the forehead with a heavy club and knocked unconscious if not killed outright, and once she was hanging completely off the ground, her throat would be cut, and the blood caught in pans set underneath. Then the flesh hewer would go to work cutting the great carcass into manageable portions for sale.

Her shoats, meanwhile, foraged around the pen for scraps of the previous kill.

"There's one we hain't goin' to take'," said Douglas in casual observation as they passed. The smell of the abattoir laid heavily around that part of the town, but the residents had grown used to it over the years. Edward and James spent as little time as possible nearby.

"Yonder's a fire," said Douglas pointing to a bright bellows-fed flame at the blacksmith shop.

"That'll work in our favor when we need it," growled Edward with his nose tucked in his sleeve. "And the roofs are most all thatched," he added, looking upward at the roofs on the single and two-story buildings, all packed in a tight row.

Douglas' hackles rippled, making him stop in his tracks. He instinctively knew something was wrong but he knew not what.

Edward turned to see why James had stopped and as he did he saw the saddler down the street pointing the two of them out to a pair of the sheriff's men, patrolling the market to keep order.

"Run James! RUN!" he shouted as he turned to run himself.

Douglas ran close to Edward's heels. As they turned the corner they ran into and toppled a cart of vegetables onto the muddy alleyway. A small, almost plump, woman began to caterwaul and nearly the whole population of the corner turned to see the commotion. A number of the men in their aprons and several shopkeepers' helpers gave chase, as much for the excitement on a dull day as for the damage to the woman's wares.

After a few more turns, Douglas peered around a corner to see if they were still being pursued. They were. The trailing crowd had grown larger.

"They're comin' fast," said Douglas as he nearly caught up to Edward, already down the street and away from the market. Edward quickly dodged into the doorway of a house on the far corner.

Douglas, thinking Edward had turned the corner, and with the guard in hot pursuit, cut to the left at the next street.

The guards and shopkeepers and their helpers followed, hurling threats and shouts and curses upon the two hapless Scots, when suddenly they realized they were chasing only one.

Some of the "rear guard", winded and tiring, turned in time to see Edward standing firmly behind them, arrow nocked and string pulled taut between his fingers.

With a shout of warning to the others, the English began to scatter. Edward loosed his arrow on the slowest, then slung another barb onto the bowstring and let it fly. The second shot was not so fortunate and landed in the next man's leg. He cursed and the Englishmen began to throw rocks and axes at the Scot.

The townsmen grew all the more angry when Edward began to laugh at their pitiful attempts to get back at him and off he ran.

Douglas spryly darted in and out of alleyways, pushing citizens and barrels and other standing things in the way of the self-appointed hounds chasing him. Determined not to lose him they persisted tightly on his trail.

By toppling a display of tinware and baskets as he passed he got some feet ahead. Then for pure deviltry, he stopping suddenly and drew his sword, shaking it at the discombobulated soldiers climbing over his hastily made barricade. Then, with a whistle, a smile and a "follow me" arm-wave, he disappeared around the corner.

Douglas returned to Gillygate by way of a midtown cross street and found Edward quietly leaning against a post munching an apple.

"Where ye been?" asked Edward, as if he hadn't only just returned a moment before.

"Damn near to London by my reckonin'," quipped the slightly younger man.

"I thought ye might'a got lost," gainsaid Edward, smiling.

"Got a mob of angry whoresons that'll be here directly," Douglas said, motioning down the street from where he had come.

Edward picked up his bow saying, "And as ye say, yonder they come."

Beckoning the mob again to the chase, James and Edward ran back through the market to where they had first entered the town not much earlier that morning.

Their pursuers began dropping off right regularly, winded from too much town life.

The Scots sprinted to the edge of the wooded park in which they had left their own contingent of men.

Out of breath, Douglas laughed between gasps as the English suddenly realized they were terribly outnumbered. It also occurred to them that there was something far more afoot than the ejection of two hooligans from the town.

They twisted and turned to reverse their course, doubling back into the marketplace screaming, "Scots! Scots a'raidin!"

Douglas was still chuckling when he climbed aboard his nimble horse and gulped down a couple of swigs of water from the skin carried on his saddle. Edward mounted his own horse, drew his sword and sauntered toward the town with Gillygate on his mind.

"Ye can't go any faster?" said Douglas, joining him.

"Givin' them English time to whip the citizens into a lather," said Edward.

Douglas smiled. Soon they could hear many voices yelling and creating much ado within Durham's fine market.

Edward dug his spurs deep into his horse's belly and whooped.

The rest followed.

The sheriff's men had run a straight line for the castle some streets over, screaming their warning to the utmost power of their lungs. They barely had crossed the drawbridge on the dry moat before it was raised in defense of the castle itself.

The king's soldiers were quickly summoned to the ramparts, drums pounded and horns blared, bringing news of the impending raid.

Edward and James drew their men to a line beyond arrow-range of the castle and loudly announced the Brus' demands for two thousand pounds in coin, cattle and grain. For that the Scots would avoid their town until the next June, like the others.

The castle warden refused to hear their words, instead telling them and their "so-called king" to go to hell.

"What ye reckon to do now?" asked Edward.

"We have them just where we want them," laughed Douglas.

"'Tain't funny!" retorted Edward, "We cannot take the castle, which they'll figure out right soon, and come out and beat the hell out of us!"

"Ye're surely right," agreed Douglas and he wheeled his horse toward the marketplace. "Come on!" he shouted, and the Brus men followed them around the tightly spaced streets back to Gillygate, where the citizens had grown bold in their absence and stood in a mob with weapons as were at hand, shaking and hooting menacingly.

"This hain't all that good," yelled Edward to James.

"Hain't all that bad, either," said Douglas as he made a straight line to the blacksmith shop.

Edward grinned and followed.

Douglas took great delight in tying a rope to the corner of the smithy's roof and pulling it down upon the heads of the smith and his helper, and dry grass fell in abundance upon the white-hot forge at which the pair had been at work. Within seconds it flared up and the thatch was soon a roaring fire, from under which the smith struggled to get away. Somewhere within, his helper screamed for aid, but the heat mounted so rapidly that none could get near him. His screams were mercifully short.

Several in the mob realized that the other roofs would indeed be alight if something weren't done to prevent it, and started yelling for water to be brought.

The rest, seeing the smith with his hair and tunic aflame, crawling from beneath the heavy, burning grass, angrily moved in on the mounted foreigners, but quickly scattered as the tough Scots methodically hacked to pieces those toward the front of the pack.

The commander of the garrison, standing on the ramparts, heard the commotion on the street and shouted to his lieutenant, "The shopkeepers have that little bunch of hooligans trapped in the market. Open the gate and sally forth to their rescue!"

The officer and his contingent gathered their weapons and left the castle on foot, heading toward the marketplace with swords drawn and blood revenge on their minds. The garrison's commandant went back to the parapet to watch his men put an end to the overreaching raiders, but upon his arrival at the wall saw instead a column of thick black smoke and flame rising above the heart of the town. "Damn!" was all that came to mind as he watched his soldiers trotting toward the conflagration in the marketplace.

As the English merchants and their customers sought buckets to carry water to douse the fire at the forge, Douglas and several others picked up burning embers and fiery clumps of thatch and flung them onto the thatch covered shops surrounding. Within minutes a half dozen other buildings' roofs were ablaze, and the rising heat carried fiery sparks to their neighbors. The whole market area would be burning shortly.

"Soldiers!" shouted one of Edward's men. The Scot quickly directed them to leave by the lower end of the street, and he and Douglas followed on their nimble horses as the English foot soldiers entered at a trot at the upper end.

Passing the saddler's, Douglas drew rein to slow his horse. The saddle still remained on the rail where he had first seen it. He leant to his left and grabbed it by the bow, swooping it onto the neck of his horse.

The saddle maker ran to recover the purloined saddle, swinging a long knife.

"Hie, Jemmy!" shouted Sir Edward, seeing the soldiers making their way around and through the burning shops and smoke filled alleyways.

Douglas freed his right hand with which he held his sword and swung it at the saddle-maker's knife hand. Fingers went flying, as did the knife, and the man ceased to have an interest in the saddle. Instead he began to yelp and hold tight to the stubs of his fingers to keep his blood from flowing to the ground.

Douglas spurred his horse deep to catch up with his men and they rolled out of town and disappeared into the woods.

The soldiers from the castle being on foot, the lieutenant called off the pursuit rather than approach the forest.

By the time the flames were conquered, most of the market area had been reduced to a blackened chasm of char and ash. Warehouses, shops, animal pens, and several of the merchants' homes had ceased to exist.

Knowing from the Corbridge ambassador (he who was beaten and sent home earlier) the demands made by King Robert, the bishopric remitted 2,000 pounds to the de Reymes manor house where Robert was staying, thus buying the town of Durham safety from Scottish raids for almost another year. The citizens of Durham couldn't imagine that King Robert had dared come so far into England in spite of the might of the English army. Nevertheless, when he demanded that one of the elements of his treaty with Durham and the surrounding areas must give him the right to ride peacefully through their territories to similarly make treaties with towns and villages farther south, such was granted.

Keeping his men from random pillaging and harassing individual farms and villages insured a long association with the northern English, and they began to think of themselves as under the protection of the King of Scots instead of their English king who had failed to protect them. Consequently, they quit sending their tax money to London and used it to pay Robert.

King Edward was furious but impotent to act for change because so many English magnates were against him.

ÒECEMBER 14th 1312
CASTLE WARWICK

Thomas Plantagenet, Lord Lancaster, led his entourage up the pathway toward Castle Warwick where he and his carefully selected group of renegade Ordainers had shuffled the hated and defiled Piers Gaveston off to his glory some six months earlier. The day of Lord Cornwall's execution did provide an occasional moment of hazy sun, but on this wintry day there was but a constant, miserably cold drizzle.

All of those who served as Gaveston's judges had survived, at least physically. Some of them had been absolved of their participation in Gaveston's trial and subsequent execution, while others yet remained rebellious and staunchly against their king. Edward, low as he was on political power, was nearly helpless at the hands of the Lords Ordainers in general, and certainly at great odds with Lord Lancaster. It could even be said that Thomas, himself a grandson of King Henry III, coveted his dear cousin's throne with a distinct passion.

The Earl of Pembroke, whose relinquishment of his sworn duty to Lancaster resulted in his word being broken, he being thus dishonored and his life put in jeopardy, uncharacteristically confessed his sins against the crown and begged the king for forgiveness. Furthermore, he distanced himself from those earls who were more directly responsible for the murderous execution.

As instructed, the castle inmates lined the last hundred feet to the steps of the castle entrance and cheered at Lancaster's arrival. Lord Guy of Warwick stood at the top of the short flight of stairs awaiting his fellow earl and conspirator. Pleased with the contrived reception, Thomas thought how his arrival was similar to the one Gaveston received, only then these same citizens were throwing piggery slops instead of cheers. He smiled at that bit of difference.

Earl Thomas climbed down from his saddle and bowed formally to Earl Guy who returned the bow, as did his wife, who curtsied at his side, and the general household servants gathered behind their earl as welcoming host.

"Well come Milord Thomas," offered Lord Guy with extraordinary joviality.

After the traveling entourage was dried and warmed, and served a feast that was small, but fit for any king in all Christendom, the two earls left the great hall to a private anteroom for a sub-rosa conversation.

Wine was poured into two ornate silver cups that rested on the table before the two men, after which the servant placed the nearly full flagon on the table and left quietly, closing the door behind him. The anteroom was left darkened. Only the warm glow of a single candelabra warmed the immediate tabletop and the faces of the two men as they leant, each toward the other in a manner that added to their conspiratorial ambience.

Thomas breathed deeply as he thought how to start the conversation.

"You've had a long day, Milord," said Guy. "Would you care to postpone this tête-à-tête until tomorrow?"

"Today we shall have our say, tomorrow we shall plot," answered Thomas, looking across the table at his dusky friend whose eyes virtually leapt from their sockets with curiosity.

"Plot?" questioned Warwick.

Sir Thomas smiled. "How I shall be made king," he quipped.

"King is it, you want to be?"

"I should be a better king than he has shown himself!" shot back Thomas, louder than he should have.

Sir Guy held his hand up to indicate his disinterest in the possibility of an argument.

Thomas calmed his enthusiasm and spoke in a barely audible voice, "You know the queen birthed a male child last month at Windsor?"

"I have gotten the news," answered Guy with a sardonic smile. "Is that your worry?"

"I thought the little sodomist would never get around to bedding his queen, shall we say... successfully," murmured Thomas, still almost under his breath. He drank a great gulp of wine, picked up the flagon from the center of the small table and poured more into his cup.

"Who said he managed the deed?" said Warwick mysteriously.

"He proclaims it for himself!" growled Thomas, his anger and disgust seething in his bosom. "He has even made the boy Earl of Chester. Would he do that for another man's child?"

Guy de Beauchamp settled back against the leather of his chair and took a sip from his own cup. Then he chuckled way down in his throat.

"He has an heir! I fail to see the humor in that!" hissed Sir Thomas.

"Think back ten months, my friend," goaded Guy.

"Ten months?" asked Thomas. He was tired and a bit irritated at de Beauchamp's coyness, but nevertheless asked, "Why?"

"Because ten months ago, the little piece of shit was runnin' all over the north of England hidin' from us and trying to save Gaveston's wonderful arse!" reminded Guy humorously.

Thomas sat nonplussed for a moment before his whole demeanor changed to one of astonishment. "Damned right, you are!" he exclaimed aloud, his eyes alight.

"Damned right I am," said Guy, again with a wry smile.

"How then could it have happened?"

"I have found there is only one way fornication occurs, Milord. A man and a woman meet and lie together," flatly stated Guy. He chuckled again, "However, 'tis likely the 'man' in this case, was not our revered king!"

"Good God!"

The two men sat in silence for a long moment as Sir Thomas abstractly stroked his beard and his mind ran through various perspectives on the event of this boy's nativity. Sir Guy enjoyed watching the earl's emotions play upon his countenance.

Thomas suddenly flattened his hand and slammed it down upon the table three times, hard. "If I can get my hands on whoever fathered that child I will have his head *and* my reason to be king!"

"Perhaps you have already had his head, Milord," he paused, "in a box."

Thomas stared at Lord Guy for a long, long moment, his eyes then moving toward the lighted candles. "It is impossible. They *both* were in the north *together*... always together," he said without blinking.

"Can you think of another man in the world who could have squirted that child from his cod and have it be accepted by Edward?" offered Earl Guy rhetorically.

Thomas's rough-hewn mind reeled at the potential for the relationship.

"Gaveston is reaching out from his shallow grave on Blacklow Hill to undo us, My Friend," said Guy. Thomas remained transfixed on the four flickers of flame to his left.

"How far must we go to kill that goddamned Gaveston?" finally said a disheartened Thomas. "His seed will do us in yet."

"Long years lie ahead, Milord, afore the seed becomes a man," prophesied Earl Guy, trying to ease the dark mood, come so gently upon the pair.

William Oliphant

ðeceɑbeꞅ 20ch 1312
Che Coᴜᴎ ꝍꝚ peꞅCh

"My King!" shouted Cuthbert just ahead of the flight of arrows that, like a handful of pebbles thrown into a pond, pelted the ground only feet from Robert's back as he hunkered about the fire with several of his knights. All sat just beyond the farthest distance of the archers' reach, though some of the Scots had their shields at their backs, just in case.

To see if there were more missiles in flight, Robert stood and peered at the wall through the haze of dusk. "Looks like they would be done for the day by now," he said. A grim smile crossed his lips.

"Maybe they just can't stand doin' nothin', Sire," said Cuthbert, "with us a'settin' here a'starvin' 'em out."

"If they put their archers on the towers they could probably get to us," mumbled Robert.

"Hope that ain't their thought, or they'd do worse than vex us, I'd say, My King," returned Cuthbert. "We fixin' to go out again tonight, are we?"

Robert nodded affirmatively. "See to the collectin' of the arrows soon as it's dark, and distribute them to the archers," commanded Robert as he quietly turned back to the fire and his conversation with his knights.

"Aye, My King," answered Cuthbert, and he swung his arm to beckon his friend Fergus to join him at the chore.

"Just trickin' us, they are," grumbled Fergus as he timidly neared the barbs.

"Trickin' us?" questioned Cuthbert.

"Just want us in closer, says I," Fergus muttered.

"Why?" exclaimed Cuthbert, "so they can shoot us!? Why us when there's real knights hereabouts?"

"I hain't a 'Sir', but I still don't want to be dead," argued the good-sized man. Fergus winced as he bent down to pull the shafts from the ground, for his back often got stiff in the area of the scar he carried from having been slashed years before by the sword of a Swan Knight.

"S'pose ye be hopin' for our king to go collectin'," offered Cuthbert sarcastically.

"King's don't be pickin' up arrows," replied Fergus, sourly.

"That's why we be doin' the pickin'," gainsaid Cuthbert, venturing into the edge of the killing range from the nearest walls of the town of Perth.

For two weeks Robert had held the city of Perth tightly bound. The River Tay, flowing at its back, fed a wide moat on the other three sides making the whole town an island fortress defended by four well-placed towers.

The old King Edward had taken the then moated but wall-less city of Perth seventeen years earlier, and murdered most of the Scottish population. The battle was already over when he gave the order that the townspeople be killed, and they were, in such numbers and with such viciousness that the slaughter of men, women, and children went on for days, not stopping until Edward responded to an appeal by clergymen of Perth. He had made sure that Perth would never again lift a hand against him. A master at planning and building defenses, he then personally directed construction of the curtain walls and other fortifications that the Brus now found so vexing.

The King of Scots had no siege machinery with which he might force a fight, thus the siege was reduced to a matter of patience, of waiting it out. Inside, they could be dining on fancy meats, or eating rats or boiled shoe leather, or nothing at all; Robert would have no idea which, until the English capitulated or suddenly dropped their drawbridge and came out prepared to fight for food.

"'Tis supper, My King," said Christina when she came to the hunkered knot of men.

Robert stood and smiled at her cheerfully.

"Slight wind from our backs toward the town," she offered almost casually. "Time to roast a pig."

Robert looked at her, then back toward the tall town walls, where he could easily see men with pikes walking their posts. Others gathered in groups of twos and threes along the parapet, watching the Scots in their camps and no doubt discussing how best to rid the front lawn of that evil scourge Robert the Brus and his band of outlaws.

"Cuthbert!" Robert called the fellow from the field where he was still looking for additional shafts.

"Aye, My King," he yelled back.

"Ye've a pig to kill!" Robert shouted, trying not to keep it a secret. "Fetch Gelis to see to the cookin'!"

Within an hour, the pig had been killed, cleaned, gutted, and spitted, and had begun roasting slowly over a hot fire. Crackling sparks and the delicious smell of cooking pork about to be consumed warmed the army's general constitution. Light winds soon picked up and carried the scent across the open field to the men on the wall and beyond.

Sir William Oliphant, commander of the garrison, mounted the long flight of stone stairs to peer over the battlements toward those who surrounded him.

"Smells like pig a'cookin'," said Oliphant filling his nostrils to their fullest extent.

"Hain't had pork since they took Dundee back in April," offered one of the guards as he stood, his head pushed outward between the merlons for a better sniff.

"Hain't had much of anythin'," said Oliphant almost in a whisper.

"We givin' up?" asked the captain of the guard who was a fellow Scot.

Oliphant paused thoughtfully, "Not for a meal of roast pork, we hain't."

The captain drew the commander aside and confessed, "I know we gave our word to fight for the English, but by God, I like not a whet of it!"

"Bound by that word we shall remain, ne'ertheless," growled Oliphant and raising his fist toward the lesser man threatened, "or I will have yer yellow locks swingin' off the wall where ol' Wallace's left arm bones be danglin' yonder!"

The captain's eyes grew large and he was sorry he had taken such a candid approach to the conversation with his superior.

"We'll not be givin' up this command for the likes of that pig," he mumbled to himself. Then he stopped in the midst of his thought. "Tain't me that needs a'tellin'," he scolded. "'Tis that Robert the Brus!"

He leant over the wall as far as he could manage without falling and shouted with all his force. "We'll not be givin' up the walls of Perth for the likes of a whiff of roast pig!" Ye a'hearin' me, Robert the Brus!?" but the wind was against him.

Robert heard not a word.

• •

At that time of year the pale sun limped across the welkin in about one-third of a measured day, after which the long stygian darkness set in for the other two-thirds. As the fires burnt low, and Robert's men settled in for a long winter night's sleep, the cold seeped into their clothing, their tents, and their bodies. Sleeping bundled together under shared blankets was often mere survival when bitter, wind-hurried cold stalked the camp.

Robert lay dozing on a bed of wooly sheepskins when Christina slipped quietly under the covers and snuggled close to him, resting her head comfortably on his massive shoulder.

Thus disturbed, he heaved a long sigh and began to stir.

Christina made room for him to move as he began working off the long, heavy shirt of mail that he wore always when on campaign. The Scots' camp was never entirely immune to a surprise attack, even on the darkest of nights, like this one.

"Where ye bound?" she questioned quietly.

"The moat," he answered.

"Ye can't see," Christina protested.

"They can't see me either with the clouds a'coverin' that quarter-moon," he returned.

"Ye takin' Cuthbert again?"

"Aye." He laced up his heavy boots and stood to pull a thick, fleece-lined jerkin on, and hang a dagger and sheath off his wide belt.

"I'll be a'waitin' for ye, Robbie."

Robert pushed the flap of the tent open and silently disappeared into the darkness. Christina lay back on the fleeced sheepskins, absorbing the heat and the smell left where he had lain.

Within little more than a quarter of an hour, Robert and Cuthbert were working their way along the edge of the moat. Cuthbert carried a contraption he had devised from a length of light line on one end of which he had secured a stone the size of his two fists. The thus weighted line ran along the shaft of a long lance to which he had fastened a forked branch cut from a tree, the line passing through the fork. With this device the pair had set out to measure the depth of the moat ringing the city walls.

When they reached the part of the moat that Robert wanted sounded, Cuthbert would drop the stone off the end of the lance into the middle of the moat and wait until the stone hit bottom. Having tied small knots in the line at regular intervals, Cuthbert could then pull the line back, count the knots, and thus gauge how deep the water was at that spot. So far, all he had managed to say was "too deep", which meant anything of a depth that Robert could not ford.

After a time of dropping and retrieving the stone to the forked tip of the lance, the pair began to think there was no spot less deep than "too deep." Cuthbert's back and shoulders began to burn and ache from holding the lance pole out over the water at the same height and pulling the line back each time. By then the stone felt like a boulder.

Still, they persevered, until he dropped the stone and heard the splash, as did the men above them on the parapet wall.

"I heard somethin'!" said one. The two Scots at the moat's frozen edge stopped any movement.

"Ah, it's just a fish," offered his companion looking over the parapet wall into the inky darkness and listening for any other sound. With torches burning at intervals along the wall, on dark nights it was difficult to see anything beyond the wall unless it was also lighted. Straining to hear, he could barely discern the gentle ripple of the slowly running stream that was the city's moat.

"Like to catch a nice fish for breakfast," averred the first.

"Reckon you would," the other returned with a chuckle, and they moved down the wall toward the corner, leaving everything silent once more.

Cuthbert retrieved and dropped, retrieved and dropped, each time measuring the depth as unsatisfactory for fording.

Splash! The stone hit the water yet again. At that point, after searching for two agonizing nights, Cuthbert whispered, "Hain't so deep here, Milord. Might be shallow enough."

"Are ye sure?" asked the king.

"Can't be fer sure, but I think it is, Sire."

Robert looked at the ice-encrusted bank and the slithering black liquid and knew what he must do. He left his sheathed dagger with Cuthbert and slid gently down the bank and into the icy water, determined to make sure of its depth. He had to check it himself because Cuthbert was afraid of deep water.

Slowly, trying not to make the slightest audible plash, he forced himself to walk toward the center of the stream encircling the city, feeling his way along the slippery bottom with his toes. He knew his time in the moat would be limited. Already his legs were beginning to cramp from the extreme cold.

He felt renewed discomfort as each additional inch of his skin was assaulted by the shockingly frigid liquid, but he would not allow it to drive him back. Finally, he reached the midpoint, and though he was beginning to shiver unwillingly, his determination made him continue to the far bank. The maximum depth reached only to his neck.

Turning around, he started back, but his toes were no longer telling him where he might safely step. They were so cold they had lost all feeling. Still, he tried to hurry; the aching cold would soon become unbearable, and he realized that he could become immobilized and drown. He remembered well how painfully stiff his knees became when he and Andrew waded in the burn to avoid the trap laid by the Lord of Lorne. *God in Heaven, that was a long time ago*, he thought.

His reverie broke his concentration on the present danger and upon his very next step he slipped. Unable to regain his balance, he splashed loudly into the gelid moat.

On the wall the two soldiers couldn't mistake that noise.

"Gotta be a damn whale a'jumpin' to make that big a splash!" said the first loudly.

"Cease your prattle and listen," commanded the second.

Robert sank low in the water so that just his eyes showed above the surface. Cuthbert lay on the ground as still as if dead.

"Can't see... can you?" one asked the other.

"Lower a lantern, fools," said the guard captain, having heard the conversation and come to take charge.

"I'll get a rope," someone said, and footsteps could be heard running along the wall walk.

Robert sighed. He knew they would be discovered if he didn't get out of the water fast. Though his teeth began to chatter and his muscles no longer obeyed his every command, he stayed up to his chin in the water and struggled to the bank.

The guards worked frantically and lowered the candle lamp into the darkness.

"I see somethin'," yelled a guard. He lifted his bow and nocked an arrow onto the string, pulling it back and letting the arrow fly, a bit too quickly perhaps. It splashed into the water near Robert's shoulder, but failed even to nick the king.

Cuthbert had better luck. He, too, had loaded an English arrow into his bow and let it fly, straight at the swaying lantern. The glass shattered and the flame went out, immediately returning the darkness. The captain cursed and told his archer to pepper the area with arrows. Within a minute there were four thuds as arrows nearly buried themselves beside the spot where Cuthbert had stood, but he had moved remarkably quickly, and now sent arrows toward the archer atop the wall. He was gratified to hear the shout of someone in pain. That bought them a few minutes.

Robert had kept his feet digging at the muddy walls of the moat and had managed to pull himself out of the water. Cuthbert came to his side, and helped him stand.

"Hie to the camp," commanded Robert stumbling along as best as his nearly frozen extremities would allow. Cuthbert kept up with his king, but faced backward toward the city wall most of the time. When the English brought up another lantern to lower, Cuthbert stopped and put a couple of arrows between the merlons nearest the soldiers, causing them to drop the lamp into the water, dousing the light and wrapping the moat in darkness once more.

Shooting blindly, the English sent several deadly shafts whizzing by the fleeing Scots, but none close enough to worry them. What concerned Robert most was that his knees were locking up as they had before, and he could barely walk. He felt so cold in the light wind that he was sure the water had been warmer.

On the city wall, Oliphant arrived to find out what the hubbub was about. He carried a lantern like the one Cuthbert had broken, and it shed a warm light upon the clutch of men gathered about the wounded captain.

"What's happenin'?" demanded Oliphant, seeing the captain holding his forearm, which was skewered through by an arrow shaft.

"We fell under attack, Milord," stated the guard captain through a grimace.

"Did they breach the walls?!" Oliphant asked looking first one way and then another to ascertain the extent of the incursion.

"Nae, Sir William, they were comin' across the moat, they were," again reported the captain.

"They can't get across that moat!" growled Oliphant in anger, but he looked down upon the quiet water all the same.

"They ran off, Sir, soon as we saw them in the water," nodded one guard.

"In the water?!" asked Oliphant in disbelief. "Their mail would sink them!"

"Perhaps they came without armor," Groaned the captain. "All I know is that they were comin' across the moat and when we tried to get a lantern down to the water, whoever they were broke the lamp and ran off layin' arrows up here by the score. One of 'em put this shaft through my arm." He held out the bleeding forearm for Oliphant to see.

After looking at it, Oliphant cast his gaze out over the edge of the wall, but could see nothing moving through sleepy, tired eyes. Off in the distance he could make out the fires in the quiet camp of the besieging Army of Brus, but he could see no movement about them. It was not an army on the move in any direction.

"Ye men are truly addled! Those whoresons are asleep, which is where I should be but for your alarm," he complained in a snorting manner characteristically Oliphant. "Frozen stiff they'd be," he mumbled.

"Then who pierced my arm like this?" the injured captain asked testily, forgetting his place. He realized right away that he had spoken out of turn by the look on Oliphant's reddening face.

"Very well, Captain! If you say we are under attack, then call out the garrison!" commanded Sir William, "We'll stay ready all night if need be!"

Robert and Cuthbert had made it back to the camp without being seen from the wall, but his own picket caught sight of the two figures right quick since he was expecting their return.

"That ye, My King?" he loudly whispered, his poleax at the ready, in case.

"Come and help, ye lackwit!" shouted Cuthbert, no longer intimidated by the possibility of being caught.

Three large men moved toward the darkness to locate the two men, fearing to carry a lantern within the killing field. Reaching the pair, they quickly assessed the situation. One man wrapped his dry cloak around the shivering king and with the others, hefted him off his frozen feet to carry him to his tent.

While awaiting his return, Christina had warmed several heavy blankets by hanging them close to the fire outside the tent. With the wind blowing coldly and Robert's past illness, she thought it best to prepare a warming wrap for him. Little did she know that he would be soaking wet as well, and when she saw them carrying him, her heart as well as her mind began to race.

She opened the tent flap and the four men placed Robert upon the bed of fleeced skins.

"Help me take off his wet clothing… and get his boots off, the muddy things are holdin' the cold against his feet," she said, knowing she alone couldn't handle the task with him almost unconscious from the cold. Cuthbert began undoing the leather laces while the other men removed his jerkin, shirt, and trews. While they worked at moving the large dead weight around, she retrieved the warm blankets from the fireside and came back.

What now?" Cuthbert asked as he pulled the second boot from Robert's foot and a streamlet of water ran out onto the ground.

"Be obliged if ye'd stoke up that fire behind ye," she said, "and hang his wet clothes on the sticks I left by it." Cuthbert took the dripping clothing with him as she shooed them all out of the tent. Quickly, she folded the warmest blanket in half, rolled him onto his side and put it against his bare back so that when she let him down again, he lay flat atop it. The second blanket she folded as well, and laid it over him from his chin to his feet, then covered all with the third and tucked it in around him until he looked like a swaddled babe. She went quickly outside and retrieved a smooth rock from the fireplace and wrapped it in her woolen shawl, then brought it in and placed it against his icy feet.

Kneeling beside him she gently rubbed a warmed oil on his forehead and his cheeks. His skin was so cold she whispered to him as she touched him, "Ye've 'bout killed yerself, Robbie! Ye grand fool! Why d'ye not let one of these other fools do this sort of thing for ye, if it must be done," her eyes brimmed with great tears as she tried to get him to speak though she knew he had no answer. And he was again shivering.

Returning to the fire outside the tent, she retrieved a cup of hot broth and brought it in to him. Again, she tried to rouse him, at least enough to sip some of the strengthening liquid. Eventually he opened his eyes and she held the vessel to his lips. After a couple of sips he whispered through chattering teeth, "I found the way, Christina! I found the way."

"I hope 'tis worth it," she said. He closed his eyes again, and she worried as she rubbed the shaking hulk as vigorously as she could manage through the blankets, trying to get him warm.

Cuthbert had left the interior of the tent and done as he was bade, hanging Robert's wet things on her sticks. He had then hunkered for a while near the flame as he stirred it, as much to warm himself as to build the flame, and having added a few sturdy sticks to the embers, left to wander on toward where he and Fergus had laid a bed for themselves and their pixie-like woman, Gelis. She always saw that both men were fed and warmed, and blessed by the little people each night.

Christina worked her way into the covers keeping Robert as warm as possible. Soon the shivering and the chattering ceased.

"Oh Robert," she sighed, talking to him though he was sound asleep, "I am right... ye know. Ye are a fool." She clutched him tighter and soon they were both warm and asleep.

The pickets enjoyed listening to all the commotion at the top of the walls of Perth in fear that the Brus Scots were going to cut off their ears and split their guts in a secret raid. Before long, that involved flying across the moat and up the wall, wielding swords and axes in their pure state of nakedness.

• •

Next morning, the sun made a valiant effort to appear through a mostly clouded sky. Robert awoke to the sounds of the camp already involved in surviving another day of siege against the walled city. He discovered that Christina was sleeping closely to him, and he was unusually warm. His second discovery was that he was totally nude beneath the blankets. He had some vague memory of being wrapped in warmth after having been so terribly cold, but that detail evaded his wit.

Christina awoke at his movement. She looked at his face and kissed him on the closest part of it she could reach, his bearded jaw. He turned and replied with a kiss upon her lips.

"Good day to ye, My King," she whispered.

"And to ye, Milady," said he, smiling at his good fortune to have her by his side on campaign, but she felt a hint of sadness in his reply.

In truth, so she told herself, she would have liked to be on her farm, breeding and tending her horses with Robert by her side, but such was not possible she knew. Thus, she accompanied Robert to ward off a recurrence of the dreaded illness that had kept him down for most of the winter of '07 and '08.

In fact, she had been deeply in love with Robert since their time together more than fourteen years earlier, after Robert's wife Isabella de Mar died. Their two children were a testament to the love she held for him then. It had not diminished, at least on her part.

"I see ye are yet alive this morn, thank God," she quipped as Robert sat up.

"Aye, barely, and thanks to you as well," he muttered and turned to look at her, lying on the soft sheep hides, her hair splayed framing her beautiful face. He smiled somberly, then stood with much effort, only to bump his head on the ceiling of the low tent ceiling.

"Ach!" She realized she had left him naked and said, "Ye need dry clothes, Robbie!" She felt the chill of the absence of mutual warmth. She retrieved the dry clothing for him and he put it on, but spoke hardly a word to her. She wondered why he was so taciturn, and asked, "Are ye feelin' unwell, Robbie?"

Realizing that he had not spoken for some time, he said, "Pardon, Christina. I am disturbed by a dream I had o'er the night. Left me unsettled. Brought back many old memories I thought were well gone."

Christina came and put her hand on his arm and asked, "It was probably because of your night's adventure. You were nearly frozen when you returned." She looked into his face and saw sorrow, and perhaps even what she would call despair. The look worried her greatly. "Tell me, My King, of your dream," she said softly.

"'Twas yonder then," said Robert, imagining back nearly seven years. He flung the portal flap back and pointed to the main gate to the town of Perth. "Yonder we stood before the gate, proud and full of chivalry. With me were Randolph, Seton, and Edward, all sittin' our destriers like proper knights, our lances lifted so that the pennants on them fluttered in the late day's breeze." His eyes misted.

"Earl Pembroke offered us a fight on the morn of the next day... we believed his sincerity and accepted. Went to Methven Park as he suggested... Pembroke attacked us that evenin' when we were layin' about by our cook fires not expectin' hell to come 'til the morrow." His voice was near a whisper by the time he said, "I saw them all in my dream last night, Nigel, Thomas, Alexander, Seton, Scrymgoer the flag bearer... the bishop's squire... all that are now dead rode again with me, but then... they were no more, and I was back at the gates of Perth, but this time they were opening. And when I looked at who it was that opened it," he looked at Christina, "...none was there but me..."

Christina sighed in sympathy but she knew it was not sympathy for which Robert was searching... it was justice for Scotland as a community and perhaps a tinge of personal revenge for losing so many of his family members and friends to the war.

Robert gazed at the great gate of Perth for a long, contemplative moment before announcing suddenly, "We're leavin' this morn!"

"While ye have them mostly starved?" she asked.

"They're a ways from starvin'," he said matter-of-factly. "Reckon they hain't e'en et the dogs."

"They set great store by their dogs, Robbie," she replied. "'Twas the dogs that kept ye from takin' Berwick month last, if ye recollect."

"Aye," he returned, "I recollect it all."

• •

Robert and his small army did pack up and leave that very morning, riding past a happy throng of hooters and jeerers shouting from the top of the city wall. His men liked it not one whit, but Robert was king and they did as he commanded.

Sim of the Leadhouse

◌ECℇ(ⅢBEℛ 21ₛᴄ 1312
ℛOℵBURGɦsɦIℛE

Near dark in a small village in Roxburghshire, the winter wind whipped the thatched roofs of the dozen or so villeins' huts and cotters' hovels as a lone rider made his way to the only blacksmith shop for miles around. He tucked his hood tight to his face once again as he came the last few feet to his destination, easily found by following the measured pounding of hammer against hot steel from within. As he wearily climbed from the saddle of his destrier and pulled open the door to the shop, he stepped over the threshold and asked loudly in an unmistakable man's voice, "Sim of the Leadhouse?"

A wiry, white bearded man with high cheekbones and a head with black, but sparse hair sprouting from the top of his pate, looked up from his work with piercing, deep-set blue eyes. "Aye," he growled in an unfriendly voice.

Andrew Stewart stepped forward into the light and pushed his hood back, giving the smith a view of his own plentiful, unkempt hair and youthful face, and placed his hand on the pommel of his still-sheathed sword.

Sim stood erect, his hammer remaining well in his hand. "What ye want, boy?"

"King Robert sent me," the king's squire said sternly.

His crotchety expression unchanged, Sim studied Andrew a moment trying to understand why such a young man was sent on such an important mission. But Andrew's stalwart presentation of himself at last convinced him that the young man was who he said he was, and he smiled, giving the hot iron on his anvil another lick. He quickly frowned and fussed at the iron.

"Ach!" said the smith. "Ye're too cold now. Back in the coals with ye!" and he shoved the metal into the hot fire and pumped his foot up and down a few times to work the bellows, building the heat.

Andrew knew he had come to the right place.

"King Robert sent ye, did he?"

"Aye. Ye have somethin' for him?"

"Two things, My Laddie," said Sim, and he reached over to pull Andrew closer into the light.

Andrew, not yet trusting Sim, slipped his dagger from its sheath and held it to the ready beneath his surcoat.

Sim saw the movement and said, "Ye'll have no mind to use that on me, Laddie, for I have great pride for our king and his army... poor souls roamin' the countryside in spite o' the freezin' we'll be havin' these long winter nights." He smiled broadly, and taking the boyish face between his hard blacksmith's hands, drew him closer and bussed him lightly on the cheek.

Embarrassed, Andrew blushed and pulled back. Sim let him slide easily from his fingertips, leaving sooty black smudges on both sides of his face.

"Tell our king that Sim of the Leadhouse be fixin' for him 'til one of us drops to the dirt dead."

"I shall relay that message to him," replied Andrew.

Sim wrapped his work into two gunnysacks and tied them together at the throats. "Ye can throw these o'er the rump of yer horse and ride off," he said handing the lot to Andrew.

"What do I tell the king about when he can send for more?" asked Andrew.

"A moon's worth," was the reply as Sim went back to poking and stoking his fire, reheating the piece he was working when Andrew walked in. He spoke not another word.

The young man took the heavy sacks and put them over his broad shoulders. He glanced at the inviting pile of hay, wanting to lie in it and sleep at least until dawn but one glance at Sim, throwing hot sparks from the white hot, glowing metal with each blow, and he felt safer taking his chances in the forest.

He did reach down and pick up a handful of fodder for his destrier, who would find foraging on the way back to King Robert difficult at best.

ÒECEMBER 21sτ
MEτꝪVEN PARK

Robert, by a serpentine path, arrived in Methven Park only a few hours after he had unceremoniously left the walls of Perth. Methven was now devoid of trees except for those defining the edges, and the ground rose up slightly on the far side where Robert had set his headquarters tent those many years ago.

His men began to pitch their tents and build their lean-tos on the site, for the wind was strong and cold. Others worked on a stable of sticks and other debris for the few remaining horses and mules that had not died of the cold or starvation to be subsequently eaten by the men. They had neither wagons nor wains. Everything was carried by the men or by pack animals.

Robert and Christina dismounted. His mind was full of the battle that had happened there soon after he took the Scottish crown and became king. Their horses followed as the pair walked slowly along.

The details were vivid in Robert's memory. He had mulled it over and over in the air trying to understand why, even with Pembroke's deceit, why he lost so badly. It was the one battle that had convinced him without a doubt, that pitched battles were not the way to win his war against the English. His entire battle strategy was subsequently reworked.

This was the battle that cost him at least two thousand men immediately, and the potential for many thousands more in the future. He was marked as being weak and ineffective against the hated English, making many fearful who would otherwise have thrown their lots with Robert. After Methven, they needed to see more "victory trophies" hanging from his banner.

Christina could see that he was in agony as he looked over the ground. She moved closer to him and put her arm around his waist. His eyes remained transfixed on the ground even though his men and women went about their business before his sight.

"Ye must not torture yerself so, Milord," she said gently.

Robert sighed deeply, knowing that she was trying to comfort him, but somehow it wasn't working. He felt terrible and he knew not what would save him from the anguish.

As they walked upon the once blood-soaked field, Robert espied a bit of dirty white within a swath of dried leaves. Knowing that it was not a patch of left over snow, he moved toward it slowly, and stooped to examine it better. Christina paused at his side. As he swept away some of the wet leaves, she gasped. It was part of a skull and neck bones, all that remained of one of his brave warriors of that day, now washed out of his shallow grave with a faded bit of plaid cloth still visible about his neck.

Robert picked up the broken skull and wept.

Christina wept, too, for Robert as well as for the dead Scot. How bitter were their tears, and how strongly those tears forged their resolve.

Some of the men and women at their chores stopped at the sight, and realizing the significance, offered prayers and reverence for their fallen predecessors.

Robert struggled to his feet, suddenly worn and heavy. "We must set our camp t'other side of the road," he ordered, not wishing to disturb the site where so many valiant Scots yet lay, just beneath the surface.

None complained as the small army pulled their stakes and moved across the road where the trees grew tall.

• •

Two days later, Andrew Stewart walked his tired destrier into Methven Park expecting to find the army bivouacked there, but it was deserted. He thought Robert must still be at the walls of Perth and had not been able to keep the time table laid out for him at the beginning of his mission.

As he rode a little ways more, however, he heard the crackling of wet wood burning at campfires, and drawing closer, people talking in low tones.

He dismounted quietly and crept closer to determine if these people were friends or foes. Seeing Robert walking among them, he shouted, "My King!"

Robert turned toward the familiar voice. "Andrew!" he replied cheerfully.

Andrew waded through the underbrush to Robert's side, and Robert smiled at the sight of the youth who was much like a son to him.

"Ye bring a package from Sim?" asked the king.

Andrew held up two fingers and smiled. Robert returned the smile and slapped Andrew on the back. "Ye hungry?" he asked.

"Ye have victuals, Sire?" asked Andrew in return, as he relaxed for the first time since being sent on the mission to Sim.

"A plenty we have, for it bein' wintertime."

JANUARY 6th 1313
The Town of Perth

It was as black as the darkest pitch except for the occasional brief shaft of moonlight darting through the scant spaces between fast moving clouds. In spite of the occasional showers of tiny, stinging ice pellets falling from the clouds, the small Scots army stealthily moved toward the walls of the town with Robert at its head. Andrew followed directly behind, dragging Sim's work in one of the gunnysacks while Cuthbert dragged the other. They all crept quietly, without so much as a cough, not knowing whether the cold wind blowing from the northwest was carrying or masking the sounds of their movements.

Reaching the icy edge of the moat, Robert used the breaks in the clouds to find the spot on the moat where he wanted to cross. This foray was the reason he had inched across the moat two weeks before, and he purposely remembered just where he was then.

Had the wind been calm the choppy water they faced would have been covered with a smooth sheet of ice, perhaps thick enough that they could have walked across. As it was, the frigidly cold moat water would have to be crossed as Robert had, a fact about which those with him had been more than dubious.

"We'll all drown!" was the most common objection when Robert announced the plan in camp, hours before. He had selected the tallest men in his army to make the crossing with him, and each man could cross without his mouth being under water, at least if the water were not too rough. After a passionate exhortation from Robert and Cuthbert's assurance that Robert had crossed without difficulty, the men agreed to the venture, though some still grumbled.

So, as Robert paced down the bank, his men awaited in their chain mail and helms, as nervous about wading across the moat as about the battle itself. The air was cold and crisp, and they were not looking forward to being wet as well.

In only minutes Robert had found the spot he sought and slipped into the water resisting the urge to gasp at the cold.

Andrew quietly opened his gunnysack and removed a rope ladder similar to the one Robert had designed to be used at Urquhart castle in the winter of 1307. With Sim of the Leadhouse and his smithy, improvements had been made to enhance its stability.

Like the old one, the new ladder was made of stout hemp rope, knotted at every foot to hold wooden steps in place, and every third step had a wooden fender to hold the narrow boards away from the wall. At the top the ropes were secured to a cloth-wrapped iron device that extended the width of the wall and angled down ninety degrees on either side to assure that the ladder would be firmly anchored in place atop the wall. The bigger the men who climbed it, the more solidly the ladder would hold.

Robert quickly took the ladder's top and a long spear-like pole that had been fashioned for the chore, and ventured deeper into the moat as the others watched in awe at his determination. Dreading the cold bath, Andrew clenched his teeth and slid down the bank, carrying the ropes and boards ladder in its stout sack.

About halfway across Robert was up to his chin in the water. He turned to look at Andrew who was at least three inches less in height and was bouncing off the bottom to keep his head above the surface. Robert back-stepped several feet and handed Andrew the pole, taking the lad's ladder in trade and kept moving toward the wall. Lightened significantly, Andrew found it easier to keep his nose above the surface, though occasionally resorted to touching bottom and pushing off to move ahead.

The men on the edge of the bank watched wide-eyed as their king moved quietly in the ever-changing light. They knew he must be close to exhaustion from the icy water, and admiration inspired them to follow him. Looking from one to another of his companions, the first screwed up his courage and slid down the steep decline as Andrew had done. Then another followed, and another, until one-by-one, every man had slipped quietly into the murk and was making his way across the ditch, carrying his weapons.

Robert and Andrew, on the bank at the foundation of the wall, pushed the tip end of the pole into the socket on the iron bracket as the others completed their crossing in absolute silence. The king and his former squire then raised the ladder's bracket to the top of the wall and forced it across the floor of the crenellation. It dropped into position with perfection.

Robert motioned for Andrew to go up as Fergus came with chattering teeth to join the pair. Andrew drew his sword and ascended the ladder. Robert and Fergus moved about ten feet farther down the wall and placed the second ladder.

Robert started up. His hand picked men were now all in the water or standing on the narrow bank dripping wet, and truly anxious to get up the wall as quickly as possible.

Andrew was first at the top. He slowly stretched over the wall, leaning on the ladder's iron- work, and peered up and down the wall walk. When he saw Robert peering back at him and no one else in sight, he slipped across the wall and hunkered tight to it.

As soon as his cold feet were again under him, Robert slowly crept down the wall walk and saw the guards wrapped in blankets and sitting on up-turned buckets at the far end, their weapons leaning casually against the ramparts. The Scot smiled.

When his twenty and two shivering and dripping men were all gathered on the wall, Robert drew his sword in one hand and his axe in the other, a signal to the others to draw their own weapons. Robert then strolled down the wall walk unimpeded to where the worthless guards kept warm. They awoke quickly enough when they felt cold steel on their warm necks.

Half a dozen men followed Andrew down the stone steps to the gate tunnel. The near darkness covered their presence and the guards at the tunnel were killed with daggers, without warning.

Andrew pulled a torch from its wall bracket as the others in his party lowered the drawbridge and freed the great gate of its large iron bolts. The doors were thrown wide open and Andrew waved the torch over his head in wig-wag fashion. Suddenly, the fields came alive with Robert's men who quietly crept across the drawbridge and poured into the narrow streets like floodwaters gushing from a breached dam.

Robert's men easily had the sleeping town subdued with very little resistance.

There was neither castle nor keep within the walls of Perth. There were houses of every description, from a multitude of hovels to a very few larger more substantial houses, but in the largest stone house near the gate, Robert knew, he would find William Oliphant.

He purposefully opened and strode through the front door alone, with only his axe held by his side. The servants obviously had not yet awakened Oliphant, but were wide awake themselves. When Robert asked where he might find their master they nervously pointed up the stairs to the second floor.

Robert ascended the stone stairs and opened the bedroom door. There lay Oliphant sound asleep, not knowing his town had been overrun by Robert's small band of men.

Robert sat on the edge of the bed, his clothes yet dripping from his agonizing trek across the moat. For a moment he watched the hefty man sleep in his heavily laden bed and wished he had received such a good night of peaceful sleep for himself. He put his sword to Oliphant's throat and slightly pushed the point inward. Oliphant squirmed at the uncomfortable prick but awoke not at all. Robert gave his stout leg a rough jiggle and the sleeper at last awoke.

He gasped at the vision of a dim shadow of a warrior in helm, sitting on the edge of his bed with a long blade pointed at his throat. At first he thought it was a nightmare, but when he told himself that he must awake, he could not. He secondly thought the shadow was an evil spirit, come to take his soul to hell. Then his leg grew cold and he was sure he had already died.

The cold water from Robert's clothing and armor was uncomfortably soaking through to Oliphant's leg. He backed away from the eerie figure and nervously asked, "What ye want?"

"We have yer town," said Robert quietly, "Ye should not have gone to the English, Sir William." Even in the dim light he saw the man's eyes grow wider.

The King of Scots allowed Oliphant to gingerly push the blade away as he sat upright in his bed. "Ye're Robert the Brus!?"

"Aye," said Robert calmly, "and ye are my prisoner."

"Damnation!" was all Oliphant could utter as he stared intently at the dark shadow.

With the dawn, the city of Perth had new authorities over the citizenry, and they were wary of what this meant to them. Most were truly subdued after seeing Oliphant, trussed in ropes, walking through the streets loudly acclaiming that Perth was a captive city and all further resistance to the Scottish king was forbidden.

Not a single man of Robert's army lost his life in the taking.

The town's six English burgesses were brought to the market place.

Robert arrived among cheers from both his army and the townspeople who were grateful to be out from under the thumb of English rule. They also remembered when old Edward of England took the town and had most of the population executed.

"The English are our enemies," said the king loudly. There were cheers and Robert stood alone with the tied burgesses before him. "These are your enemies," he said pointing to the six. More cheers and Robert knew the town was not at fault for holding out against him.

Oliphant, standing behind the king, swallowed hard for he could see the events were going to unfold against him.

"I want these men hanged," said Robert, "by noon."

He walked to where the burgesses stood and thumped each one on the chest over their heart showing who was meant to die by hanging.

A shiver went up Oliphant's back when Robert walked to him. "Ye should have known better," scolded Robert.

Oliphant dropped his head in shame.

"Ye are not the only one the English have turned against his own country," continued Robert looking at Oliphant in disgust. He thought of Thomas Randolph who had gone to the English and returned. *He is faithful now,* thought he in his quiet rage.

He hesitated to pass sentence on the commander of the garrison. Oliphant was a good Scottish warrior who had defended Stirling castle against the old Edward many years earlier, but after spending four years in an English dungeon he agreed to turn.

"Take this one back to the gaol," he abruptly said at last.

He sighed deeply when he saw the English garrison strung in rows before him. They were enemies all, in Robert's eyes. He sighed again for he hesitated to destroy this much life, yet they would kill Scots had they had the opportunity. He remembered how Edward had treated the citizens whom he considered enemies. Robert wanted not to be the kind of king known for such wholesale murder, but he had to maintain order and fear among those who would have him dead.

"On yer knees!" he ordered the English knights and soldiers.

"Those of ye who want to live must swear ye will ne'er set a hand against another Scot for all the days God lets ye dwell on earth," said Robert. "Ye who give oath can return to England as free men... but break yer oath and ye will be cursed and die that very day!"

Many of the men said, "I swear," and stood. They were escorted to the gates to walk back to England.

Several men stubbornly remained on their knees. On Robert's order the men were immediately executed by single sword slashes to the backs of their necks.

The Earl of Strathearn was Robert's next consideration.

"Strathearn, why are ye among these English?" asked Robert.

"At this point, Milord, I know not," said Lord Malise.

"My King, hear me, I pray," said a voice behind the earl.

"Who speaks?" asked Robert.

A young man who had just helped Robert wrest the town from the English stood forward. "He is my father, My King," said Malise, named after his father.

"He is for the English and ye... are in my army?" asked Robert not realizing the son of a Scottish earl was a knight in his own ranks.

"Aye, My King," said young Malise, "He is my father and I plead for his life."

Robert stood back. He looked at one then the other. "certainly a similarity," he said mostly to himself.

The earl stood forward. "Milord, ye have my son's fealty, would ye accept the fealty of the foolish father as well?"

"Given in earnest?" asked Robert.

"Most humbly so," was the reply.

The king put his hands together and Earl Malise sank to his knees and pledged loyalty to king Robert for as long as he lived.

The tribunal was over.

Robert sent Oliphant and his Scottish Captain to Angus Macdonald of the Isles for incarceration hoping the good Scots would come to Robert's peace sooner than later.

Robert ordered the remaining arm bones of the patriot William Wallace, placed there by the old Edward of England eight years earlier, to be removed from the wall above the gate and given a decent Christian burial.

The people of Perth were pleased with their "new" monarch, at least until he set them, under his master mason's auspices, to razing the outer walls of the town into the moat that he never wanted to cross again on foot, winter or not.

Lord Dungal Macdouall

FEBRUARY 6th 1313
DUMFRIES CASTLE

Lord Dungal Macdouall peered through the glass window of the solar. Below, a skiff of fresh snow covered the planting grounds and the scattered peasant hovels stretching over some twenty acres before him.

A little more than seven years earlier, Lord Seagrave had been in command of Castle Dumfries. King Robert, in a critically decisive moment, overtook the castle by rushing the gate after the killing of John "The Red" Comyn at Greyfriars Kirk. The elder King Edward had been quick to retake the fortress after Robert's crowning at Scone and subsequent thrashing at the battle of Methven. This loss and other, lesser such losses, helped to form Robert's policy of razing captured castles as soon as was possible.

Lord Macdouall's eyes wandered beyond the hovels and across the field to the myriad tents and campfires just beyond arrow range at the edge of the tree line. There the white banner emblazoned with a blue lion rampant, red tongue and claws, fluttered in the light chilled wind that punctuated the overall grayness of the morning. It was the banner of Edward de Brus, who had recently been handed down Robert's inherited former title of Earl of Carrick. Edward was also designated Lord of Galloway by his brother for subjugating the southwest of Scotland and for chasing Lord Dungal from his dark Castle Buittle.

Some weeks before this gray day, Lord Edward Brus laid siege to Castle Dumfries. Macdouall, though a Scot, had remained loyal through it all to the crown of England, unlike a number of Scots nobles who had changed sides, some more than once. Buffered and pumped by his companion at arms, Sir Ingram de Umfraville, Dungal had led a valiant fight against the Brus rebellion.

The one thing burning in his depressed mind, however, was his capture in 1306 of the Brus' brothers Thomas and Alexander, and his surrender of them to Longshanks' cruel torture and horrific executions. He was sure that the King of Scots and his brother Edward held him responsible for their brothers' suffering and deaths. That made him a marked man, doomed to be subjected to something of equal measure to his offense against them.

It was never a hair's breadth from being uppermost in his mind.

He pressed his nose tightly to one of the small panes of warped glass thinking he might see more of the siege camp, but it remained just as silent and foreboding as the moment before, the day before, the week before. Hunger gnawed at his gut like a cancer and anger seared his heart at the success of Brus' siege. Within the castle, cut off from resupply, even the laying hens, house cats, hunting dogs, the sheep and goats, milk cows, and all horses had already fallen to the flesh hewer's cleaver. Though his men were far hungrier than he, all he thought of was his own danger of starvation, impressed so keenly on his mind because he was now forced to think of his own mortality.

A low guttural moan escaped his lips. Fear now mingled with the anger welling in his being. "Goddamned Brus!" he erupted.

The rumpled covers on the luxurious bedstead behind him moved at his words. The tumble-tossed locks of the hefty nude blonde woman seemed to wave back and forth like a field of grain ready for harvest as she tried to establish her balance while getting upright in the bed.

"What say, Milord?" she questioned in as clear a voice as she could utter.

Dungal turned. He had forgotten he was not alone. "Goddamned Bruses!" he repeated, balling his fists as he did so. He then crossed and sat in the large chair before the meager fire, and put his cold bare feet all but in the embers. "Goddamned Edward! Goddamned Robert!"

"Ye et?" she questioned without thinking.

He turned in his chair and glared at her. "With that surplus ye carry ye'll live longer than most," he remarked, alluding to her plumpness.

Remembering their predicament she closed her mouth. After a few moments of being reticent, she arose from the bed and walked to the washstand near the fireplace and bent over splashing the cold water on her face. The cold made her shiver, but she proceeded to repeat the process several times.

Dungal watched her nude buttocks thinking how delicious they might be roasted on a spit.

Suddenly there was a loud cheer from the outside and Dungal rushed to the small window to see. The scene through the glass was too blurry and he opened the window to view the field before him with clarity. "Goddamn! It's Robert!" he cursed again. "Doomed we are for sure, now."

Edward seemed agitated that Christina, riding at Robert's right, was yet in the king's party, though he said nothing. Following them was Andrew, carrying the red and yellow lion rampant flag, and the hundred or so knights and warriors that had taken the town of Perth only days earlier.

Robert climbed off his destrier to meet Edward and give him a brotherly hug. "How goes the siege?" he asked.

"Ne'er can tell about sieges," said Edward smiling. "When they lower their banners and come forth with their hands in the air, the siege is over. They must be hungry by now, but their guards still man the parapets."

"Once we have Dumfries we'll raze it and move on. Caerlaverock will be next," said Robert more seriously. "Then I want Stirling."

"Ye're the king. 'Tis yer say," said Edward jerking his head and stiffening his backbone against what he interrupted as chastisement for Dumfries' not having fallen.

"This afternoon we will plan for an attack tomorrow," said Robert.

"Aye, My King," he huffed sardonically.

The new arrivals began pitching their tents and starting fires. The whole field suddenly came alive as Dungal watched from his window. He was enraged and he hollered and ranted at the top of his voice.

Robert turned toward the donjon to see Lord Dungal in his nightshirt shouting and cursing, crazed in his bellowing. *Ready to capitulate,* thought Robert and he smiled.

Dungal's woman suddenly screamed behind him. He quickly pivoted thinking someone approached him, only to see her standing in the middle of the room, bedcovers drawn about her body to ward off the chill of the cold air blowing through the open window.

She froze in place when she saw the look of violence on his face.

"What in hell are ye screamin' about?" His eyes were wild with the sudden fear her shrieking caused him to suffer. She found it difficult to respond, but finally said, "I... I couldn't get ye to hear me any other way!" He became more and more aggravated and she became more panicked. "'Tis freezin' in here, and I wanted to close the window, My Lord!"

"Close the window?"

"Aye, My..." she stopped speaking and covering her head fell into a heap on the floor, awaiting the expected blow. But instead of striking her, he picked up the heavy chair in which he had been sitting and in his strength and rage, threw it against the window, shattering the glass panes and the mullion strips between them.

"There!" he yelled, "I've fixed the window for ye, ye worthless whore, and now I'm goin' to fix ye!" he growled, and jerking the blanket from her trembling body as she tried to crawl away, he moved closer, his fists again clenched.

Later she lay fearfully motionless and silent on the bed while Dungal paced back and forth nursing his knuckles. He would feel faint from time to time, which he ascribed to hunger, and he would hold to the back of the large chair, returned in its spot by the fireplace. The fire itself was almost exhausted for lack of fuel, but he paid it no heed. Instead his thoughts were on long ago images of Robert de Brus standing on the opposite side of the creek in the moonlight, his red eyes glowing and his silver blade flashing to end the life of every good knight Dungal ordered across the creek after him.

He suddenly jerked open the heavy door to the solar, and the two guards without jumped to a more alert posture. None wanted to tangle with Lord Macdouall when he was in one of his violent paroxysms. Strangely, when he opened the door, he merely barked, "Tell the kitchen I will be there directly and I want somethin' killed and cooked proper when I arrive!"

"Aye, Milord," said the senior guard almost meekly, and he left at a trot for the great hall and its kitchen, on the opposite side of the bailey from the donjon.

Dungal slapped his whore playfully on the rump. She cried out and tearfully whimpered. "Get up from the bedstead woman and get yerself dressed in yer finest gown," he demanded.

Slowly she rose and gingerly placing her feet on the floor moved in awkward and calculated measurements trying to minimize the pain from Dungal's beating. She knew there were broken bones in her hand, sacrificed in trying to ward off the heavy blows. The rest of her ached as if she had been trampled by a horse, and her face exhibited purplish marks of his repeated strikes upon her once pleasant countenance. She dressed, but not very attractively. Her hair remained a mess and all her powdering couldn't cover the bruises.

Dungal dressed himself in his finest attire and announced, "Perk up, My Dear, for we are goin' to sup grandly on this, the last day of my life."

She was astonished. "Will... will," she stammered.

Dungal sighed and groused, "Out with it, woman!"

She began to cry. "Will this be the last day of *my* life, too?"

"As hungry as I am, My Little Harlot... yesterday should have been yer last," he answered.

She looked at him quizzically but understood him not.

On reaching the ground floor of the donjon, Dungal snatched a groom's lead from its peg by the door and fashioned one end into a large loop. He matter-of-factly slipped it over her head as if she were an unbridled mare.

"Ye fixin' to hang me, Milord?" she asked in all innocence.

"Nae, woman!" he grumped. "'Tis just a tether to keep ye from gettin' et as we cross the bailey."

"Et?" she asked.

"Aye," said he, "for ye look purely delicious, like a sow what's been fattened for the table. And there's some who was uglier than ye have been et already!" And he laughed, knowing that his troubles on this earth were soon over.

She smiled slightly, for she thought him to be softening against her and in spite of all her freshly acquired bruises, she wanted to be appealing to him on his last day. He was after all, her savior.

He tugged on the rope around her neck and she followed swaying in her misery like a cow, thinking it was his little joke. But joke had not entered his mind. About them lay diverse inmates of the castle in various stages of starvation. One man approached on his knees, begging for a morsel of anything to eat. "Tomorrow!" said Dungal gruffly, and back-handed the man across the face to get him to move away. "Ye will be eatin' the Brus' victuals on the morrow!" adding under his breath, "maybe".

The great hall was empty of the castle's inhabitants, for they had thought the hall cleaned of every edible morsel some days ago. The servants were scurrying about setting the table for the lord and his woman, whom Dungal led to the dais and sat her on his right with a bow as if she were his queen. Taking his own chair he pretended the hall was alive with knights about to enjoy a grand feast. He even heard the musicians playing in the background of the imagined ambient cacophony of the dining room crowd.

A squire quickly appeared and poured goblets of thinned wine for the pair. They eagerly drank having previously thought the supply of wine was well gone. Another, older, squire came to the front of the table and knelt before them setting several small four-footed animals in front of the lord and began to disjoint the meat. Another brought two trenchers of the top crusts poured heavily with a spicy sauce ready to receive the wonderfully smelling meat.

"This truly is a feast," she said smiling, the tether still dangling from her neck.

"Ye think I, lord of this castle, would feed ye anything but my very best?" he questioned snobbishly at the same moment he wondered how and what it was that he was about to devour.

"I thought ye were fixin' to have me for yer supper," she said giggling, even the much diluted wine on her very empty stomach beginning to affect her head.

He grinned and said in his gruff manner, "Ye'll be my sweet after the supper," and he dipped his hand deep into the top of her camisole and squeezed her generous breast.

She again giggled, relieved that she was not on his table menu.

• •

The winter dark arrives early in the day. A candle lantern flickered in the tent where Robert sat cross-legged on his pallet.

"Ye look weary, My Robert," said Christina as she pushed back the tent's opening flap and peered in.

Robert smiled at the comforting face. "Come," he offered, gesturing slightly with his hand.

She entered and kissed him sweetly on his lips. "I have porridge for ye," said she and suddenly produced a large wooden bowl from behind her back to just under his nose.

He flinched backwards, surprised to see hot vapor rising toward him.

"Porridge, eh?" he rhetorically asked taking the bowl.

"And a spoon," she said pulling a wooden one from a pocket and thrusting it toward him.

"Well civilized," said Robert as he dipped the bowl of the spoon into the upper level of the steaming grain mush and began to eat.

Christina sat and watched him enjoy his meal.

"Just as good cooked this way as dried oats mixed with sheep blood," he remarked casually between bites.

"I like it better," she said, "'cause ye don't have to chase down a sheep. They shared a laugh at the thought.

Outside, Edward saw the shadows playing on the sides of his brother's tent and poured another cup of his just brewed ale and drank it down hard. He had been drinking his foamy, dark supper all afternoon, and this cup went down about the same time as he sank to a squat and sulked, always with his eyes jealously fastened on the tent. Another cupful and he finally fell over in a drunken stupor on the snow-covered ground.

"Looks like Sir Lord Edward be deep in his cups again," said Cuthbert.

"Good we happened along," chirped Fergus reaching to pick up the unconscious knight.

"Aye," said Cuthbert, "plum froze to the dirt by morn, he'd be." The two men shook their heads and sniggered as they hauled Edward, head and foot, off to his tent to sleep 'til the dawn.

Dungal sat by the broken window and watched Brus' army going about the mundanities of life in a siege camp. While he surveilled their movements about the field he saw two men pick up a third from the ground and carry him to a tent by a blazing fire. He could even smell the light aroma of cooked food wafting across the field, but he told himself they had nothing better than his early supper. His battered woman was fast asleep after having had a fine feast, followed by a grand romp with his lordship, whom she forgave. Still, she moaned in her soreness when she moved in the bed.

He knew not whether he was insane or just seeing things clearly for the first time in his life, but there were angels playing harps before his eyes. Their sweet music enchanted him so that he swore to amend every wrong he had ever wrought against any other human being of any stature in the community. He at last felt sorrow for his wrong doings and wished he yet had more time on earth to make those wrongs aright. That was uppermost on his mind until the angels denuded themselves and danced and entertained him.

He then rudely awakened his woman for another round, so that he would have something pleasant he could think about as he was dying on the blade of King Robert's dagger, morning next.

•   •

There was not a bit of yellow or rose or any other color in the sky. At the time the sun would rise, the stark grayness all around merely grew lighter. Mantlet shields of split logs were pushed across the field without a single arrow being slung in their direction. Robert, Edward, and fifty knights in mail walked casually behind the advancing heavy shields as they were moved foot-by-foot across the bristly farm field. As they came within hearing distance a bellowing voice roared from within.

"Hold right there!" came the loud shout from the open solar window in the tower. Robert stopped and looked in the direction of the voice as it continued. "Robert de Brus! Ye wait right there... I'll be down directly!"

"Who speaks for Castle Dumfries?" shouted Robert, his breath billowing visibly before him.

"Lord Dungal Macdouall!" the lord of the castle bellowed, "I'm comin' down to surrender!"

"Told ye it was that ol' Macdouall I ran out of Buittle," gloated Edward still a bit thickheaded from the previous night.

Robert said nothing in response to Edward's comment, thinking instead of Thomas and Alexander, and Dungal's part in their terrible deaths. *Revenge would be in order,* he mused.

Robert brought his archers to the fore behind the mantlets with orders to shoot anyone who showed himself on the battlements with a bow or a spear. He then brought his remaining knights and his foot soldiers forward to man a long line, anticipating the possibility of deviltry from Lord Macdouall.

The drawbridge cranked into its down position as they heard the portcullis being lifted behind the closed gates.

A woman wailed loudly from the open solar window as the main gate slowly creaked open and Dungal timidly emerged. His angels danced all around him and his empty hands shook as he held them out from his sides as a sign of surrender. "Come to parlee, I have," he said in short breaths.

"Move forward," commanded Robert to those of his knights standing closer to him and he drew his axe from the loop on his belt. Then to the humble lord of the castle he barked, "Open those doors wide!" He wanted them to have no opportunity for any surprise attack from within the walls.

The gate doors were opened fully by several thin and staggering men. Robert knew the siege set by Edward had worked well. Robert assumed his position at the fore of his men, axe in hand.

Dungal saw the king standing tall with his army behind him. He winced. His eyes rolled in their sockets. A shiver traversed his backbone and tightened his buttocks and it was an effort for him to hold his courage within. He would have turned and run for his life but his feet would not cooperate. *I am doomed,* he thought.

Robert waited while two knights dragged Dungal in front of him.

Dungal stood before his destiny and shook with fear. "We are done," he said and awaited Robert's dagger to stab in his gut or the axe to strike his neck.

Robert stood and stared at the surrendering man with eyes as hard as flint. When the king made no move to strike him down immediately, Macdouall shook the more. Unable to bear the king's silent hatred any longer he thought there might be a chance for his survival. Thus he spoke in a surprisingly steady voice.

"I swear to ye that ye be my liege for the rest of my days, My Lord King," groveled Dungal.

Robert stared down at him in pure disgust but still said nothing.

"Kill the whoreson, Sire!" yelled Edward as he came to the transfixed pair.

Robert turned and looked soberly toward his brother.

"If ye're not to the task, My Lord King, I shall strike him dead with a joyful heart!" growled Edward, and he took a position with his sword held high, ready to strike, not totally unlike a fighting cock viewing his next challenger.

"We are here to take this castle," said Robert. "Stand aside!"

Edward hesitated a moment, then obeyed.

Robert turned back to Dungal whose head was bowed. "Why did ye turn to the English?" he asked sternly.

Dungal was oddly struck by the question on this day of his death. He thought a moment. He could hear his woman still loudly crying above his head. "Why did *ye* turn *against* the English?" he return asked, his voice shaking.

Robert said simply, "Because this is the land of the Scots, not of the English. These are our people the English killed and enslaved... even you, Dungal Macdouall." He sighed deeply and turned to motion for his army to occupy the castle.

"Ye a'killin' me now?" asked Dungal, his throat parched so that he could barely speak.

"Nae," replied Robert, sadly, feeling that he was betraying his dead brothers, but knowing that Dungal's death would affect many people. "Leave this place... one day, ye and yer people will come to the king's peace on yer own. Then ye'll not falsely give troth to yer liege lord."

Macdouall stood dumbfounded, knowing not what was the meaning of Robert's say.

"Yer free," repeated Robert, and he walked past the puzzled man, through the gate tunnel, and into the bailey of Dumfries Castle.

As he came to realize that he was going to live, Dungal's angels suddenly disappeared. No one stopped to place him in irons or strike him down. The men of Brus walked by him and followed the king into the fortress without even a curse cast upon his head. None paid him any attention at all.

With bare feet he stumbled across the rocky, snow-dusted terrain to where the destroyed solar window overlooked the field and shouted up to his woman, "They hain't goin' to kill me!" He smiled weakly. She wailed all the more.

Figured she'd be happy about that, he puzzled.

That day, nothing went as Lord Dungal Macdouall had thought it would.

march 22nd 1313
carrick

King Robert was worn to the bone. Alone and trudging laboriously toward the coastline of Carrick in the dress of a vagabond archer, his axe well concealed beneath layers of rough cloth and a long bow strung around his body so that the arrows in his quiver remained in place as he walked, nothing about him showed that he was King of Scots or that he had any stature at all in the community of the realm.

He had sent his brother to lay siege to Stirling castle and Edward's closest friend, Walter of Ross, to siege at Caerlaverock under Lord Edward's command and had held there for the last couple of months. The great ring of Scottish castles yet in English hands were falling one at a time to Robert's armies and then to his masons, who razed them. Few were those the English yet held by this date.

At the king's behest, Christina was at the siege camp outside Stirling under the protection of Lord Edward. Robert had a solitary mission to fulfill and wanted no word of his whereabouts to reach the ear of any lurking enemy. Thus had he left his destrier and a retinue of knights seven miles east to await his return. Andrew Stewart was among them.

His good friend Sir Robert Boyd had been sent ahead to Ulster to make preparations for this meeting, one of great import. With him were the two stalwarts Cuthbert and Fergus, who were told to defend Boyd with their lives and give him whatever aid he required. Other than that they were to speak to no one of their journey or what they observed along the way.

Robert stopped to pull the leather glove from his hand with his teeth, reach into an inner pouch, and draw out a portion of his dried meat and began to eat. He found his skin of water as well and drank deeply of it. The sleet-laden wind whipped violently across the dormant field and blew the falling ice into his beard where it began to gather. He shivered and pulled the ragged hood tighter to his face. Somewhat faint and dizzy, he hoped it was just from his hunger and thirst rather than a return of his debilitating illness. Without Christina tending to him with her medicines, he feared that the cursed malady might return.

As he ate, he searched the sky's constant gray cover to locate the sun's position so he could make sure he remained on his westerly course. Finally he saw it, a pale, perfectly round whiteness behind the diaphanous cloud that covered it. From that sighting he reckoned where he was and the direction he must take. *The coast is not much farther,* he mused, and biting into the salted, dried meat again, he trudged onward.

It was late afternoon by the time he reached the waves washing fast ashore from the Irish Sea. He went south and walked along the narrow strip of reddish sand, turned a muted dun color by the overcast welkin, until he came to a place sheltered by an outcropping of rugged rock. This was the place at which he was to meet the craft that would take him via the rough waters to the rocky coast of Kintyre, and Dunaverty Castle. However, the boat was not there and no sail was in sight.

Wrapping himself in his woolen rags he sat alee of the great stone projection to await the boat's arrival, and to rest after his long walk. For most of an hour he scanned the horizon for a sail until it was completely dark, and when he could no longer see, he soon fell asleep. He was aroused from his slumber by the sound of a horn drifting across the surf. Standing, he pulled the small hunting horn he carried strapped to his belt and put it up to his lips to respond to the call with two long blasts, a short, and another long.

He listened, but heard nothing. After a time he blew his signal again, two, one, and one.

He waited for a while more. From the south, and fairly near, he heard the return of three short blasts. He paced quickly down the coast until he walked right up to the beached galley, recognizing Cuthbert, who stood at its bow gazing up toward the looming black hills.

"Ye men ready?" Robert asked in a quiet voice.

Cuthbert's head nearly spun off his shoulders as he turned to see his king so near him.

Fergus stood quickly and exclaimed. "King Robert, 'tis!"

"Ye fixed for yer ride to Dunaverty?" shouted the captain who seemed to be covered head and ears and moved not an inch from his tiller.

"Aye," said the king as he removed the bow and quiver of arrows from his back and handed them to Fergus to stow along the gunnels. Then he and Cuthbert quickly pushed the small vessel off the sand, leaping into it as soon as it floated free. Robert sat in the bow, looking toward the stern. Cuthbert and Fergus sat in the middle, their backs to Robert, and manned the oars that would push the boat farther out into the water where it would better catch the wind in its single black sail. Once the wind picked up, the oars were quickly shipped and the captain ordered the sail set to carry them west into the absolute blackness of the deepening night.

Robert saw that Fergus had wrapped rags around his hands to fight off the cold. He pulled the warm gloves from his own hands and gave them to the oarsman.

"Yer gloves, My King!?" he asked not knowing what else to say.

"For now," said Robert pushing his own hands into the folds of his layered sackcloth, "Ye have them for now."

Fergus smiled as he unwrapped the well-worn rags, tossed them over the side and donned the king's gloves.

"I have King Robert's gloves," he said to Cuthbert, who snubbed his friend in envy.

The two men would again be called upon to row when the boat neared Dunaverty, but for the meanwhile they were thankful that God had sent them a good steady wind to push them before it while they rested. It would be a long ride to the cove by the high promontory on which the castle stood, but it would be much longer if they had to row all the way.

The captain kept his instincts sharp for there were no stars to follow and no shore light until they were farther west.

For a long time Cuthbert had nothing to say, and Fergus couldn't get him to come out of his resentment over the king's gloves. Finally, Fergus took off one glove and held it toward Cuthbert. At first he refused, but when Fergus started to put his own hand back inside it, he quickly accepted it and put it on one hand. That way they both cheerfully rode, each with one hand warmly gloved, and the other held in his armpit.

Robert's exhaustion took its payment and he fell dead asleep well before they neared Dunaverty.

• •

Robert opened his eyes but slightly. He could tell immediately that he was not on the galley, but that was the last moment he remembered. His clothing felt smooth if not slick, and the covers beneath which he lay were of fine linen. Though it was a struggle at first, the king propped himself up on his elbows and looked around.

He was in a large, well appointed room with plastered walls and handsome, even elegant, furnishings. Several brightly colored tapestries depicting scenes of French bowmen hunting stags and beautifully dressed ladies and gentlemen at court covered the walls. He remembered seeing some works similar to them when he last visited in Normandy.

Robert's attention turned to the oak door when it creaked while being opened, and daylight flooded the room, making him wince from the painful sudden intrusion of the light into his eyes.

The door closed and Robert sat up on the edge of the pallet. He was again dizzy. After a few moments the door swung wide and a large figure silhouetted itself within the opening. Robert searched his clothing and the bed for his axe.

"No need to fear!" announced the man as he moved into the room.

"Angus?" asked Robert, still blinking from the light but seeming to recognize his old friend's voice.

"Aye," replied Angus, "'Tis, for sure."

The king relaxed and fell back on his bed.

"Dunaverty, I presume," said Robert, groggily, snuggling back to his pillow.

"Safe as ye can be," said Angus. "Glad ye're awake after listenin' to three days of yer infernal snorin'."

"Ye put this silk robe on me?" asked Robert rubbing the material covering his chest.

"'Tis one of my best," replied Angus. "What more would ye expect from a Macdonald?"

"What more would be expected from the ol' slave trader, says I," gainsaid Robert with a chuckle.

"Good profits in slaves these days, Dear Robert," said Angus as he sat beside his friend and returned the smile.

"Lord Richard here?"

"Arrived two days ago."

"Graham?"

"In residence, My Liege."

"Why wasn't I awakened before?" groused Robert.

"Ye would not arouse!" explained Angus. "Believe me, Rob, we tried!"

Robert sighed deeply. "Where's the garderobe?"

Angus pointed to the trough with a seat at the wall opposite the door. "Goes directly into the sea," he said, getting to his feet. "Ye tend to yer necessaries. I'll send ye suitable clothes around shortly, My King."

"Ye feedin' me, too?" joked Robert.

"Eggs and a rasher of bacon?"

"Be at hall directly," he said, shaking slightly as he stood.

Angus pushed a chair in his direction and Robert used it to steady himself as he walked.

• •

Richard de Burgh, Earl of Ulster and sometimes known as "The Red Earl", stood from the far side of the trestle table in the great hall of Dunaverty castle and bowed slightly as King Robert entered. Richard was awed by his son-in-law's battlefield prowess and his kingly manner. Robert respected Richard's own prowess as a warrior but knew as well the English crown owned his fealty, as he was old Edward's top lieutenant in the pursuit of England's war against France.

The exchange of greetings was cordial after which Robert sat heavily across the table from the Irish earl. There was a long silence between the two men as the breakfast of, not only eggs and bacon was served, but mutton, fish, cheese, and breads graced the table. The moment that both men were risking a great deal of personal and political danger to bring about had come to fruition.

"Have ye heard the whereabouts of Elizabeth?" was Robert's first question.

"Only that she is under house arrest," replied the earl.

"Do ye know where?"

"Nae," said Richard, but his eyes belied his tongue.

Robert calmly ate some egg and studied the slice of bacon he held between his fingers. "I have yet to find a part of the hog that is not pleasant to eat, My Lord Ulster." Robert ate the bacon and said, "Thus, pigs get slaughtered for their goodness."

"Do ye threaten me, Sire?" asked Richard.

"Nae, just sayin' one should not be too good, or he might lose his own skin," said Robert without smiling. Richard de Burgh studied the man before him and decided the Scot was entitled to know why he had lied.

"She wants ye not to know," said Richard plainly, and ate of his own meats and bread.

"Fear I'll die tryin' to get her?"

"She is too deep into England," said Richard. "They want ye to try a rescue and she knows it."

Robert's fists tightened until his knuckles showed white, but he knew Richard was telling the truth, and that Elizabeth was right. The English would gain much from killing or capturing him. Besides, the important knowledge was that she still lived, though a hostage these seven years.

After a moment of watching Robert torturing himself with guilt, Richard asked, "Why have ye sent for me?"

Robert ate, mulling his say. "I need an army to capture the Isle of Man."

"Why Man? Why now?" asked the earl.

"The 'why' is the same reason as the Vikin's wanted it for, so many years ago," the king answered, "… to control the sea on the western coast. The 'now' is because we 'now' control the southwest of Scotland, but we cannot get others to trade with us there unless we guarantee their safe passage."

"Have ye forgotten that John Macdougall was made Admiral of England's western fleet?" asked the red-headed Irishman.

"Angus and his galleys can hold him at bay," returned Robert confidently, and he waited for his father-in-law to mull over what he wanted out of the situation. They ate in silence for a few moments before the earl told the king what he wanted most to hear.

"In the long run," he said, "I'm only interested in gettin' the English out of my bailiwick."

"This *can* be a first step to Ireland's bein' free of 'em, as Scotland soon will be," said Robert hoisting his pewter mug, indicating that he wanted more wine.

"What do ye expect of me?" asked Richard.

"Men... and money to feed and pay them... for the takin' of Man," said the king.

Richard reared back on his chair interlacing his fingers behind his head, elbows akimbo at his ears. He took a deep breath. "And nothin' will come back on me until I am ready?"

"Nothin'," was the answer.

"It is possible," said the Irish warrior.

"Let's get the English out of Scotland, then we will work on getting them out of Ireland," Robert proffered.

Richard thought through the ramifications of the proposal and nodded in general agreement.

"Good," said Robert devouring the remaining bites of his only meal for the last four days. Turning to a nearby squire he ordered, "Send for Lord Angus and Sir David de Graham."

The squire bowed and left.

"We will make a plan that we can all agree upon," said the king, smiling. At this point he had accomplished all he had hoped for this trip. *If only the rest of the plot falls into place,* he worried. *But I must risk leaving the mainland to take Man. The isle is critical to taking back the rest of Scotland. If we succeed, we win all.*

Walter Stewart

CDAY 17th 1313
RACDSEY BAY ON Che ISLE OF CDAN

Twelve galleys owned and commanded by Angus Og Macdonald made their way toward the relatively small but strategically important island of Man in the Irish Sea, just off the southern coast of Scotland.

Robert stood at the bow of the lead galley holding tight to the mast line as the rectangular sail billowed behind him and the waves rhythmically tossed and thrust him at their caprice. The wind whipped his hair about and raced across his bearded face leaving behind a salty mist that he could taste on his lips. It was tremendously exhilarating and he felt, for a moment at least, like a man without a trouble to his name.

The sixteen men who came aboard with him were accustomed to solid ground under their feet and now hung head and shoulders over the gunnels between the oarsmen. At first the tough seamen merely laughed at their passengers' weak stomachs. The Macdonalds' experienced crews had withstood many a storm in all seasons and never felt a flutter in their midsections, but after being alongside those poor creatures in the throes of their mal de mer for much of the trip, even those old salt sailors began to suffer a twinge of nausea.

The vessel's captain worked his way through the warriors and sailors from the stern to where Robert was standing. "These keckin' whoresons hain't a'goin' to be worth a fair turd when we land...uh, My King," said he in a voice loud enough to be heard over the pounding of the waves against the hull and the creaking of the mast and lines.

Robert turned and looked at the old sea dog in such a way that it caused him to drop his eyes and slink back through the melee of sick soldiers and oarsmen and return to the stern to reclaim the tiller from his second. The captain knew better than to speak his notions about Robert's men thereafter.

The trees on the low sloping hills surrounding the cove were well into view and the sun made its appearance from time to time in the massive, fast moving clouds. The invasion of Man was about to be.

Within a moment's time the captain gave the order to strike the sail, and his second released the lines that held the huge sail aloft. The rowers manned their oars and began to pull in unison to a uniform rhythm, making the craft noticeably leap forward with each stroke. The steerboard was less than accurate in adjusting the boat's subtle changes in direction, and much of the steering as they headed toward shore was done by the oarsmen. Moments more and the captain gave the order to ship oars and the galley's keel pushed its way onto the sandy beach.

Robert jumped from the bow yelling for his men to follow quickly. Regardless of their sufferings onboard, they spread rapidly into the trees to see if there was a lurking army or even spies about.

The king waved the other galleys ashore and one-by-one they slid onto the beach alongside the first.

Angus rolled his hefty body over the gunnels and splashed into the water, sword in hand. Comical it was to witness, but no one dared laugh at the Lord of the Isles, knowing that he who did would soon find his head detached from the rest of him.

He was well wet as he slogged ashore, and asked the king, "Ye catch any lurkers?"

"None hereabouts," answered Robert. "Get these others into the trees."

"Fast as they can crawl out," replied Angus. "We should get all three runs completed by dark."

"We'll bivouac among the trees at the top of that rise yonder," said Robert pointing up the slope.

"I'll send them up as we bring them in," replied Angus.

"Tell them to watch their backsides," warned Robert.

"Not exactly like slave tradin', is it?" said Sir David de Graham, the former Templar, as he strode to the pair and gave Angus a hearty slap on the back.

Angus frowned at the friendly gesture, then answered in kind, saying, "Not all that different neither."

Andrew Stewart climbed from the fourth galley and came straight to the king. "Ye reckon we need a flagstaff right off, Sire?" he asked.

"Aye," replied Robert smiling, "I want ev'rybody on this island to know the Scots are here with their king."

"Do I have yer permission to let my younger brother Walter carry the Saint Andrew's Cross?" he asked.

"Aye," answered Robert, "if ye're sure he is ready for the task. Have ye well trained him, Andrew?"

"Aye, Sire. He knows what to do and is a bright lad," said Andrew. "I would be right surprised if he did somethin' dull-witted."

Well on the horizon Angus saw the sail of the last of his twelve galleys in the little fleet. He quickly ordered the captain of the lead galley to shove off and return the fleet to Scotland to pick up the next three hundred men and women, weapons and supplies.

Robert turned to de Graham. "Take some men and scour the farms hereabouts. We need horses and saddles. And impress the pigs and chickens and the like into the Scottish army," he said.

"We returnin' the horses?" asked Graham.

"If they hain't killed," said Robert.

"Then I'll have to recollect who'll be givin' us what."

"Good notion," replied Robert, his mind reeling with tasks to be done.

Graham bowed and retired to choose a foraging party starting with Cuthbert and Fergus, certainly the most experienced scavengers in his army.

The archer MacKie was just sliding into the water to come ashore when Robert called his name and beckoned him to come to him.

MacKie bowed slightly as he came to Robert.

"How's yer mother?" the king asked.

"She's failin', I fear," said the archer sadly, adding, "Still speaks the world of ye, My King."

Robert smiled wistfully as a flood of memories filled his mind. MacKie's mother, a feisty little widow, offered her sons to her king for his army, and MacKie and his older brother Murdoch, the best archer Robert had ever seen, had fought with him through all the hard times for the next few years. His heart was saddened to hear that the tough little widow was in decline, and he told MacKie so.

"Take a few of yer fellow archers into the woods yonder and get us up a goodly supper," instructed Robert, adding, "and if ye see any English... kill them, too... they'll cook up tasty with enough onions." Angus and MacKie smiled at the jest.

"Anything tastes good with enough onions," answered the lanky Scot as he again bowed slightly and turned to leave.

"Good to see ye back," said the king.

MacKie turned again to Robert and tipped his head in acknowledgement then did as he was bade.

"I'll be leavin' ye now, Rob," said Angus.

"Get the rest of us here, then sail for Ireland," instructed Robert. "See ye in Douglas Bay in two days. None of yer crew must know what ye're fixin' to do 'til ye've done it."

"Aye, My King," said Angus, smiling eagerly to be back in the thick of the action. Life had been rather dull since the taking of Castle Urquhart. On the other hand, his treasury had grown fat on the transport of galloglass, exotic silks, and quaint tasting wines from the Mediterranean Sea. He was a most successful merchant of opportunity now that he was no longer under the taxing thumb of England.

The sparse farms and tiny villages within the neighborhood yielded three horses with saddles, two without, and a variety of chickens and several goats and one pig.

David de Graham still had feathers floating about him as they dislodged from his chain mail when he walked about.

"Ye remind me a wee bit of a molting chicken," said eighteen-year-old Walter Stewart thoughtlessly.

"Mind yer tongue!" growled the veteran warrior.

"'Twas but a tease, Milord," said the youth, chastised.

"When ye're blooded, Stewart, then ye can jest," said Graham sharply, picking as many of the feathers from his armor as he could and slinging them crossly to the wind.

Walter was certainly much younger than Graham and his profound respect for the knight's achievements brought forth a sincere apology. Graham accepted it, just as a feather fluttered out of his hair and wafted its way onto his nose. For a moment neither one breathed, but then Graham burst out laughing, unable to hold it in longer, and Stewart joined him. Afterward, though, Walter Stewart knew his place in the pecking order, and treated his blooded superiors with their due respect.

Walking up the hill to where his men and women were setting up camp, Robert searched for his squire. His paraphernalia would be on the last galley to be put into shore today, but still there were things he needed to do. He scanned the hilltop with no success, and finally resorted to shouting.

"Andrew!" he called and his squire appeared, having been close at hand all along.

"Aye, My King?" he said.

"Fetch me bow and a full quiver," he said then walked toward the higher elevations to the south. "I want to see more of this country."

Andrew grabbed the weapons and hurried to catch up to the king.

• •

Before dawn the next morning the army arose and ate quickly, then folded itself into a traveling caravan. Following the soldiers, the horses were used as pack animals. The other animals were designated to be food while the Scots laid siege to Rushen Castle, on the south end of the island. The soldiers expected to gather more by traversing the length of the island as the army headed for its objective.

Meanwhile, a local farmer named Golvan, finding it distressing to have had his horse and sow removed from his farm, saddled a second mount he had pastured in another field when Graham was in his area, and rode like the wind toward Rushen, twenty miles away.

On foot, Robert led his army of four hundred eighty-nine over the island to Douglas Bay, where he encamped on the gently sloping front lawn of the nunnery. It provided a perfect view of the sea and particularly of Douglas Bay.

Robert waited.

• •

"Scotland is upon us, Milord!" said the captain of the guard as he opened the solar door and approached the commander of the garrison at Castle Rushen.

The beefy man rolled up from his pallet and blinked at the captain. "Who did you say?"

"Scotland!... The Brus, Milord!" repeated the man louder and more enunciated.

"Brus?... Brus is here?!" asked the commander.

"They carry the banner of Brus accordin' to the one who brought us the news. He says they stole his horse and pig!" he said.

"Must be a trick," said the commander. "Bring this man to me!" Then he went to the washbasin and threw cold water on his face and shook it so that droplets slung in every direction. "That goddamned Brus!" he grunted, staring into the pool of water before him.

A knock on the door turned the commander to face it. Light from the window behind him silhouetted the hulk and his long nightshirt, hanging awkwardly to his knees. "Enter!" he thundered.

The door opened and there the captain stood holding a smallish man by the scruff of the neck. They entered the room and the captain pushed the man to the floor in front of the commander. "Says his name is Golvan and the land he works is in Ramsay," said he.

"Tell me exactly what you saw!" ordered the commander.

"Knights in chain mail, and men... lots of men... and cook wives...

an' they was a'stealin' whate'er they wanted... ravagin' and pillagin', a'headin' this way, Milord," stammered Golvan. Ye must stop them!... Milord!"

"The Brus with them?" questioned the commander, frowning.

"Yellow banner with a red lion leads them," whimpered Golvan thinking he had made a grave mistake in coming to Rushen.

"You know how many been killed?"

Golvan was stunned by the question. He knew not about numbers but he had not seen even a single murdered person either. He stayed motionless with his jaw dropped, not knowing what to say.

The commander was impatient at Golvan's silence and walked past the man who was on his knees to the captain. "Prepare half the garrison to sally right away, and send word to John Macdougall in Ireland to bring his fleet quick... we are bein' invaded by Brus... again!... Say that!" he ordered.

"Why not bide here with the whole garrison?" asked the captain.

"I want you to destroy this army ere they get here, Captain!" he loudly growled. "I'll not have Robert Brus starvin' *me* out again, king or no king!"

The captain swallowed hard at the prospects of his task but agreed and left to fulfill his orders.

Sedric the Irish Chieftain

"Sails a'comin', Sire!" yelled Andrew pointing toward the bay.

Robert took notice and stood from his hunker. Coming across the sea from the west were the stout galleys of the Macdonalds, as expected.

There was a mix of light rain and mist that morning and the king's freshly sanded chain mail would soon be turning a light rusty orange again, he knew.

Robert turned to David de Graham and said, "There is a man on one of those vessels that I would have ye go down to the shore and meet, David. Call him not by his name under any circumstance. Tell no one who he is, now or ever. Ask him no questions but bring him directly to me inside the walls of the nunnery. Take Andrew and his brother with ye," said Robert, hunching his shoulders in warding off a chill.

"What *is* his name, Sire?" asked the knight, at a loss.

"Ye will know him." The tall knight nodded, a bit puzzled, and turned to the shore, hailing the Stewart brothers as he passed to accompany him.

Robert had prepared a place inside the nunnery walls for the two men to lay plans. It was a small room but plenty adequate, and he had two cups of warmed wine brought to the room. Soon he heard the approach of several men in mail and leather.

"Robert," said the earl in recognition as he came through the door. Graham stepped into the room as well, but Robert signaled that he should remain outside, and so he stepped back and closed the door behind him.

"Richard," was Robert's reply. He stood and greeted his father-in-law. "Have any troubles getting together the men?"

"None," said the Earl of Ulster.

"How many men ye bring?"

"Hundred twenty-five plus their chieftain, Sedric," said Richard.

"And the money?"

"English pounds."

"How quick can yer men be ready to leave?"

"Just give 'em enough time to get their haunches off the boats. Might be good to let them stretch their legs."

"They'll stretch them plenty on the way. 'Tis a few miles south to the castle. We'll hie directly. We can follow the coast right well I figure," said Robert, and he lifted his cup of wine to his kinsman.

Richard brought his cup to match and the two men drank to the venture.

"Forget not my want, Robert," spoke Richard bluntly.

"I know yer ambitions," Robert answered, setting down the cup. "Have Sedric run his men along side of mine, fifty paces to our right and two abreast," instructed Robert.

"And where will ye have me?" de Burgh asked.

"At my side."

• •

By mid-afternoon the raiders were nearing Balisaly Towne just about a mile and a half north of Rushen castle.

"Ye reckon they know we're comin'?" asked the Earl of Ulster.

"Hain't made a secret of it," answered Robert, cautiously looking at the tightly grouped hovels with rough mud sides and thatched roofs. The tiny stone kirk was on the far side and the landscape seemed linked with planting fields all around. It was the farm for the castle.

Robert suddenly said quietly, "They're in the town awaitin' for us!"

He quickly turned to Graham with orders. "Take some of the men and MacKie with half the archers, makin' sure they have flints. Move them well around to the left... when ye get into position let go with fire arrows on these hovels." He held up his hunting horn and said, "Wait 'til I signal with a string of short blasts, then attack with all force."

"Aye, My King," agreed Graham, and he slipped with his men through the wood to get into position.

Robert next turned to Earl Richard. "Take yer Irish and the remainder of the bowmen to the other side where the foe will have to retreat, and stay out of sight 'til they start to run back to the castle... use the archers on them first... then rush them where they run," he instructed.

Richard's eyes raised in mild surprise. "Ye're not fightin' accordin' to the code of chivalry?"

"I'm fightin' to win!" said Robert, his brows knitted low over his eyes.

Richard stood tall, sighed deeply, and went to Sedric who listened intently to the instructions he was being given. His eyes widened and he peered around Richard to look at Robert. He smiled approval and even delight at the strategy.

On Sedric's, head every hair grew out in its own direction to be met at his ears by an equally wild beard that hung to his thin but muscular bare chest. Around his waist were strips of various animal skins twisted into a belt from which several knives in their sheaths, and one desiccated human arm dangled. There was also a finely made wide leather belt with a great silver buckle that he used to keep a plaid cloth wrap from falling from his lower body. Silver and colored stone amulets hung from his neck on multiple beaded thongs. Tattoos adorned his arms and lower legs.

It was apparent that Sedric held his position by force of fear.

Richard, the Irish chieftain, his knights and the Scots archers disappeared into the western part of the wood in haste.

The trap was set.

Soon, arrows tipped with naphtha fire pierced the gray afternoon sky in long arcs, trailing tails of dark smoke as they flew. One after another the flights of firebirds hit the thatched roofs of the hovels, which quickly began to smoke and burn, even in the mist. The men hiding inside began to cough. Soon the "would be" ambuscaders fell from the doorways holding their throats and gagging, each falling over the others.

Robert put his horn to his lips and blew his series of short blasts, and the armies from both sides charged into the forsaken Manx troops.

Smoke and fire were everywhere in the village. Robert, with his axe, then led the charge from his side, killing and wounding any in his path as he fought his way through the town. His men followed in his wake and the foe coming out of the hovels on the far side of the town where the kirk stood began to run back toward Castle Rushen.

The kirk disgorged its Manxmen as well, anticipating that it would be next to be on fire. Neither did they run into the battle, but down the lane toward the castle.

Blood was everywhere splattered. Acrid smoke from the fire rolled about, blowing low to the ground, causing even more confusion upon the battlefield. The dead and dying were lying all about but none of them were of the army of Brus. Some were merely farmers from the village, forced to fight against the attacking soldiery with no weapons but their farm tools, sent among the castle garrison to make the Manx numbers appear many more.

The escaping warriors had no better time of it. The single flight of arrows hit them hard and there was yelping and groaning as they fell over or ran faster. The archers had done their work and then moved in to finish off the wounded with short swords and battleaxes, and to retrieve arrows that might be saved.

Farther down the lane, Richard gave the signal and Sedric stood and gave such a blood-curdling scream that those fleeing from the scene of battle seemed to jump from their skins in panic. Drums beat fiercely all around them, adding to their distress.

Irish knights and soldiers rushed in fast with swords and axes flashing. He who ran fastest got away. The rest fell upon a quick death.

The Irish chased the men as best they could and cut them down as they caught them. As the flight moved away from the hamlet in which the battle began, Robert strode up to Richard. Both men were winded and sweating, and spattered with blood.

"Ye won the battle, Robbie," the earl wiped another man's blood from his face.

"By unholy trickery, would ye say?" asked Robert.

"Ye won the battle," he repeated. They stood together and watched the attack progress.

• •

"They have slain us all!" said the first man to clear the portcullis at Rushen, though he bled nowhere.

Others followed huffing and holding their sides from too much running. They were worn and collapsed as they got into the bailey.

Rushen Castle was a large tower soaring a good six stories against the sky with a courtyard at its core. A wall walk was surrounded by high crenellated battlements. The meager curtain wall formed the bailey, and the moat filled with water from the bay beside the castle. There were few outbuildings, and those were mostly for the storing of farm implements, grains and roots.

Magnus, the Viking king of Man had abandoned the castle to England only forty-five years earlier, and little had been done to improve its defenses since then.

The commander of the garrison stood stoically at the battlement staring down into the bailey as twelve escapees straggled in and the bridge was drawn, the gate closed and bolted, the portcullis dropped, and defensive positions manned. He looked north to see the Brus army pouring from the outlying trees and thick smoke billowing from the village beyond.

Robert kept his men out of arrow range and with his shield at the ready walked within the deadly circle alone, save Andrew who went in his wake proudly carrying his banner.

"Give up the castle and go free!" shouted Robert.

The commander growled and gritted his teeth before he spoke, "Ye'll not run me from *this* keep, damn ye Robert de Brus!"

Robert turned to Andrew, "That voice sound familiar, Son?"

"Sounds like the one at Dumfries, My King," replied the squire.

"That ye Macdouall?!" shouted Robert.

"Aye!" answered Lord Dungal defiantly, "It be!"

"Damn!" cursed Robert under his breath.

"Reckon ye hain't goin' to let him run free this time, Sire," said Andrew in a low voice. Robert heard the say but chose to not comment.

Dungal turned to the three archers standing beside him. "Shoot him down!" he demanded. "A silver pound to the first man who draws his blood!"

Robert saw the drawn bows releasing their arrows. He stepped back to get closer to Andrew and threw his shield up. The three arrows hit low on the shield and Robert told Andrew to step backwards with him. He turned to his archers and gave the signal to run inside the castle's killing zone and loose their own flight. Shield bearers ran in as well to shield the archers since they had made no mantlets with which to approach the castle, and those high on the castle wall could send their shafts a much greater distance than Robert's archers from the ground.

As they retreated, one of the arrows aimed at Robert instead hit Andrew in the leg and pierced his chain mail.

The bowmen firing from the ramparts got but one more flight into the air before they were on the receiving end of a flight landing in their midst.

Seeing that Andrew was hit, Robert held his shield with one arm and pulled the arrow from Andrew's calf. "Run, Andrew!" he ordered. Andrew scrambled to his feet and half ran, half limped until he had exceeded the arrows' range, trailing droplets of blood all the way.

Robert and his archers continued to back up until they too were out of the reach of the deadly barbs.

Andrew's leg wound was already being tended when Robert came to see about him. His teeth were clenched tightly together in his effort to stave the pain, and he would not have dared shed a tear before his king.

Robert smiled at Andrew and patted him on the shoulder, though it saddened him that his long-time squire was injured. Without a word to Andrew, he turned to Graham, then standing behind him, and said, "Get the camp set, we're goin' to be here a while."

Meanwhile on the wall, Lord Dungal Macdouall appointed a new captain upon the news that his former captain was dead at the hands of Brus' army in Balisaly Towne. His orders to his new captain were to ration the food, keep a sharp lookout, especially at night, and wait for John of Lorn. He would most assuredly come immediately from o'er the sea and save them from having to surrender yet again.

"You've not looked over the water as yet?" asked the captain.

"And what would I see?" asked Dungal harshly.

"Galleys, Milord. Galleys that aren't Lord John's," said the Englishman.

Dungal walked around to the south wall and peered out to sea, and there were two kinds of square sails, some yellowish, and some white, both festooned with black profiles of galleys. "It's them damned Macdonalds and Maclaines!" he griped loudly. Then he followed with a softer bit of sarcasm, "Should be easy fodder for the Admiral of the great 'Western Fleet' when he comes!"

MAY 19th 1313
The Tower in London

It was a pleasant enough day in terms of weather. The meager garden spots around the white tower were blossoming in preparation for another season of survival. The bustle inside the tower was very different. All was being made ready for the king, his queen, and Prince Edward, the king's heir apparent, now six months old, to visit the royal family in France. King Edward, however, was like the plants in the garden, for he too was plotting his own survival for another season.

"Here are the parchments you will need to show King Phillip," instructed Hetherington, waving the documents toward Edward who seemed not to be listening. He sat at the window and stared aimlessly toward the trees below, his cheek resting on his fist.

King of my world and yet I might as well be a pauper for all the freedom I have, he thought as he contemplated the Ordainers and how they totally dominated his life and his realm.

"Earl Thomas of Lancaster," announced a booming voice that shook the king back to reality.

Edward looked with alarm at Hetherington. "Why was I not informed?"

"Lord Lancaster is on your docket for this morn, Majesty," offered Hetherington obsequiously.

Edward huffed. "Show Lord Lancaster here," he instructed the herald and turned to Hetherington. "Let us be!" he ordered, put out that he had not expected his cousin.

The king's chief administrator picked up the dozen or so scrolls lying before him with the intention of tucking them safely away from curious eyes while the king was otherwise engaged, but his liege lord thought otherwise.

"Leave them! We shall talk again as soon as Lancaster departs," said Edward, and the older man bowed and walked to the door where he bowed again as Lancaster suddenly appeared between the jambs.

Edward turned to greet the earl as the door softly closed behind his guest. He stood and approached airily, the precise opposite of what he felt at receiving Thomas. "Cousin! What brings you to my chambers this day?"

"Sent by the Ordainers, My King," said Thomas acidly after a brief, but formal bow.

"To *spy* upon me, My Lord?" asked Edward returning the barb in kind, but Thomas ignored it and went about the business for which he came.

"There is much of import that needs to be done here, My King, as I'm sure you agree. On the other hand, your queen's brother will soon be knighted in France, an important event in a young noble's life. Question is," he started in sarcasm, "which is the more important matter to England? Fighting to win a war of already long duration, which has to date cost thousands upon thousands of troops and countless treasure? Or, the personal *trivia* of attending a kinsman's ceremony, and a *French* kinsman at that! Which is so important that you must traverse the channel and be gone from here for weeks if not months?"

"We would not want Phillip to get too emboldened with our Scottish brother, Robert de Brus, would we, *Cousin*?" asked the king just as sarcastically, and sitting in a large chair he gestured for the earl to take the seat opposite him.

"So, this is merely an arse kissin' mission?" quipped the earl.

"I have had to kiss arse before, Sir," said Edward.

"So I've heard," said Thomas, and left the jab to fester. "France will never come to terms with Scotland against you. Your French queen assures it."

The king paused, then said, "I'm unaware of all the queen assures but the queen and I are closer now than ever we were before... before you cut..." he slightly sobbed, "...murdered poor Piers... an act for which I will never forgive you no matter how you may beg or how many earldoms may come to you!" His eyes, brimmed with tears, were fiercely glaring at Lancaster.

"I have confessed nothing of the sort," said the earl. "Besides England lives today, better and stronger for what was... happened!"

"By 'better' you mean it is preferable for us to be on the brink of civil war, as we now are?!" gainsaid the king.

Thomas began to fume and he loosened the collar to his tunic, "I should have..."

Edward cut him off sharply. "Tread carefully, Dear Thomas, my power is again waxing."

"If you think King Phillip, sitting on his gilded throne in France will save your crown, you should rethink your purpose in life!" challenged Thomas. He was sitting forward in his chair and anxiously tapping the pommel of his sword with the palm of his hand.

Edward watched the hand. "You want *my* head as well, Dear Cousin?"

Thomas realized the signal he was giving and stopped. "The Ordainers want you not to go to France."

"There is far more at stake than a knighting," offered the king.

"And the arse kissin', too, I suspect," said the earl snidely.

"There be a'plenty of arse to go around if you would but lend your lips to the task, Thomas," replied the king.

Thomas swayed to and fro on his haunches. "Our strenuous objections will be written in the records!" he spat as he stood, thinking his chore of putting Edward's neck a little bit closer to the hangman's rope had been accomplished.

"Write in those selfsame records, that the Lords Ordainers don't always know what kings must do to keep a kingdom for them to rule over! I bid you good day, My Earl."

Thomas threw his head so that the hair lying on the front of his shoulders slung to his back. He raised a haughty brow in Edward's direction and left the room without so much as a nod.

"Damned whoreson! Damn him!" cursed Edward as the door shut. "Hetherington!" he immediately shouted.

The scribe and advisor reentered at the sound of his name, bowed, and sat at the table in front of his scrolls and began searching for the one containing the next subject to be discussed. "Here is a manifest of the rents from your Gascony lands, My King," he said pushing one of the scrolls to Edward.

The king glanced at the figures for a moment then asked, "Is there no other way?"

"It is the only practical way," he answered. "In order to personally borrow money from the Pope, you must offer the rents from your Gascon lands to him as repayment."

"Damned Ordainers," Edward fretted, twisting his face to a scowl. He threw the scroll back across the table to Hetherington. "For six years?"

"Yes, Sire. For six years only. Don't forget to speak to King Phillip of your continued harassment of his enemies, the Templar Knights, and of the hundreds you have put into dungeons and put to death," said the advisor. "Phillip *and* Pope Clement set great store by those who are helping keep the Templars at bay."

"Phillip!" Edward snorted. "Doing 'God's work' he is. He piously accuses the whole bunch of heresy and takes their castles, their fortunes, and their lives. A brilliant play to gain riches, and with the Holy Father as ally, who is to stand against him?!" Edward smiled sardonically and shook his head in admiration for his kinsman's coup. "Now 'Philippe le Bel' controls most of the moneylendin' in Europe, and all done in God's name. A brilliant strategy!" He looked at Hetherington and added, "Remind me never to play chess with him."

"I would advise that you not mention that viewpoint of his actions to

King Phillip, Your Majesty," the counselor replied.

"You have always told me well, Hetherington," said Edward genuinely appreciative of the man.

Hetherington got to his feet and bowed low. "I will have the legalities reviewed and the scribe's work completed on the morrow, My Lord," he said.

"Good," replied Edward. "Our ships leave in two days." Edward stood. "I'll be in the queen's chamber for the remainder of the afternoon. Do not disturb us there."

Hetherington was amazed at how much the child had changed his monarch.

Philip de Mowbray

JUNE 14th 1313
CASTLE STIRLING

He grimaced as he opened one eye to the day. The morn was almost despairingly chilled despite the fact that the sun had been up for hours, and he dug deeper into his blankets to warm his ears. Lord Edward Brus was alone in his tent and he didn't like being without a woman when he awoke.

The wan light made for a gray beginning, just like the many gray beginnings there had been in the eight weeks or so since Robert had sent his brother to this godforsaken edge of a boggy field.

High on the creagh above him rose the foreboding Stirling Castle, which had been in the possession of the English for nine long years. All but impregnable, the fortress fell to the old Edward because of his superior war machinery. After three months of terrible bombardment, the Scots garrisoning the castle at that time had sent word that they would surrender, but Edward refused to allow it. He waited until his massive new trebuchet, nicknamed "The Warwolf", arrived on the scene so that he could try it out on the beaten defenders he held trapped within the castle.

For most of a day he subjected the Scots on the rugged mount to a devastating barrage, like none any had ever experienced before. The Warwolf lived up to Edward's expectations, blasting the already battered castle with huge rounded stones that broke down the walls and exploded from force of impact into deadly shards. When he tired of his game, he allowed the Scots to give him his prize, though it was essentially destroyed. The fifty or so Scots who lived to the end he was dissuaded from disemboweling, instead sending them to prisons in England.

Having no siege engines, much less one of such power, King Robert relied on the old method of taking castles: starvation. The reconstructed and formidable Castle Stirling was no different in that regard from any other. It was necessary only to stay out of arrow range and confiscate all supplies before they could enter, a simple premise.

About a mile and a half away toward the village of Bannock lay Saint Ninian's Kirk where Edward kept his supplies, particularly victuals he protected as much as possible from the constant change of weather, which caused foodstuffs to rot or become riddled with vermin. As a rule he did very well at preserving the army's provisions.

However, there were sacks of grain, primarily barley, which he set aside with the idea that every one of the grains should be left warm and moist enough to green up and start to grow. Behind the kirk was a small outbuilding once used as a sheepcote that Edward had converted into a makeshift distillery.

"How comes the barley?" he asked that afternoon as he walked through the door to his clandestine operation within the siege of Stirling.

"Sproutin' good, 'tis, Milord," replied the squire Baldred poking with a stick into one of the five kettles. The smoke to the fire that kept the concoction warm and working was inefficiently exiting via the hole in the thatched roof, leaving the whole building filled with acrid haze, and Baldred, his eyes red, coughed almost constantly.

"We'll be fixed for spirits from this batch of mash in another two days, Sir Edward," explained the stripling as he handily continued the tending of the mixtures. "Ye be gettin' us more grain?"

"Aye," growled Edward, poking his finger into the warmed mixture and licking it. "Sir William know ye be helpin' me make spirits?"

"'Tain't spirits as yet," reminded Baldred, grinning broadly and ignoring the question.

Edward nodded, "Just ye keep it warm, Lad, or it'll ne'er be spirits!"

The Lord of Galloway mounted his horse and sauntered slowly down the hill, watching for movement or changes to the area anywhere around. Reaching the bottom he started to slog back across the boggy field to his headquarters tent. He was almost there when he espied fifty or more riders on the horizon, headed in his direction from among the trees of King's Park.

Throwing his horse into a gallop he shouted, "Riders comin'! Arm yerselves!" as he went splattering through the mire below the encampment.

Sir Gilbert de la Haye dropped his pan of eggs into the fire and, grabbing his sword and axe, came quickly to meet the younger Brus.

"Riders a'comin' this way fast from the park!" Edward said in haste, "Put some archers on the hillside... get these destriers saddled and men on their backs!"

"Aye, Milord!" replied Sir Gilbert, and leapt to the task as six more lieutenants came to their commander.

"Array for battle!" shouted Edward pointing to the horsemen quickly closing the gap.

The camp was busy for the next few minutes with swords and axes, pikes and guisarmes, helms and targes flying as the men dressed themselves in the regalia of war.

Christina hurried from the surgeon's hovel wherein she was trying to help with a man dying from an infected leg wound. She looked in the direction of the charging men and smiled. "Sir Edward's fixin' to get himself surprised," she spoke aloud, and waited to see the invaders' arrival.

Edward, attired in mail and leather armor held his ground, cursing within his own mind since his army was in various stages of readiness and the enemy would be fast upon them. The chargers came ahead at full gallop.

"We chargin' them?" asked Sir Gilbert, fully arrayed with his broadsword in hand.

"They'll be winded by the time they get to us," said Edward, trying to put the best face on a harrowing situation since his knights were only now straggling to him. "Then charge, we will!" he insisted.

He no sooner got the words from his mouth than he espied the van flag. It was of a blue field with three white lions rampant, and Edward sheathed his sword and removed his helm. He took in a great breath and let it out again as his excitement decreased. Then he laughed and shouted, "It's a'right, men!" before he kicked his destrier to meet with the oncoming force.

Sir Gilbert's usual pleasant disposition soured and he returned to his burned eggs, now mere cinders in the cook fire.

"Walter, ye baseborn high land lout!" Edward greeted with a broad grin.

"Thought I'd give ye a wee scare," said Walter of Ross, laughing. "Did ye shit yer britches?"

Edward laughed louder still. "Nigh on to it, damn yer hide! How'd ye get here? What about Caerlaverock?"

"Fell two weeks ago," said Walter. "Sir Ingram de Umfraville was warden. He hadn't been there long at all when we ran him out. The masons are afixin' to take the walls down, now."

"So, why are ye here?" asked Edward as the men dismounted and handed the reins to their squires.

"Yer brother sent a message," said Walter.

Edward's mien immediately turned dour, and he asked, "Sent *ye* a message?"

"Aye. I was closer than ye."

"He still in Man?"

"Aye," nodded Walter.

"So, what's the message?"

"He said I was to repair here to spell ye."

"Couldn't handle the job on my own, I reckon," said Edward feeling insulted and unsure about Robert's possible intentions.

"Message ne'er said such as that," replied Walter, surprised at his friend's turn of mood.

"Aw, hell!" exclaimed Edward throwing his helm to the ground and turning to look at Walter, changed his dourness to a smile. "Let's have a drink!"

Walter smiled, "Ye got spirits?"

"Aye," returned Edward, his hurt over the content of the message masked by a seemingly pasted on smile. "New made, it is."

The two men got astride their horses and rode toward Saint Ninian's Kirk.

"Sure is 'whores' work' to sit out a siege," mumbled Edward with a deep sigh.

The two men got into the converted sheepcote and wasted no time in sampling the goods of young Baldred, who was on loan from Walter of Airth, he having taught the youth the distillers' art. Airth had recently taken him on as his squire.

After a jug of the spirits disappeared between the two of them, they sat spraddled out with their backs against the outer kirk wall, seemingly to be in a contest as to which one knew the worst bawdy song and could sing at least a part of it.

. .

More than two hundred feet above, at the top of the oppressed creagh was the Scot Philip de Mowbray who had for nine years faithfully served as the English-appointed warden of Castle Stirling for both King Edwards. A brave warrior, he tried too hard to second-guess the wishes of his liege.

"See anythin', Captain?" asked Mowbray as he came to the officer commanding the soldiery standing guard over the ramparts of the massive walls.

"Yes, My Lord Warden. Them damned Scots..." at this faux pas he stumbled a bit but went on, saying, "...have been joined by another bunch. Ye can see 'em yonder." He pointed out Walter of Ross' men. "Even afore they arrived, the others was takin' our supply shipments. Took a heavy farm wagon not a quarter league from our gate!" replied the captain.

Mowbray looked down over the lush green undulating countryside that drifted into an edge of fog at the horizon. Standing here, as he had regularly since becoming warden, he oft-times thought of himself as a master of a gigantic, strangely shaped vessel sailing upon a sea of grass and trees, and other times he would imagine himself as a bird winging its way above the clouds. He looked to the southeast and saw the tidal River Fourth that flowed into the Firth of Fourth. That watery ingress was responsible for the proximate carse, a land of watery grasslands and miry streams.

The castle itself was surrounded by a massive and constantly refurbished stone curtain wall with an impressive gate tunnel and portcullis. The courtyard and keep and all living spaces within were well protected behind heavy, ironbound solid oak doors. The keep and attached buildings were primarily built of stone and wood, and outbuildings of wattle covered with mud, the same as the village buildings that seemed to meander down the steep volcanic upthrust of solid rock to the bottom of the castle road. At the base were a variety of hovels with mud walls. All had roofs of thatch except the main part of the castle keep, which had a roof of wood shingles.

The local farmers would normally bring their foodstuffs to sell in the streets of the village at Stirling on market day. Now those streets lay as fallow as the homes of the villeins in the surrounding landscape. Only a few of the farmers were brave enough to approach Edward's siege army to offer their wares for sale, even though most of the time they were paid a fair price for their goods and asked to return when they had more.

Not a morsel of food, however, got through to the castle inmates.

Edward had run the villeins from their homes and shops into the castle when he first arrived. If nothing more it would be additional mouths in the castle to feed, meaning it would be sooner rather than later that he would have them starved out.

Mowbray and his inmate warriors tried to break the siege several times in the beginning, some weeks earlier, but were beaten back into their lair each time.

"I think they're afixin' to attack and that's why they're gettin' in more troops," replied Mowbray, trying to figure out the Scots far below. "Maybe as soon as the moon shines!"

"Nae," replied the captain, standing taller and facing his superior, "they'll not, Milord. They know all they need do is wait us out. It's as sure as death. No need to spill blood to try and hasten it. Their commander would be a fool to attack us here."

Mowbray looked hard at the man. His dread of just that inevitability made him perform a kind of a nervous waddle as he stood on one foot and then the other. He looked over the side to study their configuration, though he knew what they were doing would be irrelevant when the castle starved. Watching the tiny figures going about their normal business made him wonder, "What ye reckon would happen if we made a truce with them?"

"The king would have yer head, I'd say," replied the captain. "I was at Dundee when the warden tried to make a parlee with a Brus."

"What happened?" asked Mowbray anxiously.

"Nothin'," said he, "The king swore to cut off his head as a traitor if he did anything but protect the keep."

"They were starved out in the end, I recall," mumbled Mowbray, plopping his hands atop one another on the wall and resting his head on their backs. He stood humped like that for near a quarter of an hour.

The captain left to check on his underlings. The day was hot and they had a tendency to hide in some of the crevices of the wall and sleep and dream of an abundance of food waiting at table for them. He didn't really blame them but he couldn't have them sleeping either.

As the captain withdrew from him, Mowbray suddenly rose up from his hands and smiled. He had a brilliant idea that he hoped would allow him to keep his head *and* the castle.

．　．

It was dusk but the hour was late when Edward suddenly awoke with a stare of fear across his face. Shaking his head he sat on his haunches. He was inside the kirk where the stores were kept. His eyes adjusted to the dim light when he rubbed them and he saw Walter facedown on the floor several feet away.

"Walter!" he said bluntly.

Walter moved not.

"Walter?!" he said again, louder.

No move.

Edward panicked. He crawled on his hands and knees toward his friend. He turned him over.

Walter giggled in his stupor.

"Baseborn drunk!" growled Edward releasing his friend's shoulder and allowing him to slump back to the floor.

Edward turned his back to Walter and used his sleeping body to rear back on. Picking up the jug that the two had been nursing last, he drained the contents onto his parched tongue and tossed it aside.

"Time for a piss," he muttered to himself and tried to stand. After three tries he was successful enough to stagger to the door. Beyond were the two horses they had left grazing on the hillside near the sheepcote. Edward headed there for another crock of spirits but the men had found and consumed it all. Nothing was left save the barley makings. Nature would be denied no more and Edward then was reminded of his mission when his britches were suddenly soaked.

"Goddamn it!" he screamed. He had no control of his overburdened bladder.

He was angry all over again, and sat on the ground to remove the wet clothing. As inebriated as he was, the task was well beyond him, and he grew more and more frustrated the more he tried. Finally he flopped over onto the grass and lay there half naked. The one thought in his head by then was, "Why does Robert not trust me to do his biddin' on my own?!" He shouted, hoping the gods or the angels would hear him and give him an immediate answer. He then wept and moaned like a beast caught in a thicket.

Moments later he got the notion to show his brother king just how much he *hated* him for placing him in this predicament. His britches were tangling his feet so that he fell, hitting his face hard on the ground, bloodying his nose. He laughed for a moment as he touched his nose and saw the blood on his fingers. Then it came to him why he couldn't walk, so he yanked at his britches until he managed to get them back up. Eventually he staggered to his horse and managed to seat himself in the saddle. For a moment he sat astride the animal and stared at the horse's neck as if he had gone to sleep with his eyes open. But he soon remembered for what purpose he had started, and set off to ride the mile and a half until he was in front of the surgeon's hovel.

He was not a quiet drunk and when he arrived at the place in which he knew Christina slept, he attempted to dismount and fell instead, his buttocks brushing against the hilt of his sword and scabbard he had tied to the saddle earlier. Cursing the fall, and cursing his horse for having caused it, he again found his way to his feet and shambled to the door.

Christina had been asleep, but was no longer, having heard the approach of the horse. Rising from her pallet she looked out the small window toward the drunken Edward and saw him fall from his mount. As he rolled around and finally stood, she was not concerned that he had hurt himself, and stifled a laugh at his buffoonery.

Seeing him approach the door, she opened it and surprised him, causing him nearly to lose his balance, but he quickly put his hands on the doorjambs to steady himself. He blinked his eyes and tried to focus on the blurry figure before him, finally calling her name in greeting her. She smelled his heavily laden breath and the strong odor of urine, and realized he had thoroughly wet himself in his drunkenness, again.

"Good morrow, Lady Chrish-tina," he slurred and bowed as low as he dared.

"'Tis not yet the morrow, Lord Edward," she said pleasantly, but stood in the doorway to prevent his entering. "The sun set only a short time ago. Why are ye here at this late hour?" He took a moment to organize his thoughts, a formidable task when it was difficult for him just to keep himself from falling over.

"To see ye..." He acted as if he were going to say more, but lost the notion.

"About what?" she coaxed.

"I've come to see ye!" he repeated.

"Yes, Edward, I know. What did ye want?"

"Ye are beautiful, Chrish-tina."

"That's what ye came for, to say that?" She still kept her amusement from breaking forth into laughter. He gently reached to take her hand in his, to which she responded by trying to jerk it away, but he had acted faster. Too late she realized that his grip was like a vise. He smiled and pulled her closer, raising her fingers to his lips where he kissed them tenderly, at the same time slipping his arm around her waist and forcing her against him.

Intoxicated or not, he had lost none of his strength, and she knew now that she had more than just a drunken fool on her hands.

"I would not hurt ye, Chrish-tina," he said softly, and tried to kiss her lips, but she turned her cheek to him instead. His foul stench was so repulsive that she could hardly breathe as he pushed her against the wall and roughly took her hair in his large hand and made her turn her face toward him, where he placed his mouth completely over hers in a passionate kiss, at least on his part.

"I need ye, Chrish-tina," he whispered softly in her ear after the kiss. She almost gagged on a whiff of his breath.

"Ye don't need me, Edward," she returned. It was useless to struggle against the muscular knight. She must try something other than force, for he would win without the least exertion on his part.

"Aye, I do," he insisted, enveloping her in his arms and kissing her about her neck and ear. "Ye know I could be good to ye, aye?" he continued kissing her, making love to her, and his hands wandered clumsily all over her body as he grew more excited. She had to wait until he loosened his smothering grip before she acted, and she would have but one chance to get away.

"Do you like this, Crishtina?" he asked, moving his lips down her neck and onto her shoulder. She said nothing, remaining immobile and as dispassionate as he was impassioned, though she knew she was about to be raped. Then he said, "I'll give ye a night that ye can remember and weep, next time ye roll into ol' Rob's bed."

Oh, God, that's what this is all about! He's standin' here slobberin' all over me to get back at Robbie! The insight slammed into her wit giving her a weapon that could inflict more distraction and more pain than the knife she usually carried beneath her skirt. It must be used sparingly.

"Perhaps so," she said quietly, relaxing in his arms. "But Robert would never hurt a woman, or make her do anything against her will."

He stopped his inept wooing, and looked into her eyes, progressing down to her breasts, which he caressed. "I'm not goin' to hurt ye, I already said."

"Aye, but ye have kept me so tightly fastened to this wall that I cannot move. I am trapped!" He stepped back and she acted as though she were released from chains, straightening her hair and her shift, which he had twisted all around her with his groping. She sighed, "That's so much better," and for the first time, she smiled, in spite of the fact that her shift was wet with his urine in places. "Now, we can get more relaxed and have a little wine, and then," she touched his face and ran her hand down his torso all the way to his crotch, "I'll give *ye* a time to remember."

"Ye do like wine," she asked without asking as she turned to the storage shelves in the corner of the small room.

"Aye, I like it. I like stronger spirits better, and ale, I like ale better, too." He watched the way she moved within her loosely flowing shift, though his blurred vision left much to his imagination.

"I have no ale or spirits, just wine," she said, reaching for a quaiche on the shelf over the small chest.

"I like wine well enough, too." He sat on the edge of the pallet in which she slept, and loosened the belt that cinched his kirtle in, dropping it to the floor.

As she brought the quaiche down to the table she opened one of the tiny drawers in the medicine box there, and took a pinch of fine powder within it and dusted it quickly from her fingertips into the drinking vessel. Reaching up for the other one, she took another pinch from the drawer and added it to the first. She closed the drawer and filled each quaiche with a ruby liquid she poured from a bottle kept beneath the table.

Carrying one quaiche in each hand, she sat on the pallet beside him and handed one to him. He was more interested in nuzzling her neck than in drinking the wine, and set his quaiche on the floor. She had to think of something to make him pick it up again, before he lost all interest in it.

"I thought ye said ye liked wine." She sipped at hers.

"Aye, I do."

"Ye're not drinkin it."

"I am fair drunk already, Chrishtina, and all I want now is to bed ye, and show ye that I am the best man ye e'er had lie with ye." He reeked so badly that she could barely stand his breath upon her breast, which he was kissing awkwardly. She purposely spilt her cup on his face and across her dress, and immediately jumped to her feet.

"Oh, now look what ye've done!" she fretted with the front of her shift, stained with red splotches. "Ye have spilt my cup!"

"Ye can have mine, Lass! Come back here with me!"

"Nae, I've plenty more. I'll get the bottle whilst I wipe the spill from my shift." She went to the corner and purposely delayed returning, picking up a cloth and dabbing at the stains. "Ach, ye've ruined it, for sure. I've a mind to make ye leave without even so much as a drop of Robert's finest wine!" she fussed, and glanced at him to see his reaction. It was as she had hoped.

Edward took the cup from the floor, downed its contents in two quick gulps, and tossed the cup on the bed. Rising from its edge he crossed to and grabbed her, turning her to face him.

"I am tired of waitin' and I'm tired of hearin' about 'King Robert'!" With that he lifted her off her feet and carried her to the bed and tore the shift open down the front. "I'll have ye, Lass, with or without yer leave!" he said, hastily removing his own shirt.

Out of the darkness at the other end of the room there came a voice saying, "Let the lass be, ye whoreson!" Edward reached down at his belt for his dagger, but was stunned at first that it was not there. His mind reeled. Never was he out in the world without his blade at his side. By the time his addled wit remembered the dagger and the belt going to the floor when he dropped them, Christina had taken it and hidden it beneath the bedclothes.

"Who are ye?!" Edward said threateningly as he glanced about the floor for the blade.

"Leave him alone, Edward! He is wounded and cannot fight ye!" Christina shouted, scrambling to pull her shift closed and get to her feet.

"Then he needs to mind his manners and stay out of another man's pleasures!"

"Edward!" she shouted, and grabbing his arm, whispered, "He is dying, leave him be!" The great Scot warrior in his drunken rage turned his strength on Christina and slapped her so hard that she spun around and fell on the bed face first.

"I can relieve his sufferin' right quick if I can but find my *dagger*! Oh, the hell with it!" he strode the several steps beyond the light, intending to beat the fellow to death, as Christina, her mouth bleeding and the whole side of her face beginning to swell, searched the bedcovers for his knife. Finding it, she pulled the blade from the scabbard and hid it in the folds of the skirt of her rent gown.

"Edward! If ye touch him, I'll kill ye myself!" she yelled. He turned to look at her, her garment in tatters, her mouth a smear of red to his alcohol-obscured vision, and he started to laugh derisively.

"Ye'll kill me? Ye, my brother's half naked trollop will kill me?" and he started unsteadily back to where she stood when suddenly, in the midst of his cruel laughter and hurtful words, a strange look came across his countenance and he bent double.

"Aaagh!" he groaned holding his midsection.

"Ye're poisoned, Edward! Ye had best go outside and drink as much water as ye can hold to try and weaken the potion…" Christina said no more as Edward dashed out the door and could be heard retching, time and again. Holding the dagger, she went to the bed of the dying man and asked if he were alright.

"Oh, aye," he said, "but I'll be better anon, Lass. Yer lip is bleedin' bad. Ye had best be tendin' yer own wounds." He reached up and touched her cheek, adding, "I'm glad ye killed the baseborn lout!"

Christina smiled. "He won't die, not from what I gave him."

"But ye said he was poisoned…"

"Aye, and that he is, but he'll not die from it. He'll soon be wishin' he could die, and drinkin' cold water will only make it worse. But I told him true. It will also make it over quicker." She went to the door and dropped the heavy bar, just in case. Only then did she put the blade back in its sheath and wrap a shawl around her shoulders.

"Would ye like a dram Clyde?" she asked as she poured her quaiche full. In spite of the brave front she had proffered to Edward, she noticed her hand shook as she poured. Getting no answer, she went to the pallet on which the valiant soldier lay. "Clyde, would ye like…" His hand was off the pallet's edge and on the floor. She looked into his face and saw that his eyes were all but closed, and his mouth relaxed into a pleasant, satisfied look. *That's what he meant when he said he would soon be better*, she thought, and closed his eyes before placing her head on the dead man's chest in sorrow.

Then Christina wept. All the emotional strain of the event poured out on her bruised cheek and upon her arms and upon the corpse of the warrior Clyde. And when she had vented all the anger, frustration, and fear, she slept, right there, kneeling over him.

When the cock crew at first light, she woke and began to put her things in a poke for a long journey. Her medicine chest and all its herbs and potions went along, too, and the foodstuffs she had laid by. Her good heavy cloak she flung around her, and she picked up her bundles and a good-sized water skin, and glancing once more at the departed Scot, Christina walked out of the hovel, mounted Edward's horse and rode off in the direction of Dundee, where her children were abiding with kith.

When Edward returned, later in the morn and saw that his victim, his horse, *and* his sword were missing, he cursed and slammed the door and threw everything that came to hand, except the bottle of red wine Christina had left upon the table. His anger spewed out as he cursed Christina, the dead soldier, the day, and his aching head. He lay upon Christina's palette, having been up most of the night as consecutive waves of nausea and dry heaves forbade restful sleep. It was not long before his tired, aching body gave in and he nodded off.

• •

Along about noon Philip de Mowbray had his squire saddle his horse. The youth stood staunchly by the beast as the warden approached the nether bailey to meet up with the ten best knights he had available to him. All eleven mounted their bony destriers and rode through the gate tunnel and down to the village. The sad condition of both horses and men was concealed beneath the brightly colored and handsome trappings they wore.

"They're comin'! 'Tis another raid!!" yelled the man closest to the street leading down from the castle.

"Shit!" grumped Edward. "Afix to fight!" he bellowed loudly, knowing he had less than a minute before the oncoming warriors arrived.

"What d'ye want me to do?" asked Walter trying to shake the cobwebs from his drunken mind.

"Get yer men in a defensive posture. Mine's agoin' to charge them head on!"

The cavalry, including Haye, stood ready for the charge but something was amiss. Mowbray and his knights parked their horses at the foot of the street and calmly waited.

"What ye reckon their trick is?" asked Haye as he came abreast of Edward.

"I know not but they hain't starvin'. I see plenty of horseflesh standin' there that hain't been et!" growled Lord Edward. "I wish they would come on... I feel like killin' somethin'!"

"Not today, Milord," said Haye. "Seems they have parlee in mind."

"Damn 'em!" said Edward, "I hain't wantin' a parlee!" Drawing his sword, he kicked his horse toward the awaiting castle warden and his show of knights.

Mowbray advanced to meet Edward.

Seeing that Mowbray was armed with neither sword or dagger, Edward jerked his rains, stopping his destrier almost in mid-gallop.

Mowbray then sauntered his horse to Edward.

Edward raised his sword to render Mowbray's deathblow, which he dearly wanted an excuse to deliver.

Mowbray did not flinch. He was fearless in Edward's shadow.

Edward was hung over from his drinking bout with Walter and his 'poisoning' by Christina. He had been thwarted in his attempted rape and his own brother Robert did not trust him to finish the siege. He yet smelled of urine, alcohol and vomit, though his trews had dried from pissing his britches. He was in a foul mood and ached for some female company, but he could not bring himself to strike the unarmed knight down and Mowbray had counted on exactly that.

So, upon the neutral ground of the road between the castle and the besiegers, the two men talked as if of a private matter.

It was very far from that.

JUNE 16th 1313
RUSHEN CASTLE ON THE ISLE OF MAN

It was going on four weeks since the Scots under King Robert laid siege to Rushen Castle. The king used it as a triggering mechanism, hoping to bring the entirety of the island under his control. While the pro-English inmates commanded by Lord Dungal Macdouall were held to their keep by his army, Robert had Angus Macdonald patrolling outside the bay abutting the castle. He waited, if nothing more expecting England's western fleet under the command of the escaped John of Argyll, known as the Lord of Lorn, to challenge the Macdonald fleet.

On the other hand, perhaps Lord John was still smarting from his last entanglement with the Brus, and yet awaited a more advantageous confrontation that would enable him to reap a tastier revenge and soothe his vexed pride.

Lord Macdouall, meanwhile, felt abandoned by King Edward, his liege lord. No help was forthcoming for him, no fleet from Ireland and no army from England.

"Where is that goddamned John of Lorn!?" swore Dungal, standing at the bars of the small open window and gazing seaward. His earlier rash defiance was plumb whipped from his spirit.

He slowly slumped to the floor. "Why does Brus persecute me? No matter where I am settled I escape him not," he muttered. He raised up the wine bottle he held in his hand and set it atop his thigh. He wrenched the cork from its neck and drank a healthy draught, after which he gasped and wiped his mouth with his sleeve.

He sat in a stupor and dozed for a long while, until he fought himself awake from the horror of a repeating dream in which Robert de Brus was attacking him with that axe he held in hand when Dumfries was lost. When the castle fell he had been prepared to die, but now he was newborn, with the mindset that he was freed and given this new life by Brus. With this nightmare recurring, it seemed to him that Brus would come to take his life back, but Dungal could not figure out why. Where had he gone wrong?

Wanting to break his thoughts and realizing he was sweating, the castle warden rolled up on his knees as a first move to getting to his feet. Once a strong, lean warrior, he had languished in fear of Robert's revenge, and thus had grown much overweight for his medium-sized frame, and standing from his seat on the floor was a great effort.

As he stood and walked toward his solar, the tip of his sword dragged the flagstone floor. The corridor was dark despite the small window, and he wandered back through the castle by keeping his fingers to the wall for stability.

The guards at the solar door opened it for their lord to enter. Across the room near the window sat his woman. She had been with him at Dumfries as she had been with him at Buittle and even before. But she knew he always had others he would visit in bedrooms throughout the castle. He occasionally let other men have her to themselves if he were of a mind to curry their favor. She was warranted to please them, and would not have been allowed to disappoint.

She loved him, if any woman could love a curmudgeon of Dungal's ilk. She was as close to a wife as ever he had.

Speaking not a word, she remained seated in the half-darkened room, wrapped in her best silk mantle, and awaited his pleasure. But he ignored her, instead flopping himself on the high, soft bed.

"Ye want me?" she at last asked, throwing her cloak back to reveal herself completely naked.

"Ye are the meanest woman I e'er have known," he said grouchily. "Leave me be!"

"Ye have let that Brus betwixt us," she complained in a low voice.

Dungal raised himself up on his elbows. "If e'er ye say that again..."

"Ye're too ruined to do anything," she taunted, standing and blocking out a great majority of the dying light coming through the window.

Dungal fell back on the bed, exhausted in his melancholy. Even anger failed to summon him any further.

She walked enticingly to his bed and tried to excite him, but the more she tried the more he shirked. He was not accustomed to his women being aggressive, though not holding her for so long a time was unusual as well. He acted almost fearful of her.

She climbed upon the bed, straddled his legs and began ripping at his loose clothing. His bottle of wine fell to the floor and without its cork, dribbled its contents onto the heavy woven rug beside the bed. Dungal felt nothing. The wine induced stupors came and went. She lay upon him and pushed a nipple from her ample breast into his swollen, cracked lips, but the gesture was wasted. He made no response. Her whole seduction was proving hopeless.

She rolled off him and sat on the edge of the bed. "Ye are lost, My Lord, e'en to yerself," she lamented. Having lived with him for all those years, she realized full well her plight. Her protector was in a poor condition to protect anything.

He tried to sit up but fell back upon his pillows.

She gently massaged his genitals in hopes of getting his interest waxing. "What grand pleasures ye have brought to the likes of me, My Lord Dungal."

He turned away from her and drifted off to sleep.

She began to sob piteously.

• •

"How are ye lad?" asked Robert coming to the tent in which his squire was convalescing from the arrow wound he had suffered. Andrew started to get to his feet but Robert motioned for him to remain on his pallet of straw.

"The leg is tolerable, My King," said Andrew.

"Can ye walk?"

"Aye," said the lad, "I can, some."

"Goin' huntin' presently," said Robert, "Ye up to a hobble?"

"Aye, Sir!" he said excitedly. "Be fixed for it!"

Robert left and sent a message asking Earl Richard to join in the hunt. Within the hour the two nobles and the squire, limping along with the aid of a wooden staff, set off to a nearby wood on the opposite side of Castle Bay to find their supper.

On the far tip of the spit of land, out of sight of the castle, the trio came upon several galleys that had put ashore there. The men were cooking fish over an open flame and the conversation was lively and boisterous. When they saw the king they jumped to their feet and a silence fell over them.

"Ye men Macdonalds?" asked Robert.

"Aye, Sire, 'cept for the Maclaines among us," one answered stiffly. Robert scanned their faces, until his eyes fell on one that was different from the rest.

"That one hain't a Macdonald or a Maclaine," said Robert, peering through the others to the squatting man eating the flesh of a fairly large fish.

Sedric laughed, half chewed fish falling from his mouth onto his hands and the sandy beach.

"Where's yer league, Sedric," asked Lord de Burgh.

"Yonder, where ye wanted them," said Sedric still gorging himself.

"Reckon ye ought to be with them?" asked the earl.

"Ye hain't with yer'uns," replied the chieftain without even looking up from his feast.

"He is my guest," said a voice coming from behind.

Robert turned to see Angus grinning broadly.

"And why hain't ye invited the rest of us, Lord Macdonald?" the king asked cheerfully extending his hand to his friend.

Angus laughed. "Not enough fish, I reckon."

"Yer sailors do nothin' all day 'cept fish," said Robert. "Ye got plenty."

Angus smiled and nodded at the truth.

"Angus, have yer men move this party around the point, where the castle is in plain view," adjured Robert.

"Want them to smell the fish a'cookin'?" asked Earl Richard.

"Wind's in the wrong direction," Robert answered, "but we can hoot and laugh a lot while we stuff ourselves from Angus' larder."

In various stages of preparation, the fish were all loaded onto one galley and the men rowed it the short way around the point where they were no more that five hundred yards from the castle.

"Make the fires much bigger," said Robert. "We'll be cookin' up some mighty bellyaches."

Andrew Stewart sat on a large rock on the shore and ate more fish than he had ever eaten in one sitting in all his life. They all laughed and ate and the accompanying wine had them all hooting in no time.

"Ye surely hunted us up a grand dinner, today, My King," said Andrew, his face and hands oily from the repast.

Robert, too, was pleased with the evening's fare and company, but he would have been more pleased if the castle came to its senses and surrendered.

• •

The distant wild, strange clamor coming through the solar window deep in the chilly night finally awoke Lord Macdouall. Thinking it was all part of another nightmare, he opened his eyes to mere slits, letting only the barest bit of light enter.

Trying to move he found he could wriggle his arms and legs a little, and was able to get to the edge of his bed, where he sat with his feet dangling.

Where's she, he wondered, scratching under one great arm. He vaguely remembered that she had crawled atop him in her nakedness and that he had been unable to move. He wondered why. *If she were to do that now, she would for certain get a different response,* he grinned to himself. Stretching his arms away out, he wondered, too, why the solar was so dark and he looked toward the window, speculating that the hour was late and the sun was at last setting.

He gasped at what he saw. There, hanging by her neck, silhouetted against the window's reddish light, was his woman. Dressed in her finest gown and jewelry, her hair curled and piled prettily atop her head, and one foot shod in an embroidered silk shoe, she hung still as stone.

He got to his feet and tottered to her. "She is not dead, she is not dead!" he said desperately. Reaching out, he shook her legs and she was all but stiff. Now her body swung gently back and forth. Turned over on the floor nearby was the chair from which she had slipped her feet to bring the rope taut around her neck. Beneath her was the other silk shoe. He picked it up and held it to himself as if a found treasure.

He slowly and laboriously righted the chair and sat in it at her feet. After staring at the brilliant sunset for the longest time, he suddenly said, "Wake up, woman!" and slapped her slow turning legs. The body swung to and fro and the rope creaked as it stretched on the overhead beam. "Wake up and get my supper!" he ordered.

A few minutes later he repeated his demand in such a loud voice that one of the guards entered thinking he had been called. One look and he quietly closed the door.

"Lord Macdouall has gone witless!" said the English guard. "Send for the captain!"

Rushing to the solar the English captain threw open the door and was stunned at the scene. He could not figure what to do. Of course the poor woman's body must be taken down and she must be buried. "Send for the priest," he said, making the sign of the cross upon himself as one soldier ran toward the stairs.

Turning to the second man he ordered that none but the priest be allowed into the room. The man shut the door and stood before it, his pike at his side.

The guard captain's mind was awhirl with panic, with the myriad things that must be done, with... he was now in command of Castle Rushen! He stood in deep thought and waited in the middle of the hallway for the priest's arrival, all the while running his fingers across his mustache and beard.

He must not dare disturb the commander of Castle Rushen; insane or not, if he yelled an order it would have to be carried out unless the priest arrived and confirmed that the lord was completely mad. Then he could... do what?

The castle was surrounded by enemy forces and the people inside would soon be starving. Stores were woefully inadequate since, thinking he could stop the attack before Brus' men got to him, Lord Dungal had ignored the two days of warning he had received.

Wrong, he had been, on a number of accounts, poor wretch.

The captain showed the priest into the solar when he arrived and the guardsmen had to take the woman down from her gibbet and lay her on the bed. Not at all sure that her death was by her own hand, but not daring to suggest otherwise, the priest prayed that God would forgive whoever hanged her, but could not perform the last rites upon a suicide. She was then carried down to the keep's small chapel to await burial. Dungal walked beside her and talked to her as if they strolled together.

• •

Along about sunup the captain send a messenger to King Robert asking a truce for parlee. The two men met just about at the same spot Andrew was shot on the first day of the siege. He stood behind Robert again this day, proudly holding the great yellow banner, the tastes of the previous night's feast still in his mouth.

The captain dismounted and walked to where King Robert stood.

"Lord Brus, we shall relinquish the castle," said the captain of the garrison.

"Where is Lord Dungal, yer liege lord?" asked Robert looking at the captain suspiciously, and searching about the battlements for signs of trickery.

"Lord Dungal," said the captain swallowing hard, "is gravely... he has gone mad, Sir."

"Ye speakin' for him?" asked the king.

"Lord Dungal is the only overlord, Sir. I am but a knight and captain of the garrison in the service of Edward, King of England. Other than Lord Macdouall, ye have killed all those of higher rank," he explained.

Robert nodded, somberly.

"Here are my terms," said the king, convinced he was talking to the most able and superior authority within the castle. "Of all within the castle, ye and yer men will swear before God ne'er to lift another weapon against a Scot, abandon yer weapons, and ye will be ferried across the sea to the Irish coast. As will Lord Dungal, to whom I have already given his freedom. Local people who bend their knees to Scotland shall live and stay on this land. The remainder will be put to death by the sword."

The knight again swallowed hard and, knowing King Edward would be harsh on his decision, agreed to the terms. If he wanted to live, he would have to hide in the wilds of Ireland, never to return home to England again.

Sedric, who had overheard the terms spelled out, was particularly interested in the garrison being sent to Ireland. He came to the captain and felt his arm as if he were a carcass on a butcher's shamble. He smiled, all the while staring at the man's arm. Insulted, the captain looked the fellow up and down, and seeing the petrified arm hanging from Sedric's belt, gasped. Quickly he pulled his own arm away and looked with wide eyes at Robert, who shrugged and smiled, but only slightly.

• •

For two days the woman lay a corpse and Lord Dungal Macdouall, unaware of anything happening on the grounds, sat in his same chair, brought to the tiny chapel for his use. Now and again he demanded that she wake and give him service. When she was buried, he wept, but later continually asked her whereabouts.

Not one local failed to swear allegiance to King Robert. His fight for the Isle of Man was finished, at least for now.

Isabella de Strathbogie

JUNE 23RD 1313
PEEL OF STRATHBOGIE

Once he and Mowbray agreed upon their covenant, Lord Edward Brus wasted no time in abandoning the siege at Castle Stirling. He had been miraculously saved from that odious chore by what he considered Divine intervention. He knew that Robert would at last be proud of him, and that "Simple Philip" Mowbray would not realize how badly he had been hoodwinked for at least another year.

Lying twelve miles north of Castle Kildrummy was a modified "motte and bailey" made mostly of wood, known as the Peel of Strathbogie. The tower house was sited atop a hill, and surrounded by its bailey, it overlooked a wide valley and beautiful forested hills in the wild country of Garry. Rivers Deveron and Bogie wandered below and that made the peel strategically placed for the protection of certain of the northern areas of Scotland. It was the home of the Earls of Atholl and at that time occupied by Earl David de Strathbogie, recently come to King Robert's peace rather than lose his earldom.

Eight riders crested the hillock south of the peel. The men were moving slowly for they had traveled six days over the mountains to reach their intermediate destination. A warrior guard ran his squire to alert Earl David to the oncoming riders. Twenty armed men came from their barracks at the sound of the clanging alarm bell in the bailey.

"Reckon they know we're here?" said Walter sarcastically, his broad grin displaying his usual good humor.

"'Ppears so," agreed Edward.

As the octet moved at a walk across the fields toward the stronghold, a young woman ran from the house, her feet bare, her hair gathered up in braided fashion around her face but streaming long and loose down her back. Seeing the riders she recognized one in the party and screamed with excitement, "Open the gate! Open the gate... quickly!"

The eight riders were ploddingly closing the gap.

Hearing his sister's scream, Earl David came into the bailey, still chewing the last bite of his midday meal, and saw his sister demanding the gates be opened. Searching out the approaching riders, he, too, quickly recognized them by their pennants. "Open the gates!" he commanded.

The gates swung wide and Isabella, skirt flowing behind her and legs flashing brightly in the sunlight, ran with abandon toward the men.

Joana came to the side of her husband. "Who's comin'?"

"Blue lion on a white field, Edward Brus come courtin' again." He replied sourly.

"Too bad he hain't yet been killed, him and his murderin' brother," said she, just as disagreeably. The couple stood in the warm sun and watched the joyous girl run toward Edward and his companions, who moved not any faster.

"Them two might be gettin' married one of these days, ye better get used to the thought of it," he hypothesized. "Be in line to be queen, she would... if somethin' happened to Robert."

"Hain't married as yet," gainsaid Joana, "*ye* better get used to the thought of that!" and she turned to go back into the house.

"Hain't ye stayin' to greet our guests?" he asked.

"I think not!" Joana said haughtily. "Ye can do all the kissin'. Jist say I'm ailin' with the pox!" At that, she disappeared through the doorway and David was left alone in the center of the bailey to meet Lord Edward and his entourage.

"Where ye been, Edward!?" asked Isabella breathlessly and fully excited as she came to the side of his horse.

Edward stopped. "I have been sittin' on my backside outside Stirlin', Isabella, My Love. Ye know, ye're as pretty as a glen full of heather," he said flirtatiously, and handed her a sprig of the purplish blooms he had just picked after he glimpsed her running.

She took the proffered branch and said overtly, "Take me up with ye, Milord, and I'll show ye the difference 'twixt me and heather." She smiled brazenly and held her hand up to his.

He took her hand and cleared his foot from his stirrup that she might place her bare toes through it, and hoisted her onto the horse behind his saddle. She squealed with girlish excitement. Edward turned to Walter and grinned.

"Reckon we'll see ye two in a bit," said Walter, and Isabella and Edward started off in the direction of her waggling finger, he kicking the horse into a faster gait.

Isabella squealed again.

Walter and his six knights sauntered up the slope and into the bailey to draw rein in front of David.

"Hail to ye, Milord Strathbogie," greeted Walter.

"I would judge that ye are a Ross from the looks of yer colors," said David, in as friendly a manner as he could muster, "but ye seem to have lost the one belongin' to those." He pointed to Edward's flag.

"Lord Edward?" asked Walter, knowing full well the earl's meaning.

"Aye," said Atholl, "Lord Edward."

Not far from the peel was truly a glen of heather, its lavender tips blowing softly in the light summer breeze. Isabella scampered from the horse's back and began running up the hill toward a small stand of pine trees. Edward slipped from his saddle and teasingly ran after her, catching her just where she wanted him to, within the closeness of the trees.

He spun her around, cutting short her laugh when he pressed his lips to her mouth. Her excited squeal was muffled. She hugged him tightly around his neck and threw her legs about his waist. He dropped to his knees and laid her on the soft bed of pine needles.

There they spent much of the lazy afternoon, until at last Isabella stood and straightened her long dress and brushed the pine needles back to the ground from where they had been collected. Looking over the field of heather that stretched away down the hill, she sighed deeply. "So, ye think me to be as pretty as all that?"

Edward sat up and looked. The sun was getting low in the sky and the whole valley had been transformed to a reddish hue. "It be rightfully beautiful, Milady," he said, "but I warrant that ye're e'en more pleasin' to my eye."

Isabella laughed and fell full on Edward's large frame. "Ye're more pleasin', yerself," she exclaimed softly, and kissed him again.

It was late and nearly dark by the time the two lovers returned to the peel. Edward walked his horse into the stable and stood him beside Walter's and the others'.

She kissed him again. "My Lord Edward, ye hain't asked for my hand as yet, and my brother is askin' when ye might."

Edward's mood changed. He had found her a willing companion and pure delight for the afternoon, but now, she had turned serious. After a moment's consideration he said, "When we get the English whipped. We'll talk of such then."

"Ye hain't a'goin' to beat the English and the Comyns," she flared.

"Ye had best hope we do," argued Edward as he dragged the saddle from his horse's back and threw it on the crib.

She realized she had spoken imprudently. Hoping to change the subject she said, "This doesn't look like yer horse."

"It got killed," he lied.

"This one looks all worn out,"

"It'll ride to where I'm goin'," he picked up a curry brush and an old rag, and thus did not see the look of horror on her face.

"Thought ye came to see me!" she yelped.

"Well, I've seen ye!" he said smartly. "But, tomorrow I must to go to Ross!"

She balled her small fist as tightly as she could and hit him squarely on the jaw as hard as she could.

He was surprised and staggered back against his horse.

"Ye damned misbegotten Brus!" she yelped and turned to run into the peel.

Edward didn't watch her go but kept currying his horse. "Reckon I'm sleepin' in the stable loft tonight," he growled to himself.

The next morning all eight men saddled their horses and rode toward the northwest and Ross. Not one of the Strathbogie family came from the keep to see them off.

"Reckon we hain't stayin' the night there on our way back," said Walter with a look over his shoulder.

"Aw," replied Edward assuredly, "she'll be a'right directly."

July 10th 1313
Castle Caerlaverock

Robert departed Man saying goodbye to his father-in-law. The earl secretly pledged his support for Robert's war against the English and Robert pledged to support Richard in his yet undeclared war against England to free Ireland from tyranny, sometime in the not-to-distant future.

The king sent a message to Edward and Robert Boyd to meet him at Castle Caerlaverock as soon as could be arranged. Walter of Ross had been in command of the siege of Caerlaverock and when the castle capitulated Walter was sent north to help Sir Edward in the siege of Stirling castle.

Caerlaverock was built on Solway Firth, which protected the southwest entrance into Scotland and was a convenient stopping place for Robert to rest and contemplate his next moves to remove the English from his homeland. Behind the castle was a great marsh of willows making the fortification a perfect defensible position. Starvation and the lack of will of the inhabitants to sacrifice themselves for that particular piece of ground were the ingredients in the fall of the castle to Scotland's favor.

Boyd had arrived two days earlier than did Edward, who had to be chased down far to the north in the wilds of Ross to be given the message. He had returned with Walter and their small retinue of knights and immediately informed Robert of the terms of his agreement with Philip de Mowbray, which allowed him to abandon the siege of Stirling and go to Ross.

Caerlaverock was being dismantled around them. The main keep was still intact, but coming closer every hour to the mason's wrecking bars.

"DAMN!" growled King Robert in pure frustration, "Damn! – Damn! – Damn!"

"But Robbie, I figured it would be a good thing!" countered Edward in a pleading voice.

"Ye figured wrong, Brother!"

"How was I to ken ye didn't want Stirlin'?"

"Oh, I want Stirlin' bad, but riskin' the whole of our entire labors for these last eight years just for Stirlin' is pure folly!"

Edward sighed. He hated to be fussed at by his brother, especially when he thought he had done what he reckoned was right.

Robert fumed and puffed and paced the course of the room, trying to fit together the pieces of the puzzle Edward had laid at his feet. He certainly didn't need the English coming north again. He turned back to his brother and declared, "At Dumfries, I said for you to go to Stirlin' and lay siege... naught more!"

"Layin' siege is borin', Robert!" griped Edward.

"Borin'?!" replied the king. "What was more entertainin' than doin' my biddin'?"

"Strathbogie's sister?" answered Edward meekly and with a slight smile of victory.

Robert sighed again. "Ye're playin' with pure fire with that Isabella."

Edward smiled, "Aye, Brother, she's fire a'right."

"And what is it ye have to say about yer friend Ross's sister?" asked Robert.

"Well," said Edward half bragging and half embarrassed, "She'd be the one I'd marry... if I had my say."

Robert threw his hands up and plopped himself down into a large chair facing toward the window. He sat, his legs tight to his body as if he were cold. He put his elbows on the chair arms and interlocked his fingers under his chin.

Edward, hoping to explain his position better, stood to his side. Frustration born of self-pity welled in him and he said, "I try, and I try, and I try, but I ne'er can please ye, Robbie."

There was a long reflective moment of silence before the king again spoke. "Do ye recollect two years ago, when that whelp of Longshanks sallied into Scotland with his grand army and all of the ships full of supplies and all the might he could muster?"

"I remember," said Edward, furrowing his brow not knowing where Robert was going with his story.

"Do ye recollect, they harried us on the east coast so bad we had to feign a raid on Man to get them to shift their interests to the west?"

"Aye."

"We skirted their army all o'er the southeast, but we ne'er let them trap us into a pitched battle!" said Robert trying to remain calm.

"Ne'er did," replied Edward.

"Do ye know why?"

"'Cause there were a lot more of them?" replied Edward.

"'Cause we can't win fightin' their kind of fight!" said the king looking up at Edward.

"Well, damn it, Robert!" growled Edward throwing up his hands in frustration, "did ye expect me to just sit there?"

"I did."

"Thomas Randolph would have..."

The king cut his say short, "Thomas would have minded my word 'til hellfires burned his feet from his legs, Edward!"

Edward hung his head.

Robert continued, "I have made ye Lord of Galloway, and I have bestowed on ye the earldom of our ancestral Carrick. I have given Randolph the earldom of Moray for he knows those high land folk and speaks their language. Ye have no reason for jealousy!"

Edward was mute. Anger welled in his heart, but his mind held it in check. For all his physical strength, he felt powerless. The anger melted as the thought of powerlessness overtook him. He became sullen, wanting only to escape his dark mood into his jug of spirits.

"Ye have given the English the perfect excuse to invade us with all the might they can muster," said Robert returning to his gaze out the window. The sounds of men razing the walls of stone were clearly audible.

"What do ye want me to do?" mumbled Edward emotionless.

"There is naught to do at this point," sighed Robert. "The English will be returnin'. Ye've invited them!"

"Not 'til year next! By then, I figured they'd have forgotten about it," said Edward, "... from what I hear they're close to civil war in their bailiwick."

"This truce ye have struck is the stuff that mends the troubles of warring cousins. They will come," replied Robert as he waved his hand in dismissal relieving Edward the pain of listening to additional abrading and him of listening to additional excuses.

Edward hesitated trying see if there was anything else he needed to say. It was another awkward silence. He heaved a long sigh and left the room with the notion of putting hand to his spirits, hoping he had enough to make the pain go away, at least for a little while.

As the large wooden door closed behind the errant brother, Robert stewed all the more. Everything seemed to be going so right, and now this "fly in the honey jar" stupidly brought on by his own brother. *How could it be?* he questioned.

He looked across the room to where Sir Robert Boyd sat observing. "Edward's a great warrior," said the king, "a battlefield is where he belongs. I ne'er should have put him to the task of layin' siege."

"Perhaps ye should send him to northern England where they hain't been payin' yer due all that regular," suggested Boyd.

"Good notion," said the king and suddenly changed the subject. "I want ye to go to Dundee with me. I want to see Christina."

"Ye ailin'?" asked Boyd knowing her servitude to the king's health.

"Hain't fully pert these days," he replied.

"Ye are king. Ye will prevail," came back Boyd in good humor.

Robert smiled. "Christina will know how to keep me prevailin'," he said.

"Ye want to leave in the morn?" asked Boyd, now on his feet standing over the emotionally spent figure.

"Aye," he answered, "in the morn... I need sleep now."

Robert Boyd placed a blanket over the chest of the drowsing king hoping another bout of illness like Slioch could be avoided. "I will make all preparations," said Boyd.

The sleeping king heard not a word.

Hetherington

July 17ᵗʰ 1313
The Tower, London

King Edward and Queen Isabella had been home from their trip to France for only a day. The trip itself was considered a great success. Edward's personal loan from the papacy had been accomplished through Isabella's uncle, Phillip the Fair, King of France, and by working together, the two kings had consolidated the bonds between the two countries more tightly than had they been in many years.

Phillip had also sent an envoy to act as mediator between Edward and the revolutionist members of the Lords Ordainers, led by Thomas of Lancaster, who were in virtual control of the government. The French king saw a dangerous precedent being set in the lords' mutiny, and it was thus something he wished to quash before French magnates decided it might be a good idea for their own country.

With those things having fallen in his favor, Edward's world was his oyster once again.

But then he got the bad news: the Scots had taken the Isle of Man and Rushen Castle.

"What happened?!" yawped the king as he came into the room and threw the fancy feathered hat he had acquired in France onto the highly polished table. Edward clutched at his chest as if pained at the news and said, "I gave that island to Piers."

"My King," said Hetherington, his arms full of scrolls as he followed

Edward into the room. He had come prepared to talk about the many subjects that had come to the fore in the king's absence. He put the scrolls on the table and said, "My King, Lord Gaveston has no further use for it."

The king's brows knitted into a scowl. "But he should yet be here and using it!" he said angrily.

Hetherington knew there was no answer for that and stood silent.

Edward sighed. "Was Macdouall slain?"

"No, Sire. Vexed of heart, he was sent to Ireland, I am told," replied the man obsequiously.

"Vexed of heart?!" asked Edward, "What does that mean?! That he was drunk... or crazed?"

"Both, one could imagine," returned Hetherington.

"Then pluck the damned Scot's name from our register, Hetherington," he said as if he were requesting a bruised apple be removed from the dinner table.

The two men worked in cloister for more than an hour before another message was brought to them. Hetherington unfolded the paper and read.

"*More* bad news?" asked the king with the accent on 'more'.

"Warden of Castle Stirlin' is within, Sire, and requests an audience, at your earliest moment," reported Hetherington. "He is here under a safe passage from Robert the Brus, and says it's critical that he see you."

Edward breathed deeply. "Those Scots ne'er give an end to their whinin'!"

"Then you will see him not, My King?"

"Of course I shall see him! Show the man in! Curiosity allows nothin' else, especially when it's 'critical'," said Edward.

Hetherington left to fetch Philip de Mowbray from the anteroom in which he had been temporarily placed.

Hetherington entered the anteroom with armed guards at his back and said, "The king will hear your report now, Sir Philip."

The group walked down the halls of the castle. Mowbray listened to their footfalls echoing off the walls. The surroundings were lavish but not as bizarre as he had imagined when being told stories. Perhaps the castle's lower dungeon levels were where all the tales were woven that told of human lives gone fatally sour. He hoped the decision he made at Stirling would not include such a final phase of his own destiny. He swallowed hard.

"Sir Philip de Mowbray, Sire," Hetherington introduced as the warden entered the large room and bowed deeply. He was willing to go to a knee if necessary to impress the king with his devotion.

"What have you for my ears, Castellan?" asked Edward, looking down at the back of the man.

"Your Majesty, I have made an agreement concernin' Castle Stirlin'," said Mowbray as he returned to his full height. The day was quite warm and his face glistened with perspiration that glued his hair to his forehead, though all may not have been caused by the heat.

Edward still looked down on him. "An agreement!?"

"The Brus forces had us under siege! We were ambuscaded at ev'ry venture outside the walls! We were fast runnin' out of victuals, My King!" he explained.

"It is your command! You are bound by your oath, Sir, to protect my property with your life!" said Edward, flaring his nostrils and flailing his arms to fully illustrate his meaning. "You, sir, are not dead! You don't even look hungry! So why do you foul my keep with your traitorous presence?!"

"My Lord King!" said Mowbray, retreating to the floor on one knee and sweating profusely.

Edward liked groveling. It kept him puffed beyond his actual size as a man.

"My Lord King," repeated Mowbray nervously, "I am alive and here to tell ye, by yer leave, that I have made a pact with Sir Edward Brus... that if, by midsummer next, Stirlin' Castle is nae relieved by an advancin' English army comin' within three leagues of the castle mount..." he almost held his breath for fear of saying it, "...I will turn the castle o'er to him or his brother!"

"And I will have you skewered on a stake!" said the king maliciously.

Mowbray chose his words carefully, seeing that the king did not understand the potential in his agreement. "I mean to say, Majesty, that it thus gives ye rightful cause to come full force into Scotland, and the Brus will be obliged to meet ye head on in battle or lose Stirlin'! He can nae refuse! Was that not yer interest when ye last sallied into Scotland?"

Edward paused and looked at Hetherington who raised his brows at the possible opportunities being presented to the crown by this warden.

Edward's temperament changed abruptly, and after a short contemplation during which he absently tapped his lips with one finger, he looked at Mowbray and smiled graciously. "My Good Sir Philip! I charge you to continue your wardenship and repair immediately to Stirlin', from where I expect you to send me constant messages of the comin's and goin's of the Scots in your neighborhood. Do you understand?" he said as if talking to a child.

"Aye, My Lord King," said Mowbray, going to the second knee and bowing his head to the floor as if a Muslim at prayer to Allah. Grateful, he was, that his was not a one-way journey to London as so many others had made. Hetherington signaled him to rise and leave, and he did, bowing deeply as he backed all the way out the door.

This could equal father's conquest of those Scottish whoresons, thought Edward elatedly.

"You must take this to parliament next month, Majesty," suggested Hetherington.

"Yes! I shall. *This* will vindicate me with those damned 'Ordainers'!" he shouted and laughed and clapped his hands with delight at the stupidity of Edward Brus, who knew not what he had given him. It was a challenge into which Edward of England could sink his teeth deeply... and fatally, straight to the heart of the Scottish rebellion.

July 18th 1313
Christina's Croft
Near Dundee

The time was hot and the rain fell intermittently in drizzles.

A woman living alone is in a dangerous position, and so Christina had invented a husband-protector, a warrior of great strength who was away at war much of the time. No one knew more than she told of him, but no one bothered her for fear that her illusive husband might seek revenge in the dark of night, if anything bad should happen to Christina or her children. He roughly looked like Robert in her descriptions.

Dundee had fallen to Robert in March over a year past, at a great expense to him and his treasury. But razing the castle had been a mighty boon to him since it closed off English supplies headed to Perth, and had made it easier to bring that town to its knees. With the English out of Dundee the region was more or less in the hands of the Scots and traveling in and out of that region became a much easier task.

Into the glen they rode. Robert Boyd, Andrew Stewart, and four knights were with their king. The men's weapons were the only evidence that they were more than they appeared on the surface by their clothing.

The farm lay quaintly on the hillside. The typical thatched roof and the smoke rising from the chimney on the large, one-story house were welcoming comforts. The dwelling was accompanied by a byre large enough for the many horses and few cattle she had raised. The mixture of bovine and equine livestock dotted the countryside within her post and rail fences.

Though he had seen Christina shortly before he invaded the Isle of Man, Robert's mind drifted to his last visit to her farm, more than two years before. It was winter then, and he remembered seeing drifts of snow contrasted by dark barren trees. Now the hills were green and fresh looking, and as he got closer he saw the children playing about a stack of hay in the field. Wooden swords clacked as the two jumped around and swung their arms.

Somehow he felt he was coming home.

Suddenly a rider came into view over the hillock. Upon seeing Robert's retinue of knights the rider stopped quickly. The horse reared and danced with excitement, and the rider slapped the reins against the horse's rump and at a gallop, came straight for them. Watching the lone rider approach, they soon recognized her.

"Christina?" asked Boyd.

"Looks to be," answered Robert, a soft smile coming to his lips as Christina came to the men.

"Robert, are ye sick?" she asked worriedly.

Robert laughed. "Ye think I come to see ye only when I'm ailin'?" She reflected concern and hastily looked him over before she answered.

"I ne'er know," she smiled. "Come ye, all of ye, to the house and rest!"

Robert nodded weary approval and she turned her swift stallion toward the byre.

"My God," said Boyd, impressed with her horsemanship, "she *can* sit a saddle."

A few hundred yards and the travelers drew rein in front of the stable. Once dismounted, Christina rushed to Robert and put her arms around him tightly. He was awkward in responding to her affection in front of his men, but she knew he was glad to see her.

"Ye like my newly fenced garden?" she asked proudly pointing to the vegetables growing within.

Robert looked around. "'Ppears ye've been addin' more outbuildin's to yer croft."

"Byre and stable," said she smiling.

"Saw the bairns a'playin' in the rain yonder," he said pointing down the hill. "Might catch a misery don't ye reckon?" he said.

"Then why are ye standin' out in it?" she replied tugging on his tattered surcoat to move him toward the door to the house.

Robert laughed and said casually, "Why do ye have Edward's horse in yer stable?"

"Borrowed it for a wee bit," she said and again smiled, for she was truly glad to see him.

One of Christina's highlanders came to the king, as he was about to enter the house. "Milord, we have good news about yer herd of horses."

"Good news?" he asked.

"We have near to three hundred either broke to saddle or bein' broke," he reported.

"I was fixin' to tell ye of the horses, Robert," said Christina, scowling at the highlander who impatiently bragged to the king instead of allowing Christina to tell him in her own time. The youth was sufficiently chastised by her glance and said no more.

"We have had much luck with the breed, Robert, and the herd has grown faster than we reckoned it would." Nodding toward the lad she said, "Ellic is a wonder with the horses. I couldn't have managed this herd without his help... even though he can't hold his tongue!"

When it began to rain harder the children came running in from the field to see the new arrivals. They were soaked through in their thin summer clothing.

"I remember ye," said Christian, almost out of breath.

"Do ye now?" said Robert bending over to be more on the child's level.

"Ye are Father King," she whispered, "but we are not allowed to say anythin' about ye to anyone we meet, else they might tell the English tailed dogs, and then they would come and take us far away!"

"Ye speakin' for sooth?" he whispered, knitting his brows.

"For sooth," answered Nigel coming to Robert.

The king looked long at his son. He had grown since his father last saw him, and had developed a perfect, if young, soldier's body. He was handsome and strong of arm. Robert was very proud.

"Come in and get dry by the cook fire," pleaded Christina.

"I would ask if I could be yer squire, Milord," blurted Nigel bluntly.

Robert stood and looked at the boy, and then at his mother. He had been taken aback by the question, but apparently Christina was not surprised. Without saying a word she turned and went into the cool darkness of the house.

Robert said, "Andrew here, is my squire, but ye can be my page, and when I make him a knight, then I shall consider yer request. I am proud that ye want to be my squire, Son." He ended with a wide smile, but Nigel's smile had faded. He wanted a promise that he would be a squire in the service of his king and father.

"We will speak of this later, Nigel," said Christina from the doorway. She hailed the lad to come change his wet clothes, but Nigel stood his ground and looked at Robert.

"Mind yer mother, Nigel, we'll speak of this later," said Robert.

"I have been practicin' with uncle Edward's great sword," said Nigel still refusing to budge from his spot.

"Edward's sword?" asked Robert, looking at Christina. Borrowing Edward's horse was one thing, his sword was another.

"Go!" demanded Christina to Nigel. "I will tell ye later," she whispered to Robert as Nigel finally went into the other room to change his clothes.

Andrew beamed at the prospect of being made a knight, but he dare not ask the king when. He did feel he had handled his own in the battle on the Isle of Man, however, he did not want the king to think he was overreaching himself.

Christina and her helper prepared a fine feast of chicken in sauce poured over hot bread in wooden trenchers. It was far from the multicourse feasts of the castle barons, but it tasted perfect to every hungry man in attendance. Christina announced it was a feast in honor of Robert's thirty-ninth birthday. It was a complete surprise to the king, he having forgotten about birthdays and the like.

Christian and Nigel were allowed to eat when the men were finished. There was certainly plenty to go around.

After the meal, Boyd and the four knights drifted toward the byre to make themselves pallets of the clean straw there. Robert encouraged Andrew to take Nigel under his wing and start the process of teaching him how to handle a sword and shield.

"Will he be yer squire's squire?" asked Andrew, grinning.

Robert smiled, "sort of."

"What shall I teach him first, My King," asked Andrew.

"That which I taught ye at the first," instructed the king.

Andrew thought back to the days when he first came to be the squire of Robert de Brus, Lord of Annandale and Earl of Carrick.

"Come Nigel," said Andrew, "this evening we sleep with the knights."

Nigel smiled. He was pleased. The honor meant that he had been accepted by his father, though he was just not sure how this would lead to his becoming his father's squire.

Christina was silent watching the transformation. She had not considered the prospects of Nigel being anything other than her young son. Her emotions were mixed and she needed to sort them out. On the one hand, she wanted her son to grow up and be manly, especially in the ways of protecting himself and the realm, while on the other, she feared losing her bairn to the world. As she turned away, Robert saw tears shining in her eyes.

• •

It was August. Robert rested, sleeping as late as he could bear and eating well of Christina's ample larder. Some days were better than others as far as his vitality was concerned, but Christina's constant care and daily feeding of herbs and honey mixtures kept him from his bouts of pure exhaustion.

He sent for Edward, Thomas Randolph, and James Douglas, and gave them each instructions on what he wanted him to do. He gave them every confidence that he was delegating more of the fighting to his younger lieutenants, who truly were the backbone of the rebellion.

He chastised his brother no further about the Stirling siege abandonment, but again warned that next June Twenty-fourth would be their day of reckoning. There was much that needed to be done before then, and the approaching winter could not stop their plans. The life of Scotland as a nation would hang by a thread.

Robert returned Edward's horse and sword with the warning not to lose them again, though he felt Christina had not told him the complete story.

Edward took them and thanked her, in all humility, for returning them to him.

AUGUST 23RD 1313
CHRISTINA'S CROFT

"Rider's a'comin'!" shouted Andrew to Nigel. The boy was mucking out the byre when he heard the call and promptly threw down his fork and ran to the door. Over the ridge came a clutch of armed men, some wearing mail, others in a variety of military paraphernalia and clothing. Nigel got the chary feeling that they were a danger, and his father had only yesterday sent the knights who had escorted him to the farm, to Dundee on an errand.

Andrew said, "Wait here, Nigel. Don't come out 'til ye are sure it's safe, Aye?" Nigel nodded, his eyes locked on the approaching horsemen.

Andrew trotted directly to the house and entered, not bothering to close the door behind him. "Riders a'comin', Sire," he repeated to the king, who lay resting on a pallet at the back of the room where it was dark. The king frowned at the light.

"How many?" he asked Andrew.

"Five or six," came the reply. "Look to be English from here, Sire."

"Leave yer sword inside and go see what they want," said Robert.

"But, Sire..." he started to protest, "if they be a threat..."

"Aye, but if ye are not armed, they may be less wary."

Andrew did as he was bade and stood outside by the front door, uneasily watching the men approach. Christina came to the front of the house from the kitchen garden and asked Andrew where Nigel was. Told that he waited in the byre, she stood beside Andrew as the riders drew near and reined their mounts before them.

"What ye men want?" asked Andrew, stepping closer to the riders so that Christina was behind him.

"Tax collectors!" declared the first rider, apparently the leader. "Ye owe tax money."

"To... ?" asked Christina.

"King Edward, o' course," said the leader, sniggering and glancing back of him at his amused cronies.

"Here we pay taxes only to King Robert," said Christina coming up beside Andrew, to his dismay. "Ye do know ye're in Scotland?" she added sarcastically.

"I know where we are, wench! I'll have no dealin's with ye! Where's yer man?" demanded the English soldier, gruffly.

"He'll be back directly, but until then, ye deal with me."

"He'll be back direc'ly," the leader mocked her. "King Edward wants his tax money now, whore!" He glanced about the farm buildings and seeing no one else, dismounted and came toward her, attempting to cow her with his size and apparent strength, but Christina gave not an inch. "The money, whore. Now!" he was almost against her.

"I'll pay naught to England, nor to any of Edward's dogs!" she replied.

The knight grabbed her with his great rough hands and held her tightly. She immediately began to struggle, and Andrew jumped forward to aid her just as Nigel screamed, "Mother!" and came running forth out of the byre toward Christina. Two of the horsemen maneuvered themselves between the boys and Christina, cutting them off before they could reach her.

"Let me go, ye English devil!" she shouted. Frustrated by the horseman's maneuvers to prevent his reaching his defenseless mother, Nigel ran back into the byre.

"We'll be havin' our tax money, ye harlot, one way or another!" he whispered in her ear. The words had hardly left his tongue before the door opened and Robert casually ducked under the lintel and stepped outside, his sword sheathed.

The man turned Christina loose immediately. She turned and slapped his startled face so hard that her hand stung mightily, and left a reddening handprint on his cheek. It angered him, but he held his temper as he rubbed his cheek with the back of his hand and watched Robert to see what he might do.

"What is it ye men want?" asked Robert in a quiet voice.

The 'collectors' were taken aback by his size and calm demeanor. "We come to collect the taxes owed to King Edward of England," said the man in as official a voice as he could muster. "Yer... woman said ye were not to home!"

"I'm here now," replied Robert. "How much ye reckon we owe?"

Caught off guard, the leader looked at the large sword hanging from Robert's belt, but he saw, too, that the others had no weapons. He mentally calculated the risk of five against one as he stammered, "Uh... 'bout... we can take your land for the crown... best pay as much as ye can." His eyes would not stop looking around from place to place, he was so nervous.

"In gold or steel?" asked Robert, his voice eerily emotionless.

The man paused. His eyes widened as he realized they had to fight this giant. He swiftly drew his sword.

Robert still held his place, watching how the Englishmen arrayed themselves, which the three of them started by dismounting and drawing their weapons. The fourth man held himself nearer the byre and grinned.

He was anxious for his companions to get on with their killing of the big man.

Christina moved quickly away from the spokesman and stood to the left side of Robert. Andrew, too, slipped behind Robert and thus closer to the door where he could retrieve his weapon, propped just inside against the wall. At the same moment the Stewart's hand touched the sword, young Nigel ran from the byre with his fork and stabbed it as hard as he could into the leg of the horseman who had blocked his way. The fork completely ran through the fleshy part of his upper leg. He howled in pain and grabbed his wounded thigh, which was spurting blood profusely. Nigel jerked the fork from his leg and attacked him again, ramming two of the fork's tines into the fellow's rib cage. He stopped his agonizing moans and fell off his mount.

Stunned, the others hesitated, but the leader ordered them to go at Robert. "Don't be killin' the woman!" he said, "She's mine!" And with a grin on his face he, too, started for the tall one with the sheathed sword.

Robert breathed deeply, and in one instant he stepped forward drawing his blade, and had the closest man dispatched before he'd had the notion to respond.

Andrew came to Robert's side with his sword handle in both hands, and deftly prevented one of the 'tax collectors' from attacking Robert's back.

Within no time, all five English were dying or dead on the ground and Nigel came running to his mother, the bloody fork in his hand. She hugged him tightly and kissed the top of his head, greatly relieved it was over and none but the miscreants had bled.

"Where is your sister?" she asked Nigel.

"Oh, aye! I put her in the straw and told her not to come out until ye or I came to get her!"

Andrew said, frowning, "'Tis good that one of ye listens when ye're told to stay where ye'll be safe!" Nigel grinned sheepishly, and ran to the byre.

As Andrew collected the weapons from the fallen, Robert looked through their kits. The first to die had only small coinage and jewelry in his bag. The rest had clothing and trinkets of little worth they had robbed from innocents.

"Probably English deserters," said Robert as he handed the kits to Christina, adding, "Dundee fell to us quite a while back. These men turned to lootin' and thievin', looks like. By their actions here, I would guess they were murderers as well."

The old man and the horses' groom came running in from the hayfield to the south. The older man carried his scythe, ready to do battle, and the younger, Ellic, had picked up a pruning pole with its sharp blade and hook, much like and precursor to a soldier's guisarme. The fight was over by the time they came panting into the garth.

Nigel ran to them and told of the short skirmish in as much detail as he could remember in his elated state, especially the part about his wanting to help his mother, though the only weapon he could find was the fork he had been using to spread straw on the byre floor. He then took them over to the dead knight he had killed. They were suitably impressed and he beamed.

"Where shall we bury them, Sire?" asked Andrew.

"On the hillside, yonder, among those trees," answered Christina pointing the way. "I'll have my men help ye dig the graves, Andrew," she said, and she left to tell the pair so.

"As Lady Christina has said," Robert instructed and walked back into the house to remove his sword belt and sit wearily on a bench. Nigel followed on his heels, still bubbling over with the event in the yard.

"Ye killed three of them, Father!" he said admiringly. The king shook his head sadly.

"I was but defendin' yer mother and ye children, Lad." He looked into the shining eyes of the child. "I was much pleased with the way ye behaved in defense of yer mother and yer home. Ye showed great bravery in attackin' the rogue."

"I want to be just like ye when I'm full grown!" He took an imaginary sword and mimicked his father's swordplay in the garth. Robert smiled.

"'Tis in the code of chivalry that the innocent must always be protected by a sworn knight," he said, "and sometimes that means ye must fight against those who would do harm, even to the death." Christina walked in at just the right moment to hear that bit of philosophy and her pleasant mien was replaced by one of worry.

"Aye, Sire! Like ye did those men in the garth!" The youth continued to practice with his imaginary weapon, making the sounds of swords clanging together, until suddenly, he stopped and came to the king, and rested his hand on Robert's shoulder familiarly.

"Father King, are ye goin' to be takin' me on as a squire?" he asked.

Robert looked up at Christina who was fraught with dread for her son's safety, but reluctantly nodded approval.

"Aye," said the father to his son, "we will see to yer proper trainin'."

"Trainin?!" Nigel quickly rebuffed, "Sire, I'm not fearful! I can ride horse as fast as the wind, and swing a sword... and today I killed a rogue, Father!"

Robert smiled again. "Ye must train to acquire a knight's discipline, My Son."

Nigel knitted his brows. "What say?"

"Discipline," he repeated. "Ye remember when Andrew left ye in the byre and said for ye to stay?"

"Aye," said the boy softly. "But how did ye know that?"

"I know many things. The point is, ye showed great courage and strength, but by leavin' the byre, ye showed a lack of discipline." The boy still wasn't understanding, so Robert added, "Ye did not obey yer orders from a superior."

"Aye," said Nigel softly.

"Tomorrow we travel," announced Robert, "Ye get Andrew to help ye pick yerself a horse, and a sword and a dagger from those left by the dead in the front yard."

"Aye, Sire." Nigel was more somber until he went out the door and closed it. Then he smiled and ran to find Andrew.

At last... an adventure, he thought.

Andrew Stewart

AUGUSC 27ch 1313
SCIRLING

The king's retinue of Sir Robert Boyd, Andrew Stewart, two young knights, and his newly acquired page, Nigel, made its way from the Dundee area more than forty miles to the region of Stirling. Robert was nearly exhausted but he felt he must see the possibilities of the landscape before winter set in. His on-again-off-again malady allowed him no room for false beginnings. They returned to the south side as they had left: in disguise and insignificant.

As the men and the boy were approaching Stirling castle along the mile of causeway across the surrounding low-lying carse, Robert asked Nigel, "See yonder bridge?"

"Aye, Father," replied the boy.

Robert paused. Time to start Nigel's training. "From now on, ye can refer to me as 'My King' or 'Milord' when in public... but nae as 'Father'."

"Why, Fath... My King?" Nigel looked directly at Robert over that curiosity.

"'Tis proper," said Robert. "That's what any page, squire, or knight calls me and ye shall, as well, before others. Save 'Father' for private times."

"Aye, My King," said Nigel with a smile, and returning to the original question, said, "I see the bridge, Sire. And on t'other side, a great castle atop that creagh," he said. "Looks like 'tis floatin' on a cloud!" Robert looked at Castle Stirling, its base surrounded by a heavy fog that did make it seem that the top of the whole rugged mount was floating effortlessly on the cloud.

"'Tis Stirlin' Castle, and the bridge is Stirlin' Bridge. Do ye know about Stirlin' Bridge and the great battle there?" The boy shook his head. "Just two years ere ye were born, Sir Andrew Murray and Sir William Wallace won over a great host of English, there." Robert continued telling the story of the great victory, answering the boy's questions and trying to get him to see that sometimes, even strength can be defeated by cleverness.

Finally, the first of the group came to the wooden bridge and started across.

Robert stopped his horse and turned in his saddle to see behind them. He signaled Nigel to do the same. "The Scots lurked on that mountain yonder, called Abbey Creagh," said Robert pointing his hand. "That's where The Wallace and The Murray waited with their band of well disciplined but otherwise ordinary men, and watched the English cross the bridge at this very spot. Ye remember our talk about discipline?"

The lad nodded and his lord continued.

"The English were yonder, at the foot of the castle, wantin' to bring an end to the Scots' independence, and so were anxious to get the deed done. But they made a mistake. Instead of takin' their army upstream a couple of miles and fordin' the river there, they ordered their men across this bridge and onto the causeway, just about where we're standin' right now."

Nigel's eyes widened to realize he was in the midst of a famous battlefield.

Robert continued, "The Scots held their positions up yonder on the creagh, and allowed about half the English army and its mostly armored and mounted knights to come across this bridge, and when they were told to advance, the Scots came off the creagh on foot with their long spears and screamin' and howlin' ran to meet the enemy."

"Only half?" asked Nigel curiously.

"The English had far more than twice the men the Scots had," explained Robert and turned his horse to come to the bridge. "So, that 'bout made the numbers even."

Nigel slowly followed Robert onto the wooden bridge as his father continued. "The English knights on this side of the bridge tried to get arrayed for the fight, but the Scots' pikes drove them back onto the others. When they tried to spread out to meet the runnin' Scots, they got onto the boggy carse that laid on both sides of the road. Their warhorses bein' so heavy, they couldn't move around, and that made 'em easy pickin's for the unmounted Scots and their long spears."

Robert stopped. He became enchanted by the vision of the battle taking place in his mind's eye.

"What then!?" asked Nigel wanting to hear more.

The king came out of his reverie and continued. "When the fightin' started, the English knights comin' north across the bridge tried to get more horses across faster, and crowded the bridge so that nobody could move much. The Scots went into the water, and clomb the legs of the bridge and over the sides to get at those trapped on it," he said.

Nigel looked down. Beyond the edge of the sides he could see the deep, swift-flowing water of the River Forth below, and he was fascinated. The look on his face urged Robert to tell the rest.

"Comin' up from both sides of the bridge, the Scots gutted the horses and the riders were thrown off into the river, or the blades of the Scots got 'em. While all that was happenin', the bridge couldn't stand neath the weight and the whole middle collapsed. "The English on the south side," he pointed ahead, "couldn't get across to help those who were fightin' the Scots and their long spears, and about five thousand were killed back yonder. The English south of the bridge turned and ran, not knowin' other Scots troops were waitin' near the Torwood. When the English tried to run and get back across the border, the men in Torwood jumped 'em Weren't many who escaped the Scots."

"Were ye with The Wallace and The Murray?" asked Nigel.

"It was a great victory for the Scots, " he replied, "'Twas a terrible end for many a warrior on both sides, includin' Sir Andrew Murray. He died later from wounds he got here. War is a terrible thing… but bein' slaves is a heap worse."

"But were *ye* here?" Nigel pressed for an answer.

"Nae," replied the king wistfully, "I wasn't. Wish I had been... but I wasn't."

"So why are we still fightin, My King?" asked the boy.

"'Cause the English want to take away our freedom, Son," he explained. For almost as long as I can remember, the English have marched across our border and tried to conquer us. First it was old King Edward, and now it's his son. They want Scotland to belong to them."

"Did ye know old King Edward, Fa… Sire?"

"Aye, I knew him. In his day he was a magnificent soldier, and a great commander. We would have had a much worse fight on our hands if he had been a younger man, and in his prime."

"Have we always hated the English?" asked Nigel.

"Nae, bad blood comes and goes," said the king.

Nigel thought on that as the entourage finished crossing the long-ago repaired bridge and drew closer to the castle in the sky.

The travelers went north of the castle through the fog cloud and around the back of King's Park, where Scotland's King Alexander III hunted wild game. They arrived back at the Roman road as the fog slowly lifted. Below them lay a beautiful, peaceful landscape filled with the water-laden carse, the serpentine River Forth fed by numerous meandering burns, and fertile grainfields. The rocky creaghs several miles away served well as background for their idyllic scenic vista.

They then went down the long slope where the fields of corn were about ripe for the scythe, then across the carse and the Bannock Burn.

Soon the travelers came to Torwood, where the old road sliced through the middle. At the southern end, Robert halted and looked over the lowlands to the south and east.

"Reckon yonder's the three leagues Mowbray measured when he made that truce with Edward," he said, clenching his teeth in annoyance.

"Knew how to get us all killed for sure," replied Robert Boyd, sitting his horse beside Robert.

"Aye," remarked the king craning his neck around, "Five more miles and we'd be in Falkirk."

"Falkirk we don't want," said Boyd.

"Falkirk we hain't havin'," gainsaid the king. "No wonder Mowbray can still scratch his nose when it itches."

Boyd grinned. "His nose, aye?"

"Aye. His nose could have been miles from his hand by now, if Edward had taken a notion," Robert smiled and wheeled his mount about, to head north again. His entourage followed.

"What about Abbey Creagh?" asked Boyd.

"They'll not be fallin' for that trick again," replied Robert thinking beyond the question. "Has to be somethin' 'twixt here and Stirlin'."

"Hain't much in the way of solid ground and woods betwixt, Robbie," said Boyd, "And it'll be within the three leagues of the truce terms."

"This battle will not be about Castle Stirlin'," said the king solemnly, "'Twill be the battle for Scotland. What ye see below us is where Scotland lives or dies."

The travelers stayed in the vicinity for two days looking at the grounds. The villeins within sight of the castle were curious, but none of them asked questions of the men for they wore swords and rode great destriers. In the vicinity's several small hamlets, however, they talked quite a bit amongst themselves about the suspicious strangers.

William Bunnock

SEPTEMBER 13th 1313
Linlithgow

Lothian, being such a large area in Scotland's southeast and bordering on the southern coast of the Firth of Forth, became an extremely important area of interest to King Robert. Edinburgh and Linlithgow would serve well as important support centers for an English army coming north to relieve Castle Stirling.

The citizens of Lothian were torn between their support for Edward of England and that for Robert of Scotland. The more successes the Scots had, the more the inhabitants of Lothian were enticed to migrate their loyalties in Robert's favor.

However, the problem was knotty, to say the least, for the English still held castles, and thus had troops there to enforce their demands that Lothian pay taxes to Edward. Robert's men required that the gentry pay taxes to Robert or risk being burned out of their houses and chased off their English granted lands. The wealthiest landowners had holdings in Scotland as well as in England, and wanted not to give any lands back to the crown of *either* side.

Among the harried residents of the region was one William Bunnock, a farmer of extraordinary size and strength. With nothing to lose but his very life and much to gain, perhaps even a piece of land, he hatched a plot to fulfill his notion of his own freedom.

Only once had William seen King Robert, as he rode through the area some three years earlier. Though the king never stopped or said a word to any person, William was impressed with the belief that the king would prevail against England. It was upon this faith and the desire to be a part of Scotland's struggle to regain her liberty that he proceeded with his plan.

In the middle of the few dark morning hours of August, Bunnock, as he had done a thousand times, yoked his oxen in the byre and led them to the front of the large wain of hay he had spent the previous hour loading. His friend and conspirator, a neighbor by the name of Hearn, worked on the opposite side of the wain making sure everything was correctly hitched.

"When will the others be a'comin'?" asked Hearn.

"They'll be along directly," said William not looking up from his purpose.

"Reckon this'll work?" asked Hearn.

"Reckon," said William, smacking the ox closest to him affectionately on the rump.

"Well, I hain't scared," offered Hearn.

William smiled knowing they both were scared. "Got yerself a sword and a dagger?" he asked his friend.

Hearn pulled out a well honed, but slightly skewed sword with one hand and a rather rusty dagger in the other. "Got both, just as I said I would!" he nervously growled trying to grow steel in his backbone. "This'n I had buried neath the manger in my byre." He held up the dagger.

"Wee bit rusted, I'd say," said William.

Hearn looked at the blade. "Course, it was buried a long time, as I said. Still cut a'right," he replied, but he looked worried, and Bunnock tried to allay his fears.

"I already sent a message to the tower," he said. "I've taken hay to Linlithgow Tower more times than I can count... don't worry so! They hain't a'gonn'a turn us out!"

"Hain't, aye?" said Hearn still unnerved.

"Ye just drive and cut the traces when I holler," he instructed.

"A'right, Will," said the small-framed farmer.

They suddenly heard footsteps coming purposefully toward the byre.

"Reckon it's the English?!" whispered Hearn ducking behind the ox's rump.

"Reckon not," said William in a rather disgusted voice. He was beginning to think he had picked the wrong man to help drive the team.

Twelve men from the surrounding crofts came into the byre.

"Where be the others?" asked William, looking at the sparse crowd.

"All that's a'comin'," said one. Bunnock was disappointed, but didn't let on to the others.

"Each one's just a'gonn'a have to do more," he said sternly.

"First six lads will stay in the wain all the way through the gate and portcullis. The rest of ye, hide outside until ye hear a signal," instructed William.

"They all have swords?" asked Hearn, beginning to sweat even in the night air.

"Aye, they all have 'em," spat William, irritated at Hearn's continued trepidation.

"Just askin'," returned the man, timidly.

"Everybody know the plan?" asked William so that each man could hear.

'Ayes' were heard around the group and some of the men got onto the back of the wain of hay in which they would ride to the attack.

Hearn asked hopefully, "Reckon King Robert himself will be a'thankin' us?"

"First we have to do somethin' to be thanked for! Now, drive these beasts as ye're supposed to! I'll walk beside the off-ox," said William. He slid his sword under the hay at the front of the wain, and made sure it was covered. Hearn took a long stick called a goad, as big around as his thumb but not as long as he was tall, and whistling and tapping the lead ox with his goad, started the cattle trudging toward their destination.

The team strained at first, until the large flat hay cart, with naught to hold the hay in place except several stout poles placed along each side, started rolling apace down the path toward Linlithgow. These same oxen had hauled many a load of hay along the well-worn trace, but there were also men to be hauled, this time.

Nearing sunup the group rolled close to the peel tower. Six of the men slipped away from the moving wain and walked through the edge of the dark wood to the rushes that ringed the peel's moat on three sides, and worked their ways as close to the drawbridge as they could. There they lay quiet and still and hopefully unnoticed until called, when they could easily join their fellow conspirators inside the wall.

Those who would ride through the gate wriggled themselves under the hay so not to be seen, and the slow-moving wain rumbled noisily across the drawbridge.

"William Bunnock, a'comin' with a load of hay!" he shouted as usual to the porter of the curtain wall gate.

The man looked out of his "spy-hole" and saw the customary wain on the bridge as expected.

"Raise the portcullis," shouted the porter, receiving no answer.

Out on the drawbridge the oxcart stood, the animals patiently waiting, but the time passed very slowly for the farmers. This was the critical moment. Without the portcullis being lifted, and without the heavy doors being opened, they were defeated before they could draw a blade.

Suddenly there came a loud clunk as the brake was released, and a slow rumble as the mechanism's massive chain wound around the barrel of the windlass inside the gatehouse, and the heavy, iron-bound latticework gate rose, powered by two large, not-so-sweet-tempered English guardsmen. They cursed all the while for having to raise the barrier for "the wain that could have waited to come when other folks came, during the full light of the day."

The portcullis was up and the gate doors were opened. Hearn smacked the lead ox on its broad rump and the yoked pair moved up the grade toward the inner bailey. Just as planned, Hearn drove the team off to the right and struck the wain's wheel against the track, stopping the wain exactly under the hanging portcullis. Bunnock was surprised, but pleased at the current unfolding of the attack.

"What's your hold?" questioned the porter, coming from his small office in the gatehouse with his brows knitted into a frown. *The first cart through the gate, and it gets stopped in the opening. It portends to be a bad day,* thought the porter.

"The wain's struck yer gate track is all," William explained, pretending to examine the problem.

The porter moved to see for himself.

William hesitated to spring the trap as the porter moved around the hay cart and looked at it from several angles. "'T'aint stuck, just... move yer animals back and it'll come free!" He barked irascibly, but he noticed the hay move and calmly took out his dagger. "Stop! Yer hay's full of vermin!" he said and began poking it with his blade. "Ye'll have to back out of here, we don't need no more rats in here!"

"In a pig's eye," said William stepping to the man.

"What say?" he asked, turning his blade to William.

No answer to his question was forthcoming, for William pulled his sword from it's hiding place in the hay and gutted him.

Well, he thought, watching the man's blood running downhill between the cobblestones, *Naught else to be done but finish it! 'Tis murder on my soul, now!*

The oxen, smelling the foul odor of the awful death, bellowed in fear and again strained to move the wain forward with the effect of jamming it harder into the track. The team had succeeded in wedging it in securely, but continuing to pull, they threatened to tear the wain itself apart.

"Cut the traces!" Bunnock ordered Hearn.

"I'm a'tryin'!" The little man replied, rapidly sawing on the leather straps with his dull dagger.

"Rusty blade, is it?" barked William, angrily.

"It's a'cuttin'! It's a'cuttin'!" yelped Hearn in panic.

William rousted the men under the hay to scatter across the bailey and do as much killing as possible. Swords drawn, they were ready for the action that fell upon them swiftly as the two men manning the portcullis gears came around the corner to see why the porter was wasting so much of their sleeping time.

"On them!" shouted William, but the pair saw the men coming and jumped back into the guardhouse, locking the door, and within a few beats of William's pounding heart, released the brake on the heavy portcullis. It fell like a clap of thunder, just missing Hearn. One of the tough oaken wheels collapsed and the wain creaked as it buckled under the heavy blow.

"Call all! Call all!" screamed William, and the remaining six men ran to the gate tunnel to find the wain and its load of hay held the portcullis about two and a half feet from the ground.

"Crawl under!" William hollered and the men got on all fours or bellies, and rolled or crawled through the gap.

William wedged a piece of the broken wheel against the guardhouse door so the English inside could not escape, but they didn't try. Instead they manned the murder holes, shooting arrows down on the incoming crofters.

The last one under the portcullis was a young farmer, and he was hit in the back while crawling through. When he screamed with the pain, Hearn grabbed the youth by his armpits and dragged him into the bailey. Two arrows barely missed the ox drover, but his efforts were in vain. Another flight from the murder holes struck the wounded man, drilling his heart and rupturing it. He never knew he had not been saved.

Hearn laid down the lifeless farmer and shook his head, having tried but failed, to save the boy's life. *What am I a'goin to be tellin' the poor lad's mother?* he wondered numbly. The shouts and screams around him faded to a mild hum as he felt anger building in his heart and mind. He suddenly heard a scream come out of his belly and into the air as the roar of a wild beast, and he rose with a new sense of determination and invincibility.

With his rusty dagger in one hand and his crooked sword in the other, he had found the backbone he was afraid he never had.

The two English guards had begun yelling at the tops of their lungs, trying to get the attention of the garrison in the peel tower, but it was no use. They tried to get out the door, but William had wedged it tightly with the piece of oak from the wain.

William quickly led his band into the large hall wherein the warriors were at the morning meal. The twelve poured through the open portal with great speed, and without hesitation hacked and stabbed their way into the room, with every stroke maiming or taking life from the unsuspecting soldiers sitting at the tables eating their pottage and drinking their ale.

Chaos enveloped the hall as men and women scattered in every direction, wailing, bawling, keening. Some few of the men drew their swords and knives and began to fight back. Others ran in shock, not knowing what was happening.

The lightening strike had surprised the garrison completely.

One of William's men was stabbed in the throat, but he kept on fighting until he fell to the flagstone floor, dead. The abandoned bowls of pottage were covered with splattered blood.

Cups overturned and the tables ran awash with ale that intermingled with the blood of those who had been drinking. All was then dashed overboard in the melee as the trestle tables were thrown aside.

The fighting was thickest on the entrance end of the long hall, but the men on the far side could not join the fracas. They stood on the tables and benches cursing the invaders until one man recognized William and shouted, "It's the hay man! It's the hay man!"

Scots in the contingent, themselves neighbors and relatives of the attackers, separated from the English and backed against the wall.

"I hain't fightin' kin!" exclaimed one. The other Scots agreed in near unison and joined with the attackers in killing their erstwhile garrison mates until those left alive, wounded or on their feet, yielded their weapons and surrendered.

It wasn't long before the remaining escapees and other inhabitants of the peel were rooted out of their hiding places and gathered in the bailey.

The women were immediately thrown out to go where they would, leaving the warden of the castle, the captain of the guard, and the surviving English soldiers at bay.

"What ye reckon we do now?" asked Hearn urgently, "Kill them?"

William noticed his friend's new demeanor and smiled satisfaction.

"I have no use for the bastards!" interjected one of the turned Scots, fearful that if they were left alive, they would bear witness against him and the others.

The two gatehouse guards, sure that the quiet meant that the English soldiery had repelled the invaders, began to pound hard on the jammed door.

Seven large men went to see to their release. The Scots of the tower house hated the English who had held sway over them, thus the two were dragged to the group and thrown among them.

By then the sun was up and starting its climb. The colorless sky turned from light gray to a soft blue. Still the debate continued, until one of the Scots from the garrison shouted. "They deserve to be burned to a crisp!"

Puzzled, Hearn said, "But, Lad, ye were just at breakfast with them... as comrades in arms!"

"No English whoreson is my comrade!" replied the man, daring Hearn to challenge him further, which he wisely chose not to do.

William stood between the two men as the Scots were all shouting for blood and revenge. "We mustn't let our victory turn into a massacre!" he shouted to deaf ears.

"A'ready a massacre," yelled another garrison Scot, his face red with anger and the lust for more blood. "*Ye* saw to that when ye came upon us!"

William was overcome and put out of the peel by the enraged men. Wanting revenge, the mob then fell upon the English survivors and killed them, every one.

The whole raid was suddenly diminished for William, who stood back helplessly and watched otherwise good men taking horrible revenge on those who had abused and treated them with such evil. Two of the men he had brought with him raised the portcullis to its height and locked it in place.

Hearn found a dagger in the hand of one of the dead in the bailey and took it for his own. He thought to throw his old rusty one onto the dead body, but then decided differently. *Now I have two daggers,* he thought.

The peel tower was stripped of anything of value, or of anything anyone wanted, including weapons, clothing, food, and livestock. The spoils were divided among the living and the tower set ablaze.

Using his yoke of oxen, William pulled the broken wain out of the passageway and started the long walk home with his beasts, home to the byre, where the adventure had begun only a few hours earlier. The sun gave way to fast moving clouds. The rains were coming.

Many of the Scots of the garrison, having taken up arms against their English overlords, melted into the landscape, back to their homes for fear of reprisals. Others vowed to seek out the Brus and join his army, to exact more revenge on the English.

Word was sent to King Robert of the ordinary citizens who so wanted their freedom, and taking up their courage and their weapons, conquered the Linlithgow Peel in his name. They took it from the hands of the most powerful army in the known world. The King of Scots gratefully accepted the gift and presented gifts of his own to the leaders. He also sent his masons to bring the charred stones of the tower to the ground.

King Edward, hearing of the fall of Linlithgow Peel, passed it off as an easy target taken by a few traitorous farmers who had attacked in the manner of wolves, not men, not worthy of any chivalrous consideration.

Robert Keith
Mareschal of Scotland

sepτemBeR 27τh 1313
manor house, dundee

In the wake of the taking of the castle in Linlithgow by William Bunnock, the whole of Lothian was stirred to action. The English were of necessity more on their guard within the strongholds they held there. Their suspicion of everyone with whom they came in contact kept them uneasy.

King Robert constantly sent tax collecting parties into the countryside to trade "truces" for goods, and those landowners who did not pay Robert's men in hard currency, grain, cattle, or other goods useful to the army, would be subject to being killed or burned out. The citizens around the English held castles also had Edward's tax collectors circulating among them. Many of the Scots in Lothian were willing to go along with Robert as king. On the other hand, they asked themselves, how well could the King of Scots protect them from depredations of whatever sort committed upon them by the English garrisons in their midst.

The garrisons needed to keep their own interests surviving in progressively more hostile Scotland while getting little to no help from King Edward, who remained embroiled in his own domestic troubles.

The decision to remove one's fealty from the most powerful liege in the isles and place it with the Brus was a difficult and dangerous one, even if Edward were weakened by his own foibles.

Lothian was the last large hotbed of insurrection against the crown in Scotland, though not the last hold-outs to bend their knees to Robert. There were others, but they were scattered across the width and breadth of the kingdom. They wanted not to lose their lands and titles that the English crown and bygone Scottish kings had bestowed upon them. One such group traveled north on the road to Dundee, where King Robert awaited their arrival.

Sir Robert Keith, oldest and most renowned of the group, led the procession. His neighbors knew him as a worthy warrior, and King Edward had high regard for his military skills. This trip would certainly end 'His Majesty's' esteem and consideration for Keith and his companions.

Following Sir Robert were his good friend Sir William de Vieuxpont of Langton in Berwickshire, and Sir Edmund Ramsay of Dalhousie, Sir Peter of Pinkie, Sir Aymer of Hadden and Sir Godfrey Broun of Colston. A retinue of thirty-two lesser knights, made up from the various districts in Lothian and Berwickshire from which they hailed, accompanied the six noblemen.

The men were dressed in light armor including chain mail covering their upper bodies, unadorned saffron yellow tabards, and surcoats, swords, and battleaxes. However, none carried a pennant. This was not a mission the men wished to have well observed, or at least it was a journey on which local spies would have to be diligent to identify the group's members.

"Dunbar hain't goin' to like this atall," said William de Vieuxpont riding beside Robert de Keith.

"He's had a'plenty of chances to come to the Brus' peace," said Keith. "There's no reason he needs to be mollycoddled by the likes of us."

"Just meant he'll be riled up when he finds out," replied William, wrinkling his nose in partial jest at his friend.

"Ye wantin' to see the 'Army of Brus' tramplin' o'er yer land and killin' yer kinsmen and villeins, takin' yer livestock and firin' yer house and fields?"

"Nae," replied William, "Nor do I want the English to do as such, and they just might when they hear what were about."

Robert sighed thoughtfully, "Tied at the tails of two horses, we are for a fact."

"Seems to be the habit of Scots," gainsaid William.

"Yonder's Dundee, Sire!" interrupted the van-knight.

The two friends smiled to each other like children, not knowing which power was likely to gobble them up first, and hoping they were making the right choice. They would have to live with the consequences of their decision to the very hours of their deaths, which they hoped were yet far off.

• •

Robert stood on the quay in Dundee talking to the captain of the large trading galley tied up alongside.

"See that this gets into the right hands, Captain," demanded Robert as he handed the man a fur covered pouch.

"Aye, Milord," he replied, bowing unnecessarily low.

"Bring me an answer to the letter and I shall see ye to a reward," bribed Robert.

"Aye, Milord," he again said, shedding another bow in Robert's favor.

"If ye fail to get that letter into the hands of King Phillip," Robert warned, "Ye'll be banned from these docks fore'er. Ye ken?"

"Aye, Milord," returned the obsequious man, "Into the very hands of the king himself, Milord, I will lay the pouch."

Phillip the Fair had written a letter to Robert offering a truce, primarily because he wanted to open regular trade between France and Scotland. Scotland had, in addition to other desirable commodities such as lumber, the finest wool in the world, which they were already trading to many of the other European countries. As long as the Brus had no trade agreement with Phillip, France was forced to buy its Scottish goods from other countries at a much higher price.

His secondary purpose, however, was to inform Robert on behalf of King Edward, that the monarch expected the Scots leader to lay down his arms and walk away, thus ceding suzerainty of Scotland to England. This made no sense at all to Robert. Why bother to negotiate for a trade agreement with the same man whom, in the same communiqué, you are exhorting to surrender?

It was all politics and games. Pointless exercises. Sitting at court puzzling how to best the other monarchs in their realm of influence. Building up the one to topple another. Edward himself had offered terms for a truce to Robert several times, but each one was rejected out of hand because the principal requisite for any negotiation with Robert was that he be unconditionally recognized as 'King of Scots'. So far, that condition had not been met.

Robert gave the ship's captain a coin in payment, knowing full well that the man would have to find a local official at his French port of call and deliver the letter to him, then have faith that it would somehow find its way to the hand of King Phillip. It was a gamble, but Robert did not have time to set up a system of envoys. Besides, Robert had no idea what trickery Phillip might have afoot. He was, after all, the father of the English queen, and she was, for the time being at least, in good stead with her husband.

The meeting with the courier was interrupted by Sir Robert Boyd with news the king was expecting, "My King, the Lothians have come." At that, the two men started back up the shallow hill toward the manor house in which they were staying.

The captain, at last realizing he had been talking directly to the King of Scots, went a bit faint and squeezed the pouch tightly to his chest. He was honored by Robert's presence.

His second mate came to him, "Ye know that was the king of all Scotland?"

"Aye," lied the captain, twisting his mouth to a wry smile, "I knew him long since." He then turned to his crewman and said, "Well, hie and make ready to set sail! We have an important task to accomplish for him!"

• •

King Robert greeted the nobles from Lothian with respect even though they had been fighting on the side of England for some years. Together they formed a loosely tied nucleus of the Lothian people, but certainly did not represent all. These were the very kinds of Scots Robert wanted to come to his peace.

He desperately needed to drive the English from their strongholds before Edward's massive army came north, for they would be seeking succor and support wherever Robert failed to prevent its being offered. He was determined to have as many English castles rendered useless to them as he and his lieutenants could manage by spring next.

Alongside Robert was Gilbert de la Haye, the King's constable. Haye fulfilled his duties as best he could, although the title was mostly hollow. There were many other fires in the realm that needed tending that were not in the strictest sense within his purview. The king was constantly sending him hither and yon to accomplish sundry deeds on his behalf.

The men from Lothian came to King Robert and bent their knee to his will, swearing fealty to him and to Scotland, thus accepting him as their king and liege. Then the entourage of knights, one by one, swore their fealty. After the ceremony, as brief and simple as it was, the men were served a supper of plain, but hearty fare. As they gathered at the trestle tables they began a din of small talk regarding the ways of the realm.

"The name of William Bunnock is on ev'ry waggin' tongue, Milord," said Edmund Ramsey to Sir Gilbert.

"Ye fearful of a commoner?" asked Gilbert, one brow arched as he awaited an answer to a question he should not have asked in polite company. Such was possibly meant to suggest that the man lacked courage, and conceivably could have sparked a heated argument, if not actual swordplay.

Everyone within earshot stopped his chatter.

Sir Edmund, known for his sagacity, paused... certainly not wanting to offend his host after just breaking his fealty with Edward and accepting the Brus. "We all fear the common folk, do we not?" he answered with great politic. "They are the many that hold us few together."

Haye smiled, "Rightly so, Milord."

"And William Bunnock performed a brave deed, for sure," added Ramsey, suddenly finding his wit warping to the opposite side of situations once thought evil, but now suddenly praised by him as proper and good.

"Rightly so, again," said Haye.

There was some nervous laughter all around and the diners continued their meal.

Afterward, the nobles gathered in a small anteroom where every man was elbow to elbow with his neighbor. Robert confided that a great battle was sure to be fought mid-summer next, and he outlined the responsibility he was expecting each man there to accept. They all, to a man, agreed.

Robert then appointed Sir Robert de Keith to be King's Mareschal, subordinate to Sir Gilbert de la Haye, who had been with him since the beginning.

The house in Dundee was large, and next morning from the eastern windows, the newly appointed mareschal could see the sun rising over the great heap of stone and rubble that had been the English-held castle there, before being razed by the king's masons. *This*, he thought, *was an appropriate setting for the occasion of our meeting and giving allegiance to the king.*

When he was properly attired he came from the bedroom as quietly as he could and asked a servant when King Robert might awaken. She answered that the king had been up and gone for hours.

*Humphrey de Bohun
Earl of Hereford*

OCTOBER 13th 1313
WESTMINSTER ABBEY, LONDON

Louis, Count of Evreux, brother to King Phillip of France, was entrusted with the negotiations between King Edward and the noble murderers of Piers Gaveston. At the behest of King Phillip, Louis had made many trips among the various parties, detailing each boastful demand and each painful conciliation, and at last had reached a settlement suitable to all, provided all sides remained in the rarified atmosphere of rational behavior.

October in London had a definite chill in the breezy air that whipped the two Earls as they led their procession of witnesses toward the doors of the abbey.

"Why must it be at the abbey?" complained Hereford, tightening his surcoat holding the cold air out.

"It is a confession on our part, is it not?" said Earl Thomas, almost humorously. "Edward wants not only him to hear our little say, but he wants witnesses, and the abbot, and God Himself to hear what depraved, evil villains we were to have executed Cornwall."

"Reckon our sins will be thus washed clean?" asked Hereford with a sigh of resignation.

"Feared of goin' to the burnin' fires of hell with your soul in hand, Sir Humphrey?" quipped Thomas.

Hereford's eyes widened, his brows knitted. He stopped the procession of witnesses the two men were leading and said, "My Lord Thomas...

have you no fear of sportin' me in that manner whilst you are standin' at the very door of God's house?"

Thomas laughed at his partner in conspiracy, "If this trick with Edward doesn't work for us, you'll see a rope around your neck and the flesh hewers at your limbs well before you see the hell fires!"

"Might be worth it, if for no other reason than to see the hewers at your hulk first!" growled Humphrey.

"Remind Our Dear Lord King that you are married to his sister," again teased Thomas, "perhaps he'll go light on twistin' you to death."

"And you are cousin to himself!" spat back Humphrey. "Such has little practical use in these matters!"

Thomas snickered at how Humphrey was riled.

The men continued their walk.

Humphrey de Bohun breathed the air in deeply, as if trying to cleanse himself of the heretical and hateful sayings of his peer. He tremendously feared Edward's wrath despite being close kin, and had had many nightmares since the four earls murdered the despicable Piers Gaveston on Blacklow Hill. He feared God's wrath far more than any living person and knew that getting out of his skin and into the arms of Heaven could be an ordeal in itself. That fear shook him to his core, yet he wanted not to heap misery on top of misery when his soul came face to face with his God... or with the Devil. Sir Humphrey was the only one of the four who was sincerely ready to confess his part in the incident and receive forgiveness. His soul ached for it.

The doors were opened wide by two pages as the procession approached. The two earls were ushered into an anteroom near where the king was to enter, while the witnesses on the part of the earls filed into the main part of the building and assumed their pre-assigned places.

Guy de Beauchamp, the Earl of Warwick, was already standing on the far side of the small room awaiting the others' arrival.

He bowed slightly to show a measure of politeness to his fellow earls. They returned the gesture and the door closed behind them, leaving the three alone.

"Anyone heard news of Arundel?" asked Hereford quietly.

"Never took the bait like the three of us pitiably doomed fish, I reckon," said Lancaster brashly.

Hereford was silent but glared at Thomas.

Earl Guy saw the abrasion and asked, "You two at odds, are you?"

"Not I," said Lancaster, "Sir Humphrey has a bone in his arse because I shed no tears for 'poor Gaveston'!"

"He is a heretic!" barked Humphrey, boldly taking a stand in front of the larger man.

Thomas crossed his arms in front and ran his finger nervously up and down on the hilt of the dagger he carried high on his chest. Humphrey made no move to back down.

"My Lords!" begged Earl Guy, "We must save our quarrels for better purposes!"

Thomas retained his scowl.

Humphrey retained his stance.

There was a long moment of silent bravado.

Suddenly, Thomas laughed, "Guy is right, why do we fight amongst ourselves?"

Humphrey relaxed his stance and turned to the small dark faced Warwick. "You had best be shed of him!" he warned, realizing Thomas would be one who would drag those around him down with him, when once he began his inevitable fall from his high horse.

Then Humphrey was silent again. He began looking around the room thinking of what the men in the main room had been talking about, and suddenly got the idea that spies were watching them and would be ready to bear witness against them. King Edward had tricked them into confession without proffering else to the agreement than his forgiveness. They would be hanged without benefit of even having their say, as they had allowed Gaveston. He began walking around the room and lifting the tapestries to see the integrity of the walls. He found no spy holes.

"Don't reckon there's a listenin' ear, do you?" whispered Lord Hereford.

"You're goin' daft," My Lord," said Thomas.

Humphrey again stood staunchly glowering.

"We've all been driven daft by this... this, Gaveston muddle," inserted Earl Guy.

"Speak for yourself, Sir Guy!" replied Thomas with a growl as he sat on a bench along one wall. "We are daft, I reckon, but for lettin' little Edward put us through this farcical exhibition!"

"Or driven daft by the ghost of Gaveston, speakin' evils in our ears and comin' before us in vision form," said Humphrey wringing his hands mournfully.

"I believe that not!" scolded Thomas. "Ye had best have a care with such drivel, else ye're fixin' to be named a heretic for talkin' to dead folk!"

"I never said I spoke to any dead folk!" shot back Humphrey.

"I hear that Edward's plannin' a great campaign into Scotland summer next," said Sir Guy, trying to change the dialogue that had taken a definite bent toward the morose.

"Scotland! Again!?" said Thomas jumping from his bench.

"Certainly," said Humphrey rejoining the conversation of the living. "I heard the same rumor."

"He will be chasin' his own tail all over Scotland, just like the last time, or so I heard," grumped Thomas.

"We had best stick to our confessions," advised Hereford. I hear them comin' down the hall to get us."

Not a half-minute passed and the door swung open. The three earls, dressed in their finest, most formal clothing, filed out ready to give the confessions of and for their lives. None of them liked the terms, all despised having to 'confess' and grovel before Edward, but in exchange for their say they were to be forgiven by the king for their transgressions in the killing of Piers Gaveston.

Each of the three had his own reasons for accepting the truce offered. Only one was sincere in his words.

Nevertheless, there followed the ceremony a grand banquet in honor of the reconciliation, and on the surface everything seemed like the frosting on a cake... all very smooth and sweet. No one gave a thought to the notion that the cake might soon be broken into crumbs.

Within the week, Thomas of Lancaster had reciprocated and invited to his castle all the attendees from the king's celebration for another round of drinking and feasting. He showed the king that he could entertain in an even grander fashion than could the king himself.

Humphrey de Bohun, Earl of Hereford, sent his regrets. Having developed an aversion for such ostentation and deception, he repaired to his castle in Essex and found himself more at home in the chapel communing with his God in atonement than even continuing with his former daily life at overseeing the tending of his fields, or playing chess with his eldest nephew, Henry, a daring and brilliant tactician. His greatest weakness being his lack of caution, the young knight was yet a formidable opponent who always assured a dangerous, exciting game.

OCTOBER 20th 1313
hexham, northern england

Whether through deliberate avoidance or poverty, various communities in the north of England would not or could not pay the ransoms King Robert had levied on them. Though he had always been even handed in his dealings with the English towns, he had strict rules, both in the collecting of the funds, and in the treatment of the townspeople. He never allowed any region to go unpunished for outright rebellion against paying him his due, but he never punished the innocent either.

The burgesses of many northernmost English towns, getting no protection from King Edward against the border raiders, had begun refusing to pay the taxes levied upon them by him. A number of them chose instead to pay those monies to King Robert, who did protect them, especially by bringing an end to raids from across their border with the Scots. This worked well for all except the English sovereign, who was impotent to enforce payment of taxes by his northern towns because of his troubles in London.

After a while of enjoying the peace purchased with those 'taxes' paid to the Scots crown a few localities became complacent, and in their false security, their burgesses made the decision to stop paying the Scottish king as well.

Hexham was typical of the spotty rebellion against paying the exacted amounts to either crown. But though the prosperous town received no consideration from their English king, the citizenry had been stirred by a local clergyman who was yet headstrong for the English and did not believe in rendering "unto Caesar the things which are Caesar's" if the Caesar in question was Robert the Brus.

Unfortunately for Hexham, the Scots king desperately needed the monies and stores that the town had previously agreed to pay and had been paying. With the expected battle for Stirling foremost in his mind, Robert knew he must force the payment of the levies before the idea spread that they need not be paid. He could not leave and head south to make the collections personally, but he could send someone else. Edward might fulfill his wishes, though his current moodiness allowed little patience for debate, and a great deal of latitude for action.

Thus it was that Lord Edward Brus was sent to talk sense into the offending citizens, and with him went one hundred mounted knights and eighty soldiers of foot in case diplomacy failed.

After the trek of some miles into Northumberland, the small Scots army collected to rest at the edge of a broad field outside the village. The abbey tower could be seen rising above the thatched roofs of the neat houses and shops surrounding the market in the town's center. Smoke from a hundred hearths rose straight and silent into the brilliantly blue sky as the men from the north prepared themselves for their task.

In the quiet village people occasionally could be seen going about tending to their daily chores. For them this was just another day until someone glanced up the road or across the low rolling countryside and saw the silhouettes of Edward's army.

"The Scots! Run! Run!" spread through the town along with shrieks and wails and tears as those citizens closer to the edge of the town grabbed whatever small valuable was at hand, be it child or coin, and hied for the wood thinking that the Scots' searching them out one-by-one would be tedious and uninteresting considering the poor spoils to be garnered. Others barred their stout doors and prayed that the invading horde chose not to come after them. Those nearest the abbey fled there and asked for shelter.

Edward stoically watched the people scatter like a flock of frightened birds.

"Ye got the townspeople bestirred, Milord," said one of his knights. "They know what we're here for. Do we now ride into the town and collect our due?"

"Hain't started as yet," said Edward, shaking his head slowly and gazing at the town. He intended to show Robert that he could collect the monies and other 'offerings', on his own, without any of Robert's 'advisors', which he thought were more like spies, riding with him. He would also make the burgesses rue the day they decided not to pay their total assessment.

Turning in his saddle and with hand signals indicating to his lieutenants where he wanted them to enter the town, he drew his sword. That done, he suddenly whooped a blood-chilling cry and spurred his stallion across the open ground toward Hexham, followed by every one of his hundred and eighty-four, all yelping their loudest.

The Scots swarmed across the distance to the town like a great wave washing onto the shore. The men on horses quickly reached the shops and houses of the merchants and craftsmen who had made Hexham town into a prosperous and thriving market and began their pillaging.

The larger, wealthier houses near the market square were broken into and ransacked first, and anything of value was swept away in saddlebags or kits while Edward rode up and down the streets laying claim to whatever he wanted to present to his brother. He ordered any horses or cattle or pigs, goats, or sheep to be driven out of town and to the field they had just traversed, leaving only the breeding stock behind. All grains were to be loaded into wains or carts and taken out as well and place along the road north.

Children hiding in the town were to be ignored, anyone offering resistance would be slain, all else were to be turned out of their houses and businesses to stand in the street and watch as their town was looted and set afire.

The tidy place was being stripped bare and humiliated and beaten, and would have a terrible, hungry winter ahead. So it must be to prevent their ever wanting not to pay what they owed the Scots crown again, to Lord Edward's mind.

He rode the cross-town paths and alleyways, from the river to the farthest reaches of the dwellings and saw that his men were refusing pity to anyone. Already there were several bodies laying where they fell as their life-blood pooled about them.

Still, he noticed that what they had accumulated included little in gold, though the merchants should have been able to pay the entire amount in coin. And where were the burgesses, those rotund and self-important men who had decided not to pay?

Edward knew the wanton abuse of the town was counterproductive to his mission, and it dawned on him that when his brother found out he would have hell to pay. The only way he could save himself from Robert's ire was to take back the gold.

"Where are the burgesses?" he began asking. "Where's our tax money?"

Here and there, in the finer homes especially, fires had been set and the smoke rose in great columns. That meant that the homes had been plundered of all valuables and the Scots should have been ready to commence their return journey. But Edward could not without a quantity of gold with which Robert could buy arms and weapons for the summer campaign. He remembered the estate outside of town that he had seen as he rode the town's cart paths and lanes.

Thinking that the burgesses might have holed up there, he took a handful of knights and went to investigate.

It was a fine, two-story dwelling, with two byres and sheepcotes, coops, and a flower-edged garth. It was far nicer than the house Robert dwelled in, or his own, for that matter.

Two knights stepped down from their mounts and rushed the door to the unfortified house, only to find it bolted. They went to work with their axes as the others scouted around the house to find another entryway.

"See that nobody leaves! We want them rounded up and unharmed as best as ye can manage!"

"Aye, Milord," answered one of the knights assuming command of the others.

The door was broken through and there were women's screams from inside, but there were no burgesses, nor the baron whose house it was. Upstairs, though, they found a cleric's robe on a bed, and began looking for the man who belonged in it. They found him, naked, hiding behind a heavy curtain that separated one room from another. The curtain had betrayed him, as it was not quite long enough to touch the floor, and his bare white toes could be seen under its edge.

The women of the house were already lined up in the front yard, soon to be joined by the wives and servants from another house nearby, brought and made to stand in the group.

The cleric, who had taken to his hiding while in the midst of his ablutions, was dragged naked before his flock. There were nervous giggles among the women despite their dire circumstances.

Edward got from his horse and, looking very dour, approached one of the women.

She fell to her knees screaming, "Don't kill me, My Lord! Don't kill me!"

"Quiet, Biddy!" growled Edward. "I want to know where yer men are."

"Don't ye say!" yelped the cleric, "God has his eye on you! You will pay dearly..."

To the gathered prisoners' surprise, a nearby knight made short work of the cleric's yapping with the pommel of his sword. The fellow dropped to the ground without another utterance, holding his bleeding and broken mouth.

"Praise God," whispered one of the several women with cooler heads in the group. Others dropped to their knees and folded their hands for fear of being struck dead by God for the mere thought.

Edward asked the one again, "Where be yer menfolk?"

She hesitated. Fear and tears welled in her eyes. At last, seeing there was no escape she whimpered, "Gone to market, they have."

"'Tain't a market day," said Edward.

"They said it was market day this morn when they all left," said the woman with a shade of doubt in her voice.

"Damn," said Edward. "Got wind of our comin' and left the villeins and their women here to be receivin' us!" He called one of the knights to his side. "See if ye can pick up tracks headin' out," he ordered.

Edward with the surrounding knights and the hostage women stood until the searching knight returned within the half hour.

"Went west, Milord," reported the man.

Edward growled and wheeled his horse to the west to collect the spoils that were due Scotland, his knights trailing after him.

Several miles down the road they espied the scoundrels, "Yonder they are!" shouted a knight as they caught up to the errant burgesses with their mixed herd.

The burgesses and their herdsmen panicked and tried to flee. Some of them ran with heavy sacks in their arms. Others ran with tethered sheep and kine.

Edward drew his sword and the other knights followed. He cut them down as he found them whether they had sword or axe in hand or not. It was the massacre Edward had wanted from the beginning and none other was there to save them.

The baron was not among the dead. Some said afterwards he had the most English coin of all, and he failed to return to his once fine home, reduced to a stone shell before the Scots departed.

Twenty men were chosen to take the plunder back to Scotland while Edward and the other knights led the procession to the next delinquent town. As word spread of the incursion at Hexham, collecting became a matter of picking up the waiting payments and sending them to Robert. The gold he did not get from Hexham he more than made up for in the later towns until he had enough that he would not be scolded by his brother, and was in fact, congratulated for being such a proficient tax collector.

NOVEMBER 7th 1313
CHRISTINA'S CROFT

The hard won levies sent from Hexham by Edward Brus were placed in the hands of the exchequers at the castle in Ayr by Thomas Randolph, Earl of Moray, who also received a complete report of the terrorism inflicted upon the people there. He, with two knights as companions, then traveled across Scotland to Christina's farm where he knew King Robert was secretly holed up.

By the time Randolph arrived at the house the weather was bitterly cold and rainy. The king's guard of four protective knights showed themselves prominently until they recognized the visitor as the Earl of Moray, after which they returned to other duties in the byre, where their scrawny horses were again growing sleek on the fodder in Christina's loft.

Andrew and Nigel sat close by the fire as Christina opened the door wide to greet the earl. "Come in, My Lord Moray," she shouted cheerfully into the blowing rain.

Thomas climbed stiffly from his horse and handed the reins to one of his knights, telling both men to take shelter in the byre.

"I thank ye, My Lady. Is the king about?" he asked as he entered her door, at which she offered a modest curtsy.

"Asleep, Milord," she answered, "he'll awake directly, I reckon."

"I'll wait," he replied.

"Of course ye'll wait!" she came back. "He's been expectin' ye to be here for a day or two, Sir Thomas."

"Expectin' me?"

"He has his means," said Christina, smiling. "I ne'er question them." She was well aware of the messenger who brought Robert the news of Thomas' coming, but as usual, said nothing more of it.

Christina showed him to a bench beside the hearth, where Andrew stood as Thomas approached and exchanged greetings with him.

Thomas sat face to the fire and put his cold hands toward the flames, rubbing them vigorously. The squire resettled himself next to the earl and returned to oiling Robert's leather armor, showing Nigel, who was in awe of his famous Randolph cousin, how such was done properly. Robert's chain mail coat and coif were at their feet, ready for their attention next.

The earl breathed deeply and asked Christina, "How is he?"

She paused thoughtfully and answered, "He has good days and bad days."

"Is he battle worthy?" asked Thomas.

"On his good days... very much so," she answered.

"And on his bad ones?" She thought about that before replying.

"I... hope the war can wait 'til spring, Milord," she said, answering the question indirectly.

Thomas concentrated his gaze into the crackling fire and wondered if the rebellion could last without the king. The whole of the years of effort rested on the person of Robert, Thomas worried, and another cold winter or prolonged exposure like that suffered at Slioch could bring the rebellion, as well as Robert's life, to a close. He shook his head as if to clear it of the cobweb-like fears.

Suddenly Robert stood towering over him, wrapped in a blanket, his feet bare. "Thomas?" he greeted.

Randolph's fears melted when he looked up at his uncle. "Sire," he said, smiling as he stood. The two men hugged each other warmly, and Robert sat on a stool before the fire.

"I'm thankful that ye arrived safe, Thomas."

Christina arose from her place across the hearth from the men and gathering up Nigel pushed him, over his protests, to the rear of the house where the entryway was attached to the separate kitchen.

"'Tis a bad day for bein' out," said Thomas, to which the king agreed that it was and leant closer into the warmth of the fireplace. They then sat in silence for a while, each thinking of what to say. Robert had a great deal on his mind and did not know *where* to start, and Thomas only one thought on his mind and did not know *how* to start.

At last Robert sighed and said, "Thomas, I am glad ye have come as I have a weighty task for ye. Are ye willin'?"

"Aye, Uncle?"

"I need ye to take Edinburgh."

"Edinburgh?" said Thomas quizzically, his face reflecting the sudden change in his mind. Like Stirling, Edinburgh Castle stood on a great upthrust of a creagh hundreds of feet above the surrounding lands. The very look of it would give sane men pangs of foreboding. To assail the fortress would take masterful planning and leadership, and Thomas was not sure he was up to the challenge. He was less a commander of such an undertaking and more of a second in command, in his own mind. Not only that, but it would possibly take a year or more. His mind whirled from one negative thought to another.

"'Tis time our English visitors are told to leave, Thomas. Our hospitality has been too long abused, I fear," replied Robert, trying to take away some of Thomas' struggling with feeling overwhelmed.

"Edinburgh is as well fortified as Stirlin'," Randolph said, nodding to agree with Robert's statement, though his thoughts were at Edinburgh, "... just as high up, too!"

"Higher, and it must be taken ere summer," said the king.

Thomas nodded in agreement but knew not how he could possibly accomplish the feat.

"Gather one hundred knights and two hundred foot soldiers, and just take the castle!"

"Mighty small army for the task," replied Thomas, again facing the fire and returning his hands to their former outstretched position.

"Ye are my best, Thomas," pleaded Robert. "Ye can... ye must do it!"

Thomas sighed, knowing he couldn't refuse the assignment. "I can take Douglas?" Robert shook his head.

"Nae. He's still in the Forest harassin' those folk... they're comin' 'round," he then added, "Haye is in Dundee so... he can't go. Boyd's here with me, doin' my bidin'."

"Boyd's here?" asked Thomas relaxing his hands.

"Hain't here right now," explained Robert. "I've sent him to hire all the blacksmiths for miles around. But he is workin' here with me. And Edward... well ye know where he is."

Thomas hesitated for a moment then blurted out what he had wanted to say all along, "My Lord King, I have received reports on what has been happenin' with the collections." Robert looked at him curiously. "Sir Edward's runnin' wild through Northumberland!"

"Wild?" questioned Robert, sitting higher on his stool.

"Aye, Sire, plumb wild, I'd judge from what I hear," said Thomas hanging his head a bit, knowing the king would not be happy to hear such news. "He's killin' folk that don't need killin' ... and burnin' what don't need burnin'..."

Robert leaned forward and put his elbows on his knees. "Not surprised," he said in a quiet voice. "Hard to know where to put him. Hain't got the patience to stay with a siege. No patience." He stared into the fire until Thomas felt compelled to say something in Edward's favor.

"He is a strong warrior, My King," Thomas tried to assuage the king's hurting for his brother. Robert thoughtfully nodded.

"Hope he survives 'til summer," he said finally. "I'll have a mighty task for him, then."

"Stirlin'?" asked the earl.

"It's all goin' for Stirlin', Thomas," said Robert almost whispering. "Edward's folly makes it all for Stirlin'."

Thomas could not believe his ears. The king was not defending his brother? His worries for the last hundred miles were for naught?

"But," started Robert, "ye said it true, he is a great warrior... one I am proud to have by my side in battle..." the king turned and looked Thomas in the eye. "He'll bring the northern English to our way of thinkin'... He cannot be patient, and so we must be."

Thomas nodded. That was closer to what he had thought he would hear, and was not disappointed. More to the point, he was satisfied that his own wit had guessed rightly, and relieved that the king had taken the report so well.

Robert sighed; a sense of resignation to Edward's temperament gave him some peace.

"Blacksmiths, Uncle?" Thomas said, suddenly realizing the subject had been lost without explanation.

Robert nodded his head. "Aye, blacksmiths... armorers in fact."

"For?"

"Spear points..." said Robert still gazing into the embers, "... axe heads, daggers and such."

"Hain't the ones a'comin' to the battle bringin' their own?" asked Thomas.

"Most will bring their personal arms, but I have somethin' else in mind, and they'll nae come prepared for that," answered Robert.

Thomas shook his head. "Ye puzzled out the battle?"

"Some," he replied, obviously troubled.

"What happens if ye let Stirlin' stay in English hands? What happens if ye just don't appear to stop its bein' relieved?"

Robert heaved a great sigh and considered what the results would be if he failed to meet the army of Edward on the fields before the castle heights. He pulled his blanket tighter around him and spoke thoughtfully and deliberately.

"If I were Edward the Lesser, I would come with everythin' I could bring north. I would arrive with a terrible force, well armed, well supplied... even greater than the bunch that I had brought a few years ago. And if I found no Army of Brus to throw my legion against at Stirlin', I would turn it loose on the rest of the country, because I would know that Brus had surrendered to his fear of my strength, and that I had won. The butchery wrought at Perth by the first Edward would pale beside what I would do to the entire population of Scotland." He paused a moment and added, "By the time I finished with them, Scots from the Orkneys to Galloway, Islay to Edinburgh, would curse the name of Brus and rue the day they called him king." His voice was barely a whisper by the time he said, sadly, "If I were Edward."

The bleakness of the description left Thomas silent and in further despair. After a moment more, Robert again spoke.

"If, on the other hand, I were met by the Army of Brus before Stirlin', I would do my utmost to destroy ev'ry semblance of Scottish manhood my horde could reach. I would sacrifice whatever was necessary to win, though it cost me a dear portion of my grand army. I would then not send the remainder of my forces abroad in the land, because I would fear that all of Scotland would resist like the men at Stirlin', and I would leave my own kingdom weakened, providin' an opportunity for Thomas of Lancaster, or perhaps even my father-in-law, Phillip the Fair, to seize my throne."

"Can we not win?" asked Randolph.

"I cannot say we can win, Thomas, I can only say we shall be cut to pieces if we meet Edward's knights in fixed charges across open fields. He has hundreds of barded knights. We have none. He has wealth enough to buy the best weapons, the finest horses, an excess of provisions. Boyd is bargaining with local smiths to make iron pike heads and blades because we cannot afford steel blades."

"That's why Edinburgh has to come down, Thomas. We must forbid them shelter and comforts, supplies, a place to defend... we must make them as weak as we possibly can."

Thomas nodded again. "Figure on my high landers?"

"Aye. All we can. Barclay, Wiseman, Frasers, and the Bishop... all of them and their resources. Ye need to get word to Lennox as well. I'm countin' on yer men from Moray to make up at least a fifth of our army!"

"And Campbell, too?"

Robert nodded agreement, then said, "I've signed a proclamation, Thomas, that says the earls and barons who don't come to my peace and send their allotment of warriors and supplies to me at Stirlin' by late spring next will forfeit all of their lands and titles in Scotland forever. Use that to convince those who would hold back... if ye must."

"Last chance?" said Thomas reinforcing Robert's say.

"From now to the Feast of St. John the Baptist... 'tis a long last chance," he replied, a tinge of grit coming back into his voice. Thomas was pleased to hear it.

Andrew had long since stopped his oiling task in mid-stroke and listened in fascination to the litany of dire consequences that could befall the Scots at Stirling. After the two men left he stared off, wondering if he might gain his knighthood at the great battle of summer next.

He, for one, could hardly wait.

Hugh le Despenser

NOVEMBER 28th 1313
The RIVER THAMES

Ten brave souls wrapped tightly in quilted robes walked in their bare feet on an icy wharf beside the Thames. They had come on this wretchedly cold London morning to test their manhood by swimming with their king in the river's frigid, wind blown, choppy brown water. It was far from the coldest day the king could have chosen for his swim, a habit he enjoyed regularly year round, but it was near freezing.

Hetherington hunched nearby, his slouch hat meeting his heavy woolen surcoat at his ears. He shivered as the wind cut across the stone dock where the ten, King Edward leading, were making their way down the steps toward the water. Squires, following their masters, were fully clothed as their only participation in the ordeal was to hold their masters' robes as they were shed.

The king's guard lined the upper part of the dock as a burgundy boat hovered close within the vicinity in case one of the knights got a cramp from the cold. At its mast was a rectangular banner snapping sharply in the wind with three gold leopards emblazoned on both sides.

Edward faced the water and, smiling as though in his glory, breathed deeply in the damp air. He then removed his robe and held it so that it draped from his highly held hands, and dramatically dropped it to reveal his completely nude, very palid body.

His sycophants clapped appropriately.

He was pleased and so turned to show his admirers his full self. Again they clapped, except one, Edward noticed. The young Hugh le Despenser watched the king display himself to all with greater interest than the rest, having found the king more than a way to the higher echelons of the chosen. He thought the well-proportioned and fit king sexually attractive.

A squire gathered Edward's robe from the wharf floor while the king bowed, as if a thespian before an audience in his own court. With fists propped on his narrow hips he issued a dare, one which he was sure would bring them all into the water. "Follow me, gentlemen, if you have a taste for adventure... and the ballocks!" Then he jumped in making a great splash.

Eight of the nine candidates ready to show the king their courage fought for their turn to doff their own robes and join the king as, to countermand the shock of the cold water, he let forth a strong whoop that echoed against the stone.

The last one, Hugh le Despenser, strode casually toward the edge of the dock, his eyes transfixed on Edward, whose head and arms flailed about in a kind of horseplay with his companions.

Sir Hugh dropped his robe every bit as brazenly as had the king, all the while keeping his eye on Edward until the king espied him standing so grandly upon his stage.

Having caught the king's attention, the young knight jumped into the swift current and swam once around the group huddled about the central figure, then climbed out of the water onto the dock. One glance back toward the swimmers told him what he wanted to know. The king was looking. Hugh turned his back to the king, took the fairly dry robe his squire offered, and left the wharf ahead of the rest of the king's companions, who believed the longer they could keep abreast of the king's escapade the greater the chance of gaining Edward's favor.

They were mistaken. As he watched Sir Hugh ascend the steps Edward suddenly tired of the game and swam to the wharf. Pulling himself from the water onto the dock he was shaking and shivering, not knowing whether it was the cold water that caused it, or the excitement of observing Sir Hugh, who had boiled his blood.

He quickly went to the top of the steps and peered around as casually as he could manage, but Sir Hugh was not in sight.

Hetherington stepped forward anticipating the king's need.

"Did you see that young man leave before I decided to leave?" he asked arrogantly.

"Sir Hugh, My King?" asked Hetherington, hoping to gain a more exact description.

"Yes," said Edward gruffly, "Sir Hugh!"

"I know him *and* his father," said Hetherington.

"Have him arrested," growled Edward, "and brought to me, immediately!"

"Arrested, My King?!" the servant asked.

"For leaving ahead of me... without my permission... I liked it not," said Edward throwing his robe over his shoulders and walking toward his horse.

"I shall have it done, My King," said Hetherington trying to keep up with the fast paced king.

"What more do we have on the agenda for today?" Edward snapped, drying his dripping hair on a cloth.

"The letter to Earl Dunbar, Majesty," answered Hetherington. "It has been put off for some days now."

"Dunbar, hmm?" asked Edward rhetorically as he climbed onto the barebacked destrier. "We'll tend to it immediately!"

"Today, Sire?"

"Yes, Hetherington!" he barked, "This very goddamned day!"

He kicked the horse in its ribs and galloped off toward the Tower, the eight aspirants following.

• •

It was mid-afternoon before Hetherington was summoned to the apartment of King Edward, where he entered prepared for any possibility of the king's affairs, but not for the strong smell of French-made perfume permeating the whole of the residence.

"Is the queen still at Windsor?" asked Edward casually from his inner room.

"Yes, Sire," called Hetherington, and he bowed as the king cheerfully entered the room and crossed to a large table where he sat.

"Then let the harlot stay there! The farther she remains from me the better! By my arse, if she were taken by that whoreson Brus to the realm of Scotland, I should let him keep the place and make no further adventures for it!" He sniggered at that thought.

The king and queen had exceeded the limits of their toleration for each other, and their short-lived honeymoon period after the birth of their son had concluded. Things were once again as they had been when Lord Gaveston lived... intolerable.

"Ready for the letter to Earl Dunbar?" the king asked, taking a small drawer of jewelry from a chest on the table.

"I am, My King."

"Tell My Lord Dunbar that I shall be comin' by midsummer next with the greatest host of men-at-arms ever seen by the Scots, to destroy Robert Brus and all who support him." He chose one of the rings from the drawer and slipped it onto his finger, observing how it looked as he moved his hand around in the light.

"I shall see to it, My Liege, and have it ready later this afternoon," said Hetherington, bowing.

"No, not this afternoon... in the morn will be soon enough." He took off the ring and selected another, repeating the process as before. "I wish to attend to no more business, today," said the king, but he stopped as if something occurred to him suddenly. "Oh, except... bring me the prisoner arrested by the wharf this morn!"

"Sir Hugh, Sire?" asked Hetherington, graciously.

"Sir Hugh," replied the king as he tried on another ring from the drawer.

It was another one of those one-on-one meetings that had developed into Aymer de Valence, Earl of Pembroke, being King Edward's closest confidant. In his obsessive drive to invade Scotland under the pretense of relieving a single, albeit important, English-held castle there, he grew enthralled with what he considered to be his greatest opportunity to settle his troubles with the Scots, and with his imperious lords, in one blow.

"I *will* have my Scotland back!" expressed King Edward forcefully through gritted teeth. "It is mine by God given right and I *will* have it back!"

Earl Aymer waited for the king to calm himself.

Hetherington pretended to be committing it all to ink and paper, immortalizing the king's every word.

Edward huffed. He fumed. And at last he sat in his large, overly festooned chair at the head of the rectangular table. Sometimes he envisioned it being a round table as in the King Arthur stories he had heard in court and from his father when he was a child. He looked to the ceiling and strained his eyes for a sign that he was doing right, saying the right words to the right people, making the right decisions. He imagined his father looking down upon him from above, putting his ghostly finger of approval on his every plan.

He suddenly leveled his eyes on Pembroke's as if he had been struck by spiritual inspiration and said, "You, My Lord Pembroke, will repair to Berwick immediately!"

Pembroke sat higher in his chair to match the king's height. Edward was tall but he had lessened every chair at the legs, except his, to make anyone sitting at his table feel they were in an inferior position.

"We need you in Berwick," he again said, a tone of insistence permeating his demeanor. "I shall make you my Viceroy... you need to be there!"

"My King," started Pembroke, "I was Viceroy under your father and yet failed to capture Brus." He remembered well that he had greatly feared for his head as the result.

"You shall not have to capture Brus, this time, Pembroke, I shall handle that myself, come mid-summer."

"Then what is to be my purpose there?"

"You will collect and organize stores for the venture, Milord Earl," said the king, gently biting his lip as he thought the command through.

"You can see to the gathering of grains and animals from neighboring areas."

"Northumberland?" asked the earl.

"All of the north of England," he replied, starting to smile as his thought blossomed full-blown. "They have been perpetually raided for years by Brus... they will be glad for the relief."

"Takin' their goods and stores is goin' to be considered relief, My King?" returned Pembroke.

"Well, take the goddamned 'goods and stores' anyway!" ordered Edward. "The people never know what's best for their own well bein'... they will come to thank us later."

"What about Lothian?" asked Pembroke.

"What about it, Sir?" said Edward, "Leave it for Dunbar to deal with."

"Dunbar is fixin' to turn against you, My King," said Earl de Valence, sighing at the possibility Dunbar would not last the winter considering how fast the other earls were coming to Robert's peace.

"He *shall* be there. He *shall not* forsake England!" said Edward vehemently. "But you must play to his pride... to the utmost... and to the pride of every Scot who still is loyal to England, for that matter."

Pembroke balked at the thought. "You'll not catch *those* flies with such honey as that."

"It's because of... of Brus!" yelped Edward. Pembroke frowned, not understanding. "Brus has issued an edict that any noble not comin' to his peace by end of spring, next, will lose *all* rights to their lands in Scotland!" complained the king.

Pembroke then discerned the bellows that heated Edward's fire, and he also knew when to keep quiet. And so he did.

"Put this to parchment, Hetherington!" instructed Edward, pointing his finger upward, accentuating his words. "Send writs to each of nine earls, the present earl, Lord Pembroke, included."

"Yes, My King," said Hetherington, and began to scribble on the paper before him.

"Lancaster, Hereford, and Warwick have just been pardoned by me and should be quite willin' to show their appreciation for my nobility in so doing!"

Pembroke knew the three had been forced to bend their knees to the king and confess their sins to obtain the 'noble' pardon, and he also knew that they did not take lightly their embarrassment at the doing. Again, he said nothing.

"And the others, Sire?" asked Hetherington.

"The others?"

"Earls... for writs?"

"Yes, of course," continued the king. "Surrey, Gloucester... and Arundel..."

"Arundel?" questioned Hetherington, "Your Majesty, he came not forward with a confession."

"Arundel will be sent a writ!" exclaimed Edward. "I shall place him at the forefront of the worst of the battle, as King David did Uriah the Hittite! That will show him that he should have come begging forgiveness of me as did the others!"

"Yes, Sire," said Hetherington and put the three to the paper.

"Send writs to Ireland... to Ulster, and to the erstwhile Lord of Lorn with our fleet. Tell him we will have a second invasion of Scotland from the western coast."

Hetherington obsequiously answered, "And are there instructions to Ulster?"

"He is to invade Ayr on the twentieth of June with all his might," said Edward, "as my father did."

"Sire, Ulster never showed the last time," objected Pembroke, referring to Edward's similar plan of three years earlier.

"He will this time, or he risks losin' his earldom... and his life!" said Edward pounding with his fist on the large table.

"The Earl of Angus is yet beholdin' to you, is he not, My King?" asked Pembroke.

"Yes! I had not considered him since he is a Scot. Send him a writ as well, Hetherington! Send writs to all our barons, too!" he ordered. "Instruct them to be at Berwick on the tenth of June with their allotment of men-at-arms... and be ready for our most glorious battle... at least of our lifetimes. Promise them they shall all have rewards at battle's end... land and titles in Scotland once we have the fight won and Brus' head piked before my tent!"

Pembroke contemplated his own promise of a possible reward. Then with a notion to hasten the undertaking he said, "When will Your Majesty seek permission from Parliament?"

"I am *king*! I need no such documents or 'permission' from Parliament or those damned Ordainers!" he insisted grandly, having already asked and been denied permission by Parliament.

Pembroke questioned the prudence of that decision, and again spoke not... to prevent riling the king when he was glorying in his own imagination... and thus dangerous. Under his circumstance of chivalry, duress, and guilt over Gaveston, he was compelled to follow his king to the ends of the earth, even to the very hinges of hell.

Roger de Mortimer

JANUARY 10th 1314
CASTLE WINDSOR

Marcher Lord Roger de Mortimer stood silently in the garden at Castle Windsor and shivered in the cold night. He smiled at himself for wondering whether he shivered from the cold, or from the chilling thought that what he was about to do might ... no, would ... cost him his head if he were caught, or later betrayed to the king. *Mortimer,* he mentally admonished himself, *you are a fool of the first water!*

Still, he stood in the dark shadows produced by the brilliance of the full moon and continued to wait for the signal, a small candle in a particular window of the castle's residential wing.

The clouds in the sky poured across the full moon making it almost impossible to keep his eyes sharply upon the landscape, but he continued to watch and hope. The moon was quite high in the sky before the signal came, and he shivered again, this time for excitement.

Soon a hooded female figure showed herself at the edge of the garden near the door from which she had just exited the castle. Lord Roger held his position lest this be someone other than whom he expected. He watched her moving across the terrain as if she knew well where every bush and bump was located.

Then she saw the darkened figure of Roger, so stalwart, his broad shoulder and a part of his head contrasting against the brightly lit stone wall across the grounds.

"This way, Monsieur, vite!" said the woman in a whisper.

Roger followed the woman across the garden and into a small postern door. Once inside she stopped and whispered for him to take off his boots so he would not make noise on the stones when he walked, which he didn't quite understand with her accent and whispering, but finally she said simply, "Boots!" and pointed to his feet. He removed them.

That done, they crept along the hallway and up the narrow, winding staircase to the third floor. Turning down a darkened corridor, they felt their way along the wall until they heard footsteps coming toward them. Quickly opening the first door she came to the woman pulled him into the room, and told him to remain quiet. She then quickly stepped back into the passageway and closed the door behind her.

So this is the way Roger Mortimer's life ends, hiding barefooted and freezing in a pitch-black room listening to my own heart pounding... until the king's guard pulls me out to arrest me and throw me into the dungeon! He remained absolutely still until he heard the woman speaking to someone down the hall. It was a man, but he couldn't understand what they were saying in their informal French. He could tell they were drawing closer to the door behind which he stood, and his heart jumped.

She has betrayed me to the guards! he thought, and pulled the dagger from his belt. Much to his relief, the voices went past his hiding place and continued down the hall. As they reached the stairway, he heard them laugh, and again he started breathing.

At the same moment, someone behind him opened the curtain at the window and bathed the whole room in the cold blue of moonlight. He spun around, blade at the ready.

"Oh, Roger! I have wait for you, Mon Amour," said the woman softly, and she ran to take him in her arms. They stood wordless in the chilly room, their arms wrapped tightly about each other, happy just to be touching, embracing, kissing.

"You nearly stopped my heart!" he said into her warm ear. "I had no idea you were here in the room." He looked down into her dark eyes, smelled the aroma of her hair, her perfumed body, her sweet breath. "I have so longed for you, My Darling Isabella!"

"I feared I would never see you again," she whispered, "Merci, Mon Dieu! Merci, Merci..." and she nuzzled her face against his chest as tears of joy fell upon his leather jerkin. He gently brought her face up to see her tearful eyes, and laughed tenderly as he kissed the tears from her face. "Do not laugh at me, Roger!" she protested.

"I would not laugh at you, My Sweet. I am laughing because I am so happy to hold you in my embrace again. Please scold me not for it!" He hugged her again.

"I have be so alone without you, Mon Cher, since we have part I have cry every night that I do not touch you."

"Then why did you not send for me long ago?" he asked, whispering in her ear. "I thought you were turning from me... that I had somehow displeased you." She shook her head.

"Non, we have go away... in France," she kissed him passionately again.

"Never been," said Roger as they released their lips.

"You must go there with me, one day."

"We shall, one day. We shall sail away and go to Paris to live and make love and have babies and..." he glanced about the room and asked, "Where are we?"

"Does it matter?"

"I want desperately to lie with you and feel your heart against mine as before, but I don't want to put you in danger."

"Roger," she said, kissing him again.

"Yes," he answered.

"Is anywhere safe from the eyes of 'Le Roi'?" she asked, somewhat bitterly, and taking him by the hand, led him to the bed in which she had been awaiting his arrival.

Roger flung off his cloak, unbuckled his sword belt and hung it on the corner of the headboard, and removed his jerkin, untying the leather thongs, and dropping it upon the cloak. But looking about him, he stopped and asked, "What of your servants, your ladies-in-waiting? Are they to be trusted not to expose us to Edward or his servants?"

"Mon Cher, my ladies are not mere servants. They have be with me since I am come here, to England, and even before, in France. We are friends. I know their secrets. They know mine. They feel about Le Roi the same way as I feel... they hate him!" she began trying to help him remove his heavy mail coat. "They would never betray us to him! Mon dames d'honneur are... Francais, you know? Non Anglais... Elles... non, 'they,' are ... um," she searched for the right word and said, "fidele, you know? Fidele?"

"Fidele... like fidelity?"

"Oui! Oui! They are fidelity!" He laughed again and she smiled and continued helping him remove his short mail shirt. "Mon Dieu! How you can wear this..." she pulled at the heavy armor, and he finally wriggled himself out of it. He then removed his quilted short armorer's coat, and stood before her in only his linens. She climbed into the bed and watched as he removed all else, shivering with the cold and the excitement.

"I love you, My Lord Mortimer," she said in a whisper as he slipped between the covers and pulled her to him. She looked into his eyes and said, "Please, Roger, Mon Amour... let us never bring Le Roi into our lieu de rendez-vous, oui?"

FEBRUARY 27th 1314
CHRISTINA'S CROFT

The king stood in the doorway of the sturdy, simple farmhouse and watched the two riders approach steadily across the sere winter grasses of the broad meadow. He recognized the larger of the two riders as Sir Robert Boyd, but the smaller man he could not place. Still, he knew the purpose of Boyd's arrival, and his spirits alternately rose and fell as he contemplated the news his friend might be bringing.

Christina came to see what held the stout door open on such a cold day and found Robert almost completely filling its place, though he had to bend down some to see beneath the lintel.

"Robbie!" she scolded, "stand out of the door and let me close it!"

"The Boyd is comin','" he grinned sheepishly as he turned toward her. "I was tryin' to see if I know the fellow with him." She stood beside him and stared at the distant riders against the snowy hills.

"I can't make him out either. Now, get out of the doorway and try to keep *some* of the heat on the inside 'til they get here!" She tugged at the big man's arm and he gave way readily, chuckling at her ordering him around. She shut the door tightly and shivered at the chill. "Ye'll be ailin' afore ye know it, standin' in the cold with nothin' on yer feet! I'm surprised at ye, Robbie!" she fussed.

"I'm alright, Christina," he insisted.

"Aye, and no thanks to ye! Here, put this around yerself!" she said, offering him a warm cloak.

"Christina, I'm not an invalid," he insisted, but he crossed to the fireplace and sat on the stool there at the front of the blaze. "Now, is that better?" She followed him and draped the cloak over his shoulders.

"Ye'll keep warm under that!" she said softly.

"Ah, Christina, ye look after me like a hen with one chick! Ye must not worry about me so!"

"And if I don't, who will? Ye certainly don't worry about yerself!" She insisted. He decided to change the subject.

"Wonder who the little fellow is with Sir Robert..."

"Ye'll find out soon enough. Can I get ye some broth or somethin' warm to sip?" she asked.

"It would be good to have somethin' warm for our guests to drink. D'ye have some mead or mulled wine we can offer 'em?"

Beaten, she said, "Aye, I can fix somethin', but only if ye will have some, too!" He grinned and she went to prepare hot drinks for the men.

Robert opened the door when he heard the pair of travelers arrive.

"Sir Robert, well come! Ye and yer companion come in from the wind and the cold!" he said, and Boyd and the other man stepped into the welcome heat of the house.

"My Lord King," said Boyd and started to bend his knee when the other fellow dropped to his knees and bowed his head. Boyd grinned and said, "Sire, may I present to you the hero of the battle for Castle Roxburgh, Sim of the Leadhouse."

"Stand, Sim!" said the king. "We cannot have our heroes restin' upon their knees on the floor!" But Sim stayed on the floor, head bowed as if in church. Robert looked at Boyd and Boyd shrugged and lifted his eyebrows, not knowing why Sim behaved in such a way.

"Sim, Boyd said, "our king has said for ye to stand and meet him. Ye cannot refuse." And so, Sim stood, but kept his head low.

Robert grew tired of the fellow's timidity and asked Boyd outright, how the battle went. "Is Roxburgh ours, then?"

"Aye, Sire," grinned Boyd, and Robert hollered a great whoop and reached out and hugged the messenger from sheer excitement. "Roxburgh fell to Sir James Douglas on the night of Shrove Tuesday." Boyd started removing his heavy surcoat and cloak just about the same time Christina entered the room in wonderment as to what was going on. Seeing all was well, she again left.

"Oh, my apologies, Sir Robert, come, sit! Ye, too, Sim," he led the knight to a trestle table with benches on each side set at one end of the room. "Lady Christina will bring us something to warm our bellies while ye tell us about the battle."

Sim didn't sit. "'Twouldn't be seemly," he said, unusually humble and quiet.

"I insist, Sim. 'Tis seemly if I tell ye to do so," said the Brus, and finally, Sim of the Leadhouse sat on the bench beside Boyd, across the table from the king.

"Tell me, Sir Robert. I want to know exactly how Douglas managed to take the castle in such a short campaign. Were there many casualties?"

"We lost but few, Sire. We caught the garrison completely off guard, celebratin' and firmly in their cups as they were." Seeing Christina approaching he stood and exchanged greetings with her as she came to the table bringing each man a mug of warm wine sweetened with honey and flavored with spices. Boyd introduced Sim to her after which she stood at the end of the table and listened to the tale of the taking of Castle Roxburgh as the men resumed it.

"How did ye get inside? Roxburgh has no easy way up the mount, much less into the castle itself."

"We climbed up some o' Sim's rope ladders. Hooked 'em o'er the top o' the wall and clomb right on up before the guard knew we were there. Sim got atop the wall afore anyone else, met up with a pikeman and slit him from his ballocks to his adam's apple!" Christina winced at the thought.

Sim then spoke up saying, "Th'owed him off the gatehouse wall, I did." It was hard for Robert to imagine that this slender, quiet man could do such a thing, but Boyd nodded in agreement with the statement. Astounded, Robert shook his head, though he smiled as well.

"But ye... how did ye get to the gatehouse wall? Surely the guard saw ye comin' long afore ye got to the mount!"

Boyd nodded again. "Aye, they did, but they thought we were a herd o' loose kine, a'wanderin' in the dark."

The king laughed aloud. "Whose idea was that?!"

"'Twas Douglas," said Boyd with a grin. "He's right smart in thinkin' of such trickery. Thought if we could get close enough to use Sim's ladders and mount the wall, that we could surprise the guard and overrun the castle before they could stop us. And that's the way it was!" He slapped Sim on the back in praise.

"Did no one mount a defense?" asked the king, to which Boyd shook his head.

"Not much of one. The only place we didn't control within a short time was the governor, a Frenchman named Fiennes, was caught in his solar and refused to surrender the castle, yellin' curses out the window. He was wounded in the face when an arrow went in on this side and poked through 'bout here." Boyd pointed at the equivalent spot on his own face. "The shaft was in between his teeth so he couldn't close his mouth. He surrendered the castle shortly after that."

"Did he live?"

"Last I heard."

The trio sat quietly sipping their wine. Robert had another question.

"Have we started razin' the castle yet?"

"Aye, My King. 'Tis movin' fair to well since we have the locals to help," said Boyd.

"Sim," started Robert, "I recollect I gave ye forge work for five hundred pike heads and a like amount of caltrops ere this spring."

"Aye, My Lord King," Sim came alive, "Ye did, for sure."

"We goin' to have them by spring?" asked the king.

"Aye!" snapped Sim smartly.

"I'll be sendin' a man to look in on ye 'bout then," said Robert.

"Said he needed a ton of iron," said Boyd, "I sent orders to Ayr for them to get that much to him over the next few months."

"Will that be enough for the task?" asked the king of Sim.

"It might take another few hundred stone, but we'll see, Lord King. Don't want to be sparin' on such pieces as weapons," said Sim the authority, pleased to the marrow that the king had asked his opinion. "Don't ye worry, My King, I'll be havin' 'em for ye," stammered Sim, "ev'ry damn one ye be a'wantin'! And if ye want more, ye need only tell me!"

Robert invited his guests to take supper with him, which they did. The next morning Sim got on the horse he had ridden to the farm from the stable at Roxburgh, and headed south toward his home and his forge. It was time to produce the pike heads and caltrops, and spring would be upon him before he knew it. King Robert promised the smith that he would have a bit of land in return for his valorous service at Roxburgh and at his anvil. A patriot, the king had called him. A patriot!

The blacksmith was a newly made man as he rode away, and Robert was sure he could depend on the full amount of pike heads and caltrops needed from him for the battle at Stirling.

Two days later Robert got word from Douglas that the entire English garrison, formerly of Roxburgh, had been safely escorted to the border with northern England and set loose in little more than their linens and footwear. However, the one time governor of Roxburgh, Sir Guillemin de Fiennes, who had bragged on many an occasion that the Brus rebellion would never take his castle, had died a painful death from infection of his wound. He was buried in the south of Scotland in an unmarked grave.

The King of Scots then sent a message to his brother, Edward, who was wintering in the manor house of Robert de Reymes near Corbridge. The Earl of Carrick left immediately to carry out the king's bidding that he oversee the complete razing of Castle Roxburgh.

Sir Robert Boyd was then dispatched to Edinburgh Castle, where Lord Thomas Randolph was laying siege, with the news that young James Douglas had taken Roxburgh. The King of Scots hoped that Boyd's story of the battle would help spur Randolph to gain the upper hand in his own siege. The anticipated midsummer battle was coming closer to their doors every day and the king wanted there to be no succor available once the army of England left the land of Berwick to sally into the land of Stirling.

In spite of the fact that the next morning was cold, Robert climbed aboard his own horse and rode the forty miles south toward Stirling, once again to look over the field on which the battle would be fought.

Christina handed up a pouch of dried meat, oatmeal, and medicines to Robert and wished him well, cautioning him to remain wary at all times.

"If the English know for a minute that 'tis ye they see treadin' about the plains and hills around Stirlin' they will surely kill ye where ye stand!"

Robert had leant out of the saddle and kissed her on the forehead, had sat up straight and said, smiling, "They might try."

William Francis

cn&RCh 10ch 1314
eÐINBURGh

Sir Thomas Randolph had been at the unpleasant task of starving the inhabitants of Castle Edinburgh for six weeks. The fortress was obviously well stocked with victuals for they made no move to surrender or even to negotiate a peaceful settlement. The manor houses and hovels at the base of the upthrust had been taken over by Thomas and his army of one hundred and forty-three men-at-arms, including twelve knights other than himself. The cook wives, squires, and craftsmen such as fletchers, masons, and a blacksmith and his helper, added another thirty-five to the number.

It was the tenth of March before Sir Robert Boyd reached Edinburgh. Its basalt upthrust had been built upon even before the Romans arrived on the island.

Boyd, by way of a local's directions, rode up to the large manor house on the road below the castle. To the left of the house was the causeway leading to the curtain wall gatehouse, three-fourths of the way to the top, and beyond that the sally port leading to the gatehouse of the large, historical castle.

Lord Thomas' immediate guard kept a tight hold on the entrance for he wanted no traffic on the roadway leading to the castle, whether going or coming.

Boyd climbed off his mount and approached the sturdy men at the door, who immediately recognized the warrior as being on the close staff of the king and allowed him quick entrance.

"Robert!" greeted Thomas, just coming down the stairs from a second story bedroom. A shy wench followed him and silently passed the two men as she made her way to the postern door and exited.

"Old tricks?" said Boyd.

"New tricks, old habits," replied Thomas, casting a glance toward the departing woman. He then ordered wine to be brought for the both of them, and settled on a bench beneath the window that looked out upon the causeway.

"Just came from Roxburghshire," started Boyd as he sat on the other end of the bench.

"Ye see the Douglas?" asked Thomas. He smiled, thinking he was about to hear that his young friend was sitting in a cold tent in the field near Castle Roxburgh, awaiting the surrender of the fortress, as he waited at Edinburgh.

"Aye. We took the castle there over a week ago," came back Boyd, and he watched the smile suddenly disappear from his companion's face.

"Aye? Roxburgh?!" finally said Thomas. He was greatly surprised, knowing it to be no small accomplishment.

Boyd nodded and slyly smiled as he said, "Robert sent me to tell ye."

"How many men with him?" asked the earl, his interest piqued.

"Forty-five," answered Boyd, "and me."

"And what did ye do?" asked Thomas, thinking Boyd's participation might have been the secret ingredient to the fall of such a strong castle.

"Let me tell ye the whole of it," said Boyd as the flagon of ale and two cups were set on the bench between the men.

It was a good half hour later when the telling was done and questions answered. Thomas leaned against the wall and rubbed his bearded chin. "Cows hain't goin' to be a likely ruse for takin' Edinburgh," he said.

"Well, starvation takes too long," commented Boyd matter-of-factly. "We'll be sittin' here waitin' when the English knock on the gate at midsummer. We must think of some other way; we must somehow get atop that rock and take that castle!"

The two men sat in silence and sipped their wine for a while as the thought settled on Thomas' mind.

"Ye bring any of them rope ladders with ye?" Thomas asked at last.

Boyd shook his head, "Take a month to get one here," he answered.

Thomas sighed deeply in frustration and stretched his legs out straight before him.

"Put yer wit to it", said Boyd, standing. "I'll be here yet a few days."

"I'll see to yer ev'ry comfort," remarked Thomas still contemplating his problem.

"I'm sure the accommodations will be comfortable," he kicked the earl's boot and teasingly glanced toward the postern door through which the young woman had disappeared into the town.

"Oh, aye," replied Thomas as he stood. He smiled, reminded of the woman Diana, in Aberdeen. He suddenly asked, "Ye ever hear of Graham, the Templar?"

"With Robert at Man, he was," Boyd replied. "Was sailin' with The Macdonald ere that."

"And what about his woman?" asked Thomas.

"They are together. She is with child, so I hear tell," came back Boyd.

Thomas sat again and reared back against the wall. "Ha!" he smiled. "So the bastard Templar is goin' to sire a colt after all! HA!!" he exclaimed loudly. "Well, we must toast the Templar and his expected wee bairn! More wine!" he called toward the rear of the house and with a sweep of his hand directed Sir Robert to return to his seat on the bench.

"May not be a colt," cautioned Boyd. "Could be a filly."

Thomas shook his head. "Nae, 'twill be a colt, with courage and willin' to fight!"

"Could be a filly with courage and a fightin' spirit," argued Boyd, "I've known quite a few lasses who would have made fine warriors!"

The two old friends talked and bickered into the night about one thing and another, finally laying money on whether or not the Templar's offspring would be a lad or a lass. At some point in the bleariness of the long evening hours they hit upon the notion of spreading the word to the townsfolk that there was a prize to be awarded for the best way to get inside the castle walls. 'A contest of sorts', as Lord Thomas had put it.

The next morning Thomas quietly circulated the rumor that a reward was being offered for information on a way to get into the castle. By noon he had four such proposals but none of them seemed to have a whit of merit. By early afternoon there was a William Francis admitted to the inner rooms to see the Earl of Moray. Straightforward, he did not stammer or fidget when he talked as a couple of the others had.

"When I was a strappin' lad...," he started and Thomas was already bored, "... my father was keeper of the watch house of the castle. One day, while in the village with some other lads, I met and fell in love with a beautiful young woman and she fancied me as well." Before he could take a breath to continue, Thomas interrupted.

"Is this goin' to get us into the castle?"

Boyd, however, was listening intently. "I think I see where he's goin', Milord."

Thomas waved his hand for the man to continue with his dull tale.

"Well, Milord, her father spoke to mine and said that I should not come 'round to see his daughter again, and then my father forbade my leavin' the castle." Thomas looked at Boyd to indicate that he thought they had heard enough, but Boyd hung on the man's every word.

"I went to the parapet wall ev'ry day and puzzled the steep rock on its north side," he related.

"Did ye find a way down and back?" asked Boyd, sitting forward in his chair. The man thought a moment before answering.

"It's been some years since I last clomb the rock, but I figure I did it 'nough to recollect the way," admitted the man.

"Will ye guide us in?!" asked Thomas, "'Twill be in the dark of night."

The man paused. "Milord, I promised my woman I'd ne'er climb it again if she would but be my wife, but I can point ye to the way."

"I must know the way, Man! D'ye not understand?" Thomas fumed thinking to clap the man in irons lest he agreed to guide them up the creagh, but for once, he kept his temper and thought a better stratagem. He plowed his hand through his drawstring pocket and brought forth a single gold English coin. "Friend Francis, take this to yer wife and ask if she will release ye from yer promise for just this one last climb!"

The man's eyes widened and his imagination soared to think of what she would say receiving such a fine coin. People of their rank in the society had seldom seen coins of gold. He cautiously reached out to take the treasure that Thomas had perched on the tips of his fingers when Thomas let the coin drop back into his palm and closed his hand to a fist.

"There will be more coins comin' if ye make this a success," coaxed Thomas earnestly.

"Aye, Milord," said William bowing slightly and keeping his eye on the closed fist of Thomas of Moray. "We will need to build a scalin' ladder twelve feet high, exactly."

"Twelve-foot ladder?" suspiciously asked Thomas, thinking the man wanted more money at the beginning.

"I may already have the materials, but if not I'll get them with the coin ye have offered," explained the man.

Thomas looked the villager squarely in the eye and smiled slightly. He wanted to believe the man a 'wee bit', which was far more than his usual trust level with strangers. He handed the coin to the man straightaway and asked if he could be back with the ladder two nights hence. William Francis avowed that he would do his best and clutching the prized coin, went home. Still, Thomas was not entirely trusting; he sent a man to watch the fellow to his home so that he would learn where the coin resided should its new master fail to return.

Three men who later came with ideas for climbing the mount were seen in the afternoon to keep any suspicion of having chosen a 'contest winner' already. He listened to their schemes with some feigned interest, all the while thinking of what he would do once he reached the summit of the mountain and the wall that, for the time being, kept the English safely in and the Scots out.

• •

On the fourteenth of March William Francis sent word to Randolph that he had constructed a wooden ladder suitable for scaling the north wall from which he once dangled his rope ladder to go secretly to town. His wife did not like the plan or William's part in it, but was well satisfied with the coin he brought to her for the bribing of her consent.

The scheme was all set. Randolph at last had a way to compete against young Douglas' grand capture of Roxburgh. Thomas would follow Francis up the north rock precipice with thirty handpicked highlanders, who were more accustomed to such strenuous climbs, while Robert Boyd would lead the remaining army in a frontal attack on the main, or east, gate as a diversion.

They reviewed the climb as William had relayed it to them, wrapped themselves in dark, warm layers of clothing, and honed their weapons to a sharp edge, knowing the kind of fight it was going to be. The garrison employed a good many archers using both long and cross bows, and skilled swordsmen manned the walls in addition. If Randolph and his men should be discovered climbing up the precipice so tightly arrayed, the archers would easily overwhelm them with flights of arrows that can find a man's heart even in the dead of night.

"'Tis dark enough, aye?" asked Boyd of Randolph as he peered out of the small window.

"'Tis," Thomas said, calmly donning a heavy coat over his chain mail and fastening it with a thick leather belt. From the belt he hung his broad sword in its sheath, and a dagger. Andrew Grey, second in command of the troops under Randolph, similarly dressed and the three men left the manor house to join their respective troops.

"Ye men ready?" asked Randolph quietly as he came to his highlanders.

All mumbled their agreement knowing any sign of exuberance would tip off the inmates of the castle that an attack was soon afoot.

Sir Thomas had been watching the skies all day and was thankful that it portended to be dry rather than a night of rain. The water would have made the rock face too slippery to attempt the climb, necessitating the whole mission being called off for another, drier, night.

"We will follow ye," Randolph said when he called William Francis to the fore. At Randolph's command, the guide started off to the north face of the creagh hoping he remembered the way to the top. For three nights, before going to sleep, he had mulled the climb over and over in his mind, reviewing in memory every move he once made by instinct. When he slept he dreamt of the trek, climbing carefully, getting nearly to the top, but fear would then consume him and he would fall, being saved from a fatal impact only by his cold, sweaty awakening.

The small army trudged silently.

Boyd led his one hundred and twelve around the creagh and surreptitiously up the east side's gradual slope. The men quietly crept up to the outer curtain wall. Sir Robert and his men then waited for Thomas to be in position on the north side.

Meantime, Thomas and Andrew and their men, following William, continued their grueling ascent. Their terrain was a mass of solid, hard volcanic rock, so sharp on its edges and so fierce to climb that the designers of the castle's defenses considered it unapproachable and therefore easily defendable. The simple twelve-foot wall on the north side of the mount was more for appearance than for protection against invasion. Still, it was there and needed to be conquered.

At the beginning of the climb William knew every handhold and ledge, but the higher he scaled the torturous rock the more like his nightmare the ascent became. Looking down all he could see was blackness, a vast abyss that lay open beneath his unsure feet. Now and again in the dim light he would catch sight of Lord Thomas, who was only a few feet below him and trusting his directions. Feeling the weight of his responsibility for the well being of the men who followed him, he carefully felt for familiarities in every crevice as he moved his bare, cold, bleeding hands over the rocks. He whispered key words to Thomas about the holds, but at every move, fear tugged at his wit.

Thomas had his men whisper and show each other where the handholds were as they moved up the face of the basalt cliff. The invaluable short ladder was handed up from one to the other as the men ascended.

The night watch along the overhead battlements could easily be heard talking between themselves, when somewhere along the queue of climbing men, there was a sudden and audible scrape of a sword hilt on the stone face.

The guards immediately went quiet. Thomas and his men froze in place. The guards listened for any follow-up to the sound. Thomas listened too, wondering if they had been discovered. After several long moments the two guards laughed at their own jumpiness and tried to make themselves feel less frightened. One threw a stone over the wall and shouted, "Away! We see you well!" but his arm was too anxious and the rock sailed over the heads of the Scots to bounce down the basalt below them.

Finally, one said "If there's any poor sods out there in this black night, I say 'piss on 'em!" They both laughed, and agreeing it was a good thing to do, proceeded to throw great yellow arcs of urine over the wall and down upon the heads of anyone there.

William and Thomas silently took the brunt of the assault upon their bare heads.

Feeling better about their courage, the two hitched themselves up and continued on with their circuitous route somewhat reassured that the noise was but a wild bird or rat running along the rock.

Thomas breathed a sigh and tapped William's leg as a signal for him to continue.

William hesitated, his breath fast and choppy. His fear of the climb had blossomed full-blown as he had stood listening to his enemy casually discussing mundane subjects over his head, and enduring the watery assault on his person.

Thomas tapped on William's leg again.

William forced himself to breath deeply. Thinking of how he had made the passionate climb in his youth, though for entirely different passions than he now endured, he pushed his fears aside. Soon his fingers released their desperate grip on the knob he held and searched out his next handhold. Of sheer courage in the face of his fear, he lifted himself a step higher toward the wall.

Another score of such minimal progressions and William Francis reached a narrow ledge, barely wide enough to stand on, and there was the base of the wall. He clambered along the ledge as far as he could, making room for the rest of the men to accumulate.

The thirty-two Scots and their ladder gathered on the rock face and rested.

Above them again there came voices approaching the wall, this time with torches. "Damn!" thought Thomas.

"We were right about here when we heard it, Constable," said one as the voices located directly above Randolph and his men.

The constable held up his torch and peered out into the darkness. The light was so pallid by the time it reached the dark stone that it was swallowed up, reflecting little back to the constable. "Don't see a damned thing," he said.

"Not what we saw, Milord," said the guard, "'twas what we heard!"

"Well, my wit says it was a night creature of some sort. An owl, perhaps, or a bat. God knows nothin' else could see to wander about in this blackness!" remarked the constable passing on the incident.

"Sorry we bothered you to come out in the night for no reason, Sir," said one of the pair.

"Not at all. It is good that you men have such fine ears, with those damned Scots layin' about at the base of the mount," he said, not wanting to discourage their astuteness. He quickly left the guards and the cold for the great hall and a cup of warm ale.

The guards having left the immediate area, Thomas was at last able to move his men. Some were shaking so hard from the cold that he knew they would be of no use to him as fighters if he did not get them engaged in battle before long. Up went the ladder.

Relieved that his nightmare had failed as portent, and charged with excitement, William Francis was the first to scramble up, with Thomas on his heels.

The men went over the walls and hunkered in the shadows until all were over and ready, then ran quietly into the bailey and up the hill toward the buildings, hoping to get well into the area of the keep before being seen. As soon as they neared the courtyard, however, an alarm sounded. Grey took his men and went shouting and screaming onto the parapet to face oncoming wall guards while Thomas and his contingent went to seize the main gate and open it for Boyd's men to enter. Still others went to attack and confuse the garrison.

Thomas Randolph made it to the front gate, and with several men raised the portcullis and opened the large wooden doors while some of his men held back the English defenders. Boyd's one hundred and more men poured through to meet the enemy.

The constable of the garrison shouted orders for the hobelars and crossbowmen to sally in defense of the castle. Word was passed through the hallways to the sleepy men, but Randolph's and Boyd's highlanders were on them before they were able to get far from their beds. One group of archers was sliced through as they were reaching for their weapons.

The harried constable managed to have one brave resistance against the incoming Scots when he had archers mount the wall walk and send flights of arrows into the bailey at the invaders. The men who were the targets of the arrows were able to avoid them or use their shields against them for the most part, though several were hit and went down. Boyd's archers returned fire to greater effect, dropping most of the constable's defenders where they stood in a line on the parapet wall. The English crossbowmen could not load fast enough even to defend themselves. Many of them jumped over the wall rather than face the attacking wildmen.

One Englishman ran through the courtyard screaming, "Treason!... Treason!" as the Scots, having dispatched or run off the night watch, began searching out other English to kill.

The castle governor, Sir Piers Liband, awoke with a start at the first alarm and looked out onto the commotion within the castle bailey, but could make out little of what was happening from where he was. He barged out his solar door, sword in hand, throwing a terrible fit. Someone had interrupted his sleep and they were going to pay dearly for their deed!

The constable, whose duty it was to inform the governor, left the wall and went in search of him.

"Milord! Milord!" shouted the constable as the passageways filled with smoke from the fires Thomas' men were setting to run the scoundrels from their holes.

"What's afoot?!" screamed the governor when he at last met with the constable.

"The Scots are within the castle, Milord!" said the constable hastily, his eyes tearing from the smoke.

The governor's eyes darted back and forth as he tried to think of what he must do.

In the bailey, things were beginning to come around for the Scots. Boyd walked through the open area, sword in hand, knowing the men could take care of themselves.

Inside, Liband grew fearful of what would become of him if the Scots captured him, and the defense of the castle was crumbling before his eyes.

"Hie for the dungeon!" he ordered the constable.

"Dungeon?" asked the constable.

"Quickly!" he replied and pulled the constable along with him through the acrid smoke toward the staircase into the bowels of the castle.

The English and Welsh garrison was subdued within the half hour. The dead and dying were scattered throughout. The fire in the keep fairly gutted the interior but contained itself to that building alone, and spread only through the upper floors.

The prisoners who could walk were rounded up in the courtyard. Some of the wounded begged for mercy and got it in the form of a merciful clout on the head with a mace. All of the other inmates were rounded up, except for the people in the dungeon.

Andrew Grey came to Thomas Randolph and said, "Milord, ye must see the dungeon."

Thomas groaned and resisted the thought. He had hated dungeons from when Lord Pembroke held him in one after the battle of Methven.

"What is it I must see?" he asked, not wanting to follow.

"The governor of the castle," said Grey.

"Bring him to me!" ordered Thomas. "I see no need for me to go to him!"

"He's in a cell," relayed Grey, "and..."

"And?"

Boyd came to the two men and heard what Grey was saying.

"The governor is locked tight in his cell, Milord, and the constable of the garrison lies on the floor just beyond the governor's reach, with the keys in his hand and his neck cut wide open," explained Grey, adding, "Or so they have been identified."

"Hain't that a puzzle," said Randolph scratching his beard and not much caring one way or the other.

"I'll see about it," offered Robert Boyd and he followed Andrew Grey to the dungeon where Piers Liband stood, newly released from the cell, seemingly shaken, and feigning appreciation for having been released.

Boyd said, "Ye the governor of the castle?"

"I was," said Liband rubbing his neck as he looked at his handiwork lying dead on the floor.

"Were ye the governor?" asked Boyd being more specific.

"Until this man rose up against me and put me in the gaol," said Liband, vehemently pointing to the sprawled corpse of his constable.

"Why did he take over?"

"Because I wanted to surrender the castle and he refused!" blurted the lying man as he dropped to his knees, his hands pushed together, praying for his life.

Boyd, finding his story suspect, grabbed the man by the collar and dragged him in front of Thomas.

Piers Liband made the performance of a lifetime, begging forgiveness and swearing fealty to King Robert forever and ever.

The castle had been taken, and the surviving English and Welsh of the garrison were allowed to leave for England upon their oaths they would never return.

Sir Piers Liband was presented in court at Dundee to Robert, who accepted his pledge of undying fidelity to the King of Scots, and granted him several estates in Scotland for his loyalty.

Edinburgh Castle was subsequently undermined by the conquering Scots' masons, and every building brought down with one exception: The Chapel of Saint Margaret of Scotland was left standing. It was said that, generations earlier Saint Margaret stated that 'Francis' would cause the walls of the castle to fall. Though reared from a small child within the castle grounds, William Francis had never known the divination existed.

In return for his most valuable service in the taking of Castle Edinburgh, King Robert granted William Francis lands in Roxburghshire, near to the lands he had granted Sim of the Leadhouse for his participation in the taking of Castle Roxburgh.

The southeast of Scotland was about as cleared of English-held castles as was possible to achieve before the summer battle. Preparations had to be completed in a very short period of time, and Robert was still not at all sure he wanted to take the gamble of a winner-take-all battle, especially since he would most certainly be outmanned by an army of far superior numbers and arms.

King Edward was dumbfounded. His eyes remained transfixed to the table before him on which lay a scrap of parchment, a missive from Pembroke telling him of the loss and subsequent destruction of the castles at Roxburgh and Edinburgh. There would be no refuge for him at either place while on his way to Stirling. *I must hurry and get to Scotland before every castle in the land is destroyed!* he thought.

At long last he mumbled the poor news to Sir Hugh le Despenser the younger, sitting to his right, and Hetherington, sitting at the far end. He said simply, "Edinburgh Castle has fallen to the Scots and has been destroyed, as was Roxburgh."

Hetherington sighed in resignation and said, " We still have Jedburgh, Dunbar, and Berwick in Lothian. The Earl of Pembroke is in Berwick; he will not let Berwick fall into their hands."

"For now," replied the king gritting his teeth. "But then again, he sent this letter!" The parchment crumpled easily in his angry fingers.

"I was in Edinburgh only last year, it seemed defensible enough," said Sir Hugh.

Edward smiled at his newly acquired paramour. "But you have yet to see a major battle, Sir Hugh."

"I work at my sham fights, Milord," said Hugh who, only nineteen and a perfect physical specimen of young manhood, had his degree of pride though he knew he was as yet untested in battle. He was a calm and nonabrasive individual who carried a secret agenda of his own design close to his heart.

Sir Hugh stood and with great oratorical emotion said, "I shall go to this battle in Scotland with you, My Brother, bringing a great host of men with me... and I shall fight... and die for you... if need be, Your Majesty."

"Dear Hugh, you have always been strong for me," said Edward. "I have no doubts concerning your loyalty."

"Thank you, Your Majesty," fawned Hugh with a grandiloquent bow.

"As a matter of fact, I shall have a special reward for you when we reclaim Scotland," teased the king coyly.

"May I know what it is?" queried Sir Hugh.

"Not now," said Edward, smiling and thinking what a grand surprise it was going to be for his favorite. The thought and immediate pain of the loss of Edinburgh Castle had passed.

"Our docket for the day, Hetherington," said the king, suddenly changing the subject.

"The earls of Lancaster and Ulster have been summoned to your side this day, Your Majesty."

"Let me know when they arrive," said Edward in an official voice.

"Yes, Your Majesty," said Hetherington standing and bowing low before leaving the king's apartment.

As the door closed Edward looked at Sir Hugh. "You will make a great battle hardened warrior," he promised.

Sir Hugh reached across the corner of the table taking the king's hand in his and squeezing it affectionately.

• •

As it happened, the two earls summoned by the king that day had met by chance as their respective entourages were entering the barbican to the Tower of London.

"The Earl of Ulster, I spy," hailed Lancaster, bowing from atop his large Frisian mount.

Richard cordially smiled. "And a good day to ye as well," greeted the Irish earl as he returned the bow.

At the behest of Lancaster, the two men came astride of each other at the head of their followers, entering the barbican tunnel together and starting around the left angle turn when a lion roared from one of the cages within the walls. The horses jumped and whinnied and would have bolted had their masters not reined them tightly.

"Just as you would have imagined, eh, Sir Richard?" said Lancaster trying to keep his mount quiet as the growls continued.

"Imagined?" asked Richard.

"Edward the Lesser keepin' his father's toys," remarked Thomas.

"Ye mean the beasts from Africa?" came back Richard.

"Among others," said Thomas slyly.

The two men cleared the tunnel barbican and started over the drawbridge, already down and in place. As they came to the gatehouse on the far side of the bridge the porter, recognizing the men stepped forward and greeted them. He ordered the portcullis to be raised and the heavy iron studded doors opened.

"You have apartments in the tower, Milords," said the porter, "Your men-at-arms must stay in the warden's quarters with our own garrison, off the bailey.

The more than thirty men making up the two earls' entourage went as they were instructed.

"The king likes to keep us unarmed when we come into his presence," said Thomas.

"Why would he?" questioned Richard, having a good guess as to the answer on his own but wanting to hear Lancaster's explanation.

"He trusts us not at all," came the reply.

Earl Richard breathed the cold spring air deeply and blew a long plume of vapor before him. "But ye're his own cousin, Thomas, surely ye..."

"With ambitions to be king, so he imagines," said Thomas alighting from his horse.

"And have ye?" asked Richard.

"To God in Heaven, by my oath I have not," lied Thomas putting his right hand over his heart then into the air at his ear.

Richard smiled knowing the earl to be fraught with such ambitions.

"Five earldoms do I now have," bragged Thomas. "I am truly greater than the king!"

"The news of the fortunate death of yer father-in-law reached my ears all the way in Ireland," said Richard, dismounting the destrier he borrowed from the king's stable in Bristol where, twelve days earlier, he disembarked the galley he had taken from Ireland.

"You know, you and I can be of service to one-another, My Dear Earl," said Thomas as if the thought had only just occurred to him.

"Speak ye so boldly of treason?" asked Richard.

"Not so much of treason as of destiny," said Thomas. "Our destiny."

"Our destiny or our ambitions?" gainsaid Richard. "I remind ye, Milord, that I am a close lieutenant to the crown."

"Personal ambitions, political destiny," replied Thomas. "And I fear not your position with the crown, Sir Richard."

Grooms from the stable came to the men and took their horses to be stalled. The two were quiet while within their earshot.

"Besides," Lancaster said returning to his thought, "Edward still holds your daughter hostage."

Richard was stopped cold.

"We both want the same thing," said Thomas, getting to the nub of his purpose.

"We do?" baited Richard.

"We both want to keep Robert the Brus alive," whispered Thomas, "even if, perhaps, for different reasons."

Earl Richard was certainly in favor of that, but admitting to it was an entirely different matter.

Thomas continued as they saw the king's keeper of the wardrobe come from the main gate to the castle to greet them. "If I were king," he said quietly, "your daughter would be home in Scotland with her husband where she belongs, and you would be left to your ambitions in Ireland... your... Celtic alliance, shall we say, My Dear Ulster?"

Richard was aghast. He always knew Thomas was a prideful man, but now, with five earldoms in his pockets, he could afford to seek higher glories. He also wondered how Thomas had guessed his most tightly held secret, the Celtic Alliance that only he and Robert had planned.

From the window, high above the men, King Edward peered down on them and off-handedly said to Sir Hugh, "Wonder what those two evil blackhearts plot against us today?"

From nothing more than idle curiosity, Hugh looked.

• •

Richard de Burgh, Earl of Ulster did indeed meet with the king, who told him of the great battle to take place at midsummer for Castle Stirling. He gave the earl a writ describing his demands of four thousand men-at-arms, including at least three hundred barded knights, to be transported to Ayrshire by the galleys of the Admiral of the Western Fleet, John Macdougall, erstwhile Lord of Lorn.

Leading that invading force, de Burgh would first take Castle Ayr, where Robert's exchequer was amassing Scotland's treasury. Then he was to form a full-fledged western front, creating an anvil on which the king could strike his hammer from Stirling, after winning the battle there.

Richard agreed, also bargaining for a visit to his daughter Elizabeth, yet being held under house arrest in Holderness. Edward's private war chest was opened and Richard was handed a thousand pounds sterling, with which to raise his Irish army and obey the king's commands in a timely manner.

His meeting with Earl Thomas on that same day was not so successful. The earl informed the king that neither he, nor Warwick, nor Arundel, would attend the king at Stirling upon midsummer. His reason was, or stated to be, that the king had failed to get the permission of the Lords Ordainers and the Parliament for the expedition. They would, however, send their respective quotas of men and knights to his use. King Edward, knowing Lancaster's political strength, did not contest the earl's decision. Besides, he greatly, and reasonably, feared that Thomas would murder him, or perhaps have it done by others, in the tumult of battle.

Elizabeth de Burgh,
Queen of Scots

April, 2nd 1314
The Royal Manor,
Burstwick-in-Holderness

Richard de Burgh left London the next day and headed north toward Holderness, north of the Humber Estuary in the east of England. As with most spring days, it seemed, the sky wept a steady drizzle across the already soaked landscape. Perhaps it was because his daughter was held prisoner there that he thought of Holderness in such terms, but to his mind, a drearier piece of sod would be hard to lay hand to in all of England.

The old King Edward had placed Elizabeth de Burgh in that God forsaken terrain. Being the daughter of one of his most effective lieutenants, she had not been killed outright, but hidden away from her husband and family in a place in which she led a life as drear and dull-witted as possible. Edward had seen to it.

Young King Edward had left everything at Holderness just as his father had arranged it, not wanting to think about it further.

Lord Richard drew rein at the gatehouse of the manor, where he announced himself and showed the guard his permission papers from King Edward. The guard, having no idea how to read, waved him on after making a cursory glance at the official looking yellowed sheet with the royal seal.

A groom took Richard's horse. The two canvas bound bundles riding the haunches of his destrier were handed to him at his request. His ten men-at-arms took their own mounts to the stable and warmed themselves by the fireplace in a small room on the back of the shelter where the English grooms tarried and gambled at casting lots.

He entered the foyer of the old and neglected royal hunting lodge, put the bundles on the floor, and was met by the warden who had recognized him from his many trips over the years.

"How is she?" asked Richard as he doffed his heavy wet cloak.

"Some days ill, some days almost cheerful," answered the warden who did not relish his position of gaoler of the Scottish queen.

"She know I have arrived?" he asked. The warden nodded.

"I expect she'll be down, directly," answered the warden again. "I will leave you alone."

"Good day to ye, Warden," said Lord Richard respectfully.

The man nodded and returned the blessing, then left.

Within a moment Elizabeth came down the creaking steps. The dress her father had brought to her on his last visit was beginning to look shabby and worn. She smiled and tears welled in her eyes at the sight of the only human being that connected her to the life she once had.

"Father!" she said with muted delight.

He smiled and held his arms wide. They embraced and she held him for a long while, not wanting to let go.

She suddenly jumped back and said, "My handmaiden Mary died about the time the leaves changed, Father!"

"I am sorry, Elizabeth," said Richard sympathetically, though he knew that both handmaidens had been elderly and not of sound mind all the time, and were more a matter of her taking care of them, than them taking care of her. At least the poor woman had been of some company to his daughter, and now there was hardly anyone with whom she could hold a conversation, the other so-called "handmaiden" being almost totally witless.

"Of the two, "Dour Mary", as I called her, snored the loudest," said she.

"So, ye're sleepin' better these days, then?"

"Seldom at all," she sighed and looked off wistfully, "Reckon we'll all be dead afore long."

"Get such from yer mind, Daughter," growled Richard wanting to put back into her backbone some of the steel she once had.

"'Tis a weary place," said Elizabeth, "and would be wearier still if it weren't for yer sparse visits, My Lord." She sat quietly for a moment, just looking at his face. He had aged much recently. The lines in his brow and around the corners of his eyes were deeper, and his reddish hair had grown noticeably grayer than it had been when she last saw him. She wondered if Robert had aged in like manner, and asked, "Have ye heard anythin' of my Robert?"

"I have, just recently," he said. "King Edward is makin' plans to meet your Robert in battle at Stirlin', come midsummer." He wanted to tell her that he had seen and conversed with Robert nearly a year before, but he dared not. Even here he could not let anyone know of their meeting lest word reach Edward's ears. "Which says that Robert is yet at large and able to lead troops. That is good news, aye?"

"No!" she cried in angst and started pacing around the room. "He will be killed! Robert should not! Must not! Edward will never meet him in fair contest of arms! Holy Mary! Let this not come about!" she prayed aloud.

Her father tried to soothe her fears, saying, "But Robert is bound to reclaim Stirlin' unless the English relieve the castle by midsummer. This is what Robert wants!"

"Oh, no, Father, it cannot be what he wants! He has so few men and weapons! He will be totally overwhelmed in such a match!" She continued pacing so that Richard could not approach her. "It will be the end of ev'rythin', Father! Ev'rythin'!"

"My Dear Elizabeth, ye are rememberin' things as they were before! All is changed with Robert and his army, now!" he lied. "He has an army equal to Edward's, and more arms! There will be little difference between the two armies except in the matter of command, and Robert is a far cannier commander than Edward at his best!"

Elizabeth shot a look at him that told him his lying had not assuaged her fears the least bit. "I promise ye," he continued glibly, "Robert the Brus has nothin' to fear from King Edward in battle, at Stirlin' or anyplace else! Elizabeth, listen to me! I would nae tell ye a falsehood, I warrant ye!" She continued to pace, but her father's words were beginning to make her allay her fears somewhat.

"As a matter of fact," he tried another approach, "I have great doubts that Edward will dare to go through with the battle. He lacks his father's abilities on the battlefield, and will not wish to leave his own country to make war to the north, especially since he failed even to find the Army of Brus the last time he crossed the border."

Elizabeth looked at him and was torn. It was not that she took to heart what he was saying, but she so wanted to believe his words that she was reluctant to say they were not true. Suppose they were true and yet she held no faith in Robert. Would God punish him for her lack of believing? With great warm tears streaming down her face she stopped and looked at the man who was her warrior father. Surely, with all his experience in war, he would know what to expect of both men once the battle was on. Her mind was struggling with what her father had said, and she finally gave in to his logic.

"Please, Father, be right!"

Richard de Burgh crossed to her and put his arms around his daughter. She held him tightly again and tried to stem the flow of tears.

"Of course I'm right, Little One! Your father is never wrong about such matters. Wait and see. 'Twill be a'right. I promise!" And if things turned out not a'right in the end, it would be no worse for her, except that she would probably never forgive her father his lies. But for right now, he wanted her to be less frightened and his words had helped that.

She dried her tears on his jerkin and kissed him on the cheek as she had done when she was small. Finally, he let her go. As she moved away, he remembered that he had the packages.

Smiling he said, "I have brought ye *two* presents this time, Daughter," he said, "dresses! I hope ye like them."

She looked into his eyes and smiled. "How would I have survived this long without ye?"

He retrieved one of the canvas wrapped bundles from the floor, shook out the folds to the first dress and held it to himself. "What do ye think!" he said merrily, trying to raise her spirits.

Her calm demeanor was sundered and she sank to her knees, pulling the dress with her, hugging it and sobbing. "It's blue," was all she could choke out.

Richard, who had not been on his knees for quite a while, went down and comforted her. *This has got to have an end, and soon, or she'll surely go mad,* he thought.

It was on his way back to London that Richard diverted his travel to meet one day with Thomas, Earl of Lancaster. He then returned to London to pick up the thousand pounds sterling provided to him by Edward.

He was back in Ulster two weeks later laying *his* plans for midsummer.

Әpꝛιℓ 7ċḅ 1314
ℓοɴδοɴ

The large framed Sir Giles d'Argentan and twenty of his fellow knights, all of whom had been ransomed, arrived in London by ship from Byzantium just as King Edward had planned. Months in a foreign prison had done little to his generally strong physique but his mental fortitude, his will, had hardened beyond its already tempered steel crust. He looked upon himself more as an inanimate machine of war than a man. A man who owed his freedom, if one could call it such, to the English king to whom he was bound, and had arrived to pay his debt of honor as best he could.

It was Hetherington, along with the exchequer, who met the men on the dock and welcomed them home to England. It had taken months of effort and a large sum of money to bring their return to actuality. Ever since Edward became aware of Mowbray's 'deal' with Edward Brus, he had written letters in pursuit of the release of Sir Giles and his many knights then held in the dungeon of the Emperor of Byzantium in Salonika. The Byzantium Christians had captured Sir Giles and many other European knights when they sallied to the rescue of fellow knights in Rhodes.

Sir Giles and his company were not unique in Edward's quest for his knights who were held for ransom in various places on the European continent, and beyond into Asia.

Edward had also sent invitations to many diverse places on the continent for knights seeking their true destiny to join him, and they would partake of the fortunes soon to be made at the Scots' expense. Scottish estates were parceled out as these mercenaries gathered like vultures over carrion, which is how Scotland had been described to the knights in Edward's letters, a dead country, ready to be revived by the victorious English king.

The nearly endless possibilities of the spoils of war were on all their lips.

Foreign free lance knights also appeared from everywhere, including France, Brittany, Gascony, Poitou, Guienne, and even the far north-eastern lands of Europe lent the services of four very blond and fair Teutonic knights.

All was coming to fruition in Edward's mind, except for Lancaster's rebelling group of earls, but he failed to care so long as they sent their quota of men for him to command.

The once proud knights he ransomed had been stripped of everything save the virtual rags on their backs. They were taken within days to the armorers and fitted for armor, and to the blacksmiths to choose their weapons and have them fitted for their respective uses. They were then taken to the saddler for their tack and trappings, and to the horse merchants where they selected their destriers.

The exchequer was reeling from the costs of outfitting the twenty-one knights, all for the battle to reclaim the castle at Stirling. An experienced negotiator, the exchequer had squeezed all the merchants for better deals, but in the end it still had been a very expensive week, with the grand total being nearly three thousand pounds sterling.

Each knight had been assigned a squire and two troopers to see to their every need as they traveled north to Berwick. On the road the seasoned knights stayed to themselves and many times were found in clusters quietly mumbling, so that their squires and troopers felt, in a single word, shunned.

april 18th 1314
cumberland, northern england

The various hostages taken from Cumberland, England, were being held in suitable quarters in the town of Dundee. Having a great ransom value they were being well cared for, as Robert had instructed, though if all else failed he would have them killed, a not unusual occurrence on either side of any dispute between nations. Not wanting to resort to murdering the hostages to extract the as yet unpaid monies and goods pledged by the people of Cumberland to ensure the hostages' wellbeing, the king sent Sir Edward Brus south to Cumberland with his men-at-arms.

It would be Edward's task to make a good impression on the citizens of Irthington.

Without coercion, the people of the village brought two wains of grain and a few small livestock, mainly goats, with a few sheep and chickens, to the village square almost immediately. They were allowed to hold back only their breeding stock.

Edward and Gilbert de la Haye left the village with the goods accompanied by promises of additional chattel within the month, and pleas that the Scots not kill their kin. Haye and Edward were both fairly disgusted at the pitiful offerings, but at least they had something to show for their trip.

Not far out of sight of the miserly town, they entered a wood, wherein they stopped at a small stream to water their horses and the small animals they had on tethers. The chickens were tied by their feet to the warriors' saddles. One of the men got off his mount to make water and saw fresh kine tracks along the bank and leading further into the thicket.

Without making a sound Gilbert dismounted, and took several of the other Scots warriors and slowly followed the tracks wherever they would lead. Before tracking the cattle very far they heard distant voices... English voices... and the crackling of green wood burning poorly. Gilbert held his men there while he listened to understand the situation into which they might be walking.

Presently the men heard the lowing of cattle as well.

"I think we might have more than a few goats and chickens to take to Stirlin'," he whispered to one of his men.

"How many ye reckon there be yonder?" asked another.

"We'll see," said Gilbert. "Ye, take two men and circle around to that direction, but make nae move 'til I do," he said to one of his men, and as he and his mates drew away, Gilbert turned to the others, "Ye and ye, come at 'em from yonder, but wait 'til ye see we've made our move. There can't be many, but if there are, they're but locals and won't stand against a surprise like we're about to give 'em."

They separated from Gilbert, leaving him with one man, and he pulled his sword from its sheath and crept softly toward the voices. It was only about twenty paces forward that he saw a few men seated by a struggling, smoky fire. Beyond them was a small herd of fat cattle, standing in a clearing, grazing on the spring's first green shoots of grass. He glanced at the man with him, and together they stood in the open and charged toward the herdsmen with cries that could be heard all the way back in the town.

The men at the fire were taken aback but turned to face their attackers, only to find themselves flanked by more men from left and right. Quickly they threw down whatever they held and dropped to their knees with their empty hands in the air.

Edward, hearing the calamitous uproar within the wood, drew his sword and held his excited destrier tightly in check. All grew quiet as quickly as it had grown noisy, and he began to wonder if Haye and the others were slain or yet lived. He started his horse across the narrow creek when he heard cattle bawling and barging their way through the wood in his direction and backed his horse off the creek bank to allow them passage.

Gilbert and his men trailed behind the cattle, being herded by the downcast townsmen, who prodded the four-legged creatures none too gently. They had become Scottish beeves.

The sacks of grain were thrown across the haunches of the larger cattle and the goats and sheep walked behind. Keeping the chickens for their supper, Edward sent twelve men to take the cattle and wheat back into Scotland while he and the rest of his men continued to visit Cumberland towns that had reneged on their promised monthly 'rents'.

Just beyond the border of Scotland relay troops were stationed to escort the goods and livestock on to Stirling, where King Robert had enough men to protect his investment and keep Mowbray of Stirling Castle wondering what was coming next.

Giles d'Argentan

ApRil, 23rd 1314
BERWICK CASTLE

The castle at Berwick had become a busy place, the center of English activity as the king prepared to relieve Castle Stirling. In preparation for that imminent day, Aymer de Valence had been sent to Berwick to see to the gathering of various materials in support of the grand army Edward was amassing in the south. Those knights who had little else to accomplish meandered toward the castle at Berwick knowing they at least would have a place to sleep and meals served to them that they didn't have to purchase or hunt in the wilds.

Sir Giles d'Argentan and his twenty newly outfitted knights, along with their entourage, had gone north to Berwick far ahead of the June First deadline decreed by Edward, ostensibly to hone their long neglected skills of battle before the June showdown. They lamented that Edward had assembled such an overwhelming array, making the outcome foregone. No matter, it was an opportunity for a knight to earn his keep, to improve his fortunes, to have an adventure.

As they rode through the gateway of the wall that surrounded the town the inhabitants, quite accustomed to the sight of traveling knights arriving, paid little attention. The knights and their squires proceeded straight to the castle gate and requested admittance. They were met by the porter who, upon finding out their identities, sent a runner to the keep to ask whether the formidable troop of men could enter.

The great square stone keep and its courtyard stood high above their heads on top of a steep slope, much of which had been formed by the River Tweed below. Its high curtain wall at the base of the knoll had nine towers built into the wall at various key points along its perimeter. Inside many buildings for various castle activities and sleeping quarters of the crown dotted the slope.

The runner, a squire of fourteen years, was breathing heavily as he entered the great hall of the castle and told the steward the name of 'd'Argentan'. The steward's eyes widened and a smile played across his lips at the very thought of entertaining the famous Sir Giles of the Holy Wars.

"Fetch them here, quickly!" spat the steward with a wave of his hand.

The youth ran back down the road toward the castle wall gate.

Sitting behind a large table, the Earl of Pembroke was listening to a merchant hawking his wares when the steward hurriedly came to him and whispered of the arrival of Sir Giles and his company.

"Return tomorrow!" said Pembroke as he abruptly stood. All the waiting merchants stood as well, bowed almost in unison, and departed the room as quickly as they could gracefully manage. The earl turned to the castle steward and uncharacteristically ordered that a feast be prepared for the evening's repast. At last! He would have someone to talk to besides the damned boring merchants and his beautiful, young, exotic-looking Spanish wife, Marie. The merchants cared only for their profits, and she only for her domestic duties, and neither cared about great and exciting events from far-flung regions of the world.

If only her mind were as pleasing as her beauty, he thought as he scurried to the apartment he shared with her in the castle.

The crowd in the hall was excited and thick, though Sir Giles was far from the only knight who had arrived in the past several weeks expecting to be treated like royalty. Most knights, even some with august reputations, were housed in the homes of the townspeople, but Sir Giles and his company would be housed in one of the barracks on the castle grounds and paid much attention.

From the minute they got the word of the feast the kitchen folk were harried, having to abandon their planned menu for the day to start on the banquet. It would be far from the usual affair, which had been planned in advance, but there would be plenty to eat nevertheless. The chickens' and pheasants' necks were rung, and the birds were plucked and cleaned and cooked to perfection, to be served with breads baked and served with rich, pungent sauces to top it all. But it was the desserts selection, puddings, pies, and those delicate little pastries, first prepared to please the queen, that would cause even these Scottish outlands to appear to be in the midst of the finest of French cuisines.

The Earl of Pembroke sat at the head table in the middle of the dais, Sir Giles to his right. The earl's pretty wife, Marie, sat at one of the women's tables on the main floor, but was not all that pleased about her position. She found Sir Giles an attractive and interesting man, and closer to her own age. With pleasure, Lord Aymer took note of the numerous times she casually tossed her head and looked in his direction, not realizing that her eye was not exactly on him, but his table companion.

"How is it, Sir Giles," asked Pembroke, "that you were snatched while in the Holy Land?"

Giles paused before giving an answer as he finished chewing a portion of a pheasant joint. He was also trying to think of a way to put the situation in as innocent a light as possible before he spoke.

"'Twas pure ill luck... I say to you Lord Aymer. We were helping some ladies in dire distress when we were overtaken by a pack of dark and evil villains who claimed to be Greek Christians. They raided the house in which we were staying and captured us all individually, whilst we had no way of defending ourselves."

"You had not your weapons?" he asked.

"They were... off our... not close at hand, Milord."

Pembroke smiled in understanding. "You were naked?" he leapt.

"Takin' to bathin' we were," replied Giles knowing his interests had been compromised but having the honor of not wanting to tell a lie to any man.

"Takened a bath myself, once or twice," said Aymer before he drained his cup of its wine and pounded it on the table in a demand for more.

Giles smiled slightly to the viceroy thinking he may just keep his secret.

As the evening wore on, the feasting tapered off somewhat to those tiny and delicate, deceptively light pastries. Those who could suffer to hold no more excused themselves to slip unobtrusively to private places or to the guarde robe to purge themselves of the feast, in one way or another.

At the end of the evening, it was the exotic Marie who retired to the solar before her husband. He arrived somewhat later and far more intoxicated than was she. Seeing that his wife had already retired and was asleep, he desired for her to waken and so slapped her hard on her well-rounded rump that was tucked under the heavy covers.

She screamed at the sudden swat and flung herself around to face her attacker. The candles in the room were few and the light dim, but she realized it was Pembroke and knew his wants and her duty.

Aymer awkwardly and with drunken difficulty pulled off his trews as she wiped sleep from her eyes and stretched. Unbound, her dark hair fell across her pillow and down onto her shoulders. Unbound, her young breasts besotted her older husband beyond even what drink could manage.

"Sir Giles, he was very cordial this evening," she said sitting up higher on the pillow.

"Sir Giles?" he said, "I reckon you're right... he was ...cordial."

"Un hombre muy guapo. ¿sí?" she said casually, lapsing, as she occasionally did, into her native language.

"What?"

"Oh, um... he is very pretty, yes?" she asked with her Spanish accent.

"Didn't note that," said Pembroke frowning.

"I have made... a memory of it," said she.

"What in the goddamned hell for?" he blurted loudly as his jealous nature overwhelmed his calm inebriated state.

Her eyes widened in surprise and fear.

"I only say he is... handsome... a handsome man!" she stumbled with the English.

"I'll tell you about goddamn 'handsome' Sir Giles!" he said, trying to demean the man. "Had the great hero and his men not stopped off on their way to Rhodes at a roadside whorehouse to get some swivin' done," he gasped as he pulled the second boot from his foot and dropped it in the straw on the wooden floor, "...they would never have been caught with their britches about their ankles, and they wouldn't have been settin' in that damn prison all that time, awaitin' for some poor whoreson to ransom 'em!"

The secret was out.

Marie blinked. "He is with woman?" she asked, meekly trying to mask a tinge of anticipated excitement in her voice.

"Move over and I'll show you what he did with 'woman'!" commanded Pembroke abruptly as he threw up the blankets and rolled his substantial bulk in next to her.

The conversation portion of the evening was ended.

April 27th 1314
Oldfleet Castle
Curran Peninsula, Ireland

Oldfleet Castle belonged to the Bissette family who had built it many years earlier. It had been passed down for several generations and was being constantly improved, turning it from the original wooden structure to a strong stone one.

In its solar Richard de Burgh paced back and forth. The Red Earl's host had provided him with the very best he had to offer, but even though he appreciated the luxury and comfort, Richard had his hopeful meeting uppermost on his mind.

Within the third hour of the morning he saw across the watery horizon exactly what he was looking for: the black sails of the three galleys wavered and lingered on the open water for most of an hour before they came closer and inspected the coast once again, making sure there were no secret traps in which they might get snared.

"Bring her about!" shouted the captain to his crew, then cupped his hands to shout orders to lay offshore to the two other galleys.

The sails were furled and the oarsmen swung the craft around so that it was headed into the bay. Near the shore the vessel was anchored and the esquif was put over the side. One oarsman and three knights wearing light armor and swords accompanied a fourth man. They rowed to the shore and all but the oarsman, who stayed with the esquif made their way up the rough and rocky hillside to the castle overlooking the bay.

Richard left the solar to greet his guest and his party at the small gatehouse on the far side of the bailey.

"John!" he hailed, smiling broadly.

"I hope this meeting is worth my trip," said John, frowning as he usually did.

"I can assure ye it will be worth yer while, since ye are Admiral of the Western Fleet," said Richard.

The two retired to the solar for a private conversation while the admiral's men-at-arms were allowed to go to the great hall for a meal. Richard had wine, bread and joints of meat sent to the solar so the two of them could converse without interruption.

Five hundred pounds silver money was laid out on the large table to the side. John opened the small glass window and looked out to sea contemplating his options. He thought it was very suspicious, and worried that the Red Earl was setting a trap for him, knowing Robert de Brus hated him as much as he hated the Brus.

Having asked several hypothetical questions of the earl and received hypothetical answers, he had no doubt that the arrangement would aid the Scots king. He hated that, but he certainly liked the pile of silver being offered. As they finished eating he wavered back and forth as to whether or not he would enter the conspiracy against King Edward. At last he agreed and ordered his men up to the solar to gather up the silver and put it into the esquif to be rowed back to the galley with him.

Richard of Ulster watched as John of Lorn hauled his loot into his galley, hoisted his esquif onto the deck and set sail to join with his other two galleys and disappear south into the afternoon shadows of the Irish Sea toward Dublin.

Richard was apprehensive about the hot tempered and spoiled John keeping his mouth shut, but he hoped that the small fortune the admiral was just handed would be enough to assure that he would at least try.

Marie de Saint Pol
Countess of Pembroke

APRIL 28th 1314
CASTLE BERWICK

The morning clouds moved swiftly in the fresh spring air. The sun was bright and unusually warm for April. The grass had begun to sprout forth in tufts, brilliant green against the sere dead grasses of the winter now past, and birds of various colors were flitting and singing and nesting in anticipation of bringing forth a new generation of their kind.

Sir Giles d'Argentan lay casually on the side of the slope within the curtain wall, enjoying the warm sun upon his face. Totally unlike the hot, straight overhead sun of some eastern Mediterranean states, the Berwick sun shone gently on the skin, barely warmer than the skin itself. He had forgotten much about his home island while he had been in the Holy Land.

The castle rose behind and above him, and the roofs of the barracks buildings were below him, but it was neither of those things that arrested his eyes and wit. His interest carried him far out to sea as he thought of things past and wondered about things that were about to be. His seemingly endless days in the dungeon at Salonika had taught him to appreciate life even more than had the realities of battle.

As he lay daydreaming, the wife of Aymer de Valence whether by design or by coincidence, walked along the hillside and saw him contemplating the nature of man and of earth.

"Good day to you, Señor," said she in her charming Spanish accent.

Giles turned and with one hand shaded his eyes against the sun so that he might see her. When he realized who she was, he jumped to his feet, losing his balance and nearly tumbling downhill, but he regained himself, if not his composure. Somewhat flushed he came to her side quickly, bowed appropriately for the wife of the earl, and kissed her extended hand.

"Please grant me pardon, Milady. I saw you not before you spoke."

"Sir Giles, I am seeking a chance meeting," said she smiling, her dark brown eyes looking into his light gray ones, "but one did not occur. Therefore I am take it in my own hands."

Giles had no answer for such an abrupt and frank woman but said, "Chance meeting, Gracious Lady?"

"!Si! I have marriage to the viceroy, the Earl of Pembroke," she cheerfully explained.

"Yes, I know who you are, Milady," he said. "Your beauty, of which I've seen mere glimpses since arriving, is difficult to ignore."

She smiled sweetly and he was glad his meditations had been interrupted. She was delightful company for an hour or so as they sat on a low stone wall and talked. The view of the North Sea was pleasant enough, but neither of them made a single reference to it, speaking instead of many ordinary subjects that were important to their lives. And then she stood and extended her hand to him as she made her goodbyes. He formally bowed and kissed her hand again, and watched her as she walked back up the hill and out of sight.

Sir Giles had never met such a captivating, beautiful woman in all his worldly travels and she never met such a magnificent, brave and gentle knight in her small world of the privileged nobility. He was thoroughly smitten, in spite of the inconvenience of her marriage. She had been equally charmed by him.

• •

It was three days later that d'Argentan was summoned to the great hall where Pembroke had been holding court, trying to be Solomonic concerning several local quarrels over land boundaries and the prosecution of two petty criminals who had been caught stealing chickens. The thieves promised they would never steal another chicken and Pembroke made sure they would make good on their promise by hanging them in the town square with a crowd of chicken owners cheering them on into the hereafter.

Sir Giles entered to find Pembroke alone with his cleric scribe trying to sort out what Pembroke had deemed as his rule of law.

"I don't give a goddamn how you put it to paper... just write it!" he growled taking a long sip from his cup of spirits.

The nervous cleric lost the notion of trying to find out exactly what was said, and more importantly, what Pembroke meant to say.

Giles came to the front of the sitting Pembroke and stood erect.

Sir Aymer looked up when he realized someone stood before him. Seeing that his visitor was Sir Giles, he bluntly waved his hand for the frustrated cleric to leave, at which the man was most happy to oblige, taking all his paraphernalia in the hopes that he might yet make sense of the earl's pronouncements.

"Sir Giles!" Aymer fairly shouted, so that his voice echoed off the hall's welkin. "Come, join me in a cup of spirits!"

"You wanted to speak to me, My Lord Pembroke?" said Giles.

Aymer pointed to the stool before him on the opposite side of the table and poured another cup, full to the brim with the fiery drink, and sloshed it grandly as he set it in front of Sir Giles.

The knight sipped only a small amount and returned the cup to the table. Aymer drank more. Giles sipped more.

"I wanted to speak to you about my wife," started Aymer, giving Giles a sudden jolt.

"I can assure you, Viceroy that I..." said Giles straightforwardly, but Pembroke cut him short.

"I aim not to accuse anyone. I don't give a pig's eye for that!" he growled.

Giles was puzzled. "Then what, Milord?"

"It's good... uh... between us, my wife and me," said Pembroke fishing for words to express what he really wanted to say in his drunkenness. "What I mean to say is that she is... we are..." he lost what he wanted to say.

"I understand," said Giles not understanding.

"Prob'ly don't," blurted Pembroke drinking deeply again, "I know she talked with ye on the hillside the other day... and I know that's all ye done. But, she hain't gone on talkin' her usual nonsense about things like... why do I wear holes in the seat of my linens and how lazy the servants are and ... and... and *all* that shit for three days now! And she's more agreeable to me in..." he stopped and eyed d'Argentan before blurting, "...if ye must know, she's more agreeable in my bed!"

Sir Giles nodded but felt a trifle stupid for the conversation even happening. Wanting a quick escape before his embarrassment grew greater he asked, "I understand, Milord. Are we done?"

"Hell no!" said Pembroke standing. "In the battle..." and there fell a long pause in his statement as he thought of what it was he wanted to say.

"Yes, Milord?" said the knight trying to fill in for him.

Pembroke cleared his throat and continued. "You and me... the two of us, are to be at the left and right sides of the king!"

"And the king's household knights?"

"Under command of Sir Edmund de Mauley, the king's seneschal," explained Aymer and at his behest the men drank again.

"You have had the *only* successful battle against the Brus, Viceroy. Will you not have your own division?"

"No, don't want it," said Aymer bluntly, shaking his head.

"But this can be your time of *glory*, Milord!" said Giles enthusiastically. "You are the hero of Methven!"

"Methven, harrumph!" mumbled Aymer thoughtfully.

"The only true battle against the Brus?" said Giles wondering why Pembroke wasn't bragging to high heavens about it. "It is a triumph, Milord!"

"'Twas no triumph! I, uh..." stammered Pembroke, "... I won alright, but I did so without honor!"

"You, Milord, behaved dishonorably in battle?" asked the knight, incredulous at what was being admitted.

"I led the Brus to believe we would not arrive for the battle until morning, and attacked him before vespers!"

"You lied at Methven?!"

"To save my arse," confessed Pembroke solemnly, and he sat there mentally reliving the slaughter until he recovered himself. "I have never told anyone before. You must tell nobody what I have said... but Brus had no chance when we fell upon him."

"That's how you won?"

The earl nodded somberly, "The damned Scots are fierce little whoresons. I wanted nothin' to do with the whole mess. I asked for none of this... this... *glory*... but old Edward kept pushin' me for more. Always more. At every success he wanted another, bigger, success. I never knew whether I was more fearful of King Robert or King Edward!"

"Why do you speak these dark thoughts to me?" asked Giles, seeing the man's regret. "You hardly know me."

"You are third best knight in Christendom," answered Aymer with a shrug. "I'm lesser."

"Third best is still next best *after* the Brus," said d'Argentan. "Besides, such things have little meaning on a battlefield."

"Reckon the Brus thinks of it that way?" asked Pembroke staring directly at the knight across the table. While he watched, Giles magically made himself into two men! Aymer shut one eye to see which was the real Sir Giles, then traded eyes to see if the other orb could see him better. His vision was just as bad one way as the other.

"I think King Robert thinks of it, not at all," answered Giles.

Lord Aymer was struck silent for a long sobering moment before repeating his orders. "Nevertheless, you will ride the king's dexter, I his sinister.

"And we are expected to protect the king in the midst of the battle?" asked Sir Giles folding his arms at his chest.

"I don't trust another livin' soul with the task," confided the viceroy.

"I don't understand?"

"Too many enemies at court," he replied in a whisper, "Some I hain't goin' to let trick me again."

"I fear I have been in the Holy Land far too long," said Sir Giles, referring to his ignorance of the current politics in London.

"Then I will tell you... keep a close eye on the men of Lancaster, Arundel, Surrey, and Warwick. Enemies all of the crown."

"Enemies... all?"

"I ken what your thinkin'," said Pembroke, "Ought to take some heads in England 'fore comin' all the way to Scotland to take others."

Sir Giles sighed and nodded agreement of a sort.

"You'll not betray my confession?" asked Pembroke then feeling he had been heard by a priest in a most uncharacteristic weakened moment.

"I shall never betray your secret, Milord," promised Giles.

• •

Two days and a night later, the moon was a mere sliver in the deep black sky. Sir Giles was sound asleep in his private quarters after a hard day's training when he was suddenly awakened by a tender kiss upon his lips.

He opened his eyes to see only shadows of Marie's beautiful face and strained to see more detail, but the faint light coming in the open window was insufficient.

She didn't speak but ran her fingers through his long hair, and he reached to touch hers. Her very scent excited him.

She breathed deeply and his long held passion was no longer restrainable as his hands went from her hair, down her slender neck and across her bare breasts.

She bit him gently and playfully on the chest and he threw back his covers and drew her near to him.

• •

As the comforting arms of the night gave way to the harsh reality of the dawn she quietly slipped from his gentle embrace, kissed his sleeping lips for the last time, and whispered her most grateful and sad goodbye.

MAY 2nd 1314
DUNDEE

The war drums and bagpipes assaulted Robert's ears as his men from Dundee gathered about him, preparing to go to the battle. The king climbed aboard his great near-white destrier, and the crowd of townspeople cheered ceaselessly. Behind him Andrew carried the king's banner, followed by Nigel, riding his palfrey gelding. The one hundred and fifty-three men from around Dundee, who had either volunteered or were conscripted, joined in the parade behind.

The men's eclectic weapons were a tribute to their agrarian lifestyle and to Robert's daring challenge to turn them into a cohesive fighting force within mere weeks.

Despite King Edward's threats of economic ruin for the various countries on the continent that sold weapons and armor to the Scots, their multitude of pack animals were heavily laden. In addition, the women traveling with the men of Dundee led more mules carrying victuals and cookware and other necessities. A rear guard of ten warriors on horses brought up the back. The town of Dundee, standing for an independent Scotland, was off to war and their spirits ran high.

Having gone to the mountains to retrieve the horses being raised there for the king, Sir Robert Boyd, Christina, and her highlanders would return with them to the battlefield at Stirling. The horses' training and conditioning had been accomplished in the rough environment to ensure their easy footing over almost any kind of terrain. Being a hybrid blend of Hackneys and Arabians, the horses could not carry great weight like the Friesians or Belgians, but were quick and nimble.

Christina's daughter, Christian, had been taken to her nearby kin for safekeeping with instructions that if the battle went badly against the Scots, no one was ever to know that she was also the daughter of Robert the Brus.

The battle thus began... not the first blood slashed from the enemy's flesh, but the first step was taken toward a point of destiny.

One hundred and six heavy wagons, each with the four horses necessary to pull them, and one hundred and ten eight-ox carts and their teams, temporarily confiscated on order of King Edward, were to be in London on the twenty-first day of May for the purpose of hauling victuals for the immense English army. Tons of barley and oats, sides of bacon, mutton off the hoof, dried fish, and a great deal of wine with which to wash it all down, were to be transported north. War supplies, pole axes, twelve-foot lances for the knights and spear-like lances for the infantry, short swords, maces, daggers, shields and bucklers, longbows with thousands of arrows, and crossbows with thousands of bolts, all headed to Scotland.

Then there were quilted coats to be worn under the armor, gloves, coifs and shirts of chain mail, and helmets for the infantry, not to mention four thousand horseshoes and the sixty-four thousand nails to attach them to the draft animals and to the pampered destriers of the knights, the lesser horses belonging to the knights, their squires and troopers. And there were multiple tons of hay and a variety of corns for the horses.

The king also put an embargo on the export of all foodstuffs from the country so that he would have plenty to feed his army of twenty-five hundred fully armored knights and twenty thousand infantry, and more thousands of cooks, stock handlers, hostlers, and other support people from not only England but from Wales and Ireland as well.

Taking advantage of the lengthy summer days, Edward expected the army to move forward about three-fourths of the day, every day, and figured it would take twelve such days to travel the three hundred-fifty mile distance, at the rate of twenty-eight or more miles per day. He expected to arrive on the twelfth of June at Wark-on-Tweed, where his rendezvous with the remainder of his military force was to take place.

With his seneschal, his household knights, and the remainder of his retinue, Edward planned to ride ahead of the long train, thus avoiding its slow and cumbersome pace. The entourages of the earls of Gloucester and Hereford, who traveled with him, would keep to his pace by virtue of His Majesty's wishes.

His loyal right arm, Hetherington, was unceremoniously shuffled to a lesser position within the administration suddenly, while the father of the young Hugh le Despenser, also named Hugh, became more important to Edward as a close advisor.

Hugh de Ross,
Earl of Ross

CDAY 7ch 1314
BANNOK

On a day of sometimes misting and sometimes pouring rain that clouded the day on the Balquhiderock carse, Robert, Edward, and Gilbert trudged the bottomland with its endless watery pows honeycombing the entire flat, from Pelstream Burn on its north to Bannok Burn on its south. The burns fed the carse's pows, or pools, and the fast running Pelstream emptied into the larger Bannok Burn very near the point of highest tide. From there Bannok Burn snaked its way northeasterly to flow into the River Forth less than two miles away.

"This land will ne'er be suitable for a pitched battle," said Robert as their three horses slogged knee deep through the grass and ankle deep in the mire.

"I figured we should fight them in the Torwood, anyway," said Edward.

"Reckon?" said Robert.

"Got a plan, I have," he replied. "D'ye want to hear it?"

"Let's go to Torwood," said Robert, "Show me how ye would do it!"

Edward was elated that his brother was giving such attention to his idea. It was not that Robert didn't give him his due, and even conceded to his plans at times when marginality wore heavily on his instincts and common sense.

Robert had visited the region three times within the past year, playing scenarios in his mind over and over again. He had already considered Torwood as a battleground and disposed of the thought, but perhaps Edward just might have a notion he had not contemplated.

The three men trotted their horses south, crossing the Bannok Burn at Milton Ford where the water, which came to their horse's bellies, ran swift and muddied from the heavy rain.

"If we did engage them in Torwood," said Robert, "this would be our only escape route."

"We can escape anywhere," argued Edward, kicking his horse to climb the bank on the far side of the stream.

Robert and Gilbert followed.

The rain had let up and the men rode on, reaching the hill of the Torwood and making mental notes of everything they saw. It had many attributes that would suit them very well. The trees were dense enough without being too dense. The large outcrops of rocks throughout reminded Robert of Glen Trool where they had hidden behind the rocks as the English were stealing toward them. The scattered boulders and outcrops had certainly been their allies that day.

On the south end of the wood the land sloped downward toward a gentle valley below.

"Yonder's where Mowbray wants us to do battle," said Robert, pointing downhill. There they could see the route followed by the old Roman road as it cut through the valley to the castle.

"How ye reckon that?" asked Edward incensed.

"Yonder's six leagues," answered Robert.

"I don't understand," Gilbert admitted.

"No reason ye should, but Edward ought to."

"Six leagues from Castle Stirlin' is the distance Mowbray set when we made the truce," said Edward, seething at the thought of it.

"We cannot possibly fight them yon," said Gilbert, a look of distress on his face.

"Ne'ertheless, if Edward's forces get within that range, the castle is considered... relieved," said Robert.

"How about somewhere beyond, such as Linlithgow?" asked Gilbert, "Or e'en Falkirk?"

The men could almost see Falkirk, even in the misty rain.

"Tweren't too good for Wallace," said Robert, "We have the same kind of army that Wallace had when went against the same kind of army Edward'll be a'comin' with," Robert inferred there could be the same result.

The men were silent. The wind blew shivers on them.

"So, how would ye see the battle bein' fought in the Torwood,

Edward?" asked Robert, facing his brother.

The earl wheeled his horse toward the edge of the trees and his brother. "I would hold the high ground with the schiltroms and let the English have to charge uphill against us... and if it goes bad for us, we can fight from the trees.

"That's better than flat land, would ye not say, Sire?" queried Gilbert.

"Certainly better than flat land," agreed Robert. "Might e'en be a possible plan."

Edward smiled slightly, withholding a broader one until he was sure his brother was sincere about considering his notion. Robert sat for a long while looking down on the scene where so much would be decided in just about six weeks. If they held the high ground as Edward suggested, the advantage would be theirs. But the English would be so many!

"One single throw of the dice," he remarked as he thought it through. "A single throw and ye win... or ye lose... and our years of struggle and the many who have given their lives to our freedom will have been for naught."

"A'right, goddamn it!" shouted Edward. "'Tis my fault! There! I've admitted it! Are ye happy?!" his anger exploded. In a rage he kicked his horse to an immediate gallop and rode around the hill and toward the ford across the burn. He would hie back to New Park where he had some strong spirits to help him forget.

His brother and Gilbert silently watched him descend into the broad valley, but Robert also closely observed his route.

"See how easily Edward gets to New Park?" he asked.

"Aye," said Gilbert.

"If we were encamped in Torwood, surrounded, we'd be," said Robert.

The sun was beginning to show through the thinning clouds.

• •

Earl Edward got to New Park in a hurry. He was drenched to the bone as he climbed from his horse and threw the reins to Baldred. Catching the reins, the squire immediately started cooling down the wet and sweaty horse. Edward hastened to his lean-to and dropped to his knees inside it. Taking his kit off a peg he started pawing through his possessions looking for a wine bottle he had refilled with stronger spirits. Finding it, he pulled the cork and took a great swig of the contents.

He felt the warmth spread down his gullet and leave behind a trail of fire on his tongue and throat. It wouldn't be long before he could forget Robert's constant harping about his agreement with Mowbray. He looked at the bottle and gauged its contents at just about as much as it would take to get him staggering, if not immobile.

But then, Robert would come and find him. And he would be angry about Edward's drinking.

"Bring my horse!" he suddenly shouted and crawled out of his tent with the bottle in his hand. "Baldred!" he shouted, "… my horse!"

The young squire, just pulling the saddle from Edward's horse, sighed and rolled his eyes skyward. *Of course, Sire! Right away, Sire! Never mind that the poor beast is worn out and in need of a rest and a rubdown, Sire!* the servant grumbled within his own mind.

He re-cinched the girth and calmed the objecting animal with his soothing voice and manner. "I hate to do this to ye, but he is yer liege lord, same as mine," he whispered in the stallion's ear.

"My horse, Baldred!" shouted the earl.

"Aye, Milord," said the squire, and he led the mount to Edward and handed him the reins.

"Give me a blanket!" he demanded of the youth.

Baldred yanked the fairly dry blanket from under the canvas where he had secreted it for himself, and willingly gave it to the knight hoping it would get the abusive earl from his area sooner. Having known Edward for so long a time, he could feel a black mood coming on in the earl's wit and wanted to be well away when it took full effect.

Edward saw Gilbert and Robert riding down the long slope toward camp. They were the two he certainly didn't want to see at that moment and gored his horse's ribs with his spurs. The abused horse jumped, and galloped out of the camp, over the hill, and into the glen, where the woods could cover a multitude of indulgences.

• •

By late afternoon the sun was glazed over with high thin clouds and the temperature had moderated, creating a warm spring day. Sleeping soundly, Edward lay upon the blanket, shielded from the sun except for lambent lights and shadows cast by the newly sprouted leaves. He had emptied the bottle entirely and was blissfully unaware that he yet remained in the world.

It was in that condition that Thomas Randolph happened upon him while leading a large host of highlanders toward the battlefield. He spotted the earl's horse grazing at the edge of the lea and came to investigate. It didn't take him long to find the snoring earl.

Randolph did not come down from atop his horse. "Is this the Edward Brus I know?" he said in a booming voice loud enough to wake Edward, and the dead.

Edward's eyes opened slightly, thinking he had been dreaming. He wondered where he was before he opened his eyes a bit more and saw Randolph looking down at him. His memory returned as to where he was and why he was there.

"Lord Edward, arise I say," teased Thomas, thundering like the voice of doom.

Edward rose from his prone position to a seated one and quickly grabbed the sides of his head with both hands, for it suddenly felt as if his crown were about to split in twain. His first thought was, *Well, Edward, ye made another great mistake!* And he slowly lowered himself backward to his former position, still holding his head.

Thomas recognized the symptoms and sighed. "Damn ye, Edward!"

"Ye whoreson! What air ye doin' here awatchin' me? Ain't ye nothin' better to be doin'? Polishin' Robert's halo, or writin' the gospel accordin' to Saint Robert, or somethin'?" asked Edward sarcastically as he agonizingly rolled on the blanket and moaned softly.

Thomas threw him a waterskin. "Drink some o' this," he said coldly. "When was the last time ye et?"

"Don't remember."

"I have some bread and some goat cheese. Will ye eat some?" Thomas started to open his kit, fastened behind his saddle.

"God! No!"

"Might help yer stomach," said Thomas, but Edward shook his head.

"Ye alone?" asked Edward as he rolled over and got up on all fours.

"The retinue is behind me less than a quarter of a mile," said Thomas.

"Retinue?"

"A great host from the high lands," explained Thomas, smiling because he had a secret.

"Who might they be?" asked Edward, struggling to his feet, his whole being suffering with the pounding pain in his head. Finally he stood almost erect, before he bent down and braced himself with his hands against his knees.

"Sir William Wiseman for one," teased Thomas.

"Ye bring the bishop, did ye?" asked Edward.

"Aye, I did. Ye know, maybe the bishop can marry ye," he added.

"What the goddamned hell ye speakin' of?" growled bleary-eyed Edward, tiring of the game. He picked up the blanket and folded it roughly as he and Thomas continued to talk.

"Why... yer fiancée, Isabella, is here to see to yer well bein', ye lucky sod!" further teased Thomas.

"Isabella?"

"Aye."

"Which Isabella?"

"Isabella de Ross," said Thomas, "Came with her brothers, she did... to see ye."

"Oh shit!" exclaimed Edward as he gathered the reins of his still saddled horse in his hands and started walking while he looked about for an escape route.

Thomas followed Edward for a few steps and said, "Ye'll ne'er guess the *bad* news I have for ye."

The Earl of Carrick looked back through bloodshot eyes at his nephew. The followers could be heard coming through the woods. "Weren't that already the bad news?"

"Not the worst," chided Thomas as he shook his head.

"Ye're enjoyin' this hain't ye?" asked Edward growing angry.

"Just bringin' ye the news from the north, Uncle," he responded.

"A'right, what's the other bad news?" he asked.

"Isabella de Strathbogie, yer other fiancée," he said, "Expects ye to marry her!"

Edward's eyes widened. "I ne'er promised to marry that wildcat!"

Randolph's entourage was drawing closer. Edward could hear them talking to each other, so he got on his horse and was about to give it a kick when Thomas said, "She wants ye to marry her 'cause she's birthed ye a son!"

"Ye're a lyin' bastard!" said Edward, wheeling his horse and heading in any direction except New Park, where Isabella of Ross and his good friends Walter and Hugh Ross, brothers of Isabella, were headed. Randolph watched his flight until he was well gone, and turned to see Isabella's brother heading his way.

Earl Hugh rode up to Thomas and asked, "Was that not Lord Edward, yonder, Lord Randolph?"

"Can't say," said Thomas, chuckling in his beard.

Isabella de Ross

CDAY 11th 1314
SCIRLING

Though the sun was shining brightly, there was a chill moving out
of the north. Thomas Randolph had brought about eight hundred men-
at-arms with him from the highlands, along with Sir William Wiseman,
Bishop David de Murray of Moray, and the Frasers, Sir Alexander and
his temperamental brother Simon, on whom Randolph kept a wary eye
at every turn.

Thomas had personally visited Sir Reginald Cheyne and found him
willing to fight for King Robert, having recently come to his peace, but the
older knight was in ill health and sent the fifteen knights and a number of
yeomen he would have brought. They were among the eight hundred.

The house of Ross also traveled with Randolph. Lord Hugh, who had
inherited the earldom upon the recent death of his father, his younger
brother Walter, who had been the closest of friends with Edward Brus,
and their sister Isabella of Ross, who would be married to Lord Edward,
if he would but agree to a date.

Robert personally welcomed the knights and many of the ordinary
soldiers beside whom he had earlier fought. The new arrivals went about
setting up tents inside New Park and were issued victuals to cook at their
own fires with the admonition, "Don't burn the woods down!"

"Ye seen Edward?" asked Robert joining Thomas and sitting beside
him on a rock ledge.

"Nae, hide nor hair," quipped Thomas taking another bite of a twist
of dried beef.

"Hope English spies hain't got him," Robert added, a tinge of worry in his voice.

"I would nae worry, Uncle. More likely 'twas Isabella got him," said Thomas.

"I think not. She has asked of his whereabouts a number of times in the last three days," said Robert, pulling one of the dried meat sticks from Thomas's offered pouch. Biting down hard, he twisted it to separate an edible piece from the hardened strip.

"Somethin' ye ought to know, Rob," said Thomas looking across the valley.

"'Bout Edward?" asked the king, chewing the leathery meat.

"Aye, 'bout Edward," he replied. "Strathbogie's sister Isabella has birthed his child."

Robert stopped chewing for moment. This was not welcome news. "What is she goin' to do?"

"Well, I don't know *why*... but she wants to marry him," said Thomas, biting and twisting his stick of meat again.

"Damn! He's already promised to Isabella of Ross that they will marry," said the king. "One way or the other, we'll be losin' a friend."

"A friend with men we may be needin'," Thomas replied.

"No wonder Edward ran away," said Robert in frustration at Edward's cowardice in the face of this circumstance.

"Heard her brother David is mighty upset," said Thomas.

"He was supposed to arrive here with his men on the morrow," said the king.

"Get set for a fight if he does," warned Thomas.

"Damn it, Thomas, why had ye not told me this bit of news afore?"

"Figured it was Edward's bit of news to tell," he replied quietly.

"Aye, rightly so. Problem is, instead of tellin' me, he ran off!" Robert spat the tough wad of beef onto the ground and standing up, was silent for a moment before he said, "Even so, we must tend to our purpose for bein' here." He turned back to Thomas.

"Put Wiseman and Fraser in charge of a troop," he instructed, "and take those first few hovels at Stirlin' village..."

"And not let anybody in or out," said Thomas, guessing the stratagem.

"Aye," said Robert, "Somebody's always lurkin' about tryin' to count our people or weapons, or some such," he said in an aggravated tone. "They think we don't know they're there."

"A'right if I send both those Fraser lads?" said Thomas. Robert nodded.

"Be sure ye tell Simon to stay out of trouble," said the king knowing the man's penchant for fist fighting.

"He'd be the first little bastard I'd throw in if there was a fight," said Thomas, remembering the long ago brawl he had with Simon.

Thomas left and gathered up Wiseman and the Frasers and the other lads to go on a daylight raiding party on the village of Stirling. The forty-odd warriors swooped into the village, already accustomed to sudden violence. The villagers scattered like chickens with the fox upon them, fleeing as fast as they could up the hill toward the castle, as they had done the previous year when the Scots began their siege commanded by Edward Brus.

This time, the attackers were more restrictive in their aims, and took only the houses farthest from the castle gate. Going through them to make sure all were gone, they found something they hadn't expected, and soon the Earl of Moray had ridden at a gallop back to the New Park.

"My King!" shouted Thomas urgently as he reined up his mount in the camp.

Hearing the intensity in his voice, Robert rushed from the trees where he had been planning the building of some houses on the back side of Cockshot Hill.

"What?!" he shouted. Thomas rode to him.

"Sire, 'Tis Lord Edward!"

"Edward?"

"He's in the village."

"Is he alive?" asked Robert not being able to contain his fear any longer.

"Aye," said Thomas, "alive he is!" he dismounted, "...but gravely drunk, Rob!"

Robert sighed deeply. "If the English had known he was there," growled Robert, "he'd be in the dungeon of Stirlin' keep... or dead!" He whistled for Andrew to saddle his horse so he could see the condition of his brother first hand.

As quickly as the horse was delivered to the king he got aboard and rode downhill as fast as the horse could fly. Baron Fraser directed him once he got near the hovel wherein laid his brother, and he entered immediately, finding Edward lying on a too-small pallet.

"What have ye done for him?!" asked Robert, trying to judge his brother's condition.

Alexander shrugged, "Nothin' My King," he said blinking owlishly.

"Help me get him to his feet!" said Robert, taking one of Edward's arms over his own large shoulders.

Alexander got the unconscious man's other arm.

"Call yer brother!" said Robert.

Simon Fraser came in and the three of them raised Edward to his feet. They dragged him into the sunshine and tried dousing him with cold water. He came to himself somewhat, but it was not sustained. They took him back inside and laid him on the bed and Robert drew a bench to his side and sat watching and listening until the late dark when he said to a soldier, "Take those full jugs out and smash them on the rocks!"

Thomas arrived to see if his uncle wanted supper, but Robert could not eat. Patting him on the shoulder in solace, Thomas took another bench on the opposite wall of the one-room house to sit the sad vigil.

The next morning Edward growled loudly for the alcohol his body craved. "Ye'll ne'er again get a drop of spirits from me!" Robert growled back at him. Edward's eyes tried to focus as he took a swing at Robert, but it was an errant blow easily dodged, and he received a smack from his brother, who hoped vainly for some sense to return.

They tried to get him to drink some water, but he sipped a little and pushed it away. He threw up what he had taken and went back to sleep. Far into the afternoon he awoke and wept, sorrowful for having gotten drunk. Yet he wanted more spirits, saying, "I'll ne'er drink another drop, if ye'll just give me one good swig more!"

Robert sternly refused him any alcohol, but Thomas gave him more water, which he drank and it quickly it came back. Then he passed from craving to sleep.

"Ye takin' him out of the fight?" asked Thomas.

"We'll see when he comes to himself. Ye get some sleep if ye can."

The next morning they were suddenly awakened by a loud banshee's scream from Edward, who was fighting his blanket and struggling to rise, scaring the daylights out of both men. Robert calmed him down after a bit and Edward wept more.

The king gave his brother a small cup of water which he slowly managed to down, and shortly he drank more. Sitting on the edge of the bed, he cried like a child who had fallen and hurt himself. "I swear to ye, I will ne'er drink again," he promised the king.

"If I see ye another time like this, Brother," Robert said through clenched teeth, "ne'er again will ye be more than one of my squires, I give ye my oath!" Robert closed his eyes and sighed, wanting everything for Edward and fearing everything was killing him.

Robert said not another word but in his heart he was just happy Edward yet lived.

When he returned to camp Edward went through periods of violent shaking and wrapped himself tightly in a blanket to try to control them. He would kill himself, but having second thoughts knew the English would be quick enough to accomplish that for him at midsummer.

Walter of Ross suddenly stood over him and said, "Got yerself messed up, I see."

"Feels like it," replied Edward, trembling terribly.

"Ne'er forget that we're here to fight, and maybe kill a few English!" he tried to encourage his friend. "Got big brother with me and... ye'll like this..."

"What," interrupted Edward attempting to smile.

"... Isabella's here," he finished, grinning.

Edward's eyes went dour. "Why ye bring her along to a war, damn yer hide!"

Walter's mouth lost its smile. "'Cause she wanted to see ye and take care of ye!"

"I don't need takin' care of!" insisted Edward. "Keep her away from me!" He dropped his head to his knees, drawn up before him. "Sorry, Walter," he sobbed, "I am a dead man."

"Still talkin' with the spirits in yer head," said Walter kneeling to be on the same level with his friend.

"Ye rest for a few days, then come see Isabella," he advised. "I'll tell her ye've been a'scoutin' and are worn to the bone."

Edward, his hands perched on his closed knees, his forehead atop his interlocked fingers, agreed that he would and Walter left him to his agonies.

"Douglas! It's Douglas!" yelled the picket, creating a momentary flurry of excitement in the camp.

"Hope that was loud enough for Mowbray to hear," said Robert under his breath.

"Now, why should Mowbray be a'feared of The Douglas?" Thomas joined the king.

"Didn't know ye had such keen ears, Nephew," said Robert, keeping an eye on the valley to the backside of Cockshot Hill. "He fears James because James has the name of bein' bloody and unyieldin' in his purpose."

"He is fierce, alright, but not ruthless… well seldom, anyway."

"Perhaps, but I'm glad we fight on the same side," gainsaid Robert.

"Yer army is comin', Rob," said Thomas. Though he said nothing, seeing the Scots army gathering with all their disparate families, joining to fight a common foe instead of each other, was a sight that always filled him with wonder, if not exactly pride.

"Not near enough," sighed Robert, "But, glad I am for ev'ry one."

"Ach, ye still have o'er a month," said Thomas, "Plenty of time for more to come."

"We need 'em to be here in time to be trained," replied Robert.

"Trained?" asked Thomas surprised. "Huh! I ne'er knew a Scot who couldn't fight!"

"As a man, aye. As a family, aye. Scots fight, and fight well. But we'll not win against the vast host we'll see at midsummer if we cannot fight as an *army* and work *together!*" Robert turned and looked directly at Thomas, "Else they'll fall before the English like wheat before the scythe… and their great courage won't save them."

Thomas' countenance grew as serious as Robert's thoughts and he began to muse about the English being so numerous. "How many ye reckon we have here so far," asked Thomas.

"Don't know," the king replied. "Reckon… two thousand with what Douglas is bringin'." He watched more of The Douglas' men comin' into the camp and said, suddenly, "Tell ye what I want, Nephew. Get Douglas and his men o'er to the Torwood and have them set up their camp there," ordered the king.

"To keep away from pryin' eyes at the castle?" Thomas surmised.

"Aye," replied the king.

• •

After James "The Black" Douglas, his four hundred twenty-three men, and at least fifty camp followers of every style had moved to the Torwood and were officially greeted by the king and the other earls who had already arrived, Robert ordered four beeves be slaughtered and the meat distributed among the ranks of his army. The people needed a good and hearty meal to let them know that they would not be subject to the added hardship of starvation while fighting for their freedom.

Around the various campfires, stories were told of how men fought in earlier battles with the Douglas, the Brus or the Randolph. Some tales of their brave deeds varied from veteran to veteran as they related the events, sometimes because their experiences actually were different, and sometimes so the tellers became the heroes in their own eyes. Tales of Perth, Roxburgh, and Edinburgh were prevalent in stories of recent derring-do.

As it neared darkness and the fires were falling into ashes, a man approached Robert as he sat on his haunches listening to one of the stories from a man who was with Randolph at Edinburgh. At the end of the tale the fellow stepped up to the king and asked, "Ye recollect me, Sire?"

Robert said without hesitation, "Sim!"

"Aye, My King," said the white bearded smith as he smiled in delight.

"Ye got my pike heads and caltrops, smith?"

"Ev'ry one ye wanted, My King," he said bowing.

"Let me see them," said Robert as he stood from his hunker.

The two men walked to where stood a long string of over a dozen mules, heavily loaded with gunnysacks in large, woven wicker panniers, one on each side, lashed across their backs. The tired animals stoically looked at them as they drew near.

Robert hefted one of the cumbrous sacks, was astonished at its weight enough to ask, "Ye load these sacks on yer mules, Sim?"

"Aye, ev'ry one."

"Alone?"

"Aye." The much smaller man began pulling sacks from the top of the heap in the pannier. "The weight don't bother me much, My King. I'm as used to workin' with heavy iron and steel as ye are. Maybe more," he cackled. "But ye must be careful wi' these caltrops, 'cause if ye don't load 'em right, there is goin' to be points stickin' out. Mules get poked, they stop in their tracks and won't go 'til ye fix it! And no matter what ye do, some points come through the baskets... a wagon's what I need, if there was a road to run it on, My King."

The whole time he talked he was lifting sacks from the pack mule's load, and by the time he stopped he had unloaded the basket on one side. The king had nearly unloaded its opposite.

Robert dropped the last sack on the ground with a loud clank. "How'd ye get these animals to move under that much weight?" asked Robert truly amazed.

"'Tain't too much for a mule to carry, My King. Not near so much as yer horse carries... you or one o' yer knights with yer armor an' all, not near," he replied with a toothy grin.

Robert opened the first sack, carefully put his hand in, and smiled as he brought a perfectly formed caltrop from the sack. He threw the hand-sized four-pronged spike on the ground. A single point stood straight upward. He picked it up and threw it once more. Again a single point stood upright. "Perfect star-thistle," he remarked, "Pity the horse or the soldier that sets foot to it."

Sim gave a little laugh, pleased that the king praised his work. "Got four hundred pike heads in the sacks on them other mules," he said.

The smith called two men, who seemed to be curious, over to help with the unloading. The three men heaved the dead weight from the backs of the other mules and dropped them on the ground.

Sim opened one of the sacks and pulled an iron pike head out. The metal was still darkened from the fires and many hammer blows that forged it. It was somewhat flat and over a foot and a half long, the forward half being teardrop shaped tapering to a sharp point. The butt end had been flattened and curled around, large enough to receive the long handle that it would need. The curled iron had a hole on either side through which an iron nail would be driven, turning a wooden shaft into a deadly pike or spear.

With him, Sim had brought along four hundred and twenty-five forged nails that would be driven through the wood and bradded on the backside. The pike head seemed strong enough not to bend, even when hitting hardened leather armor.

Robert ran his fingers over the killing blade envisioning the charging horses and men that were bound to come to his land and be impaled on this fine bit of blacksmithing. The king's specifications had been followed very closely.

"Ye help me plant the caltrops in a couple of days?" suddenly asked Robert.

"Help any way I possible can," said Sim of the Leadhouse.

"Stayin' for the fight?" asked Robert off-handedly.

"Chance to kill English, hain't it?" Sim smiled.

"I Reckon."

• •

The cock crowed at the first instance of light from the yet unrisen sun.

"Damned rooster!" complained Thomas, his eyes barely slits, "I'll have him for supper tonight. Then I can sleep later tomorrow!"

A second rooster began to crow.

"Have two, I will," he complained more as he got to his feet and exited the tent. The dew drenched everything and the wind was as still as death. A dense fog lay about in the valley. Thomas stretched every muscle and scratched everything he had, watched in amusement by a woman some twenty feet away, who was stoking her nearly extinguished fire. She blew on the embers and brought them back to life after which she added increasing amounts of dry wood chips. Soon there was a flare and she added heavier kindling.

One fire started for the morning is all we need, thought Thomas, and he headed over the hill where a ditch had been dug as a latrine.

On his way back he drew a ration of dried beef from the quartermaster and put it in his pocket for later. His task today was to get the more or less two thousand Scots out of New Park on Cockshot Hill and set up to survive in Torwood.

He woke the constable, Sir Gilbert, but it was a while before he was as lively as Thomas. Still, he was ambulatory despite his having to wipe the sleep from his eyes.

Thomas got a hunting horn from a picket coming off duty and bestirred everyone at almost the same instant.

• •

"Good morrow, James!" said the king as he came to Douglas.

"Aye, Sire," said Douglas, and he stood from kneeling at his fire.

Robert took him aside, out of earshot of others, and spoke to him. "Ye brought a great deal of supplies with ye," he started.

"Compliments of the English at Roxburgh, Robbie," he said bowing slightly as much in jest as in reverence.

"I want to reserve some of these victuals... for later," said Robert hesitating to spell out the real reason.

"In case we have to hie out of here?" guessed Douglas.

Robert smiled at the young knight's astuteness. "In case."

"Where ye figurin' would be a safe place?" asked Douglas.

Robert pointed down the valley. "D'ye know of Cambuskenneth Abbey?

"Aye. East of Castle Stirlin', across the bridge o'er the River Forth.

Around to the right side in sort of in a crook of the river."

"That's it. The abbot there will receive ye well. Take one out of ev'ry ten of the foodstuffs ye brought and cache it there," instructed the king. "Pick men to help ye, have them keep it secret. And go quickly while the fog is thickest."

Douglas nodded as he ate.

"Sir William of Airth will be waitin' at the abbey with men of his own." Said Robert.

Douglas nodded and picked up his meal, continuing to eat as he touched men on the shoulder to do his bidding.

• •

Thomas told the few that were gathered nearby that their task for the day was to move the entire camp from New Park to the Torwood. They were to tell others so that the whole of the camp would know what was to happen. In a short while, the men and women of the Army of Brus packed their belongings and headed downhill where they turned south on the old Roman road toward Milton Ford, then uphill again to the Torwood. They were a ragged looking gang, with no group discipline, but of self-determination they had plenty.

Robert watched them proceed under Thomas' command. He wanted to see how his nephew conducted the task of handling folk.

With his knights and other troops and a retinue of squires and villeins, Sir Giles led the procession of the first load of supplies to the castle in Wark. He had only to follow the south side of the River Tweed to find his way. He had requested the duty in order to remove himself from Berwick and temptation in the desirable form of the beautiful Marie, wife of Lord Pembroke, with whom he had already sullied his conscience, and endangered his knightly soul.

The men could easily see the castle from the village of Coldstream before they got to Wark. It had an impressive gray stone facade that stood high on a hill overlooking the River Tweed and the village that hovered in its shadow. Wark Castle was one of the various strongholds along the border from which many raids on Scotland had been launched, thus it was a natural choice for King Edward to make in preparation for his grand invasion as well.

The castle was one large keep rising as much as five stories with a crenellated wall at the top. It was surrounded by a very high curtain wall, pinning the bailey securely within its bounds.

As Giles came into the town he saw a large group of farmers and local landowners arguing with the sheriff of Wark and being held back by guards brandishing menacing spears. Giles stopped his train to hear the cause of the complaint.

"Yonder's our goods," said one farmer angrily, having spotted the wagon train loaded with supplies. Appearing to be threatened, Giles and his knights hastily pulled their weapons and aligned themselves before the wains in a formidable wall to confront the agitated men. They spaced their destriers just far enough apart to allow maximum clearance in case they had to swing their swords and axes. The squires and troopers drew their weapons as well but remained with the wains.

Giles held his sword high for silence but the hubbub of the crowd continued. He then pushed his destrier into the closest men so that they could not possibly have ignored him. Cursing and shouting, the men began to pull at his horse's trappings and at d'Argentan's legs and stirrups. He kicked at one man, catching him squarely on the side of his face and knocking him down.

"Next man to lay hand upon me will lose it!" shouted Giles. He was willing to do whatever it would take to perform his duty, and he would not suffer being put upon by a pack of petulant rowdies. In spite of his dire warning, one man grabbed at the knight's foot and with one deft stroke, his dare was paid for by the loss of his hand. The man screamed loudly and, grabbing his arm above the red mass that had been his wrist, he ran from the crowd slinging blood on all who were standing close to his pathway. None other doubted at that point that the knights would protect the wains.

One man moved out to the front of the crowd and the others shirked from him, not knowing what the berserk knights might do to one who actually would deliver demands on the king's fearsome warriors.

"What do you want?" asked Giles, harshly, thus recognizing the man as a spokesperson for the group.

"We have always paid our taxes to the crown, Sire. Even so, we have not received the crown's protection in any measure. First it was the Brus who raided all our lands demanding his share of what we have not, then it was Lord Pembroke, who choked us to near death. As we speak, our kine rest in the bailey of the castle yon. Ye no doubt carry our corn in your wains and our families are hungry!" argued the man.

Giles listened to all the man had to say but replied, "My understanding is that these grains are paid for."

"I were ever paid for mine," said one in the crowd.

"Nor was I," shouted another, and several others agreed.

Giles raised the weapon that had commandeered a great deal of respect by lopping the hand to the dirt. "ORDER!" he shouted loudly and the demonstrators obeyed.

"Please," pleaded the man, "for the sake of our families!"

Sir Giles was sympathetic, but his duty outweighed his own feelings. He stood his ground and said, "Ye men know that we are but the beginning of a great army heading this way, led by King Edward himself, who will again seize Scotland for England!" The crowd cheered. "I am sure the king will return to you ten times what Lord Pembroke has taken to feed his great army, which is fighting for all of us!"

"He never came to chase the Brus from our doors!" yelled one from the crowd.

The crowd cheered in support of the statement.

"We hain't heard from him in years!" yelled another heckler.

"I am Sir Giles d'Argentan, and I pledge to you that you will get returned that which has been taken from you and more, when King Edward has succeeded in killin' the Brus and all of his unholy followers! As you can see by our presence, it will be soon!"

"Sir Giles, you seem to be a man of honor," said the spokesperson. "We shall be here when you are done killin' the Brus!"

"Then open the way and let us pass without further trouble!" demanded Giles keeping his sword handy for those who did not agree.

The sheriff and his men began pushing against the farmers, encouraging them to break up and go away.

Giles called his wagoners and wain drivers to move on toward the castle. They cracked their whips and the large oxen lumbered forward, up the hill and into the bailey of the castle.

The farmers were not totally satisfied with their answer but did not want to personally feel the sting of the knights' blades, and so went home, grumbling among themselves over how much they might have won, and how much they had definitely lost.

"One here…" said Robert as he dropped a stone on the ground. "One here…" he repeated after Andrew handed him another stone and he dropped it on the ground. The fifteen men stood with shovels in their hands and Sim stood a few feet away with his hefty gunnysacks.

"I want holes dug everywhere there lays a stone that I dropped," instructed Robert. "I want them on that side of the road, he pointed behind him, "and on this side of the road." He pointed in both directions from where he stood.

He took a shovel from one of the men and pushed into the mushy ground, and had quickly dug a shallow hole about a foot in diameter.

"My King, let me dig the first!" said Andrew. Robert handed him the shovel.

Young Nigel Brus watched his father with fascination.

Andrew dug straight down to a depth of about three feet and called Sim over to hammer a sharpened stick into the bottom of the hole. He then took his knife and reshaped the stick's fine sharp point.

"When ye're done, spread the dirt around and throw twigs and grass and some such over the holes, then Sim will set the caltrops hither and yon to suit his fancy," said Robert for the benefit of those who had not prepared such 'pots' or laid star-thistle traps before.

The men nodded their heads and Sim said with good humor, "We laid a'plenty ere this day, My King."

Robert smiled and, with the two boys, walked away to let the men set to work. The traps were to be laid thickly on both sides of the road north of the Bannok Burn, but south of New Park. They were spread widely throughout the open ground and some even into the bog. The road itself, however, was not to be disturbed.

"Didn't we do about the same thing at Loudoun Hill?" asked Andrew as the men walked toward the road. Their long strides kept Nigel almost at a trot to stay close behind them.

"We didn't have star thistles at Loudoun," said Robert as the three walked up the hill on the Roman road through the Torwood. "But ye are right in that we then had the same problem we now have… more field than we could defend. With his great army, Edward could easily overrun us and slay us all on such an open ground. So, we must make the battlefield smaller, as we did at Loudoun with the ditches that forced Lord Pembroke's army to meet us head to head at the place of our choosin'."

"I think I understand," said Andrew.

Nigel was taking it all in.

• •

One thousand two hundred and nine additional pike heads arrived from various blacksmiths who either brought or sent their commissioned quantity of pike heads to Torwood, and there were others who were yet expected with their lots. The new pikes were distributed among the men who had arrived and settled in. Their instructions were for each man to cut a stout staff exactly fourteen feet in length and affix his pike head to one end with the supplied nail. Each pike would have to be as well made as its owner would be willing to bet his life on in battle.

Fletchers by the score came to Stirling with quivers filled with as many arrows as they could carry, and were immediately put to work making more. When they ran low on feathers, the geese were eaten for supper. Some jokes were made around the cook fires but nobody complained about having to eat the roasted birds.

MacKie drew a ration of arrows and put up a tight twist of hay so none of the precious shafts would be harmed while he and his archers honed their skills.

Robert was expecting several hundred archers from the Ettrick Forest in Selkirk to come within a few days' time. They had never before agreed to fight with Robert as a full regiment of archers, but had done so in twos and threes and even dozens. They had fought alongside of the master bowmen MacKie and his brother Murdoch, the latter having been killed at the battle of Dunstaffnage, six years earlier.

• •

The Roman road, marvel of engineering that it was, had been built more than a thousand years earlier by the hard work of Roman soldiers. It originated at Edinburgh in the east and made its way through the rolling Scottish countryside to Stirling and thence north across the Forth. It being the only road capable of holding numerous heavily laden wains and wagons, and thousands of horses and other animals, not to mention the tens of thousands of men on foot, King Robert knew that the English would have to traverse that route to Stirling. As the road went through Torwood, consideration had been given to another of Edward's plans, to lay an ambuscade for the advancing English knights as the vanguard made its way toward the battlefield.

Per the plan, the archers would hide behind the trees and rocks through the wood, ready to release flight after flight of arrows at close range, killing both men and horses. In the plan's second phase, the armored knights would be pulled off their destriers with billhooks. Once flat on the ground, they would be vulnerable to foot soldiers moving in and killing them with their daggers and short swords.

Unable to effectively maneuver their horses between the trees and around the large boulders for which the wood was famous, the survivors would have little recourse for revenge.

Robert rejected the plan because the battle hardened English knights would never be so foolish as to travel in easily attacked clusters, and it was too fraught with risk, even for him. He could not see a victory, but a mere "bee sting" of an irritant, from such a venture.

"I'll tell you my wit, Brother," said Robert as he and Edward sat in the warm breeze at the southern end of the wood overlooking the peaceful valley between them and Stirling.

Edward moaned lowly. His rejection was quite complete at Robert's negative reaction to his last proposal.

"Yer plot was what would have been... expected," explained Robert. "But it has usefulness to us for just that reason. It will be a simple matter to make them think that is what we intend to do."

"I don't understand that, but I will do as I promised," said Edward, "and follow yer orders to the last."

"Speakin' of promises," said Robert, "Have ye talked with Isabella?"

"Which Isabella?"

"Ross."

"Aye." Edward spoke quietly, his head down and his gaze averted.

"Does she not as yet know about yer child by Strathbogie's sister?" asked Robert, and Edward shook his head. "Ye'll have to tell her, Laddie," said Robert speaking more like a father than an older brother.

"I will tell her!" said Edward belligerently.

Robert looked at Edward sternly. "Ye must look to the truth, Edward!" After no response for a spell he decided to move on to another issue.

"Spies tell me that the English plan to launch their invasion into Scotland across the Tweed at Wark."

"Not Berwick?" asked Edward, grateful for the change of subject.

"The supplies are bein' moved from Berwick to Wark, so we're thinkin' that will be the place," said Robert, adding, "Thomas is sendin' out two parties in the mornin', one to Berwick, the other to Wark. There will be twelve men in each party to be sent back to us two at a time with reports on the progress of King Edward's long train of wagons and men-at-arms."

Edward sighed deeply, "I am sorry I brought all this upon ye, Brother."

"We are not yet ended, Edward."

Thomas hurriedly came to the resting brothers and said, "See the rider below headin' fast for Stirlin'?"

Robert and Edward looked northward up the glen and saw the rider.

"He English?" asked Robert.

"Might be from the castle, My King," said Thomas.

"Spy?" he asked.

"Reckon," opined Thomas. "He's on one of our horses. Ye want me to go after him?"

"What ye reckon they think they know that's worth tellin'," said Robert standing for a better look.

"That we await 'em in Torwood," said Thomas. "Might know about the pots ye dug today." As they watched the figure grow smaller in the distance Robert smiled.

"Perfect!" said the king.

Marmaduke de Tweng

CDAY 26ch 1314
CDORPETH, NORThUCDBERLAND

Traveling ahead of his slow moving baggage train, King Edward, his two participating earls, his seneschal, the household knights, several high ranking barons, each noble's contingent of knights, the knights' gangs of squires, scullions and varlets, and a renowned English poet took their time in wending their way to Wark-on-Tweed. They had progressed somewhat north of London, but were far from their destination where they were scheduled to arrive no later than the fifteenth of June.

In middle Northumberland the Wansbeck Valley, named after the Wansbeck River and nestled in the protective crook of that stream, was the tiny and charming hamlet of Morpeth, no doubt named for the extended moors north of the village. The ruins of an old motte and bailey castle overshadowed the few houses like a nurturing mother, her vacant windows like cold eyes warning outsiders to beware.

At the foot of the castle mount by mid-afternoon, King Edward decided to camp for the night. The king's tent was large and gaudily designed with wide bands of red and white canvas, easily enough to make sails for ten of His Majesty's largest galleys. There were perimeter tents serving as kitchen and servants' areas, and even a small tent with a bench set over a deep hole for use as the king's garderobe. This paraphernalia alone required two large wains for its transport.

Three large wains held nothing but those things the king needed for a comfortable journey, including a large oak table, elegant china, ornate silver settings and utensils, and a variety of French wines and domestic ales packed in heavy layers of straw to prevent breakage on the rough roads. Bedsteads, feather mattresses, pillows, bedclothes, embroidered tapestries, his clothing and jewelry, his armor, his horses' armor and trappings, and a dozen other appurtenances, all were necessary for the comfort and resplendence of His Majesty on the road and in the field.

Then there were the things that were for his attendance to the affairs of state, his desk, his writing pens, his parchments, his privy seal, his sealing wax, his sand shaker, his ink wells.

The pots, pans, bowls and other things necessary for the king's food preparation accompanied the cooks and cooks' helpers on a separate wain. It was Whitsun and a feast was in order. Thus, at the moment it was decided they were stopped for the night, the cooks put their helpers to setting up the kitchen while they went to the villagers and bartered for fresh fish and vegetables, milk and butter, to delight the king's palate with their culinary arts.

Lamb and dove were the king's choices of menu items for the evening, and two lambs and forty doves were slaughtered and prepared for the evening's repast, replete with breads, cheeses, sauces, honey, appetizers, desserts, and of course, wines. Both earls and other select guests were to dine with the king, whilst the other contingents were told to prepare their feasts as they would have them.

The earls and barons busied themselves with setting up their own tents and putting their entourages in order before dressing to attend the king's fete.

Once his tents were up and livable, Edward went to prepare himself for the evening's gala dinner.

"This will please your sensibilities, My Brother," said Edward as he laid a long bejeweled chain around the neck and upon the chest of Baron Sir Hugh le Despenser, the younger.

Hugh fingered the overworked and expensive piece on his chest and was pleased with how his monarch fawned over him. There were other men of his age that were seen holding hands with the king, but it was Hugh for whom he constantly asked. Perhaps it was that Sir Hugh's father was now the king's closest advisor. Or, perhaps his father had the position because the king was fascinated with young Hugh.

"Thank you for allowin' me to wear it, Your Majesty, it is lovely," gushed Hugh.

"It is yours," said Edward putting his hand affectionately on Hugh's sparsely bearded cheek.

Hugh smiled not knowing what to say.

"It belonged to dear brother Piers... once," he said wistfully. Then smiled.

"Thank you, again, Your Majesty," said Hugh in a low almost reverent tone that excited the king's conceit.

"I have a surprise in store for you this evening, Brother," said Edward primping in a mirror.

Hugh's eyes widened in anticipation and his heart pounded with excitement. "After the gift of this necklace, what could be more of a surprise?" baited Sir Hugh, fishing for a hint.

"The necklace is but a sentimental bauble," said Edward, "...nothin' compared to..." he stopped, purposefully and smiled, meaning Hugh would have to wait.

In the forward part of the tent, separated by a canvas wall, they heard Sir Humphrey de Bohun and his nephew enter, ready for the feast.

"We must see to our guests, Sir Hugh," said the king, in a particularly sociable mood.

The late evening sun came through the open west side of the tent, rolled up and pinned to catch the light breeze mitigating the heat of the day. The king emerged around the canvas wall with his grand robes of red and purple, his many jewels virtually dancing in the sunlight. The outer perimeter of the tent was festooned with elegantly dressed knights serving as guards. Their colorful tabards added gaiety to the festive occasion.

The Earl of Hereford, Sir Humphrey de Bohun, hung his shield of blue and white with six gold lions rampant in front of his tent. Having readily confessed to his part in the slaying of Piers Gaveston, Sir Humphrey retained his position as Constable of England after begging his brother-in-law, King Edward, to return it to him. The king did so, and by way of a prearranged agreement, forgave him.

Henry de Bohun, nephew to the earl, was a well-trained but hot-blooded, sometimes ill-tempered, young knight who was bound to be an asset on any battlefield where rage motivated or propelled the action. The de Bohuns had their own contingent of knights, squires, troopers, and cooks, wagoners, and grooms for the many destriers and lesser horses. They had set their tents and their own pickets forty yards away from the king's handful of tents to allow him the privacy that he demanded.

"Your Majesty," said Humphrey bowing low to greet the king.

His nephew bowed as well, with his own like greeting.

"Well come to my castle of the hinterlands, My Lords," said the king, ushering them to a table of wines. "Choose whatever you wish to drink."

The cupbearer was showing the various wines to the men when Sir Marmaduke de Tweng was announced and entered. The king turned to see the older knight come swaggering through the door. He had the dubious honor of having distinguishing himself at the first battle of Stirling, in which the English were routed by Sir William Wallace.

Close on the heels of Sir Marmaduke was an even older knight, Sir Thomas Berkeley, who had no more entourage with him than his son, Maurice, and two grandsons, the latter pair not invited to the king's feast. Sir Marmaduke had for many years, ever since his youth, campaigned with Edward's father at every season until the king's death.

Within a moment arrived Sir Gilbert le Clare, Earl of Gloucester, who entered talking to his stepfather, Sir Raoul de Monthermer. Both men had their yellow tabards graced with three large red chevrons. Gilbert was the son of King Edward's sister, Joan of Acre, by her first husband, also Gilbert le Clare, nearly three decades senior to her. When he died, she secretly married Raoul who had been squire to her late husband. Her father, the first King Edward, had Raoul put into prison for marrying Joan without his consent, but soon released him and granted him the title Earl of Gloucester in right of his wife.

Raoul held the title until his wife died, and released it to young Gilbert when he had grown to manhood and was able to take on the duties and responsibilities expected of him. It was Sir Raoul who warned Lord Robert de Brus that the old Edward was coming for him, thereby saving his life eight years earlier.

Sir Edmund de Mauley, the king's seneschal, next entered the tent, and lastly to come to the Whitsun feast was the renowned poet Robert Baston, a member of the Carmelite order, who wrote poetry in Latin.

There was but one long large table at which all the attendees would be seated on the same side, and Edward took his place in the center chair. To his right, respectively sat Lord Humphrey de Bohun, Earl of Hereford, Sir Henry de Bohun, Sir Thomas Berkeley, Sir Maurice Berkeley, and on the end, Sir Edmund de Mauley. To the king's left sat Sir Hugh le Despenser the younger, Lord Gilbert le Clare, Earl of Gloucester, Sir Raoul de Monthermer, Sir Marmaduke de Tweng, and finally, Friar Baston.

Being the only attending cleric, Friar Baston was asked to bless the meal. This he did in a drawn out manner by blessing each of the animals that had given their lives to make the feast possible, and so forth. And of course he uttered it in Latin. Sir Marmaduke sat during the prayer calmly drinking his wine by the gulps and pouring more.

Without warning the blessing was cut short by the impatient king. The friar decided to have brief prayers in the future over anything short of the king's death, when he felt he could drone on for as long as his heart desired. He positioned his chair around the corner on the end of the table so he could see along its length and keep an eye on his dinner companions.

The harper, sitting behind the table of men, began to play softly.

The squires and pages brought the first course to the sideboards on a large ornate platter that was set before the king. It was roast lamprey with tiny carved wooden daggers protruding from every slice of the eel.

Edward was surprised at the unusual dish.

Hugh spoke up, "I hope this is to the likin' of my liege. It was my notion," he confessed.

"Of course I like it," said Edward wanting to please Hugh.

The harper's music took on a tone of drama.

"'Tis a representation of the rebel Robert de Brus," said Hugh, "... impaled on your blades, Your Majesty."

Edward laughed heartily, an infrequent occurrence, and so did everyone sitting except Sir Marmaduke, who drank his laugh.

Edward picked up a slice in the middle by the dagger handle and swished it through the sauce surrounded the eel and had a goodly bite of it straightway. Hugh watched the king chew to see his pleasure.

"Exquisite!" pronounced the king. "Brus has been devoured!"

Two more plates of lamprey were served, one at either end of the table to be shared, while more wine was poured and platters of thinly sliced, roasted and jellied pike were served. As the shared plate of eel got to the Friar he refused to partake stating that the Carmelite order does not eat meat.

"The Friar," announced Edward proudly, "is writin' an epic poem in honor of our victory at Stirlin'!" He led a round of polite applause as the friar beamed, albeit humbly.

"And if we have the battle at... say... Edinburgh, will you write a poem about that as well?" Edward teased.

The table laughed, more from the wine than the wit.

The poet lifted his wine glass to the king in merry response.

"This will be the battle of all battles!" bragged Edward effusively, taking another slice of the lamprey. "He shall write about whatever happens... and we shall forever be glorified in history!" Then he deliberately put his teeth around a slice of eel and took the whole of it into his mouth at once. His jaws were packed as he chewed for the sake of demonstration for the table.

"Will you be writin' a line in your poem about the king eatin' eel?" asked Sir Hugh with a broad grin.

"Of course," lied the Friar smiling cherubically.

"Who in hell is fixed to read such a poem?" blurted Sir Marmaduke.

The table was quiet for a moment.

"Well?..." he asked gruffly before adding another question, "None of you can read Latin, can you?"

The king finished his lamprey demonstration as quickly as he could choke it down so he could speak, "It matters not!"

The table went quiet once again.

"Scholars in far off days will know, by study, what we are about to do," said Edward.

"We are to be famous among scholars?" argued Marmaduke with a drunken air of pseudo wisdom.

The Earl of Hereford stood to speak, "My Good Sir, you are bold to a fault, but of discretion you have none!"

"Who cares a fig for that philosophy?" bantered Marmaduke, biting another slice of the eel that he had wrapped in a slice of the jellied pike. The juices squeezed between his fingers and drooled from the corners of his maw.

"I will not have you speak poorly of my king's choice to document the battle," came back Hereford.

The harper played on as if fomenting the argument.

Edward at last stood saying, "My Lords, My Lords, we are here on a *happy* occasion. Need we bicker among ourselves on small matters?"

Marmaduke figured he was speaking from his goblet, said no more and focused his attention on the rings of spilled wine his silver wine cup made over and over on the table.

Hereford, not wanting to continue the argument as well, said, "Every man here well admires your past adventures in the name of the crown, Milord!"

Marmaduke nodded approval though still gritting his teeth. *Been muzzled, I have,* he thought.

The harper hushed his strings.

The squires brought in the second course and presented the first offering to the king.

"Dove," announced the king as the roasted bird glistened on the glazed ceramic plate.

The table reacted as they were served their portion of doves. The squires knelt across the table from the nobles and proceeded to serve the steaming birds.

A plate of disjointed dove was slid under the nose of the Friar, who smelled the succulent flesh bathed in rich sauce served atop the upper crust of bread and could not refuse. He began to eat.

"Are we to expect the Scots to attack us as we come to battle, Your Majesty?" asked Sir Gilbert, "or shall they hide above the Forth as they did four years ago?"

The king, searching for an answer where there was none, hesitated. He delayed by making much of eating the tiny, luscious birds, pulling bits of meat from the sauce with his fingers and using the damask table cloth to cleanse them. Then he spoke, "We can expect *any* sort of roguery from that devil."

"I should like to get my sword on him!" said Sir Henry pounding the table to punctuate his level of desire.

Up jumped Gloucester drawing his blade; "*I* shall be the one to put this very dagger through the bastard's heart!" he avowed.

Sir Henry pushed his large chair over as he quickly stood. It fell on the heavy Persian rugs strewn about as ground cover. He glared at Gilbert. Gilbert was slightly more mannerly with his chair but kept his dagger pointed upward.

"Do you think an earl can take a knight?" yelled Henry drawing his own dagger.

"Sounds almost as if you are playing... chess, Cousin," quipped Gilbert.

"I play at nothin'," growled Henry.

The king was enjoying the conflict in a way, but wanting both knights beside him on the field of battle, jumped to his feet between the two men saying sternly, "Easy, Cousins, "We are not yet upon the field! Why spill good English blood for no gain?"

The two men glared at each other as Sir Humphrey stood to talk sense to his nephew and Sir Raoul stood before Gilbert. Eventually both men were appeased by those with more common sense for the moment and each returned to his seat. However, young Gilbert could not quite let it go saying, "We shall see who is the most valuable to the family when we are faced with the real enemy!"

Young Henry jumped to his feet once again but was coaxed back to his chair by Hereford with a whispered, "Show him on the battlefield, Henry, where it will certainly not be called... murder."

Having no axe to grind and no one he wanted to impress, Raoul remained quiet after the incident. He thought of his dead wife and wanted only to do his duty to her Plantagenet family and go home. He had little use war or for the men who waged it.

"I thought the Friar couldn't eat meat," said Hugh in all innocence, staring to the end of the table at the slightly rotund man licking every finger that held a drop of anything on it. The glazed plate in front of him was as clean as if a hungry dog had done it.

All of the supper guests looked at the small poet, and he in turn looked up at the others as if he had been completely alone in his breaking of vows and yet was caught by the rest of the world.

"I never said I didn't *like* dove, did I?" said the sheepish man, his face glowing red.

The table laughed at the cleric's foible.

Bowls of water and hand towels were set before each man and the emptied lamprey and pike platters, and the trenchers were taken away.

The two lambs were brought to the sideboards and garnished with green leaves and cooked apples. The first serving platter was placed on the table across from the king and the servitor went to one knee and deftly sliced into a hind leg, putting a thin piece on a plate and setting it in front of the king. He then waited for the king to approve the taste.

The harper played softly as the carver squires plied their skills on the carcasses. The inner steam escaped to waft into everyone's nostrils, and more wine was poured for each of the men, satisfied they had shown the king the depth of their devotion to his cause.

The king seemed to be pleased with all except Sir Marmaduke, who showed his more brusque side. Sir Thomas Berkeley, who was simply enjoying the fact that he was alive and active, was a puzzle to Edward, who thought the old warrior should have stayed at home in his garden instead of going off to war with his children. Yet, he was once a great supporter of Edward's father, and thus warranted a certain earned respect.

During the third course the king thought it a good time to spring his promised surprise on Sir Hugh.

"Are you ready for your fortune to be revealed?" asked Edward, his beard glistening with droplets of sauces and fats oozed from the meats.

Hugh smiled coyly, wiping his mouth on the towel, "As you will it, Your Majesty."

The king stood and clanged two silver cups together so that his dinner guests would cease their chatter and pay him attention.

"I would here make an announcement, My Lords and honored guests," he started. "As you know, there are many of our lands and estates in Scotland that will need to have new liege lords in attendance, once we have routed those who currently pretend at holdin' them."

The men laughed at the denigration of the Scottish lords, and straightened up to pay closer attention, each hoping the king would mention his name.

"One of these is the northern high lands of Moray, which requires a new earl," said the king, knowing he was rousing the hopes of almost every one of his guests. He enjoyed the moment of anticipation to its fullest, looking each contender in the eyes before announcing his decision.

"It is upon Sir Hugh le Despenser and his father that I jointly bestow the noble title of Earl of Moray!"

The men clapped resignedly, but were not happy with his choice.

Sir Hugh was flabbergasted and sunk his face into the crook of his arm and cried with joy.

"What does he know about bein' earl?" whispered Sir Gilbert to his stepfather.

"Mind your manners, Boy!" advised Raoul quietly. "There is much land in Scotland to be parceled out. Besides which, one might note, it is not yet his to divide."

Gilbert seethed that he had not been given a Scottish earldom and swore to himself that he would show the king that he too was certainly worthy of such favor.

Lord Bohun and his nephew were likewise inspired to show their flair when the time was ripe and the eye of the king was upon them.

The king observed that Gilbert was vexed at his choosing and that the Earl of Hereford and his nephew were the first to leave at the end of the evening, and knew he had been successful in his ploy to rile his knights to a high anger and riskier warring.

Alexander Fraser
of Touchfraser

ϿϠAЧ 29cb 1314
ϿΟRϢΟΟϿ

Beneath the trees Thomas Randolph stood, and before him the men from the highlands of Moray. Alongside the earl were Bishop David de Murray of Moray, and Alexander and Simon Fraser. William Wiseman sat on a downed log to the rear of the leaders, honing his knife to a fine edge and listening to what was being said.

Thomas took a spear from one of the men closest to him and held it aloft. "All ye men fixin' to fight on foot have a spear?"

The men roared "Aye!"

"I ken some among ye are good at ridin' a horse," said Thomas, "I need ye to go stand yonder if ye figure ye do better on the back of a horse."

"Can't ride what ye hain't got!" yelled a man from the middle of the bevy of Scots.

"But, can ye ride?" shouted Thomas.

"Ride anythin' with hair!" came the reply, at which his companions burst out laughing heartily.

"Then ride ye will," shouted Thomas, "What's yer name?"

"Johnson!"

"Wait yon." He pointed to his right. "Any more?"

From among the assemblage of about twelve hundred, a good hundred men slowly drifted and stood with Johnson.

"That all?" Thomas asked.

Twenty or more came forward and joined the potential equestrian group. Thomas surmised he had pulled all from the crowd who could sit a horse, and turned to the others. He inspected the pole of the pike he yet held and noticed that the long wooden shaft had not been trimmed smoothly. Some of the tree's branches were still nubs. "Anybody want nubs like these a'scrapin' up yer back?"

"Nae," the men said.

"Come here, I want to show ye somethin'," said Thomas, pointing to the man from whom he took the spear.

The rawboned highlander sauntered forward to Thomas.

"Aye, Milord?" he said.

"What's yer name, Lad?"

"Nab."

"Turn around, Nab," instructed Thomas.

The man turned and Thomas laid the spear over the shoulder of Nab. "This is what yer goin' to do," he said. "And ye'll be fightin' from this position for as long as ye can hold out." He shoved the spear shaft forward so the protrusions scraped across the man's shoulder and Nab yelped.

"See why ye must whittle these nubs from the trunk?"

"Aye," said the man, rubbing his shoulder and frowning.

A low murmur went up from the mass of pikemen as they discussed the matter amongst themselves and felt the nubs on their own pike shafts.

"We'll be fightin' four deep, maybe more, wi' yer pikes pointed outward. To the English, we'll be lookin' somethin' like a hedgehog, and we'll have very sharp and deadly spines!" The earl walked a little ways to his left, to speak to them directly awhile.

"The knights comin' against ye will carry twelve-foot-long lances, but only about seven feet of 'em will reach beyond the knights and their mounts. We have fourteen-foot pikes, be stickin' out about ten feet, givin' ye three feet more than the knights on horse. Now, this is the way ye're to aim yer weapons... the ones on the front row will aim for the horse's chest... the middle two rows'll aim for the man's chest or gut... and the fourth row for the horse's head."

"Hain't this the same as they did at Falkirk with Wallace?" asked a man from within the group.

"They used long pikes, for sure," explained Thomas, "but we have a different notion to the hedgehog... this one will be movin'!"

"Movin'!?" asked one, who no doubt was asking for all of his companions.

"We'll be movin' from one place to another... not just stand in one spot!" said Thomas, moving about in a more or less square pattern while he spoke. "Instead of waitin' for the bastards to come to us, we will attack them!" He stepped forward and thrust the long pike at an imaginary horseman.

"How's that?" asked another.

"We're goin' to get trained to do it," said Thomas, "Train over and over again, 'til we are movin' like one great big hedgehog."

The men began to mumble displeasure and shook their heads, and looked from one to another in disbelief.

"Give me five days, try yer damnedest, and I promise ye that e'ery one of ye will come to ken the way," he said assuredly.

"It's foot against mounted knights!?" asked a man somewhere in the crowd.

"Foot against knights," said Thomas, and the men grew more disconcerted.

That's when Bishop David de Murray stepped forward and said, "O' course, it's *English* knights against *Scots* foot... Makes it about even!" The men laughed, enjoying the insult to their enemy, even though they were not comfortable with the thought of facing charging horsemen with nothing but sticks in their hands.

Thomas stepped in at that moment and gave them an order. "Whittle down those nubs and meet me on the downhill slope yonder," he said and once the men started moving in that direction, he turned to Alexander. "Ye know anythin' about trainin' men?"

"Yer doin' right well," said the Fraser, knowing even less than Thomas about such things and being unwilling to admit to it. "I generally just stir them up a bit with talk and set them loose to charge the bastards, of whatever ilk they are."

Wiseman chortled at the statement.

Thomas turned his attention to the hundred or so who had withdrawn from the group after saying they knew something about riding horses and remaining on top. "Ye men go to New Park by way of the road after dark this night. Should be a good moon out lest clouds cover it, and when ye get there, tell King Robert that Randolph said ye're the ones who can ride horses."

"Aye, Milord," nodded the first man who had been chosen.

"Watch out for the pots, Johnson!" warned Thomas, adding, "Make sure yer men stay on the road!"

Late that night the men walked down the road toward New Park with Johnson leading, and crossed over Bannok Burn at Milton Ford.

As the men headed up the hill for some fifty yards, one of the younger ones jokingly tripped another with the butt of his staff, causing him to step off the road. They laughed, and the man off the road pronounced a playful curse on his mate for putting him amid the caltrops, one of which he could plainly see near him. With care he avoided the vicious iron star thistle, but at his next step the ground fell from under his foot and the stake at the bottom of the hole pierced his thin-soled leather shoe, impaling his foot, breaking bones and tearing flesh.

The man howled in pain and several of his friends rushed to try and to rescue him from the forbidden field without getting caught in one of the traps themselves, but Johnson ordered them to stay back. At last the wounded man extricated his punctured foot and crawled to the road, keeping his comrades from going in harm's way. They then wrapped his bloody foot and helped him up the hill to New Park where Robert was bivouacked.

"Put him down here!" commanded Robert as he saw the men half-carrying their friend up the slope. "Where's he hurt?"

"In the foot, My King," said Johnson with serious mien.

Robert hunkered beside the man, pulled the thin shoe from the injured foot, and examined the wound as best he could by light from a torch. He wiped away the blood with his fingers and saw the fresh blood pouring from the triangular gash.

"Tread off the road, did ye?" he asked quietly, already knowing the answer.

"Aye, My King," the man groaned in agony.

"Bring some wine!" said Robert to no one in particular.

Somewhere from the middle of the large gathering a wineskin was produced. Robert removed the plug from its spout and poured some of the contents into the wound. The young man squawked loudly as the alcohol seared the flesh within the open cut.

"Don't let the English hear ye, lad," said Robert, trying to calm the injured fellow.

The man quieted himself and weakly smiled, but continued to writhe in pain.

"Call the midwife," said Robert, and Andrew scampered off into the dark wood to find her. "Who are ye men?"

"Lord Randolph sent us, Sire. He said to tell ye that we can ride."

"D'ye ride well?" said the king.

"Some of us are mighty good," said Johnson.

"Meanin', some are mighty bad?" asked Robert.

"Not too awful bad," spoke another from the crowd.

"We'll see about that tomorrow, I reckon," said Robert.

Andrew returned shortly with the small-framed midwife in tow, "Here she is, My King."

"Work on this lad's foot," Robert told her as he stood from the task and looked at the hundred. "Ye men go get some rest! Set up yer camp down yonder but not outside the wood." He scanned the size and stance of as many men as he could make out in the moonlight and decided they would do. "Ye can get fire from any of those ye see up the hill, and pick up yer provisions from the cook tent. Andrew will show ye the way."

"Thank ye, My King," said Johnson. Robert nodded and walked away.

• •

The next day the first of the horses arrived with a party led by Robert Keith and including William Vieuxpont, Robert Boyd, Walter Stewart, and a handful of knights of lesser rank, each in control of a line of mounts for the army. It had been a long trek from the highlands and Christina's farm where the horses were bred and raised, but the herd was a fine healthy bunch and the 'cavalrymen' could hardly wait to throw saddles on them and test them out. Christina, who had ridden to New Park with the herd, would not permit it until the horses had at least one night's rest, some proper attention, and time to graze.

The second group to arrive came in later the same day, a herd of nineteen well-trained mounts belonging to the Moffetts, whose fame for having excellent horses for battle had long been established. Not only would the Moffett horses obey every command of their riders, but they would kick, bite, rear, stamp, whatever was necessary to fend off attackers.

The next morning early, even before Robert and most of the other knights were awake, Christina went to the pinfold and watched the combined herd to see how the animals had reacted to having been mingled, and to see if they were rested enough to begin training with the army's riders. When she arrived the horses were calmly grazing and showing no signs of hostility toward each other. The hostlers gave her a complete report; it had been a quiet night with no signs of disturbance from any of the new mounts.

After watching them a while she grew a little concerned about several of her younger horses, and told the hostlers to hold them back for the day lest they get broken down for lack of rest. The others she approved for beginning training with the caveat that they were to be ridden, but observed for signs of fatigue until they were fully rested.

After the men had breakfast, Robert had every man whom Randolph had sent ride one of the highland horses to determine their prowess on horseback. Almost to a man they rode as if the horses were extensions of themselves, or they were extensions of the horses, which was exactly what Robert wanted. Even the man with the wounded foot showed well in the saddle, but he could put no pressure on the foot when it touched the ground, though the midwife had tried to align the snapped bones, applied a poultice, and wrapped it heavily to keep the foot immobile.

Johnson proved most proficient of the lot, and Thomas began to rely on him to help with the training. Robert was concerned that the other horses had not arrived, but Christina didn't seem worried.

"Don't be concerned, Rob. The rest of my herd will be here within the next few days, and in all ye'll have four hundred thirty-six of the most agile horses I've e'er seen."

"I'm runnin' out of trainin' time, Christina! A few days more means I have a few days less!"

"Ye have three more weeks, My King," said Christina. "And the horses have been trained almost since they were foaled."

"I'm less worried about the horses' trainin' than I am about their riders. I have but three weeks to train these wild men and instill some discipline," sighed Robert.

The man with the wounded foot hobbled toward them with the aid of a stout stick and was greeted by Robert and introduced to Lady Christina, though Robert had to ask his name.

"Darach, My Lord," answered the man, removing his leather armorer's cap and giving a slight bow to Christina.

"What happened to your foot Darach?" she asked.

"Two lackwits, Milady. Me and one other, actin' like fools," he grinned. "Put my foot into one o' them traps down near the ford and the stake came right up through shoe and all." Christina frowned and shook her head in sympathy for his painful injury.

"Oh, but it's a'right, Milady. I heal quick. 'Twon't be but a short while and I'll be walkin' without my friend here," he said, indicating the staff on which he leant. "But, I want to ask ye a question, Sire, if ye don't mind."

"What's that, Darach?

"Will ye be lettin' me ride? I saw ye watchin' us this mornin' and... I need to know if I did a'right."

Robert looked at the man and then down at his foot, "Aye Laddie, ye ride... but take care of that wound!"

The young highlander yelped with excitement. "Thank ye, Milord... uh... My King. Thank ye, thank ye!" he said, and with another quick bow to Christina, hobbled downhill until, too far off balance, he fell. He laughed and purposely rolled and tumbled the rest of the way until one of his friends helped him up and steadied him to the fence rail. "The king's a'lettin' me ride!" he grinned.

"Don't see why not," said his friend, "ye always was the best rider."

The highlanders spent a long while looking at the horses; pointing out the ones they would like to ride, or the ones they thought would be fastest. Before long, the sentry announced another herd was approaching, and the men all cheered.

Robert knew then that he had the backbone for his light cavalry. He hoped the four hundred and thirty-six and the few he already had would be enough once the battle started, but he would have to wait and see what happened in the next three weeks.

• •

That evening Christina fixed a supper of meaty stew from a ration of the beeves that had been slaughtered that afternoon. Nigel and Andrew joined her and the king for the repast. Nigel was happily excited to see his mother and rattled on to her about all the things he had learned from Andrew and his father, and his many friends he had made around the camp.

After supper, having learned that Isabella of Ross was in camp, and of the emotional dilemma that had been wrought by the overreaching Edward, Christina decided to pay her a visit.

"I am Christina of Carrick," she introduced herself upon entering the small hovel Isabella's brothers had made for her.

Isabella was sitting on a chair made of tree limbs and rope and covered with an old cape Walter had used for his trip to the battlefield. "I ken who ye are, Milady," she said coolly.

Christina remained standing. "I know Edward de Brus has done ye a great disservice, and the king has said he is truly remorseful that his brother has dishonored himself and his family in dishonorin' ye. He also said that, in yer heart, ye cannot forgive him."

"I cannot," she replied looking to the blank wall, away from Christina.

"Then why are ye still here?" Christina asked.

There was silence. Isabella then put her head into the palms of her hands and began to sob. Christina at first hesitated to comfort her but quickly took the two steps to her side and placed her hands on Isabella's shoulders letting her know she understood.

"I remain here because love him," the young woman finally whispered through her tears.

"So it is," Christina sighed, knowing that loving a Brus was both a joy and a burden. So while Isabella cried copious tears, Christina tried to comfort and reason with her. "I know that Edward has declared his affection for ye and proposed marriage, and if ye insist upon his living up to his word, what have ye? A man who is legally bound to ye, but will emotionally always be elsewhere. Ye will ne'er know where he is or when he'll return... or if he'll return."

"My advice to ye, Isabella of Ross, is that ye leave him here and return to yer home now, before the comin' battle."

"I'm afraid to," Isabella shook her head. "If I leave, he may be killed and I'll never see him again!"

"If it is God's will that he shall die, he shall die... whether ye are here or in Ross. Will ye be any happier if ye are here to watch him die?"

"How cruel ye are!" the heartbroken noblewoman said.

"Believe me, child, naught will be better for him because ye stay. There is nothin' ye can do here except, perhaps, get yerself killed..."

"I'm not afraid!" Isabella said resolutely.

"Ye should be! What d'ye think happens to the 'small folk' when their men lose a battle? Ye will be just another camp follower to the English! Pretty as ye are, ye'll not die quickly! Yer family's lands and titles will be lost and of no benefit..."

"Stop!" She shrieked and jumped up. "Why are ye tellin' me this, to make me afraid? Why?"

Christina stood from where she had crouched to talk to the tearful woman. "No, child, not to make ye afraid. But ye are a hindrance to him, here. He knows what will happen to ye if things go badly on the battlefield, and his mind could be on ye, rather than what he should be thinkin' about. Ye could get him killed, just by bein' here! And yer brothers! What about them?"

The woman was sobbing heavily, and Christina had no stronger argument to make. "Isabella, go home! If he truly loves ye, and he lives, he'll find ye there. If not... ye'll be no worse off than ye are." She went to the door and turned, adding, "If ye need to talk, I'll be here."

As she walked out into the darkening evening, she heard Isabella crying inconsolably.

Adam Gordon

JUNE 5th 1314
CASTLE BERWICK

"My Lord?"

"What?"

"Have you any... childs?" his wife Marie quietly asked Aymer de Valance as he sat on the bed trying to catch his breath after lying with her.

"Hell of a question to start the day with, I'd say," he mumbled in a low voice.

"You are full awake for long time, mi esposo, ¿verdad?" said she.

"So I am," said Aymer, yet dodging the question.

"Well, do you have child?" she said turning over to be closer to him.

"What the goddamn hell do you care?" he griped, "You hain't takin' care of them!" He stood and began getting dressed. Having taken his boorish response as an affirmative answer to her question, Marie lay wordless for a short while, thinking about it before broaching the subject again.

"Where are your bastard children?"

Pembroke sighed and wanted not to play the game. He had almost forgotten the twins he sired from one of the two innkeeper's daughters from Aberdeen some years back, but he had done right by them, in a way. He had left money that they should not want for life's necessities, which was more than he had done for any other offspring he might have had. Actually, he had no notion as to how many others he might have sired and didn't care, figuring that they were fortunate to get his royal blood wherever they were.

"You have any children?" he shot back at her angrily. She was shocked at his question.

"Had I... children, other than yours, My Husband, I would be a whore!" she replied. "As you plainly know, I have none."

"Children are snotty little pests, anyhow," said Pembroke finishing up his dressing.

"No, don't say this!" she admonished. "I would like to have child, I would like to have your royal blooded childs."

"It's children, not 'childs'! An' what in the name of the devil are you talkin' about!" he huffed. "We hain't been abstainin'!"

She sadly turned her face away from him and a tear made its way down her cheek and across the bridge of her nose before disappearing into the pillow.

•   •

When Pembroke entered the great hall he saw a man nearly as large as he, sitting on the far side of the room hunched over his trencher of victuals, his eyes lowered. The yellow tabard and chain mail he wore gave no hint as to his identity, except that he appeared to be a warrior.

After asking several denizens who the man might be without receiving a satisfactory response, Lord Aymer got two good-sized guards to approach the man with him.

"Harrumph," started Pembroke loudly while standing beside the man at the table.

The stranger slowly looked up from his wooden trencher and Pembroke's jaw went slack as he noticed the man's eyes. One eye, the left, to be exact. It was not dark brown like the other one, but blank, that is white, with neither opening nor iris, and the upper lid lazed about halfway down over the eyeball though his good eye was wide open. The whole of his putout eye was situated in the path of a deep scar that ran from his scalp to his left nostril, leading Pembroke to quickly surmise that a single blade stroke was responsible for the entire disfiguration.

"Lord Pembroke," said the man, recognizing de Valence readily, "Good ye could get from neath yer warm covers so late in the day to have a bite of food with me!"

"Late in the day?" growled Pembroke, annoyed.

"Aye, Lad," quipped the man. "I've been here quite a while a'waitin' yer comin'."

"*No*body said *nothin'* about *no* arrival of *no*body lookin' like you!" asserted Pembroke.

"Passin' strange, 'tis," he said, his left eye twitching slightly. "Sent a message by my own courier, I did!"

"Must have got hisself killed on the way here!" grumped Pembroke motioning for the two guards to haul him off to the castle gaol. "'Tain't safe these days for a Scot to be wanderin' about Berwick!"

Realizing what was happening the man said, "Lord Aymer, I am Sir Adam Gordon, if ye'll give me a wee chance to explain. I am Justiciar of Lothian!"

Pembroke nodded and stayed the arrest, signaling the two guards to back off, adding, "I'll need you not."

As they left he admitted to the man, "I *have* heard of you."

"Of course, ye have," said Gordon, getting back to his cooling victuals. He straightened to make more room in his belly and Aymer saw the large red *fleur de lis* on his tabard.

"What do ye want, Gordon?" asked Pembroke sitting on the bench across the table from the man.

"Come to fight with ye, I have," he said, "Yer king knew I was a'comin'!"

"He's still idlin' about in the goddamned bedstead," said Aymer deprecatingly. "You can tell him how goddamned lazy he is, too... when he gets here."

Gordon smiled, knowing that he had gotten to Pembroke and Pembroke didn't like it.

"You and Dunbar was comrades... I remember," mused Pembroke trying to keep his own eyes from migrating to Gordon's bad one. "Always hid out when I was in town, I reckon."

"Nae, Good Lord," he replied, "Just missed ye, as I was off somewhere or t'other."

"What can I do for the likes of you?" asked Pembroke after a long sigh and a pause.

"Ye got wenches to this here castle?" he asked, going back to his eating.

Pembroke shook his head in disgust. "Town's full of wenches if you have coin."

"Lookin' for the ones ye take for nary a coin, Laddie," said Gordon, his mouth agape, his half chewed pottage tumbling forth upon his beard, and his one good eye shining out at Pembroke with a hopeful twinkle.

"Go to town, damn you!" growled Pembroke.

Just then loud horns blared close by and the double doors to the hall swung wide open to allow the king to enter through them unimpeded.

"Here's your chance to tell the king your wit." Said Pembroke.

Gordon jumped to his feet and went brazenly toward the king. Pembroke, who knew not what the man might do, jumped up and followed. Gordon bowed low before the king and Edward acknowledged the man's presence in a vague sort of way before trundling along.

"He don't seem to have remembrance of you," said Pembroke, standing behind Gordon with his hand on his blade, just in case the man had murderous intent.

"Sure he does," Gordon, smiling, contradicted Pembroke's slur. "Just speaks to me thus 'cause he knows me so well!"

"Aye," sarcastically agreed Pembroke, "and you're goin' off to war with him."

"O' Course I am," the one-eyed man grumped as he returned to his half-eaten crust. "Gettin' my lands in Lothian back from the Brus!"

• •

That afternoon the hall was cleared of people and a large table was set in the middle of the room. Benches were placed on three sides and one large chair at the head, awaiting their summoned occupants.

The men for whom King Edward had sent soon arrived. Pembroke, Hereford, Gloucester, Hugh le Despenser, Henry de Bohun, Marmaduke de Tweng, Raoul de Monthermer, Robert de Reymes and Adam Gordon. The poet Baston declined, feigning fatigue, fearing boredom.

They sat with little interaction for more than a quarter of an hour before their king decided it was the perfect time to join them. He made his entrance grandly in full armor and pranced boldly to the head of the table as Sir Hugh rolled out the large hand-drawn map upon the table.

"Now!" said the king pointing to the area of Stirling Castle, "... this is Stirlin' Castle."

No one dared to suggest that he was pointing out the very obvious to men who mostly knew the area better than he.

Accompanied by his pointing finger to various points on the map, the king chattered on about going to Wark-on-Tweed and launching from there into Scotland through Lauderdale to Edinburgh, from where they would take the Roman road through Linlithgow and Falkirk to relieve the castle at Stirling. Pembroke remembered that Adam Gordon had been summoned to the meeting, yet Gordon's place at table across from him remained vacant. The king had not even noticed, apparently.

Bastard went to town, thought Pembroke while the king exhibited his knowledge of the planned assault.

Then Pembroke suddenly realized that the king had said, "Sir Adam Gordon strongly recommended that the coast route be completely abandoned. The troublesome roadways there would impede our train's ability to follow."

Pembroke seethed. *The whoreson must have seen the king earlier so he could go to town while we're a'settin' here,* thought Pembroke. But an afterthought reminded him of that Scotsman's nature, and it came to him that the king had supplied Gordon with a wench, and that they were still in the castle. *What's the point of bein' Viceroy if that sort of behavior is goin' on right under my very nose without me even knowin' about it!* he ruminated angrily.

As Pembroke's mind returned to Edward's discourse, he heard the king saying, "…spies tell us that Brus is bringin' his paltry so-called 'army' to the Torwood and a'waitin' our arrival."

"How are we fightin' him in exactly the places he likes to fight?" queried Hereford.

"We're not goin' into the wood after him… *if* he's still there and… has not yet run off," replied Edward snidely.

"As I recollect, that is a long slope for an uphill charge," interjected Sir Marmaduke, not at all sure about the king's plan as it was explained.

"We can, if we so choose, bypass the whole of Brus' army and ride directly to relieve Stirlin'," said the king, as if he had hit on a brilliant bit of strategy.

"But should we do that, Sire, we shall not achieve our main objective," said Hereford, "to eliminate Brus."

Edward sighed deeply. He kept losing track of important elements among the reasons he was to go there in the first place.

JUNE 8th 1314
TORWOOD

Every day and for much of the day, the men who were present trained to the sound of their commander's voice. As more arrivals came to the field they were integrated into the body already there and learned quickly from their peers.

Old traditions and tactics were so ingrained in some of his men, that Robert and his chief lieutenants found some few could not be otherwise trained, and were thus unsuited to the disciplined schiltrom. The 'wild men' as Robert called them, would be used in other capacities, where they could do the most good.

The nearly three thousand that were gathered practiced with the fourteen-foot-long spears as Robert had dictated. Some of them drilled with plain sharpened sticks, not knowing if, when the time came, they would be facing the English with what they now had, or with the more effective metal pike heads.

The schiltroms in training would move up the hills, across the hills, and down the hills. They would form a straight line of six men deep, their fourteen-foot pikes barely edging over the tops of the forwardmost line of men. On command they would form a circle, an ellipse, or a square three men deep, their spears bristling outward in every direction.

Another order would bring them into a smaller formation of four men deep. Though their formations were unwieldy and awkward at first, they trained until it was second nature to them. The old Scottish charge of banshee-like screams had no place in their new discipline.

The several hundred archers who had come from the borders, practiced shooting targets and foraging for game to the west of Bannok, where they were not likely to get into trouble with roving bands of English soldiers seeking to kill Scottish warriors coming to the battle.

The cavalry trained as well, riding in unison and quickly moving left or right as they were commanded. They fashioned boiled leather armor to protect the horses' chests and necks.

Robert sat his mount on the sloping plain of Bannok just below New Park wood, watching a group of riders coming along the causeway on the far side of Stirling Castle. He could not tell if they were friend or foe at first, but when they reached the near side of the bridge he saw their colors and knew who they were.

"Andrew!" he called and the squire soon appeared with his young protégé, Nigel, tagging close behind.

"Aye, My King," said Andrew.

"Yon travelers appear to be lost," said Robert. "Go and fetch them to Torwood and I'll be there directly."

"Aye, My King," said Andrew and started off.

"Andrew?" said the king.

The lad turned, "Aye, Sire?"

"On your way, tell Lord Thomas to have his men start whittlin' more spear shafts."

"Aye, My King," said Andrew as he ran to saddle his horse.

The procession was lead by many warriors wearing the yellow tabards of the men of the isles, and the column from them to the stragglers stretched a full mile back.

"No doubt lost on dry land," mused Robert, smiling.

Riding through the gouge between New Park and King's Park, he looked to the back side of Cockshot Hill where men were unpacking newly arrived pike heads, quilted jerkins, gauntlets of canvas with portions made of chain mail, short swords, axes, and daggers. The just arrived materiel was being distributed to the men of the schiltroms who had no gear of their own. Robert's planned line of supplies seemed to be falling into place, albeit, not a moment too soon.

• •

Angus Og Macdonald sat on the saddle that he had gladly taken off his horse and set on the ground. Far from being accustomed to riding a horse, he much preferred the tossing and rolling of a galley under his feet to a horse's back under his arse. Yet he seemed to be pleasant enough company when Robert rode up.

"Yer trip was uneventful, I trust," said Robert as he climbed from his mount and stood before Angus.

"We got lost," said Angus, "thanks to that damned guide we no longer have!"

"Ye killed yer guide?" asked Robert.

"Kilt him, roasted him, and et him," said Angus not cracking a smile as if it were not a jest.

Robert hesitated to hear the rest of the tale. Then he asked, "Was he good?"

"Nae," answered Angus, "rotten through and through. But we et him all the same."

They laughed at that.

"Got yer men foragin' for shafts?" asked Robert hunkering to see Angus in the eyes.

"Oh, aye! Sir Thomas saw to that right off," he replied.

"Appreciated yer help at Man," said Robert.

"Helped for the time bein', but I don't trust that damned stinkin' John of Lorn," said Angus, "He'll spell trouble for ye later on, Robbie."

"Thanks for the warnin' but I already figured that," said Robert as a large shadow loomed over the two of them. Robert turned to see the cause of the shadow. "Templar?!" he said.

"Aye," said David de Graham smiling as much as anyone ever saw him smile.

"Ye bring those other Templars with ye?" asked the king.

"Downhill cuttin' spear shafts, eight of us in all."

"All our men are fitted out, ready to fight," said Angus.

"Good," replied Robert. "Our supplies are thinnin' except for victuals; we have a'plenty for now.

"So we'll be fed proper?" asked Angus whose round belly was growling loudly.

"Ye'll eat, My Friend," replied the king. He turned to Graham, "I want ye and yers to ride horse."

"We can probably manage that, most of us havin' grown up on horses the way Macdonalds grew up on ships," said Graham with a tinge of sarcasm. "Horses are much easier to manage than either the Macdonald or his ships." Angus grinned, knowing that Graham had no great love of being on the sea.

Another figure, this one female, walked up behind Graham and wrapped long slender arms around his waist.

"This the brave lass ye ran off with?" asked Robert.

David pulled her around to his front. "Dianna," he said."

Robert stood in respect. "I remember her well," he said, "She saved our backsides at Dunstaffnage."

"Aye, she did," said David, smiling down at her.

"My King," greeted Dianna with a shallow curtsy.

"Lady Dianna," replied Robert noticing her fully round belly. "Ye are soon to give birth! Is this your first child?"

"Aye, Sire," she answered, surprisingly shy. She even blushed.

"Are ye sure ye wish to bring *another* Graham into yer life?" he teased.

"'Twill be different, Sire, for *I* shall train up this one," she set her open hand on her swollen abdomen, "... to be a farmer or a carpenter... or anythin' but a Templar knight!" She smiled up at David, who raised one eyebrow at the thought.

"Any more of ye Templars here'bouts willin' to fight?" asked Robert returning to his intent.

"None," said David. "Only the eight of us that I mentioned."

"Too bad, we could have used a hundred... ten hundreds!" said Robert, who had hoped for more of the well-trained knights.

"But we few will fight for ye... to the death if need be," said David.

Robert smiled in gratitude, but Dianna's face remained serious.

"We have brought some of yer sea-goin' kin along, too," said Angus from his seat on the saddle.

Robert looked at the men down the hill. "Is that Malcolm Maclaine?"

"Aye," replied Angus, "Right good friend in a fight, so I have found on an occasion or two."

"Did a'right for us at Dunstaffnage," agreed Robert.

"Speakin' of Malcolm..." said Angus, "... Lennox is about a day behind us."

"How many does he bring with him?" asked Robert anxiously.

"Some hundreds," said Angus vaguely. "Exact numbers are unknown to me... just saw a'plenty when we ran across them three days back."

"Strathbogie's bringin' about a hundred, or so I'm told," said Robert as he sat back on the ground beside Angus.

"I need to see to our horses. By your leave, Sire," said David Graham.

"Ye eight... ye all have horses?" asked Robert while shading his eyes with the cup of his hand.

"Aye, Sire, complete with battle armor," said David smartly.

Robert nodded and watched him and Dianna walk downhill toward the others. He stopped where Malcolm Maclaine was chopping branches off a long, straight, slender sapling and said something to him. Malcolm looked up at Robert and threw up a hand in greeting.

"Templar's lady 'ppears to be ready to have that bairn," remarked Robert to Angus, while he hailed his kinsman in return.

"I tried to convince Graham to leave her behind, but he would have none of it... if somethin' goes wrong here..." he breathed a great long sigh, "...I argued and argued... but..." Angus shrugged his shoulders as a sign of frustrated helplessness.

From where Angus and Robert were sitting they could see a caravan of warriors below, heading out of the glen and eastward down the road.

"That Lennox a'ready?" asked Angus, squinting to make out the arms.

"Nae," said Robert, "'ppears to be Robert de Umfraville... almost the last Scottish earl to hold out against us."

"Where they headed, ye reckon?" asked Angus.

"To catch up with England, I would reckon," said Robert, almost sadly.

"Ye want them headed off?" asked Angus.

Robert shook his head forlornly.

• •

The next day, as foretold by Sir Angus, Sir Malcolm, Earl of Lennox did arrive with his knights and all in splendid array. With him came one hundred and fifty-seven of the Camerons led by Sir Ian, and Henry Sinclair bringing several hundred more from his family.

Had I this many with me always, I would have had the whole of Scotland come to my peace, and much sooner, thought Robert. He stood watching the newly arrived men file across the edge of the dry valley floor where it transmogrified into the watery pows that made up the miry carse beyond.

"How are ye feelin', Robbie?" Christina asked, coming up behind the king.

"Like a great beast about to rise!" replied Robert.

"Beast?" she asked, a hint of a smile at one corner of her mouth.

"Power to do great tasks," he declared, "as in a Greek drama that once I read about in a French manuscript."

"Expectin' *that*, I wasn't," she replied with an eyebrow heightened.

Robert turned to her, took her shoulders, smiled and said, "Today, I'm fixed to *win!*"

"Because ye got more men, today?"

"Nae woman," he said frowning.

"Yesterday ye had doubts and today ye have sure triumph swirlin' in yer head?" she said putting her arm around his waist. "Dear Rob, keep to yer trainin' and to God. That's where the battle will be won or lost."

He reached across his chest and held the back of her hand that she had wrapped around his waist. "There is still so much we don't know," said Robert, taking her advice. The temporary wind of expectation was taken from his sail, but it was replaced with a more pragmatic engine of inner strength that was stronger than it ever was before.

"There came a runner this morn," said Christina after a long moment of reflection.

"Runner?" he said looking at her, "What runner?"

"Jemmy Douglas has gathered many from his region and will be arrivin' either late today, or on the morrow," she said.

Robert nodded, obviously pleased, and said, "Almost too late for the trainin'."

"Still time a'plenty for willin' folk," she replied.

• •

It was within Castle Stirling that anxiety about the looming conflict was most rampant. Only fifteen days remained before the deadline on his cleverly bargained truce with Edward Brus.

Sir Philip Mowbray stirred among the various lists and figures he had so laboriously kept ever since it was noticed that Brus had begun assembling his troops. He added and he subtracted, which was the extent of his knowledge of numbers. With all his accumulated reports he was confused and could not tell how many or what kinds of troops the Scot had at his command. Robert had moved his men hither and thither many times and, at the Brus' instruction, most had arrived at Bannok from the west where, from his two hundred-foot high eyrie, Mowbray could not see them.

His own spies, who scaled the steep unguarded rock incline on the north side of the upthrust, had brought him insufficient news of the plans of the English army. King Edward only sent Mowbray vague and generally known 'news', fearful that the message runner would be caught and tortured for the practically useless information.

Philip started to envy his erstwhile peer, the debauched Dungal Macdouall, who knew how to use spirits and women to allay his worries and fears. However, Philip was an honorable man, and honorable men often suffer alone, and in silence.

Raoul de Monthermer

JUNE 12th 1314
WARK-ON-TWEED

Followed by Aymer de Valence, Earl of Pembroke, Gilbert le Clare, Earl of Gloucester, and Humphrey de Bohun, Earl of Hereford, the English king arrived in grand array. After him and his earls came the lesser barons, knights, squire bannerettes, various men-at-arms, squires, and troopers, and a multitude of foot soldiers, all attired in chain and burnished leather armor, with steel helms, colorful shields, and amazingly varied and lively banners that rippled against the light breeze.

Trumpets blared and drums hammered their thunderous cadence announcing the arrival of the great host of thousands ready to do battle against their northern neighbor.

Once all had caught up to the king's van, the nobles took up residence within the castle, and the lesser troops pitched tents and drew rations from the castle larder and made their own cook fires. With the heraldic arms, striped tents and fluttering flags and pennants of every description, the encampment looked like an enormous tournament gathering, fair day, and market town rolled into one, from the fortress at Wark to the fortress at Coldstream, about three miles down the River Tweed.

Purveyors of all manner strolled with their wares through the newly formed lanes and mews of what had suddenly become one of England's largest cities, hawking their fresh produce, fish, eggs, milk, and breads several times a day. It was a financially fortuitous event for the locals, as all of the burgeoned populace had to be fed, as did their animals, and despite the fact that the king's stores were adequate to the task of fending off starvation, those with the resources would always buy a bit extra, or something different, to delight the palate.

Next afternoon the king called a meeting in the great hall for the participating nobles and higher ranking knights, those who came with him, and those who had arrived previously. Word had come that the great wagon train traveling from London would be in Wark in three days, after which they would have one day to rest, resupply, and repair before going across the Tweed River ford at Wark into Scotland.

The king then abruptly left the hall and made his way to the solar where he had planned a private meal with Sir Hugh le Despenser, the younger. He had tired on the tedious trip from Berwick the day before and was looking forward to the pleasures the sleeping hours provided.

Those whom he left in the great hall were encouraged to enjoy the freely flowing ale provided by the castle, and each other's company. Thus it was that men gathered, for the most part, in groups according to their peers.

Sir John Comyn, son of the murdered 'Red' Comyn, stood with Sir Robert de Clifford, appointed warden of Douglasdale after James Douglas' father was executed by Longshanks. Clifford still considered himself Lord of Douglasdale even though he had neither been there nor drawn his rents from there for the past several years.

Just moments after the two began their commiserations they were joined by Sir Raoul de Monthermer who had fought alongside Clifford in many a battle.

"Hail to you, Sir Robert," greeted Raoul. "And to you Sir John."

The two men responded in kind.

"Reckon that 'king's grant day' is close at hand," said Raoul, more because of having little other to say, than as sarcasm.

"All I want is what's due me!" said Comyn feeling stung and knitting his brows to a single one.

"No offense intended, Sir," replied Raoul thinking the response was somewhat overly sharp.

"His Majesty has promised me the earldom of Badenoch," growled Sir John angrily.

"And I, Douglasdale," Clifford stated.

"You've had Douglasdale all along," said Comyn dismissively.

"Had to build the damn tower back twice because of that Douglas whelp bringin' it down!" barked Clifford. "Burnt it to a cinder the last time! Ye need not remind *me* of that problem bein' mine all along!"

Raoul, feeling misplaced in the conversation having had no such promises from the king, drank his ale and listened until Clifford said abruptly, "And what about young Gloucester?!"

"Gilbert?" asked Raoul.

"What lands has he been promised?" asked Clifford.

"Why… none, Sir," replied Raoul politely.

"Then why is he here with such a great host of men?" interjected Comyn in an accusatory tone.

Raoul had no other answer except a very simple one. "My Lords, he is the king's cousin!"

Clifford smiled cunningly. "Let's see… Hereford and Pembroke are here because of guilt. We…" he indicated Comyn and himself, "are here for lands. If it were but a matter of bein' kin to Edward, we'd have half the realm packed into this hall tonight!"

"'Tis the only reason I know, ne'ertheless," said Raoul. He then excused himself and walked away, choosing to withdraw from the over-heated, and fast becoming dangerous, conversation.

In the corner sat Sir Marmaduke with three empty ale glasses before him. He was pounding one of them on the table to get the attention of a serving squire as if he were in a rowdy public tavern.

Raoul did what no other in the hall would do, he sat across the table from Marmaduke and pushed his own cup of ale to him. "Tide you over 'til you get another."

Marmaduke frowned at Raoul. He didn't trust anybody who would give up good ale without at least a threat of a fight.

"I'm not thirsty," explained Raoul.

Marmaduke looked at the man and then the half empty cup. He drank it down in two gulps and wiped his mouth and beard on his sleeve.

Curious, Raoul asked, "Why have you come to war on the Scots?"

Marmaduke then wished he had not drunk the man's ale for he felt obligated to give an answer in payment. "I'll get you another ale," he suggested.

"No ale," said Raoul, "Nor do you have to answer."

Marmaduke was eased as a squire came to his table with more ale. Marmaduke snatched two additional goblets from the tray as the surprised squire took a quick step backward.

"So, that's how you get three at a time," said Raoul with a wry smile.

"The squires don't come often 'nough," said Marmaduke. "Need to take fate into your own hands, at times."

Raoul nodded and stood to let Marmaduke enjoy his ale. He saw the shy, retiring Sir Robert de Reymes standing at a small port looking across the Tweed River. He looked pensive as if contemplating the philosophy of the heavens.

"Sir Robert," said Raoul concerned he was shattering a fragile glass.

Robert was shaken slightly as he withdrew from his own world but was cordial. "Sir Raoul," he said.

"Pleasant evenin'," came back Raoul.

"'Tis late, yet the sun is far from settin'," said Reymes. "The winters are completely opposite."

"The way of the northern lands," offered Raoul.

"I know the reason," said Reymes quietly, "It never ceases to astound me, ne'ertheless."

"You are a merchant of London," said Raoul in the tones of his conversation companion, "... may I ask, why are you joined in this venture?"

"God."

"God?"

"God called me to the task,"

Raoul was stumped by his answer. A religious and prosperous merchant off to war?

"Not for lands or glory?" said Raoul.

"In those terms..." Reymes answered turning from the window for the first time since Raoul had approached him, "...I must admit, it is for my region of Corbridge which has suffered from the raids of Brus so. Personally, it has devastated my income from there. "

Raoul nodded and said, "I remember, not long back, when the men of Corbridge often raided into Scotland."

"But they gave that up!" objected Reymes.

"Because they could not accomplish the task?" asked Raoul. Sir Robert considered that for a moment and decided to ignore that which he could not answer.

"They gave it up... as I want the Brus to do," said Reymes.

"I understand," said Raoul but understanding only from knowing how Sir Robert was understanding it. Otherwise, it made little sense to him.

Robert turned back to the portal and Raoul took his hint and wandered elsewhere. Spotting two Scotsmen among the English he decided to ask his questions of them.

"Good evening, Sirs," greeted Raoul cheerfully.

The two brothers, Ingram and Robert de Umfraville, greeted him in return.

"Not ale-in' tonight?" asked Sir Ingram noticing that Raoul had no goblet.

"Do you mean drinking... or sick, Sir?" asked Raoul smiling, thinking Ingram was making a pun jest.

The question was ignored.

"Tell me, Sir..." Lord Robert de Umfraville, Earl of Angus, stopped his question as he fished for Raoul's name.

"Raoul," said Ingram supplying the name for his brother.

"Yes, of course! Sir Raoul!" He started again, "Tell me Sir Raoul, since ye are so close to the king, bein' that ye once married his sister, do ye ken his disposition of my earldom of Angus?"

"I know little of such, Lord Umfraville, but if you want my opinion, I would reckon that you would be retained for the earldom." he said.

Robert smiled broadly at his brother. "See what I told ye?"

"It's just that events don't always work out quite as ye think they would," said Ingram de Umfraville. "Take Pembroke yonder," he said, pointing his finger across the room in the earl's direction, "He was Viceroy of Scotland and had Brus pinned down at Loudoun Hill eight years ago, and I stood ready to lead the men against him... but Pembroke stayed my hand."

"You would have beaten the Brus as he stood?" asked Raoul.

"We would not be here havin' to do this o'er again if Pembroke had turned me loose that day," said Sir Ingram gritting his teeth. "That's what I mean!"

"Aye, 'tis too bad," said Raoul, "Too bad."

"Too bad for England," Ingram grumped. "Makin' him Viceroy... again?" he shook his head in disbelief.

"Now Ingram," explained Robert, "Ye ken he's a Scot lover."

"I ken Thomas Randolph was in the man's very hands, yet he squandered his luck," said Ingram angrily. "And how was it that poor Macdouall got chased all o'er the south of Scotland whilst Pembroke did nary a thing to stop it?" added Ingram rhetorically.

Raoul knew the answer he sought from the Umfraville brothers and they had not realized that they had been questioned.

JUNE 19th 1314
EDINBURGH

"My God!"

Awestruck, King Edward reined in his horse as the castle mount came into view.

"What a terrible pity!" he said, agog.

Staring up to where the great castle had stood, he saw only destruction, great stones and timbers scattered about wherever they landed when the walls and buildings of the fortress were tumbled off the volcanic upthrust. He had been told of its capture and subsequent destruction by the Scots, but he had not realized the devastation was so absolute.

"How could they have wrought as terrible a thing as this in such a short time!" he wondered aloud.

"Gravity," answered Lord Pembroke, coming alongside the king and viewing the scene. "Gravity brought it down."

"How is that possible?!"

"They undermined the ground underneath and pushed over the walls."

"What is that structure that yet stands?" asked Edward.

"The chapel, Your Majesty."

Edward nodded pensively before saying, "I imagine letting the chapel stand is supposed to bring God's forgiveness upon Brus' soul after all the evil he has done, but in such an unholy creature as he, one tiny glimmer of light can hardly escape to reach God's heart!"

Pembroke wondered momentarily what God would think of Edward's soul, or his own, but said nothing.

"Are the Scots still about?" asked Edward.

"No, Sire. They capture, raze, and melt into the landscape like snow in July."

"A second pity," lamented Edward. "I should like to have avenged the death of the castle. 'Twas one of my favorite places in all of Scotland.

The king and his earl were joined by Baston the poet at this time, and Edward wanted to say something dramatic expressly for the friar's ear. "We shall camp in the shadow of yon dead castle and weep! Upon this rock will I bring her back to full life, just as my father would have done!"

"We need to get the stores off the ships moored at Leith, Majesty," prompted Pembroke, knowing that the king was a bit saddle weary and wanted to rest, though he had been pushing the rest of the army hard to make the midsummer deadline at Stirling.

Truthfully, Pembroke was ready for a rest himself, having led the caravan out of Wark with a van of fifty or so horsed knights and several hundred Welsh soldiers of foot, primarily pikemen. Edward and his seventy-six household knights later set out leading the rest of the twenty-five hundred barded knights and approximately twenty thousand lesser knights, troopers, pikemen, archers, squires, and at least another two to three thousand camp followers.

The army had been on the move for two long days, all under the observant eyes of Robert's spies for the entire journey. The King of Scots had been informed of the English king's advance to Edinburgh and the fact that Pembroke led the van. He was also told which earls were with the king's forces ... and which were not.

Robert knew that his Scots were outnumbered by a ratio of at least three to one.

"I would suggest that we seem to have plenty of stores at present," mentioned Sir Hugh, at the king's other elbow. "Perhaps pressin' on now and doublin' back for the supplies on the ships would serve our needs better, Your Majesty.

Edward lowered his head and raised his hand high in the air. They all knew his meaning; he was king and it would be done in his manner with no further conversation. He spoke, again for the benefit of Friar Baston's composition, "If we tarry here for an hour or two more, then the Scots will be allowed an hour or two more to vex themselves with useless toil."

The friar was not impressed but feigned attention.

"I'll order your tent raised, Sire," said Pembroke and rode off, glad to be shed of the posturing king if only for a short respite.

Sir Giles d'Argentan followed Pembroke for the same reason, leaving Edward's household knights and their commander, Sir Edmund Mauley, well within earshot of his banter, which was lively, but pretentious to distraction for those who curried no favor.

The king's tent was pitched and a fine delicate meal was served to the monarch and his favorite, who lolled about all evening on pallets as if at a Roman feast, as the king noted in jest. At the king's order, soldiers went out and confiscated wains to drive to Leith and offload the tons of victuals and other supplies from the eight ships laded before Edward left London.

FRIDAY – JUNE 21st
TORWOOD AND BANNOK

Robert rode his white highland-bred horse into the Torwood, sighted Thomas Randolph and walked his mount toward him. "Any word?" he asked as he approached.

"So far, 'ppears to be blessedly quiet," said Thomas looking up at his liege.

"And are ye well, Thomas? We've been so occupied with preparations, I hain't seen much of ye... or Edward, for that matter."

"I am well Uncle, except for the heat. Sure wish the weather would cool a bit."

Robert scanned the valley below. "'Twould be good if we were to have rain."

"Oh, no 'twouldn't!" replied Thomas. "Chain mail's uncomfortable enough without havin' your hacqueton and kirtle gettin' wet as sops."

"Well, Laddie, for my battle plan, I'd like to see good steady rain for the next couple of days," said Robert. "Then it could clear off and be dry for the battle itself so ye don't get yer hacqueton wet," he teased.

Thomas smiled and nodded, "Those big English destriers hain't all that manageable on a watery field. That yer thought?"

"Get 'em goin' on muddy ground and they slide about right much," returned Robert. There was an air of melancholy in his demeanor, a calmness that comes with inevitability as he sat for a moment watching the clouds move across the sky. Finally, he took a deep breath as if having come to a conclusion. "But, I think it more likely that ye'll get yer dry weather than that I'll get my rain."

"'Tis the good Lord's work, Sire, and we can only take what comes."

"True enough," agreed Robert. "Probably a good thing that no man can excite changes in the weather, for good or for ill." He started to leave and then reined in his mount. "Have a feast here, tonight," instructed the king. "Meat as well as bread."

"Ye mean slaughter more of our kine herd than usual?" asked Thomas making sure he understood his sometimes ambiguous uncle.

"Want ev'ry stew pot we own to be filled, tonight," insisted Robert.

"The men will surely like that, Sire," said Thomas.

"Small folk, too!"

"Aye?" Thomas asked.

"I want none to go hungry this night... Sunday is the vigil of Saint

John and there'll be nae meat that day. And get them to drinkin' plenty of water, Thomas," he said.

Thomas nodded. "'Twill be done, My King." Thomas had the feeling that Robert wanted no man to die with an empty belly.

"And... Thomas," said Robert, "blockade all routes into our camp from the south and west, and set pickets," he said.

"But, there may be more men comin' to fight on our side," protested Thomas.

"No more time to train them in the ways we've trained the others," said Robert, "They'd be a hindrance instead of a help to our plan."

"Aye, Uncle." Thomas hated to turn away any willing to fight.

With that, Robert wheeled his horse and returned to Cockshot Hill by way of the road across the burn. As he passed by he looked over the lands on both sides of his path for that was where his men had dug the pots and scattered the caltrops. Though not obvious in the lush grass, one could make out where some of the holes had been dug, and some of the caltrops could be plainly seen, and he smiled to himself. It would not be a bad thing for the English to know the dangers were there, for his entire purpose in creating the hazards was to frighten Edward's commanders into staying away from this route.

As he ambled along the road he wondered how the young highland fellow, Darach, was healing from the wound he accidentally received from one of the pots early on. He had not seen the spirited and agreeable man for the past several days.

When he reached the park he climbed from his horse and Andrew came to the king to take the reins from him.

"Tell the pinfold gillies that this is my horse for now, Andrew," said Robert.

"Aye, My Lord," said his squire as his shadow, Nigel, stood a few feet away observing Andrew's demeanor.

Robert walked to his newly acquired page and tousled his hair. "Nigel, ye appear to be a Vikin' child with that blonde hair," he said, and Nigel beamed. "Is Andrew teachin' ye to tend a squire's tasks?"

"Aye, Sire," the boy responded. "I can clean chain mail, polish yer helm and boots, and... did ye know that the bog yonder can grab a man's boots and hold 'em 'til they pull right off his feet?"

"I'm glad to know that ye are learnin' such; could save yer life one day," the king said approvingly. "Now, Page, I have a question for ye..." the boy's face grew serious, "... do ye know where yer mother is, now?"

"Oh, aye!" the boy grinned. "I thought ye meant to ask somethin' about my schoolin'! Lady Christina is o'er the hill, at the infirmary, My Lord," said the boy, formally. Andrew handed him the reins to the king's horse and pointed in the direction of the pinfold, and the boy started walking the stallion in that direction.

Watching Nigel walking away the king was reminded of Squire Andrew at that same age, though Andrew's hair was much darker. "Andrew," said Robert.

"Aye, My King."

"Ye must make a decision ere long, ye ken?"

"'Bout what, My King?" Andrew looked puzzled.

"Bein' Steward," said Robert.

"I like bein' yer squire better," he replied and heaved a great sigh.

"'Tis nae the point, Andrew," replied the king. "'Tis time for ye to accept the Stewardship of Scotland as it has come down to ye."

Andrew almost winced at the notion. "I think Walter should have it, Sire. It suits his temperament far better than it does mine, for sure."

"I understand it's a weighty decision for a young man such as ye. But 'twould be best for ye to consider it more," replied Robert putting his arm around Andrew's shoulder. "Yer father has been gone for more than five years, and Scotland needs a High Steward of his strength and good sense. I would have ye take the position."

"Aye, Sire, I know ye would. And I have thought about it, off and on, takin' my father's place at court," spoke Andrew, looking up at his king. "If ye have made me in that image, and figure me to be Steward, then I will do as ye wish."

"Yer father was my good friend and I swore I would see to your upbringin'," said Robert. "I'll nae force ye to take the stewardship against yer will."

"Thank ye, My Lord. I am grateful for yer havin' me serve ye as squire, and I know that my time as such is soon over. I did my best to serve ye well." Robert took a deep breath and stepped away to look at Andrew directly.

"Yer father would be proud of ye, as I am, nae matter which pathway ye choose, Lad," said the king, "But, givin' up yer birthright is a serious matter, and nae done lightly."

"Men are killed in battles," said Andrew trying to rid himself of the subject, at least temporarily. "I shall give ye my decision when our battle here is done, My King."

"Ye will fight in this battle as a knight," announced Robert with no trace of emotion, but a look of great pleasure broke across the face of the squire.

"Nae man is more fitted for the honor or the task... ye *are* ready," said Robert, a slight mist in his eyes denoting a surrogate father's pride.

"I must be away to the kirk, My King, for I am bound to pray for a full day ere I can be knighted," he said. "By yer leave, My King, I would go now."

"Ye have my permission," said Robert, and the young man turned to walk away.

"Sir Andrew," the new knight said, trying out the sound of how he would be addressed after being made knight. He grinned back at his liege lord.

"Begone, Sir Andrew," laughed Robert, and the two men separated company, Andrew to tend to his prayers, and Robert to go to the infirmary, the small temporary shelter of wattle and daub where Christina spent much of her time tending various wounds garnered in training.

Robert came to the doorway and peered into the nearly dark room. Christina looked up to see who was blocking her meager light source. "Robert?" she asked. He said nothing but nodded and backed from the doorway and she knew he wanted her to follow.

Within a moment she emerged with a cloth on which she was wiping her hands, still bloody from sewing a man's face back together. He had been in the way of an overzealous swing of a pike earlier in the day.

"Is that lad ye were doctorin' bad hurt?" he asked, looking at her sanguine hands.

"He's goin' to have a bad scar across the side of his face and one ear's been cropped a bit, but barrin' infection he'll be alright."

"What happened to that lad of Randolph's... Darach... who fell into the pot?"

"Inside," said she softly, "sufferin' greatly... with gangrene, I think. He'll nae last long without heaven's miracle." she said. "He must be delirious, for he's talkin' of ridin' a horse in the battle... when it comes. I doubt he could even sit a horse, now."

"Ach, I'm that pained to hear it! I like the lad... and his only wish is to be on a horse and ride with us to drive out the English!" said Robert sadly.

"They're supposed to be here when?"

"Today... on the morrow... but no later than this comin' Monday, Saint John the Baptist Day," said Robert, "...if they give a damn about the terms of that truce of Mowbray's. Takin' his own sweet time gettin' here, Edward is."

Christina sighed. He looked at her, tired and worn, as if she carried the worries of the world in her heart, and he tried to change the subject, to take her mind off war and death, and dying lads she couldn't save.

"Ye know, that chain mail coif pulls at my beard sometimes. Think I need to take a shave," he said, casually stroking his hairy jaw. "And even if I had no coif to wear, I'd not want Edward to give my beard a yank!"

She laughed a little, trying to appear relaxed with his jest. "I'll shave it for ye," she said, and disappearing for a moment, reemerged with shears, a razor and soap, and a stool one of her recovering patients had made of sticks and rawhide. She motioned him around to the shady side of the hovel where she set the stool near the outer wall, leaving enough room for her to work from behind.

He lifted his chin as she began shearing his abundant auburn beard that was too soon laced with gray, especially around the chin.

"Ye recollect the years we were together," asked Robert trying not to wriggle his jaw.

"I do," she said.

"They were right good years, aye?" he said.

"Aye, Robbie," she said softly, all the while continuing to work the shears and tossing the trimmings into the light wind.

"Easy days," he reminisced.

"War surely wasn't topmost on yer mind then," said Christina, wondering if this conversation had purpose beyond his feeling vulnerable. But then, what other purpose would there be?

Suddenly Christina gasped.

Simultaneously Robert smelled a foul breath close on him and opened his eyes to stare directly into the wild eyes of Sedric the Irish chieftain.

"My God," said Robert, more than a bit startled, "Sedric, where'd ye come from?!"

"Ulster sent me to ye, he did," said Sedric, his enthusiastic eyes darting from one point of interest to another as his smile uncloaked his many rotting teeth. His variety of armament, a drinking cup, and a petrified human arm dangled from a belt around his waist, swaying as he moved.

"Yet kilt all the English, yet?" asked Sedric, fingering the cloth on Robert's yellow tunic.

"There are probably enough left to satisfy ye and yer Irish lads," answered Robert.

"Ye got victuals for mine what come with me to fight?"

"How many are ye?"

Sedric shrugged knowing the king wanted a number and he had no idea what to say.

"Where be yer men?" asked the king as he stood from his seat to tower over Sedric.

"In yon wood, they are, a'waitin' to see if ye kill me or not," said Sedric tingeing his say with a snicker.

"Give them a wave to show we hain't kilt ye as yet," suggested Robert looking toward the wood.

"Shall we finish this later, My King?" said Christina.

"Wait," he asked her.

Sedric waved and danced a little step, and the wood came alive with about a hundred Irishmen, all armed to the teeth.

"How did ye all get here? I gave orders for the west and southwest flanks to be sealed off from more fighters wanderin' in. Did ye see any pickets?"

"Oh, aye, we seen yer pikemen, we did. But we didn't bother 'em none. They be still there a'right." Robert was astounded. A hundred men or more had managed to get by his pickets without raising an alarm.

"Did they not try to stop ye?" the exasperated king asked.

"No, no. They ne'er seen us! When me and them lads want to, we can be so ye can't see us, or hear us, or nothin'. Kinda like ghosts," Sedric's eyes twinkled; he was having a fine time with the king. Robert looked helplessly at Christina, whose mirth was written across her pretty face.

"Well, Sedric, the rest of the army is down at Torwood, to the south," said Robert.

"And we're to be goin' there?" asked Sedric, pouting.

"Go there or stay here," said Robert. "Suit yerself."

"We like to eat by ourselfs," he replied.

"Then do, Sedric," and he added, "I have just the task for ye when the battle comes."

Sedric smiled and repeated, "Ye have victuals?"

Robert pointed down the hill to where the cattle, goats and sheep were penned. "Go yon and tell them that I said for ye to have an animal."

Sedric looked. "Any animal?" he asked, eyeing the variety that was penned.

"One kine only, or two or three of the wee kind... if ye like," said Robert.

"Ye have a goodly heart, King," said the Irish chieftain and slapped Robert hard on the chest, never dropping his relentless smile.

"Goodly *ye* are, as well," said Robert after him as the chieftain made his way downhill and his hundred came to meet him in the middle where their supper, unbeknownst to them, awaited.

Robert returned to his stool.

"Who are they?" Christina asked as soon as she thought Sedric was beyond her voice.

"Wild Irish, My Sweet Love," he said, not realizing he had not called her that for quite a while. She, however, savored the endearment and began to hum a little Irish tune she had learned at the knee of her mother long ago. Tears came and went as she worked but Robert yet had his mind on other notions.

Soon she was finished and she rubbed his almost smooth face with her hand. "Been a long while since I've seen ye beardless, Robbie," she said, feeling the passion of her younger years for the man.

Robert rubbed his own face. "Do I look strange?" he asked.

"Just younger," she replied shaking her head, and gathering her tools she went back into the dispensary where the lad with the gangrene foot was lowly moaning. Robert brought the stool and set it inside the door.

"Can he ride?" asked Robert.

Christina looked at the young man a moment and turned to the king. "He surely has the will, Sire, but ye can't make him ride on what could be the last day of his life!" she pleaded in a whisper.

"Make him?" said Robert, "If we *have* a spare horse or mule, I'll have him put aboard so that he can ride for the sake of his honor... the last day of his life." She looked at him with great round eyes, not believing what he was saying.

"Men!" she spat out, still glaring at him. "Ne'er will I figure ye out Rob Brus!"

Robert was surprised when she turned away from him and to her patients.

"Women!" he muttered under his breath as he left the hovel.

• •

There was a second hastily constructed shelter uphill about thirty yards, near the ridge. There the Bishop of Moray held regular masses for the men, and when he saw Robert walking in his direction, he thought to take advantage of the opportunity to talk to him and so stepped into Robert's path.

"My King!" hailed Murray.

"My Bishop!" returned Robert. He was always glad to see the bishop and greeted him with a smile.

"Ye have gone beardless, aye?" said David.

"Not against God's law, is it?" replied Robert.

"Nae, of course not, Sire," said David, "but, I wanted to tell ye that Abbot Maurice of Inchaffray and Abbot Bernard of Arbroath are within."

Robert pointed to the shack serving as a chapel, the bishop nodded, and they started walking toward it as the king said, "I know both men well. Inchaffray helped us escape after Methven. Why are they here?"

"I sent for them, My King," said Murray.

"Good," said Robert earnestly, "we can use all the spiritual help we can get."

"Arbroath is here havin' brought the Brecbennach," explained the bishop, "... and Inchaffray has brought a relic of Saint Fillan."

"Ye mean like... bones and such?" said Robert lowering his voice.

"Very powerful relics of our blessed saints, they are," insisted David, "a finger bone of Saint Columba and the left arm of Saint Fillan."

The men went into the small shanty and crossed themselves as they faced the roughly made altar. The abbots turned their attention toward him and recognized the king. They bowed slightly, as did Robert.

"Good to see the both of ye once again," said the king quietly.

"We are right glad to see ye as well, My King," said Maurice, beaming.

Abbot Bernard said only, "Sire".

"The king would like to see the reliquaries," said David, and the abbots quickly stepped aside to reveal the sacred boxes atop the small table that was serving as altar. The Brecbennach, was a small, rectangular silver box with a top like a pitched roof, and having reinforced edges, festooned with simple gold designs incorporating several small jewels. The reliquary of Saint Fillan was a highly polished oaken box inlaid with silver and brass, well over a foot in length.

"Would ye like to peer inside?" asked Maurice.

"Nae," said Robert touching the boxes, each in turn.

"I have asked the abbots to help me in saying mass to the many we have here," offered David, at which the king nodded, seemingly deep in thought. "I have a request, actually two requests, Sire." Robert looked up. "First, I ask that when the drums of battle are sounded that I be among the warriors of Moray, My King," said David.

"Ye may fight anywhere ye like, My Bishop. I would ne'er stay yer hand at anythin' ye wish," said Robert.

"And this is my second wish," started David, "that Abbot Maurice lead the army into battle..." He paused and waited for his answer.

"If there is a battle such as he can lead," said Robert, "I would be glad to allow it."

"We shall see how the English array themselves," said David, gratified that he had won accord as far as the king could, at that moment, agree.

"Now, I have an immediate request," said Robert.

"Aye, My King?" said the bishop.

"There is a young man, brave and strong, who is now at Saint Ninian's kirk, laborin' with his day of prayers before knighthood."

"Aye," said the bishop.

"I have taught him much about war, but little about prayers," said Robert. "I would ask that one of ye clerics go teach him how to pray."

"I shall go," volunteered David Murray, "The lad's name?"

"Ye know him... 'tis my squire, Andrew Stewart," said Robert almost reverently.

Pain Tiptoft

SATURÒAY – JUNE 22NÒ
EÒINBURGĥ

The English were more than two days transferring stores from the ships to the confiscated wains. The soldiers had been restlessly mauling the town, building by building and townsperson by townsperson as they drank every drop of anything alcoholic they could unearth, and ate from any table they could find resting a single ort.

Only one full day, Sunday, remained in which to relieve the castle at Stirling, and it was shaping up to be a long, grueling trek with very few respites for men or beasts. There were eighteen miles between Edinburgh and Falkirk and another fourteen to Castle Stirling.

"'Tis a'ready hot and the sun's not a tenth in the sky!" growled Earl Gilbert le Clare.

"The king has not yet aroused," said Raoul, standing beside his horse, as was Gilbert.

Sir Robert de Clifford overheard the men and walked his horse to them so they could all three actively commiserate. "We should have left hours ago to reach Falkirk by dark!"

"We'll never achieve due glory if the king lays abed longer!" mouthed the impatient Gilbert.

"Glory?" said Clifford.

"For what more does a true knight endeavor in battle?" asked Gilbert, surprised.

"Lands, Milord Gloucester!" Clifford replied. "With lands, one has power!"

"I have all the lands I want," Gilbert said, "I want the glory won in battle!"

"Impatient *and* vainglorious," chided Raoul, who knew he would not be challenged by his own stepson but wanted him to realize the errors of his wit.

Gilbert grew full of fury at the remark and climbed aboard his destrier. "Tell the king, when he finally awakes... that we shall meet him in Falkirk!"

Raoul was under Sir Gilbert's command, and thus did as his lord ordered him to do. He mounted and bade follow the five hundred men-at-arms who wore yellow tabards with three red chevrons, as did the earl.

Clifford backed his horse to remove himself from the path of Gilbert and his contingent. He admired the young hothead in many ways, but he was not sure the king was going to be pleased about following Gloucester to Falkirk.

No sooner had the dust settled from the many hoofbeats of the exiting Sir Gilbert than two trumpets sounded and the king emerged from his tent dressed in his finest armor and tabard, especially tailored for the occasion. There was an obligatory roar of approval as Edward walked his few feet to climb a two-step mounting stair and gracefully sat upon his destrier, which was also fully dressed in flagrantly elegant trappings and fallalery. Another round of applause resounded. Sir Roger Northburgh handed the king's shield up to him and he pranced his horse forward, leading his pack amid cheers of the townsfolk happy to see the army leave them.

Behind the extravagant king, his knights, and men-at-arms, the wains, groaning with abundant supplies, lumbered laboriously at their usual two miles an hour. When muddy, the road was scarred with deep ruts by animals and wains alike, but the weather had been dry for several weeks and the hard-baked ruts had become harsh impediments to negotiate with heavily laden wagons. Despite the victuals consumed by the ongoing army, the additional supplies taken on at the docks at Leith had done nothing to hasten the long train, but instead had made it longer and slower.

The soldiers would have eaten better had they time to stop and prepare meals, but 'Falkirk by nightfall' was the tenor of King Edward's wit and will, and he was not to be daunted.

Symonds first spotted the yellow tabards of Gloucester progressing up the road toward Falkirk at a fast pace. "Wonder why Lord Gloucester's so eager that he hastens to the battle," he said aloud, but softly, as if speaking to his companion, who was sound asleep. The pair were hidden in a small bit of wood along the edge of a farmland outside Edinburgh.

"Wake up, David!" he loudly whispered.

David snapped his eyes open. "What!" he said loudly, causing Symonds to put his hand over the offending mouth.

"Hush!" said Symonds, "just look yonder."

David turned his wiry body over, wiped the sleep from his eyes, blinked to get the haze from them, and gazed across the hundred yards, where Gloucester and his men were riding.

"What ye reckon that is?" asked Symonds.

"Heap of English pushin' their horses too damn hard," offered David casually.

"We had best send word to the king," suggested Symonds, the senior member of the duo and therefore the commander. David rolled onto his back and lay there. "Get up and mount yer animal and get to Torwood!" Symonds ordered.

"Shit," whined David. He much preferred going back to sleep since he had kept watch for much of the overnight. "The king's got a'plenty o' lads to take care of that wee pack."

"Get yer goddamned arse on yer horse and ride!" Symonds demanded.

David reluctantly got to his feet and began to saddle his horse. "Why in hell's name does it have to be me?" he said.

"Just get, damn it!"

David finished his saddling and while bridling his horse asked, "Ye got anythin' I can eat, at least?"

Symonds pulled their supply out of his kit and divided it in half, handing one share to David who took the proffered dried meat strips, putting one between his teeth and the rest in his pocket.

"Hurry, and tell King Robert that it's Gloucester and a troop of maybe five hundred, all mounted!" demanded Symonds as David slowly swung his leg over his highland horse and poked out of the wood. "Ye must get there ahead of the goddamn English! And keep yer distance from 'em!" he warned.

Symonds turned his attention back to the road once he had seen David away on his mission. Within a reasonably short while his vigilance was rewarded as the van under the command of Lord Pembroke brought renewed activity upon the roadway. As he watched, the main body of knights and foot soldiers arrived, traveling in the heat on the hard, jolting Roman road to Stirling. Still, he lay waiting, believing that there would be more English soon following.

His suspicions proved out nearly an hour later.

Flags fluttering, horses prancing in expectant liveliness, and armor and weapons glittering in the bright sun, the distant caravan of Edward of England crawled its way along the far end of the road, slithering toward Symonds' hiding place. He held his position only long enough to espy Edward's flag of three gold leopards on a red field, and heart pounding, he threw the saddle across his horse's back and scrambled atop it. As quickly as he could manage, he picked his way through to the back of the copse, so not to be seen by the English, then rode full tilt across country toward Stirling and the waiting Scottish army.

SATURDAY ~ JUNE 22ND
TORWOOD

Robert spent much of the morning with the members of many families who had come to fight by his side: the Robertsons, Macquarries, Macintoshes, Macfarlanes, Mackays, Menzieses, Grants, Macgregors, Munros, Mackenzies, and Macphersons, among the many others that showed up in ones and twos or scores. Grateful, he was, for every warrior who had come to stand on the field with him against what was shaping up to be a vastly superior force, in both men and materiel. It was his intention to look in the eye every man who volunteered to serve with him in this most dangerous, most crucial time, and to grant each one an unspoken sense of his appreciation and his pledge that their beloved Scotland would, at last, be free.

He soon found himself addicted to staring across the south end of Torwood, searching for any sign of the enemy coming forward.

"Ye have spies out, My King," said Robert Boyd noticing Robert's multiple recent glances across the valley below. "Let them bring ye the news!"

"Might have been found out and captured, or killed," said Robert transfixed on his vigil.

"We'll know!" advised Boyd. "Symonds especially seems to be a fellow with his wits about him."

"Aye, but even clever fellows can sometimes be spotted by a sharp enough watch. If ye would, Sir Robert, have Keith and Douglas come to me, mounted... in traveler's clothes and ready to hie," he ordered.

"Aye," said Boyd. He immediately got on his horse and started for the pinfold on Cockshot Hill where he knew the two knights to be.

"Tell Edward that I want to see him, too," shouted Robert after Boyd, who slowed his canter a bit and waved his hand to let Robert know he had heard the message.

The shade formed by the trees edged across Robert while he was silently sitting, still overlooking the valley, contemplating his plan. He had gone over it in his mind many times and every single time he changed some action or placement along the way. The pieces were coming together like one block set against another will eventually build a wall. Each hour, each block, had its own unique character based on its task. If the English were coming this far to kill Scotland, Robert Brus was intending to give the invaders the fight of their lives.

On the other hand, contingencies had to be made to allow Scotland to continue her struggle... if that should become necessary.

Edward Brus, Robert Keith, and James Douglas came to the king together. Robert stood to greet the men, among his most loyal supporters throughout the long years. After some trivial conversation, Robert got to the meat of his purpose.

"James, Robert... I want ye to go off toward Falkirk, but keep to the wood. Spies hain't reportin' back as I figured," he said. "English should have easily been in Falkirk ere now."

"We'll let ye know, My King," said Robert Keith, and he and Douglas turned to leave.

"Want me to go too, Rob?" asked Edward.

"Nae, ye stay. We have much to speak about."

Edward frowned.

The Keith and the Douglas mounted and rode into the wood, where they picked their way down the hill avoiding the obvious road and taking their own path to prevent the enemy from detecting them.

Edward slid off his destrier as Robert sat cross-legged, still watching the two in the distance before they disappeared into a clump of wood.

"Well?" said Edward impatiently.

"Ne'er one to waste a drop of time," said Robert not looking at his brother.

"Yer waste, I was already engaged," he replied still standing.

"Get Thomas," said Robert feeling his brother's glower.

Edward shrugged, left and within a few moments, returned with their nephew in tow. The two men stood downhill from Robert and waited to hear what he had in mind to tell.

There was a long bit of silence before Robert again spoke.

"I will have the bishop write this to parchment this afternoon," started Robert, "but the gist of it is... if I should be killed in the battle, I would have Edward be king."

Edward was shocked that the thought had even been spoken into the air. He looked hard at his brother. He had never wanted to talk about Robert's possible death. To him it was an avoidable subject, for he believed that his own survival would be short lived if his brother died. Brave in battle he was, but he had not the political skills and understanding that Robert so clearly possessed. Edward finally said, "This is ridiculous, Brother! Ye cannot die!"

Spoke the king in a low tone, "We all will die when our time comes, and my time *can* be today or tomorrow."

"I will not believe it!" said Edward.

"Ye been talkin' to the conjurers and witches?" asked Thomas. "Has some auger told ye ye're about to die?"

"I hain't figurin' to die," growled Robert.

"Sounds like it to me," huffed Thomas, earning a quietly exasperated glance from Robert.

"If Edward should go down along with me, then I want ye, Thomas, bein' our sister's son, to be king," continued Robert.

Thomas shrugged, unaffected by the declaration. "That all ye wanted to say, Uncle?"

"That's it," said Robert.

"Then, by yer leave, My King," said Thomas, and he turned and wandered back up the hill to his contingent of highlanders.

"Why must ye think of such a prospect?" asked Edward glumly.

"Because someone... someone that we know will take up the fight to regain Scotland's freedom... *must* be given claim to the throne if I... or we are killed. We have no immunity from death, Edward, nor any notion of what is about to befall us in the next few days," spoke Robert softly, "The future is shrouded."

"My future hain't!" said Edward. "I'm gettin' married to Isabella!"

"She havin' yer bairn, too?" asked Robert pointedly.

"Not yet!" was the answer. The sarcasm was completely lost on his brother's wit and Robert didn't pursue it.

"I expect the Strathbogies will show with their contingent at any time. They're late by some days," said Robert. "Reckon to see Lady Isabella of Strathbogie... showin' up with yer bairn, Edward?"

"She won't be a'showin'," growled Edward.

"But, if she does," warned Robert, "we'll have two wild harpies and both families to fuss with."

Edward shook his head trying to will that possibility from happening.

"Ye'd best see if Walter of Ross has a knight he can send to take his sister safely to the high country," suggested the king, "'til this affray is done."

"We need ev'ry knight we can muster here!" Edward protested.

"One knight will neither win nor lose the battle, Edward," said the king, pushing his brother to make the decision on his own.

"A'right, goddamn it!" shouted Edward going into one of his explosive rebuffs.

"Then, do it now, before we close all the routes... in and out," demanded Robert.

"In and *out?*" asked Edward.

"Aye, we want all ways sealed unless and until we need them as escape routes," whispered Robert.

"Escape routes?" said Edward, not having thought, with his faith in his brother, that they might need such. Robert sensed that all hope had seeped from Edward with his comment, and hastened to replace it.

"If the battle goes badly, ye must take yer men and hie for Lennox. Make sure ye take Earl Malcolm with ye," said the king.

"And where will Thomas flee to?" said Edward sarcastically.

"High lands."

"And ye?"

"The village across the bridge. If any give chase we can defend ourselves at the bridge and head for Dundee."

"That's why ye put our extra stores at the abbey?"

"Aye, that and..." Robert stood, "...if we should get overrun, I don't want to leave the English anythin' that they didn't drag here from London. We have not fought a pitched battle since Loudoun Hill, and that was a stalemate. It's possible that..." A motion on the road caught Robert's eye as he glanced down the glen. "What ye reckon that might be?" he asked.

"Rider comin' mighty fast, I'd say," opined Edward.

"Mighty fast," the king repeated.

As the two men watched, six barded English knights emerged at a gallop from beyond the hill chasing the one, who rode a sorrel horse. All galloped at break-neck speed. "Looks like one of our spies has got himself a problem," said Robert. "Get us horses! Quick!"

Edward hurriedly did as he was told and Robert continued to watch the chase grow closer to him. Suddenly, the horse of the front-runner stumbled and threw the rider, who landed hard, losing both shield and helm.

As the pursuers closed in on him, the downed rider raised himself up and slowly gathered enough strength to climb back atop his nearly exhausted mount, but without his shield, it having skittered irretrievably away. He kicked the animal repeatedly to make it go faster, but the spent beast had little left to give in response.

Edward returned with horses and handed the reins of the white one to his brother at the same moment Thomas arrived. As Robert clambered aboard his mount, the other two took off down the long slope toward the lone rider as the English horsemen neared him.

"Not goin' to make it!" said Robert as he quickly followed, but his fear was lightened as Keith and Douglas tore out of the woods below them and toward the rider.

"Great God!" yelled Thomas, delighted to see the pair, who were far closer to and riding fast at the English.

"As I reckoned... 'tis our spy!" yelled Robert Keith when he was close enough to identify the sorrel rider. The Bruses and Randolph were still relatively far behind them.

"Looks like Gloucester's knights," yelled back Douglas, referring to the yellow tabards with three red chevrons.

Keith and Douglas soon passed the single rider, who reined in his mount and wheeled around. He sat for a moment just trying to catch his breath, and rode after them.

Keith had pulled his axe from its loop on his saddle and Douglas his broadsword from its sheath. Symonds, the spy, pulled his short sword ready to do whatever damage he could muster to the six.

Seeing that the odds had dramatically changed, the English knights' confidence lessened and their gallop slowed, but Keith and Douglas continued at top speed, reaching the six and attacking as if in a joust, engaging them whilst riding through their midst. Keith's axe struck the first blow, hacking deep into the arm of the first man he came to, felling him to the ground where he lay dazed and profusely bleeding.

Douglas' buckler deflected the sword of one knight as he passed by him and he leant underneath another man's sword arm, striking him just under his ribs with nearly the force of a lance, though it almost threw Douglas to the turf at impact. The metal rings of the man's chain mail ripped open before the sword point and filled the air with the tiny polished ringlets as the sword ran the man completely through. He never had a chance even to scream. His falling body wrenched the sword hilt from Douglas' hand, leaving him momentarily disarmed.

No matter. He swung his mount in a quick turn and charged back toward the remaining four, as had Keith.

Just one of the Englishmen continued on his original quest and tried to silence Symonds before he could report to his king. The barded knight held his lance steady as he went straight for Symonds' heart on a tightly controlled run. Having no shield or even a buckler, Symonds could only veer away before the knight got to him. Better trained than the hapless Scot, the English knight quickly adjusted and caught Symonds with a glancing blow to his right side, but it was enough. Blood gushed forth, bathing Symonds' whole side and most of his leg in scarlet. He twisted and doubled over, hanging on desperately, his horse seemingly riderless as Symonds lost its reins while trying to hold his wound together.

Keith had tried to catch up to the knight before he could reach Symonds, but the man was too close. Having wounded Symonds the knight turned about to strike again, only to meet Keith's deadly axe.

Seeing how fast their companions were dispatched and with Robert and Thomas quickly closing upon them, the other three turned and hied in the direction from whence they had come.

Robert pulled his throwing axe from his belt and with deadly aim, threw it, taking a fourth man to the ground.

Thomas and Edward continued after the remaining two, but Robert called them back, thinking they were being led into a trap.

"They are out of reach," said Robert, "and we must see to our spy."

Other knights arrived and placed themselves between the king and the retreating English at Edward's direction.

Symonds was still holding tight to his saddlebow when Keith and Thomas got to him. The sorrel was skittish and they had difficulty catching him at first.

"Struck in the right side," observed Thomas as he took hold of the horse's bridle.

"He goin' to live?" asked Robert. Thomas, experienced enough to know how much blood a man could lose and yet live, looked at Robert and shook his head while Symonds remained hunched over.

"Symonds," Robert put his hand on the man's shoulder, "what have ye brought to us?" asked Robert straightforwardly. Symonds, pale as death, raised his head to look at his king but said nothing.

"What about the English?" Robert pressed.

"They're movin', Sire! 'Ppeared to be headin' for Falkirk, left Edinburgh this mornin'."

"Falkirk today, here tomorrow," said Thomas.

"If they got an early enough start... the van could be here today," opined Douglas.

"Late start," gasped Symonds, who was beginning to gurgle.

"Get him off this horse," said Robert, "Get Lady Christina!" he shouted to one of the just arrived knights, and the man took off up the hill at a gallop while Thomas, James, and Edward dismounted and took Symonds from his bloody saddle and laid him on the soft green grass.

"Ye two," Robert spoke to Douglas and Keith, "can hie for Falkirk and let me know exactly what is goin' on with the English!"

"Aye, My King," offered Keith as he wheeled about. James Douglas quickly climbed aboard his horse and followed Keith south.

"It's all over, men," said Robert to the remaining latecomers. "Strip the dead and fetch back their horses!" He then knelt beside Symonds as the man continued to talk.

"Found David, Sire... with me at Edinburgh... dead on the trail at Winchburgh... the six were layin' in wait for me." His lips continued to move, but no sound came forth, and Robert took Symonds' hand and began repeating a prayer he had learned from his Celtic mother.

Robert de Umfraville,
Earl of Angus

SATURDAY ~ JUNE 22ND
FALKIRK

In the village of Falkirk stood a tavern wherein the Earl of Gloucester, his stepfather, and others of his best knights had gathered, knowing they were far ahead of the pack led by Sir Aymer de Valence.

Gilbert le Clare stood drinking his ale while Raoul sat nearby at a table with two knights who had been in his service when he held the earldom.

Suddenly burst through the door two of the earl's men, panting like wolves run hard. "They've killed the rest!" loudly announced the first through the door.

At that Raoul stood, ready to act in his own and others' defense, as did every man within the room. Stools and benches overturned and loudly clattered to the floor as swords and daggers were unsheathed.

"Who was killed?!" demanded the young earl.

"The ones you sent to kill the spy, Milord!" the knight quickly responded.

"You appear to be lively enough," said Earl Gilbert, acidly.

"Of our six," the knight gasped between breaths, "we two are the survivors!"

"You run into a mighty force?" their liege lord asked.

"Four," the second man answered, adding, "...five countin' the spy."

"Let me get this rightly... five killed the other four of your troop, but spared the two of you?" asked Gilbert as if pondering the odds.

"We fled after the others fell, Milord, for then we were but two against five," explained the knight, hoping for understanding and not expecting to be exemplified.

"Why were you not also killed?" asked Gilbert chiding his men. "Are you such cowards!?"

The knights looked at each other and bowed their heads.

"How many of the five were killed?" Raoul asked.

"Perhaps one, Milord."

"What do you mean, 'perhaps'! Was one Scot killed or was he not?!"

"One of them was probably killed, Milord. He was terrible hurt, for sure!" the second knight hastened to add.

"Was it the spy, at least?" queried Raoul.

"Aye, Sire, 'twas the spy," declared the first.

"It was the spy who was gravely wounded," nodded the other, hopefully trying to escape the earl's ire.

Disappointed, Gilbert cursed them before their peers and told them to begone from his sight.

The roomful of drinkers, some of whom were thankful they had not been on the ill-fated ride, righted the benches and soon resumed a normal social din and braggadocio.

Shortly, the door opened once again, to be entered by one large man and another of average height and weight. It was the Earl of Angus, Robert de Umfraville. The brawny man loudly greeted the smaller Gloucester. "We've been here for days a'waitin' yer arrival, Sir."

"My compliments to you, My Lord," said Gilbert bowing slightly to the man, whom he had met at Wark and disliked immediately. He was dead set against any whom he considered a turncoat, and Earl Robert appeared to him to be one, though he was almost the last of the Scottish earls to yet be outside of the Brus' 'peace'.

"Ye remember my brother, Sir Ingram, I trust," offered Sir Robert alluding to his companion. "Many times he has fought for and against these same Scots we be now against. He was at Loudoun Hill," bragged Robert for all to hear, grabbing his brother by the collar and pulling him to the fore, "... where he would have killed that damned Robert Brus had that damned Pembroke not stayed his hand and rode off... sneakin' coward that he is!"

"Brother!" Ingram flushed, displeased and embarrassed.

"'Tis sooth!" insisted Robert.

"We know well of Sir Ingram's reputation," said Gilbert, taking a swig from his cup.

Several snickers were heard around the room by those who listened, but if heard, they were ignored while Ingram left the presence of his boastful brother and went in search of ale.

"Hain't seen the king, as of yet," said Earl Robert glancing about as the innkeeper placed a cup of ale in his hand and stood expecting his coin. Robert tried to ignore the quiet man but the fellow defied the earl by standing in front of him, no matter which way he would turn. Finally the earl reached into his drawstring pouch and pulled forth the least coin he had and slapped it into the wordless man's hand. After examining it carefully, the innkeeper left the substantial earl in peace.

Whilst the two earls stood in proximity to each other and discussed the imminent battle, the Earl of Gloucester finished his ale and called for another... his fourth. By this time the English earl's caution diminished and his opinions increased, and he was less inclined to keep his own council.

"King'll be along directly, I reckon," he said. "We're the van."

"Van, aye," said Angus.

"Grew tired of waitin' for that goddamned king!" admitted Gilbert, causing Lord Angus' eyebrows to lift in surprise. In order to protect his stepson, de Monthermer was compelled to take the Scottish earl by the arm and walk him to the other side of the room before the hot headed Sir Gilbert's ale-soaked wit left him sinking in his own lack of political insight.

• •

At the edge of the wood and slightly uphill from the small tavern, Sir Robert Keith and Sir James 'the Black" Douglas lay scouting for information on the disposition of the expected English army. It was immediately clear that most of the gathered troops about Falkirk wore the Earl of Gloucester's tabard, though there were also quite a few of Lord Angus'.

But those were all. None of Edward's, none of Lancaster's, Pembroke's, Hereford's, Warwick's, or of any of the major knights' arms were seen, though the pair knew that Edward and Pembroke had left Edinburgh.

Keith and Douglas lay in the dark shade of the trees and moved little, observing who came and who went about the tavern and village.

"Wonder how long before Edward gets here," spoke Douglas in a hushed whisper to Keith.

"Gloucester's been here for a while... and those Umfravilles. Some of those men have been drinkin' long enough that they barely can stand," Keith pointed out. "Even if Edward delayed more at Edinburgh after Gloucester left, he must be nearin' Falkirk anon."

"He must arrive ere long or he won't make it to Stirlin' in time," said Douglas.

Hardly were the words out of his mouth when there was the slight rustle of distant movement on the ancient roadbed. As time wore on, the faint but continual murmur grew louder until it became a rumbling of hundreds of horses' hoofbeats mingled with the steady rhythm of an army in motion, leather saddles and armor complaining of the stresses, metal weapons and fittings jangling, horses' whinnies, officers occasionally shouting at their troops, scores of flags and banners fluttering constantly in the dry breezes.

As the two Scots watched, the contingent of weary knights, horses, and retinue of the Earl of Pembroke slowly ground its way into the village of Falkirk after an exhausting journey of twenty-three miles from Edinburgh, made longer and more tiring by the whim and caprice of their king. Thrice they had been halted on the road to allow the king and those following to rest or to close the gap between the forces.

"Looks like Pembroke's wore to a nub," said Douglas, and they both quietly snickered. "God knows, I'm glad I hain't on this journey with Edward, but Pembroke's bit off what he can't chew, this time."

Pembroke dismounted with much difficulty and held onto his saddlebow a few moments before letting his squire take the poor, tired beast to feed and rest him, and before Aymer could get to the door of the tavern, he was stopped by three different subordinates requiring orders or instructions. By the third, Aymer de Valance threw his hands up in rage and cursing loudly, stormed into the tavern.

Though they could not hear any of his words except his cursing, the spies at the edge of the wood knew the gist of his displeasure, and that he would be unfit to be in polite company for a good while. Within minutes of his entry, their suspicions were confirmed when men began drifting out of the small confines of the tavern. While some tarried in the tavern's vicinity, others meandered away to get themselves bedded down for the night or to take some supper.

"Poor ol' Pembroke," chortled Keith. "I hear he was made Warden of Scotland."

"Pfagh!" said Douglas, "Surely Edward wouldn't do that again! Scotland didn't much like it the first time he did it," and he paused. "Uh oh! That lad's headed this way!" Keith looked in the direction Douglas pointed and saw a knight on horseback heading directly for them. Both men quickly moved farther into the trees where they couldn't be seen, but pulled their weapons.

Douglas and Keith stood silently with perspiration beading on their brows, knowing that if they were spotted by the knight and he were able to sound an alarm, they could not possibly get away before some of the thousand or so knights in the area caught up to them. They had left their horses a few hundred yards away in a small valley behind the copse so that the animals could not give their presence away. It might as well have been miles.

The knight's fatigued horse slowly plodded up the long hill and picked its way into the tree line, stepping carefully among the detritus of the forest. The sleepy knight could barely keep his eyes open, but as he passed over the area in which the two men had been lying, he noticed that there was something amiss and stopped his mount. He couldn't understand what was disturbing him, but his wit finally told him to draw his sword. That he did, and looked all about him without seeing any danger. Still, he was uneasy, as if a spirit looked over his shoulder. His own discomfiture unnerved his horse, and the animal began to dance about.

It was then that "The Black" Douglas leapt on him and introduced his dagger to the man's throat, precluding all his efforts at calling an alarm. His eyes wide with the knowledge of his doom, the knight looked helplessly at James until his eyes rolled back into his head and he fell to the forest floor.

The knight's panicked horse sidled away from James but was caught by Keith before he left the deep shade of the thicket. Keith held the steed's bridle tightly and talked softly to him while he stroked his face and neck, calming him down with the instincts of an experienced horse trainer.

"Wonder why he wouldn't let me touch him," Douglas said.

"Probably because of the smell of blood about ye, Lad. Yer whole arm and sleeve are soaked with the poor bastard's blood," Keith opined. Douglas looked down at his arms, and the right one was soaked, as his companion said.

Leaving the horse in the midst of the wood they returned to look all about the area where they had lain to spy on the tavern, but found nothing that would have indicated their presence. Yet the man lying dead nearby had seen or sensed something that told him there was danger there. After failing to find a reason for his fear, they all but concluded it would probably never be known.

A familiar sound broke into their consciousness as they stood scratching their heads at the mystery, sending them to lie down again into the lair from where they could see the road south. A great horde of mounted knights were approaching, led by flags and banners of myriad colors and devices, including the red banner and three gold passant leopards guardant of the king of England. Beyond the pageantry of the flags were mounted trumpeters and drummers, who heralded the king himself, with Sir Giles d'Argentan riding at his bridle, his shield of red displaying three white cups, covered.

Near the king rode Hugh le Despenser, the younger, his shield quarterly white and red fretty with a black bendlet; Edmund de Mauley, the king's seneschal, a gold shield with black bend; Robert de Clifford, blue and gold checky with red fess; Humphrey de Bohun, Earl of Hereford, a blue shield with white bend cottised gold between six gold lioncels rampant; his nephew Henry de Bohun, a shield like his uncle's, except with red bend; Henry de Beaumont, a blue shield with gold semy de lys, a gold lion rampant, and a bendlet of white and red over all; a gold one with a red fleur de lys, belonging to Adam Gordon. The two Scots recognized most of the banners or shields.

Some they did not. A red banner with a white chevron, a white one with a red fess and three green popinjays; a red shield with three gold sheaves; the variations were so numerous that it was impossible to name them all.

"That's John Comyn," said James Douglas.

"Seen enough?" asked Keith. "The column seems unending."

"Aye. Edward has arrived," Douglas commented dryly. "But there are some whose forces are here, but they are not. See yonder?" he pointed to scores of men wearing the red tabard identical to the king's, but with France's blue label and said, "Thomas of Lancaster, though he rode not with the king, nor is he with his knights."

"Nor is Warwick, though yonder are his men," agreed Keith, indicating tabards of red with a gold fess and six gold crosslets. "What does this mean to us?"

"Don't know. Let's get out of here and back to King Robert with what we have. This whole place is soon goin' to be overrun by Edward's army. We leave now, or ..." The two men cautiously arose from their shaded places and stole away into the depths of the coppice. They retrieved the dead man's horse they had left tied to a tree and took him with them. "Can always use another warhorse," they agreed.

Behind them, the sea of men continued to swirl around the town until there was hardly room for the men to lie down to sleep in the whole of Falkirk. The wains and wagons continued to wend their way along the road though it would be well into the next day, after Edward would arrive at Bannok, before the last of the train would come by the small tavern.

Wanting to relax amid the comfort of his own surroundings rather than being subject to those in which he had placed himself, the king was forced to wait an hour or so for his 'things'. He wanted to have nothing to do with the tavern and had little interest in the people of Scotland, thinking of them as the least of his subjects, if at all.

Soon the wains with the king's kit and caboodle arrived in good order and the men of the royal household started pitching his tents.

The large canopy was well up, the over-sized table was assembled inside the tent and easily within sight of the tavern, when Pembroke and d'Argentan were seen pouring over maps and drinking fine wines from the king's rolling wine stores, and within a half hour word spread to the other earls and barons and the king was suddenly inundated with opinions over the same two maps which had been, at one point, very clear in his mind.

Warm wine at the end of a hot day burned what good sense any of them might have had to an alcoholic cinder.

Straight from Falkirk, Sir Robert Keith and Sir James Douglas rode. By the time they drove their mounts hard up the hill into the Torwood, their horses and the dead knight's were all three well lathered with the strain of the long run.

"Where be the king?!" shouted Douglas to the closest man they encountered.

"Saw him yon, Sire," said the man, pointing to his right and thus deeper into the wood.

"Here, take this horse to the pinfold and have him cooled down and fed." Keith threw the reins toward the man and the two riders quickly hied in the direction he had indicated.

Robert stood when he saw the two men coming toward him.

"What be the news?" asked Robert as soon as they neared.

"Sire, they're at Falkirk a'right," said Keith, swinging his leg over the horse's back and stepping down from his saddle.

"There's a'plenty of them, too!" added Douglas, who freed his feet of the stirrups and slid around and off his mount.

"When ye reckon they'll be here?" asked Robert as Thomas came to stand with the knot.

"On the morrow," said Douglas.

"Day after's the last day of the pact, aye?" asked Keith.

"We'll be ready, My Friend," said Robert, a strong resolve in his voice.

"The men have had a stout meal with plenty o' meat, a'ready," said Thomas, "What do ye want them to do?"

"Tonight, we sleep in New Park," said Robert.

"What... just pick up our cook fires and walk o'er there?" asked Thomas, his brows forming a serpentine line.

"We have a reasonable time ere the sun is set," said the king, "but hasten we must."

"Ye mean we've got to get this done afore dark?!" asked Douglas.

"I have given Mowbray safe passage to go meet with Edward, a'ready," replied Robert, "ye two must have passed him on his way there."

"We saw nobody, My King," said Keith.

Robert pulled a parchment from his pouch.

Keith frowned and asked, "Ye want them to think we're still in the Torwood?"

"I do," replied the king, searching for a nib.

Edward saw that something was happening and came to join the meet.

"Glad ye're here, Edward," said Robert. "We're movin' the army to New Park, now."

"Glad I happened by," said Edward sarcastically. Robert caught the jibe, but yet hoped that Edward would keep his promise.

"King Robert!" Cuthbert shouted as he rushed to the meeting place. "Yer man from the castle just passed us by, Sire!" said the Scot, and leaned over putting his hands on his knees whilst he gasped for breath.

"Take that sorrel, yonder and go back to the village. Tell them to let nae more leave," ordered Robert.

"Aye, Sire," said Cuthbert, "right away!" Gratefully, Cuthbert untied the horse's reins from the tree and, putting his foot into the stirrup easily mounted Symonds' horse. Seeing there was dried blood on the animal and the saddle, he asked, "This horse wounded?"

"Nae, he's nae wounded," said Thomas. "Just get to the village with him!" With a sharp kick from Cuthbert, the horse fairly jumped off toward the castle mount, Cuthbert hanging on, which garnered a few amused grins and chuckles from the men in the meeting.

Robert recalled the attention of the commanders and referred to his small parchment as he spoke. "Thomas, ye will line yer high landers up on the road facin' Cockshot Hill. With ye will be Ross and his men, and Sutherland and his..." he continued to read, "and those here from the northwest... Elgin, Nairn... Forres... Campbells... and Frasers. Should total around five hundred."

"Aye, My King," said Thomas.

"Edward," said Robert looking at his brother, "ye will be the second to line up."

"Beside Thomas?" asked Edward now getting more enthused at the prospect of the battle.

"Aye," replied the king.

"Ye'll have the men of Galloway ye got here'bouts... the earls of Lennox and Strathern and their men..." he looked up at Edward, "... make sure Strathern's fightin' alongside his son..." he looked back to his list, "... and men from Angus... Buchan... and the Mearns and Menteith," concluded Robert.

"Douglas will have the next division," he continued, "... along with Walter the Stewart, Robert Boyd... and the men from Renfrew, the borders, and Strathclyde. Understood, James?"

"Aye, Sire," Douglas agreed.

"And me, My King?" asked Sir Robert Keith.

"As ye know, and how we've trained, ye will lead the cavalry which is a'ready on Cockshot Hill," he said. "Ye have a mix of ev'rybody who can ride, includin' those Templars who arrived with Graham.

"Vieuxpont with me?" asked Keith. "There was some word about him bein' elsewhere."

"Aye," said Robert, "He'll be with ye."

"And who's with ye, My King," asked Edward.

Robert read down the list: "Men from Carrick, Bute, Kintyre, Argyll, Fife... and Strathmore... and the archers will be under my command."

Then he added, "Put yer warriors in three ranks with all their armor and weapons... tell them to remember their places in the line. They will march o'er to New Park in good array. The small folk can come later."

"Be prepared to move at a moment's notice. We've had word that the English king is now in Falkirk and should arrive by way of the road on the morrow. I pray that we have used our time well. God be with ye all."

The Scottish lieutenants scattered to the various parts of the wood to gather their commands as the king had assigned them. As the word of the enemy's approach circulated amongst the men, almost all of them were keyed up that their wait for real action was nearly over. The next two days would decide their fates, and Scotland's.

Robert assigned Angus Macdonald to organize his command. His was the largest, numbering around two thousand troops, about the same as Edward's and Douglas' forces combined. Keith had less than five hundred horsed warriors and Douglas would have a small cavalry of about thirty to work in concert with his foot soldiers.

The regiments had been established rather much as the men had been trained. These were, for the most part, hardened warriors who were accustomed to fighting man on man, but now, against England's immense army drawn from all over the Continent as well as England's north, Wales, and Ireland, they would either fight together, flee, or die.

Within the hour, just as the king had wanted, the regiments were organized and standing shoulder to shoulder on the old Roman road where it passed through the Torwood. Darkness would soon be on them and they had to move quickly to get to New Park and settle in.

Robert walked the length of their lines on foot to understand their mindset. He found them strong in spirit and willing, if necessary, to die for their country's independence.

When Robert got to Thomas Randolph, calmly sitting atop his horse at the end of the line, he looked at his stalwart nephew and said, "My Earl, Godspeed." He then held out his hand to Thomas of Moray and Thomas clasped it warmly.

"Guess this is it, Uncle," answered Thomas and he released Robert's hand, adding, "I shall see ye in New Park, My King." Then he turned his horse toward his men and shouted, "A'right, Lads! Follow me!"

He turned his horse completely in the opposite direction and the men of his command turned toward him in good fashion and followed him.

"Turn to yer left," yelled Edward, as he climbed aboard his horse, and once mounted shouted, "On to New Park!" As did the first regiment, the second followed their commander in good order.

Douglas also commanded his men to turn left and led them in a march onward.

As the men walked past him, many cheered King Robert, who walked to where his regiment stood. He, too, put his foot in the stirrup and rose up to sit upon his horse and gave the order, "To yer left!" His men turned smartly and followed their king out of the Torwood, across Milton Ford, up the slight hill and another half mile into the New Park. When Thomas and his regiment reached a point within a hundred yards of Saint Ninian's Kirk, they all halted and held their place until the others joined them.

In the waning moments of the daylight Robert again reviewed the troops to see how they had positioned themselves on the field. Satisfied that the men had worked well together, he sent them off to settle down and, perhaps, get some sleep.

The king positioned his own regiment along the south end of the New Park to protect the road, just in case Edward of England had discovered this move by the Scots.

The small folk, left behind at Torwood, took another two hours after a grayed darkness set in, to get their cooking and other paraphernalia across the burn and set up in New Park. They would get little or no sleep for they would have food ready for the warriors, come Sunday morning.

SATURDAY - JUNE 22ND
FALKIRK

Sir Philip de Mowbray arrived in the English encampment at just about dark, too late to talk to anyone. The king, so they said, was asleep and none of the earls or barons had an interest in hearing news before the king for fear of incurring the king's wrath.

Aymer de Valence, his head covered with his hood, sat in the corner of the tavern drinking strong ale and finding an interest in watching his fellow warriors turning their usual unthinking ways into absolutely witless behavior. They fought or they argued over petty subjects, usually wrapped around their general cockiness, their boasting most often based on lies told to impress the tavern wenches, or as a vain attempt to make the next man seem inferior to the boaster, somehow.

It was within this atmosphere that Sir Philip Mowbray unwittingly strode in, with no place to sleep and no way of contacting the king to get one in a town suddenly swelled to fifty-fold its normal size. He had several other disadvantages as well, not the least of which were a Scottish accent to his tongue and the fact that he wore clothing of a man of poorer status than his own, lest he be accosted in his travels.

Several losels, not knowing they were in the presence of a man of import to their king, engaged him, with malevolent intent, in a conversation.

"Where be your colors, Scotsman?" asked a soldier. Just to scare poor Mowbray, the lackwit pulled his dagger.

"I need show nae colors to the likes of ye," the warden of Castle Stirling responded, coldly. "I am here on the king's business!" he stated flatly and started to move away.

The inebriated warrior held Philip's sleeve tightly in one great hairy paw and brought his blade up to where Mowbray could plainly see it. "King's business!?" He and his fellows laughed and would have felt fully justified in cutting the Scotsman's throat.

The warden continued pulling against the warrior's tight grip. "Unhand me!" he insisted, bravely in the circumstance.

The lout jabbed the edge of his dagger against Philip's neck just under the jaw line and put his own face close. Stirling's warden had no trouble smelling stale drink on the man's otherwise horrible breath, and suddenly he realized his fearful position. He didn't want to encourage the man to behave rashly, and so held fast his composure though he could feel a drop of blood trickle down his neck.

Suddenly the man was jerked backwards by a force greater than his own and thrown to the floor.

Aymer stood over him with one foot on the man's midriff, his tabard telling the drunken oaf that he had been handled by Lord Pembroke himself. Then it was his turn to squirm in fear.

"Milord, we meant no harm," he tried to spread the blame to his companions," … 'twas only playful jestin'," the man lied in vain.

Aymer kicked his foot down upon the souse's abdomen once and the fellow rolled to his side, doubled in half and regurgitating his last ale or two. His drinking companions dispersed as if smoke in a breeze.

"Reckon they called it a night," said Pembroke, his back toward the warden.

"Thank ye, Sir Knight, for havin' saved my life," said Mowbray, dabbing at his jaw with a kerchief pull from around his neck.

"D'ye not recognize me?" asked Pembroke pushing the hood from his head as he turned.

Mowbray looked the man in the face and said, "Lord Pembroke!"

Aymer nodded it was so.

"We came to Scotland together… more than… than…,"

Pembroke interrupted his thought, "eight years ago."

"Aye," said Mowbray, "I recollect standin' on the walls of Perth bickerin' with the Brus when we came to the notion of trickin' him."

"At Methven Park," said Pembroke walking back to his corner table, Mowbray following. In the wake of the two men was the tired but enthusiastic tavern keeper who was determined to stay awake for as long as the coin or the drink lasted. "Twas Umfraville came up with the thought." Pembroke paid the purveyor for two cups of ale and the innkeeper slid the specie into the palm of his hand and left.

"How did ye escape Stirlin'?" asked Pembroke in his gruff way.

"Was allowed to come," he answered, "safe passage from the Brus himself."

"Brus let you out?"

"Kindly of him, aye?"

"Wily of him, I'd put it," said Pembroke taking a swig from his fresh cup as it arrived at the table.

"Wily… did ye say, Milord?" questioned Mowbray feeling a bit duped.

"As I remember…" he wagged his finger at Mowbray as the image came back to him, "…you had the reins of Brus' destrier in your hand at Methven! Yet he lives!" said Pembroke.

"What do you mean?" said Mowbray feeling insulted and half standing.

"Drink your ale!" said Aymer, "I simply meant to say he's an illusive man. I thought I had his reins in my hands many a time... yet he's somewhere around Stirlin,' a'waitin' for this great army to relieve him, and his rebellion, from their chores on this earth."

Mowbray returned to his seat slowly, thinking all the while that a trick must have been played on him.

"Ye reckon Brus'll be there in the morn?" asked Mowbray quietly, sipping from his foam-topped cup.

The keeper's wife came with two more cups for the corner table. The strings on the top of her kirtle were intentionally loosened and when she bent to place the cups on the table she showed her bountiful breasts very well to Lord Pembroke. He laid two small coins on the table for the ale. She picked up the coins and Pembroke watched her all the way back to the casks from where the cups had been drawn. She showed the innkeeper the coins and smiled. He cursed and put the coins into his pouch. She looked back at Earl Aymer and smiled. He grinned and nodded.

"Ye reckon?" repeated Mowbray.

"Reckon what?" growled Aymer, his mind taken elsewhere.

"That Brus will be on the scene in the morn?" said Mowbray.

Pembroke drank, keeping his eye on the alewife. "How in the hell should I know?" he responded irritably.

Mowbray was perplexed. Had Brus duped him? Would all of his information be used against King Edward's army? By letting him have safe passage, was the Brus getting him out of the way so the Scots could high tail it into the rough country and get away? *How could that possibly be?* he wondered. Suddenly nothing made sense to him for all of his scheming and planning.

"What are ye a'sayin' Pembroke?" he bluntly asked.

Pembroke looked at him with a lusting twinkle in his eye and asked, "You want to share a wench tonight?"

Mowbray was tired, frustrated, and confused. He drained his cup and slammed it onto the table. "If it gets me a bed for a few hours, Aye!"

SUNDAY - JUNE 23RD
BANNOK

The Scots were taking whatever advantage they could of their tree-shaded morning coolness. They knew that it was going to be another hot June day, but they knew not how bloody it might end. After all, the English were so close that the battle could be fought at any hour.

Robert awoke and laid Christina's head carefully onto the crumpled wool blanket that served as pillow. He was thankful for the sleep, knowing that the English would be like wolves coming on as soon as they were up and able. He had posted spies at the halfway point and at the overlook on the south of Torwood, thus giving his army the most time possible to prepare.

He knew also that the English were unlikely to send snipers to kill as they might. Theirs was a stratagem of overwhelming with numbers and running the Scots over with sheer strength.

Christina opened her eyes and saw Robert sitting, putting his boots on. She smiled and reached to touch him, then abruptly recalled what day it was… Sunday, the eve of St. John the Baptist's Day. She sat up, wide awake.

"They be here today, ye reckon?" she whispered.

"I don't know," he said quietly. "If they come, we'll be ready for them as best we can."

Christina rubbed his strong arm with affection. He looked at her and smiled. "Ye need to get my new squire fit for battle."

She winced and turned her head as tears welled in her eyes. She had given much thought to Robert's placing her son by him in the path of fully armored English warriors, and yet, it was no more than Robert's father had done to him, and no doubt, his father as well. She could not withdraw him now and was terrified of the possibilities.

"He is soon to be a man, Christina," said Robert reading her thoughts by her actions.

"I understand," she replied, "and I want him to be a man like his father."

Robert smiled before he put on his shirt and turned on his knees. Christina stood and held his heavy chain mail shirt out to him.

"I won't need that 'til after I get back.

"Get back?" she looked at him questioningly.

"Aye, I'm goin' to ride over to the carse to see how deep the burns are," he said. He stood and fastened his belt around his waist.

"Suppose ye're taken unaware?" said she.

"I'll have my axe, Lass," he smiled, knowing that nothing he said would calm her fears, and picking up his axe he showed her that he was keeping it close. "Don't worry, Milady. I'll return," and with that he strode to the pinfold for his horse, soon to head toward the Bannok Burn.

Christina awakened Nigel and started him dressing. His excitement all but overwhelmed her. He talked incessantly as he put on one piece of clothing after another while her own mood despaired as his elated.

"'Twill be hot today, Nigel," she said, "dress as light as ye dare," and unable to bear any longer watching him prepare for war, she slipped out into the morning light.

He finished and came outside the tent to find his mother talking to Dianna.

"Nigel, yer first duty of the day is to hie to the kirk and fetch Andrew back here," instructed his mother. Without a word he set off for the small kirk just down the lane and over the hillock in his yellow tabard, *a miniature of his father*, she thought.

"When?" asked Christina as she returned to Dianna.

"Soon," she said, "the babe has grown lower and kicks less, and... other signs are there," she said demurely.

"Well, ye may be a long time from the birth, so ye mustn't tell David, at least, not yet!" said Christina.

"I wouldn't dare," the Templar's woman declared.

"And stay close to me, today, no matter what may happen!" said Christina.

Dianna nodded her head, not sure she would be able to keep that implied promise.

As the women discussed the oncoming labor, the rest of the Scottish camp was coming fully alive and the thousands of men and women gathered there held their excitement and fear, and hope, in abeyance as they went about their daily routines. Their fires crackled in small echoes in the clearing, and the smell of burning wood and of bannocks baking on hot stones hung effortlessly in the air.

• •

Not far away Sir Edward Brus was having a domestic quandary of a different kind.

"Ye can come back as soon as the troubles are past," he argued.

Isabella turned. "Ye'll not get me to leave!"

"'Tis only that I'm tryin' to protect ye," said Edward then turning to Walter and asking, "Can ye not speak some sense to her?"

Walter of Ross stepped forward, "Isabella, Dearest Sister, it would be for the best if ye were off to the mountains…"

"Ask if Christina is fixed to hie for the mountains!" she interrupted.

"Christina is needed here for her skills," said Edward.

"Skills?!"

"She can doctor wounds," Walter explained.

"And I hain't any skills, I reckon," she blurted back.

Edward huffed, and throwing his hands into the air, turned away from her and left.

"We'd have ye to get out of harm's way… that's all," said Walter one more time.

"I understand yer notion but I hain't leavin'," she insisted.

Frustrated, Walter shook his head and looked at his sibling. "A'right then… See if ye can help Christina today!"

He went to join Edward, whom he found standing not far away. His squire was tying his tabard over his chain mail. "Reckon she's stayin'," said Walter.

"Weren't exactly how I saw it endin'," said Edward. "Let her stay as she wills it."

"Agree," said Walter as his squire began to straighten his chain mail jerkin so he could slip it on.

"Don't ken her wit," said Edward.

"Always strong willed, she was," he replied. "Takes after our mother."

"Reckon I always had witless wenches up 'til now," said Edward almost under his breath. "Think I might have fared better with them!"

"That include Isabella de Strathbogie?" asked Walter quietly.

Edward's head snapped. "What about her?!"

"We heard," said Walter, "'Bout yer bastard bairn."

"Well, I hain't seen it!" struck back Edward.

"Our Isabella said she didn't care what ye've done," said Walter pushing his arms into the mail sleeves.

"Didn't care? asked Edward.

"She wants to marry ye."

"And I want to marry her… some day."

• •

A group of young warriors led by an older man came from the Torwood and worked their way down toward the ford where Robert stood bathing in the cold but refreshing water of the burn. He continued his ablutions as the men came closer and lined the ford across from him.

"Good morrow!" said the leader.

"Good morrow to ye," Robert replied, continuing his bath.

"Ye know where be King Robert?" asked the fellow.

"Aye," answered Robert and no more. The man awaited further answer, but none came.

"I can't decide whether he is churlish or simply a lackwit," the man said to his companions, who sniggered derisively. Turning back to Robert he said, "I would have you point in the direction that I might find the king."

"Ye *might* find him anywhere," Robert said.

"And ye might find some manners toward yer betters!" spoke a young knight in the group, though he did not wish to rile the impressive man in the stream; he looked as if he knew how to fight and carried a few scars as proof.

"Who are ye, and what's yer purpose in seein' the king?"

"I am Sir Robert Cunynghame of Kilmaurs and if it is any of yer affair, I have brought a contingent to fight alongside the king, " the leader explained. "Would ye kindly tell me, where the king be!?"

"He'll be yon, shortly," replied Robert pointing a thumb over his shoulder then splashing the water on his hair.

"Impudent lout," said Cunynghame.

"Ye need to see the abbot... he'll write yer name in the book," said Robert ignoring the insult.

"I'm sure we can find the king on our own," growled the haughty younger knight.

"Ye had best stay to the road," warned the king.

Cunynghame and his ten men spurred their destriers and dashed across the ford throwing water up on Robert.

The king smiled. *They have their own horses,* he thought, a*nd come to the battle just in time, they did.*

SUNÓAY - JUNE 23RÓ
FALKIRK

Philip de Mowbray awoke the next morning to the sounds of men and women hustling and bustling to begin their day while he, who had come with urgent information for the king, had lain a slugabed. Not remembering the circumstances under which he had gone to sleep, he was initially startled to turn over and find himself facing the rough features of Sir Aymer de Valence. Moreover, the earl had apparently grown long fair hair, which generously overflowed his bearded face.

Rising to his elbows, he was both relieved and mortified to see the blond locks across Aymer's craggy countenance belonged not to Lord Pembroke but to the alewife from the previous evening. She lay just beyond the earl, her pouting mouth making small bubbles as she slept.

His eyes widened as he tried to recollect his actions.

It dawned on him what had occurred when he realized that his person was not all intact. He carefully extracted himself from the pair, not wanting to awaken either, and finding his britches on the straw-strewn dirt floor slipped them on, one leg at a time, dancing on one foot all the while to remain upright. To his horror, he saw his most valuable pouch, containing the key to winning the battlefield, laying on the floor with the contents scattered hither and thither amidst the dirty straw.

He was shocked at his own behavior and nausea grasped his belly as he hastily gathered the scraps of paper and the folded map and put them back into his pouch. He then exited and left the pair alone. After all, his ambition to have a bed for the night had been accomplished. Just how much more might have been accomplished, he didn't know, but his head hurt and his mouth tasted foully of bad ale.

His eyes blinked at the harsh sunlight when he removed himself from the darkened den. He was confused and disoriented. Additional streets and alleyways had sprung up overnight with the English tents and he was totally lost in Falkirk, a town he knew very well under normal circumstances. Nothing was as he knew it to be. Everyone seemed to be in a hurry going somewhere, or nowhere. He wandered about through the new thoroughfares until he at last espied the red and white striped tent, which by its very appearance was known to belong to the king.

As he approached he saw yeomen rolling up the sides of the tent and tying them off so the king and his company could get a cool breeze with which to start the day's deadly business. He could see within, that the king and some of his most important advisors were just finishing a breakfast of boiled meat puddings, breads, butter, and jam, washed down with ale. Mowbray was ravenously hungry but his self-humiliation made the thought of eating sicken his gut all the more.

He approached the huge pavilion only to be stopped by the king's household knights.

"Please advise the king that Sir Philip de Mowbray, Warden of Castle Stirlin', awaits an audience with His Majesty and has valuable information dealin' with the day's venture," he begged the tall guard.

"Wait here," said the knight and called a second guard to him. "Tell the king there be a fellow who claims his name is Mowbray and wishes an audience," he told his second, and the pair of them looked at Sir Philip as if he were either a liar or a losel, or both. Had the warden been himself, and had he been dressed properly, he would never have accepted such treatment from underlings, but he was at present dressed poorly and holding a less than admirable image of himself and so said nothing.

Within a quarter of an hour the second returned with permission for Mowbray to pass into the inner parlor of the tent. He sensed as he left the guards that they were astounded that the invitation to join the king came for such an obvious unworthy, but he hadn't the courage to turn back and see them shaking their heads in wonderment.

The large oaken table and the opulent surroundings impressed Sir Philip, whose own appurtenances at the castle keep could not compare to the king's, though he resided in such richness in the 'hinterlands' of Scotland. He wondered how such trappings, appearing to be so luxurious, had been transported there from London.

"Come, come, Sir Philip!" said Edward impatiently. "We are waitin' to hear your wit."

Mowbray momentarily froze. He stood in his rumpled, slept-in clothing before the most powerful nobles in England. His had been a strange, perhaps wicked night with an earl who was conspicuously absent from the table, and his critical notes were not merely in disarray, but soiled as well.

"Have you somethin' to say, Mowbray?!" encouraged the king.

"Aye, Yer Majesty," started Philip, "I have certain proofs of the disposition and size of the army of the rebel Brus."

"Let's start off with, say," said the king sarcastically, "whereabouts might be the rebels lurkin', if, of course, they are lurkin' about at all!" he ended with a laugh.

The men around chuckled obsequiously at the inane wit.

"In Torwood, they are, at this very minute, Your Majesty," he reported.

"I knew they would hide in Torwood and try to kill us from ambuscade!" interjected Sir Marmaduke, "as they did seventeen years ago at Stirlin' Bridge!"

"This hain't goin' to be that battle done over!" growled Earl Humphrey. "There be no bridge to cross, here!"

"And how many are there waitin' for us in the Torwood, Sir Philip?" asked Edward trying to get the meeting back to the present battle before some of his older nobles began to relive that horrible day.

"How many, Your Majesty?" Mowbray answered, stalling for time to think.

"How many men to fight against their rightful king?" said Edward, growing discouraged that Mowbray had anything worth hearing.

Mowbray shamefully dumped his once meticulously organized notes all over the large map on the table, his original intention, to lay the various papers onto the table and methodically show how many men came from what directions to Stirling, gone by the wayside. The king would have someone who could add the papers together to see the total. Straw was mixed throughout the scraps covering the king's nicely laid out map of the region.

Mowbray started rummaging through the disassembled mass but found nothing of significance. His well-rehearsed speech was vacant from his mind. His attention at last arrested on the map, which he unfolded, taking his time so that he could get an inkling of what he would say.

At last the smaller parchment was unfolded and laid atop the larger one, somewhat covering the small scraps filled with tiny marks Mowbray had so carefully used to keep count of the troops that had come to the battlefield.

The king brushed a straw from under his elbow to the ground and drew his attentions back to Mowbray's map. He suspected that Sir Philip really did have the most reliable information about the Scots' arrivals and a fair idea of where the Brus was lurking in wait. After all, how could the architect of such a brilliant plot to bring Robert de Brus to a pitched battle be a dolt?

"Torwood, this be," said Philip pointing to the map. "There are some Scots in the New Park, here, but not many. Then there's some hidin' in King's Park... that's here," he pointed again.

"I *knew* he would not come to open ground to fight us honorably," exalted Edward.

"Pembroke taught him that lesson well, so I hear tell," replied Sir Marmaduke de Tweng.

"Where is Pembroke?" asked the king upon being reminded that he was not at the table.

No one else spoke up, not that they knew anything to say, and Mowbray wisely remained quiet.

"Ah, well, no matter. How many Scots in all, Mowbray?" asked Edward, coming back to the undertaking at hand.

Mowbray shrugged because he had not the skill to tabulate the number even if he had walked among them. So at length he said, "Thousands, Your Majesty."

"This is ridiculous!" grumbled Lord Hereford.

"I quite agree, Milord!" piped up Gloucester. "This tells us nothing! Let us go to Torwood and New Park and see for ourselves where the enemy hides!"

"My Lords! Calm yourselves," said Edward, "... and let us hear the man to a conclusion."

"Accordin' to the terms of the truce, ye have but to relieve Castle Stirlin' and the day will be yers, Majesty, and Milords," said Mowbray, trying to bring order back into what was fast becoming chaos.

"Meaning?" asked Edward hushing the others by a gesture of his hand.

"Ye can easily get three leagues in this single day, Your Majesty," Philip explained. "That will be close enough to satisfy the terms of the truce I made with the Bruses... well within the six leagues I specified must be reached by tomorrow for the castle to be relieved!"

"Let us run around the Torwood and go straight to the castle to relieve it," suggested Sir Gilbert. "That way there will be *no* question about who occupies the fortress."

"That should tell them they count for nothin'," interjected Sir Henry de Bohun with a chuckle.

Edward held his hand for silence once again and pondered the map.

"Sire, there is a small garrison in Stirlin' village," offered Mowbray. "Enough to hold my few men inside, but little enough for three hundred or so of yer knights to smite them."

"How so are the ways?" asked Edward.

"There is the way here," he pointed up the Roman road on his personally drawn map. "If the Torwood be avoided all together, Your Majesty," he said, "there will be no need to engage the Brus. If your knights draw them out of the wood to block the way, so much the better."

"Are there other roads or passable overland ways?" asked Gloucester. Mowbray nodded affirmatively.

"The eastern route is the way I got here, Milord," he said. "There is a ford across the Bannok Burn that is shallow enough at this time of year, especially with this spring's modest rainfall."

"I think the western route is best," opined Gloucester taking scant look at the small map before the king.

"Then you, Milord Gloucester, shall have the honor of paradin' up that route with the five hundred knights you have brought," said the king smiling, pleased he had now a plan for the day.

"My Lord King! How so that he be given the van when I am the Constable of England!" loudly objected Humphrey de Bohun, Earl of Hereford.

"Gloucester always has the van!" grumbled Gilbert as he glowered at de Bohun.

"I have spoken!" forced the king, but Hereford tried another avenue.

"Prayed hard, I have, Majesty, to bring honor back to the de Bohun name after havin' brought disgrace to my house when I made the grievous error concernin' the late Lord Piers Gaveston of Cornwall, and this I consider my duty... to relieve Castle Stirlin' this very day!"

The salient word, 'Piers', fell on the ears of the king and he was immediately grief stricken. Hereford, he knew, was truly remorseful for having participated in the murder of his lover, and if nothing more than to be an example for the other earls involved, none of whom were the least interested in remorse, he certainly wanted the earl to be able to reclaim the honor of his name.

"Very well, I shall..." the king paused looking from one to the other, "... I give you both the honor of the venture." He smiled, thinking he had judged as Solomon would have judged.

"But Your Majesty..." began the incensed young Gloucester, but Edward closed him off when he stood.

"Lord Hereford has far more experience than do you, Milord," said Edward, "and you can learn a great deal from his expertise on this sortie."

"This is an easy task," persisted Gloucester, "one that I am most prepared to achieve, Your Majesty. And further, may I remind you that I am the son of your very own sister?"

"And I remind you, Nephew, that I am king," was his curt reply. "Both of you shall lead!"

Gloucester stood and glared at Humphrey. "You will need keep up with me, old man, or I will leave you chokin' in the dust of this accursed land!"

Humphrey stood, fully primed to accept the challenge, 'here and now'.

"Milords!" barked the king, "Behave yourselves! We have vermin in the house and that we must tend to... above all else!"

"My Lord! Why do you let him get by with callin' you 'old man'?" whispered Humphrey's nephew Henry.

"Day's not done as yet," said Humphrey elbowing his nephew on the shoulder and harshly forcing him back into his seat.

"Your Majesty," offered Earl Humphrey, "… if Milord Gloucester is to have five hundred knights, then I would ask that I may take five hundred knights as well!"

"Commit a thousand knights to a small task such as this?" asked Edward with his brows knitted tightly above his eyes.

"'Twould be the fairest and most honorable way, Majesty," argued Humphrey.

"I have dedicated more men to this campaign than the likes of Hereford ever imagined, Uncle!" griped Gilbert, pushing in front of the king to again glower at Lord Hereford.

Edward sighed. "'Twill be thus settled, without further discussion! Each of ye two shall take two hundred fifty of your own knights and relieve Castle Stirlin' by way of the western path!"

Raoul could see bad blood following in the wake of this day's work. He sadly shook his head and left the tent behind his stepson.

"Has *anyone* seen Earl Aymer?" asked the king, frustrated that Pembroke did not appear.

"Oh, he's… uh," Mowbray stammered then decided on a safer answer, "… I shall seek him for you, Your Majesty." With that he bowed gracefully and left the tent.

Edward sighed but was glad that a line of action had been decided. Pembroke would show up before long, the king was sure, because he was leaving within the hour and the earl was to ride ahead of his main force to sweep the way.

*Abbot Bernard
of Arbroath*

SUNÒAY MORNING ~ JUNE 23RÒ
BANNOK

The men of Robert's army were served oat bannocks and water for their fast on the eve of Saint John the Baptist Day. Though it was possible that many of them would not live to have another, no one grumbled about the plain meal.

Coming up the hill, the king saw the Cunynghame and his contingent talking to Bernard, the Abbot of Arbroath, who cradled in his arm the book in which he wrote every name down as it was given to him by those who came to Bannok to fight for Scotland. When it was all over, assuming he would survive and be victorious, the king wanted to know who had helped win in this grand gamble. If the battle were lost, the Scots' names would not matter, for all would be dead or scattered in hiding.

The Bishop of Moray and the Abbot of Inchaffray were set apart from the rest where they heard confessions and held a mass for those who would come.

The king, dressed in trews and boots, his shirt in his hand, walked toward the Abbot of Arbroath, who saw him coming and paused in his conversation with Cunynghame to greet him.

"Good morrow, Sire," said the abbot out of earshot of the others.

"I have come to ask that ye hear my confession, My Abbot," he said, and pausing he added, "if ye will."

The abbot smiled. "My Son, I am aware that ye have nae relationship with Rome, at present, but 'tis not my place to say that God will nae forgive ye, especially when ye don't neglect yer kinship with Him. His

Holiness has withdrawn his blessings from ye, but that does nae mean that God has."

There were no solitary places to go in all of the forest. And though St Ninian's kirk was fairly close, the men had constructed an altar within their midst, where it was most convenient. By that altar Robert knelt and the abbot leaned his ear to the king's lips. Soon the abbot stood over Robert and made the sign of the cross then raised his eyes to heaven and offered a prayer of his own, for Robert's soul and for the success of the day.

Robert crossed himself and stood and the two men talked for a moment before he thanked the abbot and disappeared into the woods.

When the abbot returned to the Cunynghame knights they had waited, not all that patiently, and were compelled to speak their dissatisfaction. Sir Robert said, "That man was bathin' in the burn when we passed."

"Aye?" said the abbot, picking up his book and pen and ink once more.

"Since we waited whilst ye ministered to him, I would have ye tell us who that man is," demanded Sir Robert Cunynghame.

"That man, good Sirs, is the King of Scots," said the abbot who was tickled to make the claim knowing the minds of the men.

Their jaws went slack with the news.

• •

"Yer meal, Robbie," said Christina when he had made his way back to their tent. She handed a portion of the oat bread to him and a cup of water.

He nibbled a bit and drank. "Anythin' that says there's a limit to this meal?" He asked.

"None to my ken," answered Christina.

"I want the men to drink as much water as they can hold," he said.

"What about bread?"

"Aye, stuff them with bannocks, as well," he replied, taking another bite.

"Andrew!" he suddenly shouted loudly.

Startled, Christina jumped a bit, but Andrew soon appeared.

"Aye, Sire?"

"Have ye completed yer day of prayer?" he asked.

"Seemed nearer two days," said Andrew humorously.

"Fetch my mail," he ordered, pointing to where his armor laid.

"Rider comin'!" shouted Gilbert de la Haye.

"Our spy, Sir Gilbert?" Robert stood and asked, again loudly.

"From the halfway mark, My Lord King," was the answer.

"Gather the commanders here, quick," said Robert.

"Aye," Haye said and went quickly away.

"Call out the drummers," said Robert to Christina, "and the pipers, and then fix yer hospital for action!" The king and the woman exchanged a knowing look before she left to follow his instructions.

Andrew held Robert's mail surcoat while he slipped his head and shoulders into it, and then the squire pulled the heavy metal fabric down and helped the king get comfortable in its weight.

"Ye still want to be a knight?"

"I do, Sire, more than anythin' else!"

"Swear ye then, to protect Scotland with yer life?"

"Aye," replied Andrew handing over Robert's arming cap and fetching his tabard.

Robert tied the cap under his chin before Andrew handed him the yellow and red tabard of the Scottish royal arms, which he slipped over his head. The squire grabbed his king's chain coif from a stub of a branch within the tent and held it as the king fitted it over his arming cap. Andrew then draped the bottom of it onto the king's shoulders.

Robert turned to look at the squire who had aided him thusly for much of his young life.

"Andrew Stewart," Robert began and fought off a catch in his voice. "Andrew Stewart, if ye are half as brave and valiant a knight as ye have been a squire, ye shall make yer father and yer king very proud." He then took half a step forward and clasped Andrew in a stout, but brief, bear hug. "And ye'll ne'er again drop my armor in the mud!" he said, laughing.

"On yer knees," the king said.

Thomas interrupted.

"Get yer schiltrom together and move them into first position... the bastards'll be here directly!"

"Aye, Sire," said Thomas, leaving immediately to carry out his orders.

Robert strapped on his sword and drew its long blade, spotlessly polished by none other than Andrew, himself. At that moment Edward stepped into view just ahead of the arriving spy. He stepped aside to let the fellow speak first.

"What say ye?" asked Robert, looking every inch the formidable knight that he was.

"Knights, Sire, a'plenty comin' from Falkirk... at a fast gallop... not far behind me!" was the breathless report.

"Hie to yer regiment!" ordered Robert.

Andrew was yet on his knee.

"Andrew Stewart, I strike thee knight. Before God I charge ye always to be a man of honor, with courage to do what is right and defend the weak against the strong," said Robert, touching the lad on each shoulder with his sword.

Edward was agape. "The enemy is at our door, and ye're handin' out knighthoods?!"

"Just one," said Robert, sheathing his sword, "...because I promised." Edward looked away from his brother and shook his head. The way he saw it, the king could carry promises too far, sometimes.

"How many's a'comin'," Edward asked. "What did yer spy say?"

"The English are headed this way, but how many he didn't know. 'A'plenty' he said. Could be the whole army. Gather the men in yer schiltrom! Tell Douglas to get his and stay in the trees!"

"What about yer regiment?" said Edward.

"Have Angus muster my command across the road, this side of the burn."

"Aye," said Edward, and tore off to find the Douglas and the Macdonald.

"Ye can get up now, and get my horse," said Robert.

"We done?"

"Aye. Get my horse, An... *Sir* Andrew!" He added, "Ye'll still be the standard bearer!"

"Don't feel any different, My King," said Andrew.

"Ye will," advised the king, and he smiled.

Sir David de Graham came to the tent. "Can't find Keith, Sire!"

"Gone to the deep wood no doubt," answered Robert as he cocked his head to one side to listen. The drummers had started their primitive pounding and the pipers their long droning, calling the men to their stations.

"Get yer cavalry together and hold them inside the wood on the south end of New Park... behind where my men are musterin'. And there be some new knights, Cunynghame I think... take them with ye!"

"Aye, My King," said David and went to the pinfold where his cavalrymen were saddling horses as fast as they could.

Andrew returned, leading Robert's horse and his own. Nigel, seated atop his horse, was with him.

The king hoisted himself astride his white steed and rode out of the woods toward the south of New Park where he could see a great distance. Andrew mounted and grabbed the yellow and red standard, unfurled it, and followed.

"Pick up the pace!" ordered Robert as he passed the musicians, "Goin' to war we are!"

The drummers beat a faster tempo and the pipers played more vigorously.

Robert looked down hill to the east and north where Thomas' schiltrom was forming across the road near the kirk, blue ribbons tied to their fourteen-foot-long pikes. The length of the pikes being greater than usual, a color ribbon on the head of each helped each man know exactly where his weapon ended.

A number of them also carried short swords and axes, wore basinets on their heads, and quilted coats and armored gloves bought from France with money extorted from the towns of Northumberland. Some even had wicker shields of their own making. They were forming up in good order, heeding every bark of Randolph's voice.

Edward's troop with green pike ribbons and Douglas' with red, were forming in the wood at the eastern edge of New Park so their numbers would not be exposed.

MacKie came trotting to Robert on foot and asked, "Where d'ye want yer archers, My Liege?"

"Muster on the south edge of New Park, yonder with my regiment... twixt the troop of foot and the cavalry, inside the wood. I'll call ye out as I need ye," he instructed the archer, then wheeled southward to see how his own men were arrayed. Andrew and Nigel followed.

A lone rider came across the ford and up to Robert. "Not far back, My King," he reported, "... comin' 'round to the west of Torwood!"

"How many?"

"One man said six hundred," the rider replied, "I don't have a notion of my own!"

If they came by the way of least resistance, the invaders would come straight up the Roman road and cross the ford within a mile and a half, and another half mile they would be where he was standing. Robert would have to wait and see how many of them there were and where they headed once around Torwood.

"Our men in Torwood know what to do?" asked Robert, patting his excited horse's neck to calm him.

"Aye, Sire. We invite them nicely to come pay us a visit," the messenger replied with a broad grin as he wheeled his mount and hied south, across Milton Ford, and up the gentle slope into Torwood. Robert turned toward the southern treeline of New Park, and could see within its depths the men he would command.

"Ye men ready?" Robert shouted the question to his troops to be answered with a resounding cheer that bellowed outward as Robert trotted his horse back and forth in front of the trees wherein they stood. Their long spears with yellow ribbons tied to their pikeheads barely moved in the day's light breeze. Perspiration took on a visible flow.

Andrew came to Robert. "Yer helm, My King," he said as he handed the cuirbolle helmet with a small band of shined gold attached.

Robert smiled and put it on firmly over his coif. Off to the south they began to hear that familiar low rumble of numerous hooves pounding distant earth.

"What ye reckon'll happen now?" asked his former squire.

"We wait," said Robert, and he leant over in his saddle and whispered to Sir Andrew, "See to Nigel, My Knight."

Gilbert le Clare,
Earl of Gloucester

SUNÐAY, Ꮮ᎐RNING – JUNE 23RÐ SOUTH OF TORWOOD

It was the onrush of the prime of the English army. Large destriers dressed handsomely in long trappings of various colors and designs according to their owners' heraldic symbols. Many had quirboilly, or molded and hardened leather armor, on their chests and heads. Most of the riders were similarly dressed with chain mail, quirboilly inset with metal plates and appointed with metal discs on their elbows, shoulders and knees, and metal shin guards.

On their heads were arming caps, chain mail coifs and quite a design variety of helmets and bascinets with visors being one of the newer innovations. They were of varied designs, including some that jutted out like lower jaws, pushed forward to cover the wearers' lower faces.

They carried marvelous weapons: twelve-foot lances, swords, axes, flails, maces, and daggers. The knights' squires, following on lesser horses, carried extra weapons and many times their masters' shields. They were the best of all the armies in Christendom and they bore down on King Robert with a glory-driven hunger in their hearts and minds.

The Earl of Gloucester and the Earl of Hereford, the latter accompanied by his nephew Sir Henry de Bohun, led the van of raiders as they galloped from Falkirk and crossed the plain below Torwood with some five hundred knights and about three hundred squires. When they neared the wood they diverted from the Roman road, stopping to catch their breaths and make final preparations before continuing to Stirling.

"Well, there be Torwood," said Humphrey, Lord Hereford, enjoying a bite to eat while they rested. "I would think that's a right hard place to root the damned Scots from." He chewed a second bit of meat and continued his thoughts. "Brus chose well... since he will not fight on the plain like an honorable man." Suddenly, his companions sat forward, eyes peering into the depths of the forest.

"Ho-ho! Look there, at the edge of the trees!" said Lord Gloucester. Standing among the trees were what they conceived to be the Army of Brus awaiting the English advance, when in actuality they saw but the twenty or so Scottish warriors purposefully showing themselves to the oncoming English at Robert's order.

"Looks like Scots, armed and ready for us," said Humphrey's nephew Henry with a chuckle.

"We are sore afraid!" laughed Gilbert. "Too bad we have no time to teach them how true knights wage war." Grinning, he took another morsel of bread from the loaf and signaled for his squire to bring him the water skin.

"Perhaps after we relieve Stirling?" asked Humphrey.

"Why not?" replied Gilbert after taking a swig of the water, "We can chase them toward Falkirk and into our illustrious sovereign's waitin' arms. What a surprise for ol' Pembroke, eh? To be ridin' toward the great battle for Stirlin' and have the Scots tumble into his lap!"

"He would probably run to Edward, as he did at Loudoun!" said Henry de Bohun, and the three men had a good laugh at Lord Pembroke's expense.

The Scots, sure they had been seen, melted into the trees like will-o-the-wisps, and the next time the earls glanced toward the wood, none were visible.

"They're up there a'right," said Hereford, "and they're always ready for a trick or two, but they hain't goin' to do any serious fightin'."

"Well, we'll be trickin' them this day," said Gilbert. "We hain't goin' to fall into their 'Torwood' trap."

"'Tis a nice day for a ride through yon glen, would you agree, Milord?" offered Humphrey, indicating a dip in the landscape to the west of the hill dominated by the wood. "Accordin' to the king's maps, it leads straight to Castle Stirlin'."

The three noblemen finished their luncheon and their necessary voiding before they mounted up to continue their triumphant ride directly into the gate of the castle, thus relieving it... and defeating Robert the Brus.

• •

"I can see dust risin' up below Torwood," said Andrew.

"I see it, too," replied Robert as he sat unmoving upon his white highland horse. "Afore long they'll be at the ford, and we'll know how many they send against us."

"Good thing it hain't rained," opined Andrew.

"Good?" said Robert.

"Aye, Sire, can't see a dust cloud when 'tis wet," he replied.

"I would that it had rained, dust or nae," Robert countered.

"They near?" shouted Sir Angus, second in command of Robert's regiment.

"Nae near enough. Hold yer position, Angus!" ordered Robert. "They've got to narrow their breadth to cross the ford, and that will give us plenty of time to get set to fight. Stay well into the trees 'til I give the order!"

Andrew's breath quickened when he could begin to make out colorful banners emerging from the cloud of light brown dust.

"They're comin', My King," said Andrew.

"I see," Robert replied calmly.

"Want me to take Nigel into the wood?" he asked.

"Nae. Ye'll both stay here with me for now," said Robert.

Andrew said nothing, but stayed where he was, holding the royal flag.

• •

"Appears there's the bad place in the trail," said Sir Humphrey pointing to where the wide top of the rocky surface of the old Roman road served as ford. "We'll have to cross with but few abreast. Reminds me of Stirlin' Bridge."

The whole of the contingent slowed as Hereford and Gloucester puzzled the best stratagem for handling the ford.

"Reckon it's Brus' plan to swoop down on us as we get parted in twain at the ford?" asked Gilbert. They could see Robert and his flag-bearer beneath the brilliant yellow banner on the hill at the edge of New Park, but their concern was the troops behind them in Torwood; perhaps they were only awaiting a signal from Brus.

"We cannot become stalled here because Brus *might* attack us, Gilbert! I shall set a rear guard whilst you take your men across," offered Humphrey, but he added for the sake of glory and pride, "Just remember we are to be received into the gate at the castle at the *same time!*"

"I well remember," grumped Gilbert, feeling that Lord Hereford had usurped part of his expected splendid victory. But further thought on the subject was suddenly rent when Humphrey de Bohun's nephew Henry took a vainglorious leap and spurred his horse down to the bank of Milton Ford and splashed across without hesitation.

"Can't you keep rein on your kin?" growled Gilbert.

Humphrey threw his hands up gesturing he knew no way to keep his nephew in check. After all, Henry was no hungrier for laurels than many of the other young knights who were accustomed to fighting on a one-to-one basis.

Gilbert le Clare, Earl of Gloucester, dug his spurs into his destrier and followed, determined that the young Henry de Bohun would not steal his thunder.

• •

"Here comes one," said Andrew as he saw the blue, gold, and red trappings of Henry de Bohun's horse splashing across the ford. It disappeared for a moment as the horse was coaxed up the short span of hill that was out of sight for Robert and Andrew.

Sir Henry suddenly reappeared on the higher ground and, rather than holding there to await the others, he was gaining speed.

Robert remained unmoved. His horse nickered.

Gilbert was the next to cross, followed by his squire.

"Ye want us out of the wood, now?" shouted Angus.

Robert turned to look at the Macdonald. "I'll tell ye when, Angus!" he said roughly.

Robert, Andrew, and Nigel remained motionless and in plain view of the attackers as they drew nearer.

After closing half the space between the ford and the New Park, before which Robert waited, Henry reined up hard. He couldn't believe his good fortune! The so-called 'King of Scots' was most nearly alone. His tabard and his helm with the gold band affixed upon it indicated he was Brus. This was going to be an easier war than he could have imagined. All he had to do to make his indelible mark in history was kill that one man!

Robert watched him lower his helm visor and knew what the youth was contemplating. He hoped the young hot-head would decide better of it, but Henry pulled his blue and gold shield with its red bend from his back and pushed his left arm through the straps.

"We goin' for him, My King?" asked Andrew, who also knew what ran through de Bohun's wit.

Robert didn't answer Andrew, but gently patted his horse on the neck.

Henry took his lance in his armored hand and spurred his large destrier forward at a hard gallop.

As the gallant beast tried to gain momentum on the long climb to where he waited, Robert loosed his battleaxe from its saddle loop and, holding its handle close to its head, parked it upright on his thigh. Andrew grew anxious and squirmed himself around in his saddle, settling in a posture somewhat like a trebuchet not yet sprung, every muscle taut and every nerve afire. He pulled his sword and held it at the ready, its blade leaning against his shoulder. He looked at Robert, who showed none of the traits Andrew was feeling, instead appearing to know every thought of the charging knight and his mount.

Henry drew closer and faster, his great horse's hooves pounding the slope as he lowered his lance to the level of Robert's heart. Holding no shield, the Scot had left himself vulnerable to the intended deathblow.

Robert trotted out about ten yards and readied himself during the last few long strides of Sir Henry's charge.

Huffing and puffing in frustration, Angus gripped his spear shaft until his knuckles turned white but he remained as his king had ordered. Andrew's jaws were clenched tightly, and Nigel could hardly stand to keep his eyes open and on the scene before him.

Henry was coming close on Robert's left side, the deadly lance aimed across himself and his horse toward the center of Robert's chest. The English knight on his large destrier was executing a nearly perfect attack.

Robert watched the great horse's hooves as Bohun was close enough to strike and he quickly kicked his white forward to close the gap all the sooner. He twisted the handle of the axe tight in his fist and just as the lance point was all but upon him, the Scot jerked his quick horse to the side and the lance tip passed his chest by several inches. Rising in his stirrups as tall as he could manage, the king brought his axe down hard on de Bohun's basinet as he passed, cleaving his light helm and his skull to his shoulders.

Henry's body tumbled heavily from the destrier, taking the axe head with him, for the butt of the oak handle was all Robert had left in his blood splattered hand.

The wood behind him erupted into a tumultuous cheer as all present saw at least part of what had happened. Coming out of his state of total concentration, Robert's mind was instantly on the other knights who were fast approaching.

Realizing what had happened, the Earl of Gloucester reined his horse to stop just past the deadly fields of hidden pots and caltrops that neither he nor the several other knights accompanying him noticed. They, too, reined their mounts and came abreast of him.

"There are more Scots yonder, in the trees," said Gilbert, nodding his head in the direction of the Brus. "I heard them shoutin' when Hereford's nephew was unhorsed."

"Will he live, Milord?" asked the tallest knight of the three.

"A corpse, or so it appeared to me," replied Gloucester.

"Lord Hereford's goin' to be vengeful!" said a second, broader knight. About that moment more knights, having followed the path across the ford, ganged behind and beside Gloucester.

Robert stood his ground, watching to see if the English knights were heading up the hill.

"I know damned well that the Scot has men waitin' in the wood," Gilbert argued with himself over whether to attack or retreat.

"All of us will be across the ford ere long," said the second knight.

Robert cast his shattered axe handle to the ground and drew his broadsword.

"Is he takin' all of us to battle ridin' a mere pony?" asked yet another knight as Sir Humphrey de Bohun, having come across the ford and up the hill arrived at the place where about a hundred knights and some squires had amassed around Gilbert le Clare.

When Hereford got to Gloucester he anxiously asked, "What's the business here? Where is Henry?"

"I regret to say, Lord Humphrey, that your brave nephew lies dead at the feet of Brus, yonder," he announced.

Humphrey gasped in horror. He had been talking to him only moments earlier. "My God!" he wept. "The foolhardy youth... so eager for glory... charged ahead without reason!" The older man had tears yet streaming from his eyes when his teeth clenched in hatred and he growled, "I'll avenge you, Henry!"

"I think that would be unwise, Lord Hereford, for Brus' army hides not in Torwood, but behind him in the wood yonder," asserted Gilbert.

"We can take any army the goddamned Scots can muster!" Humphrey declared, speaking more from hate than wisdom.

Seeing that they hesitated, Robert turned in his saddle and said firmly, "Angus, now!"

As Robert had earlier ordered, two of the four ranks came out of the wood and formed a schiltrom.

"As I told you, My Lord," said Gilbert smugly.

"Goddammit! I sure as hell didn't think Brus was fixin' to fight us all on his own!" barked Hereford, his eyes yet transfixed on his nephew's body. The riderless destrier calmly munched grass no more than ten feet away.

Watching the two earls, Robert rested his sword across his saddlebow and waited for the English to act. Andrew arrived at his side and asked, "Is it done, Sire?"

"Nae. 'Tis but the first blow, Sir Andrew," he said.

Andrew smiled at Robert's gift of addressing him as 'Sir'. "Then I shall fight at yer side, My Liege," he said.

"Where's Nigel?" the king asked, still keeping his eye on the English.

"I put him betwixt the archers and the cavalry, My King."

Robert nodded approval then signaled to Angus to move the schiltrom farther onto the field. Angus came within ten feet of Robert's back and stopped.

"We can take them!" said Hereford angrily, his grief still thinking for him.

"Let us bring the rest of our men across the ford, Sir Humphrey," suggested Gloucester. "Then we'll more easily take them!"

"You a damned coward, Sir?" asked Hereford bluntly.

Gilbert's head snapped around to glare at him.

Lord Hereford glared back through red-rimmed eyes, and goaded him more, "Feared of yer kin?"

At that, Gilbert could take no more. Dropping the visor on his helm he spurred his destrier and followed the path laid earlier by Sir Henry.

"Advance the foot!" Robert ordered Angus, and the schiltrom moved forward, allowing Andrew and the king to pass through to the rear of their ranks. With Gloucester in the foremost of the attack, the English knights and even their squires charged up-slope toward the waiting Scots.

Sir Angus Og Macdonald stood in the center of the Scots' double-line schiltrom of about a thousand men and gave the order, "Set pikes!"

In unison, the Scots dug the heels of their pike shafts into the dirt and held them, points outward. Robert all but held his breath in hopes that the men would maintain their ranks. Unlike the slowness of time's passage as he awaited Henry de Bohun, it seemed to him that the wall of English armored cavalry was moving at breakneck speed into what he now deemed a fragile line of Scots and their wooden spears.

Dear God, he thought, *what have I done to these poor bastards...* but the pikemen didn't move a muscle in the face of the onslaught.

The two armies met with a terrible clash, the Scots, yelling, immovable, the English galloping full tilt against them on two thousand pound destriers, a horrific and bloody collision followed by the screaming and groaning of dying and wounded horses and men. Many of the frontmost destriers fell dead at the spot, their great hearts pierced through with iron pike heads, their riders tossed over their heads into the mass of pikes and those wielding them. Others, wounded, bleeding, panicked, and hurting, backed away from their tormenters, some to throw their riders and run loose, others to lie down and bleed to death on the long slope down to Milton Ford.

The pikemen at the center of the English crush suffered the Scots' greatest casualties as tons of horseflesh battered them and English lance points pierced their quilted coats and chain mail even as their own splintering pikes wreaked havoc and death on the English knights.

Gilbert of Gloucester's destrier was among the first of the charging animals to hit the bristling rows of pikes and he went down, a pike impaling it's proudly held neck. It writhed in pain and fear unable even to cry out, its air supply shut off with the broken pike shaft. Mercifully, it did not suffer long, and was dead before Lord Gloucester, who had held on and ridden the destrier to the ground, could get himself clear of the carcass and its yards of trappings.

Into the noise and confusion and blood, Sir Gilbert's squire, a sturdy and powerful youth, ran from his horse to help his liege to his feet and away from the thick of the ghastly carnage, half dragging and half carrying his armored liege lord.

Lord Hereford stopped short of the lethal spear points, and turning his mount aside struck at the pike heads with his sword. However, time and again when he was successful in beheading a pike another would take its place. He shortly withdrew to contemplate the possibility of an alternate way to defeat this rabble.

Meanwhile, the knights regrouped and tried again to break the Scottish schiltrom, to no avail, and more brave men on both sides met their doom.

Hereford, after searching from several angles could find no way around the massive "hedgehog".

"Sir Andrew, fetch me the Templar," cried Robert.

Andrew wasted no time in hieing into the wood and locating David de Graham who patiently sat astride his horse.

"King wants ye, now!" said Andrew and David immediately spurred his horse.

The pair rode through the archers, through the second line of men, out of the wood and up to the king.

Robert saw them but said nothing to either, his attention as yet on the battle. Some of the English had brought out their axes, maces, and flails to try and break or yank the pike shafts from the hands of the Scots, but were finding it a hopeless occupation.

On the field, Lord Gilbert was coming to himself. "Find me a horse!" he demanded of his squire.

"Yes, Milord!" replied the squire as his eyes scanned the hillside for a loose and unwounded mount.

As he scouted for a means into or around the schiltrom, Lord Humphrey de Bohun saw the Templar ride up to the king and quickly headed to where Gilbert le Clare was sitting on the ground and rubbing his leg.

"Get up goddammit!" he shouted. "There are more of the whoresons in the wood!"

"I hain't able to help that!" yelled Gilbert who was already about as angry as he could get.

"You misunderstand me, Milord!" said Humphrey, "We don't have enough strength to repel those we now face, and I don't pretend to know what's in store for us in yon trees!"

Gloucester's squire came running with a horse by the reins. "Milord, I have a bloodied but sound horse for you!" he said. Lord Hereford looked at the blue and gold trappings and growled.

"You cannot ride Henry's destrier, Gloucester!"

"Why not?" the younger earl replied as he pushed his foot into the stirrup. "Henry has no further need of it!"

His squire gave him a boost as he hopped off the ground to get his armored weight up on the warhorse and he sat heavily upon the scarlet stained saddle.

Humphrey growled like a dog done out of his bone, while up on the hill Robert turned and signaled to Gilbert de la Haye, and out of the woods came Robert's second wave of pikemen.

"What would ye have of me, My King?" asked David.

"Everything you have already performed," the king responded.

David and Andrew looked at each other in puzzlement.

Still with Gloucester, Lord Hereford watched as another thousand men and pikes appeared with the Scots king. "See there?" said Humphrey. "Brus draws more from the wood!"

"'Tis the whole army!" replied Gilbert, understanding their position at last.

"We must withdraw!" insisted Humphrey.

Gilbert whistled and his knights immediately began withdrawing from the fight and retreating to where Humphrey and Gilbert awaited.

"On them, men!" shouted Robert recklessly.

The two thousand men rushed forward as a horde, screaming their Scottish battle yells and running hard down the slope at their enemies.

Sir Henry's squire single-handedly held his position, his sword drawn to protect the dead body of his liege. Unfortunately for him, nine of the Scots had broken ranks with an eye toward the knight's fine weapons and handsome armor, which alone was worth a small fortune. They approached the corpse with the idea of running the squire off and taking the knight's possessions as booty.

The hundreds of English knights were simultaneously unnerved to see the Scottish men-at-arms coming straight for them in such numbers. They wheeled their destriers and forgetting that the ford was relatively narrow, were soon fleeing down the slope in pure panic. As they approached the Bannok Burn at high speed they were spread far too widely. It was then that they realized it was too late, and many of them opted to run into the grassy fields on both sides of the road, a fatal mistake for some.

Several destriers went down right away, breaking their legs in the treacherous pots or piercing one or more hooves with the caltrops. Shrieking in pain, the wounded creatures most often threw their riders who landed hard and some of them onto the injurious if not lethal starthistles.

Seeing their comrades falling in the traps, others reined hard to avoid the same fate, and tried instead to cut through the bog, not realizing that the Scots had also sunk pots within the swamp area. There the traps were less numerous and some of the frantically escaping English made it to the burn and were able to escape by swimming across. Yet others became mired down in the bog and left their weighty destriers stranded in the viscous muck as they slogged through on foot.

Robert could see the horses fall and hear their distant screams. The whole of the army commanded by the earls of Gloucester and Hereford was in chaos, swarming about the ford and the bog not knowing which way might be safe to ride through, and the Scot knew his pots and starthistles had served their purpose. Forty or more mounted knights in the army of England, had either been killed or left unhorsed by the well thought out traps. The English would not again come along that route to try and relieve Castle Stirling.

The king remained seated on his horse and blew a long blast on his hunting horn to tell his men to stop chasing the English and return up the slope before they too fell into the pots.

Gilbert and Humphrey had reached the ford ahead of the others and turned upon hearing the agonized cries of the horses in the traps. Their fine proud knights were thrashing about trying to get their expensive horses unencumbered from the pots, while others, realizing they were outnumbered by the Scots, slipped back across the ford, some leading their limping horses and kicking the caltrops into the pits to keep them from their paths, or abandoning the animals altogether to their sad fates.

At last assured that they had won the skirmish, the Scots began to hoot and jeer at the withdrawing knights. Their king, atop the hill, watched in silence as the English stragglers waded across the ford and followed their mounted fellows to the south. Robert looked at the battleground somberly, the dead and wounded lying mostly where they fell, as friends and relatives went through the ghastly scene, and stopped to help those who yet lived.

His sadness at the loss went unspoken, until he saw the magnificent destriers, dead or writhing in their death throes.

"What a waste of good horse flesh," he lamented.

"Reckon it's goin' to be hard to get their bonny saddles off," aimlessly remarked Andrew, equally saddened at the loss of life for both man and horse.

Gloucester and Hereford moved off about a hundred yards from the burn and turned to assess the damage. Most of the knights following them were unscathed, but the carnage they left behind on the hill and in the trap field across the burn was awful to see.

"This is no pathway to relieve Castle Stirlin'," griped Humphrey, and he rose high in his stirrups and shook his sword in Robert's direction while yelling his loudest, "You will rue this hour's trickery and the murder of my nephew!"

Robert made out only enough of Hereford's words to understand what he was talking about, and he waved his sword as well, as if it were an open invitation to return.

"Need to get back in position, Lord Macdonald," said Robert.

"Aye, Robbie," replied Angus.

The ambulatory wounded had gone to Christina's and the rest had mostly been retrieved and dragged or carried to the infirmary. Across the half-mile of green hillside laid the bodies of seven dead Scots. Robert, Andrew and David rode to each of them and the king mourned their loss, though not one was known to the three of them by name.

Robert's regiment, walking back to where they had begun, would pick up those dead as they came.

The brave English squire was found slaughtered at the feet of his foolish liege, Henry de Bohun. Both of them had been picked clean of their weapons, armor and clothes.

Robert climbed from his white horse and stood over the naked bodies of the young noble and his squire. The king's axe head was the only thing still attached to Sir Henry's person with which he had not been born.

"Who removed this man's raiment?" asked Robert.

Sir David, sitting his horse beside the king said, "I'll find out."

"I want both of these men redressed as they were," he demanded. "The scavengers can have the weapons and armor for booty, but they must not be left as they now are."

Sir David agreed, and Robert stepped down from his horse to retrieve his axe blade.

The English galloped out of the glen into which they had so cavalierly ridden an hour earlier, Sir Humphrey envisioning what he would tell his sister, the mother of Henry, while Sir Gilbert worried over what he would tell the king, who waited not far away to hear the report on their expected victory.

SUNDAY, LATE MORNING – JUNE 23RD
COCKSHOT HILL

The word of the short but definitive battle between Robert de Brus and Henry de Bohun spread quickly among the Scots, and the soldiers' spirits were enlivened by their king's win over a knight riding a larger horse, wearing complete armor, and using a lance, as opposed to Robert's smaller horse, light armor, and a hand weapon. Thus, when he left his men in the capable hands of Angus Macdonald, the king went to the other regiments to take advantage of his good fortune, to cheer his men, and to see to their disposition and well being.

Wanting yet to keep his army's true numbers hidden, the king ordered his troops to remain among the sheltering trees, and went to be among them in the forest wherever they stood.

"We heard of yer success today, My King," praised James Douglas from the back of his horse where it stood before the men of his schiltrom. Most of the men were on their feet, others rose when he approached, and all bowed before their monarch.

Robert smiled and graciously accepted the congratulations, knowing his defeat of de Bohun was the best medicine his valiant men could possibly have been administered. Why he had put himself at such risk he could not puzzle in his own mind, unless it was simply because he had trained for single combat at the tourneys, and it followed instinctively that he thwart the challenge and not back down… from a de Bohun or any other knight.

The affable Scots warriors spoke respectfully, but straightforwardly to their king.

David de Graham, meanwhile, went separately among the men for a different purpose.

"Who are the men who broke ranks and stripped the English knight and his steadfast squire?" asked David de Graham.

"Yonder, they be Sir David," replied MacKie.

Graham rode his horse to a half-dozen men standing off to themselves and asked if they were the ones who had stripped the two men.

"Aye, we are," said the apparent leader.

"The king wants them redressed in their own clothing," said Graham.

The man looked puzzled. "Why?" he asked.

"Respect, I reckon, for two soldiers much like ourselves, who died bravely," said the Templar.

"Armor and weapons, too?" asked the man.

"The king said ye could keep them. Fair spoils," said Graham.

"But, we gathered it all for the king…" he said, "The knight was his kill."

"Then dress the men in their clothes and give the king his trophies," suggested Graham.

"Aye, Milord," agreed the fellow, bowing to the Templar.

Graham went back to his cavalry to await orders from the king. They had dismounted to keep the horses from being overburdened and stood in groups laughing and talking in low tones. He continued to watch the six who, as ordered, had separated the de Bohun's clothing from his weapons and armor and made their way onto the field to follow the king's bidding.

Beyond them, he noticed Sir Robert Keith coming down the hill from Torwood and cross the ford.

Keith, having watched the battle skirmish from the wood, knew that some of the English had fallen into the pots, but little more. Riding up the incline after passing the ford he could see the field of pots and the results of their deadly work. Fine and well-trained destriers lay upon the field, some far from dead and writhing in agony as the remainder of their lives oozed from their wounds onto the grass.

There were men, too, not yet dead but badly injured and twisting on the ground where they landed when thrown from their horses and left behind by their fellows. There was little that anyone could do for the rest, but one sat flat-legged having propped himself up with his arms. He was a young knight wounded in his legs and bleeding some. He could not walk on his own.

"Help me, My Lord!" begged the man.

Keith hesitated, knowing him to be the enemy. His yellow shield with the three red chevrons lay beside him. "Ye of Gloucester?"

"Was," replied the man. "The earl just rode on off and left us here to die."

"Ye fixed to kill me?" asked Keith, suspicious of the man in spite of his wounds.

"I shall throw my sword and dagger asunder," said the wounded man, tossing his weapons away.

Keith said, "Ye want me to help ye leave this world? 'Twould stop yer sufferin'."

Fear made the man shake. "I just want to live," he said quietly.

"Then ye should nae have come here to fight, I reckon." fussed Keith.

"Glory was promised, and good pay and honors. This was my first battle," said the knight sorrowfully, "All else was learned at tournaments. My horse, that I raised from a foal, is a'ready dead." He pointed to his mount ten feet away, its feet and legs torn to pieces, and its throat cut, still showing a slight trickle of blood.

"Different, hain't it," said Keith rhetorically.

A man nearby who laid mortally wounded raised his head just far enough to say, "Tell the Scot to go to hell!"

"Ye are dead a'ready, John," said the knight, "but, I might get better and walk again, if this Scot will help me."

Keith looked down on the man from his saddle. "So ye want me to save yer arse so ye can come try to kill us again?"

"No! I swear," he said raising his hand toward Keith. "I'll never take up arms against another livin' soul!" he begged.

"Joinin' the monks, are ye?" asked Keith as a kind of jest.

The man looked down. He was in no mood for facetiousness. He rubbed his legs to see if any feeling was left.

His comrade John raised his head once again in his dying and tried to say something, but the effort it took to say the garbled words expended the last of his life, and he dropped back into a pool of his own blood, his eyes staring nowhere particularly. Both the Keith and the Englishman felt a twinge of sadness for him.

"What do ye reckon now?" asked Keith after a moment.

The man sighed deeply as he stared at the newly made corpse. "Did ye see his soul leave his body? I ne'er saw it," he said at last.

"Hard to see such, 'specially in daylight," said Keith. "Ye got rich kin?

The knight nodded his head.

"Then I'll save ye for the ransom," said Keith, having little emotion concerning the man's life.

"Thank you, Milord!" groveled the knight as he clasped his hands and looked to heaven.

Sir Robert Keith got off his horse and cautiously worked his way into the booby trapped area where he reached to help the man to his feet, saying, "Ye sure ye hain't got a dagger or two hidden somewhere?"

"Got none," said the wounded man stretching out his hand to his savior.

Keith's foot slipped and he came very near falling into one of the pots himself.

"See, 'tain't hard to kill yerself," said the knight.

"'Tain't hard to live, neither, if ye tend to yer own rat killin's," growled Keith as he grabbed the man by the arms and dragged him between the pots to the road. The man winced all the way but he never cried out.

Admiring that in him, Keith helped the Englishman onto his own horse, and taking the reins, walked the half-mile to where his cavalry stood.

"What have ye saved from the dead?" asked Sir William Vieuxpont as he met Robert Keith coming to him.

"Hostage," said Keith.

"Looks 'most dead to me, and I saw ye havin' a'strugglin' a'gettin' him aboard yer horse," responded Vieuxpont.

The English knight raised his head a little to speak in his own behalf, "I hain't dead, yet, but I am so cold!" the fellow shivered.

"Bear witness, Sir William!" said Keith, "my hostage is alive and if kept so will fetch a penny or two!" He took off his tabard and placed it about the man's shoulders.

Graham came to the knot and seeing Keith asked. "Where've ye been?"

"Takin' a shit and collectin' hostages," said Keith in a jocular mood. "I would nae have asked ye such, had ye gone to take a shit, Sir David."

David smiled at the levity. "Had I gone to take a shit, Sir Robert, I would nae have gone all the way to Torwood!" he joked. He looked up at the pale, shaky Englishman and said more soberly, "But, ye need to get yer friend here up to Lady Christina, afore he bleeds to death."

"I was fixed to go that way myself," offered Vieuxpont.

"Nae, I'll take him," said Keith, "I have some news for the king."

Straightaway, the two friends hurriedly left David de Graham and took the man through the New Park where they were joked about the hostage by assembled knights all the way. They soon were behind Cockshot Hill where Christina had a canopied shelter for her patients to lie away from the sun, which was slowly creeping to that side of the hill.

"Got a man lost a lot of blood," said Keith as he eased the weak man from his horse. Christina helped by grabbing the man's torn legs.

"He's English!" she said with some surprise upon seeing his true tabard.

"Hostage, My Lady, help him if ye can," he replied as they laid the man down. "Ye ken where the king might be?"

"Hain't seen him since he left this morn," she said, drawing a blade from her belt. "Yer 'hostage' has fainted, I see." They went to work, pulling the remains of the armor from his legs and Christina then ripped open his trews with her knife to see the source of the bleeding. She began cleaning the wounds as Keith mounted his horse and trotted off to find the king.

In front of Saint Ninian's Kirk sat Robert astride his horse, Sir Thomas Randolph alongside, and Andrew and Nigel a few feet behind, in case there was something the king might need. Before them was Randolph's highland schiltrom, their many long spears jutting far above the metal bascinets worn only by the first and last two rows of fighters due to the shortage of the helmets.

"Just got back from Torwood, My King," said Keith as soon as he arrived.

"Ye hurt?" asked Robert, "There's blood on yer saddle."

"'Tis English," he replied.

"Good," said Robert bluntly, adding, "How was the view?"

"Mighty bad," reported Keith, "dust cloud farther back than Falkirk."

Robert shook his head, solemnly understanding the meaning of the report. "Through here will be their second attempt to reach Stirlin' ... if they make another try," he said to Thomas.

"Where ye want yer cavalry?" said Keith.

"Yonder," said Robert turning and pointing to the top of the hill nearly directly above their position. "Yonder's where we'll want them for now... and bring them through the trees lest there be spies about."

"Aye, My King," said Keith, and he trotted off to where the cavalry stood, downhill and among the trees, Sir David de Graham temporarily commanding.

Robert de Clifford

SUNDAY, LATE MORNING ~ JUNE 23RD
SOUTH OF TORWOOD

Lords Hereford and Gloucester nearly ran their horses into the ground getting back to the main force. Each was concerned that the other would be the first to report to the king and… poorly relate, if not deliberately lie about… his part in the first skirmish.

Gloucester won the race to the king's ear.

"Your Majesty!" he addressed the king in quick breaths. "We have seen the enemy!"

"Why are you riding young Bohun's destrier?" were the first words from the king's mouth, giving le Clare a momentary jolt. However, he recovered quickly.

"Poor Sir Henry was struck down by the Brus," he cried emotionally.

"Personally?"

"Yes, My Lord King, with one cruel blow of his axe."

"He is dead?" asked the king.

"Very dead," said Gilbert, "Lord Hereford is beside himself with grief… it was most fortunate that I was there to lead the troops aright!"

King Edward observed the hundreds of knights and squires following Sir Gilbert were spread in disarray across the glen floor for at least a league and a half.

"Seems you have outrun your van, Cousin," said the king pointedly, and got to the nub of the matter. "Did you relieve Castle Stirlin' or not?"

"I had not the chance, Sire! After the death of poor Sir Henry, vast numbers of Scots poured out of hiding upon us at New Park and we were forced to fall back lest we be slaughtered! Regrouping for a counterattack in an open field, we found that the Scots had laid traps for the horses that cost us many more men and mounts, and with our numbers thus reduced, we... I felt it necessary to report back to you, My Liege." He bowed, a properly subservient gesture.

The king, deciding to have a meeting with his commanders, ordered a small canopy to be erected immediately some hundred yards off the road, to keep it well away from the dust brought up by the many traveling feet of both men and beasts that continued while Edward held his meet.

"Wine," ordered Edward as one-by-one his commanders got the word and joined the king in his shade. The contrast was not lost on the foot soldiers who continued their march north at an agonizingly slow pace.

"Ye don't need to fight the Scots!" said Sir Philip Mowbray, once again pushing his plan forward. "The castle remains in your hands, and within the hour you will be within the six leagues I specified in the truce!"

The king waved his hand to hear no more and sipped his wine. He stretched his legs often during the meeting by rising on his toes and back down again.

The Earl of Gloucester had already traded his purloined horse with Bohun trappings for one belonging to a knight from his contingent. Thus when Sir Humphrey came to the tent he boldly asked, "Where's Sir Henry's horse?!"

"My Lord Humphrey, you didn't expect me to ride a horse covered with Bohun trappings, not to mention Bohun blood... did you?" parried Gilbert.

"The horse!" erupted Humphrey.

"'Tis bein' put to good use, Milord," offered Gilbert, smiling.

"Stop! Goddamn it!" said King Edward shrilly. "Drink some wine... I want to know why you two never made it to Stirlin' Castle!"

"Your Majesty," started Humphrey, "... young Gilbert led us into a goddamn trap!"

Sir Robert de Clifford tried to change the subject. "How did ye find Torwood?"

"We never went that way!" said Humphrey shortly.

"I figured they were the thickest in Torwood," returned Clifford, "good place to kill 'em all in a bunch."

"Well they weren't, and it wasn't!" said Gilbert, "They were atop Cockshot Hill in New Park and Brus killed Sir Humphrey's nephew Henry right off... with savage trickery!"

Clifford made no reply but took a goblet and summoned a page to fill it to the brim with French wine.

"I want to know exactly what happened!" demanded the king and Hereford opened his mouth to speak when Sir Henry Beaumont, the French adventurer, rode up to the meet canopy, along with Edmund de Mauley, the king's seneschal.

"Have we made it through to Castle Stirlin'?" asked Sir Edmund, hopefully.

The tent was suddenly a beehive of talk. Edward had lost all control of his meeting and stood seething as Sir Marmaduke de Tweng rode up. Reading the situation well, he hopped off his destrier and began to shout in his heavy booming voice that seemed to penetrate the loudest of cacophonies, "All hail the king! All hail the king!"

The men soon settled and Marmaduke returned the meeting to the grateful king whose voice, rather than demanding, sounded more shrill and whinging when he wanted to be louder.

"Sir Gilbert, tell your tale!" instructed the king.

"The westward passage is not the way to Stirlin'," he started.

Sir Humphrey piped in, "The ford is narrow and but few at a time can cross."

"And the sneakin' Scots are hidin' in the wood about a quarter of a league beyond..."

"That's where Gilbert lead us into a trap," interjected Humphrey.

"'Twas *your nephew* that sprang ahead... hell driven on killin' the Brus, that lead us into the trap," snapped Gilbert, glaring at Humphrey.

Clifford shook his head at the childish behavior between the two honored earls.

"Enough!!" said Edward loudly. "I presume you agree the route is not suitable to pass?!"

"'Tis not," granted Gilbert.

Edward looked at Humphrey for his opinion.

"'Tis not, My King," he agreed.

"Then how do we get to Stirlin'?" asked the king.

Philip Mowbray stood forward, "Your Majesty, if the Scots are at the western approach then the eastern approach may still be open."

Edward's eyebrow arched with interest. "Get the map."

"Yer pardon, Majesty, but this way I clearly know, as I have told ye before," explained Mowbray.

"Of course, I recollect your sayin' such," replied the king actually not remembering.

"I will lead a force of yer design to Stirlin' castle... if that is yer desire, Majesty," offered Mowbray.

"Send a sizeable force... they wouldn't dare attack a well designed, suitable force of knights," suggested Sir Robert de Clifford, quite anxious to reclaim his Scottish lands, particularly in Douglasdale.

"We had five hundred knights and three hundred squires, Milord," said Gilbert, meaning they had taken enough of a force to accomplish the task.

"I would take four hundred knights and no squires," bragged Clifford, "That would be all that's necessary."

"By the easterly route?" questioned the king.

"By the easterly route lead by Sir Philip," he confirmed.

"And your best choices for your commanders?" asked Edward happy to have a nub of a plan forming.

"Beaumont, for one," he said reaching to touch Beaumont on the shoulder.

Sir Henry bowed slightly indicating his acceptance of the challenge.

"And a man not here... Sir Thomas Grey," he concluded.

"Know him well," said Edward, "Get your four hundred together and go in all haste!"

• •

And so it was that Sir Robert de Clifford, Sir Henry Beaumont, Sir William Deyncourt and his brother Sir Reginald, and Sir Thomas Grey the elder, with their contingent of around four hundred barded knights, left the lumbering train of overloaded wains with two very different and distinct objectives: to relieve Castle Stirling and to trap the Scots in Torwood so they could not escape to the wilds beyond the immediate area, this last at the suggestion of Clifford.

It was Sir Aymer who unwittingly threw thorns onto the primrose path of that plan when he returned to report directly to the king a half-hour after Clifford's contingent had left.

Aymer drew rein when he came to the king, wheeled around and trotted his horse alongside the king's mount.

"Is my way clear?" asked Edward.

"Aye," said Pembroke, "Clear through Torwood."

The king reined quickly and looked at Pembroke not believing his ears. "Torwood!!?"

"Scots have been there, but they hain't now," reported Pembroke.

"Lord Gloucester said he saw plenty... wavin' their blue and white flag," said Edward.

"None atall there now... Your Majesty," insisted Pembroke, "and best to take this wagon train through there, too."

"Through the wood?" asked Edward.

"Hain't nothin' but soggy bottom land on both sides of Torwood," Sir

Aymer de Valence explained to the king.

"All?" asked the monarch.

"Not all," said Pembroke, "but a mighty plenty."

Edward began to vex about how Clifford was going to fare, remembering Mowbray's part in the gambit. He was, however, passing puzzled as to why the Scots played the ruse of making them think they occupied the forest of Torwood.

He called his squire to fetch him another cup of wine and ordered the train not to deviate from the road through Torwood, hoping that Pembroke alone would be right and a deviation from the road would lead to the wagon train being bogged down.

Henry Beaumont

SUNOAY, MIO-AFTERNOON - 23RO JUNE
BANNOK

Sir Philip Mowbray knew well the eastern route around the base of the hill of Torwood. He carefully guided the four hundred elite English knights along the edges of the fields of wheat, barley, and rye in the flats beyond. Here and there a small cot of a local farmer could be seen across the wider reaches of Bannok Burn toward the wood of Balquhiderock, as could the tiny hamlet of Bannok. Otherwise the vista was unoccupied all the way to St. Ninian's Kirk, and beyond to Castle Stirling.

By taking this track the English thought the force would avoid contact with the Scots, whether in Torwood or on New Park's Cockshot Hill, and after crossing the burn they would flank the wood of Balquhiderock and regain the Roman road for an easy mile and a half march to Stirling.

However, Thomas Randolph's force, in the northeastern edge of New Park and the vicinity of St. Ninian's, had the task of protecting the road to the castle. Among those in his van were the likes of Earl Hugh of Ross and his brother Sir Walter, Bishop Sir David de Murray, Earl William of Sutherland, Sir Ian Cameron and Sir William Wiseman, both of whom had been fighting alongside King Robert for about seven years, and Sir Neil Campbell, the king's brother-in-law, who had been with him even longer.

Mustered since shortly after dawn, Thomas and his men had become fatigued during the course of the long, hot morning of waiting for the enemy to show themselves within their sector. They knew that the western approach to the area had been tried by the English and found deadly, and like all of the Scots troops, they had been elated by the single combat victory won by King Robert. In spite of all that, their exuberant enthusiasm and personal energy flagged as the oppressive day worn on.

Sir Alexander Fraser of Touchfraser ordered water to be brought to Thomas Randolph's parched regiment. Passed around until they were empty, the jugs were ordered by Sir Alexander to be taken and refilled.

Even so, Thomas pulled his horse's head right and kicked his heels into its ribs to send it up the hill toward where Robert casually straddled his small, nimble-footed white, holding a position from where he could keep a wary eye the on approaches from Falkirk.

"My men, and the others no doubt, are gettin' weary, Rob," said Thomas when he arrived beside the king.

"Aye, we're all weary," agreed Robert, keeping his eyes roving across the landscape like a wolf guarding his den.

At that moment a sentry rode up and reported, "My King, 'tis more English aheadin' this way!"

"Where?" asked Robert.

"Balquhiderock," he replied, "Saw some few a'wanderin' about in the wood, too!"

"Where's the main force?"

"Prob'ly hain't the main force, Sire, only 'bout half as many as this mornin'. But they're all barded knights from what we could see, a'comin' 'round on the eastern side," he said pointing southeastward.

Robert nodded that he understood. "Ye have done well. Get back to yer watchin' and report again if such changes," the king calmly said, and the spy rode back toward Balquhiderock.

"How long ye reckon afore they get here?" asked Thomas.

"See fer yerself," said Robert standing in his stirrups to see more clearly.

"Now!?" said Thomas, whose vision in that direction was blocked.

"There they are... comin' through the trees," said Robert.

"Goddamn it!!" yelped Thomas and wheeled his horse hard and kicked it fast. He was with his regiment within a moment.

"Comes Moray," said Fraser, and he stood to see him galloping toward them.

"Somethin's wrong!" observed Walter, seeing how Thomas was beating his mount.

"Liven up!!" ordered Sir David Murray to the pikemen.

"Comin' this way!!" yelled Thomas, anxious as he was to get his news to his five hundred as quickly as possible.

Alexander raised his hand and gave a nod to indicate they knew

Thomas' want. At Fraser's signal, the men of Thomas' regiment quickly became very animated in their preparations.

Thomas drew rein, dismounted, and slapped his horse on its rump to send it out of harm's way. "Form up!" he ordered, and within minutes the regiment stood in fairly straight lines, six deep, the stronger and more seasoned men in the first and last ranks. "Remember yer trainin', Lads, this is where it's fixin' to come in mighty handy!" he shouted to them.

So far, their training had worked well, but they had yet to see a single Englishman approach their position.

The men pulled their heavy gloves from beneath their belts and put them on. The heat of the afternoon had already caused their quilted jackets to be soaked through with sweat, but they stood stoically straight, realizing well the approaching danger.

On the hill, Robert watched the troops preparing for the English onslaught. Again he prayed that his plans and training would win against the powerful army of King Edward.

"Where be the English, My Lord?" asked Andrew as he came from behind to stand his horse beside Robert's. Nigel remained to his rear.

"They're 'bout ready to clear the trees on this side of the wood," he said pointing.

Andrew squinted but saw only bright colored banners and glinting reflections on the helms of the knights, and little else, except that they were moving. "I see them, Sire!"

"'Bout half a mile, they'll be on Thomas' ground," replied Robert.

Douglas rode up on his horse and parked on the far side of Robert, where he gazed out in the same direction as the two men.

"We got English a'comin'," said the king.

"Where?" said Douglas, not having caught the sight of them.

"Just left of the trees, yonder," replied Andrew.

"Reckon this is the beginning of the whole army?" asked Douglas.

"Another probe, I figure," said Robert, "fewer than this mornin'."

Just then, Clifford came from out of the trees and got no more than forty yards beyond when he reined in his horse. Mowbray, Beaumont, Deyncourt, and Grey, all reined fast to keep from running into their leader. Mowbray ascertained the situation, wanted no part in the potential fight, and backed his horse up into the ranks and waited to see what was about to happen.

"Milords… there's Scots in the trees, yonder," said Clifford as more knights came and gathered at his back.

On the hill with Robert, James Douglas cursed when he recognized the yellow and blue checky shield with one red bar. "'Tis that damned bastard Clifford!"

"Aye, 'tis," said Robert, who looked at the Douglas and knew instantly what he was thinking. "James, ye *must* stay with yer troops! Ye have men who are dependin' on ye, includin' me!"

"But, Sire, 'tis *Clifford!*"

"And I understand that ye want to fight the whoreson. But ye'll hurt him most if ye defeat him and his English king! That'll be when he loses control of Douglasdale and his other lands, as well." He could see that Douglas was not convinced, and added, "James, ye command a schiltrom. As long as our schiltroms keep their discipline, as long as they work together, we can win! How can ye expect yer men to have faith in ye and follow their trainin' if ye go off fightin' Clifford?"

Douglas said nothing, but Robert then knew he would stay to the plan, at least for the present. If Thomas could not repel the Clifford force, however...

The English by Balquhiderock seemed to be frozen in place. They stood their horses in a group as they talked among themselves, trying to come to some decision, until Beaumont saw that the Scots had cast the deciding vote and broke up the conference saying, "Here they come!"

Thomas Randolph had given the order to move out of the wood and into the open, with him in the lead. Only a field of unripe wheat lay between them and the English.

"I can't believe they're sallyin' out to meet us!" said Clifford in genuine surprise.

"They don't know how many we are," interjected Grey.

"They're all in a straight line," said Beaumont, "If they come a little more into the open, we can easily surround them!"

"If they come a little more, they'll have us caught on this narrow front," warned Grey.

"If you're afraid, then go to the back!" snarled Beaumont.

"You men had best get your lances to the ready," said Clifford, who was in command, "and cease that stupid jabberin'."

"Go to hell!!" growled Grey as he laid spurs to his horse and took off at a furious pace to prove his manhood against the enemy.

Deyncourt, Grey's loyal friend, was beside him when he kicked his horse, and wanting to support his comrade, he whooped loudly and followed Grey at a gallop toward the line of Scots.

Both of them had their lances aimed at the torsos of the front line of men.

"Here they come!" yelled Thomas to his schiltrom. He and the Bishop of Moray stopped, and their men passed by until the pair stood in the middle of the regiment.

At Thomas' order they halted and set their long spears into the ground. The front rank went to one knee, the second line placed their spears on the shoulders of the first, and the third rank placed their pikes on the shoulders of the second, appearing from the front like a goliath hedgehog.

Still the two knights charged headlong toward the pikes.

"Only two?!" said the bishop, drawing his sword.

"Lambs, hastenin' to the slaughter," said Thomas, grimly.

The knights' shorter lances had no chance of penetrating the schiltrom as far as the bodies of the Scottish soldiers. It was a foolish, wasteful death they rushed toward.

There was the clash of the powerful, muscular flesh of the fearless animals against hard, sharp steel, and the knights' destriers, almost as if they had been skewered for roasting, had three feet of Scottish pikes inside them. The shafts cracked loudly as the carcasses fell to the ground.

Deyncourt's writhing horse had tossed him sideways into the wall of pikes, two of them ran him through one side below his armor.

Grey was slammed hard to the ground to be pinned, unconscious, beneath the great weight of his horse.

Deyncourt's brother Reginald audibly gasped at seeing the two men and their horses drop like stones. The entire group watched as the knights were trampled under the feet of the schiltrom, which at Randolph's command had stood and was again on the move across the field.

"They're comin' toward us!" yelped Clifford, shocked.

"Take command, Clifford!" growled Beaumont.

"Goddamn you whoresons!" said Reginald Deyncourt, not to the Scots but to the expedition's commanders. With tears of anger in his eyes and frustration in his heart for Clifford's failure to act to save his brother, he put spurs to his own destrier and hied toward the bristling group.

"Come back, you fool!" shouted Clifford.

Reginald was on course with his self-made fate and no words were to hold him.

"We'll all be impaled on those damned spears, one at a time, if we don't attack them to the front and the back together!" argued a frowning Beaumont.

The schiltrom stopped once again and set the spear butts into the ground, waiting for the heavy horse's impact.

Reginald followed his brother in death. His horse was immediately killed on the Scots' pike heads, their line buckling slightly with the impact, but it held.

The dying horse reared and threw Reginald, who was knocked cold when he hit the ground. One of the men in the first rank stepped forward and obliged his death with a blade stroke to the throat.

"Prepare to ATTACK!" shouted Clifford. His common sense reeling, his emotions took over, running at full tilt at seeing fine English knights dying with no battle at all. Just death.

At his call the four hundred knights came out of the wood in almost single file and onto the battlefield. Most of them didn't know who or what they were attacking until they cleared the edge of the wood, but they would follow one another. At once they moved to surround the Scots.

Thomas barked the order to form a circle, and the last three ranks turned to face the rear. All then moved outward, turning the formation into a ring with an open core, showing deadly barbs on all sides.

"There's where the long hours of trainin' pay off," said Robert observing the whole operation from his higher position on the hill. Thomas' schiltrom had maneuvered perfectly.

"Let me take my horsemen and help, Rob!" pleaded Douglas once again.

"D'ye not see those poor dead knights who threw themselves against a wall of certain death?" said Robert. "Would ye do the same?"

James Douglas was quiet, for he had been itching to kill Clifford for years.

Andrew was fascinated watching the battle forming from the elevated vantage point. His excitement mingled with fear and fired his blood. He twitched first one way and then the other seeing the warriors playing out the life and death scenario just a matter of yards down the hill.

"How can it be, My King," said Andrew, "that ye sit with so many great warriors about ye and yet, ye don't rush down and attack the enemy fightin' Sir Thomas?"

Robert smiled. "Ye'll make a great warrior one day, Sir Andrew," he opined, not taking his eyes off the assault, "but watch, and I think ye will learn more than I could e'er say."

Thomas gave the order and the schiltrom moved more to the center of the open area so they wouldn't get forced into a position where they could not move. The other nobles with Randolph placed themselves along the inner perimeters of the ring to guide the men in the directions that their commander ordered.

Neil Campbell noticed that one of the English, having been thought dead, was now encompassed inside the ring and was beginning to stir, though he remained in a rather addled state and was yet pinned neath his dead destrier. Campbell grabbed the hapless fellow by the collar and jerked the man's own sword from its sheath with which to cut his throat, when he fainted again.

"Oh, Hell!" grumbled Neil looking at the fine workmanship of the sword. "Ye can't kill a man who carries a sword that looks like this!" He left the man lying on the ground with the idea in mind to keep an eye on him. If he lived, there would perhaps be a ransom to collect. In the meantime, he had a sword for each hand.

Clifford's knights surrounded the schiltrom. "All attack when I say!!" yelled Clifford. "These are just foot soldiers!"

"Set pikes!!" ordered Thomas.

The Scots went into their defensive positions, digging the butts of their spears into the ground and bracing for the expected heavy impact.

"ATTACK!!" yelled Clifford, and the now less than four hundred barded knights set spurs to their great destriers and drove them against the five hundred foot soldiers still holding firm against them.

Horses screamed in pain as they were killed on the pikes, their riders thrown to the ground or onto the deadly spears. Other horses balked when they came to the pikes and threw their riders over their heads. The sharp cracking of spear shafts was prevalent around the entire ring as riders and horses slammed the hedgehog.

The ring held!

The ground was soon red and slick with the blood of man and beast.

The bodies gathered so that it was difficult for the footmen and the knights to maneuver the field.

"Were the English tryin' to get to the castle?" asked Andrew.

"Aye, but we stopped them," said Robert looking toward the western approach to see if they were going to try that way again.

"Why don't they just hie out now?" asked Andrew. "They hain't winnin'."

"Pride keeps them tryin'," answered Robert. "Keeps them there... 'cause they reckon they're the masters of the battlefield... and today we're showin' them they're wrong.

"And tomorrow?"

"Tomorrow will be another day..." replied the king.

The warhorses churned up a great deal of dust in the farm field, and the men of the schiltrom particularly became choked. Their eyes watered and burned, but they held firm.

The knights were becoming increasingly frustrated, so much so that one pulled his hand axe and threw it at his Scots enemies, but it missed its mark and landed at Lord Thomas' feet. He hadn't seen it coming but was luckily unhurt.

Clifford saw what happened and knew that King Robert was watching from somewhere in the wood above him. Desperate to break the standoff by mere foot soldiers, he withdrew his mace from the loops holding it to his saddle and threw it as hard as he could at the men of the first row of pikes. Perhaps he threw too hard, for his mace came to a halt inside the circle as well.

The men of the schiltrom took their shields from their backs and held them over their heads as more and more knights flung hand weapons of any description at the Scots. Most fell harmlessly within the schiltrom, but one yeoman was struck in the face by an axe and the English exalted... they had finally drawn Scottish blood.

"Position yer regiment, Jemmy," said Robert to The Black Douglas, hedging on the side of caution.

"Aye, My King," readily replied James, and he quickly turned his horse and rode to put his schiltrom in the best location for advantage, if they were to fight, but he kept his thirty-two horsed warriors separate from his schiltrom of foot soldiers.

The ground in the center of Randolph's schiltrom was soon filling with English weapons.

Unbelievably, five hundred common soldiers of foot were holding off four hundred elite English knights before the eyes of the Scottish army, the majority of whom were the same type of foot soldiers as they. It was not lost on them that, if Moray's regiment could survive the destriers and trained knights, so could they.

Robert was more than pleased. The English commanders were flummoxed.

Thomas saw that the knights had thrown every sort of weapon they had at his regiment, and still the ring held.

Clifford's knights encircled the schiltrom, testing its integrity, yet were unable to break it. Clifford laid off at a distance for a bit, contemplating his next move, a final attack, even if born of desperation.

Suddenly, without the slightest hint of warning, Thomas Randolph gave the order to attack. The English were out of opportunities to be on the offensive. The Scots walked fast in a single direction, the men on the hind side walking backwards and protecting the formation's rear.

There were minor, and quickly closed, breaks here and there in the ring as the charging Scots negotiated over the carnage of their successes.

The knights and their mounts became more nervous as the wall of death came closer, and began to back up. The schiltrom continued to advance toward them.

Very quickly the pressed knights became separated into two confused groups, neither of which knew what to do in the face of such Scottish aggression; it was not supposed to have been like this.

Seeing his command being split, Clifford called for a general retreat and wheeled his own destrier to follow the path the knights had taken when coming through the wood of Balquhiderock to St. Ninian's Kirk.

One of the two groups fled behind him, but Thomas had the ring of the schiltrom open up and block the others from following, though they tried to find ways around it.

With the knights behind them fleeing, Thomas turned his men into a long single line sweeping toward the remaining knights, who had no longer the choice of running after their commander.

At their back was the road to Stirling castle. At their front was death, or at best, capture.

Thus, they wheeled and hied for the castle, hoping there were no more Scottish schiltroms left to challenge them while they traversed the league to safety.

Seeing the hindquarters of the English as they fled, some toward Falkirk, some to Stirling, the exhausted Scots cheered and yelped in their victory over the superior, mounted force. Then they fell onto the ground and rested.

King Robert left his vantage point immediately to go congratulate the warriors.

Andrew, Nigel, and Douglas followed.

"Great skirmish!" shouted Robert to all the men, and rode directly to his nephew. "Thomas, I am mighty proud of the way ye and yer men fought! Ye have done the impossible!"

Thomas laughed with relief.

"Bring that water!" shouted Alexander Fraser, seeing the scores of squires holding the freshly filled jugs that he had sent for before the conflict began. The squires were kept busy refilling them.

The men disrobed themselves of the heavy protective clothing, slinging helmets, gloves, and quilted hacquetons to the ground, thankful for the cooler air, which had seemed so oppressively hot an hour before.

"Ye did somethin' on this patch of cornfield that's ne'er been done before," said Robert, grinning broadly.

Thomas smiled for he knew it as well.

There was a groan behind the men.

"My prisoner!" yelled Neil Campbell, "See... I have his sword!"

The men nearest him laughed as he went to collect Sir Robert de Grey, his English prisoner yet beneath the carcass of his horse.

The fleeing knights had no trouble when they got to Castle Stirling. The Scots in the village who were assigned to protect the portal to the castle let them ride right past without challenge.

The fleeing knights who backtracked toward the main army were in far greater jeopardy for they had to answer to King Edward as to why they returned one hundred and seventy-three knights fewer than when they left.

King Edward made his way toward the forest of Torwood, having traversed that far on the road to Stirling in the immediate company of more than two thousand knights. Spread behind him was a sea of nearly twenty thousand. The horde loomed enormous upon the landscape.

The local population, as others had since the cumbersome train left London, came out of their cots when the grand procession passed and watched with amazement at the splendid and seemingly unending display of English might. It would be the rest of the day and much of the night before the ponderous, elephantine wains and the pack animals of the English supply train passed through Torwood.

Suddenly, from within the shadowy darkness of the forest came Sir Robert de Clifford and his command, all in a great hurry. The king recognized the band and kicked his horse to meet them. Pembroke and d'Argentan along with a few other knights accompanied him because there was always wariness that the king could be the target of a trap or an ambuscade.

Both sides drew rein in the middle of the road.

"Your Majesty," started Clifford, barely able to catch his breath, "Enemy forces is thick in the forest of Cockshot Hill!"

Edward sat with his mouth agape at what appeared to be a man fleeing for his life, leading a routed army. As the other knights exited the dark shadows of the wood, they spread out and acted as if they had been rescued from a dire situation, doffing helms and pushing back their chain mail coifs to remove their sweat-laden armorer's caps. Some were gasping for air and others doused themselves with water begged from the king's contingent. All were disheveled and dusty and disheartened.

Edward stood in his stirrups and estimated the count of Clifford's knights before saying, "You appear to be a bit shy of your four hundred, Milord!"

Clifford was already asweat, his face showing rivulets of moisture streaking his dirty face, but the king's statement made him more so.

"Had a bad skirmish with the damned Scottish fools!" griped Clifford.

"'Damned Scottish fools' kill half your knights, did they?" asked Edward, pejoratively.

"No, Majesty! Most went on to… relieve Castle Stirlin'!" Clifford thought to say quickly.

"And the other 'most', that would be you, Milord Clifford, came to tell me what?" asked Edward sarcastically.

"They're all soldiers of foot!" said Clifford.

"Foot?" spoke Edward, his eyes widened in disbelief. "There was not a single one on a horse?"

"Perhaps thirty, I reckon," said Clifford, shaking his head as if he didn't believe it either, "... but no barded knights."

"And King Hobbie?" asked Edward remaining hostile.

"Oh, he was there, Sire," said Clifford.

"And did you kill him?" asked the king.

"No, Your Majesty," Sir Robert replied with a hard swallow, "... but I have scouted the whole of the terrain, and... and... I can tell you the best place to alight for the evenin' so that we have only a few yards to travel to meet the Scots on the morrow!"

"Your Majesty," suggested Pembroke, "Truly, I think it would be best if we settled here on these broad fields for the night. The castle has been relieved... it is... yours!"

"You goin' with the Mowbray notion, My Earl?" he asked, rolling his eyes in indifference.

"Out of the mouth of Sir Robert de Clifford, it has been relieved... Your Majesty," said Aymer strongly.

"Clifford has misplaced half his knights, and doesn't know where they went," said Edward. "*Perhaps* they relieved Stirlin'. Or, *perhaps* they were taken by the Scots! Should we believe anythin' *he* says?"

"If ye encamp here, Majesty, ye will have miles to travel before meeting the enemy on the morrow. If ye will but come with me, I'll show you my notion as to where ye should camp and have no distance to travel at all," interjected Clifford quickly. "And there be plenty of water for the men and animals as well!"

So it was that the king and his household knights followed Clifford far around the east side of the Wood of Balquhiderock to arrive at the lush, green carse between Cockshot Hill and the pools.

"Yonder be enough land to set your cavalry, Your Majesty," said Clifford pointing to a dry field.

"I don't like it," said Pembroke frowning as he looked around the terrain.

"Can't water your horses in the field," said Clifford, and swung his arm around to point to the east in the direction of the swift and deep River Forth, "But yonder, you can."

"Water our horses in the Forth?" objected Edward, "Are you daft, Clifford?"

"No, Sire, not in the river itself," said Clifford, "but just there a ways are calm, clear pools of fresh water where men and horses can all drink a'plenty!" 'The pools' were holes kept filled by slow moving streams of fresh water that ran in every direction as they lethargically made their way toward the river.

"'Tis not large enough!" again interjected Pembroke. "That dry field's not enough land to provide for our thousands of horses, much less our men! Where will we have our tens of thousands of foot soldiers? And our supply train?! There simply isn't room for all, Your Majesty!"

Clifford was quick to rebut Pembroke's reasoning.

"We shall keep the divisions of foot, and the wains, on the south side of the Bannok, Your Majesty," he argued, valiantly trying to talk himself back to the king's good graces. "Tomorrow, we shall bring our foot up and have them root Brus' foot out of the park," said he as he pointed uphill slightly toward the west, "That's where all of the Scots are holed up!"

Edward looked uphill. The long afternoon shadows revealed little as to the size of the amassed army, though he could see men milling along the edge of the forest and an occasional rider, but nothing fearful. *Perhaps I could run the foot soldiers up into those woods in the morn and roust whatever of the enemy is there left to fight. After all, they have already been in two skirmishes with my knights. How could mere Scots soldiers of foot not have been decimated?,* he thought. *Has their loss at Falkirk taught them nothing?*

Edward turned to Mowbray who had come back with Clifford and asked, "What say you, Milord?"

"There's more in the wood than you would rightly reckon, My Liege," he replied.

"More than we have?" asked the king.

Mowbray shook his head, "Not near as many."

"Then this is the obvious place to alight," said the king.

Pembroke shook his head at his friend d'Argentan, who had no opinion because he was not familiar with the terrain of Stirling in general, and Bannok in particular.

"Have my tent pitched," ordered the king. "We'll be the first to bring order to this ground and do all that's appropriate when dealing with the deceitful beggars. These whoresons will not escape my grasp as they did before, I vow."

Pembroke kept his mouth shut.

Ordered to the carse, the English knights began crossing the eastern ford in all confidence that the Scottish army, of whatever size, would be carrion for vultures shortly after sunup.

John Comyn

SUNÐAy, EARLy EVENING ~ 23RÐ JUNE
NEW PARK

"Keepin' an eye on them?" asked Robert as he came to Andrew. The young knight had taken up a position on the edge of the park with the idea of studying the disposition of the English army.

"Aye, Sire," said Andrew, intensely eyeing something across the road.

"What d'ye see? Anythin' I should know?"

"I think they might be buildin' a trebuchet or somethin'."

"How so?"

"They set up that big red and white striped tent yonder in the middle of the field," answered Andrew purely puzzled.

Robert chuckled, "'Tis nae trebuchet, Lad. Tis King Edward's tent."

"Oh," replied Andrew and remained quiet, feeling foolish.

"Ye mean it's not a great weapon, My King?" asked Nigel who had been sitting vigil with Andrew.

"Oh, 'tis a weapon for sure," said Robert, "but not a trebuchet."

Nigel remained very confused.

"They a'comin' for us in the morn, My King?" asked Andrew.

"Don't know, Sir Andrew," said Robert, wondering if they would be coming for them when the sun dissolved into a short dusk of a few hours before it rises once again. "Ye lads get some sleep," he advised, knowing full well he would be ignored.

Robert then went over to the pinfold on the backside of Cockshot Hill. He dismounted his horse and patted him affectionately. "Have him ready afore sunup," he ordered. "And my destrier, too."

"Aye, Sire," said an older man with a limp as he took hold of the reins.

"Ye ridin' tomorrow?" asked Robert.

"Wish so, Sire," he replied, "but the ridin' days are done."

Robert nodded to say he understood, then wandered up the hill to where Christina sat on her chair outside the hovel where they treated wounded. She stood to greet Robert as he walked up.

"Horse meat smells good a'cookin'," she said.

"Not good for much else once they're dead, poor beasts," he replied.

"Tired?" she asked.

"Oh, aye," he nodded. "Just about as tired as a man can be…"

She suddenly broke, "Oh Robbie, what will become of us?" She drew him tight to her and they seemed to be somewhere else for a short while as he tried to comfort her, holding her tight.

"We will survive," he said softly.

She broke the embrace. "Not if ye pull many such foolish acts as ye did this morn!" she sulked.

"I am alive, woman… am I not?" he said.

"By a hair's breadth," she argued.

"'Tis all that's needed to have the other man dead," said he.

"Foolish," she reiterated.

"How is the lad with the foot," he asked, trying to change the subject.

"The war didn't come soon enough for him," she said sadly, and her voice caught in a sudden sob.

Robert nodded. "Reckon he'll be ridin' with us from heaven."

"From the grave, down the hill," she said bluntly, feeling more earthbound than spiritual.

Robert sighed.

"Dianna's gone to havin' her bairn," she said.

"Where is she?"

"With the Templar in the wood," she replied.

"Ye midwifin' for her?" he asked.

"Nae, one more suited to the task be at it," said she. He stood there for a moment but seemed anxious to leave. "Where are ye off to, this time o' night?"

"Many things, ere the dawn," he answered.

"Then get ye to them so ye can get some sleep!" Her eyes welled with tears, but she fought them back. He smiled and hugged her again. She hugged back then let her arms release him to do what he must.

• •

As Robert was walking back over the hill to check with Andrew, Sedric, the Irish chieftain, appeared suddenly in front of him. "Hail, King," he greeted with his usual snaggle-toothed grin.

"Where d'ye come from when ye pop up like that?!!" said Robert, taken completely by surprise.

"Ireland, as ye ken a'ready," he said smiling. "Ye said ye have a thing for me to do, King?"

"Aye, I do… come with me…" said Robert. "Did ye eat?"

"We et, once," he came back.

They went to where Andrew and Nigel were yet keeping a good eye on the developments about the carse.

"They're bringin' in a mighty plenty knights, My King," opined Andrew.

"Robert replied, "They always do. Edward likes to be cautious." He then turned and said, "Sedric?"

"Aye, King," he replied.

"When it gets dark, I want ye to take some men among the English yon, and come back and tell me all about them," he instructed the chieftain. "I want to know where the knights are, where the archers are, and the foot soldiers, I want to know where they are, particularly."

"Aye, King," repeated Sedric, "and the English king? Do ye nae want to know the where'bouts of him?"

"He's in that big striped tent, yonder," said Robert in answering Sedric's question.

"Ye want him kilt?" said Sedric smiling. He had his dagger in his hand and ran his tongue up the blade.

"Nae, we'll save him for a big ransom," said Robert. He laughed a little to himself and looked down the slope at the enviable collection of magnificent knighthood. When he turned back Sedric had disappeared. "Damn!" he exclaimed under his breath.

"What say, Sire?" asked Andrew turning to the king.

"Nothin'," said Robert. "Tell me if anythin' odd happens. And get some sleep!"

"Aye," the Stewart said as Robert walked away.

SUNDAY, EARLY EVENING - 23RD JUNE
BALQUHIDEROCK

It was a combination of greed, economy, improvidence, misuse, jealousy, obsequiousness, and downright groveling, that led the English army to camp where it did. But most of all, it was malaise and overconfidence that laid a clumsy finger firmly on that very ground.

In the vicinity of Bannok, two poor farmers and three of their five children stood outside their house as they helplessly watched the English soldiers tearing the doors and shutters from it. The soldiers went inside and brought the only table they had to the yard and stomped the legs from it. They took the bedstead, then the thatch from the roof, the rafter beams and the ridgepole. The thick sod outer walls were all that was left of the structure when they departed.

The children were fearful and at the same time fascinated at the coterie of weapons carried by the soldiers. They shivered with fear and still wanted to reach out and lay a finger to the magic hand-tools of death that always had some real or imagined enemy blood smeared thereon.

"That's it!" yelled the captain as the many warriors, reminiscent of ants gathering food, set the wooden and thatch items on their heads and walked back toward Bannok.

"On to the next house!" again ordered the captain and the workers and carriers trudged behind.

Tears streamed down the woman's face. A great deal of her whole life's effort was ripped from her cot and was walking off on the heads of strangers. She made no sound, yet her husband knew her heart was breaking. He put his arm around her for comfort. "We're no dead," he tried to allay her distress. She turned and went into the cot in which she had lived her whole life, had birthed her children, and had said farewell to her parents. As she crossed the threshold she reached automatically for the vanished door, and when it was not there for her to touch, she wept aloud.

The ill-clothed children stood silently and continued to watch with round eyes, the fascinating soldiers and their weapons made of metal.

The warriors trekked across the rivulets of sluggish water known as the pows, or pools. There were already some boards, doors, shutters, and parts of a whole house, which the owners had been unfortunate enough to have built of wood, laid across the lower parts of the area. There were several such pathways used to traverse the terrain, a devilish, damp, semi-waterscape just above the high tide mark of the River Forth.

Twice a day, the fresh waters of the Forth and its tributaries were pushed backward before the incoming tides, and the burns had no place to empty other than into the pools. That time of night on this particular day the tide was coming in. The warriors were finding it an ideal place to have their destriers drink, but a poor one on which to sleep.

More knights were ordered onto the small space as they continued to arrive. The ones already there either huddled closer to the king's tent or moved to a higher spot on the scant dry parts of the carse.

"What are your opinions, Milords?" asked King Edward as he stood within his striped tent with his earls.

Wine was poured into six pewter cups by a young squire.

"I would that we had all camped below the Bannok," declared Pembroke picking up his cup, "We are here close enough for the Scots to attack us in the night, while we sleep!"

"Then we shall not sleep!" said Edward, knowing that *he* was certainly intending to get a wink or two, even if *no* one else did.

"We have tents pitched for some knights on the far side of the Bannok, Your Majesty," returned Pembroke, "and more will be rollin' in soon."

"And what about tents for knights on this side of the stream?" sniped Gloucester, who had brought the most knights of any noble there.

"Not enough room to pitch tents on this side... lest we put them uphill, closer to the park," offered Pembroke.

"I'll not have us an inch closer!" insisted Edward. "The smell alone would keep me awake!" he added gaily. The earls, of course, chuckled sycophantically.

"Then, the knights will be spendin' their evenin' by their horses," said Pembroke groaning under his breath.

"Well then, that be the case, can we use the hours to kill some Scots?" said Edward. "There's still plenty of daylight left."

"If it please you, Your Majesty, my men are much exhausted. They have done enough today," said Gilbert, and he drank a deep draft of his wine.

"We might could kill some before they formed a goddamn schiltrom, if we act tonight!" blurted Clifford.

"You never told us how it is that you came back without Grey, the Deyncourt brothers, and some others of your contingent, Sir Robert. Tales of their demise are flavoring the camp's gossip pot," said Gilbert, snidely.

Clifford turned quickly at the accusation, his hand grabbing his dagger pommel, but he answered calmly. "They died chargin' into a wall of pikes before I gave the command... bravely, I'll warrant ye, but foolishly! What truck is it of yours, Gloucester? None belonged to you!"

Gilbert smiled at the older knight.

"I should like to hear some of the gossip of how my knights *were* killed by Scottish *foot soldiers*," said Edward as he drank.

Hugh le Despenser took a sip of his wine as he watched the potential for bloodletting unfold.

"Your Majesty," started Clifford, all eyes on him, "We were surrounded by possible thousands of wild Scots with long spears, the likes of which you could not imagine! Grey and the Deyncourts rode directly into them ere we were aligned for a proper charge," he shook his head, empathetically, "and all for naught. Then the Scots stepped right over their lifeless bodies and attacked... kept rushin' us, and drivin' us back. There were none that would come to us honestly... chivalrously... and engage."

"Sounded just terrible," sarcastically goaded Gloucester.

"And what happened to you in your little scuffle of this morn, Milord?" questioned Clifford returning the sarcasm. "The Scots were not even chasin' you... 'til you ran!"

Gloucester rose to his feet as if stung by a bee, and Clifford drew his dagger and prepared for blood, but Gloucester only hastened to try to negate what Sir Robert had snarled.

"It was not like that at all, Majesty! We were fordin' the stream at the foot of the hill south of New Park and would have charged up the hill proper and run the damned whoresons out into the open, afore they knew we were there, but that little surprise was ruined by Bohun's nephew, who rushed ahead for personal glory and foretold the Brus of our comin'!" explained Gloucester, lying only slightly. "His attack on the Brus, who, I might add, was all but unarmed and riding a pony, destroyed all chance of our trappin' the Brus *or* gettin' through to the castle!"

"'Tain't so!" growled Lord Hereford, determined that the morning's first failed attempt was not going to be written into English history as having been because a member of the de Bohun family thwarted any sallying party's duty.

Gloucester turned to Bohun, "My Earl! You know it to be sooth."

The older earl balled his large fist and gave Gilbert, Earl of Gloucester, a solid punch in the face, knocking him to the ground.

Though dazed and dripping blood from his nose, Gilbert got again to his feet and slung a fist at Humphrey, who was agile enough to dodge the expected blow.

Edward was enjoying the excitement of the brawl. Rivalry was something his father was good at fomenting to his own advantage, whereas Edward simply allowed it to happen naturally and hoped he could turn it to his benefit.

Gloucester intended to try his luck again when he was suddenly grabbed around his arms from behind. He kicked and cursed. "Cease this childish behavior," said Raoul forcefully. Hearing his stepfather's voice, Gilbert stopped his wriggling.

When Humphrey saw his opponent was being held, he was tempted to take a last punch but thought better of it. Instead he straightened his raiment and with a curt bow to the king, tromped out of the tent.

"Milords," said Edward in a soothing tone of voice, "Let us not quarrel among ourselves again this evening. I'm sure we shall have all the quarreling we want with King Hobbie!" he grinned.

"What would you have us do, Majesty?" asked Clifford, attempting to shift the subject of conversation.

"The question is proposed; do we go run them from their holes tonight, or do we wait 'til the morrow to grub them up from under their rocks?" asked Edward.

"Your Majesty, I would suggest that the morrow would be more suitable, after the men have rested," said Clifford, who looked as if he could use the night's rest as well.

"And you, young rogue?" the king asked Gloucester.

"I reckon we're all tired," he said, soberly tending his bloody nose. "Best put this off 'til the morrow... after the fast is broken and the men have a good meal."

"Lord Aymer?"

"Not a chance of doin' anythin' tonight... we all be too worn," he admitted.

"Will we have a plan for the morrow?" asked Raoul.

"We'll make one at first light," replied Edward feigning a yawn.

Clifford smiled at the obvious conclusion of the meeting. He was just as happy that he didn't have to add more to his modification of the afternoon's misadventure.

The king had the competitive blood among his lords stirred so that on the morrow, they would fight to impress him, or at least that was his notion. His immediate wants were single minded: a quiet supper with Sir Hugh and soon to bed. In the morning he would tend to the Scots hiding in the wood on the hill, if they were still there.

SUNDAY, EVENING ~ 23RD JUNE
BANNOK

At long last it was fairly dark. Sedric took only four of his Irish warriors through the wood of Balquhiderock that served as common ground between the two armies. Two of his men went across Bannok Burn to where the foot soldiers were, and where wains of materials and victuals kept rolling regardless of the hour. Even in the middle of the summer night there was still enough illumination to drive a wain.

Among the foot soldiery were Irish conscripts and Sedric's men found it easy to mingle among them with little fear of being exposed. They kept their mouths shut and their ears open.

The warriors had a fire roaring and a stolen pig spitted and roasting, almost to perfection. Sedric's men thought it only mannerly to join them in their meal, and so casually wandered inside the informal circle of warriors and sat cross-legged on the ground. The pig smelled delicious and was making the English men of foot in the near vicinity angered and envious. Unfortunately, one of their cook wagons had broken an axel coming through Torwood and had been pushed off the road to allow the able wagons to pass. Now, all they could do was eat leftover bread and water… plenty of water.

Sir Adam Gordon, who knew the terrain of the area, had hung back from the other nobles and knights who were going across Bannok Burn. He had easily watered his destrier at the burn and come back to join his Scottish men as they constructed sleeping pallets for the night.

"Pig smells good," said Sir Adam, sniffing the air.

"We 'bout had that pig but for them Irish whoresons. From our very hands, took it they did, after we nabbed it from that farm, they surely did," lamented the Scot.

"Ye a'wantin' the pig?" asked Gordon peering out of his one twinkling eye, "Then go take it, Lad!"

"There's a heap more of them, Sir," said the Scot, "reckon they'll be a'keepin' their pig."

"How 'bout the bones?" said another, "I like the bones!"

"Bones hain't no good with no meat on 'em, and ye ken them Irish'll skin off e'ery last ort, crack 'em open and suck out e'ery sweet bit of the marrow," said Gordon, so convincing that all three of them salivated.

The two Scots warriors were silent.

"'Les we got somethin' for trade," said Gordon grinning slyly.

"Trade?" questioned one, "We hain't got nothin' for tradin'!"

"Well, air ye up for stealin'?"

"Stealin' what?"

"From the English!" said Sir Adam, drawing the two deeper into his web.

From the English?!"

"I swear," growled Gordon, "Ye got dirt in yer years?"

"Just a little," offered the second man.

The first man who caught the insinuation elbowed the man hard.

"Ow!" he said as he rubbed the hurt away. "Ye had no call to…"

"What must we do, Milord?" interrupted the first.

Gordon told them of his plot and the two hapless lads went merrily on their way to commit their larcenous crime at the behest of their commander.

In the meantime, Sedric and his two moved among the standing knights with fair ease. There were men everywhere, fully armored and standing stoically by their destriers wishing they had a pallet to lie upon, even if just for a little while.

Sedric carried his over-sized dagger low and close to his leg so as to show no sense of aggression. Many a knight would have easily had their throats quietly slit if Sedric had the mind for it but alas, his was a spy mission, and he had much to report to the Scottish king.

'Twas but curiosity that drove him to work his way close to the huge, striped royal tent.

The knights standing guard were just as tired as the others. Sedric picked up a bucket from within one of the wains and threw a couple of handfuls of grain in it and, carrying it purposefully as if ordered to take it to some knight's destrier, he reached the pavilion's skirt undetected and swiftly laid himself along it's bottom edge in a shadow.

He raised the hem of the tent wall just enough to peek in.

There were low sounds like murmuring. Sleeping, he guessed. Sleeping English make strange sounds, he reckoned. He remained quiet for a little while longer and the sounds became more like the snores to which he was accustomed.

Sedric rolled silently under the tent skirt and went smoothly over the large pallet of pillows. He had never felt anything so soft. There were candles playing their firelight gently on the side of the canvas, and woven wool floor coverings with patterns and elegant designs.

He crawled low to the floor so that he would cast no shadows against the outside walls, and entered a separate room wherein two men lay side by each, peacefully sleeping surrounded by luxury such as he had never seen before. He surmised that one of them must have been the English king and he wanted a closer look.

It was Sir Hugh that he first encountered. Looking into the man's angelic face, the chieftain decided he could not be the king. *Too young,* he thought, and made his way to the other.

Edward moved and turned over as Sedric lay beside him.

The Irishman remained motionless until Edward again started his deep breathing, and he then moved closer to look the sleeping man in the face. Sedric leant his head left and leant his head right to study out the peaceful countenance. Deciding this sleeper was Edward, he pulled his dagger to the king's very throat hairs and smiled quietly. Here he had the opportunity to cut the throat of the King of England... but he was satisfied in his curiosity. He couldn't hold back a silent laugh, and when he opened his mouth his foul breath blew lightly across the king's face.

Edward's nose wriggled and Sedric succumbed to the temptation of giving the king another exhalation. The king's face then reflected that he had smelled something very unpleasant, and his eyes suddenly opened to see a grinning Sedric only inches away, and he caught the flash of a blade at his own throat.

He shrieked and recoiled, pulling his coverlet over his head. If he were going to be murdered he did not want to see the blade coming. He then heard Sedric laugh in his high-pitched voice and he asked shakily, "Who are you?!"

"'Tis I, Sire, Hugh!" the young knight next to him spoke. Edward flung back his purple silk, gold piped coverlet and rising up on one elbow, sought the mysterious visage he had just seen, but it was to no avail, for Sedric had slipped away in a blink of an eye, leaving Edward to wonder if he was not a continuation of a nightmare. He cursed the land of Scotland for making him have such a dream and soon drifted back to sleep.

Sedric had heard and seen enough. He and his two men met back in the wood, but his other two men had not arrived. Sure that there would have been much pother if the two had been found out, they set off to find them. Crossing the cold water of the burn, and by a course of least resistance and the smell of cooking pork, they came upon Edward's Irish contingent, among whom his two men sat as if they belonged.

Sedric and his two walked into the circle and joined the others, and quickly realized there were also Scots among them, and a bunged cask of wine. Soon he had caught that the big Scot near the wine was named Gordon, and that he seemed to have consumed more from the cask than any other person around the fire.

Sedric smiled as the pig was finished cooking and off loaded onto the ground. The men closest began to pick at the hot flesh with their daggers. They put it between their teeth and breathed back hard to cool the searing meat that would certainly burn their tongues.

Sedric got to his all-fours and crawled to the tail end where he separated a large hunk of the upper leg for himself.

"Have some wine w' yer piggy," said an Irish warrior, handing Sedric a cup.

"Thank ye," replied Sedric as he came back to a sitting position.

"The Scots brought the wine," offered the man as explanation. "We stole the pig!"

Sedric shook his head and began gingerly eating small bites of his roast pork at first. He found it amusing that this hunk of a pig's rump was impaled on a dagger that had been deathly close to the King of England's throat just a short time before.

"Where ye from?" asked the friendly Irishman, his mouth and whiskers slick with grease from his dinner.

"Ireland," said Sedric smiling.

The man laughed loudly. "Nae, I mean yer not our regular bunch," he pushed.

"From t'other 'uns, yon," lied Sedric.

"Then ye're well come!" exclaimed the questioner and loudly laughed more. Sedric sat back in a hunker and laughed right along with his drunken friend.

On the opposite side of the fire sat Sir Adam Gordon, who had hatched the idea to trade pork for wine. There were many others in the army who were quick to get the plot and the location of the wine wagons.

The casks were manhandled from the wains against the protests of the teamsters whose responsibility it was to keep their cargo safe. But, the lack of immediate victuals and their long forced march for two days gave them plenty of excuse to misbehave.

Rolled out of sight in diverse directions, the casks were bunged and consumed at will. Only the pockets of hooting and wassailing could identify the locations of the quickly emptying casks. Nobody cared anyhow. Tomorrow they would sweep the Scots out of the wood on the hill and return home, and of what use would all that wine be to anyone then? It would just be hauled back to London and stored in the king's cellar.

As the embers of the fire burned low, the men were generally asleep with their bellies full and their wits numbed. Sedric and his four slipped from their company, their bellies full of usurped Irish hospitality.

MONDAY ~ AFTER MIDNIGHT ~ 24th JUNE
FAR SIDE OF COCKSHOT HILL

Sedric and his four men returned safely to New Park and gave their report to Robert. He quickly called a meeting of his commanders to be held on the far side of Cockshot Hill, where he knew English spies, if there were any, could not penetrate.

"We watched ye give the English knights hell today," said James Douglas with just a hint of envy.

Thomas smiled slightly. "In truth, 'twas the men. They were the ones who held the center and minded their trainin'. They did a'right," he muttered modestly, though one could tell he was proud of the highlanders' success.

"The English lost seventy-four knights ere they figured out they weren't goin' to get through," bragged Walter of Ross.

"And what about our king?!" said Alexander Fraser. "To stand against a chargin' knight with naught but an axe!?"

"Wish I'd seen it," spoke up Gilbert de la Haye.

"Well I saw it, and nearly shit my trews!" exclaimed Ian Cameron in jest and they all chuckled.

"D'ye know what he said when we got to 'im afterward?" asked Angus, and without waiting for an answer added, "he said, 'Damn! I broke my best axe!" Laughter roared from the battle hardened knights at the end of a long day.

Robert was on his way to join them when he heard the merry laughter. He knew the likelihood was that some of these same knights would be dead on the field at the end of the morrow's battle. For a brief moment, he wondered who among them it would be... James? Gilbert? Thomas? Edward? He stopped, shook off the morbid thoughts, and offered up a prayer that the morrow would not silence the voice of a single one of them.

Continuing to the gathering he entered the circle where a fire commanded the center. His smiling men all stood out of respect, but he motioned for them to sit. They were in such upbeat spirits that he hated to dash them, but he had no choice.

"We have a decision to ponder, Lads," he began.

"I hear some are sayin' we're fixin' to hie for Lennox," said Fraser, making a joke.

"It's one plan," admitted Robert, sobering up the group instantly.

Randolph stood up. "We don't want to hie!" he growled.

"Nor do I, Thomas," replied Robert, "but we're here to discuss the realities of the facts. Across the field yonder is a greater army by far than we are, and they're ready to fight and quite determined to win!"

"We're not worried!" asserted Randolph. "We won easily today, My King!"

"Skirmishes!" said Robert, "Ye won skirmishes!"

Malcolm of Lennox stood. "We figured it would be different tomorrow than what we had today, My King, but we've been through much more together."

Robert smiled at the sentiment. "Ye men are my lifeblood, I cherish e'ery one of ye." He paused a moment to wait for the catch in his throat to leave before continuing. "Our spies tell me that the English knights are poorly fed if at all, and sleepin' on their feet," said Robert, "They're the ones around the king's tent below us."

"We hain't getting' a single wink this night, Robbie!" said Thomas Randolph laughing. "Surely that hain't the secret to winnin'?"

Robert smiled. "Their foot soldiers and wagons are on the far side of the burn from the king. Many of the men are hungry and a lot of them are into their cups. In the morn they're going to wish they were in hell rather than suffer the wrath of their lieges."

"Are ye tryin' to convince us to hie, or to fight?" asked Edward Brus a bit puzzled.

"Neither," replied Robert. "I'm sayin' what the spies have reported to me… Knights standin' by their destriers, and up to their knees in water, some are."

"What about the wagon loads of supplies we've heard about?" asked David de Murray.

"Still comin' through Torwood at last report," said Robert, then took advantage of the bishop speaking up to add, "Can ye hold a mass and make sure that all who want, go to confession?"

"We'll have to start immediately to get that many heard," said the bishop, "I'll ask the abbots to help."

"This mean that we're fightin' the English on the morrow?" asked Thomas.

"Means I hain't heard word one about hiein'," said Robert.

"So will they be a'comin' for us in the morn?" queried Earl Malcolm.

"My friends," said Robert, "we have had such good fortune fightin' the English with stealth and trickery, and I know 'taint the most chivalrous of methods. But chivalry is reserved for those more on an equal footing with one another. We *must* win. Our very lives and the lives of our families are at stake." he paused, "This will be a face-to-face battle of our pikemen against their heavy cavalry. We'll have little room for stealth and trickery."

"We'll fight them, no matter!" growled Thomas.

"And ye should!" said a stranger's voice from outside the circle.

The king turned and peered into the semidarkness as his men stood and drew weapons almost in unison. As his eyes adjusted, Robert saw who came to his back so silently... Sir Alexander Seton, who held out both mailed hands to show they were empty and he meant no threat. Nevertheless, Robert's lieutenants moved to surround the man and make him a prisoner.

"I heard tell ye were here with the English," said Robert, holding his hand up to stay his capture and wondering how he got so close to them without being stopped and questioned.

"I *was* with the English, but I no longer can abide their wit," answered Seton, a strong, tall knight who joined them to stand grandly in the firelight. Belted to his back his red shield showed a gold bend containing three red crescents, his chain mail was covered by a red and yellow surcoat, his head protected by a pointed helm.

"How so their wit?" asked Robert.

Seton replied, "There is nae battle plan. Though a right good knight and soldier, King Edward is not the commander his father was and assumes that the numbers of warriors he has brought will make the difference and give him victory. He rests securely in his pavilion and the knowledge that his great English tide will wash over us tomorrow and Scotland will then be his."

"Fixin' to come for us on the morrow, are they?" queried Robert, watching the man's eyes and demeanor.

"So 'tis said," nodded Seton.

"How be they arrayed for the night?" asked the king, knowing the answer and wanting to see if Seton spoke truthfully.

"Badly. King Edward's knights have been made to take to the field in the bog around the king's tent on the edge of the dry land, while the infantry and the supply train is across the burn where there is at least higher land. 'Tis the regiments of foot which are to be brought forward in the morn to run ye from the wood," explained Seton, and then he paused before adding, "... and I would be honored to fight by yer side when they come for ye, if ye would accept me as yer vassal."

"A man so readily eager to come to another's peace, I am suspicious of his loyalty," said Robert, reaching out and drawing the knight more toward the fire where they all could get a better look.

"It's been preyin' on my wit for a long while," said Seton. "Sire, I give ye my word, I am a Scot... and I come home."

Sir Alexander Seton went to one knee and held his clasped hands toward Robert, the sign that he thereby pledged his fealty. Taking Seton on his honor, for he had always been an honorable man, Robert decided to accept him to his peace with the admonition whispered by the king into the knight's ear, "Do not disappoint me Sir Alexander!"

The king then turned to his commanders around the fire and said to all, "He who would refuse to sally forth with me on the morrow speak now!"

There was only silence. No man even looked to his neighbor to see what others might choose. Finally, Thomas said, "All shall be with ye on the battlefield, Sire. I have looked to ev'ry heart within our ranks."

"If that is yer will… 'tis mine as well," said King Robert, and they all roared fiercely like hungry lions ready to devour their enemies.

• •

Much needed to be done before morning light. Whilst King Edward peacefully slept just down the slope from him, Robert knew there was precious little time to have his battle plan set into motion.

"Reckon ye hain't hiein' to the wilds of Lennox," said Christina, recognizing Robert walking to her as she sat in her chair.

"How ye ken?" he asked.

"I heard the whoopin' for blood at yer council by the fire," she replied as he drew near.

He sighed deeply, "We're stayin'," he confirmed. Then asked, "Are ye?"

"O' course," she said, almost insulted that he had any doubts.

"We think we can win."

"We?" she asked, "What about ye? Do *ye* know we can win?"

"I would not be here at this moment if I did not believe so," he said.

"There's a wide difference between believin' and knowin'," she said with concern.

"A man ne'er knows when he will be struck down, Christina!" he gently admonished her.

She sighed as deeply as had he. She wanted to cry. She wanted to scream, but in the end she calmly said, "Ye are right, only God knows such things."

He took her hands and pulled her up from her chair and into his arms. She always felt comforted and safe there.

"I have a task for ye," he at last said quietly.

"Aye?" she waited.

"Take yer helpers and go into the vale 'twixt this hill and the next and set up yer hospital," he said.

"Now?" she questioned.

"Aye. There'll be a'plenty more in there with ye. Sir Henry Sinclair will be in command of all in that area."

"And what will Sir Henry be commandin'?" she asked, still holding tight.

William de Airth

mondAy, after midnight ~ 24th june
cambuskenneth abbey

King Robert prudently stored additional food and supplies in Cambuskenneth Abbey in the weeks leading up to St. John the Baptist Day, and charged Sir William Airth, with a small contingent, to protect the abbey and the Scots' provisions. Sir William was a distant kinsman to the king, and in a way, so was the knight's squire, Baldred.

Those two stood beside the serpentine River Forth as it wound its way around the boot-shaped peninsula on which the abbey had been constructed. Founded as the Abbey of St. Mary by the Augustinians during the twelfth century reign of King David, Cambuskenneth included a fine stone church of nearly two hundred feet in length, a free-standing three-story bell tower at the church's northwest corner, a cloister south of the church, and off to its east, support buildings and a wharf that projected into the river.

Just south of Abbey Creigh, and thus, in close proximity to Castle Stirling, the abbey received favor from King David and his successors, and had thus become wealthy and influential.

"Looks bonny with all the lights about the carse, Sire," said an excited Baldred, having never before seen such a huge encampment.

"I suppose… a malevolent sort of bonny," agreed Sir William, looking across the River Forth toward the encamped English army. There were myriad flickering torches and campfires spread out over the slight rise to the south, easily seen even in the shadowy near dark.

"Must be a thousand of them!" imagined the youth.

"Many thousands I would say, Lad," offered the knight.

"If I were yonder and fixed to fight, would the king make me a knight, ye reckon, Sir William?" asked the squire.

"I'm sure he would if ye were but two years older," replied William, "yer studies have been right good."

"I would surely like that," the squire said.

"On the morrow we'll watch the battle from here," said Sir William seriously. "If King Robert is o'errun, we'll have to act quickly to get ready for him a'comin' this way in retreat."

"Let us hope that will not be, Milord," said Baldred prayerfully whispering.

"Aye, let us hope," the knight nodded. He looked up to the brilliant night sky and realized the hour grew late. "Whatever happens tomorrow, we must get some rest tonight. Take yer last look at it, Baldred, and let's get back to the abbey." With that, Sir William started walking toward Cambuskenneth, his squire keeping up with him most of the time, but now and again glancing toward the broad vista south.

As they reached the road leading from the kirk to the wharf, Baldred said, "D'ye hear horses comin', Sir William?"

The knight and his squire quickly walked west along the road, turned with it north and, reaching the bell tower, peered into the semidarkness.

"Can ye see anythin', Baldred?" asked Sir William, squinting into the wilderness toward the creigh.

"Nae, Sire, but I can hear them," said the boy, "... and maybe see them too, from time to time."

"Someone's out there," said William, and turning to Baldred said, "Wake the guard! Could be the English!" His squire ran off to where the men were sleeping and roused them from their beds while Sir William went to stand before the church door.

The dozen men of the garrison, most being asleep, got to their feet and tried to shake the slumber from their wits while they armed themselves.

"Hail the abbey!" came a voice from beyond their sight.

"Aye, who are ye!?" yelled Sir William to the midnight dark.

"David, Earl of Strathbogie!" the voice said.

"Strathbogie with us?" asked Baldred, his eyes large and skittish.

"He is," said the knight, greatly relieved.

"I recollect plain that he were against us early on, Milord," remarked Baldred.

"Sally in, Milord," shouted William, and then to Baldred he said softly, "He has sworn fealty to King Robert, now."

With much ado from horses and riders, there loomed before them in the light of torches ensconced on the outside walls of the church was the Earl of Strathbogie, riding a grand destrier, armored for battle. "Air we too late to fight for King Robert?"

"Not too late as yet," said William, smiling broadly, "but ye've missed the causeway leadin' to the bridge o'er the river by a bit."

Thirty more riders appeared from the darkness behind the earl and reined up beside him as he dismounted. They also stepped from their mounts.

"I see ye brought a goodly number of men w'ye," William squinted his eyes to see the armed riders. "Ye have womenfolk in yer contingent?" he asked, noticing the faces of all the riders as they dismounted. Swiftly, those who had come off their horses moved to flank William, Baldred, and the few guards.

William took a full step back, wary of what was afoot, and Baldred followed.

"This lady is my wife, Joana," said David de Strathbogie pointing to the older of the women. "She is the daughter of The Red Comyn."

William nodded shifting his eyes from one to the other.

"And this is my younger sister, Isabella de Strathbogie," he continued, introducing the younger woman with the beautiful red locks, "whose father was killed because he was friend to the Brus, and she was left carryin' Sir Edward Brus' child... when he took up with another woman!"

Sir William was aghast, that Strathbogie was there for revenge on the king. "What do ye want here?" he said, drawing his sword. His knights took defensive stances and awaited orders.

"No need to draw a weapon on me, Sir William," said Earl David sarcastically.

"All of ye... leave the abbey!" barked William. "King Robert will handle ye for this!"

Earl David laughed and drew his own sword and strode toward Sir William Airth.

Baldred, closest to Isabella, grabbed her by her long coppery hair and pulled her tight against him, yanking his dagger from its sheath and drawing it to her throat.

David's eyes bulged and he stopped in mid-stride.

Sir William and his men began to back into the kirk, their weapons at the ready, when an arrow suddenly came at him from out of the night and pierced his neck through. His scream was cut short and became but a gurgle as he grabbed the arrow and tried to pull it out, but it pierced his jugular, and within seconds he fell dead between the jambs of the grand kirk's door.

Sir William!?" yelled Baldred in shock. Isabella tried hard to take advantage of the loosening of Baldred's grip and wriggled hard, but Baldred held tight and backed farther into the doorway, the guardsmen beginning to close the double doors behind them.

"They're gettin' away!!" shrieked Joana.

David waved his sword and his men rushed into the narthex through the half-closed doors. Blood flew from both sides as they clashed. Baldred held tight to Isabella, who fought him though mindful of the dagger he yet held at her throat.

Baldred backed against one of the large carved oak doors and started to push as the other men fought valiantly against the raiders. Overpowered, the Brus Scots went down, one by one, struck by multiple weapons. When it was over, they laid dead or nearly so from their wounds, while six of Strathbogie's men were in the same condition. There was only Baldred left and he had backed with his hostage into the dark, cavernous nave.

Earl David slowly pushed open the door to the nave and cautiously peered inward. He heard the squirms and squeaks of his sister and followed the sounds. "Bring a torch!" he demanded.

His men brought many torches and their flickering light illuminated the front end of the nave. Strathbogie sent some of his men down one side while he led several down the other, looking behind each stone column as they cautiously worked their way to the chancel.

Baldred's eyes were wide with fear, but he had command of the woman.

"Ye wouldn't bleed a lady… would ye, Squire?" said Earl David in a quiet soothing voice as he moved steadily toward the altar. Every noise, every tap against the stone floor or the massive columns rose and echoed through the kirk's interior, and the earl used the sounds to unnerve the boy. He began a steady tapping on the floor, which not only told his prey that he was closing in on him, but muffled other sounds as his men moved down the opposite side.

"Ye killed Sir William!" spat Baldred, his tears beginning to flow.

'Sir William… Sir William…' the name bounced to the vaulted ceiling and back to the stone floor until it died.

"'Twas ye that killed Sir William, Lad," argued David, putting his sword behind his leg. "By takin' my sister hostage." He was drawing close to the altar, and knew he had the boy trapped. "Now, if ye turn her loose, ye are free to leave."

"I don't believe ye!" said the squire.

"I have come for revenge against the Bruses," said David, "… Robert… and Edward. I shall destroy their stores held here at the abbey… and then, I'll have done my worst… Aye?… What would it profit me to kill ye, an obviously beardless squire?"

"And I can go free?" said Baldred, thinking that, if he could get free he would be able to warn King Robert.

"Of course!" said David. "Listen, I'll send all my men outside!" He waved his hand to have them comply with his statement, and they withdrew through the nave into the narthex once again. "There! See? They're gone. Ye have no more threat to ye… save me and two women… one of whom ye have as hostage."

"We'll walk, Milord?" asked Baldred, still keeping a tight grip on Isabella.

"Aye, young squire," said David. "Now, put the knife down and watch as my wife and I also leave. He turned and walked down the length of the kirk, his wife by his side.

"I want a horse!" said Baldred.

"Ye will have to come outside to get it, Lad," said the earl, and Baldred heard the door to the narthex open, and looked out in time to see the woman walk out ahead of the earl. He jerked his head back and waited for a sound that would tell him if anyone else remained within the nave.

"Come out, Lad, and ye can take my horse!" offered Earl David. "He's a fine horse for a brave man," he added.

Alone but for the red-headed woman he held by her hair, he pulled her into the center of the great edifice, and walked slowly down the length of it, cautiously watching the soaring columns for signs of an ambuscade by Strathbogie. None came.

Holding her tightly against him, he forced her into the narthex before him, but saw no one.

"We await yer presence, Squire," Strathbogie called from outside.

The boy again had a doorway to go through. He walked closer to it and saw Earl David, standing with his reins in his hand, looking toward him. "Come on, Lad. Take the reins and be gone!"

Baldred stepped into the night with his prisoner, and saw the magnificent horse and loosened his grip to grab the reins. David quickly dropped them and Isabella jerked away. In a flash she stooped to pick up the weapon Sir William had dropped and turned to ram the blade deep into Baldred's belly as he cried out in agony.

He gasped as he dropped his threatening blade and staggered backward until he was against the abbey's outer wall. He began to slide down, holding his hemorrhaging wound and whimpering.

"Ye've killed him, goddamn it!" said Joana angrily. "Where is *my* revenge?!!" Joana shouted loud enough for everyone to hear.

"He's not yet dead, My Dear," suggested Earl David.

She growled that he was already killed, but hurrying his death was better than nothing. She grabbed Baldred by the hair, lifted his head so that his eyes looked to heaven, and stroked her own sharp dagger across his unprotected throat. Blood gushed onto his tabard with the symbol of the house of Airth emblazoned on it.

The squire pitched forward... and it was done.

Joana stood and looked down on the young dead man and said, "I wish ye were Robert de Brus...!"

"Ye have not the king so close at hand as was this lad," said David, handing her a kerchief to wipe the copious blood splatters off her hands and dress.

"Take me home!" she growled, handing the bloody cloth back to her husband. "I have one consolation... tomorrow, when the Brus is routed from the field and flees through Cambuskenneth Abbey in search of his sustenance, he will find none, and it will, perhaps, cause his death! *Then* I shall be satisfied that my father is avenged!"

The men of Strathbogie put what supplies their horses could carry upon the beasts, and threw all they could not carry into the yard of the abbey and set them afire with one of the torches.

They feared setting the abbey itself alight lest holy retribution rain upon them.

Following their plan, the Strathbogies mounted their horses and rode back to their peel in the north, taking the packed horses and the bodies of the few of their men killed in the fight.

King Robert's mind worked as if he were in a trance of sorts. Having figured out many details in advance, he yet had many to consider. Sleep was neither an option nor a consideration for him, or for any of the others who milled purposefully throughout the New Park campsite, fulfilling their immediate needs and mustering as they were instructed.

The first sojourn from their labors was to attend mass in either of three locations. It was a holy day celebrating the birth of Saint John the Baptist, certainly one of the holiest days of the calendar. Abbot Bernard of Arbroath had the Brecbennach of Saint Columba and Abbot Maurice of Inchaffray carried the Reliquary of Saint Fillan. They held early morning mass in the woods where the men and women were living, offering prayers and hearing confessions.

Robert then assembled the squires and knights that he intended to bestow the honors of knighthood upon, including Sir James Douglas, who would be struck a knight bannerette and Walter Stewart, who would be dubbed a knight.

Thanks to the warriors of Thomas Randolph's schiltrom, Robert's army had a midnight supper of horsemeat pottage, cooked with leeks and beans, and bannocks, washed down with one cup of ale per man, and as much water as they could hold.

His responsibilities having been admirably discharged considering the hour, Abbot Bernard came to Robert and handed him a single parchment. "This what ye have in mind, My King?" he asked.

Robert held it close to the fire nearby and read it. Then he nodded his approval and asked, "How many copies have ye writ?"

"'Tis the only one… I wanted yer approval first," said the abbot.

"This one will do, friend Abbot," he said and turning to Andrew said, "Fetch my destrier, Sir Andrew!"

"Ye want it dressed in trappin's?" he asked.

"Just across the withers," said the king then turned to his page and ordered. "Nigel, find Lord Randolph and fetch him here, quick!"

"Aye, Sire," said the lad setting off to find Sir Thomas.

"Ye see the fire at the abbey a while ago?" asked Bernard.

"I saw," said Robert while continuing to prepare himself for the greatest battle of his life.

"Ye figured what it was?"

"Nae notion," said Robert as he slipped his chain mail over his head and stretched his large arms into the sleeves. "I sent a spy to find out, but he hain't returned."

"I fear the worst," sighed Bernard.

"The worst will be if we lose today, My Abbot," replied the king. "All else is less than that."

Bernard nodded his head thoughtfully. "Aye, I agree."

Robert settled the snug arming cap and looked around for his mail and his helm with the crown on it. He had seen Nigel and Andrew bring it to him only a few moments earlier.

"'Tis there I believe, My King," said Bernard with a slight hint of amusement in his voice at the irony of the king's helm having been thrown uncaringly to the ground.

"I see Andrew's properly teachin' my new page how to take care of my armor," he said as he bent down to pluck up the helm.

"Aye," said Bernard still holding a slight smile.

"Ye seek me, My King?" asked Thomas as he huffed to Robert's side.

"Aye, Sir Thomas, Abbot Bernard has a parchment that I want ye to read to yer regiment... my words for the men ere the battle," said Robert. "He'll go with ye and give the blessin' in Gaelic to yer high landers." The king then asked, "Ye see to all their earthly needs?"

"For now," replied Thomas.

"Thomas, also tell them for me... that if there's any among them who are not willin' to fight to the death for Scotland... or under my command... they had best hie ere the blood starts to flow!" said Robert in a determined voice.

"I'll pass that along," said Thomas, "but we have nae deserters in my regiment!"

"I'm nae more concerned of deserters than I am that our men might lose their discipline and run toward the English! If they break loose from their schiltroms and charge off by themselves, 'twill be just as bad as runnin' away... the English will cut us down like scythes in a field o'wheat! Our lads *must* hold steady!"

"I ken," said Thomas. "Ye worry too much, Sire!" he grinned and looked reassuringly at Robert, then left with the abbot to take the cleric to where his five hundred warriors were gathered.

Robert watched the pair walk away and wondered if Randolph was too confident, or were the men really that steadfast. He turned his attention back to donning his helm and chain.

"Yer destrier, My King," said Andrew coming up from behind. The abbreviated trappings he had laid over the horse's withers hung to the its knees. It was made of heavy wool, yellow with the red lion rampant.

"Edward and Douglas got their regiments together?" asked the king.

"Last I saw they were gettin' to it."

"Where'd ye put my tabard, Lad?" he asked.

"Here 'tis," said Andrew holding the yellow cloth out to him.

"Ye're to carry the standard for me today, for the last time, Sir Andrew," insisted Robert.

Andrew smiled and bowed slightly, "As ye wish, My King."

Robert paused, looking at Andrew with pride.

"Anythin' more?" asked Andrew.

"Get our banner," said Robert as he slipped the tabard over his helm and cinched it at the waist with his great sword belt.

"And we made a new axe handle for ye, Sire, as close as could be matched to the one ye broke yesterday," said Andrew handing the weapon over.

Robert handled it for a moment and, nodding approval, slipped it into a saddle loop. As he climbed aboard his destrier, he looked about him and noticed that the sky had turned from dark purplish-gray to a paler, blue-gray. There was little color about the landscape as yet. All was gray, of one shade or another, and the birds in the forest had awakened with a cacophony of song and fluttering of wings in the treetops.

"Daylight's comin' up," he said to Andrew.

"Ye ken we'll have the sun in our eyes this morn," said Andrew climbing onto his own highland horse.

"Aye," said Robert, "but it can nae be helped."

With a click of his tongue Robert signaled his horse and the animal started off, Andrew following, and they soon were where the regiments were gathering as they had been ordered. The Abbot of Arbroath, Bernard, caught the pair at the crest of the hill and handed the parchment back to Robert.

"Go well?" asked Robert.

"Ye heard not the cheers?"

"Reckon not," said Robert, "'Twas too far o'er the hillock."

"Nae a single man withdrew," said Bernard.

"We picked rightly then, Abbot," said Robert, kicking his destrier to a quicker pace to join and command his own two thousand men-at-arms.

• •

As it turned out, Sir Robert Keith had his four hundred sixty cavalry riders busy saddling their highland horses. Whilst resting from their training sessions, each man had rigged a chest plate of boiled leather for his horse, knowing that their primary purpose was to attack archers when they appeared on the battlefield. The much smaller horses would be no match against the great destriers the English knights rode, thus the need for further armor would be but a burden on the strength of the horse, causing it to lose its agility and speed.

"Ye got that extra horse?" asked Sir David de Graham as he came to the pinfold.

"It'll be fixed directly," answered Keith. He continued routinely cinching his saddle on the back of his horse.

"Robbie said he wants it in the forefront of the battle," said the Templar.

"Aye, I know. He's takin' that lad's death hard," said Keith. "Guess he feels some blame because he's the one who had the pots dug. Sad, 'tis, that he couldn't live to ride wi' us today."

"He'll be a'ridin' with us," said Graham, smiling as much as Graham ever smiled.

"Sir David! Yer woman had her bairn as yet?" asked William Vieuxpont as he neared the two men.

"Not yet," said Graham. He shooed his squire away from his horse, wanting to rig the saddle himself.

"Hell of a Templar ye turned to be!" said Keith chuckling to himself.

Graham knew it to be but a tease between peers and ignored his comment.

"Here's yer empty saddle, Milord," said the groom as he handed the reins to Keith. Sir Robert immediately tied them to the tail of the Templar's horse. "Ye take the lad's mount, David," he said reverently.

Graham nodded. "We'll see to it," he said. The three men knew that the Templars led by Sir David would be right alongside Sir Robert in the forefront of any charge they would be making.

"We're musterin' at the edge of the wood atop the hill," reminded Keith.

"I ken," said David.

"See ye lads there," said Vieuxpont as he climbed aboard his bay.

Keith got on his stallion and kicked its flanks to sally with Graham up the hill toward their gathering point.

About three hundred other riders followed their leaders in that direction. The rest would straggle along as they finished up with their tack.

Robert Cunynghame and his contingent got aboard their horses and took off after Keith and the Templar.

David wondered how Dianna was, but tried to shake the feeling. She was in the hands of the midwife, and Christina was there as well. *She will be a'right,* he told himself. Going into battle whilst thinking about a woman was definitely a revolutionary experience for him. Up until then he couldn't have cared less about any woman as he rode into such conflict, but Dianna... had attached herself to him. Worse. She had attached him to her. She was so devoted and loving toward him that his stoic resistance was shattered. He had done something he could never have imagined; he fell in love, not that he would have admitted it.

The cloudless sky was a deep bright blue, except for a faint yellow glow beginning in the east.

• •

"If ye swear ye'll stay put," said Sir Neil Campbell, "ye can sit on this very spot and watch the battle. If we win, ye are my prisoner," he paused considering the chances of the Scots' losing, and finished, "else, ye go free."

"I understand, and I give you my word... I shall be here 'til the battle is decided," said Sir Thomas Grey, the Englishman captured the day before. He held his bandaged head in his hands as he sat on the ground, his knees hiked.

"'Tis the way of war," replied Campbell. "The English are holdin' my dear wife, Mary... If we win, perhaps I can trade ye for her."

"I hope she lives still," said Grey who was not only angry with the English king but with Baron de Clifford for botching the skirmish the day before.

"And I hope yer head quits achin' ere long," said Campbell smiling. Then he went down the hill to the edge of the trees where Randolph was giving final instructions to his troops.

• •

The men of the king's regiment patiently waited as the king made final preparations. They were nervous with excitement and ready to kill the 'dog tail-ed' English, as the Scots sometimes called their southern adversaries. Each man held his main weapon, the fourteen-foot long pike, upright in the air, the foot-long yellow ribbons laying limp in the breezeless morning air.

Robert rode his white horse up to the men, who stood in six ranks as they had been trained. Andrew was behind the king holding Robert's yellow and red lion banner. Nigel followed on a palfrey of his mother's choosing.

Flanked by Malcolm Maclaine and Gilbert de la Haye, Angus Macdonald stood proudly before the men. The chieftains of the various families stood in line with their families. Robert, alone, rode in review from one end of his battle line to the other looking at every man.

"Hail, King Robert," said Angus stepping to the fore to greet Robert as he came back to the center.

"My Lord Macdonald," replied Robert, "Are we ready?"

"We are, My King," shouted Angus and the men roared with cheers.

Robert took the parchment from beneath his sword belt. Andrew held the king's shield high.

The King began to speak, "My Lords... My People, accustomed to enjoy that full freedom for which in times gone by, the kings of Scotland have fought many a battle!"

The men who could hear loudly cheered. The ones who couldn't, cheered as well.

The king continued, "For eight years or more, I have struggled with great labor for my right to the kingdom and for honorable liberty for all of us. I have lost brothers, friends, and kinsmen. Your own kinsmen have been made captives, and bishops and priests locked in prisons. Our country's nobility has poured forth its blood in war! Those English barons you can see before ye yon, clad in mail, are bent upon destroyin' me and obliteratin' my kingdom... nae... Our whole nation of Scotland!" he paused and bowed his head, "They do not believe that we can survive. They glory in their warhorses and equipment... For us... The name of the Lord must be our hope of victory in battle. This day is a day of rejoicing..." he paced his horse a little to the left. "It is the birthday of Saint John the Baptist."

The men cheered once again.

"With our Lord Jesus Christ as commander, Saint Andrew and the martyr Saint Thomas shall fight today with the saints of Scotland for the honor of their country and their nation!" He again paused and looked over his men and referred to his parchment. "If ye heartily repent of yer sins ye will be victorious!"

Again they cheered.

"As for offences against the crown, I proclaim a pardon, by virtue of my royal power, to all those who fight manfully for the kingdom of our fathers. Scotland!" and he took the banner from Andrew and waved it vigorously before them.

Then they cheered the loudest of all.

Robert, still carrying his banner, ran the whole length of his regiment, to show his men he had every confidence in them. Then he went to Edward Brus' and James Douglas' regiments just down the hill, and repeated his speech to both of them. Each time the men cheered just as loud and just as heartfelt as had the ones before.

As the king finished, the sky was blood red but the sun had not yet breached the dark, sharp cut of the hilly horizon.

• •

"Did I hear somethin'," asked King Edward, poking his head out of his tent.

The guards closest jumped to attention. "Seems to be comin' from the Scots on the hill, Your Majesty," said one. Edward stepped from the tent and looked up the long, gradual slope but saw nothing but a single tiny figure here or there.

"Get me Pembroke, d'Argentan, Hereford, and Gloucester!" snapped Edward.

"Yes, Your Majesty," said the guard and left at a trot, knowing the three were not far afield as yet.

"We 'rousin' now, Sire?" asked Sir Hugh sitting up and rubbing sleep from his eyes.

"The damned Scots woke me. Seem to be cheerin'... makin' some big noise," replied the king. "The sun has not even risen yet!"

"Reckon they're tryin' to frighten us?" he yawned, "... make you think the lot of them are still there when they're not?" asked Hugh.

"If I know Brus... he's up to some illusion!" said the king, then called in the squires to bathe the pair.

Pembroke was first to arrive and he slipped into the tent immediately, since he was told the king demanded it. The sight that greeted him made him wish he had been spared. Edward and Hugh were stark naked, butt cheeks to butt cheeks and standing in a small tub of water. Two squires were vigorously sponge-bathing them among their giggles and twitches. Pembroke turned his head to look away and apologized, "Beg pardon, My Liege! I'll be back directly!" said he.

"Don't go, Milord!" entreated the king.

"Indeed I must, Sire," he said, throwing the tent flap away and stepping out. D'Argentan was just walking up, also having been summoned to report right away to the king. "Stay here, Sir Giles. You will thank me if you do," he said, his eyebrows peaked in an arch.

Sir Giles took the earl's advice and waited nearby for his audience with Edward. On the field before him stood two thousand excellent knights who were appallingly worn, not only from their long, two-day march to this place, but from getting little or no sleep during the scant dark hours. As the sky grew redder and brighter, they were groggy to say the least.

Europe's finest army stood unrested in a miserable, stinking field, where the knights and their two thousand horses had pissed and shat the scarce dry ground to a slimy wetness that made all wish for a breeze to blow the stench away, preferably in the direction of the Scots.

"Have you eaten, Sir Giles?" asked Pembroke.

"Too early for such," he exclaimed, "If this were winter, we would be talking in the middle of the night!"

"'Tain't winter," replied the earl. "'Tis the Feast of Saint John the Baptist and we'll soon be in a battle. You had best eat while you can."

"Just the thought of eatin' in this stink sullies my appetite," said Giles, and looking to Aymer asked, "Did you eat?"

"Sick," admitted Pembroke.

"Of what?" asked Giles.

"Guts are burnin' and piles," said the earl.

"You have herbs for such, Milord?"

"Hell no!" replied Pembroke. "Herbs just make it all worse."

"You men talkin' about holdin' the attack off for another day?" asked Earl Gilbert as he came to the knot.

"Not me," said Giles. "I'm talkin' about eatin' in this god-awful smell."

Pembroke shook his head, a slight grin was quickly seen and dismissed.

"To bad," opined Lord Gloucester, solemnly. "I had hoped you were of the same conviction as I."

"What conviction would that be?" asked Pembroke.

"We're not ready!" said the young earl.

"As the king says..." said d'Argentan, "... so will we do."

"But we three must convince His Majesty that the men are too worn, too poorly arrayed," pleaded Gilbert.

Aymer shook his head as he spoke. "That be a hopeless task, Milord. 'Twas decided hours ago that we're goin' to march our foot soldiers across the stream shortly, and they are to run the Scots from the trees," said Pembroke, adding, "if they yet be there."

"Clifford's goin' to be sent around to the backside of Cockshot Hill and kill any cowards as they flee," interjected Giles.

"Clifford!?" Lord Gloucester was incredulous. "Clifford couldn't do anything yesterday... Why would he be sent to do nothing today?!!"

"Lord Gloucester," said Pembroke, "... your rivalry with Clifford is beyond me."

"My lords, I can hear you," sang out Edward from within the tent.

"A simple discussion of stratagem, Sire," offered Pembroke in a louder voice to let the king know he was talking to him.

The three knights stood glum-faced until Edward signaled to them that the bathing was completed and they were dressing.

They entered the tent with a wary eye for things untoward, but their hesitation was proven unnecessary.

"Have some bread and wine," offered the king, as he and Hugh were being dressed by a half-dozen squires.

Gilbert accepted the invitation and poured himself a goblet of wine.

"Where's Hereford?" said Edward angrily.

"Hain't seen him as yet, My Liege," said Pembroke, wanting to sit but his affliction made him opt to stand.

"My Lords, I want all the knights to deploy higher on the hill toward the Scots, and we'll bring the foot across that stream and in behind them," instructed the king.

"That your plan?" asked Pembroke, not really caring at that moment.

"Yes!" said Edward, and putting an emphatic point on it added, "Yes, it is!"

Hereford entered and bowed to the king.

"Am I getting' trouble from you as well?" said the king, attempting to head off disagreement with his scheme.

Hereford shrugged, his face suggesting ignorance.

"Well, I have trouble," started Gloucester.

"I know, My Lord, because you want to wait until tomorrow," said Edward. "The tent walls are very thin!"

"Yes, Sire, it is my belief that we must get off this godforsaken sompe and wait until tomorrow, when we're all more rested!" pleaded Gloucester. "We are only in this distress because of Clifford's and Bohun's failures of yesterday!"

Sir Humphrey de Bohun silently riled at the disparagement of his nephew and balled his hands to fists once again. Pembroke moved between the men. "'Tain't worth it," he whispered, "Let ignorance have its say."

"Can we have some action here?!" yelped the king. "I have given an order!!!"

"Your Majesty! Your Majesty!" screamed Sir Ingram de Umfraville as he came bursting into the tent fairly dragging along two of the tent guards who were trying to restrain him.

"Let him be!" ordered the king. "What are you yelpin' about?"

"Come, Sire! Ye must see this!" he answered.

The sun had barely peeked over the range of low hills to the east when King Edward and his entourage of earls and knights trudged through the mire of dung and piss to the forward position of the standing knights.

"What?" griped the king, aggravated that his new-made boots had been ruinously soiled.

"There!" said Ingram pointing uphill, "Along the edge of the wood!"

Edward looked and saw King Robert's Scots filtering out of the trees, the sun reflecting on their pikeheads, the men yet in shadow.

At the behest of Abbot Maurice, who walked before them holding high the arm bone of Saint Fillan in one hand and a crucifix in the other, they knelt to pray. Those with swords and daggers slipped them from their sheaths and held them pommel heavenward, effectively casting shadows of crosses upon their faces when touched by the first rays of the rising sun.

"See that, Umfraville?" smirked Edward, "...we have won already!"

"Won already?" asked Lord Gilbert as he came to look up the slope.

"They kneel before me and ask for mercy," boasted the king.

"Aye, they ask mercy, Sire, not from ye, but from God in case they die on the field of battle," said Sir Ingram.

"I told you that we should wait!" screamed Gloucester.

The king turned on the earl and glowered, "Afraid of mere Scottish soldiers of foot, are you, Cousin?"

"Sir, I fear no man born of woman!" asserted Gilbert, and repaired directly to his tent.

"So, Sir Ingram! You think your countrymen mean to fight us?" said the king, condescendingly, as if teasing a child.

"These men shall fight to the death, Your Majesty. To the very last man," responded Ingram, clearly awestruck at the heroic sight of Scots, standing from their prayers and forming battle lines.

"Your Majesty," said d'Argentan, "I agree. They mean to do us battle, and right soon... We had best get arrayed."

Edward's eyes widened at the realization that the Scots were moving toward him. "Our plan is useless now!" he lamented. "What shall we do?"

"Sire, we must move these men as far forward as we dare, then bring as many mounted knights in behind them as possible," advised Giles.

"Yes, Yes! A good plan, Sir Giles... we shall bring in all the knights!" said the king as he turned and ran downhill to his tent to prepare for the coming attack.

Scottish Foot Warrior

MONÐAY, ÐAWN – 24ch JUNE
BANNOK

From the time they stood from their prayers and Edward Brus gave the order for his men to move forward, they crossed the road and began their sloping descent through the field of unripe wheat. The war drums began a resonate pounding, measuring the beat of the warriors' footfalls toward their powerful enemy.

James Douglas moved his schiltrom into position to Edward's left and paused, so that his unit marched slightly behind.

Thomas Randolph held his men back just long enough to allow Douglas to pass and then he moved forward in his farthest left position.

King Robert and his schiltrom laid back a hundred paces before he started his men down the hill, working them to the right, closer to the woods, closing off the road south as a means of English escape.

Lord Edward's leading schiltrom arrived at wider ground and at his order the six ranks merged into four, making longer, thinner lines.

Douglas gave the same order when his schiltrom could perform the maneuver, and his men complied with the same ease.

Robert smiled with pride. His plan was working perfectly, but he knew the attack was out of range for planning and required more innovation on the part of the commanders and individual men, who lived and died within the length of a foot of steel one way or the other.

"Gird for war!!" shouted Lord Gloucester as he arrived among his five hundred knights and squires and prepared to arm himself.

"At last! We're goin' for the Scots!" shouted a young knight standing hard by.

"Not quite! The Scots are comin' for *us*!" the earl seethed, and he pulled on his chain mail jerkin.

The knight could tell from the earl's voice that all was amiss; his smile faded, he swallowed hard and ran for his horse.

Gloucester's squire and groom hurriedly saddled and bridled his destrier, one of the few mounts that had not remained saddled all night. As soon as it was ready the earl climbed aboard, just as the king emerged from his pavilion. Seeing what was happening, the king was horrified and ran to forestall the earl's actions.

"Gilbert! You cannot attack the Scots alone!"

"You think me a coward, Cousin?!" snarled Gloucester.

Sir Raoul hurried to his stepson, "Gilbert, what is afoot?" he asked, panicked at all the commotion he saw around and among the troops of Lord Gloucester.

"The damned Scots have beaten us to the advantage, Father," said Gloucester climbing aboard his horse, "and my *cousin* here has decried me for a coward!"

"I never decried you as such," yelped the king. "I but asked you if you were afraid!"

"Well, that's the same damned thing!" argued Raoul to the king, forgetting that Edward was his sovereign.

Edward grabbed the sleeve of the earl's chain mail jerkin and demanded that he wait for their troops to organize their counterattack.

"Unhand me!" snapped Gilbert, angrily wrenching his sleeve from Edward's fingers, "You are a disgrace to your Plantagenet blood!!"

"You will rue this day forever!!" said Edward, his fingers smarting from having had his grip torn from the metal fabric.

Gilbert reared his horse and its forefeet came down hard on the ground, causing Edward to spring aside. One glaring dare in a look to his king, and the earl spurred his destrier hard toward the west, grabbing his lance from his squire's hands as he went.

Edward Brus saw a knight bound out toward him, free of the other knights, who seemed to be chased by a steadily growing number of knights wearing bright yellow tabards with three red chevrons.

"Set pikes!!" ordered Edward and his lines stopped moving forward. The front rank dropped to one knee and dug the butt ends of their spears hard into the ground; the second rank did the same, placing the shafts of their spears over the shoulders of the first, and the third and fourth ranks stood, holding their spears over the shoulders of the others, expecting the brunt of the force to be mostly absorbed in the first two ranks.

Gloucester, his hair whipping out behind him, picked out the place he would plow into as his destrier rumbled up the long slope at a gallop. At least three hundred of his knights ultimately managed to get mounted and follow him, and the first among them were trying their best to get in front of their liege lord. But Gilbert was angry and cursing King Edward every time he spurred his swift horse. He would show Edward that he was not fearful!

"Damn! We should have gotten farther down the slope ere they came against us," said Robert, watching from up the hill.

"The most of them appear to be plenty excited, but all are in much disarray," remarked Andrew Stewart. "Some are just now mounting and leaving camp!"

"Be ready, Lads!" shouted Edward Brus and he clenched his jaw in determination. James Douglas and Walter Stewart gave similar encouragement to their ranks. Randolph held to the left and remained somewhat separated from the other two regiments. Still, he watched closely in case the Gloucester men veered into his path.

Though the great beast was pounding the turf as hard as he could, Gloucester pushed more, trying to make his charger exceed the possible, digging his spurs deep into the abused beast's sides until they were bloody raw. His squire followed him doggedly, though not closely, holding the earl's banner high so that it fluttered out in the rush.

"Brace up!" shouted Earl Malcolm upon seeing the steed heading for his section. The men in the first two ranks thrilled with excitement and their throats went suddenly dry, not having any idea how hard they were going to be hit. They had watched Randolph's schiltrom the day before but somehow, with the destrier and knight bearing down on them, it was different. They held fast to their pikes, squinted their eyes to protect them, and gritted their teeth in expectation of the great blow's being struck.

"That fool has to be young Gloucester, a'fixin' to get himself killed," lamented Robert.

Andrew held his silence, speechless in the awe of watching the courageous knight approach all but certain death. The young knight's heart seemed to stop and his whole body flinched with the impact as Gloucester ran full force against the iron-headed spears in the center of Edward's schiltrom.

The wounded horse reared up and screamed in pain, the shattered ends of several pikes projecting out of its chest and neck. Copious blood was slung in every direction as the horse tried to escape its agony. In his last conscious second, Gilbert had gasped, realizing the horror of the sacrifice he defiantly made in the name of glory. The first spear pierced through his chain mail below his ribs on the left side, the second, through his chin. Blood erupted from both gashes. Gilbert thought to scream but his death came first. He went to the ground with his destrier. Both were corpses by the time they came to rest.

Gilbert's squire, following him at full speed, managed to stop his mount short of the deadly pikes, and he stood agape, his eyes wide in disbelief at seeing his liege thus ripped open and awkwardly still.

Raoul de Monthermer's heart broke that his son threw away his life for the sake of his petty pride. A warrior himself, Raoul understood a soldier's honor, but it was but a fool's arrogance that killed his boy.

Gloucester's men reined their animals and slowed up when they watched their liege fall so readily on the pikes. Shocked at his instantaneous death, they sat upon their horses and caught their breaths after the long gallop up the rise, and contemplated what they should do next.

Having tasted the first-drawn blood, the Scots demanded more, taunting the English with their shouts of "Tail-ed dogs! Tail-ed dogs!" The chant spread quickly across the hillside and could be heard on the carse by the English knights not yet mounted, and not anxious to ride their tired horses up the long route taken by Gloucester.

King Robert watched the exuberance of his army grow as he held his breath and set his jaw tightly. This was the most dangerous moment, he knew, and prayed that they would stay with their intensive training and await orders rather than breaking out to charge toward the English, individually or en masse, as had their families for centuries.

When King Edward saw Gilbert hit the Scots' lines, his gut convulsed and went into knots for the loss of his cousin, one of his major commanders. He cursed Gilbert as well as the Scots to mask his feelings of fear and loss from the others. "Goddamit!" he swore, "Serves him right!"

The jeers and taunts from the Scots were what it took to bring Gloucester's knights to return to their ire, having at first contemplated the horrible death that their liege had suffered.

"What must we do?" asked one pale and shaken knight of another as they and their fellows rode around on the hillside.

"We must charge the whoresons!" responded the second, "and shut their damned maws for 'em!"

"T'would be death to charge them!"

"Perhaps not, if we went in all at once," suggested the second. "The earl charged in alone, making it easier for the pikemen to stand their ground. If all of us were to sweep into their line together, how could they resist our force? How could they even think of standing against us?"

"You may be right," responded the first knight. "Of course you're right! Just seeing hundreds of us come at them will cause them to falter, and we can then break apart their schiltroms... as was done at Falkirk!"

Having thus screwed up their courage, they went to their comrades and persuaded them of their invincibility in a unified attack into the Scots' thin lines. Soon it was decided; they would hit the Scots in a massed charge all across the front, and with determination in their hearts and heads, they replaced their visors, lowered their lances, and spurred their horses to continue their assault, though they had lost much of their original momentum.

"Brace up! Brace up!" was the command passed along the lines of the two forward schiltroms.

Every man of the twenty-five hundred stood awaiting the slam of the destriers against their pikes. They had been well heartened by the killing of Lord Gloucester and held fast in the face of the rolling mass of horseflesh and armor, each one resisting the urge to run forward in a countercharge.

With a horrific explosion of impact that sounded like distant thunder to the men yet on the carse, followed by echoing screams of men and horses at the tearing of skin and muscle, the two forces met with equal determination. The scant armor in which the horses had been hastily dressed saved none of those charging. Their lances were not long enough to penetrate to the Scots before they were themselves impaled upon those of the enemy. Some of the riders went down with their dead or dying horses and were pinned underneath. Scots on the front ranks stepped ahead and mercifully cut the throats of the wounded men and mounts with swords or daggers.

Some of the horses had caught the fresh scent of death and knew better than to run onto the pikes, balking at the last second and throwing their riders head-over-heels into the fighting Scots. The English who survived the charge mostly became fodder for the third and fourth ranks, who killed those who wanted to fight and carried off the others, declaring them prisoners.

Though some of the long pikes splintered with the impact of the destriers, the lines held. Serving as bearers, the squires following the schiltrom quickly replaced broken weapons and helped Scots who were wounded, mostly from lacerations from shattering pike shafts, back to Christina's aid station for treatment. Several in the front ranks had suffered broken limbs when the wounded men and animals fell into them, but most, even on the first rank, came through the attack without harm.

King Robert's schiltrom cheered at seeing the first charge of the barded knights stopped cold by their fellow foot soldiers.

In the middle of the broad field below, Gloucester's squire, holding his dead liege's banner hanging limp in the windless air, sat his horse all alone and stared with hollow and disbelieving eyes at the carnage before the schiltrom.

Henry de Bohun having been about the same age and just as headstrong as the Earl of Gloucester, was perhaps why Lord Hereford had struck the earl earlier in the king's tent. The memory of Henry's death was again dredged to the surface of his uncle's emotions. He could not stem the flow of tears following the etched lines in his cragged face as he prayed for understanding.

"They'll attack on a smaller front when next they come!" said Robert.

"Think they'll break our line?" asked Andrew.

"That would be their notion," said Robert. "Hitting across the whole line didn't work." He trotted his destrier across the field to where Randolph had halted.

"There's that goddamned Brus!" screamed King Edward pointing uphill. "What's he fixin' to do now?!!"

"I would think he prepares to arrange his troops differently, to make it more difficult for us to attack on a broad front," said Sir Giles d'Argentan.

"That's a stupid, useless move!" said the king. "We will ride over them regardless!"

Sir Giles ignored the statement and said, "How can I serve, Your Majesty?"

"Figure how to break that line of fools!" replied Edward flailing his arms to more fully emphasize his words, but Sir Giles read it more as the jumbled state of his wit.

The Gloucester knights who had not died in the direct attack, realizing the uselessness of the method, had stopped short of the sharp pike heads and wheeled their horses to trot soberly back to their lines and await further orders from the king.

Some who lost their mounts drew their swords and tried to cut the Scots' long spears, and found out quickly that such was a vain and deadly tactic.

A swath of bloodied yellow tabards and trappings lay in a heap all along the front of the Scots' line of attack.

Andrew followed Robert across the cornfield to Randolph's schiltrom. He was proud to be the king's standard bearer and enjoyed feeling the flag tugging at his hand as the air rushed by when he rode, and he knew that many knights on the battlefield below had their eyes fixed to it.

"Tell them to move on down the hill, Sir Andrew," instructed Robert when the lad had come abreast of him as he talked to Randolph.

Andrew moved the king's banner front to back several times, a signal for the men to move forward.

The spotter saw the signal and relayed the message to Edward Brus.

"Move Forward! Forward!" shouted Edward. The commanders along the line repeated the order, and the Scots again moved down the hill, stepping or even climbing over the dead and wounded from the last English charge.

Thomas Randolph's schiltrom quickstepped to come in line with James Douglas' and Edward Brus' troops.

King Edward called loudly for his squires to get his garb and dress him for battle, and for the groom to fetch his destrier.

"They just stepped over our dead and are comin' on!" said Pembroke watching the Scots' progress toward the lowlands.

"Call out the Welsh, goddamn it!" shouted King Edward. "They'll break that line quick enough!"

The Scots stubbornly kept coming down the slight hill, their pikes held menacingly forward.

"ARCHERS!" shouted Pembroke toward the rear area.

Angry over Gloucester's death at the spearpoints of mere foot soldiers, the English knights were in a quandary as to how they should proceed against the foe.

"This is the same as they did yesterday!" called out Clifford upon riding to the king.

"How did *you* break it?!" asked the king. His squire was holding the royal chain mail so that Edward could wriggle into it.

"I could *not* break it," admitted Clifford.

The king's mouth dropped open in astonishment. "How many did you *really* lose yesterday?" asked Edward, his eyes narrow and glaring in rage at his commander. The squire held the king's red and gold tabard for him.

"'Tis of no matter now, Majesty," said Clifford, his horse dancing for action.

About a hundred Welsh archers responded to Pembroke's call. "Stop them!" ordered Pembroke, pointing uphill. The bowmen came from between the scattered knights to the front.

Seeing them taking their positions before the English encampment, Robert looked to Andrew and said, "Sir Andrew, signal a halt!" Andrew moved the flag up and down, the spotter relayed the order to Edward Brus, and he brought the line to an abrupt halt. Robert then signaled Nigel to come to his side and bade him gallop to his archers, gathered on the army's right side, near the wood of Balquhiderock. "Give MacKie this message: tell him to strike the English bowmen, now! Ye understand, Nigel? Tell him to aim for the bowmen!"

The page hied to the place where stood the Scottish bowmen, found MacKie easily, and repeated the command. "Aye, Lad, return to the king and tell him ye told me!"

At that, MacKie and his bowmen ran from the cover of the trees and into the open. MacKie quickly surveyed the scene, saw what was happening, and drew his bow and let fly an arrow in the direction of the English archers. The other Scottish archers lined up behind him in scattered fashion and watched the arc of MacKie's arrow, which missed hitting an archer all together, but hit a knight sitting his horse. MacKie then knew his distance and windage to the target.

When the knight was struck by MacKie, and without orders, the English archers stopped their flights on the Scots' schiltroms and redirected their aim toward the Scots archers, lofting four flights of arrows before they knew whether they were on the mark.

The English army's Welsh longbows had a greater power than most of the Scots' bows, even when lobbed at the target, and though the Scots saw the flights coming and drew up their bucklers to protect themselves, some of the bucklers were split when the arrows struck, and those holding them were killed or wounded. Many standing along the rear had seen the sun flash off the arrows and quickly ran backward to get beyond their supposed landing area.

"Hit 'em!" shouted MacKie, and the able archers arose and got off three flights of arrows before they, too, turned and ran for the wood, but many of Robert's Ettrick bowmen lay dead or badly wounded.

Seeing the exchange, Robert rode quickly toward Earl Edward

and ordered, "Back up the men! We've got to get them beyond arrow range!"

"Can't Keith take care of them, Robbie?" said Edward Brus.

"Not when they're thus surrounded by knights!" argued Robert.

So, while the schiltroms moved farther away from the English camp, to much hooting and jeering from the English knights, the Scots archers began shooting from the edge of the wood, thus keeping the Welsh archers diverted from their initial task of raining death on the schiltroms. Since the Welsh were commingled with the knights, the Scots targeted both with great accuracy.

"Kill those goddamn bowmen!" ordered Edward as his squire strapped his sword belt around his waist.

Obediently, the English archers responded with more flights toward the wood, but the Scots were fairly safe among the trees.

King Edward's destrier, fully entrapped with heavy red cloth with gold leopards almost down to its feathers, arrived about the same moment the king was fully girded for the field, and he mounted, ready at last to take charge of the battle for Stirling.

Clifford pushed his visor into place. The small slit was difficult to see through but it was protection. Waving his sword he yelled for others to lend him a hand in rooting out as many as possible of the 'little bastards' in the wood south of the battlefield. A score of the knights beholden to him followed him into the trees.

"They didn't wait for my orders!" shouted an incensed Edward Plantagenet.

Pembroke's squire rode up leading the earl's destrier. "And what are your orders, Your Majesty?" asked Pembroke, taking his horse by the reins and still hoping, due to his currently painful affliction, that he could avoid getting into the saddle.

Sir Hugh le Despenser came to the king holding his shield over his head to ward off any wildly shot arrows that might fly his way.

"Put your shield 'round on your back!" demanded King Edward.

"But Sire, the arrows…!" pleaded Hugh.

"It is *unseemly*," said Edward emphatically, "Put it *down!*"

Hugh drew his shield around to his back.

Clifford and his men headed straight for the archers in the wood.

"They're comin' for us!" shouted MacKie, and he and the other archers let another flight loose and tried to move deeper into the wood to discourage the oncoming knights.

Clifford's men caught up with those who fled slowest. One Scot was dispatched easily, when a knight ran up on him from behind and felled him with one swooping blow with his sword.

Another bowman nocked an arrow as he ran. Hearing a destrier closing with him, he held his breath and drew his bowstring back to take his shot, but when he stopped to turn, he was instead struck with the spiked balls of a flail. Released, the string flung the arrow into the horse's neck and caused the animal to panic and cry out.

The knight got off his wounded horse and retrieved his other hand weapons, an axe from his saddle loop and a dagger from his belt. He hadn't planned on being without his horse, but he knew that his best chance was to work his way back out of the wood. He crouched and surveyed the terrain as his valiant steed faltered, staggering about in trying to stay on his legs. But the loss of blood was too great and he fell, first to his knees, then with blood flowing from his nose and mouth, he noisily crashed to the forest floor.

That's when the knight heard MacKie shout to his fellows in an angry voice... "He's mine!"

The knight fully realized he had strayed too far afield from his fellow knights and glanced about for a safer place to hide. An arrow suddenly thudded into the tree beside his head, and he knew the Scots had him for sport. Searching for an escape route, his eyes widened and sweat trickled off his brow into them, making him blink. He tossed away his helmet and pushed back his chain mail cowl and arming cap, trying to cool his head.

"Oh, God!" he said under his breath again and again as he did not see a place to run. He thought he heard a footfall to his left and spun around to see what approached, but there was nothing there.

He found it harder to catch his breath, feeling that the air around him was hot and stale, without benefit to his lungs.

Suddenly he heard a horse coming through the trees from west, and he stood to do battle, but the horse's rider leant forward on the horse's neck, and it wasn't until the mount had passed him that he saw the rider was without his head.

This was more than the gasping knight could bear and he leapt up and ran as fast as he could along the narrow path set by the horse 'neath the headless rider. Dodging in and out among the trees he could see the horse entering the sunlight ahead of him and smiled, he was going to be out of the wood in a few more strides, and could at least see his enemy, but it was not to be. An arrow from MacKie's deadly Welsh longbow slammed into his backbone and through his heart, and he fell dead without so much as a yelp.

Sir Robert de Clifford was deeper into the forest, where the trees grew thicker and the large horses bumped from side to side between them, and his visor made it difficult to see into the deep shadows.

He halted his pursuit and raised his visor to broaden his view.

With no sign of a bowman, he found little advantage to chasing the clever fellows farther on horse and was about to give the order to hold off the attack, when an arrow hit him in the arm. He cried out with the pain and his face screwed into a grimace, and he started to grab at the painful barb when another struck him in the face through the open visor. That arrow had gone through his cheek and into the back of his throat, to be stopped only by the rear portion of his helm.

Another knight in Clifford's group seized the reins of the baron's destrier and hastily withdrew with him out of the trees in a withering hail of arrows toward safety.

"Lord de Clifford is dead, Majesty!" yelled the knight, who yet led the baron's horse.

"And where is the baron?" asked the king. "He waited not for my orders!"

"He is here," said the knight turning to show Clifford upon his horse, but instead he saw only an empty saddle. Poor dead Clifford had slipped from his destrier and was lying among the trees where he had been killed.

"Send the archers and some infantry in to root those devils out!" screamed Edward.

Andrew came to Robert's side. "Looks like a gob of worms, below, My King," he said having observed the apparent disorganization among the English troops.

"Don't ever underestimate yer enemy, Sir Andrew," warned Robert, "It can kill ye the quickest of all mistakes."

"'Ppears they're fixin' to send their archers after ours," again observed Andrew.

"Aye, they are," said the king. "Those men will have to take care of their own."

On the carse, King Edward knew not what to do to get a cohesive attack mounted, and he announced in a loud voice, "An earldom to the man who can break that schiltrom before it reaches my tent!"

"Your Majesty!" said Sir John Comyn going to one knee at the feet of the king's horse, "I'll break those whoresons from their nest!!"

"Then arise from your knee and do it, Sir John!" said Edward.

Up jumped Sir Pain Tiptoft, another baron, and asked if he would be eligible for the reward of an earldom, as well.

John Comyn growled and barked, "I'll not be sharin' my earldom with ye!"

"Sire," said Tiptoft unpleasantly, "I am askin' for my own goddamn earldom when I have broken the schiltrom!!"

"Bring up the infantry! Bring up more archers!" screamed the king, ignoring the argument going on before him.

"The infantry cannot get through, Sire!" replied Earl Aymer still standing on the ground and holding the reins of his horse.

"Do you not want an earldom, Milord?" asked Edward.

Pembroke answered, "One I have... 'tis enough."

"Am I to get my own earldom or not?" queried Tiptoft, returning to the subject of his most pressing interest.

Edward looked toward the rise and gauged that the Scots were no more than a quarter mile away.

"Your own earldom... for sure," he yelped in panic. "You and Comyn take your knights and break the damned line so that we can scatter those damned Scots! They *will* scatter, and we'll then be able to hunt them down!"

"So we shall, Your Majesty," said Tiptoft determinedly as he climbed aboard his horse and went to Comyn who was already gathering his men.

"Reckon to hit them hard in the center?" asked Tiptoft.

"Do ye get yer own earldom?" asked Comyn abrasively.

"Edward says yes!" barked back Tiptoft.

"Then we'll hit the center, together," agreed Comyn, his hardness for the argument mellowed.

"Formin' up to come at us again Lord Edward!" said Earl Malcolm of Lennox.

"I ken," said Edward Brus. He delayed only long enough to size up the coming assault, before giving the order to halt and set pikes.

Douglas and Randolph also halted their schiltroms to set spears and wait.

King Robert galloped to Angus Macdonald and ordered him to bring two hundred of his men to shore up the line.

"Where ye a'wantin' 'em?" he asked, coming to Robert.

"Most likely they'll try the center, but be ready to move yer men one way or the other as they charge," said the king.

"Aye, Robbie," said Angus. "Would feel better commandin' w' a galley deck 'neath my pegs, I would,"

Robert smiled, "Ye'll do just as well on dry land," he said.

Angus led his two hundred to back up the center of the lines, a move that was quickly noted across the field.

"You see how they rearrayed?" said Tiptoft.

"I saw," answered Comyn, "I would propose that we head for the center, and at the last, veer right to where the Douglas banner is."

"We should be able to overrun the bastards if they think we are attacking elsewhere in the line," agreed Tiptoft, and grinning at Comyn added, "Wonder where my earldom will be."

"Comyn failed to see the humor, being totally focused on the charge. "Turn on my signal!" was all he said.

"I see little use in trying the same head-on run into the goddamn pikes," Tiptoft commented, causing the hackles on Comyn's neck to rise.

"Well, Sir Pain, how do you suppose we might do different?" sniped Comyn. And Tiptoft gazed toward the Scots' lines for a thoughtful moment.

"I suppose…" he said mockingly, "… that we turn alright, but when we reach the right place, that we jump our mounts over the pikes and into the pikemen!"

"Jump!?" Comyn was stunned. "These horses weigh a ton apiece! How…" he frowned.

"Have you never had to jump over a deep rill or a downed horse?"

"Well, of course I have!" Comyn felt insulted.

"That is how," said Tiptoft. Comyn retained his frown but agreed to the stratagem.

"If it fails we shall all be slain on the pikes."

"If it isn't tried we shall all be slain on the pikes anyway, just like Gloucester."

"We should not send all of the ranks in at once, I think," said Comyn. "'Twould be better to attack in numerous waves."

"How so?" questioned Tiptoft. "The notion is to overrun the rabble with our great numbers!"

"If we engage all our force at once and, as we expect, open the ranks of pikes, who would we send into the break?"

"I understand your meaning," answered Tiptoft. "Send in one wave to make a breach for the rest to pass through. 'Tis worth a try, by God!"

Thus, with the two 'future earls' in the lead, the four hundred knights they commanded aligned themselves in traditional style across the field upon which the Scots awaited the inevitable onslaught. Many of the four hundred looked cheerless and unkempt from their night in the bog, but others seemed anxious to begin in spite of having had no rest.

Comyn kicked his destrier, as did Tiptoft, each with glory and an earldom on his mind and expecting his own determination and daring to be the coup.

"Where's d'Argentan?" shouted King Edward as the horses leapt forward whilst he watched.

"I am here, Your Majesty," Giles said, sauntering his horse to the king. "I am to be at your bridle, so expect me to remain close."

"I thought you were to figure a stratagem with Comyn and Tiptoft," said the king.

"I overheard them talkin', Sire. They do what I would do were I not by your side," said Sir Giles. Then he turned to Pembroke who yet stood nearby and, knowing full well the reason, nevertheless jested, "Why are you not mounted with us, Lord Pembroke?"

Pembroke glared at the man in silent banter.

Having watched the four hundred knights preparing to charge, King Robert said to Andrew, "We pulled Angus to the line too quick!"

"Too quick?" asked Andrew, not catching his meaning.

"Aye, too quick!" he repeated, and nudged his horse toward his bristling lines

The colorfully trapped destriers cantered up the slight slope until the leaders saw their ranks of knights well underway, when they increased their gait to a gallop.

With so many heavy horses' hooves pounding the suffering grainfield, the earth itself seemed to shake and rumble and the formidable power of the battlefield warriors was impressive to behold.

"This time our assault should break that line of heathens!" said King Edward watching his brave knights urging their horses faster as they neared the line of spears.

Robert rode to the center behind Angus.

Comyn and Tiptoft strove harder to speed toward their goal.

"They'll be shiftin' direction afore they get here," said Robert to the Macdonald, who nodded that he understood. Glancing about along the ranks of the three regiments, Angus instinctively knew, if the English swerved, where they would attack, and alerted his lieutenants to prepare for the move.

The attackers repositioned themselves as they ran, going from a straight line, as Gloucester had done, to a kind of triangle with a blunt point. Robert knew then that he was right.

"They might run us o'er this time!" said the Earl of Strathern, pulling out his dagger and swiftly cutting a corner off his leather vest and clenching it tightly in his teeth.

"Shut yer mouth," growled Earl Malcolm, "They hain't a'getting' through!! And what in the name o' God are ye doin' eatin' leather?"

"Hain't eatin' it! Tryin' to fix my teeth so I don't break more, like I did last time!" he shouted above the din as the horses grew nearer and the men in the waiting lines began to chant again.

"Tail-ed dogs! Tail-ed dogs! Tail-ed dogs!"

"Hold yer men steady!" demanded Robert at the top of his voice as he and Andrew, trailed by Nigel, moved behind the Scots' lines.

"Steady!" repeated Edward Brus, hollering to his men.

The Scots in the center braced for impact when suddenly, Comyn and Tiptoft turned and headed straight for the Douglas banner, followed by their four hundred. None hesitated.

Angus and his two hundred pikemen scrambled to their left and hastily began to set their pikes.

As the contingent drew close to the pikes, Comyn jumped his destrier on top of the Scots and Tiptoft did likewise, as echoing reports from the spear shafts snapping in half could be heard on the carse, even above the dull roar of the conflict. Brief screams from lives cut short and moans from wounded and dying men were heard as well.

The Scots did not flinch from performing their duty, even with tons of horseflesh hurling toward them. Neither did John Comyn nor Pain Tiptoft shirk theirs, and the spears of the doomed pikemen repaid them in equal horror, impaling them and most of their knights and their fine warhorses as they leapt over the hedgehog's front ranks.

The second of four ranks of English knights rode in close behind forcing the Scots to climb over their dead and wounded and the still kicking horses to fill the breach as they approached. Having seen the success gained by their leaders, the second line jumped their destriers onto the disorganized pikes and tried to drive their animals over the bodies of their comrades and the Scots, and even over the just arriving Macdonald reinforcements.

The devastation to the Scots was twice as deadly as the first assault.

For the first time in the two days of fighting, Robert realized, there was a potential for a wider breach. Within the span of mere heartbeats, three score Scots spearmen had been crushed or mauled, and most would die of their wounds before the day was out.

Andrew's eyes widened to see the horror of the scene. Many battles had he been involved in, but this was more immediately horrifying than ever he had seen before.

"Where's my infantry?!!" called King Edward loudly. He, too, had seen the potential for a breach in the Scots' lines.

"Hain't a'comin'," said Pembroke.

"What?!! Why not?!" asked the king working himself into a grand rage.

"We'll be all day and half the night gettin' 'em across the stream in ample numbers," he replied.

"Damn them to the cinders of hell!" screamed the king.

"We're goin' to have to break that line with the men we have here," said Pembroke, adding, "Your Majesty."

"We had best get a next volley lined up, Your Majesty," said d'Argentan.

"I agree, Sir Giles," said the king, and surmising that the valiant efforts of barons Comyn and Tiptoft had opened the Scots lines, he was most desirous of being there when the Brus capitulated. Then his success would be greater than that of his father, who was never able to bring the Scots, or even the Brus, to heel. Thus he announced grandly, "And I shall lead them!"

Robert's lines wavered and tore open as successive ranks of knights sacrificed themselves for England. And every onslaught made a larger and larger hole.

Angus' two hundred pikemen served as a patch, but they, too were taking a pounding.

"They just keep a'comin'!" said Angus as the one beleaguered place in the line got hit again and again. Though the men to either side moved in to fill the hole, they had no place of secure footing, and it was impossible to hold a position while stumbling and falling over the accumulating bodies of men and mounts and weapons. At the first opportunity Robert ordered a move forward and the men climbed over the dead so they could maneuver on solid ground.

The prisoner brigade and the men assigned to help the wounded off the field swooped down to rescue those who might be saved, inspecting the jumbled mass of torn and bloody warriors for survivors and putting to death those men and horses who would otherwise only suffer agonizing ends. A trail of men carrying or aiding the wounded soon left a bloody path away from the site of the broken line and toward Christina's hospital, where wounds were cauterized and broken bones set.

Aimlessly wandering and wounded destriers meandered the field or made their way back to the pows for water, and what was left of the Comyn and Tiptoft knights, demoralized over their comrades' failure to open the Scots lines completely after all the bloody sacrifice, saw no point in adding themselves to the heaps of the dead.

Though the morning was far from over, the day grew excessively hot, the men were sweating profusely in their quilted jackets and mail, and the schiltroms were beginning to lose men to dehydration and heat prostration, but still the lines held until that attack had run its course. Then Robert ordered water carried to the men in buckets and kegs, as much and as long as there was time before the next attack.

"They failed to break the line!" shouted King Edward as his seneschal, Sir Edmund de Mauley, rode to his side.

"The king's household guard are ready, Your Majesty," he announced with a hint of a bow though in the saddle.

"It is well, Sir Edmund," the king said and looking about remarked to Sir Aymer, "My Lord Pembroke, lest you intend to run into battle, I suggest you mount your horse. We are attacking."

With that, the king sallied toward the household knights, Giles d'Argentan at his right stirrup.

Pembroke, hating the notion of being in the saddle, reluctantly climbed aboard his destrier and eased his rump into the seat. The result wasn't quite as bad as he had imagined and he quickly took his place at the king's left.

Hugh le Despenser assumed a position to the right side of d'Argentan, and Mauley, the left of Pembroke, and the five rode toward the somewhat reduced lines of Scots.

The king's household knights and about five hundred more assembled behind the king. Many of them were just happy to get onto dry ground and out of the swamp, to which they had been relegated by their position in the traveling entourage.

King Robert saw the attackers arraying and ordered his commanders to move forward. The commanders brought their troops back to life along the line, and repeated the king's order. Again the Scots stood and marched toward their enemy.

"They're comin' toward us!" growled King Edward. "I would have thought the rabble would have broken their schiltroms and charged us by now!"

No one responded to the comment, especially Pembroke, who had seen the Scots fight him at Loudoun Hill under King Robert's command.

"Mauley!?" said the king.

"Yes, Your Majesty," answered Sir Edmund.

"When we get closer, you shall have the honor of leading the attack," said Edward, and Mauley bowed in appreciation.

"We shall attack where you now see the banner of Lord Brus," instructed the king. "Do you understand?"

"Yes, Majesty. I shall do my best," said Mauley.

King Edward set spurs to his destrier and began a trot as the quarter-mile distance between him and the Scots grew noticeably less with every minute of delay.

Having passed the human and animal detritus of the first battles and standing again on the unobstructed battlefield, the Scots reorganized their lines and continued to move toward the carse. King Robert ordered Angus back to the reserve schiltrom whilst he remained with the line, pacing his horse back and forth encouraging the men. He was accompanied by Andrew, who displayed the royal banner in his wake, making it appear to Edward Plantagenet, as his attack gained speed, that Robert de Brus was everywhere.

Sir Humphrey, Lord Bohun, sat his horse on the carse and observed the charge as if it were all playing out in a dream.

Nearby was Sir Ingram de Umfraville, who, though not a part of the attacking force led by the English king, began to worry that the day was not going to favor the English. It certainly was not going according to plan because there had been no plan. Had there been one, it would have been immediately scrapped when King Robert took the offensive by marching onto the field in formation, something the English had not considered in their wildest imaginings.

Knowing that there were three to four hundred Welsh archers mingled with the infantry on the south side of the Bannok Burn, Ingram wheeled his horse and headed toward the ford.

"Set pikes and hold the line!" ordered King Robert, "Here comes more than before!" He followed the line down as the men stopped and set their spears once again. He repeated his warning then went higher on the hill to about halfway between his own schiltrom and the schiltroms under Edward, Douglas and Stewart, and Thomas Randolph. Andrew followed with the banner, and Nigel followed Andrew.

From the carse King Edward saw Robert standing back from the line and it vexed and angered him, even more than losing the hundreds of his knights and nobles. He wanted to kill the source of all his problems in a single blow, and toward that end gouged his spurs into his horse's flanks and let out a cry as loud as he possibly could while standing in his stirrups and swinging his sword over his head.

At his elbows, Sir Giles and Lord Aymer galloped their destriers at a farther distance from the king, fearing the wild erratic swings of his sword.

For a moment King Edward exalted in the image of himself as the one great warrior in all Christendom, challenging the whole of the Scottish army.

But that was only his imagination working, for the hundreds of knights flogging their destriers behind him lived in their own mass spellbinding as they fearlessly bore down on the mere foot soldiers. They were far more accustomed to running against knights of their own ilk, albeit mostly in jousts, who were fully outfitted with similar weapons and rode on like destriers, each weighing a ton or more.

King Robert waited and watched the approaching tide of human and horseflesh to see any key movement that might tell where and how the attackers were going to hit. The only thing he was sure of was that Edward was not going to be the first impaled on his Scots' spearpoints.

Then he saw King Edward indicate Edward's schiltrom, and as his troops swarmed past him, he slowed his gait.

"Edward!" shouted Robert.

Edward heard the king's say and ordered, "Bear up and hold tight, lads!"

Gone were the Scots' cheerful touts of "Tail-ed dogs" of the earlier skirmishes. Too much blood had soaked the ground behind them, and too many good Scots now lay awash in it.

Again the front rank of Scots was lowest to the ground. They shivered and many crossed themselves when seeing the legs of the horses heading so fast toward them, knowing the horses would probably be jumped on top of them. Still, they set their jaws and held their pikes strongly outward, hoping to kill the beasts straightaway, before they were jumped. That way the dead horses would hamper the next assault's approach.

The second rank of pikemen targeted the chest and neck of the horse first and then the rider. They, too, knew the dangers of the destriers falling on them as they jumped. The first two ranks had trained to work together, and so far had been successful in stopping the assaults, though at great cost.

The knights came on strong as the Scots braced with all their might. They knew their fates to be in the hands of the Almighty as they took a deep breath and held against the tons of thundering horseflesh and lances coming down on them.

Again the horrific cacophony of breaking lances and spears, and the screams of horses and men in pain, was heard all along the line. The knights kept coming; one layer after another, until there was so much carnage that separated the two factions that it was difficult to maneuver any horse or man on either side to reach the enemy.

"There is yet no way to get through!" protested King Edward. The barded knights stood thirty or more yards from the schiltrom and looked at the line of bristling spears opposing them. The English had lost all sense of organization. Many riderless and wounded horses wandered the area, making it even more difficult to get a cohesive attack together.

"We could run atop of the dead horses and then jump!" impulsively growled the king.

"I don't think that would work, Your Majesty," said Sir Giles respectfully, but Edward wanted none to go against his wit.

"Goddamned well it might!" he yelled in pure frustration. He then called for his seneschal who, he knew, would follow his every word. "Mauley!!"

"I saw Sir Edmund go down in the first assault rank," said Sir Giles.

"Mauley?... Mauley's dead?" said Edward evidently truly shocked.

"Along with many other of your own knights," said d'Argentan.

Edward stood high in his stirrups again and held his sword higher and shouted loudly, "Goddamn you, Robert Brus!!"

King Robert heard the curse and knew the frustration his counterpart then felt. He smiled to himself but never let Edward know his pleasure. The only response the English king got was the line of Scots shouting and jeering at him.

Edward snarled in anger and called a challenge to Robert as way of solving his dilemma of being hindered by the dead and dying. "You hide behind yon carrion... come fight here, where *we* are!!"

"Move ahead!" ordered Robert without hesitation, and the commanders along the line gave the order. The Scots closed the gaps the battle had left in their lines, stepped over the dead and wounded, and came straight for the standing English knights.

"My God," they come!" said Edward, astonished.

The schiltroms kept walking at their steady pace and before Edward could get his men together the Scots were within ten yards of him.

"Fall back!" ordered Edward, thinking to reorganize where he had more space to get a running start for an effective charge. Those knights who were not badly wounded fell back with their king and again formed a line, this time but yards from the king's pavilion.

The three schiltroms kept coming. They were well within an eighth of a mile of the royal tent of red and white stripes, which was beginning to sag noticeably from being bumped by the men and horses trying to get into fighting positions. Most of the barons' tents, being much smaller, were simply cut down for the ground space on which they stood.

Robert's schiltrom shadowed the three forward schiltroms but still remained to the rear.

"We're not goin' to make it by running against them the same way, Sire!" suggested Pembroke, who had his mind more on the pain in his arse than on the battle.

"I know that, damn you!" Edward rebuked him.

"We must get to the men behind the pikes, Sire, else we cannot break their lines," suggested Sir Giles. "Can we not bring our own pikemen to the fore?"

"If I had brought them here, where would they stand? We are ourselves running out of room to begin a charge!" shouted Edward as more knights joined him.

Pembroke saw his erstwhile friend Thomas Randolph on his far right side and smiled, just for the sake of all the whisky they had consumed together.

The English knights, unaware that there was great debate over whether or not to charge the Scots again and to what avail, were ready to start another sally following the actions of their king.

Pembroke's charge was going to be half-hearted at best. He thought of his wife and wanted to live to get back to her. His political ambitions were dwindling at the same rate as his interest in the battle.

Ingram de Umfraville, having crossed Bannok Burn seeking the lost archers, was among the thousands of milling infantry who had heard the battle was already underway and were awaiting being called to join the action. On several occasions the knight was asked about the battle and he would lie and say, "Our knights are easily winnin' o'er the Scots rabble," and then move on, leaving the stout English yeomen slapping each other on the back in congratulatory fashion. He forced his horse through the crowd, wishing there was some way to get these thousands of men into the fray.

Sir Adam Gordon saw him coming and greeted him. "Where ye bound, Milord?"

"Ye ken where those Welsh archers be hidin'?" asked Ingram.

Gordon pointed and said, "At yon wain a'havin' a wee drink, they were, last I ken." Gordon had just left the group and was 'a wee drink' into his day as well.

"They drunk?" asked Ingram.

"Nae more than am I," said Gordon, astonished that Ingram would ask such. "And I hain't the least bit drunk, Sir."

"Help me bestir them, then!" insisted Ingram.

"Bestir them?" asked Gordon, "Needed in the battle, are they?"

"I fear all is lost if they are not engaged!" answered Ingram as if in confidence. Gordon's brows rose precipitously in surprise.

"Fetch my horse, I will... and go with ye, Milord," said Gordon, having been enlivened.

Sir Ingram's last statement also fell on the ears of two infantrymen who had an interest in news concerning the happenings on the other side of the treacherous stream. They looked at each other as if they didn't believe what they had just heard, and gossip of the dangerous kind was at that moment hatched.

"CHARGE!!" screamed King Edward with all the anger in his being, and he kicked his horse hard to make his short run to the fast advancing Scots' deadly hedgehogs.

"Set pikes!!" ordered Robert.

The commanders rapidly passed the word and the line halted and braced for another onslaught.

This time the English king held his lead and outran Pembroke and d'Argentan. His destrier's legs flew as fast as it was possible on the land that was all but flat between him and the Scots, and headed into the line of spears right in front of Edward Brus.

"'Tis their king! he shouted to his pikemen, "... don't kill him!!" he added, thinking of the huge potential for ransom.

The pikemen avoided impaling the red and gold clad figure though King Edward's magnificent horse was stabbed again and again as the king bravely tried to maneuver about so that he could chop at the shafts of the spears.

Knowing that the king would be taken for political and monetary gain if the wounded destrier collapsed so close to the schiltrom's front ranks, Sir Giles grabbed the royal horse's reins. He jerked the animal's head around while trying to dodge the swings of the king's sword.

Within a few steps the brave horse could not do more and fell to the ground and died within moments. Edward barely missed getting pinned beneath the heavy animal, and stood to his feet immediately.

"Capture him!!" ordered Edward Brus, and the men on the first rank moved forward out of their positions.

Sir Giles placed himself and his destrier between the king and the advancing Scots and wielded his sword so deftly that the foot soldiers shied back, though they still held their spears.

Impulsively, Edward Brus suddenly broke through his men and

engaged Sir Giles in a sword duel, but the well-trained destrier made it impossible for Edward to land his blows well, and after but a few strikes being exchanged, Giles took his foot from his stirrup and kicked Edward hard in the chest, knocking him to the ground. The pikemen rushed their schiltrom forward to protect their lord, and Sir Giles's destrier was certainly not off limits and was quickly dispatched. Giles rolled off the animal's back before it hit the ground and was immediately facing several pikeshafts. Hacking at them with his sword, he actually snapped the head off one and managed to back away from the other two as the rest of the English knights hit the line of spears hard.

Giles d'Argentan looked about for the king, but found that he had been rescued by knights under the orders of Lord Pembroke, who lingered back from the charge.

"A horse!!" screamed Edward, "Get me a goddam horse!!"

Sir Hugh rode to his liege and dismounted, offering his destrier to the king, the reins of which Edward quickly jerked from the gloved hands of his young lover and said, "Get another, quickly!" He climbed aboard le Despenser's horse and shouted for another attack.

The French adventurer, Sir Henry de Beaumont rode to the side of Sir Aymer and said, "Milord Pembroke, we'll soon be pushed into the swamp!"

"What?!" grumped Pembroke.

Beaumont pointed toward his rear.

Pembroke wheeled his horse and with his back to the battle saw exactly what King Robert was seeing. Anon they would be trapped with the swamp at their back, the Bannok Burn to the south, and the Pelstream to the north. They were penned in by less than five thousand Scots in spite of the fact that there were some twenty thousand English soldiers of foot just south of the Bannock.

"Damned poor placement, just as I tried to tell him," he muttered to himself. But, right now they had to deal with the Scots, so he turned back to Beaumont. "How do we flank these blaggards?!!"

"I cannot say. When we tried to surround them yesterday, with Clifford, they formed their lines into a circle... protected 'em on all sides," explained Beaumont, hastily forming his hands into a circular shape.

Pembroke knew immediately that they hadn't the ability to break down the schiltroms the way things were.

"Is there a way off this sorry sompe?" was the obvious question.

"Perhaps... far right side up by that little church is the only way I know," replied Beaumont pointing. "You extracting the king now?"

The question hit Pembroke hard. Withdrawal meant complete and utter defeat at the hands of the ragtag Scots. Hundreds of brave knights, the flower of England, and many he knew well, lay dead and wounded behind the line of Scots who stood stoically under the command of Robert de Brus.

Pembroke was not ready to give up the field as yet, nor would Edward be. Thus his first thought was of what might he do to turn this battle to their advantage, a conundrum for sure. Then, still looking toward the River Forth, he saw a string of men working their way across the far pools.

"My God, I ne'er knew we'd be getting' shed of our horses to get this done," said Adam Gordon following at Umfraville's rear.

"We're all on foot. 'Tis the only way!" said Ingram de Umfraville.

Adam looked back across the lush green boggy wasteland to see his three hundred and forty-seven archers, who were sobering up fairly well, coming about in single file. He waved to encourage them on, even though he wasn't sure to where Sir Ingram was leading them.

Umfraville suddenly sank up to his waist in a pool. Adam, who was standing only ankle deep just beside him, grabbed his hand and pulled him from the muck.

"Reckon to find a way around this pool," said Ingram fully soaked on his bottom half.

"What about 'round yonder?" said Adam pointing to a more solid appearing route.

"Ye a'wantin' to lead?" snapped Ingram.

"Ye're doin' a grand job of it," soothed Adam, not wanting to admit that he had no idea what was afoot.

"Then let me pick my own path!" said Ingram, who never liked anyone to tell him what to do. He proceeded exactly as Sir Adam had pointed it out to him.

"Thought ye ne'er liked this way," said Adam as the length of men kept following and staying fairly dry legged.

"I ne'er said I didn't like yer route… I had it in mind all along," he answered.

"Aye?" said Adam realizing the man's wit, "Then how we a'gettin' o'er *that* dry shod?" he asked pointing to the Pelstream just ahead.

"I reckon the archers need a bathin' anyhow," smirked Ingram.

Sir Adam Gordon looked at Ingram with his one good eye and had nothing to say, at least nothing over which he thought he wouldn't get smacked down. "Ye first, Milord," he said with an affable smile on his face. "I'll see that the hind end of the line gets across a'right."

Ingram growled at his comrade who seemed to be fearful of the burn, which had high sides, but far less so than parts of the treacherous Bannok. Still, their crossing point was not a ford.

Pembroke, still looking to the rear, saw that there were many more knights lingering beyond the king's tent. "Get those men into the fight!" he ordered and looked at Beaumont to carry out his command.

Beaumont nodded his head and trotted off in that direction as King Edward directed yet another attack against the Scots line, even though his dwindling horsed troops and their mounts were rapidly fading from weariness, discouragement and dehydration.

Taking advantage of the time it took the English to reorganize, the Scots commanders moved closer, step by step. They called a halt and set their spear butts into the ground awaiting another assault from the English cavalry.

Pembroke was not the only sage warrior who saw the line of archers working their way across the swampy pows... so did Robert. They disappeared into a clump of trees along the edge of the Pelstream and with no more than a glance further to his left he could see their destination.

"Call the archers from the wood!" said Robert.

"Aye, My King," replied Andrew and he lit out for Balquhiderock's forest.

Edward's attack was different than before. The knights came in close and hacked at the spearheads with swords and flails. Instead of taking the line in grand style of a single leap they were going to take the spears one at a time.

"Push them back, Edward!!" said Robert riding in close to the line.

Anxious to take advantage of the situation, Robert stepped from his destrier and grabbed a spear from the closest man to him. Making his way through the schiltrom ranks he was encouraging the men to take the advantage and go forward. "Move on them men!" he shouted loudly and he stepped to the fore and again shouted, "Ye can beat 'em back, now!! Keep movin'!!"

Edward Brus caught to Robert's want and gave his own order, "Forward, men!! Move on them!! Push the whoresons into the pows!!" Taking a spear from a young Scot who was carrying the extra weapons, he followed his brother to the fore of the fight.

The English knights, hanging from their saddlebows and swinging their weapons against the deadly pikes, were far too engrossed to notice the king and his brother had joined the conflict, but they noticed quickly that the lines of Scots were steadily moving toward them.

Robert thrust his spear out long and jabbed it through a horse's neck before its rider could block the move. The startled horse reared and threw the knight to the ground, knocking the wind from his chest.

The advancing Scots stepped over the stunned knight and continued their slow, steady advance whilst the men behind the lines took the gasping warrior and several others prisoner and shed them of all weapons and armor.

The order had raced the full length of the combined schiltroms and the Scots moved inexorably forward, battling the mounted knights as they approached to try and get at the men in the ranks by forcing themselves between the pikes. But since the English were not charging into them, the Scots no longer found it necessary to set their pikes. They could move across the cornfield at a fairly steady pace. They would soon be near King Edward's colorful tent, and thus made it their target, chanting, "The tent! The tent!" in time to their pace.

And they knew they were winning, by the scared looks on the faces of their foe, and their chant grew louder and more threatening.

King Robert withdrew and took the reins of his horse from Andrew, who had dutifully seized them when his liege jumped off. Robert remounted and immediately galloped up the hill to see what progress was being made by the English archers.

Reaching his vantage point, he was given little comfort because the long string of enemy archers had completely disappeared from view. However, his warriors were moving ever tighter to the striped tent and the knights still left to fight were getting squeezed into a smaller, tighter space of ground and were finding it harder to maneuver.

Looking to his right he saw some few of his own archers trickling out of the wood and wondered how many had survived what he thought had developed as an archer's battle within the trees. Anyway, he was thankful the English archers had lain off his schiltroms. His stouthearted lads were steadily forcing the finest mounted knights in Europe into an untenable shrunken section of the battleground between the burns.

Dead and wounded men, primarily English, thickly littered the pathway the advancing schiltroms had trod. Christina and her helpers moved from one bloody figure to another, trying to find the men they could yet help. The pickings were poor at best, for the Scots who were less seriously injured remained in the fight as long as their strength lasted.

Wounded English were taken for potential ransoming if they were expected to survive, or were mercifully killed on the spot.

MacKie ran to the king where he stood. "My King?" he grinned, "looks like we might take the field, this day!" Robert was not so pleased, knowing that the English yet had tens of thousands of troops below the Bannok, and they were fresh and well fed.

"'Tain't over, yet, MacKie. Gather yer bowmen here and keep yer eye across that burn, yon," instructed the king, pointing northeasterly, "If I figured rightly, there'll be Welsh archers there, right soon."

"Aye, Sire," MacKie nodded, and went to fetch his bowmen up the hill.

Robert called his son and page, Nigel, who had fallen under Sir Andrew's protection since the battle began, to summon Sir Robert Keith and his cavalry.

He then slowly walked his horse back down the hill, picking his way through the field of corpses until he arrived at his own schiltrom. "Sir Angus?" said the king, not seeing the Macdonald immediately. Angus emerged from within the ranks of the fourth, and largest schiltrom and greeted the king.

"Aye, My King," he said, politely. Then his entire demeanor turned to that of a man who felt affronted, and with his chin stuck out and his brows lowered he asked, "Why hain't ye a'lettin' *all* of us into the fray, Sire? We been out here all day without hardly liftin' a finger, and we didn't come just to roast on this damned field!" Robert looked at Angus and several of his stalwarts who had come to stand alongside the best sea captain in the islands, if not in Christendom.

"Here's yer release, Milord," replied Robert smiling, if a bit grimly. The men stood and looked at each other.

"He say we can fight?" asked the Maclaine.

"He said," replied Angus.

"Well? What ye a'waitin' on?" asked Robert.

Angus Macdonald, the Maclaine, and the other lads erupted in shouts and ran down the slope to where their command awaited, and within practically no longer than it took Angus to say it, the two thousand men fell into their ranks and proudly marched off to join their fellow Scots in the fight.

Robert wheeled his horse and trotted back up the hill.

"How many more men do they have comin' in?!" asked King Edward, seeing the field repopulating with men and pikes.

"They've been here all along, Majesty," said Giles as Pembroke joined them.

"We can't get any run at them at all, My King!"

"One way or another, we'll defeat this rabble or we'll keep fightin' until the last man dies on this godforsaken field!" growled King Edward loudly.

The English knights fought valiantly on as best they could, hacking at the pikeshafts, and throwing their maces and then their battleaxes at the Scots with some effect. They still held tight to their shields, swords and daggers, the most precious weapons they owned.

The Scots pressed against each other and forced the English knights into ever tightening quarters. The hindmost of them were already slogging around in the miry swamp.

Friar Baston, having fled across the burn and holed up with the unused infantry, was glad he had been paid for his poem beforehand and had sent the money to his Carmelite order.

Marmaduke de Tweng, who had seen the battle shaping up badly from the beginning, finally joined the other knights, though he cursed at nearly every breath for what he termed 'stratagem by accident and stupidity'. The celebrated hero of the battle of Stirling Bridge, which, he thought, was lost to another such stratagem, had ambitions not so highly flung as he found himself compacted with his fellow knights on a shrinking field. He merely wanted to stay alive.

The English knights were backed against their king's grand pavilion, which collapsed to the ground in stages as the large horses, their riders maneuvering to prosecute the battle, consumed the tent's space.

Robert had the whole of his trained schiltroms committed to the effort of driving the English into the bogs. The pikemen pressed hard against the constant attacks of the large horses coming against the spearheads.

The unmounted English knights were having better results as they clashed against the pikemen, who were far less trained for that kind of warfare than were the English.

Swords clashed and clanged between the spears.

Thomas Randolph and Edward Brus were the first Scots to the fore to challenge these threats to the line. The fresh troops of Robert's schiltrom took first position to relieve the men who had been struggling since just before dawn to do the king's bidding. They were worn to the bone and splattered with blood, including some of their own, but they were glad still to be alive for there were many Scots as well as English who were not.

The brothers Ross also moved forward to confront the English fighting on foot. Walter was perhaps the boldest as he ventured deeper among the English knights than many of the others. His complete focus on fighting a single knight made him an easy target to the next man's battleaxe, and he fell, to be quickly trampled by the hooves of the many milling horses.

Earl Hugh saw his brother fall and with his sword in one hand and an axe in the other he slashed his way to his brother's corpse. He stabbed and hacked at horses on one side, then another, to keep them off his brother. The English welcomed a Scottish knight who was, like Walter, willing to step beyond the schiltrom to fight their brand of war, and Hugh soon found himself in front of a frustrated English knight ready to show his prowess.

Hugh dropped his axe and slid his shield from his back and strapped it onto his left arm. Walter lay dead at his feet. The Englishman raised his sword above his head in an attack position. Hugh held his sword to his side until he could see how the man was going to fight him.

In broad strides, the Englishman covered the several steps that laid between him and the Ross, and brought his blade down hard on the earl's shield. Sir Hugh instantly brought up his own sword and pushed its blade hard against the man's gut, where it met with the man's heavy leather armor without much effect.

The Englishman smiled and prepared to attack again, raising his sword high and to his left in an attempt to flank the earl's shield. At that moment Hugh, Lord Ross, drove his sword into the man's armpit, completely severing the shoulder muscles and piercing his chest cavity.

The knight had expected to be standing over the decapitated body of Sir Hugh on the ground at that moment, but was instead gasping for the breath that the Scot's blade was denying him.

Several other English knights in the vicinity, having witnessed the defeat of their comrade, closed in to kill the earl.

Hugh of Ross backed away from his oncoming attackers and into the protective arms of the bristling spears. He would have to wait to retrieve his brother's body.

The Keith came to Robert's summons and asked, "Sire, ye wanted me?"

"Aye, Sir Robert. I think the English archers are..." no more than that got from his mouth before scores of his men began screaming in pain or falling out dead, and another flight hit them before his eyes.

"They've flanked us with their archers!!" growled Robert through gritted teeth, "Get to yer men and run them off!!"

Keith said not a word but was already on his horse hieing uphill, shouting to Graham to get in their saddles.

From their position in the wood the cavalry came to meet Keith who pointed across the Pelstream to the one element that could directly affect the battle. The more than four hundred rode quickly down the hill toward the shallow ford of the burn.

Robert rode to MacKie. "Why didn't ye yell they were there?!!" he questioned.

"Out ere we knew!" said MacKie.

"Close in as ye need, but kill them or drive 'em off!" ordered Robert clearly irritated.

On the field below, the men in the schiltroms were desperately trying to protect themselves with their woefully inadequate shields over their heads, whilst they fought on with the English knights. It would be but another flight or two before men would start retreating from the swift death that was decimating the Scots warriors.

A joyous shout went up from the tormented English knights. At last they saw the Scots taking some of the severe punishment they had themselves suffered all morning. Even King Edward found his energy renewed to fight on.

But their respite was short lived.

It took a long couple of minutes for the Scots bowmen to place themselves where they would be most effective before they started to lob flights of arrows onto the English archers. The first flights fell into the thickest center of the Welsh bowmen, and the howls and screams arising from the felled men cut through the tightly packed English knights like a dull blade.

Split into two parts, the Welsh brigade also split their direction of fire. The larger group kept their flights concentrated on the schiltroms, and the smaller began responding to their immediate threat and fired back at the Ettrick archers.

"Spread out!" said MacKie as he saw the flight coming toward him.

The barbs swished and thudded into the ground all around and took down many a Scot but those still able to nock an arrow kept shooting in rapid flights. Despite their continual barrage, more Scots were felled with practically every incoming flight. Though each man had brought with him two dozen arrows, they were beginning to run out.

Suddenly, MacKie called out, "Stop shootin'!" and the order was repeated until no more arrows were lofted. The archers relaxed their strings and watched their last flight, already in the air before the order went out, come to land, felling three of the English archers. They were perplexed as to the ceasefire until they saw Keith's cavalry fast closing in on the enemy bowmen.

Then it was the Scots' time to cheer, and cheer they did.

It was the erstwhile Templar, David de Graham, and his seven who led the attack. Hunkered low in their saddles, they spread their animals widely so they could swing their swords with impunity. Seeing them approach, the Welsh archers turned their deadly attention to them.

Arrows flew thick among the raiders. Keith was close behind Graham and his Templar knights, and after each man sent a couple of arrows in the raiders' direction, most decided it was prudent to flee. They scattered before the incoming Scots like dry leaves before a winter gust.

"Keep shootin'!!" screamed Umfraville, his sword flailing the air in every direction. This was his opportunity to save the battle for the English and he did not want it to fail.

Those archers who stayed kept up a peppering of the fast approaching cavalry.

Graham's horse was hit in the chest. The arrow penetrated through the leather armor wounding it but slightly. The second arrow struck in the animal's throat, which caused it to twist its head, but it kept running.

Two of the other former Templars were hit and knocked from their horses. Another lost his horse to an arrow, but those were among the last missiles lofted by the Welsh toward the horsed Scots.

There was barely time left to flee, and the remaining archers ran toward the swamp through which they had come; here and there one would stop and fire another arrow at their pursuers.

Ingram de Umfraville was swinging his sword around like a madman, trying to get the Welsh to stand their ground.

Adam Gordon peeled his one eye wide at seeing the oncoming troops so very near and agreed with the archers. He, like they, headed for the boggy path back to the wagons and the infantry, thinking Sir Ingram to have lost his wit.

A third arrow, thrown at random, hit Graham's horse and it fell dead, mid-stride, flinging Graham clear as Keith passed him at a gallop toward the bog.

Feeling like he had been run over by a charging bull, Graham rolled over and sat upright. Shaking his head to clear it of the darkness hiding in the corners, he took his helmet off and tossed it aside.

Keith held to his saddlebow and leaned overboard to cleave a bowman almost in two before his nocked arrow could be fired against him.

A sudden arrow whizzed past Graham's head and he fell to cover behind his dead horse.

Three Welsh bowmen, having spent all of their arrows, saw Graham in a vulnerable position and ran toward him, their hand weapons ready for action.

Vieuxpont saw the three almost on top of Graham and hied his horse toward them.

Graham scrambled for his sword, which had fallen from his hand when he went down, but the first attacker was too near. He reached Graham and took a wild slash at him.

Graham dodged it and lunged forward, hitting his attacker with a well-placed shoulder in the midsection that threw the man backward on the ground. The Templar's knife was swift to draw blood as a second attacker was close on.

Vieuxpont galloped his horse near and drew the attention of the fellow away from Graham and to himself. The man made a panicked attempt at stabbing the Scot's horse.

Graham looked again for his lost sword and in the process spotted the horse that had been tethered to the tail of his own mount before dawn. It stood not ten feet away, lazily munching on the green grassy land.

Vieuxpont wheeled his horse and again went against the Welshman with the sword, but he was quick and wily and Vieuxpont missed his stroke. The fellow caught the tail of the horse when Vieuxpont slowed to turn, and used it to move around behind the knight without his being aware. When he got the chance, the bowman slit the horse's belly, spilling its viscera to the earth before the knight knew what had happened. The horse collapsed beneath him and Vieuxpont hit the ground hard and lay there stunned.

Graham found his sword and bounded to retrieve the empty-saddled horse.

Vieuxpont tried to stand but was wobbly, and the bowman took full advantage of his condition. He stabbed the great knight in the gut as the third bowman came to Vieuxpont's back and hit him hard across the neck with his sword.

By then, Graham had his sword and a mount and turned in time to see Vieuxpont's demise. One swift kick to the horse's flank and Graham was upon the second archer and deftly took off his head.

The third man was fast to turn and flee, but Graham and his light horse easily ran him down and killed him, and he was alone in the lush green meadow.

Seeing there was nothing to be done for Vieuxpont, who undoubtedly had saved his life, Graham hied again for the fast scattering bowmen. He was back in the battle.

"Take up the position where those archers were run off," ordered King Robert.

MacKie replied, "Aye, My King." And what was left of the Ettrick archers' contingent followed MacKie as he ran fast for their crossing spot of the Pelstream.

Yet in pursuit of escaping bowmen, Sir Robert Keith was fast catching up to one of the Welshmen when the fellow turned at point-blank range and with his powerful bow fired his last arrow into the neck of Keith's stalwart horse. When the horse went down, the Scot was sent tumbling over its head and hit the ground, but in such a way that he rolled, rather than landing hard. He glanced about and saw nothing of his sword, and his cavalry was passing him by. Pulling his axe from his saddle loop he started to run toward the killing field, yelling at the top of his lungs the old Scottish battle cry.

Ingram saw him coming on foot and screaming and became oddly fearful, not of the horsed knights, who were deadly with their slashing swords, but of Keith, who had targeted him personally from the first step of his run.

Sir Ingram turned and ran as fast as he could, only to find that he was in almost as much danger from his own archers. As they ran, they would turn and shoot at those in pursuit, and Umfraville was too often near the sailing missiles.

Leaving far more than a hundred of their number lying dead or injured about the field, the last of the archers slipped back into the pools of boggy water from which they had emerged but a short time before, as the grand hope of Sir Ingram faded. Into the mire they went, hoping the Scots would let them go.

They were in no direr position than were the knights of King Edward, unable to maneuver but little on their great horses in a greatly reduced pen formed by swiftly running Bannok Burn, the lesser Pelstream, and the continually closing Scots schiltroms, at that point well beyond the trampled remains of King Edward's grand tent.

For every spear the knights had destroyed they had paid dearly, and though there were not nearly so many pikes bristling outward from the schiltroms as there had been, the knights were in no less peril from the determined Scots. No longer having a way of replacing their broken spears, they merely drew swords and axes from their belts and pressed tightly to the crowded horses and riders, gutting and hacking at every limb to which they had access. Frightened and panicking, the horses were biting and kicking in a rage of their own.

The knights had no room to retaliate against the Scots without damaging the men and horses crowded about them, and the carnage grew with every step taken by the Scots.

MacKie and his archers had claimed the ground vacated by the fleeing Welshmen, and Robert raised his hand and gave them a visual signal for them to loose their arrows into the congested English knights.

The barbs did their deadly work with surprising efficiency. Knights were falling fast on the north side of the field. Only the few long bows could reach as far as the south, but there were some, leaving the English no place to hide. The archers quit only when they had run out of arrows.

Aghast at the situation, Lord Pembroke realized that there was no further recourse. The battle to relieve Castle Stirling was beyond saving. No matter what else transpired, his duty to his sovereign was clear and urgent. He yet rode alongside Edward, who was constantly shouting irrelevant orders to knights who could no longer move more than a few feet in any direction.

Aymer pulled his reins unmercifully against his horse's bleeding mouth and forced it to back up so that he could move to the king's other side and talk with d'Argentan. Coming to him and speaking so that King Edward was unlikely to hear what he proposed, he said exactly what was on his mind.

"'Tis over, Giles! Our archers are routed, our cavalry is unable to form a line to defend itself, much less wage war," he confided, "and our grand hoards of foot soldiers lie dormant beyond the Bannok, powerless to join us on this steadily dwindling bogland! We must remove the king from danger!"

"But, that will end the battle, Milord! Would you surrender?"

"Hell, no! We'll not surrender! But neither must we allow the king to suffer bein' captured... or killed by one o' them damned archers... without tryin' to get him off the field, anyway!" Pembroke insisted. "Our battle is lost! Our only responsibility now is to Edward, and I fear he shall not go easily."

Giles d'Argentan was crushed, but looking about him, he came to realize Pembroke was right. There was nothing else they could do but retire the king.

"I'll tell him where we stand and why he must now retreat!" said Sir Aymer, seeing Sir Giles' stricken countenance.

Sir Humphrey, Lord Hereford, was just as shattered in spirit when he also realized that the battle was lost. He then gathered his knights and traversed Bannok Burn at the ford, abandoning the battlefield to the victorious Scots and men of lesser wit than he. Hereford led his men south through the multitude of infantry, and all who saw the earl and his men departing quickly realized that it meant the battle was lost, without the infantry ever having been engaged.

Humphrey found his foot soldiers and extracted them from the mass.

"Ye hiein'?" queried Robert de Umfraville, Earl of Angus, who had spent almost all morning on the east side of the burn.

"I am, Sir. Goin' to Bothwell, before we head back to England," replied Hereford.

"Battle goin' all that bad, is it?" said Earl Robert with fallen spirits.

"'Tis," answered Hereford, shaking his head.

"Mind if we go with ye?" asked Lord Angus uneasily.

"Come along," said Hereford, "'Twill be good to be shed of this shit!"

"I'm waitin' for my brother, Ingram," said Robert, standing high in his stirrups and looking over the crowd. "I'm sure he'll be along anon."

"Come as you can," said Humphrey, "We'll be slowed some by these men on foot." The contingent marched off to the south, out the 'back way' west of Torwood, the most direct route for the long walk to Lord Hereford's Castle Bothwell.

Soon, the barons in charge of the various infantry factions had a great deal of difficulty holding the men as, driven by fear, those around the edges of the camp had begun slipping away. At first there were few but their numbers increased, and atop their horses the barons could, within a short while, easily see scores of men leaving at once.

Whether because they were in unfamiliar territory, or because they thought they were less likely to be seen leaving, or because they were simply confused, some of the deserters set off toward the east, rather than the south and England.

To the east a league or so lay the tidal waters of the River Forth and the fens of the lowlands, which claimed the lives of many of the fleeing men trying to cross.

"Rob the dead Welsh," shouted MacKie to his fellow archers. They had run shy of arrows and this was one way of replenishing their supply. After foraging among the effects of the dead enemy archers and gathering their arrows, the Ettrick bowmen were about ready to rain more death on the English knights.

Lord Pembroke went back to his position at the king's left and waited until Edward finished issuing an order to a bewildered knight, who was already wounded and bleeding from his leg. When he noticed Pembroke's return to his side he threw open his visor and said, "Where were you, My Lord? You were not to leave your place at the king's side!"

Pembroke said nothing for a moment, trying to think of a way to make Edward see their predicament.

"Well!?" the king demanded an answer.

"Your Majesty, I have come... and Sir Giles has come... to safeguard you from the battlefield," said the earl.

Edward sniggered, but there was a tinge of fear in his voice when he retorted, "Whatever do you mean, Pembroke? Leave before the battle is won? You must be mad!"

"Sire, we are in an unsound position..."

"Nonsense! We have near twenty thousand men to their... what, four or five thousand? Humph!"

"... we are drowning in men, Majesty, but have nowhere for them to fight! We are herded into a pinfold of our own making from which few will escape. The battle is lost!"

"LOST??!! We're still fightin'!!" shouted King Edward, becoming agitated with the discussion. "It is you, Pembroke! You haven't the will to win! You hadn't the will to win at Loudoun, either! I see it all now! You are responsible for our failure to conquer the damned Scots! You, my most trusted commander, are a traitor, de Valence!!"

"My Lord King..." Pembroke could all but feel the headsman's axe at the back of his neck, and found it difficult to catch his breath on the oppressively hot day, even before he heard the king's next words.

"I shall have you executed for your treachery, Pembroke! By God I will!"

Pembroke was agape and without words. At that moment, Giles d'Argentan showed the courage of which he was made.

"You cannot win, My Lord King!" he said coming to assume the king's reins.

"Unhand my horse, you whoreson, or I will remove your hand from its arm," screamed Edward completely unaccustomed to being handled in such a way.

"We take no pleasure in saying these words, but you must not be captured, and if we do not retire from the field now, you will be in the Brus' hands... My Liege."

"Hereford has already left the field," Pembroke again found his voice, "We must do the same else we shall not be able to retreat... the day is lost!"

"Hereford left?!" a stunned Edward asked in disbelief.

"Your Majesty, you cannot linger to be captured!" argued Pembroke strongly.

Edward's eyes grew large as the realization of the word 'lost' filtered beyond his passion.

"Where is Sir Hugh?" shrieked the king. "Is he dead?"

"Forward in the thickest of the fight, when last I saw of him," said Pembroke.

"Get him! Make him come to me!" ordered the king. It was just at that instant that the king's horse screamed and shivered as its forelegs buckled, throwing the king forward. Only Pembroke's close proximity kept him from falling from his saddle to the front, as Edward was able to grab Pembroke's arm. A Scots warrior, having worked his way deep into the English side of the melee, had cut the destrier's foreleg tendons and was jerking hard on its bridle to pull the king to the ground.

Giles immediately swung his sword only a single time and the brave Scot fell. The king's struggling horse collapsed on top of him.

Edward fell onto his horse's neck, but quickly recovered to stand. He cursed the dead man lying under his horse for having come frighteningly close to capturing him, though he was now thoroughly convinced to leave the field.

"Hugh!" he shouted. "I want Sir Hugh!"

"I'll send a man to find him," said Giles, who stopped the closest knight and sent him in search of the king's favorite.

Pembroke, feeling the urgency of the circumstance, ordered another to fetch the troops of Lancaster and Warwick, and the king's household guard. There was no time to dally if they were to make the king's escape successful.

Edward stood alone but for Pembroke and d'Argentan in the midst of a swirling madness of his own folly. His wobbly plan, now dashed, was to have had the head of Robert de Brus piked at the entrance to his tent by that time. Instead, his tent was now thoroughly trampled into the mud and filth and gore, overrun by the yet advancing enemy, and he began to see the battle as Pembroke had described it.

His fear of imminent capture overcame him and transformed him from a fearless beast of prey to a fearful animal to be preyed upon.

Four hundred and a few scores of the king's designated bodyguard were left alive on the field to be rounded up and called to join the king. None were told that their duty would be to extract the king from the field, or that the battle was lost. Somebody grabbed a destrier, miraculously unscathed, for the king to ride. The beast's trappings were far from Edward's red and gold leopards, but on the other hand, it was still alive, unhurt, and suitable transportation.

At mid-morning, the sky was blue and the sun was becoming far hotter than usual for the time of year. Men on both sides were failing from exhaustion and dehydration, yet those who were left fought for all their worth. Now beyond pride or reward, the conflict had become an indescribable commitment within the hearts of the individuals lost in the struggle.

MacKie and his peers gathered more than two hundred arrows from the field's dead and began again to spread them into the English side of the battling mob. Suddenly the English knights were dying on the north side of the field once again, and the others pushed to the south and out of range, clogging the field even more.

"That's it!" shouted Sir Henry Sinclair with a swing in the air of his short sword blade to get everyone's attention. "King Robert has given us the signal!!"

Behind Sinclair stood about fifteen hundred men ready to do battle in the name of Scotland. Among them were men like Sim of the Leadhouse, Cuthbert, Fergus, Alexander Seton, a worthy knight in his own right who had joined the Brus only hours earlier and had not trained with Robert's schiltroms. Also, Sedric the Irish chieftain with his warriors who had done a great service to the cause by scouting out the English disposition during the night, waited for the call. There were foragers and cooks, those who had kept the army supplied and fit, hundreds of servant lads, called gillies, along with many others who supported the king and simply wanted a hand in fighting the enemy.

"Are we ready?" asked Lord Pembroke when the king's guard and Sir Hugh le Despenser had arrived.

"We must be, else we fail!" said Giles, holding the rein on the right of the king's mount as did Pembroke on the left. This not only gave them some control on the direction in which the king's horse would be allowed to go, but placed the pair of knights between the king and any assailants.

Striking spurs to their destriers, the trio, monarch and protectors, took off at a gallop to make their way along the Pelstream's spongy south bank. Sir Hugh followed closely, and Sir Roger Northburgh as well, he carrying the king's three leopards shield and like banner.

The stalwart bodyguard, knights dedicated to the purpose early on, surrounded the king as they forced their way through the crowd of stymied English knights and headed for the small opening yet between the muddy banks of the Pelstream and Thomas Randolph's regiment. There they knew was the ford, where they hoped to be able to cross and hasten for Castle Stirling.

Henry Sinclair's 'army' had a full three-quarters of a mile to cover before arriving at the battle itself, and so emerged from the wood running as they came down the hill.

Thomas Randolph, upon seeing the contingent of King Edward's knights working around to his left and thinking the knights were attempting to outflank his position, ordered his hard-working schiltrom to form their circle as they had done the day before, and wait for an attack.

Though the English rode within twenty yards of the schiltrom, Edward and his bodyguard ignored them to turn north and hie toward Castle Stirling.

Robert watched the departing knights and could have ordered Randolph to attack, but held his tongue. The King of England did not even turn his head the least bit; his loss on the battlefield was not reflected in his continued haughtiness.

Across the Pelstream, from where the archers saw the escaping riders, it was a different story. They hurried to launch their remaining arrows into the midst of the fleeing royal party before they got out of range, doing as much damage as they could by dropping five of the knights from their mounts. One of the unfortunates to fall was Sir Roger Northburgh, bearer of the king's banner and shield.

The others in the galloping procession tried to miss their downed comrades as they fled, but none dared sacrifice their duty of remaining with the king to help them. Thus the banner and the shield of Edward of England were unceremoniously trampled underfoot by the flying feet of the destriers.

The Welsh archers finally made their way back among the ranks of the infantry, who were outraged at hearing the gossip of the battle having been lost.

Ingram de Umfraville, last to crawl from the bog pools, was met by Adam Gordon.

"Too bad ye killed so few," said Adam, who had emerged from the bog but moments earlier. He tugged and pulled Ingram's hand, helping him from the last of the bog muck.

Ingram snarled at his incidental cohort in misadventure. Adam was among the first to excite panic when the Brus cavalry had arrived.

"Heard yer brother was searchin' for ye, Ingram," said Adam, blinking his one good eye to clear it of any lingering water.

"What the hell's Robert a'wantin'," he said angrily, "He might as well have stayed at home for all he's done!"

"Don't ken what he's done, but he's in yon direction a'askin'."

Some of the enormous infantry division of Edward's army began to crowd around the archers, asking some very pointed questions: "How come you to run off?", "How come you didn't kill more of the Scots?", "Why were we never called to the battle?", and making accusations: "Cowards!" "Fools!"

Ingram quietly slipped from their midst and went to search out Robert, who was not hard to find since his squire followed him everywhere carrying his great white banner with the red lion.

Before long one of the frustrated infantrymen balled his hand to a fist and hit one of the Welsh archers, who staggered backward among his peers in surprise. Another of the frustrated soldiers hit the archer closest to him and before long there was a 'free-for-all' broken out near where the archers had exited the bog.

There were many more of the English infantrymen than there were of the remaining Welsh, and consequently the English walked away holding and rubbing limbs and heads while the Welsh lay groaning and bleeding on the ground.

Seeing the banner of King Edward leave the field as others were still fighting and dying in his name caused much fear and dismay to fall upon the remaining English. There were no orders from any noble telling the lesser knights and infantry to follow, or indeed, to do anything. Those left to their own devices did the only thing they knew how… they continued to fight as if there remained a cause. However the truth was that with the exit of the king, the great army was immediately headless and bleeding lives from every pore.

Stirling was less than a quarter of a league away and looming high and commanding over the landscape. It was the most logical place from which to plan another day's continuation of the battle, and that was what Edward had convinced himself would happen, once they were safely behind the castle's stout walls.

When they had reached a safe distance from the bloody field above Bannock Burn, however, Sir Giles d'Argentan drew rein and gave a signal for Pembroke to do the same, effectively halting the whole entourage of fleeing knights.

Pembroke looked about them to see what danger had halted the mass of knights on the Roman Road, but perceived none.

"What is the meaning of this, Sir Giles!?" asked Edward, unhappy with the delay.

"Your Majesty," said d'Argentan, "I am unaccustomed to running from a fight, having never done so, and I shall not run from this one. Since you are safe from harm now, and with your permission, I intend to return to the battlefield."

"What in hell's name do you reckon you're doin', you fool?!" growled Pembroke, his bushy eyebrows hooding his eyes.

The renowned knight came to the other side of the king's horse to speak to Sir Aymer, whom he considered his friend. In so doing, however, he erred and rode across in front of the king's horse, earning a frown from the king as well.

"Sir Giles, I shall not have you abandoning me on the side of the road like a worn out nag!" protested the king.

"Sire, I fought in the Crusade for the sake of God. Today, I fought at your side for your sake," said d'Argentan. "Now, I must return to the carse and fight for my sake!"

"Holy goddamn knights!" Edward snarled. "I shall never understand the like!"

Giles had no answer for the king and bowed respectfully.

"Be sure that you don't wind up in another gaol," warned Edward, "for I'll not save your arse again!" With that, the king kicked his horse hard and galloped straight for Castle Stirling, followed by the hundreds of knights of his bodyguard, who flowed around d'Argentan and de Valence standing like stones in a rushing stream. Pembroke remained to speak to the courageous knight.

"I'll return with you," said Aymer.

"No, Milord. You must not place your life in jeopardy for my pride," said Giles.

"'Tis not for you that I would do anything," said Pembroke, "… and I do not intend to throw my life away as you seem to have in mind to do."

"I cannot say that I have in mind to throw away my life, Milord, but I must return and complete my service on the field of honor," admitted Giles.

"If you return and enter the 'field of honor' you shall be killed." argued Pembroke.

"I understand the possibility, Milord, yet I would not wish to live to hear it said that I fled the battle out of fear for my life!" He wanted to add, "and I am forever in love with your wife," but that would leave his friend angry and suspicious of his wife, and her with an unhappy husband, so he kept the secret of their one tryst in his heart, where it belonged.

Aymer admired the gallant knight and considered him more like a son than a friend. As if he had overheard Giles' thoughts, he said, "If you concern yourself with our recent conversation concerning my wife, I assure you that I hold nothing against you and in fact have reason to be grateful for your ..."

"Milord," Giles interrupted, "your wife loves you, and you alone. She is a beautiful woman and I envy you her favors. Return your attentions to her in equal measure and you shall be a happy man!"

Aymer's eyes widened. He was far from accustomed to speaking of such private matters to other men, and growled at himself for listening, but there was something in the man's words that resonated with a spark of nobility in his heart.

"Don't worry, Sir Aymer, we shall meet again... if not in this world, then surely in the next." Having said all he intended to say, Sir Giles spurred his destrier forward and went back over the hill to where the desperate battle yet raged.

He was a good fifty yards gone when Pembroke shouted, "Hold on! I said I was goin' back with you!" and he put his destrier to a gallop and caught up. The two men were momentarily bonded, but their fates were destined for entirely different roads.

Sir Robert de Reymes had dismounted and was hard against the press of men. The armies had become so tightly ensnared that the fighting was reduced to hand-to-hand. Men fought until they could no longer stand, and then, if they could, they crawled away before being trampled by those who had stood immediately behind them.

Sir Robert had been a gentle merchant in London, his wealth gotten on his own merits rather than through political friendships. His estate lands north of Corbridge in northern England had been devastated by the raids of Robert Brus and it ate at him that his once thriving lands were at that time practically worthless. His anger played on his wit as he forced his way to the killing line with the banner of King Robert in his sight.

Reymes pushed his way to the confluence of the masses and began to pike and kill with great rage. Having had little experience with such battling, when he suddenly came face to face with a large angry Scotsman he froze and failed to take advantage of the Scot's own surprise, but the Scot did, slashed at him, leaving a scarlet gash from his forehead across his nose to his jaw. Sir Robert dropped his weapons and grabbed at his face falling to the ground in shock.

"We are to remain here," ordered Sir Henry Sinclair. His rabble, anxious to get into the battle, reluctantly held their ground.

"When we bringin' Sir Henry to the fore?" asked Andrew of his liege.

"Directly," said Robert looking uphill to see if they were in position.

It was at that moment Robert noticed Lord Pembroke and d'Argentan coming back along his flank. He watched as the pair split and Sir Giles sat his horse in the middle of the battlefield and looked all around at the carnage and waste, while Pembroke headed for the eastern ford of the Bannok Burn.

"Reckon the king's returnin' too?" asked Andrew.

"Ne'er can tell," said Robert, "Best keep an eye out... they might be sneakin' around the hill to get behind us."

"Sir Henry would ken ere we would," replied Andrew.

Robert looked at Andrew, smiled and shook his head, "Just keep yer eye out!"

Pressed hard against the high steep bank of the Bannok, many of England's knights were unable to remain there but found themselves pushed off and into the burn, where the waters ran deep and particularly swift through the gorge. In their heavy armor and elaborate trappings, the knights and their horses found it a struggle to keep their heads above water as they were washed downstream. A few actually escaped from the battlefield in that manner, but most who fell down the bank were drowned when they could not make it across.

Seeing the knights escaping or attempting to, and having heard that the king had left the field, the infantry became an unstable force as the men began thinking of their own safety. Their liege lords, those not killed in the fight, were having a terrible time holding the men together. In fear and rebellion, parts of the infantry lost all discipline and ran to overturn the wains of supplies and again got into as much of the wine as they could lay hand to.

Friar Baston, having regained his own self-control by then, stood among the men shouting for calm, for prayer, and for courage to remain and fight. Even as he spoke, Sir Adam Gordon gathered the remaining men he had brought to the field and led them away toward his home in Lothian. There he hoped he and they could hole up until the heated passions of the time cooled.

Sir Aymer on his destrier sloshed through the high water at the eastern ford and was glad for every hand of height the horse measured. Reaching the far side he was completely surrounded by men anxious for some word about battle.

Sir Giles remained a long moment on the battlefield alone, watching the struggling mass at the eastern end. The knights were far fewer in number than when he left with the king, and totally cut off from escape. There were none free to join him in a glorious charge against the foe.

His hour had passed.

Or perhaps not.

He yet had his sword, and there were unbroken lances here and there on the field. He rode about the battlefield until he found one of suitable length and, stepping down from his horse, he hefted its weight.

It would do.

Mounting his destrier again, he happened to see Robert on the hill, and seemed to know that the Scots king was watching. He nodded a sad farewell to a worthy opponent, shouted a warning to the men on the ground to stand back, closed his visor, and spurred his horse.

Whether by accident or by design, he found the only remaining spears of the schiltrom line and smashed headlong into them. The pikemen had no time to set their pikes into the ground and were bowled over backwards, but they bit deeply into the horse and its rider.

Perhaps the last thoughts of Sir Giles d'Argentan were of another man's wife, which could be why he chose to honor her with his death.

There were no more barded knights to fight, they having either abandoned the field, been taken prisoner, or laid dead in the wake of the Scots' schiltroms that had fought the English to the edge of the carse.

Robert knew the battle could go on for hours yet, as tired, defeated men stood and were killed by other tired, victorious men. He decided it was time to end it and ordered Andrew to give the signal to Sinclair.

The newly made knight took the king's banner and waved it back and forth three times.

"There's the signal," said Sir Alexander Seton.

"Aye, 'tis," agreed Sir Henry, and he turned to his strange collection of an army and said, "We go, lads!!"

Being within a quarter of a mile from the battle, Sinclair's men started to make their grand charge. They even had multi-colored banners made of whatever cloths they had at hand and the banners streamed out behind them as they ran.

Their blood curdling screams while they came down the hill added to the impression that a fresh contingent of Scots had come to join the fight. The English were in dire fear and the shrieks reverberated throughout the remaining men.

Sheer panic permeated the English, and the Scots who had been fighting were greatly relieved that the arriving horde was on their side.

The whole of the English army, which had been deadlocked against the Scots throughout the morning, gave way as those who dared to flee began to scatter into the bogs and streams in panic.

"On them, they are failin'!" shouted Robert, coming closer to the line. The men picked up the mantra and started shouting with dry mouths and parched throats, motivated by sheer excitement of the win.

Within moments they were chasing the English into the rivulets of slow moving water that fed the pools. Many tried to follow the pieces of houses spread about on the fens.

The men that had fought from the earliest morning stopped their chase and let the 'fresh troops' carry their attack alone, and so they did, driving the English into the bogs and sompes and massacring any on whom they could lay hand or blade. Many of the fleeing soldiers fell or flung themselves off the steep sides of the gorge into Bannok Burn and soon the treacherous, rushing burn was choked with the dead, forcing the waters to back up onto the fields.

The schiltrom warriors sat or laid among the awful carnage in the field of unripe wheat, threw their helmets and arms to the ground and stripped off every stitch of clothing they cared to.

Eventually, they all were watered by the women and boys who saw to the filling of the jugs and barrels from the stream that washed their enemy away.

It was a hot day and the sun was less than halfway to its zenith. Within the morning, from dawn to that time, King Robert's ragtag army, at great sacrifice of lives and blood, had brought the mighty English army to its knees.

Frair Robert Baston

mondAy, lAte-morning - 24th June BANNOK

King Edward's detachment hastened across the intermittently dry and soggy field to the village at the bottom of the volcanic upthrust. At the top awaited Castle Stirling and sanctuary. Sir Philip Mowbray, having left the English camp soon after they pitched the king's red and white striped tent, saw them coming. A half-thousand men, of Warwick and Lancaster and the king's own household knights and more, traveling in great haste from the field of battle meant only one thing to Mowbray: the battle was over and the Scots had won, at least for the day.

The relatively few Scots stationed in the village knew they were no match for the hundreds of English knights and hid from their view in the houses as they galloped through, following their king.

Mowbray watched them approach and went to the gatehouse battlements about the same time the king drew a tight rein before the barred oaken doors.

"Mowbray!!" shouted the angry king as loudly as he could manage.

"I am here, Sire," announced Mowbray, pushing his body against the wall and standing on the tips of his toes to make himself as visible as possible.

"How dare you bar the gate against your king!" shrieked Edward.

"Have ye won the battle, My Lord?" asked Mowbray.

"How the hell do you dare question your king?! My knights are within!" argued Edward, "therefore I have relieved the castle!"

"Your knights, Sir, are in the dungeon as of this morn," said Mowbray, a little shake in his voice, which he noticed if no one else did.

"Dungeon?" squawked the king in disbelief. "I demand that you release my knights, immediately!!"

"I cannot, Sire. At present, they are my prisoners," retorted Mowbray. "Once ye have returned to London, however, we can negotiate their ransom."

"Ransom! Damn you, Mowbray! I shall have your head for this! They are my knights! Release them to me now!" howled Edward. "Open this goddamn gate and let me in!! The Scots will be here soon!!"

"Sire, if I should let ye in," said Mowbray, "ye would by your very words, be imprisoned here! All the Brus would have to do is lay siege to imprison us all! Our victuals are playin' out... it would be but a matter of days before we would be forced to surrender!"

Other than his father, Edward had no memory of anyone ever before in his life telling him 'no' to his face, and this was not going to set a precedent. "Open this gate to your king, Mowbray!"

"For yer own good, Majesty, I will not!" repeated Sir Philip, who knew that after this the king would certainly put him to death, even if he opened the gate immediately. He was finished in London. There was no going back.

"I *will* lend ye a guide to show ye a way around the Brus and back to Falkirk," he offered.

The king seethed. The king sighed and cursed the damn Scot for holding his castle against him. There was nothing that could be done to cajole Mowbray into removing the bar from the gate. On the other hand, Mowbray had given Edward a face-saving out; he could say that he fled Stirling to avoid being imprisoned there by the Scots, who were no doubt riding to capture him as he stood.

"Send out your guide," conceded the king.

"Very well, Sire," agreed Mowbray, glad that he didn't have to dodge arrows and thrown maces to thwart the king.

From the two hundred foot height of Stirling Edward looked back toward the battlefield where he knew the fighting was still raging though he couldn't see it. His heart said to return and fight, but if he were captured it would be worse than death for the warrior king with so much weighty family baggage to carry.

The guide emerged from the small postern gate leading a pale horse which he mounted to follow them back down the steep roadway to the village, and from there to show the king the route around the western side of King's Park and Cockshot Hill. The western trail was far from the fighting and on blessedly firm ground.

Macgregor, one of the men assigned to the village guard to see the garrison stayed penned inside, observed the direction in which the English were traveling and got aboard a horse and hied for the battlefield.

Sir Thomas Grey, Neil Campbell's prisoner, sat as he agreed to do, at the top of the hill. From there he had an objective view of the battle like few others. There were times during the fray where he felt compelled to break his word and fly into the Scots to sever their hold on the terrain. At other times, when he saw his English comrades being slain, he felt only sadness, and guilt that he had allowed himself to be captured. In the end he sat stunned, lost in a temporary inner world, his mind masking the horrors of the worst of the battle.

The killing was not done yet, though the field was heavily littered with the bodies of the brave. It no longer mattered to them whether they were Scots or English, all their ambitions for this earth were stilled.

Not far from the feet of his destrier, Robert saw an English nobleman struggling to get to a single elbow. His face and hands were so bloody they showed no sign of original skin. His eyes could not see for the blood that was liberally spread across him from the top of his head, down his white tabard decorated with a red crenellated cross. Robert could not place the symbol but saw the knight wore red spurs. He stepped down from his destrier and knelt beside the man.

"What is yer name, Sir Knight?" he asked.

Andrew came to the scene sitting his horse and looked down upon the man, who was blinded to whom he spoke but sputtered, "Robert... de Reymes."

Robert nodded and he remembered where he had seen the shield before. He put his arm around the man's shoulders to make him rest more comfortably.

"Did... we win the battle?" asked Reymes hoarsely, a deep rattle down in his throat.

"We did, Milord," answered the king, not considering his say to be a lie.

Reymes offered a slight smile before he went limp, and Robert laid him back to the earth from which he had struggled so hard to rise just moments earlier. It seemed to Robert that the man was at blessed peace.

"Who was he, Sire?" asked Andrew mournfully.

"We used his manor house north of Corbridge," said Robert. "His shield hung beside the fireplace."

"I recollect it now," said Andrew, sighing deeply. "The merchant from London."

"Aye," said Robert. He then stood and began to walk the killing field.

Christina came to the king and grabbed him around his neck and kissed him on his lips. She had seen him as she was tending some of the wounded atop the hill. Their salty tears mingled between them as he hugged her in return. Suddenly she drew back and shouted, "Ye have beaten the English, Robbie!!"

Robert shyly smiled. "Aye, woman, we have!"

Nigel came from his horse and hugged his mother.

Seeing Andrew watching them, Christina waved for him to join in, but he shook his head. Fighting the tears back he turned his horse and sauntered off downhill to where the warriors were cooling off with water and wine and swapping stories of heroism that would last for generations. He dismounted and hunkered among the men and listened.

Lord Pembroke went in search of his contingent of three hundred or so Welshmen, brought to the battle from his earldom. He found them huddled together on the south side of the massed infantry. Their half-naked bodies and bare feet showed they had dressed for a war that was already lost.

"Lord Pembroke!!" said Uther, their Chieftain, who was named after the father of Arthur Pendragon.

"Gather our men, we must leave... now!" directed Pembroke harshly.

"But we have seen no battle as yet, Milord!" protested Uther, his eyes wide with questions about the day.

"The battle is done," said the earl, "We have lost all. The king has left the field and gone home!"

Uther's eyes widened even more at the news. He could not believe the grand English army had been beaten! *What size army does the King of Scots have that could win over the English?* he wondered.

"Get our men on their feet before the Scots get here and capture us!" insisted Pembroke.

"Will they eat us?" asked Uther.

"You'll wish they had," replied Pembroke, a lie to rush them on.

"UP!!" shouted Uther and the men of Pembroke were on their feet, spears in hand, ready to fight.

Pembroke led the procession southward toward Bothwell Castle.

Other infantry regiments saw Lord Pembroke leaving with his contingent. They had witnessed many of their comrades' attempts to escape through the land of the pools, and had watched most fail. Some cursed the Scots for making the English fight on such a poor piece of ground, as if it were solely an evil notion on the part of the Scots and their own leaders had no say in it.

The Welsh archers, who had fought so bravely for Edward the younger all morning, followed Pembroke and his vassals south, having found kinship with those lads because of their common decent. Both groups had a cultural memory, passed down from their elders, of having been beaten severely by the English infantry a generation before during the age of the old Edward. It was he who brought down the last true Prince of Wales and gave the title to his son, the very same man for whom they had fought that morning.

Left to fend for themselves the majority of men remaining on the field were soon afflicted with a feeling of panic. They didn't find drowning a pleasurable prospect, yet dying at the axe blade of a maniacal Scot was equally horrifying.

"Let's just walk back the way we came. We'll get to Wark afore long," suggested one infantryman.

"I'll go!" shouted a third, having no better notion of what to do.

A great roar arose from the anxious men, and about a thousand set their feet back on the path that had brought them to the forsaken land of the Scots.

Hearing the shout, Robert the Brus was reminded that there were certainly thousands more English about, and that they were potentially dangerous if turned to any kind of command.

"Post sentries on the burn crossin's," he ordered, and no sooner had he spoken than Thomas pointed out a rider from the north.

The Macgregor from Stirling village was hieing fast in his direction.

"My King! My King!!" he shouted very loud and excitedly.

Robert raised his hand so the man would stop or at least slow. "I'm the king, what d'ye want?"

"The English king left Stirlin' just afore I did!" he gasped as he and his horse tried to catch their breaths.

"Left?" asked Robert, and his first instinct was to prepare for an attack.

"He came... he left," answered Macgregor, "and all who came with him."

"And the castle garrison?"

"Remain on the hill, Sire."

"Damn!" said Robert foully, though that probably meant there would be no attack.

"What's wrong?" asked Christina.

"King left Stirlin'," said Robert.

"Good riddance, says I," remarked Christina.

"I had hoped he would remain there, but he was too smart to get lock-holed," remarked Robert. "Nigel, get on yer horse right away and find James Douglas for me."

"Ye want him here?" asked Nigel, mounting the palfrey as he spoke.

"I do, and quick!!" emphasized Robert.

"Aye, My King," the boy said and slapping the reins against his horse's rump, galloped downhill toward where the warriors laid about on the grass.

"What's yer name lad?" Robert asked the messenger.

"Macgregor, Milord."

"Ye did well, Macgregor. Now, go back to Stirlin' and keep a watchful eye on what happens next," instructed the king.

"Aye, Sire," said Macgregor smiling, well pleased with himself for getting a 'well done' from the king.

Within minutes James Douglas came to Robert, dressed for battle and fully ready to do Robert's bidding.

"Jemmy, the English four or five hundred are hiein' south with their king... toward Falkirk, I figure," explained Robert. "Take yer fresh cavalry, and draw volunteers from Keith's bunch, and get after them!"

"My few after five hundred?" asked Douglas, raising one eyebrow inquisitively.

"The rest I want to stay with me, here," said Robert climbing aboard his destrier, "Might be they hain't done fightin' as yet."

Douglas flew uphill where his thirty-two men stood with their horses. "My Horse!!" he shouted quickly.

Soon emerged his men on horseback holding the reins to his horse. "Been waitin' on ye, Milord," grinned his second in command.

"Might wish ye hadn't," said Douglas wheeling his horse toward Keith's contingent.

"Take any ye like," said Keith, "I'm told to stay."

"I ken that," said Douglas. He shouted his need for volunteers and Graham was the first to come forward.

"Hain't yer woman 'bout to give ye a bairn?" asked Douglas.

"'Bout," he nodded.

"Then ye'll stay," said James Douglas.

"Take my Templars," said Graham, "Only five of us left."

"That, I'll do," replied Douglas knowing them to be particularly well trained for the hard-riding task at hand.

Seeing the men gathering, MacKie guessed their purpose and came straightaway to offer his hand and his bow to Douglas' service, but Douglas noticed the archer's quiver was empty.

"Ye would be of little use without arrows, Archer!"

"Get some, I will," said MacKie. "Have ye a horse for me, Milord?"

"Take this one," said Graham, handing MacKie the reins to the horse he had led into battle tied to the tail of his own. "It was good luck for me."

MacKie smiled and took the horse to find usable arrows.

Another twenty-five men volunteered as well, and all got aboard their horses and rode away down the Roman road toward Falkirk, where they hoped they could at least harass the English fugitives.

Among the English thousands milling about below the Bannok were King Edward's poet, Friar Baston, who sat on the seat of a nearby wain rather than the fouled ground, and Sir John de Foxley, a minor baron from Berkshire, sickened to distraction over the loss of the battle. They watched the chaos developing within the leaderless soldiery, and both knew most would be uselessly slaughtered if someone didn't give them direction.

The baron looked at the priest, who undoubtedly would not know how to get the men motivated to leave the wains of food and wines to attack, and so climbed himself upon the back of the wain and spoke to those nearest him.

"Men of England, hear me! We have come too far not to be given the chance to smite our enemies!" Hardly anyone paid attention to his words, and they with naught but lethargy. He could see the will to fight had gone from them, and he would have to give them reason to join him in another effort against the foe.

"We shall go into history as the greatest army in the world... and as the men who were defeated by a force far less than half our size, if we do nothing."

"As you said, Milord, we had no chance to join the battle!" shouted a man in the small group gathered to hear him. "How can we be blamed for losin' it?"

"You and I know we were never called to fight, but when we march home, our neighbors and kinsmen will hear otherwise... all they will know is that we came to the field and the enemy defeated us!" More faces stopped and looked up at him standing on the wain. Others noticed a small crowd had gathered and came to see why, and soon, he had a couple of hundred men hearing his words, though without much enthusiasm.

"You may sit on your haunches here in this filth and wait for some Scot to come across the stream with his pike or his battleaxe and put an end to your sorry life for you, or you can stand like men and refuse to be put to death like an injured gelding!" The men around him began to get roused by his words, and their desire to live and fight grew greater than their fear that the Scots would kill them all.

"Your earls, many of them, have been killed in battle with the other knights! Some have left you here to die, without having called you to fight for your king!" Shouts of anger arose from within the crowd as the baron spoke convincingly of their mistreatment. "But you now have a say in what becomes of you! You have a knight before you who can lead you into a courageous stand for your king and England!"

Many of the men cheered, and the audience grew to many hundreds as more and more men joined the throng.

"King Edward has left the field and gone to Castle Stirlin' until he can return to lead us from this godforsaken place! If they can, the Scots will surround the castle and take him captive! He is our king! Come with me, and rally to his defense!" he shouted.

As more men gathered and needed to understand what was afoot, the soldiers talked among themselves and one of them shouted back to Foxley. "What can we do to protect the king?! We have no horses and no officers!"

John de Foxley was much encouraged, not that he had a thought-out plan at all, but that he could keep the fight against King Robert alive.

"I know a back way to the castle... one that will not cross the battlefield!" proclaimed Foxley and waved his arm to show the followers which way to set their feet. "Pick up your arms and your foodstuffs and follow me!" So about three thousand men-at-arms followed John, Baron Foxley, west around the back side of Cockshot Hill where they turned north. Unbeknownst to any man among them, King Edward and his escort had earlier headed south and escaped along the same pathway.

There were still thousands more who wandered leaderless with no idea of how to get home, but that was what was uppermost in their minds. Many lamented that they should have departed with Lord Pembroke, but alas, that opportunity was long past.

"What will we do?" asked the Friar aloud to himself as he clutched the only possession that meant anything to him at that moment: his pouch containing quills, ink and parchment, instruments with the potential of being a repository for his mind, which he considered exceptional and worth leaving to posterity.

He wasn't expecting an answer to his rhetorical question but suddenly a voice came from below him. "I'll tell you what!"

The Friar turned toward the voice, "Sir Marmaduke," he greeted, relieved to have one of his acquaintance join him in this desolation.

Marmaduke de Tweng climbed onto the team-less wagon. Its cargo of fine heavy furniture, destined for a Scottish castle somewhere in the highlands of Moray, had been scattered and broken by frustrated men. Lacking direction, they took umbrage against their lieges for leaving them to maunder about ineptly while waiting to be slaughtered by the exuberant Scots, and were as much a danger to themselves.

"What will you do, My Dear Baron," said Baston sarcastically.

"Givin' up my barony, My Friar," he said without a whimper.

"Feared to lead men back to the safety of their English homes?" asked Baston.

"Brus will get his fill of killin' on yon side of the stream," explained Marmaduke, "If he gets no trouble from this side he'll just let them wither away."

"You think so?" asked Baston a brow raised.

"You've sure changed from your scaredy self, a'sittin' in the bog a while ago," said Marmaduke smiling slightly.

The friar paused a long while, then admitted, "No, Baron. I have not changed. I am yet fearful that Brus will pike my head outside his... cot," he said disparagingly, adding, "I understand he pulls down every castle he captures."

"I would advise that you look quick at Stirlin', Friar, for I understand it belongs to Brus, now that the battle is lost to him." He and the priest looked to the north where the castle sparkled in the afternoon sun atop its massive pedestal. "It will no doubt be razed. Did you see what he left of Edinburgh?"

"Yes, I did. A pity. And it grants me no faith that he shall have mercy on any of us!"

"No man I know is without fear, Friar. It is a matter of findin' where it is that each man is weakest, then he can be made to fear. Even knowin' Latin can't help that," said Marmaduke, a slight hint of admission on his part slipped into the tone of his voice.

"You know Latin! Where did you study?" asked Baston.

"Cambridge," the baron answered, "Was fixin' to be a priest, once upon a time."

Friar Baston smiled. "Figurin' on givin' up the barony and takin' back up with the church?"

"Figure on survivin'," was the answer. He loosed his wide belt and slipped his tabard off, over his head. He took a long look at the three green symbolic popinjays and red bar on the white linen cloth, then wadded it in a ball and threw it on the ground.

"How easily you shed your titles, Sir Marmaduke," said the friar.

"Shed yours," suggested the baron.

"Without mine... I confess I am completely naked," he replied raising a brow.

Marmaduke started to pull at his chain mail leggings. They were heavy, it was hot, and he felt he had no more use for them. Then he said, "I was here before, you know."

"Before what?" asked Baston.

"Years back… fightin' the Scots," reminisced Marmaduke, "We tried to run then… from Stirlin' Bridge, but the Scots were hidin' yonder in the Torwood, a'waitin'…"

"You bested them?"

"We… I escaped," he admitted, then added to explain his misspoken word, "We lost a great many that day, and this day as well. But not from a lack of bravery… from poor witted decisions and vanity!"

Sir James 'the Black' Douglas, having left Bannok by the Roman road through the Torwood, expected to catch up to King Edward's company somewhere around Falkirk. He thought the king and his men would spend the night there, as they had two days earlier. The pursuers were no farther than a hundred yards into the wood when Douglas suddenly threw his hand up and pulled rein.

Straight in front of them was a contingent of near eighty men spread across the road and set for battle.

"In the name of King Robert, stand aside!" shouted Douglas.

Their leader sallied his horse forward. "Ye men of Robert the Brus?"

"We are!" came back Douglas, "and ye are impedin' the king's business!"

"I am Sir Lawrence Abernethy of Roxburghshire," said the leader.

It took Douglas a moment to realize who the man was. "Ye are a Scot fightin' for the English?"

The men on both sides bristled and made themselves ready for war.

"We *were* comin' to the battle," said Abernethy.

"Battle's done with," said Douglas, "Ye're too late… 'less ye want to fight the likes of us!"

"And who won?" prudently asked Sir Lawrence.

"We won!!" growled Douglas, "Now, out of our way or we'll consider ye enemies!" At that he pulled his sword, prepared to back up his order.

"But we are Scots!" argued Abernethy.

"Turned Scots," spat back Douglas, high on the glory of success. Sir James edged his horse closer to Abernethy's group as his men came tight to him and stood ready with their weapons. "Fight or get out of our way!"

Lawrence Abernethy dismounted to defuse the confrontation.

Douglas sallied closer.

"If King Robert has won the battle, I and my vassals would come to his peace," offered Sir Lawrence.

"Time is wastin' away!" said Douglas anxious to get back to his pursuit.

"Time for what?" asked Abernethy.

"We are after King Edward who ran from the battle... tucked tail, he did," said Douglas with serious mien.

"Then allow me and my four score to accompany ye in yer chase," offered Sir Lawrence.

"Get on yer knees and swear allegiance to King Robert... and I shall consider yer request," said Douglas in quick syllables.

"I offer ye my hand in friendship... and to show my sincerity I have offered to help ye chase King Edward. I also deny him as my liege lord, henceforth!" The stalwart man looked the younger knight in the eye and made no move to bend his knee.

Douglas thought a moment. The deal was the same, but lacked a yielding to Douglas' will by getting to his knees. That took courage, of which Douglas was a great admirer. Further, Douglas realized that it would take more time to force the issue, letting Edward get farther away from them. He slammed his sword into its sheath and the potential ordeal was finished.

"Let's go keep England's king from his slumber!"

MONDAY, NOON ~ 24th JUNE
BANNOK

The men from Ross lifted the mangled body of Sir Walter from its death place on the battlefield onto a small pallet. Isabella de Ross stood beside Edward Brus and wept bitter tears as Sir Hugh tried to remain stalwart at their brother's death.

"I wish this day had ne'er been!!" cried Edward Brus, "Oh, that it could be undone!!"

No one had witnessed Edward Brus brought to tears before. The news of his three brothers brutally executed did not as much. Never had the death of *any* person brought a tear to his eye, but the death of Walter, Edward's dear friend and the son of an erstwhile enemy, had opened wide the flow of tears as if for all such sorrows he had ever known in his life.

"We will always miss ye," said Isabella, reaching out and running her fingers along the tattered silver lions on his tabard as the bier passed before her.

"Father would have been proud of ye," softly spoke his brother Hugh as the body passed him. Hugh saw his brother fall and tried to fight his way to save him. It was no wonder that he felt guilt, and anger because he couldn't prevent it from happening.

It was decided that they would leave that afternoon for Ross with the corpse of Walter. Earl Hugh led the procession, with Walter carried across the back of the destrier on which he had arrived, followed by Isabella and the warriors of Ross. Having lost seven soldiers in the battle, the earl decided to escort their bodies back to Ross as well.

Edward was left on his own to grieve.

Robert grieved for Walter's death as well, for the young knight was an affable lad and a great warrior. However, his immediate concern was the thousands of roving hungry and angry English infantrymen yet thick in the vicinity of Bannok. As long as they were about, none was safe in purse or person.

"Thomas?" said Robert to his nephew.

"Aye, Rob?" replied Thomas coming closer to the king.

"Many wains of supplies and much wealth lie across the burn," said Robert.

"I ken," said Thomas, "...ye a'wantin' me to run off the English and take possession?"

The king nodded somberly.

Thomas Randolph gathered a contingent of about three hundred highlanders and proceeded across the burn.

Crossing the rushing stream on his horse, Thomas pulled a stout hemp rope across and tied the end around a large tree so that his men, all on foot, could follow him across holding to the rope and not be swept downstream.

The men formed up along the edge of the water and with as many unbroken spears as they could manage to glean from the battlefield, made their schiltrom.

"Here come the Scots," said Marmaduke.

Friar Baston looked up from his mumbled prayers and the string of rosary beads he kept pushing through his fingers one at a time. Neither of them had found reason to budge from their seats aboard the wain.

"I suppose I'll be a prisoner," said the Carmelite.

"If they don't eat you," teased Marmaduke.

Baston did not take to teasing very well and remained transfixed on the approaching hedgehog. He saw Thomas on horseback in front of the men, giving orders as they went.

The remaining English infantry, who had come to the battle under feudal mandate, fixed their weapons for action but none of them were interested in picking a fight that didn't affect them personally.

The English women, who had traveled to the battlefield with their soldier menfolk or as cooks, laundresses, and servants for the army, huddled off to themselves hoping the heathen Scots would not harm them.

In the midst of the English, Thomas stopped his men and ordered them to come to a circle as they had done with Clifford the day before.

From the back of his horse, Thomas directed his say toward the largest mixed group of English and Irish foot soldiers, "We are here to warn ye off the field or kill ye!" he firstly announced. "'Tis yer choice!"

The soldiers gathered closer together and shook their weapons mincingly.

He continued, "Any who want to go back to wives and families in England and wherever else, can do so at this moment. Take nothin' with ye save the clothes on yer backs!"

Marmaduke slipped from his seat on the wain. "Must leave ye now, Friend Friar," he said quietly. He went around to the back of the wain and took his chain coif and hauberk off and threw it into the dirt at the wheel. He rubbed mud on the handle of his sword and strapped it again about his waist. He had spent at least a quarter of a year's income from his lands for the chain mail but, on the other hand, paying ransom for a baron such as he would be far more costly, even if his wife was Lucia de Brus. With a wave to the priest, he calmly walked away.

Baston sat clutching his pouch close to his chest by wrapping both arms protectively around it. He stoically waited to see what misery would be heaped upon him as a prisoner of the Scots.

At the beginning of the battle, King Robert had sorrowfully watched as the young Sir Gilbert le Clair, Earl of Gloucester, fell. Robert's grandmother was of the le Clair family, and Elizabeth, his queen, was sister to Gilbert's wife, both daughters of the 'Red Earl' of Ulster. He had the youthful corpse taken to Saint Ninian's Kirk near the edge of New Park and properly laid out on a draped table.

The body of Sir Robert de Clifford was done the same, and the king had asked the Abbots to shrive the two English knights and attend to them appropriately. Other slain English nobles were taken reverently to the kirk and placed on benches beside their shields. The lesser ranked dead were stripped of everything and laid out naked on the ground in a line, ready for mass burial.

Robert ordered a cessation of killing and the beginning of taking prisoners for the purpose of ransom or free release, at his discretion.

The Scots women combed the battlefield for weapons of every kind, such as pike heads, swords, arrows or daggers, and anything else of value, including the fancy materials in the clothing of the dead knights.

Andrew kept his distance from the king and, being no longer his squire and at his constant beck, he got on his horse and went to investigate why there had been a fire at Cambuskenneth Abbey during the night. He would get a chance to talk about the battle with his friend Baldred, who was temporarily garrisoned, there.

King Robert understood the weight he had placed on the shoulders of his erstwhile squire. He felt the sense of parenthood in many ways but the lad was now a man and had the particularly ponderous question of stepping into his father's shoes to decide on his own. Andrew said nothing as he left, and Robert knew that it was best to let him go.

He then summoned his heartsick brother to send him on a mission to chase the earls of Hereford and Pembroke, possible hostages, who were traveling toward Bothwell Castle. His thinking was that Edward needed a challenge to ease the pain over losing his closest friend, Walter of Ross.

Walter FitzGilbert

ꟽONÐAY, ꟽIÐ-AꝽCERNOON – 24Ch JUNE
CASCLE BOChꟽELL

"Milord, the banner of the liege approaches," said Lewis.

Walter FitzGilbert was a large Scot in his mid-thirties and had served as constable of the English castle since Pembroke vacated the premises six years earlier. Situated in a horseshoe bend of River Clyde, the castle was about twenty-four miles south of Stirling. There was a large tower house donjon connected to a short curtain wall, and it to the smaller prison tower. Behind was a large bailey enclosed with a log fence closed by a simple swing gate. No surrounding curtain wall. No moat. The grand plan of its initiator was lost to history, thus the castle had never been completed.

"Sir Humphrey?" asked the constable.

"Aye, Milord... Sir Humphrey," repeated Lewis, the steward of the castle.

"Must be they've been to the Stirlin' battle a'ready," assumed Sir Walter, returning to his bench trying to put his mind together to welcome the earl.

"They *are* at yer gate," reminded Lewis.

"Aye," replied Walter, "at my gate."

"Shall I allow them entrance, Milord?"

"How many are there?" asked the constable.

"A great many," came back the steward.

"Open the gate and welcome Lord Hereford to his castle," said

Walter, suddenly standing again.

The limited garrison was called out to hail their English lord to his castle, and as trumpets sounded the gates swung wide for the Earl of Hereford and his fleeing hundreds.

FitzGilbert bowed low to the horsed figure before him. There were more than three hundred nobles and knights on horseback behind the earl expecting entrance, at least into the bailey where they could get something to eat or a relatively safe place to stay the night in a hostile land.

Exhausted, Humphrey de Bohun, Earl of Hereford, dismounted and stretched his aching back.

The Umfraville brothers were immediately behind the earl and dismounted as well.

"Milord. How many do we have seekin' shelter?" asked the warden.

"What, no welcome?" growled Humphrey.

"Of course, Milord Earl... welcome to Castle Bothwell," groveled FitzGilbert. "How may I serve Your Lordship?"

"We have had some mean days, FitzGilbert," said Humphrey.

"Then ye must rest, Milord," said the Scot and gave him bad news about the castle's limited resources, "... but I can accommodate... say... the barons among ye and... perhaps fifty others at the most."

"Sir Ingram?" called Humphrey.

"Aye, Milord," said Ingram as he approached Hereford.

"Cull out fifty knights by order of rank and tell the others they must go on to Carlisle for their rest," said the earl.

"Aye, Milord," replied the man and turned to do the earl's bidding.

"My solar, Constable," demanded Humphrey.

"I'll have Lewis clear my personal belongin's," said FitzGilbert, bowing.

Earl Humphrey didn't bother to acknowledge the constable's say but trudged up the steps and entered the keep and the great hall, on the first floor. The garrison's sleeping quarters were on the second floor, and on the third was the lord's solar.

Sir Walter frowned at Lewis to stir him to action. The steward's eyes widened in realization, and he ran after the earl to attend to his wants.

"Must have been a great victory to be won so quick," pried FitzGilbert.

Ingram de Umfraville grunted as he began to remove the saddle from his horse. "Ye got grooms?" he asked tersely.

"Aye, Milord," said Walter, "Have two. Send them to ye, I will."

Old Lord Thomas Berkeley, his son, Sir Maurice, and two grandsons arrived at the tower and behind them were Sir John Seagrave and Sir

Antony Lucy.

Walter looked as the tired men filed in to dismount and enter the keep. Their demeanor was not what he would have expected. Men celebrating an early, and thus easy, victory usually were outgoing and cheerful, even though tired. These barons and knights were silent and dour, and that set Walter FitzGilbert to thinking.

• •

Turned away from Castle Bothwell, the Hereford knights followed the river south through the Clyde Valley toward the English border and Castle Carlisle. Once out of the Clyde Valley, however, there were the "fells", rough country of the southern mountains they had to traverse before reaching the Annan Valley and the descent toward Solway Firth, beyond which lay Carlisle. Thus, after four or five days' travel, they would be relatively safe and able to nourish themselves and their horses.

The countryside was roused against them well before the knights reached Cumbria, and many who had survived the battle did not make it out of Scotland. As was the custom of the age, the local populace strove to do as much damage as possible to the losing army.

Lord Pembroke had been warned that Castle Bothwell was filled to capacity and would take in no more, and therefore continued pushing south along the same track as Hereford's knights. However, all of his Welsh followers were on foot, making the trek take far longer, and the hostility of the countryside grew more so as they walked toward home. Adding to the natural harshness of the region were the Borderers, who pursued and felled the English as they fled.

MONÔAY, MIÔ-AFTERNOON ~ 24th JUNE
ON THE ROAÔ EAST OF FALKIRK

When first it peeked over the hill at Bannok in the early morn, the sun was warm. As the hours drew the sun higher into the sky, the heat increased. By the middle of the afternoon the heat was unbearable, especially to those who were attempting to escape, or were in pursuit, on their hot, lathered horses.

King Edward and his entourage were hard at their whips and spurs as they went back down the same road they had come up two days earlier.

"We're killing our horses!" cried Henry de Beaumont.

"The Scots are fast on us," replied Edward. "We cannot let up!"

"We've got to stop, goddamn it!" argued Beaumont.

The king saw a small field off the right side of the road and swung his arm to indicate they would be stopping there. He drew rein on the far side of the cropland.

"You win," snapped Edward to Beaumont, though he knew the stop was needed, "We shall rest our horses!"

"Stream here!" shouted one of the knights leading his horse.

All the knights surrounded the field with a defensive perimeter to protect the king against their pursuers or local cotters out to punish the losing soldiery. To maintain the perimeter, the knights were only allowed to leave the line in small groups to water their thirsty horses.

The king looked across the field of wheat and the trampled areas where his contingent had ambled, and noticed how it was not unlike the fields of wheat at Bannok. His first notion was that he would never eat wheat again without its leaving the bitter taste of failure in his mouth. He silently scoffed at himself for such foolish imaginings. There was no failure on his part except that he had listened to poor advisors.

"How fortunate, Your Majesty!" sarcastically said Beaumont, very disappointed in failing to get his Scottish earldom. "We can drink, as well as rest."

The king glowered at the French adventurer, "How fortunate for you that I let you live," gainsaid the king punctuating his statement with a cruel half-smile.

Beaumont knew when to keep quiet about certain subjects, and an emotional, if somewhat jesting, threat of death from the king *was* one of those subjects.

The first half of the knights watered their horses while the king and his party rested.

"Why do we run from these Scots bastards?" asked Beaumont carefully crafting his words while still angry at the king's misadventure.

"You are a fool, Sir Henry," said Edward, "How could we possibly fight with merely five hundred knights?"

"But Majesty, how many are giving us chase?" sparred Beaumont.

"Doesn't matter," said Edward, "The countryside is alive with angry Scots... we cannot fight them all."

Sir Henry looked about uneasily to see if he could espy any of the 'angry Scots' the king mentioned, but none were visible to him. "There must be some reason why the men pursuing us are not attacking!" insisted Sir Henry.

"Take a count, Henry!" growled Edward, keeping his voice down, "You'll find we are fewer than we were when we left Stirlin'... I think they trail us and kill any who fall behind!"

Sir Hugh le Despenser came to Edward and offered his horse, already watered, to the king. The king accepted the young man's offer and changed mounts and was thus able to keep his horseback vigil. The horse he had ridden from the field of battle yet wore the caparisons with Gloucester's heraldic symbols, showing it to be from one of the dead earl's knights. All such trappings were removed from the horse and he was led to water.

Sir James Douglas and Sir Lawrence Abernethy halted their own animals when they saw Edward resting his. There was little they could do except keep pushing when possible and resting when Edward rested.

King Edward suddenly began to laugh almost uncontrollably.

Beaumont frowned at the sight and went to water his mount.

Sir Hugh returned with the king's destrier, leading it by the reins. "Your horse, My King," he said quietly.

Edward characteristically turned on his favorite, "Why can't you be more like Piers?!" he ranted. "Piers would never have let me fall into such a trap!!"

"Piers is dead, My King," said Hugh in an innocent, reverent voice.

"Piers is not dead!" continued Edward, "Never say that again!" He dismounted from le Despenser's horse and stood, up to his knees in wheat. He fretfully kicked at the stalks as if he were mad. He pulled at the tops of the grain and threw the pitiful pieces to the wind.

He then slumped onto the glebe and threw his hands over his face in desperation, apparently crying.

His knights knew better than to pay him mind, though some of them looked at him askance as the horse watering continued.

"What ye reckon's a'goin' on?" asked Abernethy watching from the far edge of the field camouflaged by a line of trees.

"King's gone daft, I figure," said Douglas.

"Good time to attack them?" the knight asked.

"We're not goin' to attack, Sir Lawrence," said Douglas, "We're just escortin' them to the border."

"No attack?" said Abernethy, his brows knitted. "How about capturin' the king?"

"Ye want, have at it," said Douglas and Abernethy smiled, understanding his meaning and kept quiet.

Shortly afterward, the king composed himself and stood, leaking from his eyes and his nose as he wiped both with a single swipe of the tail of his bloody surcoat. He climbed into the saddle of the un-trapped steed and sat upright, looking every bit the regal personage.

"There shall be two disappointed at my survival," he announced.

"Two, My King?" asked Hugh who had little to say or do during the king's fit.

"My queen, of course... and that loathsome cousin, Lancaster," he said smiling slightly at the irony, trying to wrestle some victory from his utter defeat.

"And you are not put out with me?" asked Hugh in all guilelessness.

"Not you, Dear Brother," said Edward, "You are the light in my world." He reached out his hand and touched Hugh's cheek tenderly. The young man's countenance shone brightly again, knowing that he was not in disfavor.

"In which direction are we heading from here, My King?" the youthful knight asked, having been lost ever since they left Stirlingshire.

"For Dunbar, Sir Hugh. Earl Patrick, I hope, has not turned against us like that goddamned Mowbray," cursed the king. He then took account of his knights; all had watered their horses and were standing, back in travel array.

Henry Beaumont anxiously returned to the side of the king and pointed out the farmers who had begun to appear along the edge of the wood with farm weapons in hand.

"Hurry!!" said Edward not wanting to get trapped by an irate mob.

"Is this all the resting these poor beasts get?" Beaumont asked incredulously.

"For now," said Edward turning the head of his horse. "I had rather ride the damned horse to death than to chance being captured by Scottish barbarians. And there are simply no places to rest thoroughly 'til we get to Castle Dunbar on the coast."

"What about those supply ships at Leith?" asked Beaumont.

"Set sail when we left Edinburgh, I should imagine," groused Edward, and he whipped his horse to the fore of his troop.

Monday, Mid-afternoon – 24th June
Bannok

King Robert stayed on the battlefield, maundering all afternoon. Some of his men wanted to leave with their booty, others were just tired and wanted to nap where they sat. Concerned that there were yet many still hostile English in the neighborhood, he held all to the battlefield who were able to fight.

The line of dead English bodies grew longer as the day wore on. The line of dead Scots was remarkably short. Sad for the loss on both sides, Robert was, but grateful to God that the Scots had paid the lesser price.

In the shallow hollow on the far side of Cockshot Hill in New Park lay Dianna. In the small lean-to tent she writhed with the labor pains as the mid-wife busily swabbed her brow with a cooling cloth and mumbled prayers in a kind of melodic litany, occasionally breaking to give some terse direction to her.

Sir David Graham stood not far away. Templar life had not prepared him for the likes of this duty. Associating with women and the shaving of beards were both frowned upon by the sect and for the life of him he could not understand why either of those things made a difference in his abilities to kill Saracens in the Holy Land. When he met Dianna in Aberdeen, he had no intention of having a family, or of having a woman as part of his life.

She, on the other hand, knew from their first encounter that she loved him and she pursued him to every place he went and every battle he fought. She cooked for him and his fellow ex-Templars, she washed his clothes, and she was a comfort to him at night. After some time Graham came to realize how he would miss her if she were to suddenly be taken from him, and he found himself praying as earnestly, as ever he had, that she and the bairn would both live through the ordeal.

On the grainfield, there were about thirty local men who came with empty hands to Robert and fell on their knees before him. The man in the front stood, but with head still bowed, asked, "King Robert, we have come to beg a boon of ye."

"Aye," replied Robert, "Are ye from hereabouts?"

The man was surprised that the king had any interest in the lot of them. "The corn ye now stand on was planted by our hands."

Robert looked down at the blood soaked wheat beneath his feet and knew their winter staple had been ruined. "Aye, yer wheat is of nae promise this year." The king looked at the faces of the men, and said,

"On 'tother side of the Bannok are wains and wagons left by the English, some full of foodstuffs. Ye men and yer families take what ye need to get through the year. Tell Lord Thomas that I sent ye. D'ye ken?"

"Aye, Sire! Thank ye!" several of the men said with big smiles, their heads bobbing up and down in wee bowing motions.

Robert then noticed some of the women behind the men were whispering to one another, and he asked the apparent spokesmen, "What are they saying?"

"They are saying that ye are the mysterious stranger that would sometimes visit us in secret. We reckoned ye were from the little people," he said, and Robert laughed aloud.

"Do I look like I'm from the *little* people?" he grinned.

"We reckoned ye might be their giant god come among us," he answered, "... ye appeared and disappeared so quickly!" The man kept his eyes cast downward.

"I am no god... but have we taken care of yer boon to her likin'?" said Robert, aware that the day was slipping away and there were things he had to do.

"Nae, My King. We have nae asked the boon yet," the leader said.

"Oh?" Robert looked puzzled.

"Nae, Sire... we came about our houses...?"

"Yer houses?"

"Aye, Sire." said the villein.

"What about yer houses?"

"They're laying about in yon pool lands," said the man, "or parts of 'em are."

Robert looked at the pows and for the first time recognized window shutters, doors, and thatch strewn about. "Yon's yer houses?" asked Robert pointing.

"We'd like to have 'em back, Sire," said the man bowing low, "... if ye need them nae longer."

Robert smiled at the irony. "Take them as ye will," he said, seeing the Macgregor hieing toward him once again.

The group all bowed low to the king before they turned toward the swamp where the English had left parts of the cotters' houses spread across the watery lowland.

Macgregor stopped and scanned the field. When he espied the king he rode directly to him. "My King! My King!" he shouted loudly.

Robert seized the reins of the man's horse as he slung himself from the saddle. "King Robert!" he shouted excitedly, again gasping for air after the hasty ride from Stirling village.

"I'm right here, Macgregor," said Robert.

"There's thousands of them!!" said Macgregor, puffing.

"Thousands?" asked Robert, "Thousands of what?"

"English, Sire! Attackin' the castle!" he said loudly. "We all fled from the village!!"

"I don't ken yer say," replied Robert.

"They're in the trees and bushes all o'er the side of castle hill," he explained. "Protectin' their king, they say!"

Robert again smiled at the irony. "They figure Edward is holed up in the castle?"

"Aye," said Macgregor, "so we reckoned ere we ran off from the guard duty."

"We'll see to them," promised Robert. "Ye go yonder and get a bite to eat."

"Thank ye, My King," said the Macgregor as his eyes followed the king downhill to where Sir Ian Cameron and Sir Alexander Fraser stood among the corpses. Many of the men on both sides were familiar to one or both of them, and they were philosophizing over life and death and the rarely innocuous moments between.

The bairn's first cry caused David de Graham's eyes to widen with the sudden realization that the child was alive, born of his own flesh. He smiled and strode quickly to the tent where Dianna had been laboring for so many hours. As he peeked into the tent, the midwife held the child by its ankles and flopped it onto the mother's belly. She then tied a string tightly around the umbilical and, with a sharp little knife taken from her wooden box of medicines, cut the cord and separated the child from its mother.

"Ye got yer laddie, Graham," said Dianna weakly.

"I reckon," said David awkwardly, "Ye be alright?"

"I reckon," she said, and closed her eyes in much needed sleep.

The midwife wiped the child clean and wrapped it in a soft linen blanket. Handing him to the Graham she smiled with reverence, "New life for the old world."

In the absence of Thomas Randolph the king ordered Cameron and Fraser to round up as many highlanders as they could and hie to Stirling village with Macgregor to drive off the English hanging around the castle base.

He then found Sir Gilbert de la Haye and sent him to Castle Stirling to negotiate with the English and convince them to go home... and never come back.

CRONÒÀY, LÀCE-ÀFCERNOON – 24ch JUNE
BOCHWELL

Suspicious as to what had happened in Stirlingshire, the castellan of Bothwell had sent his steward, Lewis, to carry the news of a small feast to the sixty-seven men he had allowed into the castle. The banquet was being prepared, Lewis was to say, in honor of the gallant victory of the morning at Stirlingshire. FitzGilbert's thinking was that someone along the way would confirm or deny the purpose for the dinner.

Lewis found he was only a half dozen personages down his list when he spoke with Richard de Umfraville, lord of the Scottish earldom of Angus, who looked as if he were the next hog in the pen to be slaughtered.

"Supper?" queried Sir Richard indolently.

"Aye," said Lewis, "In honor of yer victory today... or yesterday."

The hefty man smiled sadly. "There was no victory, Lad."

Just as FitzGilbert had imagined, all was not well. "The Scots trounced ye?" Lewis attempted to clarify the statement, but the door to the earl's small quarters slowly closed in the steward's face.

Lewis quickly went to FitzGilbert with the tidbit.

"We shall go along with the supper anyway," said the constable. "Continue with the announcements... except don't say it's in honor of anything. Tell them it will be soon."

"I don't reckon Lord Angus will be a'comin'," said Lewis.

"Keep a careful note on who comes and who remains in their quarters," ordered FitzGilbert, "and tell no one ye know anything about the battle."

. .

When the supper was close to serving, a squire went through the halls of the nobles' individual quarters and the knights' barracks quarters ringing his small bell to let the visitors know the time was nigh. Lord Hereford, the barons, the thanes, and the highly ranked knights were anxious to enjoy their first hot, sit-down meal since leaving Wark-on-Tweed a week earlier. The food smelled delicious, the castle's beds were relatively soft, and the air was fresh, unlike the previous night spent on the carse at Bannok.

The men's spirits were strengthened.

As the dinner guests wandered into the hall the music began.

Since it was his castle, Lord de Bohun of Hereford naturally sat in the center at the head table on the dais, and as expected, Lord de Umfraville of Angus kept to his room, but his chair was nevertheless placed at the table. His brother Ingram de Umfraville, sat beside the empty chair and to his right Sir Antony Lucy and Sir John Seagrave took their seats. To Hereford's other side were places for the Berkeleys, father and son, and an empty chair for Walter FitzGilbert, the warden of Castle Bothwell.

Other tables for knights of descending ranks were set along the sides of the great hall, creating a horseshoe shape with the head table connecting the sides.

Wine was poured into the goblets and gradually the general hubbub of conversation strengthened. Sir Walter arrived and greeted his liege with a generous bow from across the table. Hereford was glum and didn't wonder why his constable had not immediately taken his place in the empty chair.

The nervous castellan walked to the middle of the hall and stood at the center of the horseshoe arrangement. Once there he gave the signal for the musicians on the far end of the hall to cease their playing. The knights around, expecting an announcement from their host, paid some token attention.

"Stirlin'shire… I ken… went poorly for ye," Walter began speaking tensely, "…and was won by the Scots…" The hall fell totally silent.

Earl Humphrey had his mind on the first day of the conflict and the death of his nephew. It was but a skirmish, really, and in hindsight the earl could see that Henry had made a poor gamble and lost, paying the debt with his life. No one could possibly blame the de Bohun family for young Henry's rash action. Though a pity, it was but his own folly.

Walter stood in the quiet hall with some apprehension, while many of the tired knights wondered why he bothered to speak if that was what he had to talk about.

"I wish to say, Milords, … that ye are henceforth my prisoners!"

The word 'prisoners' came alive around the hall, as it was the trigger word for his castle garrison to come simultaneously to the backs of the unsuspecting earls and barons with drawn weapons and prick their necks with the sharp points. The doorways were suddenly filled with fully armed men of the garrison, including archers with bowstrings drawn, ready to let fly at the first man who drew a weapon.

There were then no doubts of the castellan's intentions, or of their collective powerlessness.

Lord Hereford's eyes widened in fear and anger when the cold, emotionless dagger blade touched the back of *his* neck and his sword and dagger were quickly taken from their sheaths and from him.

The hall and its nearly seventy knights were seized within a single instant.

The earl stood as daringly as he could with a dagger pricking his neck. He pounded his fist to the table and shouted, "Treason! You whoresons! 'Tis treason pure and simple!!"

No one disagreed with the earl. It was treason against him, though not against Scotland, the once sovereign country returning to its power as an independent state. Walter FitzGilbert had seen a chance to capture the castle for the Brus, and garner favor in the eyes of the winner of the second battle for Stirling. In a moment, the serving squires were going about in the hall, removing the weapons from the sides of the seated Englishmen.

At the same time, men of the garrison had been sent to strip the weapons from Earl Richard, who yet fitfully worried in his quarters. Two other English knights were captured whilst sleeping in their open quarters on the second floor.

"I want the word of ev'ry man here that he will not try to escape, so that we can be chivalrous about this unpleasantness," said FitzGilbert in a voice grown louder and more confident. "Those who will not give their word, on his honor as a knight, will be allowed residence in the prison tower, and naught but bread and water for their suppers."

There was a loud grumble among the English knights, but as Walter circumnavigated the hall there was not a single prisoner who refused, either to give his word, or Sir Walter's hospitality.

"We can all eat now," said FitzGilbert as the weapons were taken from the hall and a heavy guard set on its portals.

• •

"Sir Walter... Lord Galloway and two hundred royal knights await down the hill, out of arrow range," said Lewis as he came to the castle warden.

"Lord Galloway!?" questioned FitzGilbert, his mind awhirl. "Ye mean Edward Brus?"

"Aye, Milord," replied Lewis, "'tis the king's own brother."

"Have my horse saddled!" said Sir Walter. "I shall ride down to meet him."

Within moments Sir Walter and his steward were sauntering down the hill before the castle. There Sir Edward Brus and his men impatiently waited, and Bothwell's archers lined the short length of the curtain wall in case the business took an unexpected turn.

"Hereford within?" were the first words from Edward's mouth.

Walter was taken aback. He thought at least there would be some polite conversation before he made his startling proclamation of such a grand array of prisoners. He stammered as he reworked his mind and at last simply said, "Aye, Milord!"

"Sandstone won't burn," said Edward, looking up at the oddly incomplete castle, "...so we'll lay siege and starve ye to the bone if ye do not surrender yer castle!" To his surprise, the castle warden relaxed and smiled.

"No need for such dramatic upheaval, Milord Edward," said FitzGilbert, "As of this night, I pledge fealty to yer brother, King Robert. He shall henceforth be my liege lord."

"What say ye?" asked Edward, frowning. He had expected a fight, not a capitulation.

Sir Walter stepped down from his horse and knelt on the ground before Edward.

"I give ye my oath that I accept Robert de Brus, King of Scots, as my liege from this day forward," said the castellan. He then asked, "Do ye require any further words, Milord?"

"Not if ye hold to the ones ye said," answered Edward. "I have come to yer castle because we're after the Earl of Hereford, Lord de Bohun. Is he within?"

"He is, Sire, as are right about three score knights and several more nobles," said FitzGilbert, rising to stand again. Edward grinned and looked at his nearer followers with a smile that told them what he had previously said was now confirmed. He then turned back to the constable.

"I figured I'd find him here since he holds this castle for the English... but that is all about to change. I am told that Lord Pembroke hied this way as well... is he in yer castle?"

"Nae, Sire. He ne'er arrived here, but we could nae have given him entry if he had. We have no more room."

"Damn!" said Edward, disappointed that Aymer de Valence had slipped his grasp. He pulled his sword and asked FitzGilbert, "Where is Hereford within the castle, and what's the easiest way to get to him?"

"Ye should have nae difficulty, Milord... he is my prisoner," said Walter proudly.

"Prisoner?!" said Edward Brus in surprise.

"Since I have just pledged fealty to the king, Lord Brus," went on Walter, "he is our prisoner, whom I relinquish to ye, along with all his party, including Lord Angus... and about sixty-five others."

Edward smiled.

Malcolm Maclaine

cpoNÒAⱩ. lACE-AⱩCERNOON ~ 24ch JUNE
CASCLE SCIRLING

Baron John de Foxley arranged his soldiers in the trees and bushes lining the bottom of the basalt cliff. His initiative was to protect King Edward whom he though to be within the castle at the top of the hill.

Sirs Ian Cameron and Alexander Fraser had arrived with their contingents of highlanders to prevent the renegade troops from forming into a fighting force that would create another battle in which to fight. Robert was well satisfied with the day's work and felt there was no reason to shed more blood.

Sir Gilbert de la Haye arrived to negotiate with the rabble's leader.

"Ye reckon to knock some sense into these dolts?" asked the Cameron.

"Reckon to try," said Gilbert.

"Leader's name is Foxley," said Fraser, "A baron in his own right… says he's here to 'save' the king."

"Not thinkin' very clear, is he," said Gilbert.

"He doesn't ken that the king has fled the country," offered Cameron.

"Let me go negotiate with him," said Malcolm Maclaine as he patted the axe hanging from his saddle.

"Ye stay out of the fray," ordered Gilbert, adding with a grin, "'Til I tell ye to go whip his arse!" The men laughed at the drollery.

Suddenly the sounds of horses' hooves were heard beating the cobblestones on the hill above them.

"Mowbray's comin' down with a contingent!" said Haye.

"Ye men get yonder!" said Cameron, pointing to the roadway leading up through Stirling village to where stood the castle.

The Scots formed a phalanx across the road and meant to hold the way.

"The king comes to our rescue!" shouted Foxley for all his troops to hear.

Down the road came Sir Philip Mowbray and a mere half dozen knights.

Foxley watched as the knights drew rein short of the Scots' spearheads and stood their ground. "Where's the king?" Sir John wondered aloud.

"Methinks they still be a'hidin' in the keep, Milord," suggested a foot soldier standing nearby.

"King Edward of England would never hide, you dolt!" argued Foxley. He then noticed the spearmen backing away as Mowbray and his knights went to meet with Sir Gilbert. He saw them bowing and talking as one chivalrous knight to another. Then Mowbray wheeled and ran a straight course for Foxley.

"One from the castle is comin' for us!" shouted the serf.

Foxley drew his jeweled sword as the soldier shirked away behind a close bush.

Mowbray stopped twenty yards out from the renegades and said in a loud voice, "King Edward came and left hours ago!"

"Sneakin' Scot!" yelled one of the men.

"Don't trust him!" shouted another.

"I have just turned the castle o'er to the Scottish crown," he proclaimed again loudly so all could hear who cared to.

Sir Gilbert rode to his side. "Give up yer weapons and live!"

"How can we trust stinkin' Scots?" came a shout from the hillside.

"Ye can trust this," shouted Haye, "… if I have to come for ye on that hill, ye'll not come off it alive!"

An axe was thrown out of the vegetation and onto the ground at Gilbert's feet.

"There's one a'comin' off the hill," said Gilbert smiling.

"But the axe barely missed ye," argued Mowbray.

"But it did miss," remarked Gilbert.

Fraser, Maclaine and Cameron rode to the two forward men and formed a line. The spearmen came to their backs and the renegades could see there were plenty more troops beyond.

"Yer king is *not* within… I give ye my oath!" shouted Mowbray. "All is lost to the English… ye must go home! This is no longer yer fight!"

Two men emerged from the bush pushing Sir John de Foxley ahead of them. "He's the one what told us to come here!"

Gilbert ordered two pikemen to take him prisoner, and said to the two who surrendered, "Ye two go home to England and ne'er come back with a weapon in yer hand!"

Foxley's sword and dagger were stripped from him and his hands tied in the back. He was led across the boggy ground on foot to where Robert was collecting persons of worth whose families would pay a ransom.

The two men struck out for King's Park where they thought to find their way back through Falkirk and on to Wark-on-Tweed, and then home. Other Englishmen followed their lead until the Scots left the rest as being harmless.

Mowbray and his few knights rode to King Robert and formally swore their fealty, passing Castle Stirling back into the hands of the Scots, where it had not been for many a year. King Robert left Mowbray as constable until it was razed by his masons.

• •

Sedric came to the king. Two of his wild Irish warriors were carrying a large iron cook pot they had found among the wagons of the English and asked Thomas if they could have it as a part of their booty. Robert approved Thomas' decision and they were last seen heading west, taking frequent turns in carrying the heavy pot on their heads. King Robert was sure that they would find another way to tote it before they got another mile.

"Reckon they'll get it home ere it sinks them?" asked Christina as she came to Robert and slipped her arm into his.

"Might sink Angus' galley!" he replied.

"Angus hasn't left?"

"Fixin' to in the morn," said Robert. "Layin' out in the wood asleep right now."

"When will ye get some sleep, Robbie?" she asked quietly.

"When it is finished."

"It was a great victory," said Christina looking Robert in the eyes.

"Depends on who tells the story," said Robert.

"Ach, Rob! Allow yerself a moment of joy! Ye have won," she repeated with a beautiful smile, "won o'er the English!"

"I just pray that I have captured enough barons and knights to trade for Elizabeth and Marjory... and my sisters," he said wistfully.

Christina was silent for a moment. Elizabeth had been gone for so long she had almost forgotten Robert was married to the beautiful, fiery Elizabeth. When his queen returned, Christina knew that she would have to give up being close to the only man she ever loved. She was very capable on her own, but somehow when Robert was away, her private and personal fabric was no longer whole.

Now, Elizabeth would take Robert away from her for the second time, and she suddenly hated her for it. Perhaps his queen had died and Robert didn't yet know! *Holy Mary, Mother of God! Forgive me! What a terrible thought,* she chastised herself.

Elizabeth was meant to be Robert's queen, and there was nothing more to do except stand aside and bless the days she had with him.

"Aye, Robbie, I hope ye can ransom them all, as well," said Christina as she reluctantly pulled her arm from his.

As it was, Friar Baston was practically ignored by Thomas Randolph when his men captured the wagon train all but intact. The only words that passed between the two men were when Lord Thomas ordered the friar off the wain. The oxen and the draft horses were penned nearby, seemingly without a care for all the turmoil churning around them.

King Edward's remaining foot soldiers and camp women had thrown down their weapons and left the area right quick. Some had stayed as gravediggers for the price of supper and a morning bannock from the Scots' larder.

Marmaduke grabbed the friar by the arm and led him from harm's way. "You hain't a'wantin' to get killed, air you?" asked the baron.

"Not wantin', and not needin' to," quipped Robert Baston.

"Poets!" teased Marmaduke shaking his head, "… hain't worth spit!"

The Carmelite smiled, something he would not have done some hours earlier. He was changed by having tasted mortal fear and the starkness of the horror surrounding the battle. Never once during the conflict had he thought to give last rites, or to simply pray over the dead, but sat instead, as if in a nightmare from which he could not escape. He wondered how he had been drawn into such a bloodbath spawned by greed and ignorance.

"Goin' to the other side o' the burn, I am," declared Marmaduke suddenly.

"Thought you didn't want to be taken prisoner?" said the surprised Baston.

"Goin' anyway," de Tweng replied, "to see the battlefield for myself."

"Weren't you there?" asked Baston.

"There… I was, but there I didn't stay… it sickened me greatly," answered Marmaduke, somewhat ashamed.

"Then why do you wish to see it now?" asked Baston.

"To see if I am among the dead," he said in all seriousness.

"Among the…!" Baston sighed deeply. "How will you get across the stream?"

"There's a rope rigged across it," he said, "I can hold to the rope and not get swept away." Then he looked at the poet and asked, "How did you get from that side to this?"

"On the rump of a lesser knight's mule," said the poet, smiling.

"Goin' to be a mite tougher gettin' back," said Marmaduke.

"I'll go with you," announced Baston.

"Me?"

"Now!"

Marmaduke nodded his head in agreement, and the two very unlikely friends trudged toward the stream. Baston could only think of how he was to keep his written poem from the fast-rushing water, and Marmaduke just wanted to check on his own state of mind.

After tying his pouch around his neck, the friar and the warrior hung tightly to the stretched rope and walked carefully across Bannok Burn and onto the water bounded battleground.

Corpses yet floated in shallow pools on the eastern reaches of the area, and beyond the edge of the escarpment, though hundreds had been washed into the firth, bodies of men and horses were yet so thick as to hold the stream out of its banks and deep onto the lowlands. Laid out on the edge of the carse they saw the long lines of naked bodies and the gravediggers hard at work with borrowed shovels to get them underground as fast as possible.

Both men were fascinated with the lines of dead.

Marmaduke looked at the face of each man to see if any among them were his kin or acquaintances. He held his tears well for the sadness that was within his heart, and the experience taught him that he was not dead after all.

Sir Raoul de Monthermer saw him contemplating one of the dead and came to him. "Lively they were," he commented.

Marmaduke jumped, "You scared the hell out of me, Raoul!" he exclaimed.

Raoul smiled a bit. It had not been his intention to startle the man. "You still have your yellow tabard on," said Marmaduke.

"I see you have slipped from behind your green popinjays," said Raoul.

"He didn't want to be captured," inserted Baston.

"What about you, Raoul," asked Marmaduke, "you wantin' to be taken?"

"I am waitin' to speak with King Robert about the body of my son," said Raoul, and a sob caught in his throat as he spoke so sorrowfully.

"Where is your son?" asked Baston quietly, not daring to glance over the dead.

"I watched them carry him to the church up yonder," replied Raoul, indicating Saint Ninian's Kirk.

As the two soldiers talked, Robert Baston succumbed to his spiritual need to take a closer look at his fear, and the dead, and he walked along the head of the line and did as Marmaduke had done. At one solitary moment, Baston was struck by his overwhelming desire to pray over these men without regard to whether they were English or Scots. He set down his pouch and got to his knees, his interlocked fingers tucked tight to his chin, and he began his Latin recitations, prayers for killed. He had found, amidst all the carnage on the battlefield, something he had lost that had made his life worth living, so many years ago. He knew he had again been called by God.

Without realizing it, the three men were suddenly taken by King Robert's immediate presence. "Sir Marmaduke, whose prisoner are you?" he asked.

Marmaduke's eyes widened to see the king standing only feet from him. He stammered a bit before blurting, "I was fixin' to be yours, Sire," he lied, but Robert seemed to believe him.

"Raoul, my old friend," Robert's eyes teared as he looked deeply into Monthermer's sorrowful gaze, "I am heartsick at your loss."

Raoul lowered his head and as tears spilled down his leathery cheeks quietly said, "I'm glad his mother has gone and doesn't have to endure this."

"Joan is gone!?" asked Robert. He had long been out of contact with the private English world into which he had once fit so well.

"Six years gone," replied Raoul, wiping his eyes with his sleeve.

Robert nodded his head. "Gilbert's o'er at Saint Ninian's Kirk," he said.

"I'd like to have him returned for proper burial at home, Sire," said Raoul respectfully.

"So long ago, ye saved my life with a spur and a twelve pence," said Robert, "How could I deny ye any such request?"

Raoul bowed to the king.

"I would have ye and Marmaduke get a wain and take the brave dead knights I have rounded up in the kirk back to England, where they can be mourned proper by their kinfolk and given a Christian burial," said Robert.

Finally Raoul asked, "What is the ransom to be paid for the bodies of the dead knights to be returned?"

"Nothing," replied the Scot.

Raoul's eyes welled. "No ransom?"

"No ransom," said Robert, "… not for them." He paused a moment and then smiled, adding, "There are two things in the kirk that your king might want to have back. Perhaps I should require a ransom for them." Monthermer and de Tweng glanced at each other and they both, with great curiosity, looked at Robert.

"Edward's shield was found along the route Edward's party took when he fled the field," he said, adding, "and his privy seal was found in his collapsed pavilion." he couldn't help but grin.

The two English knights shook their heads in near disbelief.

"What about our friend the poet," asked Sir Marmaduke.

"Poet?" replied Robert, curiously.

"The yonder friar, Robert Baston. Edward paid him to write the glorious story of the battle in verse," explained Marmaduke. "Had it most near writ before we arrived at the field."

"That's interesting... how did he know?" asked the king, a slight smile gracing his lips.

"Know what?" asked Sir Marmaduke.

"How the battle would end?" returned Robert. "How did he know we would defeat Edward?"

Marmaduke was dumbfounded for a moment. He shrugged his shoulders.

"Let me see his poem," said Robert.

Marmaduke lifted the pouch from the ground without the praying friar knowing what he had done. The poet yet remained on his knees, moving from one body to another.

Robert opened the pouch and began to read the epic poem, though his Latin was slow and not always correct in his translation. The two barons stood patiently by, all the while. Suddenly Robert chuckled to himself.

"Not all that good a poem," said Marmaduke sheepishly.

"Ye read this?" asked Robert pushing the parchment in the baron's direction.

Marmaduke nodded his head.

"I think it should say the truth about the battle, don't ye?" he queried.

Raoul asked what it said that was not true.

"Well, the biggest lie is that the English won the battle, in grand style, and drove the Scots from the field in terror!" answered the king. Raoul hung his head with a wry smile.

"When the friar comes from his prayers, tell him he is my prisoner, and that I want the poem rewritten to suit the truth," he said, "or I shall send him to a monastery on a lonely island in the Orkneys... and ye tell him that I want to see the paper ere he leaves here under yer command, Sir Marmaduke!"

"Yes, Your Majesty," fawned Marmaduke, glad that he was not going to have to pay ransom for his freedom, but only had a task to do for the King of Scots.

MONDAY, EVENING – 24th JUNE
BANNOK

It had been a very long day, and even a long two days, for those who had not slept during the short period of not quite darkness.

The field was quiet except for the gravediggers and an occasional laugh among small knots of men and women rehashing the day's events.

On the other side of Cockshot Hill, near where the pinfold held their horses, the Scots gathered in a kind of simple reverie for their own survival, and to mourn those who had been lost in the conflict. Many of the freshly slaughtered destriers were cooked and old ballads were sung in low tones with tears for their deliverance.

After King Robert had seen to the comfort of the Scots he went to Saint Ninian's Kirk to sit with the dead. His kinsman, Sir Gilbert le Clare, a brave but impulsive lad, would in Robert's mind have been a great leader of England one day, if it had not been for his rashness in running headlong into the schiltrom's pikes ahead of his contingent. Sir Robert de Clifford, a proven warrior who had been a bur under Robert's saddle many times over the past years, was also dead.

Robert had the body of Sir Henry de Bohun laid out in the kirk as well. Many brave English noblemen lay dead at his feet. John Comyn the younger, Robert de Reymes, Pain Tiptoft, Edmund de Mauley, Giles d'Argentan, Sir Robert Clifford, and Sir Dungal Macdouall, son of his nemesis in many a battle. All dead. He knew, but for the grace of God, there laid he. He also knew the English had fallen into his well-laid trap such as a spider would weave for its intended meal, enticing the much greater English fly to enter.

A shadowy image suddenly appeared at the door of the kirk.

Robert looked only briefly and said, "Come in, Sir Andrew."

Andrew Stewart walked a few paces into the chapel and paused as if having something to say but reluctant to say it.

"Sit here," said Robert, indicating the bench on which Lord Gloucester laid cold.

Andrew awkwardly sat on the edge of the bench.

"Made yer decision, haven't ye?" asked Robert.

Andrew nodded.

"Ye're not followin' in yer father's boots, I presume," said Robert in a quiet tone.

"Been to Cambuskenneth," said Andrew solemnly.

"Supplies are gone, I ken," said the king.

"'Tweren't the supplies that mattered," the young knight replied, sniffing back tears. "'Twere my friend Baldred, the squire," said Andrew almost at a whisper. "Neck cut deep ear to ear."

"I was told," said Robert.

"Did ye ken it was Lord Strathbogie?"

"Who said?" asked Robert, hearing something he had not been told.

Andrew opened his hand to reveal a bloody patch of cloth that had been ripped from a tabard of one of Earl David's men.

Robert took the cloth and opened it up. There was no doubt about the black and yellow stripes belonging to the earl. He sighed deeply, and would have cursed David de Strathbogie had he not been at a solemn wake for the brave knights. He would, however, take revenge on the young Earl of Atholl for this betrayal and the murders of his guard.

"Sire..." Andrew struggled with his words, "... I have too many questions without answers... too many puzzles about life and what it means to be alive."

"Those questions we all have all the time," explained the king.

"I want answers, at least to some of them," said Andrew, as he looked Robert straight in his eyes in the flickering candlelight. "Here we are, sittin' among our dead enemies, pushing them aside for a seat on the bench, and they would not have hesitated to kill us this morn... that's the whole of it!" He sniffed back tears again.

"I'm thinkin' to go to the Holy land, My King," he added softly.

"Mighty long way to go for answers," said Robert.

"Not the distance that matters," said Andrew.

"I ken," said the king, "Ye a'lettin' yer brother Walter take the Stewardship?"

"'Tis not for me," replied Andrew... "I would make ye a terrible steward, but Walter... is more like our father. He has a wit for keepin' up with details."

Robert smiled. "I wish I could go with ye, Sir Andrew," he lamented.

"I wish so as well, My King," he replied, "but somebody must stay and be king!"

Robert laughed a little and knew he had been stuck with the task. A government built on parliaments and proclamations and laws would come from the rich hard-won earth of Bannok.

The task was far from over, but it was also far from its beginnings.

Bibliography

Armstrong, Pete *Bannockburn 1314.* Oxford, England, UK: Osprey Publishing, 2002.

Barbour, John *The Bruce* (with translation and notes by A.A.M Duncan). Edinburgh, Scotland, UK: Canongate Books, Inc., 1997.

Barron, Evan Macleod *The Scottish War of Independence.* New York, New York, USA: Barnes & Noble, Inc., (Reprint) 1997.

Barrow, G.W.S. *Robert Bruce and the Community of the Realm of Scotland.* London, England, UK: Eyere & Spottiswood, 1965.

Bingham, Caroline *Robert the Bruce.* London, England, UK: Constable and Company Limited, 1999.

Brown, Chris *Robert the Bruce, A Life Chronicled.* Scotland, UK: Tempus Publishing Ltd., 2004.

Cosman, Madeleine Pelner *Fabulous Feasts.* New York, New York, USA: George Braziller, Inc., 1998.

Crome, Sarah *Scotland's First War of Independence.* Alford, Lincolnshire, UK: Auch Books, 1999.

Gallwey, Ralph Payne, *The Book of the Crossbow.* New York, New York, USA: Dover Publications. (Reprint) 1995.

Gies, Frances & Joseph, *Daily Life in Medieval Times.* New York, New York, USA: Black Dog and Leventhal Publishers Inc. exclusively for Barnes & Noble, Inc. (Reprint) 1990.

Lacombe, M.P. *Arms and Armour in Antiquity and the Middle Ages.* Translated from the French by Charles Boutell, with a Preface, Notes, and One Additional Chapter on Arms and Armour in England. Conshohocken, Pennsylvania, USA: Combined Books Inc., 1996. (Reprint)

LaCroix, Paul and Meller, Walter Clifford *The Medieval Warrior.* San Francisco, California, USA: BCL Press/Book Creation, LLC, 2002.

McNamee, Colm *The Wars of the Bruces.* East Lothian, Scotland, UK: Tuckwell Press Ltd. 1997.

Oakeshott, Ewart *A Knight in Battle.* Chester Springs, Pennsylvania USA: Dufour Editions, Inc., 1998. (Reprint)

Robinson, John J. *Born in Blood: the lost secrets of freemasonry.* New York, New York, USA: M. Evans and Company, Inc., 1989.

Scott, Ronald McNair *Robert the Bruce King of Scots.* New York, New York USA: Barnes & Noble, Inc., 1993. (Reprint)

Reese, Peter *Bannockburn.* Great Britian: Canongate Books, Ltd, 2000.

Scottish Fairy Tales. Edinburgh, Scotland, UK: Lomond Books, 1998.

Tabraham Chris *Scotland's Castles.* New York, New York, USA: Barnes & Noble, Inc., 1997.